INVASION: REDUX

THE ORIGINAL FIRST EDITION

THE INVASION UK SERIES

DC ALDEN

© 2006 DC Alden

First published 2006

This edition published 2022.

The right of DC Alden to be identified as the Author of the Work has been asserted by him in accordance with the Copyrights, Designs and Patents Act 1988. All rights reserved.

No part of this publication may be reproduced, stored in a retrieval system, or transmitted, in any form or by any means without the prior written permission of the publisher, nor be otherwise circulated in any form of binding or cover other than that in which it is published and without a similar condition being imposed on the subsequent purchaser.

All characters in this publication are fictitious and any resemblance to real persons, living or dead, is purely coincidental.

A NOTE FROM THE AUTHOR

Invasion: Redux is the original version of the Amazon bestseller *Invasion*, first published in 2006.

I have decided to re-release that singular work in its entirety because of the thousands of emails and comments I have received—and continue to receive—from people asking, *'whatever happened to that first version?'*

So here it is.

But take note—the original version was not in a good place. It was wounded and riddled with so many literary bullet holes that I almost gave up on it. And during that long and painful rehabilitation, I updated *Redux* to reflect the huge technological changes we've all experienced since its original release. I've also introduced a couple of new characters and scenarios to underpin the narrative, and to provide more context regarding back story, plot, and motivations.

I hope this version will make more sense this time around and provide you with a grander fictional experience than my original amateurish scribblings.

And for those who are new to my work, please note—***Invasion: Redux*** is a near-future, alternate history military thriller. Any resemblance to the current world we live in is purely coincidental.

I hope you enjoy it.

SERIES GLOSSARY

- 160th SOAR (Special Operations Aviation Regiment)
- 2IC - Second in Command
- ACOG – Advanced Combat Optical Gunsight.
- AFB – Air Force Base
- AFV – Armoured Fighting Vehicle
- ANPR – Automatic Number Plate Recognition
- ARV – Armoured Reconnaissance Vehicle
- ATC – Air Traffic Control
- ATV – All-Terrain Vehicle
- AV – Audio/Visual
- AWACS – Airborne Early Warning and Control
- Basha – A waterproof, plastic sheet used for shelter and/or groundsheet
- BTP – British Transport Police
- CASE-VAC – Casualty Evacuation
- CBRN – Chemical, Biological, Radiological, and Nuclear
- CDS – Chief of Defence Staff
- CID – Criminal Investigation Department
- Civpop – Civilian Population
- CO – Commanding Officer
- Common Purpose – Alleged Marxist cult posing as Leadership Charity
- CP – Close Protection (close protection officer/team)
- CQB – Close Quarter Battle
- CSM – Company Sergeant Major
- DEVGRU – Navy Special Warfare Development Group (formerly SEAL Team 6)
- DMR – Designated Marksman Rifle
- DVLA - Driver and Vehicle Licensing Agency
- EWOP – Electronic Warfare Operator
- EXFIL – Exfiltration (Extraction) – to escape a hostile area
- GMLRS – Guided Multiple Launch Rocket System
- Haji – Slang term for anyone wearing the caliphate uniform

SERIES GLOSSARY

- HEAT – High Explosive Anti-Tank
- HUMINT – Human-sourced Intelligence
- HUD – Head-up display
- HVT – High-Value Target
- IDF – Israel Defence Forces
- IED – Improvised Explosive Device
- IFF – Identify Friend or Foe (aviation transponder)
- ISR Brigade – Intelligence, Surveillance, and Reconnaissance Brigade (UK)
- JAASM-XR – Joint Air Surface Stand-Off Missile (Extreme Range)
- JLTV – Joint Light Tactical Vehicle (Humvee replacement)
- KIA – Killed in Action
- LAV – Light Armoured Vehicle
- LRASM – Long Range Anti-Ship Missile
- LSV – Logistics Support Vehicle
- M-ATV – Mine Resistant-All Terrain Vehicle
- M-27 – Heckler & Koch Infantry Automatic Rifle
- MIA – Missing in Action
- MilGPS – Military navigation application
- MOD – Ministry of Defence
- MRAP (vehicle) – Mine-Resistant, Ambush-Protected
- MSS-2 – Multi-Mission Special Operations Aircraft
- MTVR – Medium Tactical Vehicle Replacement
- NCO – Non-Commissioned Officer
- NEST – Nuclear Emergency Support Team
- NMCC – National Military Command Centre – Pentagon
- NSA – National Security Agency
- OC – Officer Commanding
- OP – Observation Post
- QRF – Quick Reaction Force
- PNC – Police National Computer – UK Law Enforcement Database
- REMF – Rear Echelon Motherfucker – A soldier with no combat experience
- RSM – Regimental Sergeant Major
- RTU – Returned to Unit
- RV – Rendezvous
- SAS – Special Air Service
- SAW – Squad Automatic Weapon

SERIES GLOSSARY

- SBS – Special Boat Squadron
- SHORAD – Short Range Air Defence system
- SIGINT – Signals Intelligence
- SITREP – A situation report on the current military situation in a particular area
- SLS – Space Launch System
- SRR – Special Reconnaissance Regiment
- TAC Tablet – A tablet-based navigation system
- TFL - Transport for London (body responsible for London's transport network)
- UAV – Unmanned Aerial Vehicle
- UFV – Unmanned Fighting Vehicle
- UGV – Unmanned Ground Vehicle
- UISV – Unmanned Infantry Support Vehicle
- UKSTRATCOM – UK Strategic Command – Tri-Service Command Group
- USEUCOM (EUCOM) – United States European Command
- USCENTCOM (CENTCOM) – United States Central Command
- VBSS – Visit, Board, Search, Seizure – (naval operations)
- VEID – Vehicular Improvised Explosive Device
- VLS - (Vertical Launch System)

"A conquering army on the border will not be stopped by eloquence."

Otto Von Bismarck

PROLOGUE
THE FAR FUTURE

The streets of London were dark and deserted. From the shadows of a derelict building, two boys watched and waited, biding their time until they were certain no one had seen them. They left the abandoned house and moved out onto the pavement.

Moving swiftly, they avoided the streetlights and sought every shadow, every patch of gloom, every unlit side-street. For these boys, the hours of darkness held many dangers. At any other time of day, the authorities tolerated their presence in the city. Now, after the setting of the sun, discovery could end in prison and death.

The boys were sixteen and seventeen-years-old, brothers by birth, and always mistaken for twins. They should've been at home, across the river Thames, at their ramshackle apartment in the crumbling Lowborn enclave of Vauxhall. Instead, they violated the curfew willingly. Because these young men were on a mission of the utmost importance.

They'd left Vauxhall that morning, boarding the trains at Clapham Junction station, where tens of thousands of Lowborns thronged the platforms to ride ancient boxcars into the city. The sun was already up as they clattered over Grosvenor bridge, the rusting iron crossing that straddled the Thames near Battersea Park.

The train rattled on towards the end of the line, where it shunted to a halt inside Victoria Station. Within seconds, the platforms filled with thousands of figures, a vast majority dressed in navy blue coveralls with reflective strips on the right arm and leg. The uniform of the Lowborns.

The boys followed the crowds beneath the station's huge glass canopy and funnelled through one of many checkpoints, their security wrist bands scanned by scowling guards. Once through the station, they headed below ground and boarded a seat-less tube train. Only Lowborns used the underground, a filthy mode of transport that kept them off the streets and out of sight.

The brothers alighted at Justice, the deep-level station once known as Westminster. They climbed the lifeless and poorly lit escalators before passing through an underground tunnel and into the basement of the Grand Halls of Justice, the enormous glass and marble complex where laws were passed, and people tried in its many courts.

It also housed the inner chamber, where the Supreme Judicial Council—a one-hundred strong body of senior judges and lawyers—held their gatherings. Located beneath the enormous bronze dome at the centre of the building, the inner chamber was a magnificent circular room constructed of marble terracing surrounding a raised podium.

Above the terracing, inbuilt digital panels depicted an animated montage of military victories throughout the ages, from the capture of Jerusalem in 638 AD to the sinking of the Chinese super-carrier in the Bay of Bengal thirty years earlier, and new arrivals often found themselves distracted by the digital battles raging in silence above them. The chamber represented the beating heart of caliphate power in the former British Isles, and access was restricted to members of the Supreme Judicial Council and their invited guests.

And the maintenance staff, of course.

Down in the basement, the brothers loaded their cleaning cart and headed for the service elevator. On the ground floor they set about their daily tasks, polishing floors, cleaning toilets, and buffing marble statues, until they arrived at their last and most important cleaning assignment of the morning—the inner chamber itself.

The English oak entrance doors stood sixteen feet high and were adorned with beautiful carvings. Two ceremonial soldiers wearing historic garb and armed with Jambiya daggers ushered them inside. A security guard patrolled the floor of the chamber, alternating between watching them and chewing on his fingernails.

The boys cleaned the marble walls and digital panels with long pole dusters. They navigated the circular rows of steep terracing, plumping the cushions and polishing the marble surfaces to a high sheen. One brother—the younger one—stepped up onto the central podium and cleaned the ornate speaker's lectern, dusting the wood and polishing the glass autocue until it gleamed like a mirror.

After inspecting their work, the guard dismissed them, and the brothers joined the maintenance resource pool for the rest of their long and tiring day.

At dusk, they returned to Victoria station for the journey back across the river, losing themselves amongst the thousands of other Lowborns who pushed and shoved their way onto the waiting boxcars. The boys found a space in the last car as instructed.

With a loud hiss of compressed air and a violent metal clanking, the train shunted out of the station. To the west, the sun had dipped below the horizon and the clear blue sky had darkened, revealing the first stars of the evening.

It was time.

Hidden by the crush of bodies, an unfamiliar face used a knife to slice off their security wrist bands. As the train cleared Grosvenor Bridge, the fight broke out. Fists flew, and the crowd surged and yelled.

The brothers slipped out of the boxcar and dropped to the ground, rolling away from the rusted steel wheels and hiding in the undergrowth by the side of the tracks. The train rattled out of sight, but the boys stayed hidden, using the time to turn their coveralls inside out and hide the reflective strips.

Under cover of darkness, they slipped back across the railway bridge, passing over the river patrol boats as they swept their searchlights across the southern bank. Safely across the bridge, the boys skirted the edges of the harshly lit marshalling yards and ducked through the pre-cut gap in the fence before sneaking into the derelict house.

Now the boys moved fast and silent, all the way to Warwick Square in Pimlico. The district was home to rich merchants, financiers, and other caliphate elites, and the houses were large and magnificent, built around squares of ornate, well-tended gardens.

The boys' target was a magnificent six-storey dwelling nestled between two others of similar opulence. In a top-floor window, a single light shone through the slats of a wooden blind. That was the signal.

Now they moved slower, and with caution. They slipped into a dark side passage without incident and entered the gardens at the rear of the property. Huge palms ringed the high walls, and a raised lagoon full of colourful fish dominated the patio.

A glass wall slid open to receive them and the boys stepped inside a shadowy room furnished with tall plants and expensive-looking furniture. The glass wall slid shut and climate-controlled air washed over them. As their eyes grew accustomed to the darkness, they saw the portly silhouette of a man standing in a doorway, beckoning them.

He led them along a tiled corridor to a large entrance hall lit by sweet smelling candles and dominated by a magnificent staircase that curved upwards to the floors above. The portly man turned to face them, silent in the flickering light. The brothers bowed their heads.

'Greetings, your eminence,' they said in unison.

The portly man smiled. 'Welcome, my young friends.' He gestured to an open door off the entrance hall. 'Make yourselves comfortable. Ali will bring food. Physical strength is important, especially now. Go.'

The boys stepped into a high-ceilinged room lit by more candles and ringed with bookshelves. They stared in wonder. Books were a valuable commodity across the river, and they ran their fingers across rows of embossed titles and thick spines. These were the words of their literary fathers—Shakespeare, Dickens, Betjeman, and many others. Forbidden works for Lowborns and priceless antique tomes for the elites.

Wheels rumbled, and the emir's manservant, Ali, entered the room, pushing a serving trolley laden with silverware. He removed the rounded plate covers and steam billowed.

'With the emir's complements.'

Ali backed out of the room. The boys stared with open mouths at the food, the platters of spiced lamb and chicken, the bowls of scented Jasmin rice, the peppers and roasted vegetables, and fresh bread and butter. On the lower shelf stood frosted decanters of chilled water. The boys attacked those first.

THEY RECLINED ON THE SOFAS, bellies full, safe, and content. As the candles burned, shadows danced across the room, and they spoke of their upcoming mission.

They knew a price would be paid, that lives would be lost, and families destroyed. Men would be rounded up and sent east to fight in the border wars, never to return. But not the boys. If captured, they would be publicly executed, but the risk was worth it. They were fighting for freedom, after all.

Although the memory had faded, they still remembered the attack on their home, a tumbledown brick and slate dwelling to the north of the city, close to the huge, rusted tail fin of an ancient US Air Force B-52 bomber that angled into the sky.

The gunships had attacked the estate at dawn, in retaliation for a terrorist attack their family knew nothing of. The gunships had hovered above the streets and opened fire, their missiles and guns chopping brick and wood to dust and splinters. Mother had saved their lives, throwing them into the cellar before an explosive round cut her in half.

The toddlers whimpered for hours until strong hands clawed them out of the rubble. They were sent south, across the river to the enclaves, where kindly men and women took them in and reared them under new identities.

As the years passed, elders schooled the boys in the true history of their nation, of a once-proud people reduced to an existence of hard labour and servitude. The elders explained that one day, when they were older, the brothers would be called upon to play their part and strike a blow against tyranny.

The years passed.

And the call came.

THE DOOR OPENED, and the boys snapped to their feet. The emir waved them back onto the sofa and sat opposite, plumping cushions. He settled, smiled, and spoke.

'The food was to your liking?'

The boys nodded. 'Yes, your eminence.'

'Good. Soon the sun will rise, and the day will be upon us. A day that will be carved into the memories of friend and foe alike. But there is much to do in the few hours we have. Are you ready to learn, young brothers? Are you ready to go forth and strike fear into the hearts of our enemies?'

The boys sat a little straighter and spoke with clear, determined voices.

'We are ready.'

CHAPTER 1
CALIPHATE

THE MOON SHONE IN THE NIGHT SKY AS THE BLACK HAWK TRANSPORT helicopter skimmed low over the desert dunes, rising and falling with the contours of the slopes below.

Inside the aircraft's transport bay, four men sat in silence, their headsets on, the noise and vibration of the helicopter enough to give one of them a headache.

General Faris Mousa, commander of the Islamic State's Special Operations Command, shifted in his seat as the helicopter thundered over another towering dune, then dropped like a stone towards the desert floor. Much more of this and the pounding inside his skull would develop into a full-blown migraine.

Stress, that was the problem. Too many plates to juggle and not enough time, but given what lay ahead, was it any wonder? He gazed out of the window, looking down as the desert flashed beneath them. His God-given name, Faris, meant Horseman in Arabic. How he'd love to be in the saddle of a beautiful Arab mare right now, travelling the silent desert guided only by the stars. Maybe in the future, when all this was over.

Maybe.

Yet despite the pressure, what lay ahead excited him. Mousa had been a soldier for as long as he could remember, killing his first man before he'd had hair on his balls, graduating from freedom fighter to regional military commander during the caliphate's formative years. He was a natural soldier; tough, resourceful, instinctive, and highly intelligent, qualities he'd inherited not from his spineless father but from his mother, who'd ended her life on a bus full of Jew soldiers in Tel Aviv, her fake baby bump packed with high-explosive.

Those same qualities had kept him alive during the Great Realignment and had steered his rise through the ranks to command Special Operations and Planning, a position that had brought him here, inside this helicopter on this night, as it raced low across the moonlit desert.

The pilot's voice hissed in his headphones. 'Five minutes.'

Mousa spread his fingers in a 'five' gesture to the elderly man sitting opposite him. The senior citizen, flanked by two large and armed bodyguards, smiled and nodded. He wore a simple dark robe and a traditional shemagh on his head. A trimmed white beard framed his lined face, and a pair of round spectacles rested on the bridge of his hooked nose. Through his fingers, he ran a simple band of prayer beads.

He looked like any other elderly gent approaching his 78th birthday, an unremarkable figure dwarfed by the soldiers on either side of him. But Mousa knew that one glance, one word or gesture from this quiet man would have his bodyguards shaking in their boots. For the man sat opposite was His Holiness, the Grand Mufti Mohammed Wazir, chief cleric and supreme ruler of the caliphate.

The Black Hawk slowed and banked to the left. Below them, scattered amongst the crumbling ruins of an ancient desert fort, Mousa glimpsed the marquees pitched around a lush oasis. On the other side of the oasis, he saw several military helicopters parked on the hard-packed dirt. Beyond the encampment, out in the darkness, combat troops patrolled the perimeter.

The Black Hawk settled on the ground a short distance from the old fort. Mousa yanked the door open and dropped to the sand. The bodyguards were next, moving past Mousa, their weapons held ready.

Mousa helped Wazir down from the helicopter. The waiting Defence and Foreign ministers bowed deeply.

'Your Holiness. An honour, as always,' said Defence. Both men kissed the caliph's outstretched hand.

Wazir nodded. 'Is everyone here?'

'Ready and waiting.'

'Then lead on.'

They followed a subtly lit path through the oasis, arriving at a collection of tents erected beneath the dark green canopy. The largest was a luxurious Bedouin marquee near the centre of the clearing. Guards swept aside the entrance flaps and Mousa led them inside. He saw deep couches adorned with exquisite cushions and rugs arranged around a fire pit. Oil lamps hung from the awnings, throwing the periphery of the tent into deep shadow.

Mousa took up position behind Wazir as the man himself settled into a large chair. Several men entered the tent and formed a line in front of Wazir, taking turns to bow and kiss his hands. Then they took their seats on the surrounding couches alongside the Defence and Foreign ministers. The new arrivals wore a mixture of civilian and military uniforms, and as regional governors of the caliphate, they were powerful men in their own right.

Servants poured tea and coffee and retired from the marquee. The conversation was light, and the group spoke of friends and family and bodily health. The small talk ceased as the Caliph Wazir cleared his throat.

'My brothers, it is fitting that we should meet like this, in the custom of our forefathers.' There were nods and murmurs of approval amongst the gathering. The caliph continued. 'Our fractured past is behind us, our countries now united under a single flag. Never have we witnessed such cooperation, such unity, and peace. Such strength. Now it is time to realise our full potential, to embark on our own crusade. History in reverse, my friends.' He turned to one delegate. 'Mustafa, your readiness report, if you please.'

Mousa eyed Mustafa Hassan, leader of the Turkish protectorate. Even after its absorption into the caliphate, the Europeans were powerless to invalidate the protectorate's EU membership, its leaders too frightened to speak out as the Great Migrations facilitated by the Turks continued to trample all over Europe's borders, their dishevelled ranks littered with jihadis, regular soldiers, and intelligence agents. With an invasion force of over half a million men, Hassan's troops would be the first into enemy territory on the eastern front. Nothing could stop them, and everyone knew it.

'We have twenty-two tank divisions ready to advance through Bulgaria and Serbia,' he reported. 'Their mission is to link up with our pathfinder forces who will fly into the Austrian city of Graz. Once on the ground, the airborne troops will capture the control tower and clear the air corridors for the second wave, comprising an additional eight thousand assault troops. They will secure the airfield and the surrounding area until the ground forces reach them. When the Turkey-Austria corridor has been established, the main bulk of Turkish forces will advance into Europe.'

Next, it was the turn of the North African (West) leader, who dabbed a handkerchief around his thick, sweaty neck. His brother Ahmed, France's first Prime Minister of Moroccan heritage, had ambitious plans for the initial phase of the campaign; the assassination of the President, the arrest of influential members of the Army General Staff, and the sowing of doubt, confusion and fear amongst his parliament and National Assembly.

Ahmed would then look to his EU colleagues in Brussels for guidance, but they would be too busy dying or cowering beneath their desks, leaving the Moroccan free to sue for peace on his own terms. Whether each element of that plan would work, Mousa couldn't be sure, but there would be enough political chaos to ensure that French forces would not mobilise against the invaders.

They discussed the nuclear question again, but it was agreed that with Ahmed at the helm, France would not initiate a pre-emptive launch on her own soil, nor against the caliphate itself, and the fifty-seven reactors dotted around the country would provide the fissile material required for Wazir's own weapons development program.

There would be trouble, of course; Mousa knew that many in France would fight, and perhaps their famous Resistance might form once more, but Wazir had gambled that the French had no stomach to see their country levelled again.

The same was true for Germany, a former powerhouse that had

been neutered both politically and socially by decades of progressive politics and mass immigration from Turkey and the Middle East. With the caliphate's allies working within the Bundestag to spread chaos and uncertainty, it was unanimously agreed that France and Germany would offer little resistance. The door to Europe was wide open.

He listened to the Russian foreign secretary speak next. They wanted control of their precious pipelines and peace on their southern borders. They were opportunists, Mousa knew, and he didn't trust them, but they would play their part. What the Russians didn't want was the horrors of the Chechnya war brought to the streets of Moscow and every other major Russian city. The caliph could make that happen with a single phone call. Yes, the Russians had nuclear weapons and the technology to deliver them, but nuclear war served no one. So the Russian bear had taken the deal and would continue its growling slumber behind its own borders.

And so it went on, around the table. Mousa had heard the plans many times. Hundreds had died to protect the military exercise narrative. Even the troops aboard those ships in the Adriatic were unaware that the invasion was real. Only the men in this tent knew the full scale of the operation. Soon, the entire world would know.

Militarily, some of Europe's forces would fight hard, but without clear leadership, any fightback would be disorganised and ineffective. And thanks to decades of political pressure and the introduction of divisive ideologies, the fall of Western Europe was already under way. They just didn't realise it yet.

Across Europe, the agents of change had worked tirelessly, infiltrating governments, undermining institutions, sowing division, widening the fractures, until people regarded their fellow citizens with suspicion and hatred. Europe was adrift, impossibly divided. All that remained was its conquest and subjugation.

Tens of thousands of sleeper agents across Europe would help in that endeavour. Only a tiny number, handpicked by Mousa and his team, knew the full picture and were ready. With access to weapons and explosives caches, they would be the tip of the spear when the operation began, and their impact would be devastating.

The invading force comprised eighteen strategic battle groups, numbering over two million troops. It was the biggest invasion force the world had ever seen. One week from today and we'll see if it all works, thought Mousa.

The caliph sipped his dark, bitter coffee and placed the cup on the table. 'Your preparations are to be commended, my brothers. The time for talk is now over. Continue with the exercises and prepare to execute the invasion order.' He looked at every face gathered around him. 'We stand on the edge of history. Remember that in the coming days.'

The caliph stood. One after the other, the attendees kissed his hand and left. Already, Mousa could hear the helicopters winding up, preparing to leave. After the tent had emptied, Wazir motioned Mousa to sit with him.

'What are you thinking, Faris? Speak openly, my friend.'

Mousa thought for a moment before he answered. 'I believe our forces are as ready as they'll ever be. Year in, year out, we play these games around the Mediterranean and their eastern land borders, and all the while, the Europeans smile and congratulate us. They are frightened, as they should be. Yet there are some who whisper warnings and can see with clear eyes what is coming. But those voices are few, and their detractors many. If western governments heeded those warnings, we would know. We have countless ears and eyes in their halls of power.'

Wazir nodded and remained silent for several moments. Mousa waited, as he always did in the great man's presence. Of all his high-ranking military personnel, Mousa was the only one to have the ear of the caliph.

After a few more moments, Wazir spoke. 'In my reflections, I have seen the future of Europe, and we will be victorious in our campaign. The eleventh day of June will be a day of liberation.'

Mousa nodded. 'Inshallah.'

The caliph stared at Mousa. 'In which case, your duties as my planning officer are no longer required.'

Mousa's blood ran cold, and his eyes darted to the marquee flap. Nothing moved. There were no soldiers with guns, no warning shouts, no chains on his wrists. Yet the caliph had relieved him of his command. Why? His mind raced backwards over the previous few days. Had he caused some offence? A careless word? An undetected slight?

Wazir smiled in the firelight. 'Relax, Faris. I need your skills elsewhere. I trust those paratrooper wings are more than a soldier's vain decoration?'

Mousa's heart raced. 'I am at your service.'

'Good, because I want you to lead a special airborne operation in London. For now, you will travel to Cairo, where your new 2IC, Major Allawi, will brief you on your mission.'

Wazir paused, his voice low as he gazed into the flames of the fire pit. 'Britain is a strange land, perhaps the only country able to resist us. Which is why I want my most trusted and gifted soldier there.'

Mousa bowed his head. 'I serve at your pleasure.'

Wazir smiled and held out his hand. 'Help an old man up, would you?'

A few minutes later, they boarded the helicopter. As Mousa strapped in, he ran through a mental checklist. At 44, he was still in good shape, but a 5-mile run every morning wouldn't hurt. Some refresher parachute jumps too, static and free-fall, and time on the ranges. As the Black Hawk's rotor blades reached full speed, Wazir gestured to Mousa, tapping his headphones. Mousa dialled in his own headset.

'I can see your mind ticking over,' Wazir smiled. 'Do not worry, Faris. Your troops have trained hard. They are ready. What they lack is your leadership.'

Mousa met the caliph's steady gaze. 'I will not fail you, your Eminence.'

'Of course you won't,' the older man smiled.

The Black Hawk lifted off the ground in a cloud of stinging sand and headed north towards the gleaming city of Baghdad that lay beyond the distant horizon.

11TH JUNE

CHAPTER 2
10:44AM
10 DOWNING STREET

British Prime Minister Harry Beecham ran a finger around his shirt collar and took a sip of water as the discussion continued around the conference table.

The air was warm and stuffy, and he wanted to get out. He didn't like the deep-level briefing room. The reinforced concrete bunker, buried twenty-seven feet beneath Downing Street, had been built in the 1960s, and on his first visit, someone had told him it could withstand a nuclear attack in the ten-kiloton range.

Harry was more sceptical. Some years ago, an east London tower block—also built in the sixties—had collapsed, killing over two hundred people.

As he listened to the voices around him, it was clear the COBRA meeting had run its course. Later, Harry had an important dinner with the US ambassador Terry Fitzgerald, and what he needed was a few uninterrupted hours of peace to prepare for the event. He gathered his briefing papers together and tapped them on the table.

'So, is there any other business?' he asked, raising an eyebrow. The various members of the COBRA looked at each other and shook their heads. 'In that case, let's wrap this up.'

The meeting adjourned and Harry and left the room, joined by his director of communications, David Fuller. As he made his way back up to Number Ten, Harry reflected on the recent discussion. Every year, the Islamic State held its massive war games around the Mediterranean and every year tensions ratcheted up across the UK and Europe as people held marches and rallies to mark the occasion, some in support and others against. COBRA gathered to discuss potential problems, which usually amounted to nothing more than low-level public disorder.

Thankfully, religious terrorism was a bad memory these days, and while there would always be troubled individuals with axes to grind, the threat of something more organised had vanished. Which was a miracle, Harry thought, and he cast his mind back to the last terrorist attack in the UK, the Edinburgh bomb.

TELEVISED ACROSS THE GLOBE, the Edinburgh Military Tattoo was the oldest and foremost military marching band event in the world. Held over three weeks in August in the grounds of Edinburgh Castle, the event culminated in a stirring finale involving over a thousand bandsmen from around the world, watched by an audience of over five thousand lucky ticket holders packed into stands in front of the castle itself.

Ten years ago, the massed bands of the Royal Scots, Royal Artillery and many others had marched through the castle's historic gates and onto the esplanade, surrounded on three sides by the cheering audience.

As the tattoo reached its finale, a lone piper stepped forward to sound the last post. For those watching, it was the most poignant moment of the whole festival. It was also the moment the plastic explosive, packed into dozens of scaffolding tubes supporting the temporary seating, detonated. On televisions around the world, viewers saw the blast before the broadcast was cut.

The attack killed three hundred men, women, and children and left fifteen hundred injured. The security services traced the five bombers to east London and arrested four of them. The police shot the other.

When investigations revealed the bombers were citizens of the burgeoning caliphate, Wazir had expressed his sorrow and outrage. He petitioned the British government to deport them so they may face the caliphate's justice. The media was divided on the issue, and Human Rights lawyers looked the other way.

After much deliberation, the government bowed to pressure and deported the bombers. An hour after they landed, Wazir had them beheaded in a Baghdad prison. The British public cheered him on.

Since then, the world had remained peaceful, and the caliphate had grown into a superstate. Wazir had changed everything, including the Arab-Israeli question. He'd brought them to the negotiating table where agreements were made and hands shaken.

Wise heads had prevailed, and that peace had lasted for years. It had earned Wazir a Nobel prize and the fawning admiration of western liberal elites. Including Harry.

Fuller's voice echoed in the tunnel, refocussing Harry's thoughts.

'Remember, the car's picking you up at seven this evening.'

'That's cutting it fine.'

'You could cancel Greenwich,' Fuller said.

'I made a promise. Seven it is, then.'

They parted ways as they entered the basement of Number Ten. Harry went straight up to his private apartment on the top floor, where he found Ellen in the kitchen, tapping away at her laptop. He kissed the offered cheek.

'Hello, darling.'

'How was your meeting?' she said, her fingers a blur.

'Tedious.'

'Pour yourself a coffee and sit with me.'

Harry did both, loosening his tie as he watched his wife work. She'd kept her good looks and trim figure, and the press often described her as warm and engaging. For Harry, there were not enough adjectives to express how he felt about Ellen Beecham. She was the love of his life, his soul mate. When Harry's ministerial career ended, they would start over again, far away from politics and London. They had no children, and no desire to remain in the spotlight once the car drove them away from Downing Street for the last time. Harry looked forward to that day, but for now, he had work to do.

'The car's coming at seven tonight.'

Ellen looked up from her screen. 'What time are you due back from Greenwich?'

Harry was due to open a new school wing in south London, but time was pressing. 'Sixish. Problem is, I don't feel prepared. Tonight is important.'

'So cancel Greenwich. They'll understand.'

'I made a promise, Ellen. I'll just have to work in the car.'

'I'll go,' she said.

Harry shook his head. 'I can't ask you to do that.'

'It's a ribbon-cutting. I'm happy to do it.'

Harry didn't argue. Ellen cared about people, and that shone through every time. She was a good fit for an event like this. 'You're sure?'

'Positive. What's the itinerary?'

'Speak to David. He has the details.' Harry kissed her and stood. 'Thank you, darling. I'll be here for the rest of the day. Any problems, call me.'

'Of course. Bye, Harry.'

'See you later.'

Harry left the apartment and headed downstairs.

CHAPTER 3
2:19 PM
DEEPCUT, SURREY

ABDUL JALAF ROLLED DOWN THE WINDOW AND OFFERED HIS ID CARD TO the security guard at the main gate. After a quick inspection, the guard raised the barrier and waved Jalaf through. He put his small van into gear and drove into the complex.

Creswell Armaments PLC had occupied the sprawling, well-guarded site just outside the town of Deepcut for 53 years. For the last 18 months—and after passing what the company laughingly referred to as a vetting procedure—Jalaf had worked at Creswell, repairing broken windows, fixing door locks, changing light bulbs, and a multitude of other tasks that were required of him as a maintenance contractor.

He was a familiar face around the site, always polite, always helpful. To his colleagues, he was a quiet man, never indulging in the banter and gossip that was part of daily life in the maintenance department. But he was always punctual, often worked late, and was first to cover a sick colleague.

After a year at Creswell, they promoted him to supervisor, which gave him access to the most sensitive parts of the factory, and he moved around the complex freely, inspecting fire escape doors and carrying out a myriad of repairs on everything from faulty blinds to blocked toilets.

And Jalaf's eyes roamed everywhere his swipe card gave him access to, including the restricted research and development building. With his grey overalls and clip-on ID badge, Jalaf blended in perfectly with his environment, head down, always busy, always watching.

Like a ghost.

Because that's what he was.

A<small>LTHOUGH HE BREATHED THE AIR</small>, worked, ate, and slept, Jalaf's reason for living died when an Israeli F-16 fighter dropped a single cluster bomb on his small-holding on the outskirts of Ramallah in Palestine, destroying his home and killing his wife and his 4-year-old twin girls.

On that terrible day, he'd left his farm near the banks of Pesagot Lake at six am and travelled north into the city of Ramallah, where he sold fruit and vegetables at the Saturday market in Ramallah's main square.

He was putting the final touches to his display when he heard the low rumble of the detonation in the distance. He looked around. No-one else seemed to have heard it, so Jalaf shrugged it off and carried on stacking and labelling his produce. Bombs and bullets were a way of life on the West Bank.

For the next hour, Jalaf bartered with his customers and traded gossip with the other stall-holders, until he noticed a subtle change in the atmosphere. The bustle of the market faded, replaced by an indistinct murmur. Heads turned as a group of serious looking men cut a swathe through the muted crowd, and Jalaf noticed that several of them were police officers.

They stopped in front of Jalaf's stall, and the grey-haired man in their midst stepped forward, a grim expression on his face.

Yussef Al-Mahji was a well-known and respected figure in Ramallah, a businessman and sometime politician. When people suffered and died at the hands of the Israelis, Al-Mahji would be there, standing by a hospital bed or a graveside, offering support, a few kind words, maybe some American dollars. *What does he want with me?* Jalaf wondered.

Al-Mahji stepped closer. 'You are Abdul Jalaf?'

Jalaf didn't say a word. Instead, he nodded, bewildered.

'Courage, my brother. There is bad news. The very worst.'

'What?' he whispered, his throat dry.

'The Jews struck a house with a missile. Your house.'

The colour drained from Jalaf's face. 'No.'

But Jalaf knew. A ball of ice formed in his stomach, and his knees buckled. Al-Mahji caught him before he hit the floor. They took him to his father's home, south of the city, and the next day, Al-Mahji was there by Jalaf's side at the funeral. Hundreds poured into the streets behind the cheap plywood coffins. There was much wailing at the graveside, and many condolences offered, but Jalaf was numb to it all. His beautiful wife was gone, his daughters too. What had he done to deserve this? He was not political, never had been.

After the last mourners had left, Jalaf returned to the shattered farmhouse and sat on what remained of his front porch, staring into the distance as the setting sun dipped below the horizon. He was alone. What else was there to live for?

Three years after the incident, Al-Mahji returned to visit Jalaf on his partly rebuilt farm. It was a warm summer evening and Jalaf was sitting on his porch sipping bitter coffee as he watched the Mercedes bouncing along the dirt track towards him. The powerful saloon braked to a halt in a cloud of dust, and Al-Mahji climbed out, a briefcase in his hand Jalaf stood as he approached, and they shook hands.

'It is good to see you, Abdul,' said Al-Mahji.

'You also,' replied Jalaf. 'Would you like some coffee? The pot is still warm.'

'That would be good.'

For some time, they sat on the porch making small talk and watching the chickens scratch around in the dust. The conversation eventually tailed off, and it was Al-Mahji who broke the silence. He picked up his briefcase and laid it on the table, snapping the locks open.

'They found this on your property after the attack.'

Al-Mahji held out a small piece of metal about the size of a cigarette packet. Jalaf took it and turned it over in his hands. It was dark green, with black stencilled letters and some scorch marks around the edges.

'It was a Paveway 2 laser-guided bomb that killed your wife and daughters,' Al-Mahji said. 'That fragment is part of the missile actuation system. We know who made it and where.'

Al-Mahji placed the object back on the table. Then he produced a packet of American cigarettes from his pocket, lit two, and passed one to Jalaf. 'It was the last Israeli air-strike before they signed the treaty. And they attacked the wrong target.'

'They paid me blood money,' Jalaf said. 'Ten thousand dollars.'

'An insult,' Al-Mahji said, flicking his hand.

'They took everything.'

'It is your right to shed blood.'

Jalaf wasn't stupid. He stared at Al-Mahji. 'What is it you want from me?'

'You speak English, yes?' Jalaf nodded. Al-Mahji picked up the bomb fragment, turning it over in his hand. 'I am offering you the opportunity to go to England, to the factory where they make these bomb parts, and kill as many as you can. Before you yourself are killed. Then you will join your family in paradise.'

Jalaf sat rooted to his chair, his legs suddenly weak. So, his angry words had reached Al-Mahji's ears, and now he had a decision to make. To stay here, haunted by the memory of a dead wife and the ghostly laughter of two dead daughters, or to take bloody revenge. For Jalaf, the choice was a simple one.

'I have no military training,' Jalaf said.

'You will learn the ways of warfare. Say the word and your family's deaths will not go unavenged.'

Jalaf thought about his girls and his eyes welled up with tears. But the time for grief was over. It was time to enter the House of War.

'When do I start?'

JALAF SMILED AT THE MEMORY. There had been many times since then—at the desert camps, on the long overland journey to England and his first few weeks in an overcrowded bed-and-breakfast in Dover, that his resolve had wavered, and he'd longed for the soil of his homeland underfoot and the warm sun on his face. But there was no turning back. He'd prayed for strength and God had answered him.

He parked his van outside the maintenance block and grabbed his toolbox from the back. Entering the single-story building, he turned left along the corridor towards his cramped office with its threadbare carpet, battered filing cabinet and ancient personal computer. He locked the door behind him and unlocked his personal locker. He took out the blanket from inside and unwrapped the AK-19 assault rifle. Smuggling it in had been easy, as were the 120 rounds of 5.56mm ammunition.

He slapped a magazine home and hung it on a hook inside his locker. Then he took the fragmentation grenades from inside his lunch box and primed them. He placed them back inside the foam-lined box and secured the locker.

He checked his watch—nearly one o'clock. His stomach churned with excitement at the thought of what was to come. Soon, he would avenge the death of his beautiful wife and his two little princesses.

And the Creswell scientists, the doers of Satan's work, will know the meaning of bloody revenge.

CHAPTER 4
2:58 PM
GREENWICH, LONDON

A MAN WITH POWERFUL BINOCULARS TRACKED THE ARMOURED BLACK Jaguar, sandwiched between two Range Rovers, and a quartet of motorcycle outriders as it swept through the school gates.

He was two hundred meters away, observing the convoy through the window of a scruffy roadside portacabin furnished with plastic chairs and a table covered with discarded newspapers and stained coffee mugs. Wire mesh covered the dirt-streaked windows, giving the observer extra cover.

The man had finished briefing his team, and they were now outside, wearing overalls and high-visibility vests, shovelling sand and staging cones like any other road gang. Unlike other gangs, his people had grenades (smoke and fragmentation) and automatic rifles, all hidden amongst the building materials on both sides of the road.

The convoy headed towards the main building. According to his intelligence, the British Prime Minister would give a speech, mingle with the faculty, then leave the building at five pm. His convoy would then leave the school premises via a different route approved by the Downing Street security team, one that would take them through the roadworks outside.

As the convoy slowed to negotiate the twisting traffic cone layout, the trap would be sprung, and his men would trade their tools for weapons. The directional mines, buried in piles of sand and ballast on opposite sides of the road, would detonate first, taking out the motorbikes and the Range Rovers. Then they would kidnap the British Prime Minister.

The snatch squad had practised the abduction in a disused factory in the Midlands for the last three days, and the visit to Greenwich was the best opportunity to carry out the mission. Once in their custody, they would transport Beecham to a safe house in Blackheath until caliphate troops arrived. The man had every confidence their mission would succeed.

He swept his binoculars across the school building as the convoy stopped outside. A small reception of students and staff awaited Beecham's arrival, and the man watched the security teams from the Range Rovers alight first. They watched the crowd, spreading themselves out along the temporary barriers, waiting for Beecham to appear.

One of them opened the door to the PM's Jaguar, and the shooter gripped his binoculars a little tighter. This was to be his first live sighting of the target. He had seen Beecham on television and in the newspapers many times, but never in the flesh...

The legs that swung out onto the pavement were smooth and shapely. A woman, and like most western women, she dressed like a whore, with her tanned limbs visible for all to see. The shooter lingered on those limbs a little too long, and it angered him. The woman was a distraction, a decoy sent by the devil to lure him from his divine mission. His first bullet would be for her.

Faint cheers and clapping drifted on the warm breeze as the woman headed for the waiting reception party. He switched focus back to the Jaguar, but Beecham failed to appear. He switched back to the woman, and she leapt into his vision once again. She was smiling and shaking hands, the welcome committee offering their paws to be gripped and pumped like the udders of a cow—

Beecham wasn't there. He swept his binoculars over the crowd and settled again on the blonde woman. It was Beecham's wife. She'd taken his place. So be it.

He flipped open his cell phone and speed-dialled a pre-programmed number. Using code words, he briefly explained the situation, and the voice on the other end of the phone ordered him to stand down and wait at the safe house for further instructions.

The man was bitterly disappointed. His men would be too. The voice on the phone assured him there would be many other targets in the coming hours.

At a sand-blown airstrip in North Africa, a Humvee jeep screeched to a halt next to a large turbo-prop transport aircraft.

The driver waited behind the wheel and watched two sticks of heavily laden paratroopers shuffle up its rear loading ramp. It was just one aircraft in a huge line of planes that stretched the complete length of the two-mile long runway, and each one was loading men and equipment. The noise was deafening as scores of planes rumbled past, taxiing for take-off.

The driver stepped out into the blistering desert sun and approached a small knot of senior officers conferring beneath the wing of a giant transport plane. Just beyond the aircraft, another transport thundered down the runway and lifted off into a clear blue sky.

'What d'you want?'

The driver's head snapped around and he saw the officers staring at him. One of them beckoned him. The driver stepped forward and saluted, his knees suddenly weak.

So this was him, the caliph's favourite general. The driver handed over the message slip and the general scanned it before dismissing the driver with a wave of his hand. The driver scurried away. It wasn't a good idea for a lowly corporal such as himself to get too close to these men of power. You never knew what mood they were in, and if you incurred their wrath, well, that would be too bad. The penal battalions were full of men who had crossed an officer's path.

The driver hopped into his Humvee and drove off without looking back. The message must have contained bad news. After reading its contents, the famous general had cursed and reached for a radio.

CHAPTER 5
3:07 PM
SCOTLAND YARD, LONDON

SCOTLAND YARD'S OPERATIONS CONTROL CENTRE WAS LOCATED FOUR levels below ground and was the most sophisticated operations room of any emergency service in the country.

Opened in a grand ceremony by the Home Secretary nine months previously, the OCC resembled a NASA control room, with its sixty full-time operators manning curved banks of computer consoles facing a huge, digitised map of London covering one entire wall. Each operator controlled a specific sector, with access to its myriad CCTV, traffic and ANPR systems that monitored the streets twenty-four hours a day.

It was an invaluable tool in the fight against crime, but as far as Chief Inspector David Greenwood was concerned, cameras couldn't slap the bracelets on criminals. The more money the Met spent on tech, the less there was to spend on training good coppers.

He looked down into the main control room from behind the soundproofed glass of the OCC's Duty Manager's office, a smaller room set above the main floor. He glanced at the incident board on the information wall. Quiet today, he saw. Which suited him perfectly.

At forty-six, Dave Greenwood had enjoyed a long and successful career with the Met, but the daily commute from Surrey and the politics of the job had taken its toll. He wouldn't climb any higher in the ranks than Chief Inspector for a multitude of reasons, none of which had anything to do with his effectiveness as a police officer.

So, in four years' time, he would take a reduced pension and get out.

He cleared his thoughts and focussed on the task at hand. Today he was reviewing the camera coverage plan for a demonstration in central London on Saturday afternoon. The Coalition of Foreign Workers was due to march from Speakers' Corner to Trafalgar Square, where the demo would conclude after the usual round of speeches and banner waving.

It wasn't the march itself that troubled Dave, but the predicted numbers—a million attendees, maybe more. If trouble broke out, things could go south quickly. The Met had cancelled all leave, and reserves from other forces were being brought in from as far as South Wales and Yorkshire. Having an abundance of innovative technology was great, but public order policing required boots on the ground.

Because things had changed, Dave reflected. The public had lost respect for the police, and criminals were no longer troubled by the consequences of their actions. Especially in the inner cities, where many of London's sink estates had become no-go areas for the police, even during daylight hours.

In Southall, Brixton, Hackney, Tower Hamlets, Wembley, and Southwark, the police were told to back off and allow community leaders to deal with their own problems. Criticism of the strategy was ignored, and the senior management team looked the other way.

Dave was one of those critics and his advice—based on years of experience—was also discounted. His audacity to challenge the ideology of his superiors wasn't, which is why Dave knew he'd reached the last rung on his career ladder.

He scooped up his phone and punched in a number. 'Ross, can you bring in the figures for the weekend, please?'

Sergeant Ross Taylor entered Dave's office a few moments later, a sheaf of papers in his hand. Dave waved him into a seat and gave the figures the once over. 'Any surprises?' he asked.

'West Midlands are thirty-four officers down, so they've put out a call for personnel on leave to come in. Lancashire and Greater

Manchester can only send thirty bodies between them. Seems they've had a whisper about a planned disturbance.'

Dave raised an eyebrow. 'What kind of disturbance?'

Ross made finger quotes. 'Unspecified.'

'Helpful.'

Ross continued. 'Northampton can only send fifty, so we're about two hundred bodies short. Oh, and we've also lost one of our choppers. Cracked rotor blade discovered on a routine maintenance and there's no spare. But we'll have two others up, and Surrey will send their bird over should we need it.'

The phone on Dave's desk rang. He picked it up and listened to the voice at the other end of the line. He asked a couple of questions, put the phone down, and leaned back in his chair. 'They've cancelled the march.'

Ross frowned. 'Saturday's march?'

'Correct.'

'Why?'

Dave shook his head. 'No idea. The organisers withdrew their event application. They didn't give a reason.'

'That's odd.'

'It's a result. When we get written confirmation, you can tell the other forces to stand down.'

Ross got to his feet. 'I was going to ask if I could slip away early. I need to get the bike into the garage.'

'Sure. No problem,' Dave said.

'And I'm on a day off tomorrow. I can come in if you need me.'

'That's fine,' Dave said. 'We'll cope.'

'Thanks, guv.'

Ross left the room, and Dave logged into his computer. A moment later, his inbox pinged with an incoming message. It was confirmation from the Gold Commander that the march had indeed been cancelled. Which was good news all round.

Dave wasn't afraid to get his hands dirty, and if they ever needed him on that thin blue line, he'd be there, but the truth was he felt relieved that the march wasn't going ahead. It stank of trouble, and most of those marching had expressed their distrust and, sometimes, open hatred of the police. Goaded by firebrand politicians, the crowd would've turned on the police and all hell would've broken loose.

But not anymore.

Things were quiet across the city, and thanks to that cancellation, Dave felt confident they'd stay that way.

CHAPTER 6
4:03 PM
MORDEN, SOUTH LONDON

Faz Shafiq rose to his feet and followed the rest of the congregation out of the prayer hall and into the adjoining atrium, where he took his shoes from the cubby-hole and slipped them on.

In the main foyer, he browsed the pamphlets and books on display and engaged one of the mosque workers in a brief conversation about the IS war games playing out in the southern Mediterranean and across the caliphate, all the time keeping one eye on the hallway. After a few minutes, the wait was over.

His surveillance target appeared.

Faz headed for the exit, keeping his distance from the man ahead of him, target designation BOXER. The target stopped and spoke to two unknowns before making his way out into the sunlit street. Their huddled discussion was brief, and they exchanged handshakes and cheek-kisses before Boxer left. Faz watched him hit the pavement and head towards Morden town centre. As usual.

'Boxer's on the move,' he mumbled into the tiny microphone secreted under his shirt collar. His hidden earpiece hissed in reply.

'Copy.'

Faz let Boxer drift ahead. They'd been stuck on him for three weeks now, around the clock, with little to show for the man-hours spent. Once his superiors downgraded Boxer's status—as Faz was sure they would—this job would wrap and Faz and his team would move on to pastures new. Yet his gut feeling told him that would be a mistake.

Faz was 34 years-old and had been an intelligence officer for the last five years, recruited through Cambridge University in the time-honoured tradition of English spies. Or rather, in Faz's case, British-Pakistani spies. He'd been a natural from the start. Discreet and unobtrusive—a grey man—yet with excellent observation and recollection skills. Instinctive too. As Max, his fellow operative and team driver, often said, *Faz Shafiq can spot a wrong 'un from a mile away*. Max was right.

Except, neither Faz nor his team had enjoyed little success lately because Boxer was putting them all to sleep. And that was unusual.

Faz had worked a wide variety of terrorism cases since moving from his liaison role with Customs and Excise. Those cases ranged from right-wing extremists to eco-loons and everything in between. The religious ideology threat had all but evaporated these last few years, which had pleased everyone.

Then they'd handed Faz the Boxer file.

Boxer was in his mid-twenties, a Syrian refugee, always well-presented with a slim build and a trimmed beard. He lived in a bed-sit in Clapham, on a street lined with tall Victorian terraced houses split into multi-occupancy dwellings. The kind of street where middle-class city workers lived cheek-by-jowl with large immigrant families and a person would hear a dozen different languages on a shopping trip to the local Sainsburys.

The three-storey Victorian terrace where Boxer lived was a transient place, with people coming and going at all hours of the day and night, and Faz had noticed on his first recce that security was tighter than the average flop-house. The owner—a Lebanese businessman who lived abroad for most of the year—had secured the front door with two expensive Banham locks and monitored the entire property with a network of high-spec, unobtrusive CCTV cameras.

Whenever the front door opened, surveillance revealed two large men inside the always-unlit hallway. Security, Faz noted, vetting callers, and often patrolling the street while pretending to make calls on their phones. Instead, they snapped registration plates and followed suspicious passers-by. Faz figured they had someone embedded in DVLA, running those plates against known government vehicles. Yet as keen as the men were in counter-surveillance, they'd failed to spot the government watchers in the first-floor apartment across the street.

That Boxer lived in such a place gave Faz much cause for concern. The Syrian had come to the attention of the security services after a three-month trip to the caliphate. That wasn't a crime, but the bomb dog at Stanstead Airport had detected residue on Boxer's backpack and that made him a potential player.

They gave Faz the job of watching him, but the culture inside the service was different now, since Wazir had united the Middle East. There was a reluctance to pursue surveillance targets indefinitely, an institutional hesitation to apply pressure, to be more aggressive towards suspicious foreign nationals, and that hesitancy came down from the highest political ranks, Faz had heard. In Whitehall's defence, there had been no trouble for years, attacks or plots, and no one wanted to upset the caliphate.

But Faz's gut was telling him that something was off.

The house in Clapham needed further investigation and a bigger team to monitor it. Faz had requested additional resources, and they'd turned him down. If the surveillance on Boxer uncovered something of note, then Faz could ask again. Until then, the answer was no.

A car horn blared, and Faz saw Boxer jog across the main road. Faz slowed his own pace and let him go, knowing Boxer was headed for the tube station. On paper, the Syrian was a creature of habit, but he wasn't fooling Faz.

A van drew up alongside and the cargo door slid open. Faz jumped in as another watcher, Kilo Three, hopped out and hurried across the road after Boxer. The driver, Max, studied Faz in his rear-view mirror.

'Well?'

'Nothing,' Faz replied. 'Prayers as usual, a quick chat with two unknowns and then he left.'

Max raised an eyebrow. 'Unknowns?'

'Never seen them before, but they knew each other. We need to piggyback off their CCTV, get some grabs.'

'I'll put a request in.' Max took a deep breath and sighed. 'If we don't get a result soon, we'll be packing up again.'

'I know—' Faz stopped talking.

'What's up?' asked Max, watching him.

'That moment, with the unknowns, just before Boxer left.'

'Go on.'

'They embraced. As a group.'

Max turned around in his seat. 'Is that significant?'

'I don't know.' Faz frowned and pinched the bridge of his nose. 'He's never done that before.'

'We've only been on him for three weeks.'

'Yes, but Boxer's a loner. No friends, no relatives, not as far as we know. He's a cold one. It's out of character.'

'What do you think it means?'

Faz processed what he'd seen. The handshakes and embraces were warm, meaningful. As if the parting held some significance for all three men. It was a common scene experienced by most, usually at airports or train stations, and Faz suddenly realised its significance.

He looked at Max as a sudden jolt of fear made his heart race.

'I think they were saying goodbye.'

CHAPTER 7
4:17PM

MORDEN UNDERGROUND STATION

Boxer hurried towards the station, his heart racing.

Finally, the day of days had dawned.

He'd felt his burner vibrate during prayers, and his spirits had soared when he'd read the coded text message. The others had also received their coded signals, and it was all they could do to keep their parting as low-key as possible.

But they would meet again in paradise before the sun had set.

In the caliphate, they had selected Boxer for a special task. He knew it involved driving because they'd told him so, and because he had excelled in driving skills around the ruins of Aleppo. The impending mission would also result in his death, and that filled Boxer with pride. He had recorded a parting message for his family. He had attended his last prayer session.

Now it was time.

He entered the tube station and tapped his travel card at the gate. Down on the platform, the station was quiet, but that was to be expected. Morden was the southernmost stop on the Northern line and at this hour, most commuters would travel in the opposite direction.

A northbound train waited on the platform. Normally, Boxer would enter the first available carriage, but today he continued towards the front of the train. Employing his anti-surveillance training, he turned around in mid-stride and doubled back.

There were two people behind him on the platform. One was an old woman laden with shopping bags, puffing her way onto an empty carriage. The other, a white man in his late twenties, continued towards him. He wore a baseball cap, jacket, jeans and running shoes. Boxer made a show of checking the passenger display above his head. The man veered off and hopped aboard the train half-way up the platform.

Boxer continued towards the front of the train and entered the empty carriage behind the driver's compartment. He took a seat facing the platform and presently the doors hissed shut. The train lurched forward, accelerating into the tunnel.

Glancing to his right, he searched the rows of empty carriages as they rocked and swayed through the darkness. He noticed the man in the baseball cap, two carriages down, staring at his phone.

Boxer tried to work out what carriage Baseball Cap had got on. He was sure it wasn't the one he was in now. The man must have used the interconnecting doors to work his way towards the front of the train. If that was the case, then Boxer might have a tail. Or he could just be paranoid. But his training had taught him to be paranoid.

Everyone was a potential agent of the law.

I'll know soon enough.

The train continued its journey, rattling beneath southwest London, the carriages becoming more crowded with each stop. The carriage intercom hissed and crackled.

'The next station is Clapham Common.'

His home station. Boxer stood up and glanced to his right. Two carriages down, Baseball Cap was also on his feet. The train hissed to a stop at Clapham Common. Boxer got off. Baseball Cap got off too. Boxer cursed.

He lost himself in amongst the other passengers, headed towards the stairs. Baseball Cap would be somewhere behind him. Boxer felt certain the man was an agent.

Warning beeps echoed around the concourse—the tube doors were about to close. As Boxer reached the stairs, he pushed his way through the crowd and hopped back onto the northbound train. The doors rattled closed. For a moment, he locked eyes with Baseball Cap.

They both knew.

The train rumbled towards Clapham North station. Boxer found a seat and pondered his predicament. So, he was being followed, but for how long and by whom? The police? Security services? Boxer cursed under his breath. He lived a simple life, mundane, predictable. He felt confident he'd aroused no suspicion. Yet they were on to him.

The train slowed, pulling into the next station. Boxer took out his burner and jammed the device down the side of the seat. He stood up, waiting for the doors to open.

When they did, he moved further up the platform and re-boarded the train.

FAZ TAPPED Max on the shoulder as the van approached Clapham Common station.

'I can't hear him. Put him on speaker.'

Max flipped a switch on the comms panel over his head and turned up the volume. The speaker crackled.

'—Kilo Three, Boxer is loose. I'm outside the tube station.'

Max pointed through the windscreen. 'There he is.'

He stopped by the kerb. Kilo Three jumped aboard, puffing from his sprint up the station stairs.

'He clocked me and re-boarded the train, headed northbound,' he said.

Faz's gut feeling told him something bad was in progress. He climbed over into the front passenger seat and keyed his radio.

'Control this is Kilo-Seven. Request immediate CCTV track on surveillance target Boxer, currently riding a northbound Northern Line train from Clapham Common. Next stop, Clapham North.'

Overhead, the speaker hissed its response. 'Copy that, Kilo-Seven. Wait Out.'

Wait out? Since when did control keep him waiting for a tracking request? 'Control, Kilo-Seven, requesting priority reacquisition, over.'

The speaker hissed again. The stress in the controller's voice was clear. 'Kilo-Seven, standby,' she said. 'We've lost over thirty targets in the last ten minutes. We'll get to you as fast as we can, over.'

Faz's gut turned to ice.

AT STOCKWELL STATION, Boxer left the train and took the stairs up to the busy ticket hall. A tall, clean-shaven white man wearing a hooded sweatshirt and jeans stood by the barrier, searching the faces coming up the escalator. He saw Boxer and nodded. Boxer veered towards him, pushing through the crowd.

'Hey! Watch where ya going, bruv!'

Boxer ignored the indignant black man and tapped through the ticket barrier. He followed the Hoodie out of the station and into bright sunlight, turning left onto Binfield Road. The Hoodie let Boxer catch up.

'Any problems?' he asked as they walked along the side road.

'I was followed,' replied Boxer. He described his journey, leaving nothing out.

'That's it?'

'Yes, I—'

'Oi, you!'

The voice boomed behind them. The black man from the station was marching towards them.

The Hoodie slipped a hand under his sweatshirt. He turned to Boxer. 'Don't say a word.'

The black man was in his early twenties, tall and muscular. And he was angry. Without breaking stride, he planted both hands in Boxer's chest and shoved hard, sending him stumbling onto the ground. The Hoodie stepped sideways, caught off-guard by the sudden attack. The black man ignored him, looming over Boxer, and jabbing a thick finger in his face.

'Who the fuck d'you think you're messing with?'

Boxer's eyes blazed with anger. He could smell the man's disgusting breath, felt the angry spittle on his skin. He tried to get up, but the black man raised his fist.

'Stay down, bitch! Unless you want—'

CRACK!

The bullet blew the side of the man's head out. He collapsed at Boxer's feet, the gaping pink hole pumping blood onto the pavement. The Hoodie grabbed Boxer's hand and dragged him to his feet. Behind them, a scream split the air.

'Move!'

He shoved Boxer forward. They hurried towards the next junction, crossing the road, and dodging the early evening traffic. The Hoodie pointed to a Ford saloon car parked in a leafy side street. There was a man behind the wheel and the engine was running.

'Get in.'

Boxer slid into the back while the Hoodie took the front seat, the gun still in his hand. The car pulled away from the kerb and turned down another side street, heading towards the city.

In the distance, Boxer heard the rising wail of a police siren.

IN THE OCC, Dave Greenwood was sipping his fourth cup of coffee of the day when a red icon pulsed on his computer screen. A shooting in Stockwell, one fatality, IC3 male. Two suspects involved, IC1 and an IC6. BTP officers on scene and two Trojan units en route.

Okay, good.

Dave interrogated the live CCTV feeds at the scene. He saw a crowd, and the BTP officers on scene, sealing off the street. He picked up his desk phone and dialled the assigned operator sitting in the control room below.

'Sarah, what's the ETA on that Trojan unit?'

A voice came back through his headset. 'Two minutes.'

'Play back the incident, please.'

On a separate monitor, a digital video file played. Dave watched the incident unfold to its bloody conclusion. He saw the suspects hurrying away before disappearing out of shot. The video ended.

'Where did they go?'

'Lansdowne Road. No coverage there. I'm pulling the footage from TFL and running it through Clearview, see if their faces are in the database.'

'Keep me posted.'

Dave watched the monitors as the response vehicle arrived at the crime scene, now joined by two others. *If they get hits on the cameras, we'll find them*, he thought. If not, it'll be good, old-fashioned detective work.

Dave took another sip of his coffee. *Ugh, cold*. Time for another, he thought.

This could be a long day.

CHAPTER 8
4:33 PM
10 DOWNING STREET

Harry was alone in the Cabinet Room, poring over his notes in preparation for the evening's engagement with Ambassador Terry Fitzgerald.

Although he had his own private office in the building, the Cabinet Room exuded a certain gravitas that sharpened his mind for the task at hand. His workflow was interrupted by a tap at the door and David Fuller entered the room.

'David. What is it?'

'Sorry to disturb, Harry, but something's come up. An urgent security matter.'

'How urgent?' Harry asked, still leafing through his notes.

'Security is saying a number of surveillance targets have disappeared. They're concerned.'

Harry put down his pen. 'What targets?'

'They didn't say. They want to brief you downstairs at five.'

'I see. You'd best get Peter over here, asap.' Peter Noonan was Harry's deputy PM, a close ally with a cool head in any crisis.

'He's in Mayfair, giving a speech, at the Press Club. You want me to pull him out?'

Harry shook his head. 'If he was anywhere else I'd say yes. What time is he due to finish?'

'Five-thirty.'

'Get a message to him, discreetly please, David. I want him here as soon as he's done.'

Fuller left the room. Harry speed-dialled his wife's number.

'Hi, darling. How are things at Greenwich?'

'Good. They barely noticed your absence.'

Harry smiled despite himself. In the background, he could hear the hubbub of conversation. He kept his tone casual. 'What time are you finishing?'

'Thirty minutes or so.'

He checked his watch. 'Can you wrap it up early? And call me when you're on your way home.'

There was a pause on the line. 'Is everything alright?'

'Of course,' he lied, trying to sound casual. 'A change in tonight's schedule, that's all. Can you put Matt on the line, please? I'd like a quick word.'

He waited while the phone was passed to Matt Goodge, a detective sergeant in Ellen's security team.

'Sir?'

Harry kept his voice low. 'You've heard about this security threat?'

'Just getting the details now, sir.'

'I want my wife out of there, Matt. Do it calmly and quietly, and get her back here as soon as possible, do you understand?'

'Of course.'

Harry ended the call and glanced at his notes, an untidy scrawl of talking points and bullet lists. He cursed under his breath. There was never enough time, and now it looked like he'd be unprepared for tonight's dinner. If this security meeting dragged on, Harry realised he might have to wing it. He cursed again.

The smart money said that this security scare would turn out to be a waste of everybody's time.

CHAPTER 9
5:15PM

HAMMERSMITH, WEST LONDON

Ross left his motorcycle in the garage on Ravenscourt Road and walked the mile back to his apartment in Chiswick.

It was a beautiful afternoon, and he was looking forward to his day off. When he got home, he'd grab his gym gear and go to the club for a workout. After that, he'd wander down to the pub where he'd enjoy a pleasant evening sipping a few beers by the river.

And maybe he'd ask Lara would join him.

Lara Bevan lived on the top-floor of his apartment block and she'd rocked Ross's world from the moment he'd set eyes on her. That was a while ago now, and he'd been trying to find an opportunity to ask her out on a date ever since, but fate always played a hand and screwed the timing.

They'd often pass each other in the hallway, Lara pounding down the stairs, hair wet and late for work, or Ross would be heading out for an evening shift just as Lara arrived home from her job in the city. What brief contact they enjoyed was friendly enough, but Ross felt there was a connection there.

And when she smiled at him, he was sure Lara felt that spark, too.

So, it was time to bite the bullet and make his intentions known. If Lara was home this evening, he'd ask her to join him for drinks at the pub. If she wasn't home, he'd drop a note through her door. Either way, she'd know he was interested, and Ross smiled to himself.

Who dares, wins, right?

He crossed over into King Street and headed south, cutting through the subway under the busy A4 road that carried traffic in and out of west London.

He reached the peaceful riverside path a few minutes later and made his way home alongside the slow-moving water. It was a longer route, but he wasn't in a hurry. It was a perfect day to walk.

He checked his watch and smiled as he thought about the promise of the night to come.

It was 5:20 pm.

CHAPTER 10
5:31PM
CLAPHAM, SOUTH LONDON

IN A SIDE STREET OFF CLAPHAM HIGH ROAD, FAZ PACED THE PAVEMENT, phone in hand, trying to get a handle on what was happening elsewhere.

Max tapped on the windscreen and waved him over to the van. Faz pulled open the side door and jumped in.

'What is it?'

'Got something on the Met band. A shooting at Stockwell.'

Faz called the Met's OCC, and a female voice came on the line.

'BX, go ahead.'

'My callsign is Zulu-Kilo-Seven,' Faz responded. The Zulu code would identify him as a member of the security services. 'Duty supervisor, please.' She patched him through.

'Chief Inspector Dave Greenwood, Ops Commander.'

'My callsign is Zulu-Kilo-Seven, and the day-word is Trammel.'

'Received. How can I help?'

'The shooting incident at Stockwell. I need to see that footage.'

'Standby.'

A secure link pinged on Faz's phone a few seconds later. The footage confirmed that Boxer had dumped his surveillance in Clapham only to meet another man further down the line. Alarm bells filled Faz's head. He spoke into the phone.

'The man on the left of that footage is a surveillance target. Have you got a location update?'

'A car picked them up on a nearby side street. No vehicle ID yet. We're checking the cameras on all likely routes out of there. We'll get a break, just can't say when.'

Faz kicked the side door in frustration. Boxer had disappeared. He lifted the phone.

'If you get any more info, call me. We need to find these targets asap.'

'Understood.'

Faz ended the call. One thing was certain—an operation was underway, and it wasn't just Boxer involved. There were others out there, all of whom had shaken their surveillance.

Something big was about to happen.

CHAPTER 11
5:42PM

CHISWICK, WEST LONDON

Lara Bevan wasn't sure if it was the car tyres crunching up the gravel driveway or her insistent bladder that woke her from her nap.

She pulled her knees up and shifted position on the sun lounger, desperately trying to drift off again under the warmth of the early evening sunshine that bathed her balcony. But her bladder was refusing to co-operate. She still felt tired, even after several lazy hours on the sofa, but the hangover that had plagued her that morning had melted away.

Her day had started as it always did, with a chirping alarm at 6 am. She'd dragged herself out of bed and headed for the shower. The mirror told its own tale of woe. Lara wasn't unattractive, though. With shoulder-length dark hair, olive skin, brown eyes, and a good figure, Lara knew she turned a few heads, but her morning reflection was likely to turn a few stomachs.

The after-work drinks were taking their toll, and she knew she did it because she was bored. She was tired of her job as an insurance broker, of dreary dates with good-looking but shallow men, and lately, she'd become conscious of her ticking biological clock.

Marriage and family had never featured on her radar, not seriously, but for reasons she couldn't explain, she found herself staring at other couples in the street, envious of their intimacy. Babies made her want to cry. This wasn't like her at all. Lara Bevan had always been the envy of her friends; smart, sexy, funny as hell. Compassionate and generous. *When you start work in the city, You'll be fighting them off,* they told her.

And they were right. She drew a lot of attention, and she loved it. Now those friends were married, or partnered-up, and all of them were mums. Most were happy. Lara's heart was empty. What was wrong with her?

The previous evening was a case in point. Birthday drinks after work had turned into another mid-week, late-night session. Lara had joined the birthday girl and a crowd of friends and co-workers. They'd hit the bars, and later a restaurant, then another bar, then a nightclub.

Lara knew she should've bailed after the meal, but she didn't. She wanted to meet someone, to lock eyes across a crowded room, to feel a spark, something, anything. Instead, she drank far too much. At three am she was playing pin the tail with her door key.

Three hours later, her alarm went off, and she was staring at the horror show in the mirror. Skipping work wasn't an option—she was giving a presentation that morning—so she'd showered and dressed and drank two mugs of coffee.

She'd stepped outside her Chiswick apartment block into warm sunlight. Transport-wise, the new-build block wasn't in the most convenient location, but the street was quiet, and the rear gardens backed on to the River Thames. There were worse places to live.

Sunglasses on, she'd almost made it to the tube station when her head spun and nausea gripped her stomach. She threw up next to a newsagent waste bin, cheered on by a bunch of school kids. Commuters stared in disgust. A passing van tooted her. Lara retched until her stomach was empty and hurried back home, mortified.

She spent the rest of the day in bed, watching her iPad and snoozing. Phone calls and texts went unanswered. At 3 pm, she crawled out of bed and made scrambled eggs and toast. She didn't finish it, but she felt a little better. She picked up a book, a trashy romance novel, and settled on the balcony lounger. After a few pages, the words on the page blurred. Lara was soon asleep.

Now, an insistent bladder and the sound of a vehicle in the driveway below had woken her. She slapped her book down on the decking and padded to the bathroom. As she passed the kitchen, Lara glanced at the clock on the wall.

It was almost quarter to six.

CHAPTER 12
5:49PM
10 DOWNING STREET

As far as Harry was concerned, the meeting was breaking new ground.

None of the politicians in the room had dealt with the spectre of imminent domestic terrorism before. It was an aberration from the past. And yet, here they were. Harry studied the surrounding faces. The politicians looked confused. The others looked deeply troubled. He spread his hands.

'So, we have a situation. The question is, what do we do about it?'

As the debate kicked off once more, his eyes turned to the geo-political map on the wall, and the vast swathes of green that represented the caliphate's territory, stretching from the Atlantic to the Himalayas.

Wazir's achievements over the last decade were unprecedented, and he now controlled the world's largest oil and gas markets. He'd brokered energy deals with Russian and China the west could only dream of. European leaders scrambled to pay homage whenever he visited the continent, which wasn't often, hoping to cut similar deals.

Other western politicians warned of dangerous dependency and urged their leaders to find alternative sources of fuel and energy, and fast. Publicly, Harry championed the wind farms, solar fields and electric cars of his party's donors, knowing none of them would provide what the UK needed.

The Americans used to have the same problems. Past administrations had pursued green policies that had crippled the country. President Mitchell had reversed those policies and had suffered for it, politically and economically. But no longer.

Harry had heard whispers of something revolutionary. Wall Street markets continued to spike upwards. Mystery and rumour abounded, but the White House was saying nothing.

Harry had tried to broach the subject with Terry Fitzgerald, but the man was playing his cards close to his chest. Harry wanted to see those cards or get a glimpse at least. Britain needed help, and fast. There was too much at stake, which was why tonight's meeting was so important.

Yet here he was, listening to COBRA arguing about domestic terrorism. He cleared his throat, and the voices died away.

'So, is there an immediate threat or isn't there?'

'Losing a subject isn't unusual,' said the MI5 representative, 'but today we've seen multiple disappearances. The odds of that being a coincidence are huge. Something's in the wind.'

Deputy Chief of Defence Staff, Brigadier Clive Forsythe, spoke next. 'The Islamic State's military exercises are the biggest we've ever seen,' he said. 'And provocative, as always. Granted, they're being conducted on the EU's borders, not ours, but if the boot were on the other foot, our covert special forces would be very active at this point. It's not a stretch to connect the two.'

'Have you lost your mind?'

Heads around the table swivelled towards the suntanned, balding pate of the Foreign Minister, Geoffrey Cooper. He looked at Harry. 'Prime Minister, I think we're overreacting here.'

'Explain,' Harry said, giving the man his stage and hoping he would fall on his face. Copper was small-minded and arrogant, and deeply unpopular with his staff. Worse, he favoured some international partners over others, often in publicly embarrassing ways. Harry had pencilled him in for a demotion in the next re-shuffle. Cooper had been a bad choice, and as far as diplomacy went, he was also bad for business.

Cooper leaned on the table and talked directly at Harry. 'As you know, I've built constructive ties with Baghdad. The respect is mutual. If we target their people, it could have serious diplomatic repercussions.'

'*Their people?*' Harry echoed. 'The targets are British citizens. It's no one's business but ours.'

'Citizens, yes, but culturally they're tied to Baghdad. Some might see this as profiling. Discrimination, in fact.'

Across the table, the MI5 official bristled. 'They're working to a timetable, and they used counter-surveillance techniques to lose their tails. Whatever this is, it's coordinated.'

Cooper ignored him and focussed on Harry. 'I'm urging caution here, Prime Minister. We need Caliph Wazir onside, especially now.'

'The minister has a point,' said the Metropolitan Police Commissioner. 'We've spent decades trying to rebuild relations between our communities. I'm sure nobody wants to see all that good work undone. We should think long and hard before we act.'

'Hear, hear,' Cooper said, nodding to the overweight police officer.

Harry pinched the bridge of his nose. The commissioner had played into Cooper's hands, but that was to be expected. The policeman was a political appointee and had driven a desk for most of his uneventful career. Harry pushed his chair back and stood up. The others around the table followed suit.

'Find those missing people, asap. Commissioner, what's our current threat level?'

'Low, Prime Minister. No likelihood of an attack.'

'Raise it a level. We'll worry about hurt feelings later.' He saw Cooper flush red. 'And I don't want to see any media leaks. Let's raise our guard without raising fears. Thank you, all.'

The attendees filed from the room. Harry used his mobile phone to call his wife. She answered after a single ring.

'Harry? Is everything okay?'

'Yes, of course, darling…' He saw Cooper hovering and covered the phone with his hand. 'Wait outside, would you, Geoffrey?' He turned his back, dismissing him. Fuller ushered the Foreign Secretary out of the room and Harry continued his call. 'Where are you?'

'Not far. Traffic's horrendous, as usual.'

'Okay. I'll see you when you get back.'

Out in the corridor, Harry saw Fuller trying to placate a fuming Cooper. The Foreign Secretary pushed past him and stood in front of Harry, his finger wagging.

'Prime Minister, with the greatest respect, I have far more experience—'

Harry cut him off. 'I don't have time for this. Let's leave security issues to those who know best.'

'You're making a stupid mistake,' Cooper snapped back, his face boiling with anger.

Harry stepped closer. 'Watch your step, Geoff.'

Cooper bit his lip and pivoted. 'All I'm saying is—'

'I'll see you at the Grosvenor.' Harry turned on his heel and trotted up the steps to Number Ten.

COOPER'S EYES burned into Beecham's departing back. Fuller smiled.

'Harry's under pressure right now.'

The Foreign Secretary glared. 'Don't patronise me, you slimy fucking toad. You're not even a minister, for God's sake.'

Fuller's smile didn't waver. 'There's no call for insults. We've both got jobs to do and I'm afraid I've neglected mine for too long today. Now, if you'll excuse me.'

Fuller headed for the stairs. Cooper couldn't resist a parting shot.

'He's making a mistake. If he pisses Baghdad off, it'll undo everything I've accomplished. I'm going to put this fire out before it takes hold.'

Fuller paused on the stairs. 'Don't do anything rash, Geoffrey.'

Cooper flicked his wrist. 'I'm not asking for permission, Fuller, so jog on.'

He disappeared up the stairs into Number Ten. Cooper watched him go, chastising himself for losing his temper. It was a stupid thing to do.

Especially when there was so much at stake.

CHAPTER 13
THE FOREIGN SECRETARY

Cooper marched into his private office and slammed the door behind him.

He poured himself a brandy to dampen the glowing embers of his temper and dropped into his chair. There was nothing he could do to change the current situation. He had to let it play out, but whatever the outcome, he would have to undertake some damage control.

He winced as he thought back to the briefing. It was a stupid move to doorstep Harry, and he'd overplayed his hand with Fuller. It wasn't the first time.

Cooper knew he'd made a few mistakes during his tenure as Foreign Secretary, but no more or less than previous holders of the post. He'd had to grovel to Harry Beecham twice just to keep his job, a role that Cooper was determined to keep. He enjoyed the status, the deference of others, the sumptuous banquets, the first-class trips abroad. And in particular, he enjoyed his relationship with the Islamic State.

He'd worked hard on that front, eager to ingratiate himself with Baghdad, hoping they might toss the UK a few trade crumbs. He'd managed a few minor concessions, but it wasn't much. Instead, Cooper believed he'd made progress on a personal level.

He had a good relationship with the caliphate ambassador in

London and he'd been to the embassy many times, a beautifully renovated Georgian building on Kensington Gore. Whether on business or social occasions, Cooper always took full advantage of the superb cuisine and expensive wines, an indulgence reserved only for the embassy's non-religious guests.

Yes, Geoffrey Cooper enjoyed a close, personal relationship with the Islamic State. They knew he was a man of importance and they listened to him, really listened. When Cooper was alone with the ambassador, he liked to share his personal political ambitions. And after too many glasses of the embassy's impressive Burgundy, his private dreams.

One dream, above all—an audience with His Holiness Mohammed Wazir, chief cleric of the Islamic State and supreme ruler of the caliphate. Before Harry got the chance, if they could arrange it. Because the British Prime Minister was no friend of the caliphate, Cooper had told the ambassador frequently.

It was Geoffrey Cooper they could trust.

His involvement with the Islamic State began when Harry had promoted him to secretary for trade and industry.

He'd flown to Egypt for a conference, landing at Cairo International Airport. It was the only hub that Europeans could fly into, no matter where their final destination was. From Cairo, travellers would continue their journey by state airline, bus or train.

Non-caliphate citizens could not travel without visas, which were hard to get, even for someone of Cooper's stature. They had shut down the tourist industry, and the sites at Luxor, the Pyramids, the Great Temple of Petra in Jordan, were all closed to foreigners under preservation orders. Cooper had publicly supported the move shortly after Wazir had risen to power, but his fawning tweets had fallen on deaf ears.

He refilled his brandy glass, yanked open a desk drawer and kicked his feet up. He remembered the meetings in government buildings and city hotels, all handled by emissaries, local dignitaries or other representatives. To Cooper's increasing frustration, Wazir never showed his face. The man was a virtual recluse, and Cairo a dead end.

There were rumours that the Big Man lived in an ancient caliphate fort on the shores of the Persian Gulf. Or a desert palace in the hills of Jabal Sawda. Never the same place twice, they said. Cooper figured Wazir hadn't built the enormous white marble pyramid in Baghdad for nothing, and he believed the transformed city was where the caliph spent most of his time.

Foreign governments had extended invitations to the caliph, Britain included, but he'd always refused them. Wazir's responsibilities were to his people and the caliphate. He didn't soil his hands with the grubby business of international politics.

But his image was everywhere; on roadside hoardings, building murals, bus stops, train stations, in cheap frames behind shop counters. The slight, bespectacled Wazir, head held high in profile, looking bravely into the future. Beloved by his people. And invisible. The man was an enigma, a mystery. He was also the key to Geoffrey Cooper's future.

He swallowed another mouthful of brandy and smiled, recalling the trip that changed his fortunes. The speech he'd delivered to the Alexandria conference had been a litany of flowery endorsements of Wazir, and the local delegates had applauded him. When they'd invited him to the palace resort of Sharm El Sheikh, Cooper had nearly fainted. Finally!

He'd called Harry in London, and Cooper had dangled the carrot of a meeting with Wazir. Harry fell for it, and a day later they flew Cooper into the desert by helicopter, along with his secretary and personal aide. He'd dispensed with his British bodyguard, his safety guaranteed by his hosts.

They flew over the beaches of Sharm-El-Sheikh, where coastal hotels and beaches lay empty. In the harbour, trawlers had replaced the tourist dive boats and jet skis.

Further inland, desalination plants pumped fresh water via underground irrigation networks, transforming the surrounding desert into a vast patchwork of crop fields and fertile land. Life had literally sprung up from the desert floor. Cooper recalled being stunned by the transformation.

The helicopter landed on a raised helipad above the trees of a vast oasis. As the rotors wound down, a small welcoming committee escorted Cooper and his aides into an elevator that took them down to the oasis floor.

An electric buggy waited, and it whisked them along asphalt paths beneath the trees. Cooper delighted in watching colourful birds flit between the palms, diving and swooping around the cool waters of gurgling streams and deep rock pools. One or two European diplomats had been here before, but he was the first Brit.

The buggy left the oasis behind, and Cooper caught his first sight of the palace, a seven-storey circular building constructed of enormous limestone blocks with a huge, flaming brazier at its pinnacle, rumoured to be visible for fifty kilometres. Manicured gardens surrounded a building designed and built specifically for the accommodation and entertainment of special guests of the caliphate.

Cooper knew that an invitation here meant they wanted to do business.

The buggy stopped beneath a stone portico, and caliphate officials welcomed Copper's party inside the towering glass and limestone atrium. Cooper shook hands and posed for photographs, his beaming smile genuine.

They escorted him to a private suite on the top floor, a sumptuous, ornate apartment decorated with expensive furniture. The bathroom was enormous, and Cooper washed off the dust of his journey with a long shower and jacuzzi. He sat in a robe on the balcony and saw the distant Red Sea shimmer beneath the warm rays of the setting sun.

After dressing in the black silk djellaba gown provided, a young female escorted Cooper through the ornate gardens to an outdoor dining area lit by candles. Cooper mingled with the dozen businessmen and caliphate politicians already there. They sat around a low wooden table, propped up on mounds of large silk cushions.

As night fell, the song of exotic birds accompanied the quartet of musicians performing in the background. Overhead, a billion stars created a setting that bore no recent comparison for Cooper. It was surreal. Magical.

The guests feasted on curried soups, roasted chickens and succulent fish, washed down with crisp white wines and rich reds served by attractive young women in traditional Arabic dress. His caliphate hosts steered the conversation, ensuring that stomachs were full and glasses topped up, and after dinner, Cooper found himself engaged in debate with a Turkish businessman and a Spanish diplomat. The Turk was baiting the Spaniard about his country's policies towards immigrants from North Africa and Cooper was keen to hear the Spanish line. Immigration was a huge issue in Europe.

And that's when he'd heard her sweet voice for the very first time.

'Would you like a refill, sir?'

From his nest of cushions, Cooper glanced up and saw the most beautiful woman he'd ever laid eyes on. Warm brown eyes, a face framed by dark ringlets, a smile wide and white, and flawless skin. Cooper held out his glass, speechless in her presence. As she leaned over to fill his glass, Cooper's eyes lingered on her deep, full cleavage.

'If there is anything else you require, please ask.'

Her voice was low and throaty. Cooper stared into the dark pools of her eyes and was lost. He mumbled something, and she smiled and drifted away, tending to the other guests but stealing an occasional glance at him. The surrounding conversation was no longer important. It was background noise that failed to distract him from this vision of beauty.

Then she was gone.

Cooper wanted to inquire about her but feared the offence it might cause. When he retired for the evening, sleep evaded him for hours. When it finally found him, he dreamt of her.

The next day, he joined the other guests on a guided tour to the coast. On a low bluff, they entered a foot tunnel that sloped beneath the sand to an elevator room. A lift transported them fifty metres down to an auditorium, and for a moment Cooper forgot about the girl.

The amphitheatre lay on the seabed, its curved walls and domed roof made of glass. Outside, the clear blue waters of the Red Sea teemed with aquatic life, and rock walls on either side towered above them, their craggy surfaces festooned with marine vegetation that swayed in the shifting currents.

Shoals of shimmering fish danced through the water, and a tiger shark beat its tail towards them, slowing as it passed the wide-eyed humans watching from the other side of the glass. The shark bumped its snout and Cooper took an involuntary step backwards. A killer, a man-eater, at least 14 feet long, its black eye staring back at him. Then, with a bored flick of its tail, it swam away, fading into the distance.

Cooper remembered the moment well. He also remembered when he saw the girl again. It was later the same day, after lunch. The others had gone to visit a desalination plant on the coast. Cooper had explored the oasis instead. He was deep in the trees when he saw her.

He caught a movement, and there she was, crouched in a small clearing, picking flowers and placing them in a basket. She saw him and her face lit up. Cooper's heart raced. She told him her name was Zara. She said he had a handsome face and kind eyes.

Cooper was captivated. He spent the rest of the afternoon walking by her side her, talking of their lives and what had brought them both to Sharm-El-Sheikh. Zara was there by dint of her linguistic skills. She spoke English, French and Spanish. She knew that Geoffrey Cooper was an intelligent and powerful man, and she'd seen him many times on the TV.

He was also handsome, she'd said, and felt drawn to him. By the time they parted, Cooper believed that what he felt wasn't just lust. It was love.

At dinner that night, she passed him a note. Later, he met her in a secluded glade, and they rode horses out into the nearby desert. Zara led him beyond the oasis and into the wilderness. They built a fire and drank sweet tea beneath the black dome of the night sky. Her hand found his, and she kissed him with a passion he'd forgotten existed. She told him she felt it too and gave herself to him.

A short time afterwards, he held her under the blanket as they watched the stars. They both knew their love was dangerous and vowed to keep it a secret.

Leaving the palace proved to be a painful experience for Cooper.

Zara was nowhere to be found, and he didn't dare look for her. He thanked his hosts for their hospitality, a smile frozen on his face. Inside, his heart was breaking as he boarded the waiting helicopter. Twenty-four hours later, he was back in London, as miserable as he'd ever been.

The weeks passed, and his mood worsened. But three months later he woke to the most wonderful news—Foreign Secretary Robin Ashcroft had died of heart failure, and Cooper was to replace him.

He was overjoyed and reached out to his friends in the caliphate. An official visit was scheduled, destination Cairo. Cooper did the diplomatic rounds and had to work hard to contain his excitement when he was invited back to Sharm-El-Sheikh.

The next day, he watched from his window seat as the aircraft circled the oasis helipad, his own head spinning. There was no sign of Zara at dinner that night, and as he lay despondently beneath the silk sheets of his enormous bed, he heard tapping on his suite door. He slipped on a robe and crossed the marble floor.

He cracked open the door and his heart leapt.

Zara led him to the bed, and Cooper's life was complete. For a young, unmarried girl, she displayed a surprising wealth of sexual expertise and Cooper made a mental note to get back into the gym. As the first rays of sun streaked across the horizon, they both succumbed to a deep sleep.

He awoke hours later to find her gone. On the pillow was a handwritten note—*Meet me at the oasis. Noon. By the waterfall. Love, Z.*

In the blistering heat of the day, Cooper wandered into the oasis and followed the paths to the rocky waterfall, where a crystal-clear stream cascaded twenty feet into a deep pool. Zara appeared from the tree-line and they kissed. But then she pulled away, and Cooper saw her tears. They had reassigned her to a language school outside Beirut. They would never see each other again.

Cooper was crushed. He held her close, never wanting to let go. For the first time in his life, he felt truly happy, and now they were banishing her? Despite his position, Cooper was powerless to act. How could fate be so cruel?

There must be a way, he asked her. Maybe, she said, and Cooper's heart had soared. As Zara spoke, his face drained of colour. When she'd finished, he let go of her hands.

Spying?

Not spying. Information.

Cooper's instincts told him to walk away, but his emotions held him prisoner. Zara explained her supervisors rewarded the servants with privileges for information about the guests. Sometimes it was money, or a trip to the west. Where a person could disappear.

Cooper struggled with uncertainty. Zara was ashamed. She apologised and vowed never to bother him again. Before he could stop her, she'd fled into the trees. Cooper's mind was in turmoil. *Spying.* That's what it was. He couldn't betray his country, could he?

He thought about past scandals, the damage that traitors like Burgess and McLean had inflicted on the establishment. And the others, the whistleblowers from MI5 and MI6, who'd spilled their guts all over the media. People had short memories, especially in politics. So how would history remember Geoffrey Cooper? A loyal and respected party member? Successful trade secretary? He thought not. A tough, uncompromising Foreign Secretary? Maybe. If he secured an audience with Wazir, well, things would certainly be different—

He jolted as if stung. That was it! He raced through the trees until he caught up with Zara. He was panting hard, unused to the physical exertion. She pleaded with him to accept the inevitable. There was no future for them. They should not torment themselves. So Cooper explained.

If the information was good enough, could it buy him an audience with the caliph? And would they allow her to go to London? An excited Zara said she would talk to her superior.

That night, Cooper sat alone in his suite, barely touching his food. Zara came to him just after midnight. Her superiors had agreed, but with conditions. If it all worked out, they would allow her to travel to London. And if the information Cooper supplied was good enough, an audience with Wazir would be considered.

Cooper was ecstatic. He would make his mark on history and spend his life with Zara. As Foreign Secretary, he was privy to thousands of documents, most of which had little or no intelligence value. He would throw them a few bones, maybe even cut and paste some declassified trade documents.

Whatever he gave them, he'd make sure the country couldn't be harmed. Maybe he'd throw in a little court gossip, too. Fuller was a suitable candidate for a smear campaign.

His mind was made up. Zara was overjoyed and spent the last two nights of his stay in his bed.

THE MAN'S name was Ali, and he was a trade affairs under-secretary. Cooper met him three weeks later, at a reception at the Kensington embassy. At the end of the evening, Ali had approached Cooper. He was a slim, bearded man in his early forties, and as they shook hands, he muttered under his breath.

'Zara sends her love.'

Cooper could have cried with joy. When his official car arrived outside the embassy, Ali escorted him down the steps. He grasped Cooper's hand.

'It was good to see you, Foreign Secretary.'

In the back seat of his limousine, Cooper found a letter inside his coat pocket. When he returned to his official residence in St. James's, he hurried to his private study and slit the envelope open with a letter knife. His heart raced as he read Zara's words.

I miss you terribly. My body aches for yours…

He loosened his tie. He could smell the scent of her skin, taste her lips.

Trust in Ali. He is a friend and ally. The key to our future happiness.

Cooper met Ali two days later at an exclusive health club in Mayfair. They sat in the empty steam room, and it was Cooper, a white towel wrapped around his ample waist, who broke the silence. 'So, how does this work? Remember, I'm surrounded by people most of the day. It'll be very hard to slip out.'

Ali laughed as he swiped a hand across the glass door. Outside, the locker room was empty. 'This isn't the sixties, Geoff. We won't be taping letters under park benches or anything like that.'

Cooper bristled at the informality, but kept his mouth shut as Ali continued.

'It's all very simple these days. I've got a small USB device. All you do is plug it in to whatever computer you're using and that's it.'

Despite the heat, Cooper felt a shiver as the reality of his betrayal dawned on him. He loved Zara, but did he love her enough to commit espionage? *Yes, he did.*

And the world had changed. A hundred years ago, the state executed traitors. Now they got lucrative media deals. What was patriotism, anyway? Nothing more than an obsolete notion from a bygone era. And if by some chance they caught him, he'd spin it into the greatest love story ever told. The talk shows would lap it up.

Cooper nodded. 'USB, eh? Sounds simple enough.'

Ali reached out and squeezed Cooper's sweaty shoulder. 'Any information you bring us will only be used if it's mutually beneficial. You have my word on that.'

'That's reassuring.'

The younger man stood. 'I should go. Give it a few minutes before you leave.'

'This thing in my computer, what does it do?' asked Cooper.

Ali dismissed the inquiry with a wave of his hand. 'It will mask your IP address, cover your tracks. Allows you to look at anything you like without leaving a footprint. I can give you a full technical brief if you'd like.'

Cooper shook his head, the sweat rolling down his face. 'When will I see Zara?'

'It depends on what you give us. It's a risk-reward deal. Think about it.'

Cooper left the club an hour later. Back in his ministerial office in Whitehall, Cooper locked the door and clicked the small device into a USB port at the back of his computer. A tiny green light blinked on, and Cooper used a blob of hand sanitiser to wipe his prints off it.

He sat down behind his desk. If discovered, he'd deny all knowledge of it. That would be his first line of defence. Once Zara was in the UK, he'd throw the thing in the Thames.

On the screen, the cursor flashed. He typed in his government ID and password and set about the business of the day.

A MILE away across the Thames, on the 5th floor of a commercial office building in Waterloo, two men sat behind a large desk, reading newspapers and drinking coffee, each of them keeping a vigilant eye on a single lifeless computer screen.

On that screen, a cursor blinked, the only sign that the system was drawing power. The surrounding office was empty, hired through a bogus front company on a long-term lease, and comprised a single desk, two chairs, and a telephone. The men had water, snacks and sandwiches, and there were two sleeping bags spread out on foam roll mats. They were told they wouldn't have long to wait. A day. Maybe two.

And so it had proved.

The blank computer screen sprang into life and lines of coded information began scrolling at a rapid rate.

Armed with powerful laptop computers, the men went to work as they snatched Cooper's login details and uploaded a sophisticated software program to the Whitehall network.

There it discovered the remote systems beyond Cooper's office, mapping out the LANs and WANs, the data farms and the internal file structures of the massive, integrated government and defence systems across the river. Cooper gave them the Foreign Office. He gave them Cabinet too, and the Defence Secretary. That individual gave them the MOD and the keys to the kingdom; budgets, strategy documents, briefing papers, naval and air assets, civil emergency planning, troop deployments, manning records, reservist quotas, infrastructure, munitions dumps...everything they needed.

In the following months, the transmitter connected to Cooper's computer continued to squirt enormous amounts of sensitive information through an undetected firewall and across the river to the men in Waterloo.

And from there, to the military planners in Baghdad.

· · ·

COOPER TOSSED BACK the rest of his brandy and put his glass down. Behind him, his computer hummed away, the dongle still attached to its rear USB port. Three months had passed since he'd plugged it in and since then, Ali had repeated the same mantra...

Just a few more weeks, Geoff. Zara will be here soon, Geoff. I promise, Geoff.

Until yesterday. Yesterday, Ali had said *days*.

But Harry's ham-fisted surveillance and paranoia could ruin everything. He had to nip it in the bud, push for that elusive meeting with the caliph, force Harry to back down. But first, he had to let Ali know what was coming down the pipe and limit any potential fallout.

If anyone could finesse his way out of trouble, it was Geoffrey Cooper.

CHAPTER 14
5.51PM
DEEPCUT, SURREY

ABDUL JALAF ENTERED THE RECEPTION AREA OF THE HIGH-SECURITY research block, pushing his maintenance cart in front of him.

To his left, a bored guard sat behind the reception desk reading a newspaper and ignoring the bank of CCTV monitors overhead. He saw Jalaf and waved him through. Jalaf nodded his thanks. He pushed his cart towards the security doors ahead of him. This was the entrance to the labs, the place where the devils built their bomb components.

The bombs that had killed his family.

He swiped his ID card, and the doors hissed open. To his left he could see the research engineers in their white coats, beavering away at their workbenches behind the glass wall that stretched the length of the single storey building.

One engineer, a blonde woman, looked up as he rolled his cart past. She smiled, and Jalaf smiled back. He had seen the whore many times, mostly in the lab but often at night outside the company social club, drunk with alcohol, pressing herself up against a man and not always the same one.

She would be first.

He stopped at a small storeroom and bumped the door open, wheeling the cart inside. He locked the door behind him and rummaged beneath the cleaning materials on the cart's lower shelf, retrieving the automatic rifle he'd placed there earlier.

Cradling the weapon in his right arm, he checked the magazine and worked the cocking handle to chamber a round. Then he loaded a 40mm fragmentation grenade into the underslung launcher and placed extra magazines into the pockets of his overalls.

He was ready.

Jalaf checked his watch—five minutes to go. He knelt down and prayed.

Soon, he would join his family in paradise.

CHAPTER 15
5.55PM
WHITEHALL

Boxer gripped the steering wheel to stop his hands from shaking.

A short time ago, after leaving the warehouse in Lambeth, he'd driven along Whitehall and stopped in front of Richmond House.

Looking every inch the UPS employee he purported to be, he strolled into the Department of Health reception area and handed over the package containing nothing but MRI equipment brochures. After making the delivery addressed to a random employee, he returned to the van.

Now he sat behind the wheel, looking at his watch every few seconds.

His target lay across the road, Downing Street, home to the British Prime Minister, guarded by barriers, black gates and armed cops, and Boxer praised God for the opportunity given to him.

He felt regret that he would miss the glorious days ahead, but soon his life would be over and he would enter paradise. That was compensation enough. His shaking hands settled.

Besides, he wouldn't feel a thing. Buried beneath the cardboard boxes behind him was a four-thousand-pound bomb in a crate packed with nuts, bolts, and nails. And his would not be the only attack today.

He scanned the surrounding faces; white, black, yellow or brown, any of them could be soldiers like him, waiting for the signal, the detonation of his bomb. He wanted to lock eyes with one of them, to know he wasn't alone, but it was impossible to tell. Besides, it didn't matter. He would meet those brothers and sisters in paradise soon enough.

He checked his watch again. Time was short now. Boxer reached beneath the dashboard for the small plastic cylinder with the button on top, attached by fibre optic cable to the bomb in the rear. Once armed, all he had to do was maintain pressure on the button. As soon as he released that pressure, the bomb would detonate. Simple.

The minute hand of his watch crept towards the hour.

It was almost time.

Whitehall was busy, and traffic flowed back and forth. He'd have to pick his moment well. He checked his mirrors. No one suspected anything, but that wouldn't last.

Boxer took a deep breath and held down the button with his thumb. He connected the battery box under the dash, completing the circuit. A small red LED pulsed. The massive bomb was now armed.

The cenotaph was to his left, and Downing Street was almost directly across the road.

He couldn't miss.

He dropped the van into gear as his lips moved in silent prayer.

CHAPTER 16
5.56PM
FOREIGN & COMMONWEALTH OFFICE

THE PHONE RANG AGAIN AS COOPER CLIMBED OUT OF HIS OFFICIAL vehicle. He breezed past the security office and climbed the stairs, answering the phone on the fifth ring.

'Yes?'

'Geoff, it's Ali.'

Cooper waved away his bag carriers. They scuttled back down the stairs. He watched them go, his voice a harsh whisper into the phone.

'Are you insane? I said no names.' He wanted to add *you fucking idiot*, but right now he needed Ali onside. Instead, he took a deep breath. 'You have news?'

'I've been trying to reach you for the last hour.'

'I'm the Foreign Secretary. Believe it or not, my day is often a busy one. What d'you want?'

'There's not much time, Geoff. You should check your email, right now.'

'What do you mean?'

'It's all over. Check your mail.'

The line went dead. What was over? A black cloud of impending disaster consumed him. He took the stairs two at a time, barging past his PA, Charlotte, and slammed the door to his office. He flopped into his chair. He had mail, sender unknown. Mouth dry, he clicked on the attached video file.

Confusion knotted Cooper's brow. It was a home movie, a child playing on an empty beach, the sea an emerald green, the sand pure white, the lights of a distant city glowing in the half-light.

Dusk, somewhere in the Gulf, Cooper realised, dabbing at his face with a handkerchief. The child looked young, maybe five or six, a light-skinned Arab boy splashing around in the surf. Who the hell was he?

Then the hand-held camera panned right, and his heart skipped a beat.

Zara.

As beautiful as ever, wrapped in a colourful sari as she sat on the sand, the evening breeze plucking at her dark ringlets. She stared out to sea, her face lighting up as the child ran to her and wrapped his arms around her neck. She beamed that familiar, perfect smile.

A mother's smile.

A man entered the frame and scooped up the child. He was tall, chiselled, and dressed in military fatigues. Cooper felt a painful stab of jealousy as he watched him kiss her cheek. She looked at him with the same eyes that she'd once looked at Geoffrey Cooper with—love, desire, respect. They were a couple, the child a by-product of their love. The video ended. Her face, that beautiful face, remained frozen on the screen.

For a long time, Cooper stared at her, his emotions ranging from utter despair to fear and rage. Then, with a shriek of frustration, he picked up the computer and hurled it across the room. He slumped back into his chair, crushed, his hopes and dreams as shattered and irreparable as his computer.

What had she done? What had *he* done? They'd baited him like a fish, and he'd swallowed it hook, line, and sinker. But why? And if she was a spy, he'd said nothing, given them nothing more than a few low-level briefing documents. What the bloody hell was going on?

The game was up, though. Word of the affair would come out. Maybe that's what Ali meant by *not much time*. In which case he was ruined, his career over. Cooper slid deeper into his chair. On reflection, he realised he didn't care. He was no spy, and it was losing Zara that really hurt. Without her, he had nothing. In his mind, he'd included her in his life, his plans.

Now she was gone forever.

Cooper reached for the decanter on his desk and filled a glass. He swallowed half of it, the brandy burning a fiery path down to his stomach. He heard a knock at the door and Charlotte entered the room. She observed Cooper splayed in his chair, drink in hand and tie askew.

She took a step forward, her shoe crunching on the wreckage of the computer screen.

'Foreign Secretary? Is everything all right, sir?'

Cooper tipped the rest of the brandy down his throat and refilled his glass. 'Be a good girl, Charlotte, and fuck off. I've had rather a day of it.'

Speechless, his PA backed away, closing the door behind her.

CHAPTER 17
5:57 PM
CHISWICK, WEST LONDON

Lara stepped out of the bathroom and heard car doors slamming below her balcony.

There were six apartments in her block and the gay couple opposite were the only ones who owned a car. They were on holiday in the Greek Islands, so it couldn't be them. So, maybe it was the policeman, Ross Taylor.

She hurried back to the balcony in her bathrobe. Ross was a little older than Lara, but handsome with grey flecks in his dark hair. She'd seen him lots of times, but she really hadn't spoken to him that much. He worked odd hours and was always in a hurry when they passed each other.

Yet Ross had smile that was genuine and little roguish. She liked his banter when they did meet, which wasn't often. And he didn't have a steady girlfriend, because Lara would know. So, he had potential. It was time to get to know him a little better.

She slipped onto the balcony and lay back on the lounger. She'd play it cool, glance over the railing, a subtle cough to attract his attention. *Hi Ross. Lovely evening, isn't it? What are you doing for the next fifty years?*

But it had gone quiet down there. What was he doing? Then she heard an approaching aircraft. That was nothing new for Lara or anyone else who lived in west London, living as they did under the flight path into Heathrow Airport. But the noise would give her cover, a chance to stand up and have a peek below.

Overhead, the roar of aircraft engines grew louder.

'Roger Speedbird two-niner-seven, you are cleared to land, runway one-one-four.'

Captain Lewis Ainsworth sat a little straighter in the cockpit seat of his double-decked Airbus A380, his fingers resting on the controls as the 385-tonne giant headed towards Heathrow on its automatic landing path.

Ainsworth was looking forward to getting home. It had been a long trip, from London to LA and then on to Hong Kong, for a two-night layover. From Hong Kong, he'd flown the twin-decked aircraft via Moscow, skirting caliphate airspace as was the norm these days. It meant flying a roundabout route, crawling north-eastwards up the spine of the Himalayas and across the western Siberian plain into Russia, and from there via Finland to London.

Flying the Airbus was easy enough, and nearly all the in-flight systems were automated, but one never knew when an emergency might manifest itself. So, a few more minutes of concentration would see the bird on the ground and Ainsworth could then enjoy a short period of leave.

Maybe he would take his wife away for a few days, to the cottage in Devon, or maybe Scotland. They both loved the beauty of the Highlands, and the weather looked promising. He would take Mary out to dinner that evening to discuss.

Through the cockpit window, distant runway lights beckoned. As he listened to his co-pilot giving a running commentary on their progress, Ainsworth kept his hands and feet ready, just in case the auto-landing system disengaged itself. Incidents were rare, but not unheard of.

His eyes swept the digitised control panel, noting all systems were in the green. Outside, visibility was almost perfect, and nine-hundred feet below the aircraft, the river Thames was a sparkling ribbon, snaking its way westward beneath the warm summer sun.

As Ross strolled along the street towards home, he felt the rumble deep in the pit of his stomach.

He looked up and saw a British Airways super-liner on its final approach into Heathrow. Ross shielded his eyes as the huge aircraft swept low overhead, chased by its shadow. It would be nice to move away one day, out of London and away from any major airport.

With hundreds of planes flying overhead daily, it was only a matter of time before something terrible happened.

Ross shook off the depressing thought as he neared his apartment block.

Lara craned her neck to see what was going on down below.

Someone had parked a minivan at the side of the block. Not Ross, then. Damn. So who was it? The driveway was private property, residents only. She heard feet crunching on the gravel and low voices. She peered over the balcony.

Thirty feet below, three men dressed in jeans and t-shirts were unloading long green tubes from the back of the van. Lara's gut feeling told her the men were up to no good. They were all Asian, and two of the men were fiddling with the tubes, while the third man kept looking up to the sky. She could hear them talking, but their voices were hard to hear because there was a plane coming and—

Oh God.

In that moment, Lara realised what the tubes were for, and the horror of it rooted her to the spot. She watched the men walk across the rear gardens and rest the tubes on their shoulders, pointing them upwards.

Lara stood transfixed on the balcony, unable to move, her hands gripping the rail and her lips moving in silent terror.

CHAPTER 18
5.58 PM GMT
EUROPE

ALL ACROSS THE CONTINENT THEY WAITED.

The moment they had trained for was nearly upon them and each cell, each group, each individual had planned their operations meticulously.

Some had been preparing for years, migrating westwards with bogus documentation or none at all, disappearing into sprawling communities, securing employment, infiltrating target organisations, identifying personalities, mapping infrastructure, absorbing, planning, and briefing their assault teams.

Others had received target-only instructions weeks, days and, in a few cases, hours before. Stockpiled explosives and weapons had been distributed, and targets reconnoitred. Twenty-four hours earlier they'd received the *go* signal from their handlers.

There was no going back.

Final preparations were made, clocks and watches synchronised, last-minute recces conducted, equipment and weapons checked, vehicles fuelled and readied. Nothing was left to chance. From the Baltic coast to the toecap of Italy, thousands of individuals and assault teams all across Europe moved into position.

The countdown had begun.

At air, land and sea control points, computer systems were logged into and powerful software codes secretly executed. Security guards were lured away and neutralised, or simply wandered from their posts, leaving them unguarded. Intruder alarms and CCTV systems suddenly developed 'faults' or were shut down completely. As the minutes ticked away, other teams took up ambush positions around their targets, weapons cocked, trigger fingers ready.

Transport infrastructure was a paramount objective. Railheads and major junctions, marshalling yards, airports, air traffic control centres, motorways, trunk roads, bridges, tunnels, crossing points, ferry ports, cargo docks and the Channel Tunnel itself were all targeted with specialist teams.

Laser designators were activated and placed in the grounds of buildings and installations selected for military action, their unique signals detected by aircraft patrolling high above the Mediterranean Sea. Locations were plotted, coordinates fed into computers and downloaded into fuelled and prepared missiles that waited in darkened silos.

Around the coastlines and docks of Europe, combat troops and their supporting tanks and armoured vehicles waited in the rolling gloom of cavernous cargo holds. Sailing under false papers and flags of convenience, the ships had arrived at their target ports over the last twenty-four hours. The troops inside these ships looked out through hidden viewing ports at the activity on the docks below them, and the landscape beyond. This was to be their battleground.

From Turkey to Morocco, hundreds of thousands of fighting troops and support units made final checks to weapons and equipment while they waited in huge, sprawling camps, airfields and assembly points dotted across the caliphate.

Thirty thousand paratroopers and their support units were already airborne, their transponders identifying them to European air traffic controllers as cargo or passenger planes. They flew criss-cross patterns over south-eastern Europe and the Mediterranean, adhering to well-rehearsed schedules and air traffic lanes.

On the ground, another thirty-thousand paratroopers sweated inside their aircraft as they waited for the *go* signal that would send them across the skies into Europe. The wait would be short as the minutes ticked away. An operation that had been over two decades in the planning was about to be realised.

Years had become months, weeks had become days, then hours, and finally, minutes.

The military might of the Islamic State was poised, about to unleash itself upon Europe in a show of force not seen since the days of the Ottoman empire.

CHAPTER 19
5.59 PM
CHISWICK, WEST LONDON

Lara heard the roar of the aircraft and looked up.

Several hundred feet above her, a huge Airbus rumbled over the rooftops of Chiswick on its final approach into Heathrow.

She gripped the balcony rail until her knuckles turned white. The horror of what was about to happen numbed her senses. As the shadow of the plane swept overhead, the men below fired their weapons. In a blast of white smoke, the high-explosive missiles streaked up into the air.

Lara found her voice and screamed.

The third man looked up and saw her. He leaned into the minivan and retrieved an automatic weapon. He shouldered it and took aim.

It happened so fast that Captain Ainsworth could not react.

He neither saw nor heard the approaching missiles, but he felt the shock of the double explosion and the shrapnel that sliced through the cabin. The cockpit display turned red, and then the remaining fuel in the starboard wing ignited and blew it to pieces.

Ainsworth's bloody hands wrestled with the control yoke, but he knew he was a dead man, along with the 511 passengers and crew behind him.

Through the cockpit window, the sky disappeared as the plane tipped over and plummeted towards the streets below. Ainsworth let go and closed his eyes.

Mortlake Road was busy with rush-hour traffic in both directions. A muffled boom and a growing roar drowned out the noise of the traffic and the blare of horns. In shops and homes, the background clamour of life faded as a growing pressure squeezed the air.

On the streets, the sky darkened, and a terrible scream drowned everything out as four-hundred tonnes of metal and flesh ploughed into the busy junction of Cumberland Road and the South Circular.

He was so calm about it, the way he lifted the gun to his shoulder and took aim.

Lara still gripped the rail, unable to remove her hands. Then she heard a *click*, and the man frowned and checked something on the weapon.

Lara prised her fingers off and she staggered backwards, tripping over the patio door runner as the balcony exploded with bullets, the rounds shattering glass and brick and stitching a pattern into the ceiling above her head.

She screamed and crawled inside, the sound of the gun deafening, terrifying. Scrambling behind the sofa, she lay flat, her hands clamped over her ears and her heart hammering in her chest. When the building shook, she knew that hundreds of people had just died a terrible death.

And she was next.

Ross heard the roar of the missile launchers and flinched.

He saw missiles rocket up into the sky, chasing the giant aircraft and detonating in puffs of black smoke and flame. The booms rippled across west London. He saw the wing explode and the plane tip over. Then it fell from the sky, trailing black smoke.

In all that time, he hadn't moved a muscle.

A scream and a long burst of automatic fire shook him from his paralysis. Just a few moments ago, he'd existed in another world, one where the sun shone, where an evening with and a cold beer and a gorgeous girl beckoned. But that world had gone, turned dark.

Even the sun had lost its warmth.

The pavement rumbled beneath his feet. It was the plane hitting the ground, and the tremor galvanised him. He drew the service pistol clipped to his belt, a 9mm Glock, and chambered a round. Speed-dialling the OCC, Ross saw he had no signal.

He pulled off his jacket and yanked a police armband up over his arm, advancing at a fast lope past the glass entrance doors to his apartment block. He stopped and peered around the corner.

A dark-coloured minivan squatted between the buildings, wrapped in a thin cloud of white smoke. The minivan's engine roared into life, but the driver was just a shadow behind the wheel. Two more men appeared—the shooters, Ross guessed—and they climbed aboard.

The side door slammed shut, and the minivan pulled away, crunching along the gravel drive towards the street. There was no haste, no urgency, and that shocked Ross. He stepped halfway out from cover, his Glock up in the aim.

'Armed police! Stop the vehicle, now!'

The wheels spun as the minivan sped up towards him. Ross fired twice, punching two holes in the windscreen and the driver's chest and face. The minivan collided with the wall, grinding along the brickwork, still moving and out of control.

As it drew level, Ross fired twice at the rear passengers. The van roared out from between the buildings and careered across the road, smashing into a parked estate car with a loud bang that lifted its rear wheels into the air. It crashed to the ground.

The engine roared, then died.

For a moment, there was silence. Ross advanced, his gun pointed towards the minivan. He heard a rough curse, and a man scrambled out of the side door holding an automatic rifle. There was no time for a challenge, so Ross shot him twice in the chest. The man dropped onto the road, his gun clattering beside him.

Ross moved forward, his heart pounding. All three men were dead, and he'd had no choice. He searched the corpses but found nothing, not even a wallet. He picked the gun up, a HK-416 assault rifle, and unloaded it, shoving the magazine and two spares into his pockets.

Another explosion made him duck, and he saw a huge fireball mushroom above the treetops across the river. The ground rumbled with several secondary explosions and a column of thick black smoke billowed into the sky. His mind was numb, shocked by the speed and horror of the unfolding situation.

He ran back to the apartment block, pulling his cell phone from his pocket—still no signal. He flung open the glass door, Glock at the ready, and announced his presence. It was deathly quiet.

He fumbled for his keys and entered his own apartment. The landline was dead. He placed the rifle and magazines in his bedroom gun cabinet, locked his apartment, and ran upstairs, banging on doors. Outside Lara's apartment, he heard sobbing.

'Lara, it's Ross from downstairs. Are you okay?'

The sobbing stopped. Ross stepped away from the door. Maybe she wasn't alone.

'Lara, can you come to the door?'

He heard movement inside, and the door unlocked. He pushed it open and stepped inside. Lara stared at him, speechless, shaking.

Ross took a quick look around, holstered his weapon, and marched into her bedroom. He returned with her duvet and wrapped it around her shoulders. She leaned into him, and the floodgates opened, her body shuddering as she sobbed.

Ross held her tight, noting the damage to her balcony and the bullet impacts around her walls. *Lucky girl.* He listened for the sirens, for the response units that must be on their way.

'It's going to be okay,' he whispered. 'It's over now.'

But Ross was wrong.

All across Europe, it was just beginning.

CHAPTER 20
GREEN LIGHT

...57, 58, 59....

Boxer's G-Shock watch flipped to *18:00*.

It was time.

Bomb armed and pressure switch in hand, he released the handbrake and eased the UPS van away from the kerb.

At Parliament Square, the armoured black Jaguar carrying Ellen Beecham swept past a mob of placard-waving protesters.

Ellen tried not to look, but she couldn't help herself. She saw the obscene hand gestures, heard the muffled filth that poured from the protesters' twisted mouths beyond the bulletproof glass.

What had she ever done to these people? She'd asked herself that question many times. There was no easy answer.

They turned into Whitehall. Ahead, the Range Rover's brake lights flared as the convoy slowed for the turn into Downing Street. People on the pavement stopped and stared, phones pointed at her car. The motorcycle outriders broke off and sped away up Whitehall.

Ellen reached down for her handbag as the Jaguar slowed. She pulled out her mobile phone, tapped a text message, and hit send.

I'm home. xx

Boxer swung the vehicle around and saw two Range Rovers and a fancy black limousine turning onto Downing Street. A VIP, or the Prime Minister himself. It was a sign from God.

In a moment of cold clarity, Boxer realised the enormity of what was about to happen, and it filled him with an aching pride. Gone were the nerves and the shaking hands. The fear he'd felt only minutes before had lifted, like removing a coat. He felt a sense of calm unlike anything he'd ever experienced before.

Or would again.

He floored the accelerator, and the vehicle lurched forward, cutting across the oncoming traffic.

Horns blared.

At the entrance to Downing Street, the Range Rover slowed for the rising gate.

Ellen slipped off her seatbelt and picked up her bag. A sudden, frantic blast of car horns filled the dead air inside the Jaguar, and Ellen turned around, her heart rate rising. Police officers surrounding the Jaguar began firing their weapons, the noise deafening. Ellen screamed. The driver screamed, too.

'Move that fucking vehicle!'

The Jag rammed into the back of the Range Rover. Ellen wailed as her face collided with the driver's headrest. The police officer next to her dragged her to the floor, his weight pinning her to the carpet. Blood poured from her nose.

The gunfire was constant now, hammering off the walls of Downing Street, thundering across Whitehall. She buried her face in the carpet, her hands covering her ears. The door flew open, and the horror filled the Jaguar.

Hands clawed at her, grabbing her arms, ripping the skin off her hands. She fell halfway out of the car, and she cried in pain and terror.

Boots and bullet casings danced around her head as the gunfire and screaming rose to a deafening, terrifying crescendo...

'Move her!'

'IED! Take cover!'

'Stop that fucking vehicle!'

'Kill him!!!'

She closed her eyes.

BOXER KEPT as low as possible, peering over the dashboard to keep the truck on course through the bullet-riddled windscreen. Death was seconds away.

He sat up and floored the accelerator, the truck fishtailing on shredded tyres as it headed for the gap between the Range Rover and the rear of the Jaguar.

Boxer yelled a war cry, a scream of pure exultation that was cut short by a bullet to the throat. Two more snapped his head snapped backwards, and then he was hurled against the shattered windscreen as the truck smashed into the driver's door of the Range Rover—

THE UPS VAN exploded in a white-hot blast, obliterating Ellen Beecham's Jaguar.

It vaporised police officers, tourists, pedestrians, cyclists, taxis, cars, buses, concrete, metal, bricks, and glass. The shock wave punched across Whitehall, peppering the MOD, Scotland Yard, and a dozen other buildings with fist-sized holes and blowing out every window, killing dozens more inside.

Manmade thunder rippled across the city, and an enormous cloud of yellow dust enveloped the area. A massive crater, several meters deep and filling with water from a cracked main, marked the spot where the entrance to Downing Street existed only a few seconds before.

The blast had cut the Cenotaph in half. Vehicles burned. Hundreds of people lay dead, dying, and injured across Whitehall. Those that could, ran.

Downing Street was beyond recognition, its historic façade stripped away, exposing the now ruined interiors. Roofs collapsed and tiles rained down into a street buried by rubble. Multiple fires took hold inside, and black smoke billowed into the sky as alarm klaxons split the air with their ghastly wail.

A moment later, they fell silent.

CHAPTER 21
THE FIRST CUT

Abdul Jalaf stepped out into the corridor, the automatic weapon gripped in his hands.

For the first time in many years, he felt free, liberated from the yoke of timid servitude. The mask was gone, and now the staff at Cresswell Armaments would see his true self. Through the glass wall, the white-coated creatures in the laboratory continued their evil tasks. Jalaf smiled. Finally, he would have his revenge.

The assault rifle roared and bucked in his shoulder as he raked the laboratory with explosive bullets. Screams echoed throughout the building. To his right, doors slammed open, and a security guard appeared, armed with a pistol. Jalaf dropped to one knee and fired two rounds, knocking the guard to the ground.

Turning to his left, Jalaf fired two 40mm grenades into the reception area. The detonations shredded wood and furniture, and when Jalaf charged into the smoke-filled lobby, he saw the security guard on all fours, coughing and spluttering and covered in plaster dust. He fired a single shot into the man's back. Frightened screams drew him back to the labs.

The surviving technicians bundled towards the far end of the corridor, where a panicked crowd squeezed through a fire escape door. Jalaf jammed the Kalashnikov into his hip and pulled the trigger, sending a fragmentation grenade hurtling across the floor, skittering beneath the legs of the panicked herd. Jalaf ducked as the grenade cracked. He looked up, heard the screams, saw the bodies and smoke. He charged down the corridor.

The blonde woman, the whore, stumbled towards him. In her chubby arms, she cradled the slippery pink rope of her own entrails, spilling from the gaping wound in her lower stomach. Her face was a white mask of concentration as her mind tried to cope with the horror of what was happening to her.

She slipped on a pool of blood and fell. Jalaf watched as she tried to get to her feet, floundering like a newborn colt. Jalaf stood over her. She looked up at him, her eyes pleading. He answered her silent prayer and shot her in the face.

The other survivors were scrambling around the corridor, some blinded and deafened by the grenade. He opened fire, switching aim as he mowed down the screaming, pleading devils who'd played their own part in the death of his family.

He coughed as smoke swirled around him and flames engulfed the lab. Alarm klaxons wailed, and Jalaf stepped over the bodies and headed out into the evening sunlight. Across a rectangle of patchy grass was another single-story research block. To his right, a chain-link fence marked the perimeter of the site. To his left was the distant main entrance. Jalaf saw several figures running here and there.

He heard a shout and saw a man and a woman running past the block. He recognised them as Matthew Hall, one of Creswell's directors, and his secretary Lucy. Hall was practically dragging the terrified girl behind him. Jalaf slung his rifle behind his back and called out to them.

'Mr Hall!'

Seeing Jalaf in the smoky doorway, Hall slowed, and Lucy dropped to her knees on the grass. Two large black smears of mascara streaked her face as she sobbed. Hall's face was ashen.

'I know you. You're the maintenance chap.'

Jalaf nodded. 'What's happening?'

Hall waved his arm in the direction of the admin buildings. 'God knows. Someone said there was shooting down by the main gate.' He saw the smoke billowing out from the building behind them. 'What happened?'

Jalaf smiled and swung the AK into his hands.

'Oh my God!' screamed Lucy.

She wrapped her arms around Hall's waist and hid behind him. Hall raised his hands. 'Not her, please. I'm begging you.'

Jalaf took careful aim and fired a single round. The bullet took Hall in the chest, and he fell backwards into his secretary, sending them both to the ground. Jalaf walked over to where they lay on the grass, kicking Hall's body over. The secretary lay beneath him. Her blonde head had burst open like a melon. Two for one. An excellent shot.

Jalaf heard distant gunshots echoing over the rooftops. Maybe he wasn't alone in all this. He reached into his overalls and yanked out a green headband, wrapping it around his forehead. If there were others like him out there, he'd want to be recognised as one of them.

He stepped over the bodies and made his way towards the main entrance. As he crept closer, he saw dead guards lying on the road and an abandoned car in front of the red and white security barrier. The gunshots seemed more distant now, carried by the light evening breeze.

He heard a shout behind him and turned—

The flash blinded his eyes. When they cleared, he saw the summer sky was now above him, the most beautiful shade of blue he'd ever seen. A shadow loomed over him, and he heard a rough curse. The kick to his ribs broke something, but Jalaf barely felt a thing.

He brought his hand up to his face and saw it painted with bright red blood. He'd been shot, but he wasn't sure where and by whom. It didn't matter because he expected to die today. In fact, he welcomed it. Death would escort him to paradise where his family awaited him. It had been too long since he'd seen them.

He struggled for breath. His vision blurred and the blue sky above grew smaller, as if he were falling down a well. He heard his daughters' laughter somewhere in the gathering darkness. His journey was at an end.

He saw his wife, and she smiled.

CHAPTER 22
TOMB

DAVE GREENWOOD WAS SCROLLING THROUGH HIS EMAIL INBOX WHEN HIS computer screen lit up with emergency call alerts.

He pushed his chair back and stood up. Down in the control room, most of his operators were also on their feet, shouting into microphones and punching their keyboards. Flashing red icons littered the digital wall map of London.

Dave stepped out onto the gantry, his eyes drawn to a bank of CCTV monitors below. There seemed to be something happening on every screen, a flurry of chaotic images that didn't—

The OCC went dark, plunging the subterranean room into pitch blackness. Dave couldn't see his hand in front of his face. He heard someone curse and the crash of a chair toppling over. Dave grabbed the rail in front of him and called out.

'Nobody move. The emergency lights will kick in any second.'

Dave waited, holding his breath. A minute passed, then two. Mobile phone lights swept the room, but still no emergency generator activity. What the hell was happening?

'Everybody, grab a chair and sit down. When the power comes back, we'll need to process the situation on the ground.'

He used his own phone to find his desk. He speed-dialled the number of a colleague upstairs, but the phone system was dead—

A dull boom rumbled above him, rattling the light fittings across the ceiling. Dust floated down through the upturned torch lights. He shouted for order.

'Everybody take it easy. Something's going on up there and we need to find out what it is so we can help officers on the ground.'

A bright torch beam washed around the room, revealing pale, frightened faces. 'I found a torch, sir.'

Dave headed down to the main floor. In the bright light of the beam, he hurried to the main doors. The keypad was lifeless, so he grasped a handle and pulled. Locked solid.

'Aren't they supposed to release in a power cut?' a voice asked.

'Give me a hand, someone.'

Several operators gathered around and grabbed the handles. After a few seconds of effort, they forced a gap wide enough for Dave to squeeze through.

Outside, he stood in the dark corridor. Then he called out to one of the other operators, a police constable called Mark Curran.

'Mark, you come with me. And bring that torch. The rest of you stay where you are.'

Curran was a senior operator, competent and level-headed. He was also a forward for the Metropolitan Police rugby squad, and Dave might need the muscle. Curran squeezed his large frame through the gap and joined his boss in the corridor.

Dave played the light around the walls, settling on the locker room. 'Let's get our firearms.'

They retrieved weapons and utility belts from their personal lockers. Dave checked his sidearm, a standard issue Glock 9 mm automatic pistol. He clipped the plastic holder to his belt and grabbed his body armour, strapping it to his body. Curran gave him a look.

'Better safe than sorry,' Dave said.

Curran donned his own vest. 'Do you think that was a bomb we heard earlier?'

'Could be. What did you see on the monitors?'

'Hard to say. I saw people running, smoke, a couple of big flashes. Some cameras went out immediately. Looked like chaos to me.'

Dave took out his pistol and chambered a round. 'Just in case,' he said.

'You think it's that bad?'

'Maybe. How long since you were on the street?'

Curran pondered the question. 'Three years.'

'So, we play it careful. Let's go.'

Dave led them towards the lobby and into the emergency staircase. He shone the torch upwards, the light playing over the concrete stairs that disappeared into blackness. The closest exit was three levels up, an underground car park. Right now, it was the only way out.

'Let's try the car park exit first.'

'Roger,' Curran replied.

They made their way up the stairs, footfalls echoing around the dark chamber. After climbing two flights, Curran tugged Dave's arm and whispered in the darkness.

'Can you hear that?'

Dave stopped, cocking his head. 'Sounds like someone knocking. It's coming from the car park.'

When they got to the landing, Dave shone his torch along the short corridor that led to the car park. Someone was banging on the fire escape door from the other side.

Dave placed the heel of his left hand on the release bar, holding his pistol in his right hand. He shouted through the door.

'You! On the other side of this door! Stand back! I'm going to open it!'

He braced himself, ready to give the door a hard shove.

Behind him, Curran sniffed the air. 'I can smell burning.'

But Dave had already slammed the door open.

From the wall of smoke and fire, the creature leapt at them, screaming.

CHAPTER 23
CENOTAPH

Geoffrey Cooper's vision wavered between darkness and a blurred nightmare.

He preferred the darkness. It was warmer, more comforting, but a sharp pain in his lower abdomen was denying him the beckoning shadows. He cuffed away the blood and dust clogging his eyes.

After several confused moments, he realised he was lying face down on the floor of his office. *How did I get here? Did I fall?*

He turned his head to the right and saw his computer screen, the one he'd thrown, lying in pieces on the floor. There was something about that screen, a suspicion that it was key to his present condition.

With a painful effort, he rolled over onto his back. The vast ceiling was now a work of abstract art, pitted with holes and scarred with black streaks. All the light fittings had disappeared, along with sections of plaster, exposing the rib-like timbers beneath. The supporting wall had gone, too. *How could that be?* In its place was a huge, jagged hole, and he could see all the way across Whitehall.

Around him, shattered floorboards sprouted from the floor at crazy angles, creating long, jagged splinters. Like the one in his stomach.

A foot-long wooden stake had penetrated his abdomen close to his left hip. It had bent all the way over, presumably where he had lain on his stomach in the gentle embrace of unconsciousness, yet the sight didn't horrify him.

Instead, he studied the wound with a detached fascination. There didn't seem to be much blood, which was good. Blood was so difficult to remove, and the shirt was handmade from Saville Row. *I'll probably need a tetanus shot too.*

As the pain ebbed and flowed, Cooper considered pulling the stake out. He unbuttoned his shirt around his plump waist. *Ugh.* The skin surrounding the wound was a deep bluish-purple, and thick dark blood pumped over his fingers like treacle. Cooper felt sick. Best not to attempt any amateur surgery. Better leave it to the experts.

He let his head rest back onto the filthy carpet. There was another pain too, niggling at the back of his mind, a terrible memory that bubbled just under the surface. Something to do with—

Zara's e-mail.

Yes, that was it. The pain of her message had crushed his heart. He closed his eyes, trying to recall the details. When he opened them again, he saw it, just a few feet away, lying amongst the rubble. His broken computer. The USB device, the one that Ali had given him, had led to this. Cooper knew that now, and the full weight of his culpability lay heavy on his wheezing chest.

He had to tell someone and damn the consequences.

He heard sirens, but they sounded a long way off. Where the hell were the police and the ambulances? This was Whitehall, for God's sake. Cooper wasn't certain how long he'd been laying there but it felt like quite a while. Where was everybody?

Maybe he could make it to Downing Street. Harry would be there. He'd know what to do. And Harry had to be told that this was Wazir's doing. He'd tell him about Zara and that bastard Ali, and the bug in his computer. And get the awful piece of wood removed from his belly. It was really hurting now.

Slowly, painfully, Cooper made it to his feet. His head swam, and he felt the bile rise in his throat. He leaned over and vomited, splashing a half-digested lunch over his shoes. When he'd finished retching, he wiped his mouth with his shirtsleeve. Blood in his vomit.

Better get a move on.

He made it to the landing and staggered down the stairs, gripping the handrail with both hands. There didn't seem to be much damage down here, just broken windows and scattered masonry, but he didn't see a single person.

He stumbled out onto King Clive Street, weaving through the arched portico and past the deserted security gate.

At the junction of Whitehall, he leaned against the pockmarked stone facade. He looked down and discovered his trousers were wet with blood. Fear gripped him then. He might die if he didn't get help soon.

He raised his head and, despite the growing pain, shock rooted Cooper to the spot as he absorbed the magnitude of the surrounding devastation.

It was a bomb. There was no doubt in his mind.

A few yards away, the decapitated Cenotaph stood in a sea of rubble, and every surrounding building had suffered heavy damage. Vehicles burned and bodies lay everywhere, some moving, some burning. Most were dead.

Behind him, the blast had peeled away the facade of the Foreign Office and he saw his own room exposed to the world. He was lucky to be alive.

Outside Downing Street, a fountain of water sprayed high into the air and drifted across the road. It reminded Cooper of Sharm El Sheikh, and the waterfall where he'd met with Zara. How he wished he were back there now, with that deceptive beauty in his arms.

He heard a rushing sound, and he saw another waterfall, an ugly one, comprising rubble and bodies tumbling from an upper floor of the Cabinet Office and crashing to earth in a cloud of dust. That's where the blast had detonated, Cooper realised, looking at the vast crater where once there was a pavement and steel gates and vigilant police officers. All of it vaporised.

Which meant Harry was probably dead, too.

He skirted huge piles of rubble and staggered towards the Cenotaph, leaning against its severed remains. He saw flames reaching high into the sky above the shattered rooftops of Downing Street and wondered where the emergency services were. It felt like the end of the world.

He felt cold, too. His head spun, and he slumped sideways, lying prone against the base of the monument. It felt wrong to be there, his skin touching a monument erected to honour the fallen. Sacrilege. This wasn't a place for selfish, reckless traitors like Geoffrey Cooper.

Yet there was nothing he could do about it now. His world grew dim, and he felt relieved. He wouldn't fight it this time. He closed his eyes, knowing they'd never open again.

The devastation of Whitehall was gone, replaced by a dark oasis. Cooper looked up through the treetops. It was night, but a night so dark that it frightened him. There were no stars and no moon.

He searched the shadows between the trees and called her name, but Zara didn't answer. Instead, the darkness descended towards him like a black ceiling, swallowing the tops of the palms, getting closer.

Then it devoured him, and he didn't feel afraid anymore.

CHAPTER 24
DEMOLITION MAN

Harry tried to piece together the last few moments.

He remembered pouring a coffee as he replayed the text of his dinner speech, when he thought he heard shots. As he unplugged his headphones, a tremendous flash had lit up the kitchen, followed by an ear-splitting bang. The floor fell away before rushing back up to meet him, knocking him over. The air had filled with choking dust.

Only then did his brain catch up.

Harry struggled to his feet, wincing as pain shot through his body. Steaming coffee had scalded his hands and blood from a skull gash ran down his face. Nausea gripped his stomach, and his ears rang with a persistent, high-pitched tone.

He leaned against the rubble strewn counter and looked around the kitchen. The ceiling had suffered a partial collapse, power cables swung lazily from the shattered ceiling, and the blast had stripped away the wall overlooking Downing Street.

Harry took a step backwards as roof tiles scraped over his head and sailed past his exposed kitchen, crashing to the street below. And he could smell gas. That was Harry's first thought. A gas blast.

I'm home. xx

He grabbed a tea-towel from the counter and clamped it to his head to stem the blood flow. He had to find Ellen, make sure she was okay.

He couldn't locate his mobile phone, and the wall phone lay fractured at his feet. He left the apartment and headed downstairs, frightened by what he saw. The entire building appeared to have taken a terrible hammering, as if some huge hand had picked it up and shaken it. The photographs of past PMs lay scattered across the stairs, glass and frames broken.

When he reached the first-floor landing, he heard someone coming up the stairs and Fuller stumbled into view. Harry stared at him in shock. Shredded clothes hung from his colleague's spare frame. His face and exposed flesh were grey with dirt and blood, and most of his was hair singed off. His left shoe was missing, the foot slick with blood. Harry ran down the stairs.

'David!'

Despite the obvious pain, relief swept over Fuller's face. 'Harry… thank God you're okay.'

Harry put an arm around him. Fuller vomited blood onto the filthy carpet.

'We've got to get you some help,' Harry said, revolted.

He heard shouting down in the lobby. Harry looked over the broken balustrade rail and watched several police officers wearing black helmets and brandishing automatic weapons filing through the broken arch that was once the entrance to Number Ten.

One of them saw Harry on the landing above and charged up towards him.

'Prime Minister, I'm Sergeant Morris, Parliamentary Protection Command. Downing Street has been attacked. Looks like a truck bomb. All our comms are down—'

'Where's my wife, sergeant?'

Morris looked confused. 'Your wife?'

'Look after him,' Harry said, helping Fuller to the floor. Then he was hurrying down the stairs and stumbling over the rubble into Downing Street. Two of Morris's colleagues followed him outside. What they saw stopped them all in their tracks.

A gigantic crater marked the entrance to the street. Everything else was gone, the gates, the barriers, people, as well as both corners of the Cabinet and Foreign Office buildings. Water from a broken main blasted fifty feet into the air, throwing a curtain of damp mist halfway across Whitehall, where vehicles of every description burned, blanketing the street in black smoke.

Harry saw bodies too. Lots of them. He turned away. In the surrounding buildings, fires were taking hold. It was a nightmare. He looked to his right and saw the wreckage of a vehicle at the far end of the street.

'No!'

The police officers shouted a warning, but Harry was already clambering over the rubble towards it. When he got there, he found a mess of twisted, smouldering metal and burning tyres.

'Ellen!!'

Strong hands grabbed him before he could plunge into the black smoke. A square-jawed cop pulled him close, his face an inch from Harry's.

'There's nothing you can do, sir! We have to get you out of here! Right now!'

An explosion echoed across Whitehall, followed by several distant gunshots. Harry's brain was playing catch-up again. 'What the hell's happening?'

'Get him inside!'

The cops frogmarched Harry back to Number Ten and bundled him into the lobby. He saw Fuller lying on the ground and being tended to by a helmeted police officer. Another volley of gunfire echoed through the shattered building. Harry looked at Morris.

'A truck bomb, you say?'

Morris nodded. 'That's what it looks like. Either way, we must get you to a safe place, find out what the hell is happening.'

'Where's safe?'

'I was hoping you could tell me, sir.'

CHAPTER 25
GOING UNDERGROUND

Harry yanked off his tie and threw it away.

He cleared debris from the stairs as Morris and his officers carried Fuller down through the debris of Number Ten and out into the garden, where most of the surviving staff had gathered near the far wall.

Many were cut and bruised and covered in dust. Those were the lucky ones. Some of their colleagues were lying beneath the rubble. Harry saw they were frightened. So was he. But being frightened was better than thinking about Ellen.

She said she was home. Harry could only assume she was at the gates when the bomb detonated. He felt a flash of anger and swore at the Gods. Another minute either way, and perhaps she would've survived. But he couldn't think about her now. It was too much.

Instead, he helped make his friend comfortable, Harry heard more gunfire. Sergeant Morris led him away from the others.

'Mr Fuller's in a bad way. Internal bleeding, we think. Unless he gets treatment asap, he won't make it.'

'Then we must get help,' Harry said, glancing at his stricken friend.

'My priority is to get you to a place of safety, and that's not here.'

Harry glared at the helmeted police officer. 'You mean abandon

David and the others?' He shook his head. 'We all go, or we all stay. Those are the options, sergeant.'

Harry broke away and knelt next to Fuller. He gripped his friend's hand. Fuller's face was pale and drawn and sweat beaded his forehead. The police medic had ripped open his trouser leg to reveal a large, open thigh wound. Harry looked away from the grisly mess and focussed on his friend.

'You're going to be fine, David. Help is on its way.'

Fuller turned his head towards Beecham. His eyes were horribly bloodshot, and his voice rasped as he spoke. 'I don't... feel too good, Harry. Something inside me feels all wrong.' His voice trailed away, and his eyelids closed.

Harry gripped his shoulder. 'David, listen to me. You must stay awake, okay?'

Fuller's eyes fluttered. 'Where's Ellen? Is she here?'

Harry bit his lip. Fifteen minutes ago, the world revolved at its usual pace. Now it had turned upside down and in that brief period, Harry had become a widower. Now he was about to lose his best friend. He fought to keep his voice strong.

'She's fine,' he lied, his eyes moist. 'Stay awake, David. I'll be back.'

Harry approached Morris, who was talking into his radio. For a moment, Harry's hopes soared. 'Who are you speaking to?'

Morris shook his head. 'No one. The entire network is down. That includes the mobile networks too.'

Harry pointed to Fuller. 'There must be something we can do.'

'Sir, with respect, your friend is dying. And he's not the only one. There are wounded people dying all over Whitehall, and since I've been here, I haven't seen or heard any emergency services. And we can't ignore that gunfire. I think this is a major terror attack on a scale we've never seen before, and unless we get out of here, we could all end up like your friend.'

'A terror attack? But that's impossible.' *Or was it?* Harry recalled the COBRA meeting. Those surveillance targets, all vanishing at the same time. This was the result. A bomb. But that didn't explain the lack of response, and the shooting that sounded like it was getting closer.

'Where can we go?' Morris asked him. 'There must be somewhere. A secure area or shelter. Anything.'

Harry's thought processes couldn't keep up. 'I need a moment with David.'

'Make it fast.'

Harry knelt by his friend's side. Fuller was barely conscious, and his skin was so pale, Harry thought he'd already passed. Then he saw his eyelids flutter. 'David. Can you hear me?' The eyelids opened. 'We must go, David. Help is on its way, though—' He choked on the lie and squeezed his friend's hand.

Fuller's voice was so low that Harry had to lean in close to hear him. 'Get to the basement, Harry. They'll look for you there.'

'I'm sorry I couldn't do more, David, I—' Harry's voice cracked. His friend was dying right in front of him. Ellen was dead too. He turned to the police medic. 'What can we do for him?'

The helmeted policeman showed Harry a morphine ampoule. 'I can make him comfortable, sir. He won't feel any pain.'

Harry looked at his friend. Fuller's eyes were closed now, and his skin had taken on a grey pallor. He looked awful. 'Do it.'

The medic injected Fuller, and Harry held his friend's hand. It twitched several times and then went limp. The medic checked his vitals and nodded. Harry lifted the blanket over Fuller's face and stood. A long rattle of machine gun fire echoed across St. James's Park. Harry ducked, as did everyone else. It was close.

'We have to find cover!' Morris said, grabbing Harry by the arm.

Harry shook him off and pointed to Number Ten. 'The basement briefing room. It's secure and deep below ground. There's also a tunnel that runs beneath Whitehall, leading directly to the MOD building.'

Morris turned and saw the burning building behind him. 'You mean go back into Number Ten?'

'If we can,' Harry said. 'The basement is bomb and fireproof, sergeant. And we can use the tunnel to evacuate the staff.'

Morris barked at his men. 'Round everyone up.'

In a few moments, the police had herded the survivors together. Harry turned and bid a silent farewell to his dead friend and then he was moving, surrounded by police officers, jogging across the garden and back into Number Ten. The smoke inside was thicker now, and he heard the dull roar of flames as fires consumed the upper floors. Harry led them through the building and stopped outside a heavy black door marked *Authorised Personnel Only*. Harry twisted the metal handle and shouldered it open. A wide stairwell led below ground.

'Mind your step,' he said, relieved to see the emergency lights were on. How long they would last was another matter. They switch-backed down several flights of metal stairs to a long concrete corridor. On the right was the briefing room. Harry pointed towards the end of the corridor.

'That will take you to the MOD building.'

Morris ordered two of his men to escort the civilian staff beneath Whitehall. As they filed past him, Harry shook a hand here and there, trying to sound optimistic. 'Just do what the police tell you. Stay safe. Everything's going to be fine.' He watched them go, most of them familiar faces, and he realised he didn't know most of their names. Behind him, Morris stared at the ceiling.

'Feels like fresh air down here.'

'It's the air filtration system,' Harry said. He pointed to a door across the corridor. 'There are backup generators in that room. They won't last forever, so I suggest we get moving.'

Harry led Morris and his remaining men into the briefing room. The policeman's face lit up when he saw the comms equipment along one wall. As Morris flipped switches, Harry tried the internal phone system. It was dead. After a lot of dialling and cursing, it was clear to all of them that nothing worked.

'Everything's down,' Morris said, confirming the worst.

Harry shook his head. 'How can that be? This place can withstand a nuclear attack. We should be able to speak to GCHQ at least.'

Morris looked grave. 'Maybe they're down too.'

The thought hadn't occurred to Harry. Maybe this *was* a nuclear attack? He leaned on the conference table, his head bowed, his knuckles white as he gripped the edge. *Think*, Harry. If this was a nuke and Whitehall was the target, the devastation would be total. Yet there were survivors, and sirens, and shooting close by.

'You said this was a truck bomb, right sergeant?'

'Yes, sir.'

'So where is everyone? My people, yours, the fire brigade, ambulances? They should all be here!' Harry thumped his fist on the table.

Morris shrugged. 'Maybe they've evacuated elsewhere. What's the emergency protocol? If not here, where would you go?'

'I don't know!' Harry snapped. He searched the media screens for signs of life. Where was Sky News? The BBC? They couldn't be off the air, surely?

Running feet echoed along the corridor outside, and then Harry saw Brigadier Forsythe march into the room. He wore a helmet and a ballistic vest. In his hand, he held a pistol. Four heavily armed men in civilian clothes followed behind him and fanned out around the walls. One stayed near the door, watching the corridor.

The relief was so intense, Harry could've wept. 'Clive! Thank God—'

The brigadier ignored Harry and barked at Morris. 'Take your men and head back to the MOD. Your colleagues are waiting for you.'

Morris obeyed and led his team from the room. Harry didn't have time to thank him. 'What the hell's going on, Clive?'

Forsythe holstered his pistol. 'Here's what we know. At 6pm, terrorists launched a series of coordinated across the country—'

'What?'

Forsythe held up a hand. 'Just hear me out. All comms are down, which means the they got to the Critical National Infrastructure exchanges and control hubs, or some of them at least. Before comms dropped, I spoke with the commander at Aldershot garrison. It was brief, but he said there was shooting inside the camp. Senior staff had left for the day and the situation was chaotic. The line went dead seconds later. So, it's not just London. From the roof of the MOD, fires are visible right across the city, and civilian airliners have been shot down—'

'What?' Harry said again, unable to process what he was hearing.

'This is more than a terrorist incident, Prime Minister. I believe these are the first shots of a much wider conflict.'

Harry felt sick. 'Wider? You mean…are you talking about war?'

'Until we know for sure, we need to get you out of here.'

'And go where?' Harry said.

'Prime Minister—'

Harry cut him off. 'Let's dispense with the formalities. Harry's fine.'

Forsythe nodded. 'Very well. The plan now is to transport you to Alternate One, codename Northstar, an emergency command-and-control complex out west, beneath the Mendip Hills. It's an off-the-books facility, only to be used in situations such as this.'

'I've never heard of it.'

'No elected politician has, aside from the PM who had the foresight to anticipate such a crisis. And thank God she did. That secret has been kept in-house, on a strictly need-to-know basis. Now, you need to know.'

'So, how do we do this?' asked Harry.

'We travel light and fast, just you, me and your security team.' Forsythe gestured towards the soldiers behind him. 'These men are from Hereford's Counter Revolutionary Warfare wing. Close protection experts. They'll keep you safe.'

Harry glanced at them. They carried short-barrelled weapons and had pistols strapped to their bodies. He saw magazines and knives and ballistic vests. They looked dangerously capable, and that gave Harry some comfort. But that didn't solve the immediate problem.

'How do we get out of Whitehall?' Harry looked up as a deep, seismic rumble shook the walls and floor. Dust filled the air. Forsythe continued, his own eyes watching the ceiling.

'I'll explain as we go. Mike?'

One of the SAS team approached. His hair was longer than a soldier's should be, and dark stubble sprouted around his jaw and cheeks. He wore a black rain jacket and baggy green cargo pants, and he held his automatic weapon in his right hand, the barrel pointed to the ground. He walked with an easy stride, like he'd done this a hundred times. Not a glimpse of tension, not a bead a sweat. Just a calm, self-assured manner, one that Harry found both intimidating and comforting at the same time. Forsythe did the introductions.

'Harry, this is Mike Reynolds, your CP team leader.'

'Sir.' Reynolds held out his hand. Harry shook it, noting the tough skin and firm grip.

The soldier pointed to his comrades. 'Quick introductions, then. The big blond fella is Gaz Cole, and the nasty-looking redhead is Tony Brooks. Man by the door is Sherman. If they tell you to do something, do it, okay? It could save all our lives.'

'Of course.'

Forsythe headed for the door. 'Okay, let's get moving. Follow me, please.'

Harry followed him out into the corridor and the SAS team spread out on either side of him, watching the corridor in both directions. Forsythe stopped outside the generator room. Harry frowned.

'That's the emergency power room,' Harry explained. 'There's nothing in there.'

'Have you ever been inside?'

'No.'

Forsythe nodded. 'And why would you?'

He took a key from his pocket and unlocked the heavy steel door plastered with electrical warning signs. Once inside, Harry followed him down a shallow concrete ramp. Against the far wall stood four power generators, each about the size of an American-style refrigerator. Controls panels glowed on the face of each of them. A workbench stood against another wall littered with tools, oily rags, and rolls of coloured wire. Harry turned as the door slammed behind him and Reynolds and his team headed down the ramp.

'I've jammed the door, boss. The only way in is to blow it.'

Forsythe nodded. 'Good.' He turned to face Harry. 'This is where it gets interesting.'

Harry watched the brigadier pull a plastic card from his breast pocket. He examined it, then stabbed at the keypad of the second power generator. Harry stepped back as the bottom half of the unit hissed and swung inwards, revealing a dark crawl space.

'What's this?' Harry asked.

'Our escape route,' Forsythe told him. 'It's a short crawl of about twelve feet to the other side.' He pulled a torch from his kit, snapped it on, and disappeared inside the false panel. Seconds later, his voice echoed.

'Follow me, Harry!'

Harry got down on his hands and knees and crawled inside the power unit. On the other side, he got to his feet, slapping his hands clean, the coffee burns stinging. He'd forgotten all about them. The room was a small, grey concrete cube with a steel door in the opposite wall. A single bulb sunk into the ceiling threw weak yellow light into the tight space. After a few moments, Reynolds, Sherman, and Brooks made their way through, dusting themselves off on the other side.

'Gaz has got our six,' Reynolds said. 'He'll seal the hatch from the inside.'

'Roger.' Forsythe turned and used the same key to unlock the steel door. He tugged it and it screeched open. Cool air swirled around the room. Harry followed Forsythe out onto a wide metal gantry. He gripped the rail and looked down.

'I'll be damned.'

CHAPTER 26
DEEP SLEEPER

BY GOOD FORTUNE, HE'D MADE IT INTO THE DARK WOMB OF HIS ENEMY.

It had taken years of hard work and sacrifice to get to this point, plus a reservoir of strength he'd found deep within himself, but ultimately it was luck that put him on the Whitehall duty roster for this week.

To get here he'd suffered pain and humiliation, and many times it was only hate that had kept him going, but now that sacrifice had paid off. The war had begun, and he was here, in the belly of the beast, ready to inflict damage.

He stared at the back of Beecham's head as the PM gawked at the sight before him. It would be so easy to kill him where he stood. He could take out the brigadier, and if he was fast enough, Reynolds and Brooks, too. Cole would come running and he'd catch a bullet as he stepped onto the gantry.

All dead, including Beecham. Job done. But his role was more important than that of a mere assassin.

He reached inside his pocket and felt for the micro-transmitter, the one given to him a week ago by a nameless man in McDonalds on Tottenham Court Road. It was a state-of-the-art piece of kit, half the size of a credit card and almost as slim, but once activated, it would send out a certain signal on a certain frequency that was being monitored by his comrades.

The battery would last for 72 hours, which should be enough time for it to be located and triangulated. He would attempt to slip the transmitter into Beecham's clothing somehow, or at least stick close enough to him so his comrades could pinpoint his location.

But that strategy was risky because Forsythe might redeploy him. Or he could get injured, or even killed. Death didn't worry him, but failure did. So, he needed to attach it to Beecham's person.

It was the only way to ensure success.

He'd get his chance, of that he was certain, but when that chance presented itself, he had to move fast. The good news was, his true mission had begun, and he was already in play.

He glanced over his shoulder, beyond the open door, to the dark crawl space. Just beyond it, the first transmitter was already announcing its presence to the world.

Trooper Junior Sherman had every confidence that his people wouldn't be far behind.

CHAPTER 27
SANCTUARY

Dave Greenwood crouched behind a row of stinking wheelie bins, his heart beating so fast and loud, he imagined it echoed off the walls of the surrounding building.

He hoped everyone down in the OCC had the good sense to stay put, because leaving had proved almost lethal for Dave.

When he'd slammed open the door to the basement car park, he'd seen the wall of fire, he'd sucked the choking black smoke into his lungs, and he'd felt the wave of searing heat that had forced him backwards. He'd tripped and fallen on his backside. It had saved his life.

From out of the fire, a screaming figure, engulfed in flames, charged into the corridor. Dave couldn't tell if it was a man or a woman, glimpsing only hairless, blackened skin and bared teeth as it cannoned off the corridor walls.

Engulfed in flames that reached the ceiling, the human torch staggered past Dave and ran straight into Curran. His colleague's clothes caught fire, and he screamed, stumbling backwards, the blackened creature wrapped around him, as if locked in a macabre dance of flaming death. Curran hit the landing rail hard and disappeared over the top, dragging the human torch with him as they plummeted down the stairwell.

The scream echoed up the concrete chamber and then Dave heard the bone-crunching impact below. He ran to the rail and looked over, saw their bodies far below, motionless and burning.

Dave turned away, coughing violently as black smoke filled the corridor. The stairwell was acting like a chimney, sucking the noxious clouds inside, and he knew he had to act fast. He looked up and counted—four flights to street level.

He charged up the stairs and made it to the emergency exit, crashing through the door and falling to his knees. Thick black smoke chased him away, and he stumbled around the corner of the building, coughing, and spitting.

He heard gunfire close by, amplified by the surrounding buildings, and he scurried behind a row of coloured wheelie bins, crawling on hands and knees through foul-smelling puddles and stinking rubbish. His eyes streamed and his lungs hurt, and he took deep breaths to expunge the smoke and slow his heart rate.

He pulled his pistol from its holster. He heard a distant siren, but it soon faded away to nothing. His radio was full of static. He knew he had to move, try to establish comms with central command, find out what was going on and where the threat was coming from.

He had to find some friendlies too, and that would be inside Scotland Yard itself.

His chest still hurt, but he cuffed his eyes and got to his feet. Down in the OCC, his people needed help. He had to find someone from facilities, get the elevators working and evacuate everyone to the surface. He headed for the staff entrance around the back of the building.

The security door was closed, but with the power out, it opened when Dave yanked it. Inside, the corridor was empty. The security office to his right wasn't. There were two dead bodies lying on the floor, their white shirts stitched with bloody holes, their chairs toppled over. They were security guards, unarmed and easy prey for the infiltrators who must be inside the building.

Dave gripped his gun tighter as he headed towards the main reception. When he got there, he discovered more bodies, most of them by the main entrance.

Corpses piled on top of one another, as if they'd tried to escape all at once. Pools of blood and footprints stained the floor. Bullet holes peppered the glass entrance doors, and Dave saw the impacts were internal.

As he moved towards the reception desk, his boot kicked a brass casing, sending it skittering across the foyer. It was one of dozens scattered all around him.

Behind the desk, he saw the body of a young woman, another security guard, her head horribly swollen, her face a mask of blood and surrounded by a crimson puddle. He saw her chest rising and falling, but her eyes were sightless, and when Dave whispered to her to hang in there, she didn't respond.

Brain dead, Dave guessed. Without help, she wouldn't last more than a few more minutes. He reached up and checked the desk phone. Nothing. He checked his mobile again.

No Service.

The gunfire made him jump. It boomed above his head, on one of the upper floors. It was automatic fire, a long burst, which meant it was a bad guy.

Dave's mind was having trouble keeping up. This was a terror attack, no question, but on an unprecedented scale. The confused CCTV images that proceeded the power cut had everything to do with the current situation, but what frightened Dave was the sheer lack of response.

He kept low, scampering into the fire escape. Inside the stairwell he smelled smoke, but that was all, just the smell. The fire from the car park below was venting elsewhere, thank God.

He crept up to the first floor. If all this started at six pm, most of the civilian staff would've left for the day. But there would be shift workers and cleaners and maintenance staff moving around the building, and most of the duty cops would be unarmed and unable to defend themselves.

On the first-floor landing, Dave pushed the door open a crack and saw dead bodies along the carpeted corridor. Uniformed bodies, some of them senior officers.

Then he heard voices, shouting in a language Dave didn't

understand. He heard glass breaking, and he used the noise as cover to get into the corridor and work his way towards the voices. He saw shadows rise and fall across the carpet ahead.

The noise was coming from a room to his right. Judging by the rapid speech and accent, he guessed they were Middle Eastern. That worried Dave, because if these guys were terrorists, they wouldn't stop until they were dead. He counted the different voices. Three men, maybe four.

He was outnumbered and certainly outgunned.

He thought about backtracking, then changed his mind. Fuck these arseholes. He straightened up, took a breath, and stepped into the doorway.

A breeze blew through the smashed windows, and beyond them, Dave saw the black smoke from the car park fire rising into the air. The men were watching too, three of them, but what bothered him was their causal attitude. They weren't hyped-up, wild-eyed, active shooters. These scumbags appeared to have all the time in the world to carry out their murderous rampage.

Dave raised his gun and tracked the barrel left to right, shooting the first man in the back, then the next. The last guy spun around but his wounded colleague fell into him and dragged the barrel of his AK down as he fired. The sound was deafening. Dave shot him twice, and he too fell to the carpet.

Shooters two and three were dead. Number One was coughing blood and cursing. Dave stood over him, gun pointed at his face. He saw the hole in the man's white shirt, right in the middle of his back. He'd hit the shooter's spine, which was why he wasn't trying to get the gun out from under him. All he could do was cough and curse.

Dave was horrified, not by the man's injuries and obvious distress, but by the epaulettes on the shoulders of his uniform. A serving police officer. Dave didn't know him. Probably a desk jockey.

Dave jammed his gun into the man's cheek. 'How many of you are there?'

The man's eyes rolled and settled on Dave. 'Fuck you.'

'You want help? Start talking.'

'Fuck you. Shoot me.'

He coughed and spat blood. Dave heard a shout from outside and he ran to the broken window. Below him, he saw a column of armed men filing into the building. *What the hell was happening? Where was everyone?*

He jumped when he heard another rattle of automatic gunfire from above. Threats everywhere. Scotland Yard was compromised and there was nothing Dave could do about it. He had to get out, find help, a firearms team, anyone.

He ran back down the corridor.

When he got to the stairs, he heard shouting below. He charged down, then twisted beneath the staircase, hiding in the dark recess. The voices in the lobby got closer, then the stairwell door crashed open. Dave couldn't see them, but he heard their feet pounding the steps above him. He heard the screech of the first-floor door.

In a few moments, they'd see their dead colleagues and realise someone was fighting back. Dave stood no chance. He rolled out from beneath the staircase and headed back the way he'd come, through the rear entrance. Beyond it, the spiked security gate hung open, and Dave ducked through it just in time.

He flinched as the deafening report of an AK hammered the walls of the surrounding buildings, and he heard rounds pinging off the steel gate behind him. A second later, he rounded the corner and was gone.

He found himself in a passageway that led to Whitehall. When he got there, he stopped and peered around the corner. His jaw dropped open.

'Jesus Christ,' he whispered as his eyes registered the total devastation before him.

Instinctively, he looked across the road to Downing Street, and saw the giant crater marking the entrance. The security gates, the armed police, the corner buildings that flanked the narrow street, all of it was gone, destroyed, and a cracked main washed across the road.

The facades of the Cabinet and Foreign Office buildings were gone, revealing shattered interiors, and flames engulfed the upper floors of Number Ten, belching more smoke into the clear evening sky. Closer, the bomb—there was no doubt now—had sliced the Cenotaph in two and bodies lay everywhere, some horribly mutilated while others appeared unmarked, as if they were sleeping.

Scores of cars, buses, taxis, and delivery vans lay scattered across the road. Some burned, melting the tarmac beneath them, and spewing more smoke into the—

CRACK!

Brick dust blinded him as a bullet smashed off the wall close to his head.

Dave ran out into Whitehall seconds before a fusillade of bullets chewed up the alleyway behind him. He turned left and ran towards Parliament Square, guessing he was being hunted by the friends of the men he'd shot.

He cut into the road, vaulting a man's body, glimpsing a pale, bloody face, and an outstretched hand. There was nothing he could do. It was about his own survival now. He felt the heat from a burning police car ahead of him and he held his breath as he plunged into the curtain of smoke spewing from its broken windows.

Automatic fire thundered off the surrounding buildings and Dave ducked as bullets zipped and ricocheted all around him. Somehow, he survived the volley and turned the corner into Parliament Square. There was less damage here, but cars lay abandoned and broken glass littered the pavements.

Dave's arms pumped, and he forced himself to keep his knees high, even though his muscles screamed, and his lungs burned from smoke inhalation and exertion.

But Dave couldn't slow down. He imagined his pursuers to be younger, fitter, and better armed, and any moment now they would chop him down. Dave swerved across the road, weaving between abandoned cars. He would get to St. James's Park and lose himself in the trees and bushes, then make his way to Buckingham Palace.

There would be a security force there. There had to be.

The car hurtled along Birdcage Walk towards him, swerving around stationary vehicles like a joy rider. He saw gun barrels sticking out of the windows, and Dave knew the car spelled trouble.

Turning into Storey's Gate, he slowed, unable to push himself. He heard the screech of tyres, then doors opening and angry shouts. His odds of survival were shortening by the second. If he ran into trouble coming the other way, he was toast.

He thought of his wife Rebecca and prayed she was safely at home in Guildford. She was a smart and capable lady, but if she was watching the TV, copper's wife or not, she would go out of her mind. All Dave had to do was stay alive, and that meant finding somewhere to hole up until the cavalry arrived.

That would be the army, no doubt. There were some troops stationed in London, but Dave guessed this scenario hadn't been gamed out. They were probably massing somewhere, waiting for armoured vehicles and helicopters to support them.

Until then, he had to find somewhere to hide, and fast.

He turned into Queen Anne's Gate, a quiet, elegant street of tall, Regency period buildings. He ran for fifty yards, then ducked between two parked cars. Chest heaving, he scanned his surroundings.

The street was an oasis of calm and order. It was deserted, too, and that was good. All the houses had basements that were accessible from the street. If he had to, he could hide down one of them.

Dave checked his pistol. He'd fired five or six shots, he wasn't sure. He had another magazine of sixteen rounds, but that wouldn't help him against his pursuers.

He heard them now, spilling into the quiet street. What the hell was wrong with these guys? They must have better things to do than hunt a single man. What was their mission, their objectives? Or was this it? Detonate a massive bomb and wreak havoc afterwards. Kill as many people as they could before they were gunned down.

Dave hoped the latter would happen soon.

He held the Glock tight in his hand and lifted his head. Through the windows of the car, he saw the men fanning out across the street, some on the pavements, the rest in the road, all armed with black AKs.

They were moving methodically, their guns up, their eyes swivelling left and right. Dave's options were diminishing fast. He should run now, while they were still at the end of the street. But what lay around the corner ahead? Dave had no idea, but it was a reasonable assumption that there could be more terrorists—

The sound built from a mild rumble to a terrible thunder in

seconds, and Dave glimpsed a black shape streak low overhead, shaking the ground and triggering a dozen car alarms. The thunder roared again, louder, and two more shapes flashed above the street.

Dave took a breath and scrambled down the steps of the closest basement, swinging the gate shut behind him.

He eased himself down into the shadows, conscious of the voices above him growing louder and more excited. The planes were fighter jets, but as Dave wondered what they were doing, he heard a distant *boom*, and felt the ground tremble beneath his boots.

Either a plane had crashed close by, or they'd dropped bombs. The latter was unthinkable, but his unseen pursuers above seemed excited by the fly-by. Dave could hear them cheering and whooping. Perhaps they'd forgotten about him. Perhaps they would abandon their pursuit and move on.

Either way, Dave hid behind the steep stone steps and made himself as small as possible. There were pot plants all around him, and the red-tiled floor was neat and clean. The door to the basement apartment was gloss black and decorated with a large brass knocker, but no lights glowed inside. As the voices above him grew louder, Dave considered forcing the door.

That's when it opened.

An older gent beckoned him inside. Dave didn't need to be asked twice, and the man closed the door behind him.

The hallway was in shadow, and Dave retreated a few steps, listening as the shouts above faded. The older man turned to him, his snow-white hair parted to one side, his thin lips curled into a broad smile.

'At last, the police,' he said.

CHAPTER 28
DRIVE BY

AT SIX PM, FAZ AND HIS SURVEILLANCE TEAM WERE STILL IN BINFIELD Road, close to the scene of the shooting.

While they waited for an update on the whereabouts of Boxer, they watched several police cars and vans arrive in a screeching chorus of wails and lights.

Uniforms spread out across the road, stringing rolls of blue and white tape between lamp posts. A few yards away, Boxer's assailant lay dead in the gutter, covered with a white plastic sheet.

Beyond the cordon, the rush hour was well under way. At the junction of Clapham Road, traffic had slowed to a crawl as drivers rubber-necked to see what was going on. Commuters streaming from the tube station stopped to gather behind the police tape, taking photos and footage with their phones. Selfies too, Faz noticed. What was the world coming to?

'Boss?'

Faz saw Max approaching. 'What's up?'

'Check your radio. Looks like comms are down.'

Faz twisted the volume knob on the radio clipped on his belt. All he heard was static. He changed channels, but the static remained. He looked at Max and frowned. 'That can't be right—'

Gunfire rippled across the evening air. Not close, but not far either, and loud enough to cut through the muted roar of the traffic. 'Weapons,' Faz said, and they ran to the van. Kilo Three had already opened the lock-box and handed out the Glock 26 pistols. There were compact guns that packed a hefty 9mm punch but held only ten rounds because of their size. Max grabbed the police armbands and handed them out.

As Faz pulled his identifier on, he saw the firearms officers had taken cover behind their vehicles, eyes scanning the surrounding streets and traffic for the threat. The crowd at the cordon had scattered, leaving two bodies on the pavement, and Faz darted around the back of the van.

He peered back up the street towards the huge intersection at Clapham Road. Vehicles skidded to a halt, trying to avoid the panicked pedestrians as they scattered across the intersection like frightened deer. Car horns blew as the traffic backed up in all directions. A lot of the drivers wouldn't know what was happening, and that would lead to frustration and bad choices.

He saw two firearms officers crouched behind their BMW 4x4. 'Hey! Where's it coming from?'

The closest officer turned towards him. 'Somewhere up on the main road,' he said, tight-lipped. 'Just stay under cover. With any luck, he'll give his position away.'

Faz switched his attention back to the intersection. The bodies on the pavement were still there, but the earlier crowds had gone, scattered to the four winds. He figured commuters coming up from the tube were being held inside the station concourse, but that wouldn't last given the rush-hour tube traffic.

He watched as a double-decker bus edged out into the junction, its driver pulling around a stalled vehicle. Passengers on the upper deck were staring down at the confused scene below—

The bus disintegrated in a blinding flash, followed by an ear-splitting bang. Faz hit the ground as a wave of hot air rolled over the van and shrapnel pinged off its body. His ears rang as his mind tried to process what he'd just seen.

He pushed himself to his knees. The bus was no more, leaving behind a carcass of twisted metal and billowing black smoke. Other vehicles around it burned too, and debris covered the road and pavements. Faz saw blackened bodies still sitting in their seats.

As the ringing in his ears faded, he heard screaming and more sirens. Bodies lay everywhere, many of them dismembered.

Police officers ran towards the carnage. Shots rang out and two officers went down. Gun gripped in his hand, Faz still couldn't see where the threat was coming from, but he guessed the shooter was in a building somewhere up on Clapham Road overlooking the intersection.

One thing was certain, though. Boxer was involved. Him and many others. Faz didn't believe in coincidences, not in the intelligence game. This was a planned operation, but why here? Stockwell wasn't exactly a strategic target.

'See anything?' Max asked, scrambling next to him.

Faz shook his head without taking his eyes away from the burning bus. 'I saw two cops get hit.'

Max nodded. 'You think there might be another shooter?'

'Maybe.'

Kilo Three joined them, the Glock looking small in his hand. 'What's the plan, boss?'

Faz saw the police had dragged their wounded colleagues into cover. Shots rang out. It was time to go. 'Let's get back to HQ, regroup. We can't add any value here.'

'I'm on it.'

Max yanked open the van passenger and slid across to the driver's seat. He fired up the engine. Kilo Three took the comms seat in the back while Faz hopped over into the front.

Max pulled away, flicking on the blue and twos. Faz cringed, expecting rounds to hit the van, but then they turned a corner and cleared the immediate area. Now they were heading through the back streets towards Wandsworth Road. All around them, people had gathered on balconies and street corners.

'See that?' Max said, pointing through the windscreen.

Faz saw it, and his stomach churned. To the east, columns of smoke towered into the sky. 'What the hell is happening?'

'Whatever it is, it's on a scale we've never seen before.'

'Comms are still down,' Kilo Three reported.

'Don't stop for anything, Max.'

'Roger.'

Max weaved the vehicle through the backstreets until they reached Wandsworth Road, the major artery that would take them east towards Vauxhall. Max turned right, then slowed almost immediately.

'Shit! We've got trouble.'

The road ahead was a maze of abandoned cars, most of them with their doors flung open. Faz saw more bodies lying motionless on the ground. Beyond that, a petrol station was burning, the flames engulfing the overhead canopy. Beneath it, the inferno had reduced several vehicles to blackened shells. Faz didn't want to think about the body count.

'We can't sit here,' Kilo Three yelled. 'Move it, Max!'

Max turned to Faz. 'I can spin her around, head towards Battersea, take Chelsea Bridge.'

Before Faz could answer, something pinged off the bodywork.

'Jesus, we're taking fire! Go, Max! Boot it!'

The van roared forward, swerving past an abandoned car. Faz saw a figure ahead, leaning on the roof of an abandoned car. A male, mid-twenties, wearing a desert pattern combat jacket and black jeans. He was aiming an assault rifle right at them —

'Contact front!' Faz screamed, but it was too late. The windscreen exploded and rounds punched through the skin of the van.

Faz was already down, curled up in the footwell, the Glock still in his hand. The engine roared, and then the van collided with something, the impact knocking the wind out of Faz's lungs. The engine rattled, then died.

Max was dead too, the bullet wound visible in his skull, his eyes wide and lifeless. Faz heard footsteps approaching, and guessed it was the assailant's careful tread. Faz cocked his pistol and froze. He heard Kilo Three's breathing, the rustle of his clothing.

'Don't move,' Faz whispered. It was all he could think to say. He wasn't a soldier, and neither was Kilo Three. The smart thing to do was stay out of sight until they had a clear shot.

He heard glass crunch underfoot. The shooter was right outside and Faz pressed himself lower in the footwell. He'd never killed a man, but right now he'd do it in a heartbeat if he got the chance. He heard the scrape of a footfall, and the side door flew open.

The rifle rattled and Faz took his chance, throwing open his own door and falling to the ground. He raised the Glock, arm extended, and shot the assailant in the face. The shooter dropped his gun, his knees buckling as he folded to the ground.

Faz scrambled to his feet and crouched, scanning the immediate area. It was a maze of abandoned cars, and another shooter could get close without being seen. He kept his back to the van, head swivelling, then he peered in the side door, knowing what he'd find.

The floor was slick with blood, and bullet wounds stitched a ragged, bloody pattern from Kilo Three's neck to his groin. Faz turned away. He was on his own.

To the east, the garage fire roared, the flames fed by the underground tanks. Across the road, a sprawling housing estate stretched into the distance. That's when he saw a muzzle flash from the third-floor window of a scruffy council block. Automatic gunfire rattled, but it wasn't directed at Faz. No one was advancing towards him, ducking between abandoned cars, guns pointed his way.

The evening breeze picked up and smoke swirled across the road. Faz searched the corpse. No ID, no bank cards, no phone, nothing. But dead men could still be useful.

Faz holstered his pistol and picked up the man's weapon, a matte-black AK-15, 7.62 calibre assault rifle with a muzzle suppressor.

He'd fired Kalashnikovs several times during his training. Counter-terror officers had to be familiar with their adversaries' weapons, and the AK-15 was a globally exported model. This one also had a Vortex sight mounted on its top rail. This was hi-tech stuff, expensive. Where had it come from?

He unloaded and reloaded the gun and stripped the shooter of his two extra mags. The man was also wearing body armour, a black covert model, and Faz worked fast to strip it from his body and strap it beneath his hoodie.

Feeling better protected, he moved away from the van in a low crouch, using the smoke as cover. He paused behind an abandoned builder's van and took stock of his situation. His radio was still dead, and between him and the safety of Thames House was a minefield of anarchy and armed terrorists.

Heading east along Wandsworth Road could prove deadly. The gunmen in the tower blocks had the road covered and from their high elevation could pick off anyone foolish enough to attempt passage. No, he'd have to wait until dark. He checked his watch. That was in three to four hours.

He needed a bolt hole to stay off the streets.

A short distance away, he saw an alleyway between two storefronts. It might be a dead end, but then again, it may be just the hiding place he was looking for. He checked the street again. There was sporadic gunfire, but it was further up the road.

As if on cue, the wind shifted, drawing a curtain of smoke across the street. Faz used it as cover, running to the side of the road and ducking between two parked cars.

Keeping low, he checked the pavement in both directions. Empty. The alleyway ahead was book ended by an internet café and a storefront with steel shutters. The smoke drifted across the pavement. Faz held his breath and ducked into the alleyway.

It was narrow, about thirty feet long, with a wooden gate at the far end topped with razor wire. He tried the handle. Locked. He glanced up at the razor wire, all rusty but still a major hazard —

Two or three shots rang out. Faz spun around, raising the AK. Smoke obscured the end of the alleyway, and he imagined armed figures behind it, searching for him. Reaching over the top of the gate, he threaded his hand between the coils of razor wire and found a dead bolt on the other side. He eased it back, and the gate swung open. Faz closed it behind him and slammed the bolt home.

He found himself in a small backyard. Eight-foot walls surrounded him, and discarded building materials littered the yard. There was a door to his left that led into the rear of the steel-shuttered store, secured with nothing more than a small padlock.

Faz shouldered it open, splitting the wooden door. He stood motionless, listening. In the dim light, Faz noticed the freshly plastered walls, tins of paint, and lengths of timber. There was no glass frontage or door entrance, just a wide aluminium shutter separating the newly renovated store from the street outside. Light pierced the shutters, illuminating a billion drifting dust particles, and Faz breathed a little easier. The space would provide temporary shelter until darkness fell.

He barricaded the back gate with a couple of bags of plaster and wedged the broken door with a plastic chair. It wasn't perfect, but if someone tried to gain access to the rear of the shop, he'd know about it. He found a spot against a dry wall and lost himself in the shadows. All he could do now was wait for the sun to set.

But the darkness held its own dangers. Friendlies might open fire on the dark-skinned man with the assault rifle before he could identify himself as a British intelligence operative. And how far would he have to travel before he reached the security cordon? Because there had to be one, right? And was this happening elsewhere in the city? What about other major cities? Whatever was happening, it was coordinated, and that frightened Faz. He wouldn't be alone, though.

He thought about his girlfriend, Salma Nawaz, the bright, funny, and attractive legal secretary he'd met a few months ago.

Things had been going well, and they'd enjoyed several dates together. She lived near Brick Lane in an outrageously priced one-bedroom apartment, where Faz had spent the odd night sleeping on the couch. Salma wasn't one to rush things, and Faz respected her for that.

He wondered where she was at that moment. Still at work, probably, which meant she'd be able to see the fires from her office in the city. Faz tried to remember what floor Salma worked on. The 42nd, that was it. Or maybe she was at home, watching it on the news. He hoped so. He wondered if she was thinking of him, too.

She believed he was an IT consultant working at a dreary government department in Whitehall. How would she react if she saw him now, holed up in an empty shop with an automatic rifle across his lap?

For the first time that day, Faz managed a brief smile.

. . .

AT THAT PRECISE MOMENT, Salma Nawaz was pushing and clawing at the unyielding mass of shouting and screaming bodies that pressed her against the window on the 42nd floor of the Hanson building.

She screamed and heaved, but her voice was lost, and her body was too weak to free itself. And when she twisted her head and looked out over the city, she saw smoke and fire and that made everything worse.

A short time ago, she'd been working in the document room, one floor down from her desk at Lewison-Butler and Partners, the prestigious law firm where she worked. She'd been tapping at her keyboard when she thought she'd heard a scream.

At that point, her PC died, and the emergency lights stuttered on. She made her way outside and up the fire escape stairs. When she reached the 42nd floor, the first thing she noticed was all the desks were empty and every computer lifeless. Then she heard another scream and her skin crawled. What was happening? Everyone was crowding the floor-to-ceiling windows at the far side of the open-plan office.

She wanted to know what they were looking at, but her fear of heights tempered her curiosity. She steeled herself and marched towards them.

The entire office was looking east, and everyone was shouting and pointing. Some women were crying, and that frightened Salma. One older lady broke away from the crowd and bolted. Salma watched her cross the office and disappear down the stairs. She climbed onto a desk, looking out over the heads of the crowd.

Then she saw it.

A giant airliner circled the sky over east London, two of its engines trailing black smoke. Salma watched in horrified fascination as the aircraft turned towards them, and more people bolted for the stairs. Salma wanted to run too, but for reasons she couldn't explain, she didn't move, transfixed by the spectacle beyond the enormous windows.

Without thinking, Salma clambered off the desk and pushed her way to the window. The plane was an Airbus, a double-decked, 500-seater, and as it screamed over the city, she could see its wings dipping and swaying as flames and black smoke belched.

Salma knew the aircraft was dying, and she imagined what it would be like inside. Screaming, perhaps, or the silence of acceptance. As it approached, she could see the tail fin, shattered, blackened, and trailing ribbons of twisted aluminium.

The office darkened as the huge airliner filled the sky in front of the building. Salma screamed as it thundered past the windows, the wingtip barely fifty feet from the glass. In its wake, the entire building shook to its foundations. Pictures fell from the walls, and everything rattled violently. Salma held on to a crying woman as the floor trembled beneath her shoes.

As the tremor faded, Salma ran towards the west-facing windows. The aircraft's wings rose and fell, the engines still spewing black smoke and flames. She knew it was about to crash. It banked sharply to avoid another skyscraper, the turn so steep that Salma instinctively knew the pilots had lost control. It flipped over and nosedived towards the rooftops of the West End. Salma turned away, horrified.

She had to get out before fear overwhelmed her. Home, that's where she would go. Lock the door, pull the curtains, keep the TV off, until she could cope.

She ran towards the fire escape, then stopped her in her tracks. The rumbling thunder beyond the door grew louder with each passing second. Salma backed away. Then the door burst open, and scores of people spilled out into the office, yelling, and screaming, tumbling over desks, and sprawling onto the floor.

Salma saw a woman lose her footing and fall beneath the stampede. The woman tried to get up, but someone trod on her face and then someone else fell on top of her. Salma screamed as several gunshots exploded around the office.

A man cannoned into her, and she fell. Her head cracked against something hard, and her vision swam. She scrambled upright and fought to stay on her feet as the stampede swept her across the office. Then it halted, and the resulting crush squeezed the breath from her lungs.

Her vision blurred, and she felt a cool surface beneath her skin...

Glass.

Salma's eyes refocussed, and she found herself pinned against a window. She twisted her neck to see what was going on.

Over the heads of the crowd, she could see raised arms. She heard a gunshot, and people screamed. Salma screamed too. People pressed in around her, pushing her against the glass. She pushed back, screaming, crying, and that's when she heard it.

She turned towards the window, and her blood froze.

A small crack had appeared at the top of the huge glass pane and, as she watched, the jagged finger grew another few inches.

The plane, she thought. The near miss had rattled everything, weakened it somehow, and now the crush against the glass was making things worse.

Salma tried to turn her body, but the tightly packed crowd had trapped her. Her chest hurt and it was getting difficult to breathe. She looked again and saw the crack had worked its way down across the window, wider and deeper. Grey, powdery dust poured from the corner of the ceiling just above the window.

With every ounce of strength she possessed, Salma tried to wriggle her way out, but the wall of bodies had her trapped. Horrified, she watched small lumps of concrete break away and fall on people's heads.

The man next to her realised the danger and yelled for people to move. Others joined in and tried to push their way forward, shoving and punching their colleagues in front of them. Salma felt the pressure on her body ease, but then shots rang out and the crowd backed up again, slamming Salma against the glass.

She felt the window move.

She screamed as it tilted outwards and cool air whistled through the gap. Then it held fast, and Salma saw a single steel bolt holding the frame in place. A second later, she saw it bend and knew it was going to give way.

She sobbed and screamed, pushed and clawed at the surrounding bodies, but it was no use. The bolt was bent, and dust fell on her hair and shoulders. Salma coughed and spat and screamed and prayed, but none of it would save her.

The window ripped the bolt from the ceiling and twisted away.

Salma fell with it, and the wind rushed past her ears. She saw people falling through the air around her, saw their bodies tumbling, glimpsed their terrified faces, heard their cries and screams. Salma Nawaz screamed too.

Death waited five-hundred feet below.

It rushed up to meet her.

CHAPTER 29
FIRESTORM

Across Europe, confusion reigned.

Like Britain, other major European cities had experienced widespread power outages moments before hostilities commenced.

In city centres and surrounding suburbs, traffic-signalling systems suddenly failed, causing many accidents and huge jams. Subway systems, trams and trains glided to a halt, powerless.

For a few moments, people reacted in a manner typical of the long-suffering commuter. Many complained loudly about the state of the public transport system, while others merely shrugged their shoulders and took it in their stride. Some closed their eyes and settled into their seats or buried their noses in tablets, books and newspapers, resigned to the delay. Many reached for their mobile phones to call friends and loved ones and were puzzled by the lack of signal.

After several minutes, commuters packed inside stranded carriages began to feel uneasy. For others, trapped in subway tunnels deep underground, fear had already taken control as passengers clawed at doors, windows and each other to escape the claustrophobic blackness.

In residential suburbs across Europe, people tinkered with TVs, checked telephones and repeatedly flicked the switches of lifeless air-conditioning units and household appliances. Frustrated and confused, they joined their neighbours to shrug shoulders and complain light-heartedly about the sudden loss of power.

The comforting routine of everyday life had suddenly been turned upside down, but things would return to normal very soon, they reassured each other.

And then, without any warning at all, the chaos began.

CHAPTER 30
OPEN BORDERS

GEORGI MILANOV WOKE WITH A START. HE SAT UP IN HIS CHAIR AND rubbed his aching neck. His first-floor office was hot and stuffy, and a large, late lunch hadn't helped his energy levels. And today was a slow day too.

Not just slow, Milanov observed. It was practically dead.

He tapped his keyboard and checked the system again, but the figures on the screen were the same as they were before lunch. Since eight o'clock that morning, 244 Bulgarian-registered vehicles had crossed into Turkey. Only seven had crossed the other way.

Seven.

Milanov scratched his balding head. How was that possible? As senior customs officer, he'd supervised the busy Kapitan Andreevo border crossing for four years, a dry, rolling landscape bordered by Turkey to the east and Greece to the south, just beyond the Maritsa River.

But busy wasn't a word that applied today. Normally, hundreds of vehicles would pass daily in either direction, everything from articulated lorries to single mopeds. Every day, for the last four years.

Except today.

Milanov picked up his binoculars and walked to the window. He could see the Turkish customs post a mile further down the road.

Beyond the distant fences and barbed wire, the Islamic State flag hung like a wet rag above the roof of the administration building.

There was no queue of vehicles waiting to cross into Bulgaria, no long lines of trucks, no families taking a break in the car park. It was quiet, which was most unusual. Beyond the customs post, the ground rose up, and the road disappeared over a low rise. *What was going on behind those hills?* mused Milanov.

He was about to pick up the phone and call his district supervisor when he saw several vehicles heading towards Bulgarian territory. He scanned them with his binoculars and saw they were all Turkish-registered vehicles travelling in a loose convoy.

He picked up his phone and ordered his on-duty team to divert the convoy into the customs hall for checks. It wouldn't hurt to keep his people on their toes.

Milanov watched them as they climbed out of their vehicles. They were all men, no women, or kids, and mostly suited. Businessmen assumed Milanov. They emerged a few minutes later, climbed back into their vehicles, and continued into Bulgaria.

Milanov wondered where those seven Bulgarian vehicles had got to.

Just before eight pm, a coach with darkened windows crossed from Turkey into Bulgaria and rolled into the car park. Milanov watched the passengers disembark, stretching and rubbing their cramped limbs.

They looked like a football team, all dressed in the same black track suits, and he wondered where they were playing and whom. Milanov had always been a big soccer fan. He'd played regularly as a young man, and they'd told him he had potential, until a knee injury forced him to give up the game.

Now in his late forties, he was too old to play at all. *Too old and too fat*, his wife liked to remind him. She could talk.

Milanov studied the track suits as they filed into the customs hall beneath him. The younger ones were joshing around while the older guys—coaching staff, no doubt—were a little more serious.

They wore jackets and trousers but looked pretty fit too. Just before they disappeared out of view, Milanov saw one of the older guys reach inside his jacket.

As he did, two of the younger men turned to face the car park, their smiles gone and their eyes sweeping the area. As if they were searching for something. After a moment, they disappeared inside the building.

Milanov was an experienced customs officer, with a gift for sensing when something wasn't right. Many a smuggler had fallen foul of the Bulgarian's sixth sense. And now that sense was ringing alarm bells.

He slipped his cap onto his head and left his office. He would observe the group from behind the one-way glass in the main hall. If there was a problem, Georgi Milanov would spot it.

As he reached the door to the customs hall, it flew open, hitting him hard and sending him tumbling onto his backside. Several track suits rushed past him and pounded up the stairs. He heard shouting and glass breaking. Strong hands dragged him to his feet and bundled him into the customs hall.

There, a track suit spun him around and slammed him against a wall, binding his wrists with a tough plastic tie. That's when he noticed the new arrivals were all carrying weapons. The older guys had radios and one was talking rapid-fire Turkish. Milanov heard the words *objective* and *targets*.

He glanced to his right and saw the rest of his team similarly trussed, their noses against the wall, their pistol holsters empty. At that moment, Milanov believed terrorists had captured him, and his life would soon be over.

They herded the Bulgarians outside and made them sit on the car park asphalt. Milanov watched as several military trucks and tracked vehicles rumbled along the road towards his customs post, and his heart raced. Two of the vehicles were giant bulldozers, and Milanov had a terrible vision of a tracked monster veering towards them and crushing them into blood and meat.

Instead, the bulldozers flattened the fences and barriers, clearing the way for a convoy that was headed towards Bulgaria. As his colleagues muttered and cursed, Milanov watched a never-ending procession of tanks, armoured vehicles, and troop transports roll into the European Union unchallenged.

He felt anger, frustration, and shame, because there was nothing any of them could do but watch as an army invaded Bulgaria. Dust and noise filled the air, made even more terrifying by the flight of attack helicopters clattering across the sky into Bulgarian airspace.

Europe is at war with the Islamic State, Milanov realised. *How did that happen? Why didn't anyone see it coming? What were they doing in Sofia and Brussels? Were they asleep? Or were they involved?*

Milanov was a simple man, yet he also knew how the world worked. Politicians were out for themselves these days. Most of them could be bought off. Is that what happened here? Milanov didn't know, and doubted he'd ever find out.

But as hundreds of military vehicles rumbled into Bulgaria, Georgi Milanov knew one thing for certain.

If he lived to see another dawn, his life would never be the same.

CHAPTER 31
WAKE UP CALL

As the first shots echoed across grid-locked European cities, Islamic State missile batteries finished their pre-flight checks.

Satisfied that their birds were ready to take to wing, they waited impatiently for the launch order. Thankfully, they didn't have long to wait.

Launched from locations too many to count, hundreds of AGM-200C TSSAM Super Cruise missiles rocketed into the calm evening air.

The take-off points were varied; silos deep in the North African desert, trucks in the Bosnian Hills, assault ships in the Mediterranean, and IS military aircraft flying thousands of feet above that same sea.

After achieving initial thrust, their engines trimmed power and levelled off. Once they'd achieved flight stability, the missiles' targeting computers went to work.

Retrieving pre-loaded target data, advanced processor chips cross-referenced that data with on-board guidance systems and made the required course adjustments. At twelve feet long, the Super Cruise was smaller than its legendary big brother, but it packed a serious punch and was marginally more accurate.

As the missiles entered European airspace, the onboard computers switched to attack mode, adjusting their fins, and dropping altitude. Receiving continuous updates from their quad-GPS and terrain mapping systems, the birds avoided major obstacles while flying at low Mach numbers. Time-to-target was relatively short.

In southern Europe, the missiles answered the insistent calls of the targeting transponders planted at airbases, military headquarters buildings, communications centres, tank and armour sheds, early warning radar complexes, naval bases, and hundreds of other military facilities across the continent.

The front runners dipped their noses and dropped towards their targets, and the first detonations rippled across Europe, shattering the peace that its citizens had enjoyed for several decades.

And those political leaders who'd laboured under the hope that what they were witnessing was some strange power supply event, wondered no more.

The bombs were falling.

The firestorm had begun.

CHAPTER 32
FIGHTING FOR AIR

As political leaders scrambled for information, deep cover sleeper teams went to work, seizing transport control centres and blocking strategic road and rail intersections.

Assisted by embedded human assets, or through sheer surprise and deadly force, teams of armed men and women took control of Europe's vast road and rail network management hubs. Targeted motorways were blocked, and terrified motorists encouraged to leave at the nearest off-ramp, often by bursts of automatic fire.

No-one needed telling twice, not even the police patrols who found themselves cut off from their control centres and seriously outgunned. Many major road routes across Europe were cleared and secured. The IS advance teams were expecting traffic.

Lots of it.

Meanwhile, inside Europe's Air Traffic Control centres, more deep cover agents put their long-rehearsed plans into action as power cuts rolled across Europe's major cities. Emergency generators were sabotaged, and smoke flares thrown into empty rooms and stairwells, spreading panic amongst employees.

Buildings were evacuated, and air traffic responsibilities passed to other ATC centres and airports who found themselves in the grip of their own emergencies.

In most cases, operational personnel inside the ATC buildings followed SOPs and filed outside, where they gathered in car parks and other designated safe areas to await staff roll-calls, unaware their places were being taken by Forward Air Controllers of the Islamic State Air Force, men and women intimate with European air traffic control systems.

And now it was time to go to work.

The FACs settled into comfortable chairs, slipped on their comms headsets, and quickly absorbed the real-time flight information on the consoles in front of them. They had only one priority—clear the skies.

In the air, pilots listened to new instructions delivered by unfamiliar voices. Hundreds of civilian passenger aircraft were diverted to the nearest airport that could accommodate them. But it wasn't all plain sailing for the invaders.

On the ground, at the major airports of Paris, Lyon, Rome, Düsseldorf, Amsterdam and others, police and security units stood their ground and engaged the armed men and women who attacked passenger terminals and airport infrastructure with automatic weapons and grenades. Concourses ran with blood and terrified civilians scattered across roads and motorways to escape the carnage.

Outgunned and outnumbered, the police and security teams succumbed to the attackers, and one by one, the major airports were secured.

Runways and taxiways were cleared, and specialist teams stood ready to process the flights that were already airborne, awaiting the order to descend upon Europe.

CHAPTER 33
CITY OF LIGHTS AND DEATH

AT SEVEN PM, A SERIES OF CO-ORDINATED TERROR ATTACKS RIPPED through the streets of every major European city.

Army and civil militia units suddenly found themselves under assault in their own barracks while on the city streets, police officers screamed for backup over lifeless communications networks.

In the Spanish capital of Madrid, a huge bus-bomb detonated outside the high-security National Police Station on the Puerta Del Sol. As survivors staggered out of the smoke and rubble, fourteen IS commandos from the Libyan brigades opened fire from cover, cutting down anyone in uniform. When nearby Policia and Guardia Civil units responded, they found themselves thrust into a war zone for which most were unprepared.

Similar scenes were repeated across Europe, but in terms of violence, Paris was to suffer the most.

Several hundred sleeper agents had descended on the city centre throughout the day, travelling alone or in small teams from the bleak, soulless estates that ringed the French capital.

At seven pm, the orgy of violence began. Most of the perpetrators were Algerians, and history had taught them of the Paris massacre of their fellow countrymen and women in 1961 by the French police and security forces. Protesting at the strict curfews imposed on their community by the authorities, their Algerian forebears had organised a peaceful night-time march through the centre of Paris in defiance of those curfews, only to be met with unbridled police brutality. Many were beaten, shot, and garrotted to death while others were thrown into the fast-flowing River Seine.

Now, their descendants would have their revenge.

Every police and civil guard station in the city centre was attacked. In most cases, heavily armed teams took up positions around the target buildings and bombarded them with automatic weapons fire and rocket-propelled grenades.

In others, suicide bombers entered police stations under the pretence of reporting a crime, then detonated their devices. More sleepers went to work inside the army and Gendarmerie Nationale buildings. Guards were killed, keys were snatched, doors and gates unlocked, armouries raided, and human targets identified and killed. Anarchy engulfed the city.

The gunfire and explosions echoing across the centre of Paris could be seen and heard for many kilometres. From the balconies of crumbling tower blocks in the crime-ridden suburbs, the disenfranchised, dispossessed, and displaced residents that made up the lowest class of France's social order looked out across the city and saw pillars of black smoke and fireballs rolling up into the evening sky.

But for some, the spectacle did not fill them with fear. What they saw wasn't death, or carnage or chaos — they saw motive and opportunity. And they saw a chance to rage against a society that had cast them into concrete prisons, with poverty and despair as their ever-present jailers.

At first, they were just small groups, maybe ten or twenty youths, stoning panic-stricken motorists on the surrounding overpasses. Soon the numbers grew into hundreds and the hijackings began. Having escaped the horrors of Paris city centre, drivers and passengers found themselves running the gauntlet of violent mobs and were dragged from their vehicles and beaten.

Some were lucky enough to escape, their clothes in tatters and their bodies bruised and bloodied, but thankfully still alive.

Others were not so lucky.

Across the Seine, in the western suburb of Nanterre, two quick-thinking girls, both students at the Université Panthéon-Sorbonne, had seen the distant fires and decided to escape the city.

Their plan was to make for the forest of St Germain, where one of the girls had a relative. Dashing from room to room in their small apartment, they grabbed clothing, food, water, sleeping bags, and a dozen other items they thought might be needed.

In the garage beneath the apartment block, they piled into their tired Renault Clio and accelerated out on to the street, heading north to intercept the A14 trunk road that would take them out of the city.

The girls were terrified as other cars roared past them, the laws of the road no longer observed by a city infected with fear. They both screamed as a van overtook them, then watched in horror as it turned hard right at speed and rolled over, colliding with a shop front, and bursting into flames.

Instinctively, the driver turned left. She knew she was headed away from the motorway, but fear now dictated her actions.

The girls soon found themselves driving along a residential street where grimy apartment blocks and graffiti-daubed walls lined their route. They turned left and headed north again, the road leading them deeper into a maze of dilapidated streets. Smoke drifted on the evening air.

As they passed an avenue to their left, they saw cars burning fiercely across the middle of the road, and a single body lay motionless on the ground. The girls cried in fear, the driver accelerating and wrenching the wheel hard right, careering around another corner at fifty kilometres an hour, and ploughing into a thousand-strong mob marching on the city.

The driver screamed.

Bodies were tossed into the air, some knocked down like skittles, while others were caught under the front wheels and dragged along the ground, their limbs ripped and torn, their screams drowned by the roar of the scattering crowd.

The Renault shuddered to a halt, its bodywork battered and slick with blood, its front wheels lifted off the road by the screaming, moaning, writhing heap of bodies beneath its front wheels. In seconds the vehicle was swamped, the girls dragged out by their hair and clothes and beaten savagely.

Baying for revenge, the remainder of the crowd surged in.

In the minutes before they died, the girls were gang-raped on the tarmac by a frenzied, hate-filled mob. As the assaults continued, urged on by jeering hordes, a man pushed his way to the front of the crowd. He was tall, dark-skinned, and he wore a ballistic vest, a pistol in a military holster strapped to his right thigh.

The shouts and screams died away and a hush fell over those gathered around the vehicle. There was something about this man, an air of importance and conviction that commanded respect. He drew a short, curved knife from his belt, and without warning, cut the throats of each girl in quick succession. There was a stunned silence.

He closed their eyelids as blood pumped from their necks. Moments later they were dead.

The man sheathed his knife. For him, it wasn't an act of cruelty, but one of mercy. The mob had beaten the women, violated them. It was the behaviour of animals, but that was to be expected. The crowd had morphed into a single organism that had only one purpose—destruction.

So, for the time being the man would stay with them. He had their respect now, and they would do his bidding. He would direct them against the French security forces until they were defeated and IS controlled the city. Most would die, but that was not his concern. The Renault was set alight, and he strode to the front of the mob.

The pack had a leader now, a man who urged them onwards towards the centre of Paris, where the once-elegant and historic streets had become an arena of barbarism and death.

CHAPTER 34
THE ALAMO

'Mr Ambassador, pardon my French, sir, but you need to keep your fucking head down!'

Terry Fitzgerald, US Ambassador to the Court of St. James, lay face down in a corridor on the third floor of the embassy in south London, gasping beneath a pressing mound of camouflage and Kevlar.

He had been in the same position for roughly two minutes, and it was becoming extremely uncomfortable. He tried to wriggle free, but a Marine Gunnery Sergeant in full battle gear shoved Fitzgerald's head back down to the floor.

The ambassador had enough of being protected. He pushed back and struggled loose. As expected, the Marine sergeant—his name tag said *MENDES*—rounded on him.

'Keep your head down, Goddammit!'

Above the thump of explosions and the rattle of automatic gunfire shaking the floor beneath them, Fitzgerald had to shout to make himself heard.

'I can't just lay here! Give me a weapon! I can help!'

The ambassador could see Mendes considering the request. The kid would probably know that Fitzgerald was an Afghan War vet, a platoon commander with the 82nd Airborne in oh-nine. He might've read about the battlefield citation and the Purple Heart. Fitzgerald had seen some rough times. The kid would surely know that.

Come on, kid. Stop treating me like some desk-driving bureaucrat. Use your head.

Fitzgerald flinched as fist-sized holes punched through the walls further along the corridor. Someone outside the embassy had set up a large-calibre weapon and was busy raking the building, floor by floor.

Terrorists armed with automatic weapons and RPGs were pounding the Marines defending the embassy lobby, and it was for Goddam sure that any reaction force that might be racing to their rescue would be a dollar short and a day late.

The situation was already untenable.

If this was the day of his own reckoning, he'd go out fighting. That was the soldier in him talking. Fitzgerald the diplomat was trying to work out how things had fallen apart so quickly.

An hour earlier, he'd been working in his private office on the third floor of the embassy as he prepped notes before a dinner engagement with the British Prime Minister. As he typed, Fitzgerald knew that Harry Beecham would try to tap him up about America's economic bump that was only going to go one way—skyward. But it hadn't always been like that.

Foreign wars had cost a lot of blood and treasure, with little to show in return, unless you were a major stockholder in one of the many defence companies that had profited from those so-called endless wars. And when the Caliph Wazir had risen to power and expelled US troops from the region, it had marked a turning point in history.

Later, Fitzgerald had heard rumours of shadowy figures in State wanting to assassinate Wazir and plunge the Middle East back into bloodshed and turmoil. There was no profit in peace, everyone knew. But the assassination had never materialised.

As far as Fitzgerald was concerned, US interests within the caliphate should be commercial ones that benefited both countries. Two desert wars had shattered the lives of thousands of young

American men and women and their families, and meddling in the Middle East was ultimately costly and counterproductive. For everyone.

As he refocussed on his notes, Fitzgerald's PC suddenly died, and his desk lamp went out. He picked up the phone on his desk and that was dead too. He heard a tap on the door and Maggie, his private secretary, entered the room.

'Sir, we've had a power cut.'

'Is the entire building out?'

Before Maggie could answer, a low rumble shook the building, rattling the thick ballistic windows.

'What the hell was that?' Maggie said, her hand grabbing the edge of Fitzgerald's desk. Maggie was from California, but Fitzgerald knew the shaking was no earth tremor. That was an explosion.

'Maggie, get everyone down to the basement shelter, nice and orderly please. Where's my security chief?'

As he said the words, another blast shook the building, followed by a long burst of automatic fire. Fitzgerald marched Maggie into the outer office.

'Get everyone downstairs, right now. Go, Maggie!'

As his panic-stricken secretary bolted, three men in combat uniform marched into the outer office. Major Pete Vincenzo, head of the Marine Security Guard detachment, barked at him. 'Mr Ambassador! We need to get you to the shelter right now!'

'What the hell's happening?'

'Let's walk and talk.'

The two escorting Marines flanked Fitzgerald as they headed out into the corridor. He saw embassy staff heading into the stairwell and heard pounding feet echoing off its walls. The upper floors were being evacuated too. Good.

'A suicide bomber took out the Brit cops and punched a hole in the security fence,' Vincenzo told him. 'We've got at least fifty bad guys assaulting the building, some of them armed with RPGs, but there's no response from the Brit cops and we can't raise anyone on the horn. Communications are down across the board. Standing orders are to get you to a safe place. Right now, that's the basement shelter—'

'Stand fast!'

Fitzgerald spun around as a voice boomed along the corridor. He saw Ethan Katz, the resident Assistant Trade Secretary striding towards them. Fitzgerald knew Katz was really a CIA operative working under an assumed embassy cover. Beside Katz was another Marine, a Gunnery Sergeant. Katz stopped in front of them and addressed Vincenzo.

'Pete, I need to brief the ambassador about an off-site evac.'

Vincenzo winced. 'Not a good idea. SOPs say we hunker down in the basement.'

Katz shook his head. 'Not this time. I estimate at least a hundred shooters out there and they're closing in fast.'

Vincenzo frowned. 'A hundred now?'

'At least, so what I need is for you and your people to secure this building and slow them down. How many troops do you have?'

Fitzgerald noted the use of the phrase *slow them down*. Not *stop them*.

'Thirty,' Vincenzo reported. 'They're being issued weapons and ammo as we speak. Captain Eveland is organising the embassy defences.'

Katz nodded. 'Good. I'll take care of the ambassador from here. And I'll need another four guys for close protection. Send them upstairs as quickly as you can. I'll hang on to Gunny Mendes here, if you don't mind.'

Vincenzo answered in the affirmative and headed for the stairs. Outside, the gunfire sounded louder. Fitzgerald turned to Katz. 'I thought the threat board was clear.'

Katz lowered his voice. 'I've just had word from Langley.'

'I thought all comms were down.'

'Echelon is not wired into the local power grid. A flash message came through less than five minutes ago. IS land and air forces have invaded Greece and Bulgaria and IS naval assets have engaged targets in the Mediterranean. NORAD reports multiple missile launches originating from caliphate airspace and there have been power outages all over the European mainland.' He paused, then said, 'hold on to your hat, Terry. This looks like an invasion of Europe.'

'Impossible,' said Fitzgerald. 'Unless their annual war games—'

'We don't have time to speculate,' Katz told him. 'Your safety here cannot be guaranteed.'

'The basement is secure,' Fitzgerald argued. 'And besides, the cops must be on their way. We're in London for Chrissakes.'

Katz shook his head. 'Tell him, Mendes.'

The Gunnery-Sergeant looked and sounded rattled. 'I've been up on the roof, sir. We're under attack from all points of the compass. And I saw a plane, a big passenger jet, crash into the city. It was trailing smoke, like a missile had hit it—'

Katz cut him off. 'This thing is big, Terry. You're leaving this embassy.'

'But I—'

'No arguments. We can't afford another Addis Ababa.'

Fitzgerald remembered the incident well. When Ethiopian rebels staged a coup that plunged the country into civil war, the scenes at the US Embassy in the capital were reminiscent of Saigon. But not everyone got away.

Rebels shot down the last helicopter carrying the ambassador and his security detail. The bird came down just outside the embassy walls, and the survivors, including the ambassador, were hacked to death by machete-wielding rebels. The cell-phone footage went viral. Images that Fitzgerald would never forget.

'Point taken, but there's no way out, Ethan. Our only option is to stand fast.'

Before Katz could answer, the stairwell door flew open and four armed Marines hurried towards them. One of them carried a ballistic vest in his hand. Katz took it and handed it to Fitzgerald, who pulled it on. As he fixed the last Velcro strap in place, a massive explosion knocked them all off their feet.

Two more blasts followed it in quick succession. The detonations made Fitzgerald's ears ring and the air in the corridor filled with dust. Ceiling tiles lay shattered on the carpet and light fittings swung lazily above their heads. Katz pulled the sidearm from his belt clip and chambered a round.

'Is everyone okay? Any injuries?' shouted Mendes. There were groans and curses but no injuries.

Fitzgerald cringed as a large-calibre weapon began firing, puncturing the embassy's façade, and drilling holes the size of baseballs along the corridor walls. Fitzgerald wheezed as Mendes and his Marines piled on top of him.

'Give me a goddam weapon!' Fitzgerald yelled, but Katz shook his head.

'Forget it! You're leaving, right now—'

The building shook as two tremendous explosions detonated somewhere below them. There was more dust and more dislodged ceiling tiles. Fitzgerald heard people screaming. The sound of agony and death.

The Marines kicked away the debris. Fitzgerald touched his neck, and his fingers came back red. Mendes gave him a quick once-over and reported the wound was superficial. Another Marine had suffered a badly gashed cheekbone and was bleeding heavily. Katz slapped Mendes on the arm.

'Check out the northern staircase!'

Mendes and one of his team crawled through the debris towards the stairwell at the far end of the corridor.

'We're going up?' Fitzgerald asked.

'Yep.' Katz grabbed Fitzgerald and dragged him to his knees. 'Follow Mendes! Go!'

Fitzgerald dragged himself along on his elbows, the other Marines crawling around him. A burst of gunfire from the stairwell behind them spurred Fitzgerald on, and he felt naked without a gun in his hands. Ahead, he saw another Marine crawling towards them. Mendes recognised him.

'Jackson! What the hell are you doing here?'

'It's gone, Gunny, all of it—'

Mendes grabbed the kid by his arm. 'Slow down. What's gone?'

'The command post, Major Vincenzo, all of it. They're all dead. Now we got Hajis inside the perimeter.'

Fitzgerald heard a long rattle of gunfire behind him. He looked over his shoulder and saw more Marines piling through the doors. They vaulted over Fitzgerald and the others. One of them saw Mendes.

'Move! They're right on our ass!'

Katz grabbed Fitzgerald and dragged him up. 'Get to that stairwell, right now!'

Fitzgerald took off, caught in the middle of a stampede of uniforms. Someone outside must have spotted them, as rounds impacted the walls and ceiling. He heard the big gun again, the larger rounds getting closer, exploding plaster and brickwork in their path. Fitzgerald thought he was going to be hit at any moment. He heard a scream behind him and bodies hitting the floor. Then he was at the doors, charging through them to the safety of the stairwell. Katz followed, his breath ragged. He kept moving up the stairs.

'Let's go, Terry!'

Fitzgerald hesitated. The Marines should've made it by now. He crouched down and pushed open one of the stairwell doors. He saw Mendes and Jackson crawling towards him. Behind them, a mess of camouflage and raw meat. Blood was splashed all over the walls. *Poor bastards.* Fitzgerald held open the door and Mendes and Jackson scrambled through.

Katz yelled from the stairs. 'For Chrissakes, let's go!'

Fitzgerald helped Jackson up. Mendes was wiping blood from his face with the sleeve of his combat jacket. Both men had lost their helmets.

'Did you see it? Those rounds? They just chewed the guys up!'

Fitzgerald could see Mendes was traumatised. His uniform was stained with blood and his voice shook. Jackson stood immobile, pale as a ghost. Fitzgerald shoved him hard.

'Move! Both of you!'

By the time they reached the top floor, Fitzgerald was puffing. He looked around and saw he was standing on a small, enclosed landing. From up here, the sounds of the battle had faded a little. Katz led them through another two sets of double-doors, the last of which were labelled 'Maintenance Area' and secured with a heavy padlock and chain that Katz was busy unlocking. The CIA man spoke over his shoulder.

'Mendes, I'm gonna need you to buy us some time. Ten minutes at least. Can you do that?'

The Gunny nodded. 'We'll set up a perimeter a couple of floors down. But whatever you're doing, do it fast.' Mendes held out his hand. Katz grasped it. Everyone knew what it meant.

'Just keep 'em off our tails,' Katz said. 'I'll be down as soon as the ambassador is clear.'

Fitzgerald shook their hands too, and he watched the Marines push through the double doors and disappear. He felt nothing but admiration and sadness. He'd seen too many young men die, but he never thought it would happen here, in central London.

Katz unlocked the doors to the maintenance area and ushered Fitzgerald inside. The room was dark. He took a couple of steps and stopped. 'Ethan, I can't see a thing.'

'One second.'

He heard Katz scraping around in the darkness behind him. The next moment, lights flickered on around the walls.

'I thought we had no power,' observed Fitzgerald.

'You can thank a back-up generator and solar batteries. That's how I got the flash message. Wait here.'

Katz crossed the room to a computer terminal. As he tapped on the keyboard, Fitzgerald looked around. The ceiling was high, about twelve feet, and smooth. No overhead pipes or ducting here. A large steel tank dominated the room, and Fitzgerald assumed it was a water tank. Otherwise, the room was empty—

A green light suddenly blinked on a panel built into the side of the tank. Then a loud whirring noise filled the room. Katz hurried over.

'Follow me.' Katz pushed a small switch on the panel and a recessed hatch hissed open. He ducked his head and stepped inside. Fitzgerald followed. A moment later, the ambassador stopped dead.

'What the hell?'

The vehicle mounted on a steep ramp was slate-grey and looked like a small fighter jet, with two short, stubby wings and a tail fin decorated with black stars-and-stripes decals. Inside the plexiglass cockpit, multi-coloured displays showed the aircraft—because clearly that's what Fitzgerald was looking at—was drawing power. It was roughly twenty-feet long and pointed towards the ceiling.

'It's a Boeing Systems Evacuation Vehicle,' Katz said. 'One of only a dozen in the world. It was installed a couple of years ago. You remember the re-fit?'

Fitzgerald nodded. Gangs of hard-hatted technicians and workmen had invaded the top floor of the embassy for months. Fitzgerald was told it was part of the planned environmental systems upgrade. Air-con, heating, and suchlike. It happened right under nose too.

'The system is fully automated,' Katz told him. 'Flight controls, navigation, landing, everything. There's nothing to worry about. This thing is virtually indestructible.' He clapped Fitzgerald on the shoulder. 'Lose the vest and strap in. We don't have much time.'

'Wait a minute—'

'Now, Terry. Please.'

Fitzgerald relented, dropping the body armour to the floor. He stepped up on the ramp and climbed into the cockpit. Katz climbed up after him and leaned over, cinching Fitzgerald's harness tight. He pointed to the instrument panel, which comprised a series of high-definition, multi-coloured screens.

'That's your altimeter, your nav system, comms panel, and the TV screen is a forward-looking thermal and low-light camera. There's a compartment by your left leg. Inside there's bottled water, rations, a radio, survival kit, and a flare pistol. But don't worry, you won't need any of that.'

Fitzgerald had to ask. 'Where the hell will this thing take me?'

A series of explosions rumbled beneath their feet, followed by long bursts of automatic fire. It was muted but getting louder.

'Time to go, Terry. She's pre-programmed to fly you to a classified destination. Don't ask because I don't know. But don't worry. Eyes will be watching you.'

Fitzgerald shook his head. 'I feel like an asshole running out like this.'

Katz winked. 'If this was a two-seater, I'd be leaving with you.' He lowered the cockpit cover and locked it into place. Back on the ground, he held up a finger. 'Launch in one minute. Good luck.'

Fitzgerald gave him a thumbs up and Katz disappeared, the hatch hissing closed behind him. Fitzgerald braced himself for—what, exactly? He had no idea what was about to happen, other than this small aircraft might just save his life. But his only, and that didn't sit well with him.

He ran an eye over the display. Apart from the basics, he didn't have a clue what the readouts were telling him. The TV monitor was just an opaque square, probably because the nose camera pointed at the ceiling and—damn! The ceiling! What was he going to do, smash through it? Wouldn't that damage the craft?

He felt it vibrate and focused on the controls in front of him. On the upper right-hand corner of the display, he noticed a small digital countdown...*six, five, four—oh, Jesus.*

Fitzgerald gripped the wide arms of his seat. The craft was vibrating heavily now, like an Indy 500 car on the start line, being held back only by its brakes. He flinched as four sharp bangs detonated above his head and light flooded into the room.

Fitzgerald saw the rectangle of clear blue sky, saw the counter reach zero, and the craft shuddered on its launch ramp. Then it roared upwards, and Fitzgerald grunted as g-forces slammed him back into his seat. All he could see was the blue sky above and the control panel shaking violently in front of him.

The vibration faded, and the roaring noise settled to a low hum. The craft had finished its upward trajectory, and the nose titled down. He saw the expanse of west London laid out before him, and he gripped the arms of his seat as the aircraft levelled out again and increased speed.

Now the ground passed quickly beneath its tapered nose. Across the horizon, Fitzgerald saw columns of smoke and huge fires. Mendes was right. This wasn't localised to the embassy.

As the evac craft carried him to safety above the sprawl of west London, Fitzgerald's thoughts turned to the people he'd left behind.

KATZ COUGHED and spluttered as he exited the maintenance room, now filled with smoke from the solid-fuel booster rockets. Fitzgerald had got away. Mission accomplished. Before Katz left, he pulled his pistol and fired two rounds into the launch terminal.

As he stepped out onto the landing, the sounds of battle replaced the ringing in his ears. The stairwell beyond was filled with smoke and dust, and the deafening sound of gunfire reverberated around the walls.

When he reached the seventh floor, he saw Mendes' legs splayed out on the landing. The rest of him was lying prone behind an overturned filing cabinet, as he hammered mini-gun rounds down the corridor.

Jackson lay next to him, his skull oozing blood and brain matter, his eyes and mouth wide in sudden death.

'What have we got?' Katz asked, lying next to Mendes.

'Lots of bad guys. I'm making a dent, but any minute now they'll hit us with grenades and we ain't got no cover here.'

A heavy boom shook the floor above their heads. Dust filled the air.

'That's my trip-wire up on eight! Time to go!'

Mendes got to his knees and fired another long burst down the length of the corridor. As they climbed the stairs, Katz saw a figure on the landing above. He glimpsed beards and guns and opened fire over Mendes' shoulder.

Mendes was firing too, and then a grenade detonated, and Katz fell backwards down the steps. He screeched in pain as he felt something in his back snap, and then he rolled to a stop face down on the landing below.

Mendes, bloodied and blackened, crawled down the stairs towards him. Katz saw trails of blood behind him.

The young Hispanic crawled next to Katz and grimaced through bloody teeth. 'Took some shrapnel in my legs.' He winced, then pulled his Glock sidearm. 'Lost the mini-gun, too. How about you?'

'There's something wrong with my back—'

He heard shouts above and below, foreign tongues reverberating up and down the stairwell. The enemy closing in. 'But I guess it doesn't matter anymore.'

'Welcome to the Alamo,' Mendes said with a grim smile. The Marine pointed his pistol up the stairs. Katz heard running feet along the corridor, a stampede almost. They were closing in on all sides, unopposed.

'Here they come!' yelled Mendes. 'Let's fuck 'em up!'

Katz fired as a shadow loomed behind the corridor doors. He knew he was about to die, yet he felt no fear. Katz wasn't a church-goer, not anymore, but he was a believer, and that comforted him.

He emptied his magazine through the doors.

'Grenade!' Mendes barked, and Katz saw them bouncing down the stairs towards them, three, four, five grenades.

That would do the job.

'The Lord is my—'

CHAPTER 35
DEUTSCHLAND ÜBER ALLES

At 6:59 pm local time, an articulated truck rolled along the Bielefelder Strasse towards Normandy Barracks in Paderborn, the only significant British Army outpost in Germany.

The barracks were a remnant from the 1930s, when they were used to house and train Wehrmacht troops. Now it served as the HQ of British Army Germany. This impressive sounding moniker bore no resemblance to reality, for there was no longer any 'army' in Germany.

After the Second World War, the British had maintained a significant presence in the country, but where once its forces had numbered fifty-seven thousand, now there were only two hundred troops stationed in the entire country. But they remained a target.

Surrounded by walls and fences topped with razor wire, Normandy Barracks was a mixture of accommodation blocks, administration buildings, equipment stores, a petrol, oil and diesel compound, garage and maintenance sheds, and various ancillary buildings. There were four access gates, three of which were unmanned but heavily secured.

The fourth was the main gate on the Bielefelder Strasse itself, through which all vehicular and pedestrian traffic passed. At just before seven pm on a warm summer evening, traffic in and out of the camp was light.

The articulated truck approached from the north, rumbling along the Bielefelder Strasse, and slowing before the main gate. It turned into the camp and stopped in front of a heavy red and white pole manned by two British soldiers.

One of them climbed up onto the running board and asked the driver for identification whilst the other soldier walked along the side of the low-loader, tugging at the weatherproof tarpaulin lashed over what looked like several large crates. The driver passed over a fistful of paperwork to the other soldier, all of which was in German but clearly stamped with the legend 'Normandy Barracks'.

The soldier looked at the crumpled, greasy paperwork and decided that he didn't get paid enough to sort this kind of mess out. That privilege would fall on the shoulders of the duty NCO in the main guardhouse.

The soldier ordered the barrier raised and directed the driver to pull into the parking area just inside the main gate. He walked across to the guardroom, papers in hand, and the microsecond of bright light registered by the soldier's eyes was his last as the driver detonated the two-thousand-pound bomb lashed to the back of the truck. The white-hot flash disintegrated the guardroom and everything inside it. It also obliterated the camp gates, 50 meters of walls, trees, and fencing, and shattered every window in sight.

Of the truck, there was nothing left.

In the camp NAAFI, where off-duty soldiers were enjoying a beer, the blast knocked everyone off their feet, scattering tables and chairs.

When they got back up, coughing, and swearing, the barman produced a hidden weapon—an AK-12—and opened fire on his customers, killing over a dozen, before two Royal Engineers from 23 Amphibious Engineer Squadron tackled him from behind. The squaddies pinned him against the bar, the assault rifle trapped beneath the barman's body. One engineer grabbed a broken bottle of vodka and stabbed the barman in the face and neck until the man stopped screaming and bled out across the bar.

Then the engineer took his weapon and rallied the survivors outside. They had only moments to organise themselves.

Sirens wailed across the camp, and then the power failed, and the screeching died. Gunfire took its place, and men with guns targeted the unarmed British troops as they scattered across the camp, often running into fire as they rounded corners.

Inside buildings the carnage repeated itself, and soon the accommodation and admin blocks ran with blood as deep cover IS agents cut down anyone in sight. The POL point blew in a ball of orange flame and rained burning fuel over the vehicle sheds.

The engineer with the AK led the survivors from the NAAFI towards the camp armoury, but as he reached the main door, a young soldier emerging from the windowless building with a freshly issued weapon, saw the AK, panicked, and opened fire, killing the engineer and two others.

In the ensuing melee, an IS agent cut loose from the cover of a nearby building, killing three more Brits and wounding several others.

At the main gate, cars and vans filled with IS sleepers drove around the vast bomb crater and headed straight for the same armoury. When they got there, they ignored the wounded and helped themselves to the small arsenal of pistols, assault rifles, grenades, and thousands of rounds of ammunition. They would need all of it if they were to wrest control of the city from the German authorities.

The surviving British troops—now numbering less than twenty—realised they were incapable of stopping the carnage and fled, scaling walls and fences and melting into the surrounding streets.

Behind them, their comrades lay dead, and dying, scattered across a devastated camp that now burned fiercely, sending black smoke into the evening sky.

The last remaining British military outpost in Germany was no more.

CHAPTER 36
EYE OF THE STORM

THREE HOURS AFTER VIOLENCE AND TERROR GRIPPED EVERY MAJOR European city, the attacks stopped.

Sleeper teams and terrorist groups broke off their engagements and melted into the side streets, dragging their wounded with them, and leaving the dead where they lay.

The element of surprise had worked better than expected, and the attacks had curtailed the ability of military and police forces to respond effectively. Bases and barracks were smoking ruins, littered with dead bodies, and burning vehicles.

Those who survived tried to re-establish order amid the chaos, but it was too late. Power cuts and failed communications networks ensured the collapse of the command structure, and with it, any hope of a tactical response to what was now a conventional war on a huge front.

The safety and security enjoyed by Europeans for decades had evaporated. While civilians scanned the radio waves for news and updates, their leaders scuttled into emergency bunkers, unsure of what to do and unable to do anything.

Across Europe, Islamic State intelligence officers on the ground were faring much better. Reports coming in over military satellite networks confirmed that over sixty-five percent of military and government targets had been degraded successfully. Power and utility control centres had been captured intact and major motorway and high-speed rail routes secured.

Forward Air Controllers reported the skies were now clear of civilian traffic. Only Schiphol Airport in Holland had suffered major damage when a Japanese Airlines Dreamliner collided on take-off with a Fed-Ex cargo plane being remotely landed by the tower. Burning wreckage had severely damaged one of the main runways and several planes on the ground. For now, Schiphol would be out of service.

Meanwhile, contact reports were collated from each sector of operations and uplinked via UHF radio to the senior IS intelligence officer in Europe. He sent the encrypted data east via a military communications aircraft orbiting high above the Mediterranean Sea. The data was checked and confirmed—Europe was reeling, like a tired boxer against the ropes, bloodied and breathless. But still dangerous. Scattered enemy forces remained a threat if they could somehow regroup and reorganise.

To the east, Turkish airborne troops had landed in Austria, and grounds forces deep inside Greek and Bulgarian territory were pushing west. The war had been underway for three hours and it was time to commit the main body of IS forces.

The orders were encrypted and beamed to a thousand field commanders dotted across the caliphate. The messages were decoded and verified. The first shots had been fired, the first blows had been struck. Now it was time to finish the fight.

The order was given.

Invade.

CHAPTER 37
INVASION

THOUSANDS OF AIRCRAFT CIRCLING HIGH OVER NORTH AFRICA AND Turkey finally received the signal they'd been waiting for.

Following pre-planned flight paths, they dipped their wings and increased power, bringing their aircraft around onto new headings.

These were the pathfinder units, numbering tens of thousands of paratroopers, light infantry, armour, engineering, communications and intelligence troops. All had a multitude of tasks and objectives.

The key priority for the paratroopers was to secure the airfields, bridges, roads, railways, and other major transportation junctions and control centres, and relieve the sleeper teams that held them. In sticks of twenty, the planes trimmed their engines and began a slow descent towards the European mainland. Ahead of them, squadrons of IS Air Force fighter jets went to full afterburner, their Active Element Radars scanning the skies.

Above the Spanish mainland, six Typhoon Eurofighters of the Ejercito del Aire Espanol had made it airborne, although only three planes had working missile systems beneath their wings. The others had been in such a hurry to get away from their besieged airbase, the ground crews had no time to deploy their weapons.

Now they patrolled the skies above the city of Granada, desperately trying to contact a command network that was intermittent and filled with garbled messages. Below them, huge plumes of black smoke funnelled up into the evening sky as buildings burned across the city.

A few minutes ago, an unknown voice had ordered them to land their aircraft, without delay, at the civilian airport in Malaga. The suspicious pilots had refused. Instead, they watched the skies, and their instruments, for trouble.

And trouble was coming.

Approaching from the south, a flight of IS F-22 Raptors rumbled at low-level towards the Spanish mainland. Their threat detection systems alerted them to the Eurofighters, and each aircraft launched a single AIM-160 guided missile from its internal weapons bay. The missiles dropped from beneath the Raptors, falling twenty feet before the solid-fuel rocket motors ignited, accelerating the weapons to Mach 3.

The Spanish pilots, still watching the ground below them, saw their threat boards light up and heard alarms buzzing inside their helmets. Spanish lives ended abruptly, in a storm of shrapnel and shock waves, and three of the six Typhoons exploded in the sky before any of the pilots could identify the threat. Training, instinct, and faster reactions saved the lives of their comrades.

The survivors banked, climbed or dived towards the ground, punching out flares and chaff to distract the missiles. Now it was human skill versus ruthless supersonic technology.

The first fighter banked hard to the north and went to full afterburner. A missile caught him six seconds later and obliterated his fighter from the sky. The second pilot pulled back on his stick and pushed his thrusters to the stops, sending the plane into a near vertical climb.

At forty-eight thousand feet, just before the missile exploded behind his starboard wing, the pilot noticed his radar light up with multiple contacts to the south.

When he detected the incoming missiles, the survivor pilot threw his plane to port and headed for the deck. He levelled out a mere thirty feet above the jagged peaks of the Sierra Nevada mountains and continued southeast at fifteen hundred miles per hour, crossing the coastline above Roquetas de Mar at an altitude of fifty-two feet, breaking windows and dislodging hundreds of roof tiles.

Four kilometres out to sea, the chasing missile lost track and nosed into the blue waters of the Mediterranean.

Madre de Dios, that was close.

The pilot checked his threat display. There was something else out there—

He looked up and saw two Raptors dead ahead and closing fast. They banked left and right and thundered past his wings. The Typhoon shuddered violently as the Spaniard fought for control. He twisted around in his seat and carried out a visual check. Cannon fire had shredded his port wing and his wingtip ECM pod was gone. Hydraulic fluid gushed from the impact holes and his cockpit was filled with pulsing red lights and shrill alarms.

His crippled Eurofighter was dying beneath him.

He eased the aircraft into a shallow climb and steadied her as best he could. He reached down between his legs and yanked the ejection system handle, exploding his canopy upwards and firing him out of the cockpit. His flight seat fell away and his parachute deployed seconds later.

As he drifted down towards the blue waters three thousand feet below him, the pilot wondered how long it would be before someone picked him up. His emergency transponder was already transmitting, so it shouldn't be too long. Then maybe he would find out who Spain was at war with.

The pilot's question was answered sooner than he thought.

Five hundred feet above the surface, the parachute spun him around to face due south. Several kilometres distant, hundreds of ships of all shapes and sizes dotted the sea, their wakes clearly visible even as the sun dipped towards the horizon.

And they were all headed north.

The sea rushed up to meet him and he splashed down, the water around him staining with red marker dye. As he bobbed up and down on the surface, he saw a rib bouncing across the waves towards him. Well, at least he wouldn't drown.

As he watched the boat draw closer, he thought of his wife and daughter at home in Albaicin and wondered what was happening there. Nothing, he hoped. Perhaps he was dreaming. Perhaps he'd wake up any moment now, next to his sleeping wife and their newborn daughter. He'd get up, make coffee and sit on the terrace that overlooked the old Arab Quarter. And he would thank God, as he did every day, to have blessed him with such a life.

But this was no dream.

He heard the boat's engines wind down, and he braced himself. As the sleek, black rib slowed alongside him, the Spaniard looked up at the hard, unsmiling faces of the IS Marines. Gloved hands reached over and dragged him into the boat. The pilot stared down the barrel of a machine-pistol. At that moment, he doubted he'd ever see his family again.

IN NORTHERN EUROPE, a Russian naval task force carrying two spearhead formations of the 76th and 106th Guards Air Assault Divisions steamed for the German Baltic coast.

Dozens of helicopters flew ahead, sweeping in over the coastal town of Lubmin and landing behind the perimeter fences of the Nord Stream 2 pipeline facility and the nearby Peenemunde Airfield.

With frightening speed, the elite Russian troops seized both targets before calling up the waiting landing craft and armour. Within one hour of the first helicopter touching down on German soil, the Russian troops had secured all roads south and created a defensive perimeter that was quickly reinforced with more troops, light armour and logistics equipment.

As Russian transport planes began landing at Peenemunde, UAVs skimmed across the skies, watching for trouble. The whole of the peninsular—and the vital Nord Stream 2 pipeline—had been captured without a single shot being fired.

As the sun sunk to the west, Russian troops dug in and waited. Around them, water birds called from the surrounding marshes and estuaries, and insects buzzed and flitted through the warm air. Peace had returned to the coastal plains.

The Russians had little idea of what was happening elsewhere in

Germany, where larger towns and cities were under ferocious assault, where power, phones, internet, TV and radio had all failed, where terrified civilians cowered in their own homes as police and army installations came under brutal assault. Where bombs and gunfire rattled earth and shook the sky.

A land where terror reigned.

ON THE OUTSKIRTS OF NICOSIA, Greek-Cypriot farmers looked up in curiosity—and then disbelief—as waves of Turkish planes droned overhead and the sky filled with blossoming green canopies. Some ran for their farmhouses. Others stood and watched as Turkish paratroopers landed in the surrounding fields.

Some of those farmers had long memories and knew there was nothing they could do.

To the north, the invaders swallowed the Balkans, and the Italian ports of Bari, Pescara, and Ancona lay in the path of the advancing IS warships and troop transporters. On the Italian west coast, sleeper units hit the ports of Naples, Civitavecchia, and Livorno. They blockaded the port entrances and engaged Italian security forces with small arms, grenades, and rocket fire. Their mission was to hold the port for twelve hours. IS naval forces would arrive before then and secure the strategic targets.

Out at sea, flotillas of cargo ships carrying troops, supporting armour, and heavy weapons, changed course and steamed at full speed to their targets. As Europe reeled, blind and bloodied from the earlier attacks, organised opposition would be sporadic and disorganised.

SIXTEEN HUNDRED KILOMETRES south-west of Baghdad, inside a purpose-built command and control centre buried deep beneath the Jabal Sawda mountains, Caliph Mohammed Wazir studied the enormous digital screen that dominated one entire wall of the busy operations centre. He didn't speak, nor did he display any emotion as he absorbed the information generated by the tactical display.

Behind him, senior members of his Military High Command stood by and watched the same screen. Below them, on the main floor, scores of operators processed real-time battlefield information from the Theatre-wide Battlefield Information System.

Developed by the Chinese military, the system had gone live less than a year before. There were glitches, of course, but his technicians had assured him that T-BIS would give his forces the edge against the under-funded and complacent European armies. The credit-card sized digital GPS transponders, installed on almost every land, sea, and air military vehicle, would provide status information uplinked to a network of MILSPEC aircraft and low-earth orbit satellites using encrypted microburst technology, and relay that information to dozens of listening stations dotted all over the caliphate, from the North African coastline to Pakistan. If the situation changed on the battlefield, Wazir's Military High Command would know about it in real-time.

The caliph watched in silence as the military campaign played out across the vast map of Europe, a shifting, digital dance of blue, green, purple and red icons. The red symbols were European military formations and bases. Since hostilities began, over half had disappeared from the display.

'Things appear to be going well,' Wazir said.

'Better than we'd hoped,' one of his generals replied. 'The sleeper teams have struck a devastating blow, and the missiles took out a long list of potential problems. The EU, and their leaders, will struggle to talk to each other, never mind organise what's left of their military. By the time they do, our tanks will be parked on the Champs-Élysées.'

Wazir turned and faced the general. 'We need to own the skies. Especially in western Europe.'

The general pointed to the display. 'Airborne units have already landed in Austria, Spain and France with little opposition. In the next 24 hours, the east and western battle groups will link up and cut the Italian mainland in two. As far as Europe's capitals are concerned, they're in absolute chaos. Civilians are staying off the streets, not only to avoid us, but to steer clear of the mobs as well. When they're not looting, they're attacking their own security forces. Which plays well for us, of course.'

Wazir shook his head. 'Fighting each other, even as their world collapses around them. Fools. And what of the British?'

The general flicked through an iPad handed to him by an aide. 'Invasion forces are ashore and probing deeper into enemy territory. Airborne forces are crossing the English Channel as we speak. By morning, they should have secured their objectives. We have the momentum, caliph.'

Wazir nodded. 'For now,' he said, 'but we must be cautious. We must hold the territory we've taken. Reinforce at the earliest opportunity. Control their cities, their people.'

'It will be done,' the general said, nodding.

Wazir said nothing more. His words would be noted, and his commanders would act on those words, but they didn't ensure victory.

Yet he couldn't help feeling a shiver of excitement when he saw the might of the Islamic State, a superstate that he himself had built from nothing, swallowing vast swathes of the European continent.

CHAPTER 38
LONDON'S BURNING

Ross peered around the bedroom door and checked on Lara.

The sleeping pill had worked, and he'd calmed her down enough to convince her she needed rest. As he watched, she murmured something unintelligible and turned over. After a moment, she settled down again, and Ross closed the door.

The pill was one of his own, and he only used them when shift changes messed with his sleep. It was a mild dose, and Lara wouldn't be under too deep for too long, but it would give him time to find out what was going on out there.

Since he'd been inside Lara's apartment, the overriding sound Ross expected to hear were emergency vehicle sirens, as police, fire and ambulances made their way to the incidents outside his block and across the river. He expected to hear the chop of India 99 as it hovered overhead.

What he hadn't expected was a total lack of response and an unnatural silence, as if the city was holding its breath. His mobile phone was dead, and the land lines to the apartment block were down too. The power hadn't come back on, and what he thought was a terrible day was looking like something much worse.

He'd heard the odd siren, but they were distant, and after a while they stopped too. Ross didn't understand it. The worst terrorist atrocity the country had known and there'd been no response. The streets should be crawling with cops. Instead, nothing.

As for the crime scene outside, with every passing minute, it was getting contaminated. Ross had shot and killed three men, and though they were terrorists, the memory made him feel sick. He imagined himself standing in a dock charged with their murder, and that made him feel worse. Stranger things had happened.

And those bodies were still out there, lying on the road. Ross had pleaded with Lara to let him go outside, but she'd wrapped her arms around him and wouldn't let go. So he had to wait until she calmed down and the pill kicked in.

As she drifted off, she'd been oblivious to the shouts from the street outside, the roar of speeding cars, and most troubling of all, gunfire. And not just single shots. Ross heard long bursts from automatic weapons. He didn't know which direction it came from or how far away it was, but the sound rattled across the west London sky.

With Lara still sleeping, Ross decided it was time for a recce. He closed the apartment door and went out onto the darkened landing. Glock in hand, he headed downstairs, slow and quiet, until he reached the ground floor lobby. Through the glass entrance doors, he could see the busted up minivan and the bodies still lying on the road. Like them, the street appeared lifeless.

The sun was below the horizon now, and the sky was darkening fast, casting deep shadows. What a difference a few hours can make. He should've been sitting outside the pub right now, sipping a cold one on a first date with Lara. Instead, she was upstairs in her bullet-riddled apartment, and he'd seen an airliner blown out of the sky—

He stepped back into the shadows as light washed over the scene outside. A car was approaching. A patrol car, Ross hoped, but he stayed hidden anyway. Even if it was the cavalry, he knew they'd be operating on a hair-trigger.

The lights grew brighter, and he heard the low growl of a diesel engine. Ross saw a large, flat-bed truck, and he backed deeper into the shadows. The truck's windscreen and side windows were covered with wire mesh and a dozen armed men stood on the back, gun barrels sweeping the shadows.

The truck stopped with a loud hiss of brakes, and he watched some of the shooters jump down to the road. He heard voices, but the words were unintelligible. The men on the ground lifted the bodies and loaded them aboard the truck. Someone banged on the roof of the cab, and it pulled away. Ross waited until the sound of its engine was lost in the distance before venturing outside.

He stood in the building's shadow, listening for threats. He heard a baby crying somewhere, and far away, a siren. Across the street, most of the houses had their curtains drawn, and Ross guessed the occupants were lying low. Given what had happened, he didn't blame them. Planes shot down, trucks full of armed men and no police would do that to a person. Make them frightened to go out, to even peer around the curtains.

So London was under attack, and whoever was behind it had access to serious weaponry. A state player, and Ross knew there was only one with the balls to pull off something like this.

The street wouldn't offer any answers, only problems, so he returned to Lara's apartment. He crossed the living room, broken glass crunching underfoot, and looked out across the darkness of the river. Sheets of flame towered up into the sky, and Ross could see a hole where terraced housing once stood. But that's all he could see. He needed to get higher.

There was a hatch on the landing outside Lara's apartment. Ross used a chair to stand on and pulled himself up into the small maintenance room above. From there, a door led out onto the roof.

A breeze carried the smell of burning fuel and smoke across the river, and the fires painted the sky red. Ross looked east, towards the city, and a chill ran through his body.

Darkness cloaked the whole of London, punctured by fires clustered around the city. He turned full circle, and the picture was the same in every direction. Fire and darkness. On the elevated section of the M4 motorway, cars and trucks burned too—

His eye caught a movement, four or five dots of light approaching from the south-west. Aircraft, police or army, Ross didn't care. He needed to know that help was inbound, that the power would come kick back on, that people all over the city would get the help they needed.

The dots of light grew larger, and he heard a dull roar. They turned towards him, and Ross realised the aircraft were following the river. They flew closer, banking around to pass level with the apartment block—

Ross could barely believe his own eyes. Cruise missiles, flying in a 'V' formation, barely a hundred feet off the ground. They rumbled over the river, heading towards the city. He tracked their glowing exhausts until he lost sight of them, but Ross knew what was coming.

A minute later, white flashes lit up the sky to the east, followed by thunderclaps that rolled outwards across the capital. Ross stood rooted in shock. A missile attack, right here in London. He felt his stomach churn and his legs weaken.

This was no terror attack, he realised.

This was war.

CHAPTER 39
SOUTHAMPTON DOCKS

INSIDE HIS ARMOURED COMMAND VEHICLE, GENERAL UMAR AL-BITRUJI, Commander, Islamic State Invasion Forces (Britain), stood over the T-BIS console and watched the fast-moving red blips disappear from the screen.

'Direct hits, all five missiles,' reported an operator seated at the console. Al-Bitruji ignored the acknowledgement and turned his attention to his second-in-command, Colonel Hasan Farad, who was shuffling printed message reports.

'Resistance?'

'Light, disorganised. Their communications infrastructure has been disrupted and British forces are in disarray. Any resistance is localised. Cruise missiles have damaged their spy bases at GCHQ and Flyingdales, and sleeper teams have attacked all major military garrisons, resulting in many casualties and much damage.'

Al-Bitruji raised a thick eyebrow. 'And the bad news?'

'British tanks and assorted armour escaped from Tidworth garrison,' Farad told him. 'And several fighters at RAF Coningsby managed to get off the ground and engage our aircraft but denying them their airbases will force their hand. They'll run to the north.'

Farad shuffled some more message slips.

'We've seized the BBC studios in London and Manchester, as well as Sky TV in west London. Transmission of the pre-recorded radio message will begin soon, on DAB, FM, AM, and Medium Wave. So far, the plan seems to be working.'

'Famous last words,' Al-Bitruji muttered. 'I need a smoke.'

He jumped down from the multi-wheeled vehicle and lit a cigarette. Farad joined him, and together they walked past the long column of command vehicles parked in the shadows of a massive dockside warehouse. Nearby, in the darkness of a vast car park, an anti-aircraft vehicle hummed on auxiliary power, its launch tubes pointed at the black sky.

They climbed a metal staircase to the roof of the warehouse, where they had an unrestricted view over the dockyards. They watched in silence as huge container ships were unloaded under cover of darkness. The torches and coloured wands of logistics personnel looked like distant fireflies as they swarmed all over the dockside, and thousands of tonnes of equipment crammed the water's edge as cranes swung cargo nets back and forth.

Beyond the docks, unseen on the dark waters of the channel, many more ships waited at anchor to be unloaded.

Somebody should've thought about that, the general fretted. All those ships, heavy with military cargo, lined up in Southampton Water. What a lovely target. 'Let's hope none of those rogue fighter-bombers decide to come sniffing down here,' he said.

Farad shook his head. 'Given the depth of our air cover? Doubtful.'

'Would you stake your career on that, Hasan?' Al-Bitruji smiled in the darkness. 'I didn't think so.'

The general and his battle group had sailed from Port Said on the Egyptian coast three weeks ago, hidden inside a huge container ship that was now being unloaded a short distance away. From its cavernous hold, thousands of tons of military hardware were being delivered to shore before being checked off and mated with waiting crews.

Al-Bitruji watched an attack helicopter being craned onto the quayside, where air crews waited to tow it to the assembly area inside the warehouse below them. The scale of the operation was enormous, and Al-Bitruji was relieved that so far, they'd suffered no losses. But how long could it last? He flicked his cigarette over the rail.

'Let's go.'

Back inside the command vehicle, the general barked an order to his comms team. 'Get me the Chief Landing Officer.' Minutes later, a middle-aged man in blue camouflaged naval fatigues climbed into the back of the mobile command centre. Commodore Bayan threw up a smart salute.

'At your service, General Al-Bitruji.'

'There's a queue of ships out there in the channel. We need to unload faster before the enemy strikes. How long will it take?'

Bayan's gaze never wavered.

'Your spearhead battalions and their equipment are almost unloaded, general. One hour at the most. Space is tighter than we expected. However, the logistics crews are working well. My estimate? Three days before every ship in Southampton Water is unloaded and headed back to the Med. More ships are en route—'

'Slow them down and spread them out. We can't afford to have them all bunching up. Sunken ships and bomb-damaged docks could seriously hamper the invasion.'

'I understand,' the Commodore said.

'Work faster.' Al-Bitruji waved his hand and dismissed the commodore. The naval officer snapped out another smart salute and left the vehicle. Al-Bitruji turned to Farad. 'Where are the recce units?'

Farad consulted a T-BIS console. 'Holding station at the M3 and M27 junctions. The roads are empty.'

The general checked his watch. 'Give the order to advance in fifteen minutes and get the supporting units moving up to their jump-off points. Come on, let's go!'

The air inside the command vehicle buzzed with commands issued by the four seated operators. Farad checked every order issued and its corresponding confirmation signal on his portable T-BIS device.

Al-Bitruji's eyes were fixed on the system console and its 3D map of the surrounding area, which he tapped with an electronic pencil.

'Relocate seven SAM units at my marks and confirm full coverage on deployment. And double the security perimeter around the docks. I want this place sown up tighter than an ass's backside.'

Al-Bitruji stepped out of the vehicle and lit another cigarette. The stress was building, he knew that. There was so much at stake, and failure would be frowned upon, to put it mildly. A great gamble, that's what this was. In any conflict, military plans fell apart after the first shots were fired.

The invasion of Britain would be no different.

Farad stepped out and joined him, his eyes never leaving his hand-held T-BIS unit.

'All orders confirmed, general. Spearhead units are now headed towards their jump-off points. ETA, ten minutes.'

'Good. We should move too.'

As he was about to climb back into his command vehicle, the general stopped in his tracks. He walked a few steps away from the command vehicle, his head cocked to one side. Then he heard it again, a low drone high above his head. Next to him, Farad interrogated his device.

'That's the airborne assault element en route to their targets.'

Farad offered the device to the general. Across the screen, scores of blue icons marched slowly north-eastwards.

Each one represented an Airbus A400 tactical transport aircraft capable of carrying 180 paratroopers and their equipment. The general handed back the device. Overhead, at seventeen thousand feet, the invisible planes continued their journey, their turboprop engines throbbing in the moonlit sky.

'We're witnessing history being made,' Al-Bitruji said. 'Let's get the command element moving. As soon as a helicopter becomes available, get it to pick us up en route.'

'Yes, general.'

His 2IC tapped several instructions into T-BIS, and seconds later, Al-Bitruji watched the long line of armoured vehicles beside the warehouse roar into life in a cloud of white exhaust fumes. Armoured doors slammed shut and top hatches were thrown open as vehicle commanders waited for the order to move.

Al-Bitruji beckoned the commander of the lead vehicle. The multi-wheeled monster lurched out of line towards him and rocked to a halt a few feet away.

'Awaiting your orders, general,' shouted the vehicle commander.

Al-Bitruji raised his voice above the roar of the engines.

'Get ready to move. We're heading for London.'

CHAPTER 40
ATLANTIC WAVES

Twenty-two miles due west off the rugged coast of Portugal, the *USS California* carved through the unusually calm waters of the Atlantic Ocean, its sleek grey hull almost lost against the gathering dusk.

The 240-foot-long ship represented the new generation of Windward-class stealth surface craft that had been developed by the US Navy and the *California* was at the cutting edge of that technology.

Visually, the ship resembled a B-2 stealth bomber on water. Her main superstructure was wide and low-profile, with a curved bow that raked backwards and sloped away towards the rear of the vessel. The bridge was at the very front of the ship, its rounded superstructure jutting out over the water like the nose of an aircraft.

From its sides, two large 'wings' dipped towards the surface of the sea and gave the *California* its balance and buoyancy. There wasn't a single right-angle to her design, nothing that could give a potential enemy a radar return of any significance until the ship was well within missile range.

Like her airborne cousins, the *California* relied on her advanced covert technology to avoid detection and close in on her targets. There was only one open deck, a 30-foot-long covered gantry at the rear of the ship above the centre hull. Although a vessel of the United States Navy, the *California* was unusual because she wasn't made of steel.

Instead, she was constructed of a classified material that had all the buoyancy and flexibility of a fibre-glass boat but with the strength and ruggedness of Kevlar armour. Rumour had it that during sea trials, a prototype was driven onto rocks in shallow water at a speed of over ten knots.

The resulting damage comprised some broken crockery in the officers' wardroom and a broken arm on the bridge. The officer of the watch had simply not held on tightly enough.

She was small, at just over 22,000 tonnes, and stealthy—but her real weapon was her speed. Powered by four water-jet engines, a fully loaded *California* was capable of speeds of up to seventy-two knots on light to moderate swells. In heavy seas she was reduced to around thirty-five, but she was still the fastest naval surface craft of her type in the world—and classified Top Secret.

The Navy had gone to huge lengths to ensure that their stealth ship had remained a secret during development and trials. The *California* was equipped with SAMPSON radar, a system so sophisticated it could detect multiple naval and land-based missile launches from over the horizon whilst performing complex tracking tasks on an electronic platform that was almost undetectable.

She was fast, virtually invisible to other surface craft and submarines, and could search and track simultaneous targets at any point on the compass for over six-hundred miles.

Captain Frank Schelling and his 82-man crew were on a routine patrol and surveillance exercise, tracking an extended line of 12 merchantmen tooling northwards up the Portuguese coast at 18 knots.

Schelling had noted the convoy when it had first appeared on radar several hours earlier. He'd ordered the *California* to approach before loitering twenty miles from Cabo de Sao Vicente, the point where ships leaving the Mediterranean turned north into the busy shipping lanes towards the Bay of Biscay and the ports of northern Europe.

Fifteen feet beneath the bridge deck in the Combat Information Centre, Schelling's techs tracked the evenly spaced convoy as it turned northwards. On the display screen above the bridge's long, sloping windows, Shelling watched the feed from the *California's* LongBow low-light thermal imaging camera tracking the lead ship, a Chinamax bulk carrier. He noticed the target ship was observing blackout drills, which was unheard of for a cargo vessel—

A buzzer blared across the bridge.

One merchantman had just lit off an air-search radar. It made three quick sweeps of the sky before shutting down again. CIC confirmed the radar signature was a military set, high-power.

What the hell were merchies doing with military-spec radar sets? wondered Schelling. Moments later, the SAMPSON array began picking up traffic from the Med, missile launches and radar signatures, so many that the processing computers had to recycle just to keep track.

Schelling ran down to the CIC and saw a dark room lit up with flashing red console lights. The captain's first thought was the caliphate annual war games, always provocative but contained and predictable. This was something else. This was an electrical storm of radar signatures and missile tracks—real missiles—flying in the skies over the Mediterranean Sea.

And they were headed for the European mainland.

The first shots of a war, Schelling realised.

He took two paces and reached for the overhead PA mic. 'General quarters, general quarters, all hands to battle stations.' As he re-hooked the mic, a communications officer handed him to an incoming Eyes-Only flash traffic message. Schelling read it and whispered, 'Goddam.'

Back on the bridge, his crew had donned helmets and ballistic vests. 'Mr Andrews, break us off from the merchies and secure the ship for a high-speed run to this position.'

Schelling handed the message slip to his subordinate, who passed it on to the navigation officer. The young seaman punched the co-ordinates into the navigation computer system and received a green confirmation light on his display.

'Co-ordinates locked in and confirmed, sir.'

'Very good,' replied Lieutenant Andrews.

Schelling strapped himself into his bridge seat and slipped on a headset and mic. He watched his crew do the same. Andrews picked up a handset and dialled in to the ship's PA system.

'Bridge to crew, all hands secure for high-speed run.'

Fifty-four seconds later, Andrews reported the ship ready. On his command console, Schelling saw all lights were in the green and the ship was ready. The drilling of his crew was showing results—nearly seven seconds better than their previous attempt. Except this time it wasn't a drill.

'Mr Andrews, come about to course zero-one-zero degrees. Make your speed sixty knots.'

'Aye, aye, sir.'

Andrews repeated the order to the two pilots sitting below and forward of Schelling's chair, and the captain felt that familiar, gentle vibration as the *California* accelerated. He checked his display and saw they were approaching 30 knots. After fifteen months as commander, Schelling still felt the adrenaline pumping as he watched the sea racing faster and faster beneath the nose of the ship.

'Nav, status.'

To Schelling's right, the senior navigation officer, hunched over his multicoloured displays, spoke into his microphone.

'We'll clear the major shipping lanes in sixteen minutes. There's a fishing fleet twenty-six miles north of us, target count, twenty-two vessels, scattered configuration. Recommend course change, two degrees to port to clear their nets.'

'Make it so.'

Andrews hailed Schelling on his secure headset. Although only six feet away, he was also safely strapped into his own seat as the ship rocketed across the surface of the sea.

'What's happening, sir?' Andrews asked.

'Good knows. But those IS missile tracks were real and headed for Europe. This is a shooting war, Chuck. Officially, we're at DEFCON Three. We'll know more when we get on station.'

'Those coordinates. There's nothing there but empty sea.'

'It's a search and rescue mission. A man in the water. And we're to avoid all contact with other vessels, friendly or otherwise. Deadly force has been authorised.'

'Roger that.'

Schelling glanced at his second-in-command. By the dim light of the bridge, the younger man's face had paled.

CHAPTER 41
TICKET TO RIDE

Harry was sipping coffee in the kitchen when he heard his wife calling his name. It was coming from outside, so he stood up and crossed to the kitchen window.

Down in the devastated cul-de-sac, Harry saw Ellen, surrounded by her close-protection officers. David Fuller was there too, and they were all looking up at him, waving from a mound of rubble that filled Downing Street.

Harry was confused, because they were all covered in blood, and their clothes hung in charred strips from their bodies. They waved in silence, smiling, and Ellen's smile faded.

Then she screamed, long and loud, a terrible wail that cut through Harry's chest like a spear of ice—

'Harry?'

He bolted upright on the sofa, his shirt damp with sweat and his blanket tossed to one side. It took him several seconds to realise where he was. Brigadier Forsythe stood over him.

'Are you alright?'

Harry nodded, the sound of that scream still ringing in his subconscious. 'Yes, I'm fine. Just a dream.' The Brigadier handed him a bottle of water. Harry gulped it down. He plucked the damp shirt away from his chest. 'I need a change of clothes.'

'I think we can accommodate you there,' replied the Brigadier.

Harry wasn't surprised…

WHEN HE'D CRAWLED through the false panel in the generator room, he presumed—and feared—he'd be scrambling through small, dark tunnels for the next few hours. How wrong he'd been.

Instead, he'd stood on a steel gantry high above a huge cavern, the concrete floor at least thirty feet below him. Above his head, long-drop halogen lights illuminated small-gauge railway tracks that disappeared into the blackness of two wide tunnels in the far wall. An underground railway station, directly beneath Downing Street. Harry's shock was obvious.

Down on the platform, Harry inspected the tunnels and saw there were lit by blue LED lights recessed into the smooth walls. The tunnels headed off in different directions, and Harry wondered where they went. He turned around and saw a glass wall cut beneath the gantry.

'Quite a sight, isn't it?'

Harry turned and saw Forsythe and the SAS team watching him for a reaction. Harry nodded. 'Amazing. Shocking.'

'Yes, it's hard to imagine something like this could be built with no one upstairs knowing about it. Follow me, please.'

Beyond the glass, Harry discovered a high-tech control room with lots of unfamiliar equipment and several display panels mounted across the smooth concrete walls. Forsythe turned to Reynolds.

'Let's establish comms, please, Mike. Quick as you can.'

'Roger that.' Reynolds gestured to Cole, Sherman, and Brooks. 'You three recce the tunnels. Stay close, keep in range of your radios.'

The SAS men hurried off. Harry flopped into a chair. 'What the hell is this place?'

Forsythe rolled a chair over and sat opposite Harry. 'It's an emergency transport system, for use by a sitting Prime Minister, the Cabinet, and members of the Royal Family. They built it during the Crossrail project, when engineers were tunnelling all over central

London.' He pointed outside. 'Apparently, there's a tunnelling machine buried behind that wall. It was easier and cheaper to mothball it.'

'What about the tracks?' Harry asked him. 'Do they run all over the city?'

'The left track turns due east and connects to Buckingham Palace,' Forsythe explained. 'There's a smaller platform facility there, beneath the rear gardens. From there it turns north-east and terminates near Kensington Palace. Access to ground level is via a staircase leading to a disused but very secure Royal Parks Police office. The other tunnel tees into an old Northern Line spur and goes to a government document storage depot in north London. From there, it's a short drive to Northolt.'

'Is that how we're getting to this Northstar facility?'

'Not until we know what the situation is up there,' Forsythe said, pointing to the ceiling. 'When we do, it'll be by helicopter, from Kensington Gardens or Northolt. Once we establish comms, we'll know more.'

'What about my ministers? The Cabinet?'

'An emergency message was sent to the contact list. How many of them received it is another question.'

'Are you saying I'm the only one left?'

'We'll know more when we get to Northstar.'

That's if we make it there, Harry fretted, thinking about downed airliners and surface-to-air weapons. But what choice did he have? The sooner he was back in the driving seat, the better he would feel. Losing control made him feel redundant, and thoughts of Ellen threatened to swamp him.

He stared at the dark tunnels, their curved walls dotted with small blue lights. He wasn't looking forward to entering them, but at least they would spare him the horrors on the surface. 'How is all this powered?' he asked Forsythe.

'Solar batteries fed from rooftop arrays in Whitehall. Although the power requirement is low, the batteries won't last long, especially when we use the transport cars. None of us want to be down here when the lights go out, which is why we need to establish comms and get moving.' Forsythe stood up. 'Let's go next door. Speak to Mike.'

Harry followed him into the adjacent comms room. On a large central table were several telephones, computers, and military-spec radios. Reynolds, headphones clamped over his ears, was stepping through radio frequencies.

Across the table, Sherman, Brooks, and Cole had returned from their patrol and were thumbing through directories and punching telephone numbers. Reynolds looked up as Forsythe entered.

'Anything?' inquired the Brigadier.

Reynolds shook his head. 'Everything's still down and Northstar isn't responding. I'm scanning civilian and military frequencies too, but I'm running up against a lot of encrypted traffic. Not ours,' he added.

'Anything from Northwood?'

Reynolds shook his head. 'Negative.'

Harry swallowed. Northwood was home to five operational HQs: Strategic Command, Standing Joint Force, Permanent Joint Headquarters, Allied Maritime Command, and the Royal Navy's Maritime Operations Centre. If they were unreachable, the situation was worse than serious.

'Keep trying,' Forsythe told him.

Harry stepped back into the control room. Forsythe followed and closed the door. 'How can everything fail so badly?' Harry asked him. 'Aren't there backup networks?'

'I can only assume our enemies have struck from the inside, too.'

'Spies?' Harry said. 'That can't be possible. Not on this scale—' He heard a low rumble and felt a tremor through the concrete floor.

Forsythe glanced at the ceiling. 'There's no time for debate, Harry. You might be the only senior government figure left, and the priority is to get you to safety. That means we need to contact Northstar, so in the meantime, I suggest you take the opportunity to catch your breath. Follow me, please.'

The galley kitchenette had fresh running water, a small electric hob and boxes of canned and dried goods stacked high along one wall. Forsythe opened the cupboards. 'There's tea and coffee here, and some powdered milk. Next door is a lounge with a sofa and blankets in the cupboard. There's nothing you can do until we speak to the outside world, so you should rest while you can. We must get the word out that the Prime Minister is alive and well.'

'If there's one thing I hate, it's being useless.'

'Understood.'

Forsythe left and Harry wandered into the adjacent rest room. He grabbed a blanket from the cupboard and slumped onto the sofa, kicking off his shoes. Maybe a nap wasn't such a bad idea.

He'd never felt as drained as he did right now, and he'd certainly had a bad day. But others had fared far worse. Terrorist attacks, planes shot down over the city, gunfire around Whitehall—it was a nightmare.

He thought of Ellen then, and it took some effort to force the image of her face from his mind. He had to focus on something else. Like how this started.

What had caused this upheaval? A diplomatic incident, maybe? No, he'd know about it. Unless Cooper was keeping something under his hat. And those surveillance targets all disappearing at once. That was the key to what had happened since.

Wazir is behind this, Harry's gut told him. It was the only theory that made sense, but the implications were overwhelming.

He closed his eyes, his energy spent, both physically and emotionally. The adrenaline that had pumped through his body for the last few hours dissipated. His mind drifted.

And in his dreams, Ellen screamed for her life.

THE RADIO HISSED AND STUTTERED, then a cold, clipped, English voice echoed around the room:

'This is an emergency broadcast. Do not leave your homes or workplace. Lock all doors and keep away from the windows. Conserve food and water. Do not use your mobile or landline telephones. Some areas of the country are experiencing power outages. Do not be alarmed. Unplug all electrical appliances until power is restored. Stay tuned to this frequency. This has been a government broadcast.'

'It's really happening,' said Forsythe.

THE SHOWER WAS TEPID, but it helped flush the nightmare away.

Harry also felt a little more energetic. He towelled himself dry and dressed in fresh clothes from the storeroom next door. He wasn't sure that a green t-shirt and multi-patterned combat uniform was fitting attire for a Prime Minister, but they were an improvement on his shredded trousers and bloodied, sweat-stained shirt.

Feeling a little better, he walked into the comms room, but no one looked twice at his uniform. He was about to speak when Forsythe held up his hand for silence.

Reynolds was speaking into his headset. 'Roger, Northstar. Next transmission in three-zero minutes. Out.' He slipped off his headset.

'What's going on?' asked Harry.

'Northstar is up and running,' Forsythe said.

'Thank God,' Harry said. 'Does that mean we're getting out of here?'

'There's been a development,' Forsythe told him. 'We found something on the civilian network. Mike?'

Reynolds offered Harry his headset. Harry clamped one to his ear. At first, all he could hear was the hiss of empty ether. Then:

'This is an emergency broadcast....'

Harry slipped off the headset. 'That's not the official UK emergency warning broadcast.'

'It's broadcasting on every frequency in the FM and Medium Wave bands. Anybody with a working radio will hear it.' Forsythe said. 'This feels more like a coup. Chopping the head off the government and minimising civilian interference. Makes it easier for the enemy to move around without people running around the streets.'

Harry was speechless. *A coup?* Before he could find anything to say, the Brigadier continued.

'Northstar has filled in a few blanks. As suspected, someone went after the Critical National Infrastructure exchanges and control hubs. Before the network failed, operators recorded a storm of garbled messages that swamped the networks. Shootings at various military bases, a truck bomb at Catterick Garrison, attacks on police stations and dockyards...'

Forsythe paused. 'Two civilian airliners were shot down over the capital, one in west London and one near Tottenham Court Road. And the power is out everywhere. This is a planned strike, Harry. No doubt.'

Harry dropped into a wheelie chair and ran a hand through his still-damp grey hair. 'What else?'

'Northstar thinks this the start of a full-scale military invasion.'

'Wazir,' Harry said.

Forsythe nodded. 'That's the current consensus.'

Harry was having trouble understanding how they'd got here. Relations with the caliphate were amicable, never cosy, but always respectful. And Cooper had made good progress on the diplomatic front. Yes, their annual war games were always a little provocative, and this year was their biggest ever—

Of course, it was. Now it all made sense. Or was starting to, at least. 'Who's in charge at Northstar?'

'Major-General Julian Bashford is co-coordinating the military response. There are several key personnel there, plus one or two government people, and the facility is secure. General Bashford has ordered all military personnel still functioning to head west, or north to Scotland, whichever's closest, but that message is being broadcast in clear because of the disruption to our networks. The situation is chaotic.'

'So, what's the plan?'

'We're taking the westbound tunnel to Kensington Gardens. Once we're there, we'll see what Northstar has planned for us. Mike?'

Reynolds took his cue and turned to Sherman and Brooks. 'You two, recce the foot tunnel for another exit, in case we get bumped on our way to Kensington—'

'Wait, there's a foot tunnel?' Harry asked.

Forsythe shook his head. 'It connects to a disused tube station at Swiss Cottage, but like the other train tunnel, it's heading in the wrong direction. It might also be compromised. But we need an escape route if things go bad.'

Sherman and Brooks hurried from the room. Reynolds was giving orders to the blond-haired soldier, Cole.

'Head upstairs and cover our six. Any sign of trouble, get your arse back down here, sharpish.'

As Cole climbed the metal stairs to the gantry, Harry followed Forsythe and Reynolds into the glass-walled control room. Reynolds took a folder from a cupboard beneath the control desk and sat down. Forsythe stood and watched, arms folded. Harry joined him.

'What's he doing?'

'Powering up the train. It sits somewhere up the tunnel between the stations.'

Reynolds flipped a page in the folder and smoothed it out with his hand. 'Right, here we go, then. Driving a train. Easy-peasy.' He ran a finger down its plastic-coated page. 'Step one, open power conductors one, two and three…'

CHAPTER 42
ASSAULT & BATTERY

The planes approached from the south-west at 230 miles per hour. Fifteen miles from their target, they descended to six-hundred feet and reduced their airspeed.

In the lead aircraft the Jumpmaster, listening to the aircrew instructions inside his headset, thumbed the rubber button, bathing the cargo bay in red light.

The airborne troops packed inside the aircraft struggled to their feet beneath the weight of their battle-order equipment. He knew they were glad to be standing after a flight of nearly six hours.

The Jumpmaster was relieved too. Their journey was almost at an end, and no one enjoyed flying inside a fat, heavy transport plane in a combat zone.

He watched the paras stretch their limbs and carry out final equipment checks. He gave an order to his own team, and the night air whistled around the cargo bay as the huge tailgate of the A400 transport plane lowered on hydraulic arms and locked into its jump position.

Tethered to his aircraft, the Jumpmaster walked to the edge of the ramp and looked down. He'd never been to the UK, and now he was seeing London for the first time, a landscape of dark rooftops, empty streets and occasional fires whipping below the low-flying aircraft.

He checked the skies and saw the black shadows of the other aircraft in their trailing formation. Ten aircraft flying in two sticks of five planes just under two miles apart, carrying a mixture of paratroopers, light armoured vehicles, and jeeps.

There were hundreds of other aircraft in the sky that night, all heading for various targets across southern England and the Midlands. Their job was to secure and protect the airfields, to clear the runways and provide safe air corridors for the rest of the invasion force.

Yet the Jumpmaster knew they were vulnerable, despite the intelligence that told them enemy air activity was negligible. He knew there would be rogue fighters out there looking for targets. Or troops on the ground, angry and armed with SAMs, determined to fight back against the invaders. All the Jumpmaster could hope for was a successful drop and an uneventful journey back to North Africa.

His headset hissed. The captain reported empty skies above the drop zones, and the Jumpmaster went to work, running through the pre-jump checklist with his crew. The paras stood in long lines, ready to drop from the ramp and fuselage doors, their eyes watching for the green indicator light.

Those closest to the ramp watched the ground rushing below them, but the Jumpmaster saw no fear in those hard eyes. They were ready, and for a moment, he envied them. But that didn't last long. Far better to die in the air than in the mud and blood of a foreign battlefield.

He heard the captain's voice inside his helmet. The Jumpmaster stood in the middle of the ramp and held up his gloved hands: *Ten seconds.*

The aircraft remained steady, and the cargo bay turned from red to green. At that moment, the paras didn't hesitate, streaming past him on either side of the ramp and stepping off, before being plucked away into the night sky.

When the last man had exited the aircraft, the Jumpmaster watched his team run the equipment pallets off the ramp and out into the night. When the cargo bay was empty, he radioed the captain and reported a successful deployment.

The ramp was raised and locked into position. He felt the plane turn and climb, its nose swinging around to the south, and he felt a flutter of relief.

There was still a long way to go, but the hard part was over.

BEHIND AND BELOW THE JUMPMASTER, hundreds of paratroopers floated to the ground inside the permitter fence of Heathrow Airport on the outskirts of west London.

On hitting the tarmac, the paras released their harnesses and dumped their chutes into scattered piles. They formed up into their respective units and raced towards their pre-arranged rendezvous points.

Within 30 minutes of the first boots on the ground, all five terminal buildings at Heathrow had been secured. Elsewhere, the airports at Gatwick, Stanstead, Luton, and Birmingham were captured without major incident. Combat engineer elements went to work, sweeping the runways clear for the main invasion force.

Minutes after that confirmation transmission, transport planes and their fighter escorts began lifting off from military bases dotted across the caliphate's Mediterranean coastline.

THERE WERE four other planes in the sky that night, pushing deeper into London.

Each Airbus A400 was carrying a detachment of specialist Pathfinders, the best of the caliphate's airborne forces. Over the dark suburbs of London, the four transports swept in low towards their target, jinking up and down, left, and right, as they thundered over the fires raging in central London.

The planes dropped from six-hundred feet to two hundred, the optimum height the paras would drop from. This was to be the first real-world mission using the airborne forces' low-deployment system developed two years before. Each para had trained continuously for the last three months, the aircrews even longer.

Precision flying was called for and with it, no small amount of courage.

The drop zone was the Mall, the wide, tree-lined avenue that ran from the front gates of Buckingham Palace to Admiralty Arch at Trafalgar Square, a ceremonial route used by British royalty for the last two centuries.

At almost two kilometres long and fifty metres wide, it was going to be the quickest and tightest jump any of them had ever made, but the paras were well-trained, and the mission was a vital one.

The risk was acceptable.

With two miles to go, the planes bounced up and down in the roiled air over South Kensington and then banked left to avoid a huge fire at Victoria Station. The pilots lined up on their target, raised their flaps and eased back their throttles.

One by one, the transport planes thundered over the roof of Buckingham Palace.

Inside the cargo bays, green lights blinked on—

He was first out of the lead aircraft, as he should be.

His chute deployed above him with a loud *crack*, and its layered ram-air configuration stopped his rapid descent towards the ground with a few metres to spare. He stepped on to the road and unhooked his harness before racing towards the cover of St. James' Park.

In less than sixty seconds, all four hundred of General Mousa's men had made it to the ground and were moving through the shadows towards Horseguards Parade.

Behind them, the only evidence of their arrival was the faint hum of the departing transports and the rustle of hundreds of discarded parachutes, as a gentle night breeze swept along the deserted Mall.

Squadron-Leader Bob Heywood searched for a target for his remaining AIM-120 air-to-air missile, slung beneath the port wing of his F-18 Hornet fighter jet.

He had one kill under his belt, an enemy fighter that had blown his wingman out of the sky before either aircraft reacted. What had started out as a standard training mission over the Thames estuary had turned into a fight that had already claimed the lives of most of his squadron and half of his ground crew at RAF Mildenhall in Suffolk.

The attack had started at six pm, when a car bomb exploded at the main gate. Then there were armed men inside the wire, attacking buildings and personnel with automatic weapons and grenades.

As luck would have it, a company of RAF Regiment soldiers had been queuing up outside the armoury after returning from a live-fire exercise at the Thetford Forest training area. The soldiers helped themselves to fresh ammunition and deployed to counter the threat.

As the battle raged, Heywood and his wingman had leapt aboard their aircraft, firing up the F-18s twin General Electric turbofan engines and rolling out to the taxiway. They were airborne less than a minute later. As they circled the base at low altitude, they saw black smoke and aircraft burning in their hardened shelters.

When Heywood and his wingman gained height and extended their search patterns, it was clear that RAF Mildenhall wasn't the only target.

The two British fighters pressed on towards the capital, drawn by the smoke that smudged the evening sky over London. Thirty miles out, Heywood's threat receiver lit up and an audible alarm shrilled through his headset.

Before he could react, his wingman disappeared in a ball of orange flame. Heywood banked his fighter hard over as a missile streaked beneath his port wing. He dived for the ground on full afterburner, desperately firing chaff pods in his wake, then located his attacker, a single aircraft seven miles behind him.

After shutting down his electronic warfare systems, he banked fifty feet above a small village and headed for his attacker. He powered up his systems, targeted the enemy fighter with a single sweep of his radar, and launched one of his two missiles. Seconds later, the enemy plane was blotted out of the sky, spiralling down to the ground in a fiery arc that ended with a ball of flame in a distant field.

Since that kill—his first live one—Heywood had refuelled back at Mildenhall, but rearming was impossible. The base munitions dump had also been hit and was still burning. The Group Captain told Heywood that they were abandoning Mildenhall and regrouping in

Scotland, because they were under attack by a foreign power. That had shocked the pilot.

But before they would head north, the Group Captain gave Heywood a mission—recce the situation in London, then head back to Mildenhall.

A minute later, Heywood was back in the air.

HE BANKED HIS PLANE, bringing the nose around to head due south over London.

In normal times, London shimmered from the air, a carpet of a billion lights. Now it was a surreal sight. The city below him was covered in a sheet of darkness and dotted with countless fires.

He cruised at an altitude of nine-hundred feet, his air-search radar shut down to avoid announcing his presence to enemy fighters. Only his threat receiver was fully active, and this was his third pass over London without a target.

And Bob Heywood desperately wanted a target.

He watched the ground below. On the Edgware Road, Paddington Green police station was burning like a Roman candle. The darkness of Hyde Park slipped under the nose of his fighter as Heywood mentally mapped out his route - head for Whitehall, check for distress signals, flares, anything that may show that there were VIP survivors down there, then follow the Thames east to Tilbury, then north-eastwards back to Mildenhall.

Straightforward enough, but he certainly wouldn't feel safe until his wheels hit the runway—

His radar lit up.

Four targets had suddenly appeared a mile in front of him, as if they'd lifted off from the streets of London, which was impossible because they were A400s, and now they were climbing for altitude.

So, they'd been dropping something, men, equipment perhaps, and their IFF transponders screamed enemy. Heywood lit up the lead aircraft with his targeting radar and thumbed the launch button of his one remaining missile.

It would be an easy kill.

· · ·

Inside the lead A400, the captain was reflecting on the success of the parachute drop on The Mall when his co-pilot shouted in alarm and his threat receiver board flashed red.

The other three aircraft in the formation were already firing off chaff and IR flares.

The captain stayed low and pushed his throttles to the stops.

Heywood swore in frustration as his computer registered a missile launch failure. He advanced his throttles and chased the slow-moving transport planes, winding up his 20mm cannon.

They were flying low and slow and in a nice, tight formation.

Perfect.

Carter Whitman was losing the battle to keep his wife calm.

For over three hours, they'd been trapped inside a Perspex capsule high over the Thames and she was slowly coming apart. Carter hadn't wanted to take a ride on the London Eye, but his wife had promised to stream the visit to the folks back home, live, and uncut. And good ol' Carter would be there too, smiling like a dummy for the camera and waving to her super-sized clan back in South Carolina.

How he regretted coming on the trip, but his wife had talked him into it and Carter went along with her, as he always did.

So, he'd paid over the odds for the tickets and queued with the rest of the tourist sheep, squeezing into a stuffy Perspex bubble that creaked and groaned its way to the top.

Carter liked England, and he loved all the castles and old buildings and the sheer history of the place. He'd made the trip across the Atlantic many times, but since his retirement, he thought he'd seen the last of London.

The city had changed a lot since his first trip decades ago. Now it was scruffy and noisy, and no one seemed to speak English anymore.

Everywhere he turned, there was some demonstration or other, and van-loads of cops occupied every street around Whitehall.

There was an air of... what? Carter didn't know, but it smelled like trouble. An unease on the streets. Or maybe it was his own paranoia. Either way, he couldn't wait to fly back to California, but his wife had insisted on a last spin around the London Eye.

Then the rusting iron ring had popped a cog or something. Great. Carter looked down at the ground where a crowd had gathered and several of the lower capsules were being evacuated. Of all the goddam luck. Couldn't have crapped out when Carter Whitman's shitty capsule was near the bottom. Oh no, had to be here, right at the summit, four-hundred feet above the river.

He'd forced a grin for his frightened wife and contemplated a couple of hours in a packed, sweaty capsule overlooking the dirtiest, most expensive capital city in the western world.

But then came the explosions. They'd seen some, like the one that detonated across the river in Whitehall. Carter had seen the smoke and debris spiralling into the air above the rooftops, and the shock wave had run through the Eye to their capsule.

That had frightened Carter. Others around him screamed. Then they'd heard the gunfire, and Carter knew they were all in serious trouble.

As they stood stranded above the embankment, smoke drifted across the canopy, obscuring their vision. Night fell, and people moaned and sobbed around him, including his wife. Nobody had come to their aid. No police, no fire department, nothing.

Down on the streets, it was anarchy.

All Carter could do was hold his wife and tell her everything was going to be alright.

'ENEMY AIRCRAFT! SEVEN O'CLOCK.'

The captain in the lead A400 was about to order evasive action when two hundred rounds of explosive ammunition ripped through the skin of the fuselage and detonated around the cockpit in a shower of sparks, blood, and flesh.

With both pilots dead and its flight controls shattered, the huge transport aircraft lurched to the left and lost height rapidly. Behind it, the pilot of the second aircraft flinched as the laser-like tracer rounds appeared from nowhere, shredding the plane in front of him. He also banked to the left.

That was his first mistake. His second was to increase power as he craned his neck and scanned the night sky over his port wing.

As the lead plane stalled, the pilot of the second aircraft punched through its tail fin, destroying his cockpit on the starboard side. The lead A400 military transport, its tail disintegrated, nose-dived towards the huge steel wheel below.

CARTER HEARD a thunderous ripping sound and saw the tracers flying over their heads.

He couldn't comprehend what was happening, but he knew it was all about survival now. The capsule rocked as people around him panicked, screaming, and pushing, hammering on the Perspex walls of the bubble in sheer terror.

He saw the sparks and flames in the sky above them, and in the blackness, the roar of aircraft engines and the sound of screaming metal grew louder. Then he saw it, a huge, burning aircraft headed straight for their capsule.

Carter spun his wife around so she wouldn't see. He held her tight and whispered words of comfort while inside he raged. Their lives were about to end here, now, in a dirty, piss-stained plastic box instead of their beachside home in Santa Barbara that they both loved so much.

The air was filled with the screams of dying engines and doomed humans. The sky above him blazed. Carter Whitman squeezed his eyes shut and kissed his wife on the cheek.

His last thought was of the cool, blue waters of the Pacific Ocean.

HEYWOOD FLINCHED as he watched the falling aircraft crash into the London eye, its propellers shearing off and scything through the passenger pods.

The remaining wreckage deflected off the attraction and hurtled to the ground, severing the steel backstay cables, and exploding in a massive fireball. An enormous sheet of flame blossomed around the giant A-frame supports, engulfing the London Eye in thick smoke.

Heywood turned away and banked his fighter around. One down, one damaged, two to go.

The remaining transports had broken right and headed south on full power. Heywood closed the gap, the targets bright in his head-up display. Just as he was about to squeeze the trigger, he stopped himself. If he fired now, he could send both planes crashing into residential areas south of the river. He could kill hundreds, not just the aircrews in the transports.

He swore and brought his F-18 around. There was still a wounded transport out there.

As he headed back towards the Thames, Heywood didn't see the London Eye, now blackened and twisted, and with half its capsules shattered or missing.

It swayed drunkenly on its massive steel feet, tipping the occupants of shattered pods to their deaths. Some hit the water far below, while others cannoned off the structure and disappeared into the flames. But the destruction wasn't over.

The Eye had stood on the south bank of the Thames for decades, and in that time, the river had ebbed and flowed and seeped through the walls of the riverbank, soaking into the deep foundation piles. Far below the embankment pavement, the compression foundation was slowly being reclaimed by the ancient waters of the Thames.

The remaining backstay cables sheared away from the structure, and, for a few moments, the gigantic wheel just stood there, swaying. Beneath its feet, water erosion and the impact of the aircraft combined to fracture several piles at once. Without its retaining cables, a pendulum effect built up, and the Eye rocked back and forth.

Seconds later, the huge bolts broke free from their crumbling concrete housings and sent four hundred tons of steel toppling into the dark waters of the Thames.

· · ·

'Come on! Pull up, you bitch!'

The captain of the second transport gripped the control yoke with all his might, fighting the dying plane around him. When he'd punched through the tail of his flight-leader's plane, he'd increased power and tried to gain height, activating the fire-suppression systems as alarm buzzers screamed inside what was left of the cockpit.

The co-pilot was gone, along with his seat and a whole swathe of instruments. Sparks fizzed and spat from severed power cables, and his own instruments were covered in a thin film of hydraulic fluid. He banked the plane around, desperately trying to gain height. He needed a few hundred feet, that was all. Just enough to bail out.

But he needed a few seconds of level flight to grab the chute beneath his seat and get it on, and the plane wasn't cooperating. She wouldn't last much longer, he knew that.

The plane rumbled due east, directly above the Thames. Two of the plane's engines coughed and spluttered, and the captain eased back on the yoke, the wind screaming around him. He thought about jumping into the river without a chute, but the thought horrified him.

Ahead, the twin columns of Tower bridge loomed out of the darkness as he tried to tease more power from his dying aircraft.

Heywood trailed the transport, now neatly bracketed in the gun sights of his F-18.

White smoke trailed from both starboard engines, but Heywood waited before pressing his attack. The farther east they flew, the wide and deeper the river became.

With any luck, the plane would hit the river and the only casualties would be a few fish.

The pilot had a plan of sorts.

With one hand on the yoke, he reached for the parachute beneath his backside and slipped it over one arm. Once it was on, he would push the remaining engines to the stops, climb as high as he could before stalling, and drop out of the hole in the fuselage where his co-pilot once sat. It wasn't a brilliant plan, but it was all he had.

He glanced at his altimeter as he pulled the other arm through the loop of his chute. The needle spun around the dial, first one way and then the other. Useless, but he knew he was far too low. He'd have to get a visual reference, but the windshield was cracked like a spider's web and his side window was slick with hydraulic fluid.

There was a fire to the south-east, but it was too far away to give him any idea of—

THE TRANSPORT PLANE struck the northern column of Tower bridge and disintegrated in a ball of flame.

The tower itself crumbled, sending hundreds of tons of Portland stone crashing onto the roadway below. It was too much to bear. The road bridge arches gave way, twisting and falling into the river below.

The southern tower, now fatally weakened by the loss of its sister, wrenched itself free and fell forward on top of the already-submerged wreckage of the road, the collapse causing an immense wave to wash over the riverbanks along the Thames.

In the space of a few minutes, two of London's most famous landmarks had ceased to exist.

HEYWOOD PUNCHED through the towering cloud of dust and smoke and advanced his throttles.

He turned northeast for Mildenhall, feeling drained. The adrenaline had sapped his energy, and the sight of his capital city blanketed in darkness, destruction and death had crushed his spirits.

As he cleared the suburbs of east London, he thought about the people below and what they would be feeling. Fear, of course, panic, uncertainty. Pain. Heywood considered possible casualty numbers, and that made him feel worse.

Skimming low over the Essex border, Heywood resigned himself to the fact that his country was at war, and he did not know why. All he knew was that many people had died today.

He had no clue what the future held or even if he'd make it through the night.

But if he survived the trip to Scotland, and if there was a decent airbase with a well-supplied armoury and spares for his F-18, well, he'd try to even up the odds for the people down there.

THE PARATROOPERS FANNED out across the shadows of St. James' Park and headed for their primary objectives.

One group moved east towards Horseguards Parade and secured the northern end of Whitehall. They were armed with anti-tank weapons, mortars, and heavy machine guns. Another group did the same at the southern end, taking up position at the junction of Whitehall and Parliament Square.

The third and largest of the groups left the dark and leafy fringes of the park, sprinted across Horseguards Road, and made their way along King Charles Street in two columns.

They avoided the rubble and smoking timbers, weaving their way through the destruction as fires raged in the surrounding buildings.

On reaching Whitehall, the group split again, with small teams taking up defensive positions across the wide avenue where cars, buses and bodies still burned.

The primary group of paras turned left, scrambling through the bomb crater that marked the entrance to Downing Street. They picked their way through the rubble, weapons held ready as they raced towards the most famous front door in the world, now scorched, splintered, and hanging at a drunken angle.

The assault team discharged several flash-bang grenades into the entrance and adjoining rooms and followed them in. Moments later, the ground floor was pronounced clear. More paras hurried inside and began clearing the rest of the building floor by floor. After several minutes, the all-clear signal was given.

Soldiers carrying black, shock-proof cases followed Mousa into Number Ten. Above him, he could hear the muted roar of fire extinguishers as more personnel tackled the flames on the upper floors.

He stood in the hallway and gazed around the once-grand house that had received and entertained world leaders for over two hundred years. Now it was scorched and wrecked, almost beyond recognition.

A pity. He would have liked to have seen it in all its glory.

Mousa continued into the Cabinet Room and watched his command group setting up. They swept the famous cabinet table clear of debris and cracked open their foam-lined cases of communications equipment. A captain approached, and Mousa cocked his chin.

'What is it?'

'We've found a body.'

'Is it Beecham?'

'No, general. It's a senior staff member.'

'Show me.'

The two men made their way out into the garden. Other paras were already out there, sweeping the grounds and establishing a security perimeter. The body was lying near the wall, a grey blanket draped over it. Mousa squatted down and yanked it back. A waxen face stared back at him. The captain was flipping through a set of index cards.

'It's David Fuller,' he reported, 'Director of Communications to the Office of the Prime Minister.'

Mousa took the card and studied the picture. 'Have the body removed and kept separate from other casualties.'

He returned to the Cabinet Room, already a hive of activity. Cables snaked their way around the floor and electronic data flowed across several computer screens. Operators sat around the table, faces smeared with camouflage cream and headphones clamped to their ears.

Mousa barked. 'Status report, Major Allawi!'

A short but broad-shouldered Major limped across the room.

'Voice comms are up and running, general. T-BIS is on-line, and we are active on the battlefield net. I have uploaded the initial mission report and status.'

'Security?'

'Whitehall is sealed at both ends and we'll start clearing the surrounding buildings shortly. The Treasury and Foreign Office buildings are still burning and have sustained heavy damage. We will deal with the MOD last. Our spotters report movement on several floors there. I thought it prudent to secure the rest of Whitehall before sending in an assault team.'

Mousa nodded. 'Good. The surrounding area?'

'Recce troops will observe and report. When reinforcements arrive, we will widen our security perimeter. The infantry battalion assigned to Whitehall should arrive in the next two to three hours. So far, resistance has been light.'

'MY GOD, THAT WAS CLOSE!'

Al-Bitruji and Farad brushed the dirt off their clothes as they surveyed the burning wreckage of their command vehicle.

The British Apache helicopter had appeared from nowhere and fired a couple of missiles before anyone had the chance to react. Al-Bitruji's driver had swerved to avoid the explosion ahead of them, and Al-Bitruji has thought the moment of his death had arrived when another missile streaked towards him, only to pass a few meters away.

They'd driven into a roadside ditch and tipped over as the second missile had exploded behind them, destroying several vehicles, and splashing burning fuel across the motorway. Farad helped Al-Bitruji crawl out as the ripsaw buzz of incoming 20mm rounds faded.

Al-Bitruji watched the dark silhouette of the attack helicopter bank over the top of them and disappear into the darkness. As far as the general knew, not one of his men had got off a single round in reply.

'What the devil happened?' asked Farad as both men scrambled back onto the road.

'Panic,' Al-Bitruji replied. 'This is the first time many of these boys have been under fire.'

Al-Bitruji watched as several vehicles and their occupants burned, the light from the fires reflecting off the low cloud above. He knew it was his fault. The excitement of reaching London had overtaken him, and he'd thrown caution to the wind. Convoy discipline had been lost, and they'd bunched up too tight, creating a target-rich environment for the Apache pilot.

And maybe he would be back.

'Get the recovery tanks up here and get that wreckage shifted,' Al-Bitruji ordered. 'We have to move fast!'

Already, vehicles were using the opposite carriageway to circumnavigate the burning carnage. Al-Bitruji did a quick count. A dozen vehicles gone, and their occupants. If they'd been spaced out properly, their losses would've been fewer.

A heavily armed Humvee pulled up alongside them and Al-Bitruji and Farad climbed in. The general turned to his second-in-command.

'Have the gap between each vehicle increased to a hundred meters. Every tenth vehicle will carry two troopers with SAMs. And get me some air cover. This is unacceptable.'

As Farad worked the radio, Al-Bitruji interrogated his T-BIS console. *So, Mousa was in Downing Street already.* No doubt the arrogant bastard would rub that in when they saw each other again.

Al-Bitruji was no admirer of his fellow general and thought the paratrooper a pompous ass. But he was close to the caliph, a position that Al-Bitruji himself would give anything to be in. Still, maybe the tide would turn in Al-Bitruji's favour.

Mousa's target was Prime Minister Beecham, of whom there was no news. Perhaps he was already dead and buried under the rubble of London. Al-Bitruji smiled. Or maybe not. Maybe Beecham had escaped, and that would mean Mousa had failed.

That being the case, the caliph would not be pleased. Maybe the old man would give the task to someone else, someone who had waited in the wings. He had to get to London fast, and without further incident.

The general slapped the driver on the shoulder and the Humvee lurched forward, racing towards the head of the convoy. But not too close. If the helicopter came back for another bite, they might not be so lucky next time.

And someone would have to take responsibility for the attack, for the lapse in convoy discipline. Naturally, it couldn't be Al-Bitruji. He leaned towards Farad, his voice low.

'Find me a scapegoat, Farad. A senior officer who will cough up to this debacle. Someone must pay, no?'

Farad nodded. 'Consider it done, general.'

CHAPTER 43
POLICE INFORMER

'So, where the devil is his body?' demanded Mousa.

He was conferencing with his senior officers in the Cabinet Room. Around the damaged walls, his heavily armed close protection team stood sentinel, and the air crackled with continuous radio chatter. Major Allawi studied his notes.

'We've found several casualties in both the Treasury and the Foreign Office buildings, general. We've found more remains in Downing Street itself, but we could not identify them. Casualties from the VIED blast, no doubt. One survivor confirmed Beecham was upstairs in his private apartment.'

'He's still alive.' Mousa said.

'Agreed. Beecham and Fuller were close friends. Perhaps Beecham stayed with him?'

'His people would've moved him to a safe location.'

Another officer said, 'Our spotters have yet to see any enemy aerial activity over Whitehall since the initial attacks. Nor has any convoy attempted to reach Downing Street. If he left, he did so on foot.'

Mousa let that sink in, then shook his head. 'I don't see it. Far too dangerous.'

The officer pointed to the floor. 'Then he went through the tunnel below us. The one that leads to the MOD building.'

'Highly probable. Is the assault team in place?'

'Ready to storm the building,' Allawi told him.

Mousa nodded. 'Give the order. Find Beecham. And I want him alive.'

Two hundred meters away, on the sixth floor of the MOD building, Sergeant Terry Morris was struggling with the cold reality of his imminent death.

Minutes earlier, through the smoke of burning vehicles, Morris had seen scores of heavily armed troops moving into position around the building. He saw assault rifles, heavy machine guns, and grenade launchers, and he could see they were professionals. Morris was more scared than he'd ever been in his whole life.

The system had collapsed. There was no one at the end of his radio, no operators, no shift commanders, no backup, nothing. It was just him, his team of six, and twenty terrified civilians.

Morris had taken the brigadier's advice and found a suitable spot to wait out the immediate crisis.

The sixth-floor conference room was in the centre of the building and had no windows. It had thick carpet and comfy chairs and a water cooler. An emergency torch gave them a little light and the Downing Street staff, along with a few MOD personnel, were sitting on the floor in the semi-darkness. Some whispered in low, trembling voices while others sat in silence, flinching at every tremor and dull explosion that shook the walls of the building.

A short time ago, they'd heard the roar of low-flying planes followed by an enormous explosion. Some of the group panicked as a terrible screaming filled the air. Then the earth had rumbled beneath them, shaking the building. One of his guys said that the London Eye was lying half submerged in the Thames and bodies floated everywhere. That news had done nothing for anyone's nerves.

When Morris had a look outside, he'd seen troops weaving across Whitehall towards them. That moment of joy turned to fear when he realised they weren't British troops. With the elevators out of service, he sent men to the ground floor to observe and report, while the rest of his team remained on the sixth.

As the minutes ticked by, Morris hoped the soldiers had gone elsewhere. Outside the conference room, at the far end of the corridor, he saw one of his guys, Tony Freeman, watching the stairs. He walked towards him. 'Anything happening?'

Freeman shook his head. 'It's all gone quiet—'

BOOM! BOOM!

Twin explosions rocked the building. Smoke funnelled up the stairwell and into the corridor. Morris coughed and spluttered. Freeman stared over the rail.

'They're inside!'

'Everyone back to the conference room, now!' Morris raced up the corridor. A pale-faced man in chef's whites poked his head around the door. 'What the fuck's happening?'

'Get on the floor!' Morris yelled at him. He reached the stairwell at the other end of the building and leaned over the banister. More grey smoke and dust boiled up the walls. One of his people was still down there.

'Back up here, quick as you can!' Morris yelled. He heard a muffled shout, then a storm of automatic fire. His team were all armed with HK G36 carbines. What Morris heard was something else. He'd just lost one of his team.

'Terry!' Morris turned to see Freeman running towards him. 'Simmo's down! They're coming up the stairs!'

'Same this end. Back to the conference room, quick!'

They bundled into the room. The civilians scrambled as far away from the door as possible, shouting and screaming. Morris thumped on the table for order.

'Be fucking quiet, the lot of you!' He saw their frightened faces and softened his tone a little. 'Look, we need to be calm now. We've got armed men on their way up to us, so we must be still and quiet and not make anyone nervous, okay? Deep breaths, all of you. We're going to be fine.' The panic subsided, and Morris gathered his remaining team members together at the other end of the room. He kept his voice low.

'We're not soldiers and those are combat troops down there, so I suggest we unload our weapons—'

'Fuck that,' Freeman growled. 'They might come in here and start shooting. If I'm going out, I'm doing it with this in my hands.' He gripped his carbine, his eyes hard and unblinking.

'You want to be a hero? Step outside,' Morris told him. 'There are civvies in here, remember? Talk like that could get us all killed.'

'You're making a mistake,' Freeman said.

'You know where the door is.'

They faced off, and Freeman relented. He lowered the barrel of his HK. 'So, what now?'

'Unload our guns, lay them on the table and sit down at the other end of the room. Spread yourselves amongst the civvies and keep them quiet. When the bad guys get up here, we'll put our hands on our heads. Go.'

Morris lifted his G36 over his head, unloaded the magazine, and set it down on the conference table. The others did the same, then spread themselves out amongst the civvies. Morris wedged the room doors open and sat down. His heart hammered as the sound of men moving along the corridor towards them. In the gloom behind him, someone stifled a sob.

'Easy now,' whispered Morris. 'Everyone put your hands on your head and don't move a muscle. Let me do the talking.'

A shadow loomed in the doorway, and a figure pointed a gun around the door. Then he stepped into the room, followed by several others. Morris saw the heavy weapons, the body armour, and the tough-looking faces below their helmets. The soldiers spread out, weapons raised. Like a firing squad. *Nobody breathe*, Morris prayed.

Another soldier entered the room and stood in front of Morris, the barrel of his weapon pointed at his face, and radioed a message in a language Morris didn't understand. The man reached down, hauling Morris to his feet. He found himself face to face with a very serious-looking soldier with wings on his chest. *A Para*. Morris' legs felt like water.

'We're unarmed,' he told the para. 'There are civilians here—'

'Your name?'

'Sergeant Morris, Metropolitan Police.' Morris waved his arm at the civvies behind him. 'We escorted these people from Downing Street.'

The para's eyes narrowed. 'Downing Street?'

'That's right. We helped evacuate—'

'Shut up, Terry!'

Before Morris could respond, another soldier shot Freeman with a pistol. He slumped sideways into the lap of the chef, blood from the hole in his head pumping over his white tunic. Morris turned away as the whimpering began. His interrogator grabbed him by his collar and pulled him close.

'Beecham, did you see him? Is he alive?'

'Yes.'

'Where is he now?'

'With the others. The soldiers.'

The para barked an order and Morris winced as they secured his hands behind his back with a plastic tie. Two more soldiers bundled him out into the corridor.

'Where are we going?' asked Morris.

'To speak to my superior,' the para told him.

CHAPTER 44
WANDSWORTH ROAD

THE SHOOTING HAD ALL BUT STOPPED.

At least an hour had passed since he'd heard gunfire on the street outside his hiding place and what little he heard was distant.

As he waited for darkness to fall, Faz heard other sounds, too. Harsh, urgent voices close by, English and Arabic, although it was difficult to tell what was being said. He'd heard screaming too, ear-splitting screams of anguish that made the hair on the back of his neck stand on end. Later, a car had approached at high speed, its engine roaring and its tyres screeching in protest. Then, an almighty bang, followed by an ominous silence.

At one point, several people ran past outside, their shadows flitting across the walls and their footsteps pounding the pavement. The metal shutters rattled as a body cannoned off them, and Faz had held the gun tight, but the commotion passed, and he'd sat back down against the wall.

Later, he'd heard aircraft, jets, and what sounded like turboprop engines, then a distant explosion, but that too faded. For the last hour, the only sounds he'd heard were the fires roaring and spitting outside.

Now the shadows had lengthened, and Faz peered through the shutters. He saw scores of burning vehicles out there, most of them now blackened shells. The smoke was still thick, hanging in low, oily black clouds that drifted across the darkening streets. He saw his surveillance vehicle a short distance away. Max was still slumped over, and Kilo Three's legs hung out of the side door. Just seeing them there, dead, made Faz feel nauseous.

He moved back into the shadows and wondered how far this chaos had spread. Was it confined to a few square miles in south London or was it part of a larger operation? He ran his mind back over the events of—this morning? So much had happened since then. Now he was operating in a different world.

Boxer had shaken his surveillance and disappeared. And just before comms went down, control had been swamped with tracking requests. That meant that scores of surveillance targets had dumped their watchers simultaneously, and just before the bus bomb at Stockwell station.

So, this was a major terrorist attack. Bigger than that, compared to past incidents. But how far had it spread? He couldn't imagine the SIS building at Vauxhall Cross being compromised, so help would be there, and in numbers.

But that didn't answer the question—where was everyone? Where were the firearms teams, the aerial surveillance, the sirens? This was a civil emergency, which meant the PM had powers to deploy the army. They wouldn't just contain the problem, not with so many people dead.

Faz thought about his own situation. If he went looking for help, he'd need to go armed, but if friendlies spotted him, he'd be engaged first. So maybe he should stay put? But if people came looking, nosing through the shops, looting—surely that was only a matter of time?

A voice echoed around the empty store. Faz took a few steps backwards, melting into the darkness. He heard more voices, then a shout. The voices moved away and Faz crept towards the shutters.

Carefully, he peered out through the slats onto Wandsworth Road. A group of men, maybe seven or eight, had gathered around the surveillance van, inspecting the body of the terrorist he'd shot. It was hard to ID them because they were lit only by the light of the fires, but the body armour and automatic weapons were unmissable. What struck Faz was their demeanour. They walked and talked as if they owned the street.

As if no one was coming to stop them.

One man squatted down next to the dead terrorist. A few seconds later, he stood and shouted a command. Faz took a step backwards as another group of men appeared out of the smoke. Now there were at least a dozen terrorists, and Faz saw a couple of women amongst their number. They dragged Kilo Three's body out of the van and dumped him onto the road. Max joined him a few seconds later and rough hands went to work, searching them.

Someone had killed and robbed one of their own, and Faz knew what was coming next. He heard a sharp order, and the group turned and fanned out, guns up, heads swivelling. They couldn't know if Faz was out there, but they were taking no chances. It was time to move.

Faz backed away. As he did, his foot caught the rubbish bags stacked in the centre of the room, and an empty soda can clattered across the bare concrete floor. Outside the shop, shadows froze.

Faz held his breath. The shutters rattled violently. He backed towards the corridor. They shoved something through the metal slats and a sharp light blinded him. Faz turned and ran towards the rear yard as an automatic weapon opened up. Wood and plaster exploded all around him and he threw himself onto the concrete. He reached up and opened the back door, crawling outside. He heard voices shouting and footsteps running.

They were coming for him.

He scrambled to his feet and unblocked the back gate, ducking into the alleyway. He turned left, sprinting down the narrow channel and away from the Wandsworth Road. Angry shouts echoed off the alley walls behind him. Faz found himself in a dark street of terraced houses, and he kept running until his breath came in ragged gasps and the shouting had stopped. He dropped behind a parked car and checked for signs of pursuit. Nothing.

Wait—

He squinted into the dark and then he saw them. Seven or eight gunmen were jogging towards him, maybe fifty meters away, moving methodically, checking the gaps between the parked cars. There was no time to think.

Faz sprinted from cover. A rifle barked and bullets zipped overhead, cracking off the brickwork of a nearby house. Faz turned into another side street, the same as the first, all parked cars and dark houses. He cut across the road, running as fast as he could. When he looked behind him, he saw the hunters fanning out across the street. He turned and fired his weapon on full auto, the sound suppressed to a metallic rattle by the black barrel tube. He struggled to control the burst, but his pursuers ran for cover. Faz ran too, turning another corner.

To his left was a chain-link fence and beyond it, the darkened sprawl of New Covent Garden market, a massive complex of warehouses with lots of places to hide. He scaled the fence, dragging himself over the limp barbed wire, and dropped to the other side. He ran for the closest warehouse and lost himself in the black pools beneath the wide canopy.

He crouched behind a tower of wooden pallets, his back against a vehicle loading bay, his chest heaving with the effort of his escape. Thirty seconds later, his hunters appeared at the chain-link fence. Barrel lights and torches probed the darkness, washing over the warehouse, but Faz was invisible behind the pallets. Their voices carried on the night air, but Faz couldn't work out what they were saying.

A few minutes later, the lights were extinguished, and his pursuers headed back the way they had come. Faz waited for a minute or two, watching and listening, then he moved off, creeping around the edge of the warehouse. There was litter everywhere; cardboard boxes, discarded plastic wrapping, overflowing waste containers, all testimony to that day's frantic business. Faz suspected that tomorrow would be a slow day.

He reached Nine Elms Lane, a normally busy commuter route that ran between Battersea Park and Vauxhall. What he saw there was a graveyard of vehicles, some damaged by collisions, some intact but abandoned, their doors flung open. One car burned fiercely, the white flames charring the car's bodywork. So, the incident area was far larger than he thought, and the sky remained devoid of traffic. Heading east towards Vauxhall Cross might be a mistake—all major roads converged there, and he might run into that armed group again.

So, he needed to head north, across the river. If Vauxhall Bridge was out, the next closest crossing was Chelsea Bridge. But before that, he needed a different perspective. He needed to get higher, find a vantage point that would give him unrestricted views over the immediate area, and the place that would provide such a vantage point was a short distance away.

He set off at a pace, weaving between abandoned cars, keeping low, watching, listening. Ahead of him, the vast expanse of the Battersea Power Station complex loomed in the darkness like a mountain range. It was a development of luxury apartments, commercial spaces, bars, shops, and restaurants all clustered around the original and iconic power station building that was over 100 years old.

Now, the vast complex was black and empty, the apartment blocks rising above Faz's head as he kept to the shadows of the buildings. On closer inspection, he could see the dim light of torches and candles above him, but the streets were devoid of life.

He headed for Park Heights, a thirty-storey, circular glass and steel structure that rose from the middle of the power station floor, creating a fifth tower that stood over four-hundred feet high, dominating the four original chimney stacks. It would be a long climb, but it would be worth it, he reasoned. Up there, he could see the extent of the attacks and how far the power cuts had spread. And where he needed to head to.

He avoided the main entrance and its huge glass facade. Instead, he circumnavigated the vast building until he found a maintenance staff entrance set into a dark recess. He took cover, then with careful aim, shot out the security keypad. He yanked the handle—still locked. *This isn't the movies.*

He stepped back around the corner and aimed again. He fired another two shots, and the punctured keypad swung loose. Faz yanked again, and the door opened. He used his mobile phone torch to read the wall map and took the service staircase to the Park Heights lobby. He found himself inside a plush, circular reception area furnished with smart chairs and sofas, deserted and undamaged. The trouble hadn't reached this far, not here in one of London's more upmarket residential blocks, but he kept the AK slung across his chest and gripped, his thumb resting on the selector lever.

Behind the reception desk, he found a torch, hurried past the dead elevators, and began the long climb up the stairs. Reaching the tenth floor confirmed Faz was out of shape. By the time he reached the 21st, he had to stop for a breather. On the 42nd, he sat for five minutes on the top stair, hoping his exertions would bear fruit.

His breathing and heart rate approaching somewhere near normal, Faz kicked the maintenance door twice, and the Yale lock gave up the one-sided fight. Inside the room, signs warned him to wear suitable clothing and attach a safety line. He unbolted the exterior door and cracked it open. A stiff night breeze swirled inside the maintenance room and Faz stepped out onto a circular gantry at the very top of the building. He let go of the gun and gripped the rail. It wasn't the height that bothered him—it was the frightening vision of London that turned his legs to water.

As far as he could see, darkness blanketed the city, lit only by a multitude of hellish red fires dotted around the horizon. He shuffled around the gantry, his hands gripping the rail. He looked east towards Vauxhall Cross and Whitehall, but saw only fire and smoke, and the occasional glimpse of a well-known landmark. The scene chilled him. Beyond the area of Whitehall, a huge fire burned somewhere in the West End, its flames reaching high into the dark sky. It was surreal and terrifying. He continued his circumnavigation and saw nothing that gave him hope. This was more than a terrorist attack.

He heard shots far below him, echoing between the apartment blocks. From his lofty vantage point, he saw a small convoy of vehicles, headed up by two trucks filled with people crammed onto the flatbeds. Not help, Faz knew instinctively. This was trouble. And they were headed straight for the power station.

He left the gantry and headed for the staircase as fast as he could.

CHAPTER 45
RIVERSIDE BLUES

Lara was awake when Ross returned to the apartment. She was pale, and a fitful sleep had tousled her dark hair, but she'd dressed in sports leggings and a sweatshirt and that was a good sign.

'How are you feeling?'

'Groggy. I was hoping this was all a dream. It's not, is it?'

Ross shook his head. A candle burned on the living room table, and he stepped over the broken glass and stood on the balcony threshold. Across the river, the crash site was still burning, and a blood-red hue painted the sky above. He shuddered at the thought of the carnage.

A faint noise caught Ross's attention, and it drew his eyes towards the river. As his vision adjusted to the darkness, he caught a slight luminescence on the water's oily black surface. Something moved in his peripheral vision, an object that seemed to glide through the shadows, and Ross saw a rowing boat moving upstream, oared by a single figure. It faded from view until he lost it in the darkness.

The river.

'Ross? What's going on?'

He turned around. Lara stood in the hallway, reluctant to step into the living room.

'Where are the police? The fire brigade and ambulances? There must be hundreds of people dead and injured across the river.'

'No one's coming. London's under some sort of attack. There's no power, no mobile or landline service, no TV, nothing. And there are fires everywhere.'

'So, what do we do? Stay here until help arrives? Until the power comes back?'

Ross recalled the missile impacts rippling across the city. 'No. We're getting out of here, at least for the short term. We need to be proactive, find out what's happening, prepare for a period of uncertainty. Sitting here and waiting for help that might not arrive is not a plan.'

'What about the government? Won't they send in the army?'

'Maybe, but that could take days, or weeks. The fact is, we don't know what's happening. All of our systems have collapsed, and the streets aren't safe. If we get out of the city, we might find help.'

'I don't have a car. Neither do you.'

'That's why we're going to find a boat.'

Lara looked horrified. 'A what?'

'The streets aren't safe. There are terrorists out there and no one is stopping them. There'll be bodies and not just from the plane crash. If they're not recovered, disease will spread. And what about food? This is a city of almost ten million people. I can guarantee you that shops are getting looted as we speak. Pretty soon they'll be empty, and then what?'

'You're frightening me.'

Ross stepped closer and gave her arms a gentle squeeze. 'Don't be scared. If we use our heads and act fast, we can get through this.'

She took a deep breath. 'I'm listening.'

'My brother and his family live out in the west country. They're eco-freaks, with a smallholding and a few acres of land, all quite remote. They've got pigs and chickens and grow their own veg. My brother Rob, he's big into all that off-grid living. I can't think of a better place to go right now.'

Lara shrugged. 'So, what should I bring?'

'Pack a bag, a rucksack, something like that. Wear dark clothes and bring wet weather gear, just in case. It might take us a while to get to where we're going. And bring cash, cards, and ID too. Driving license, passport. Just in case we need to prove who we are.'

'What about food?'

'Pack bread, butter, noodles, jam, peanut butter, stuff like that. And water. As much as you can carry.' He broke away and headed for the door. 'I need to get some kit from the flat. I'll be back in five, okay?'

'Okay.'

Ross headed downstairs, listening, and watching for trouble. Inside his own apartment, he changed into his police-issue black tactical trousers and jacket. He grabbed a large rucksack from the spare bedroom, packed spare clothes, torches, batteries, a compass, some dried foods, and a compact cooking stove that he hadn't used since Glastonbury a few years before. He stopped in the kitchen and stuffed several small bottles of water into his rucksack. It was a lot of extra weight, but necessary. What was the saying again? Three weeks without food, three days without water, three minutes without oxygen. After that, a person would be dead. Ross hoped none of them would ever apply.

There were a couple more items he needed to pack. From the gun cabinet in the bedroom, he retrieved the HK-416 assault rifle and magazines, and spare mags for his Glock. He adjusted the sling, so the weapon rested across his chest, then he pulled a navy windbreaker over the top.

Kitted up and ready, he shut off the gas and the mains electricity and locked the apartment door, hoping he'd find it in the same state when he came back.

Up in Lara's apartment, they carried out the same last-minute checks and left. Tears rolled down Lara's face. She'd tied her hair back, and she wore a fleece, a hooded rain jacket, and dark sneakers on her feet. The daysack on her back was stuffed to the gills, and she looked vulnerable and beautiful. All Ross wanted to do was hold her.

'Everything'll be okay,' he said. She didn't look convinced. Instead, she pointed to his windbreaker.

'That's a gun, right?'

He nodded. 'It's for our protection. Don't worry, I doubt I'll ever use it.'

Down in the lobby, Ross checked the street outside. Nothing moved. He eased open the door and moved outside, gesturing Lara to join him. He leaned close to her and whispered in her ear. 'Move around the side of the building and keep to the shadows. Head for the towpath, okay?'

She moved off, trainer crunching on the gravel drive. Ross waited until he was satisfied that no one had seen or heard them, then moved off into the darkness.

He found Lara waiting at the rear of the property, where decorative bushes bordered the public towpath beyond. Ross knew there were hundreds of vessels and scores of boat clubs stretching all the way out to Berkshire and beyond. They'd find something, preferably with an engine. Lara whispered in the dark.

'Whereabouts does he live, your brother?'

'Near a village called South Lockeridge, in Wiltshire. I reckon the river could take us as far as Reading, maybe further. It's about thirty miles from there.'

Her face was pale in the darkness. 'We're going to be okay, aren't we?'

He squeezed her arm again. 'As long as I'm here, nothing bad will happen to you. Okay?'

'Okay,' she echoed, and offered him a weak smile.

'When we move off, stay close. If I hold up my hand, just freeze. Don't move, don't talk. Have you got a torch?'

She held up a black Maglite. 'I put fresh batteries in.'

'Don't use it unless I say so. Your eyes will get used to the dark pretty quickly, so we'll rely on our night vision. Ready?'

Lara took a deep breath. 'Not really.'

Now it was Ross's turn to smile. 'That's the spirit.' He pushed through the bushes and stepped onto the towpath. As if on cue, a sliver of moon peeked from behind a bank of low cloud, revealing a damp, gloomy trail along the riverbank.

'Keep close and keep quiet,' whispered Ross. Lara gave him a thumbs up.

They followed the silent riverbank, heading west towards Kew Bridge.

CHAPTER 46
WHAT LIES BENEATH

Mousa ordered the British policeman out of the room, barely able to look at the man.

He'd begged for his life and gave Mousa everything he wanted to know before Mousa had asked him a single question. Disgraceful and cowardly was Mousa's opinion of the policeman, but in this case, that was a good thing. Now he knew for sure. The British Prime Minister was still alive.

The invasion plans had called for the elimination of several European leaders and senior political figures, especially those who had voiced concern about the Caliph Wazir and were critical of his burgeoning empire. That number was small, however. The Spanish, French, Belgian, Dutch, and Italian leaders would be spared a bullet because of their previous grovelling to the caliph, and the EU parliament had been in his pocket long before the first plans were laid. Many European leaders would do as they were told, simply to cling to the wealth and power that they and their families had become accustomed to.

The German Chancellor, a man who had publicly expressed doubts about the ever-expanding caliphate, had avoided the suicide bomber who'd detonated her vest in the lobby of the Reichstag. According to the latest intelligence, caliphate forces had found his helicopter abandoned outside the city of Rostock on the Baltic coast. He was probably headed for Denmark, assumed Mousa. He would find no shelter there.

According to T-BIS, caliphate forces in Europe were seizing their objectives with minimal casualties. The populations of major cities were heeding the pre-recorded messages and staying off the streets. Chaos and confusion ruled the day, and now the night. Yet Mousa knew from his own experience on the battlefields of Iraq, Yemen, and Afghanistan, that it was always darkest before the dawn. And often, when the sun rose, it brought fresh hope and vigour for the fight.

The British possessed that potential for stubborn confrontation. They were a warrior race, proud and aggressive, and with a long history of warfare. Many would refuse to accept their absorption into the caliphate. With their forces routed, they would be quick to organise resistance, which is why Mousa needed Beecham alive.

In recent years, the British public had showed a blind faith in the words and deeds of their politicians and public institutions. Whether those words were spoken by the Prime Minister or the familiar face of a prime-time news anchor, they were trusted words and opinions, to be accepted without question. The British had been beaten down by years of economic stagnation and crisis after crisis until they had been subdued to a point where they could be controlled easily.

Beecham was no different to past leaders, but war was often a catalyst for personal change. The fact that Beecham was still on the loose might shake the British out of their malaise and give them hope in their darkest hour. Captured alive, he would be used to provide the continuity that most people would crave. He would remain in power and do as he was told.

But where was he?

On the airstrip in North Africa, Mousa had been informed of Beecham's last-minute schedule change, which put the PM in the crosshairs of the VIED on Whitehall. Yet luck was on the general's side, and Beecham had survived the blast intact, yet he was nowhere to be found. So, what did Mousa know?

He knew Beecham had stood right here in the Downing Street basement a short time ago. He knew others had joined him, a ranking army officer and a small detachment of soldiers in civilian clothes. Special forces, tasked to extract the PM to a place of safety. But where would that be?

Most of the military secure facilities had been attacked. Others, like Chequers, were being watched. His own men had sealed Whitehall off, but that didn't mean that Beecham hadn't already escaped. If so, how? No helicopters had breached Whitehall airspace since the VIED detonated. The streets around Whitehall were filled with abandoned, burning cars. Nothing moved, not if it didn't want to be fired on.

Those British soldiers would want to keep Beecham safe. Yes, chances might have to be taken, but those would be measured choices, not reckless risks. He would be safe somewhere. And where was safer in a war zone than deep below ground?

Deeper than the basement they were already standing in.

His eye caught the heavy steel door to the generator room across the corridor. He grasped the handle and tried to open it, but it didn't budge. 'Major!'

Allawi hobbled out into the corridor, his right lower leg wrapped in a field dressing. 'General?'

'How's the leg?'

'No fracture, just some heavy bruising to the shin.'

Mousa slapped a hand on the generator room door. 'Get the combat engineers to open this door. And tell them to bring their GPR kit.' Allawi raised an eyebrow. 'Ground Penetrating Radar,' Mousa explained.

'You think there's a tunnel below us?'

'Let's find out. And whistle up a SERTRAK team, too.'

Allawi turned away, a radio already in his hand. Mousa stared at the thick door, then he rested an ear against the cold steel, listening for life beyond the presently impenetrable barrier.

FOUR INCHES away from Mousa's left ear, Trooper Gaz Cole also had his ear pressed against the steel door. He'd heard muffled voices on the other side, then someone tried to open the door. That would be impossible, given that Mike had jammed the mechanism from the inside with a thick steel bar. Yet if the people on the other side wanted to get in, they'd find a way.

Cole backed off and ducked through the false generator panel, sealing it from the inside. Thirty seconds later, he was down on the cavern floor.

CHAPTER 47
DAVY JONES' LOCKER

'Contact! Transponder bearing 044 degrees, range 175 miles, altitude 1100 feet. Transponder ident is alpha-seven-one-one. That's our bird, sir.'

'All engines stop,' acknowledged Captain Schelling. 'Mr Andrews, let's get the rescue party on the water, but keep them close. This thing might land anywhere.'

'Aye, aye, sir.'

In the dimly lit belly of the ship, a watertight hatch slid back to reveal the waves twenty feet below. Suspended above the open hatch, six crewmen sat strapped into a rigid-inflatable power launch. Each man wore a survival suit and ballistic helmet, and two of their number carried light machine pistols. On the Chief's signal, the boat was lowered down onto the water. As its twin propellers bit into the waves, the launch accelerated from under the hull, then bobbed on the surface close behind, waiting.

On the bridge, Schelling registered the new blip on the master radar display.

'Launch is in the water.'

'Thank you, Mr Andrews.'

As the minutes ticked by, Schelling pondered the new orders received since arriving on station 47 minutes ago. He'd briefed his officers and made a general crew announcement over the ship's PA system. He removed the message slip from his breast pocket and read it again:

*** FLASH MESSAGE ***

PRIORITY ONE: USS CALIFORNIA TO HOLD STATION AT 6.56 49.85—AWAIT IMMINENT ARRIVAL OF AIRBORNE EVAC CRAFT —RECOVER VIP PASSENGER AND SCUTTLE CRAFT—MAKE ALL POSSIBLE SPEED TO MID ATLANTIC RIDGE—GEOHASH EQGFCDXU84436—RV WITH TASK FORCE 87—ALL NON-US CONTACTS TO BE CONSIDERED HOSTILE—ALERT STATUS DEFCON THREE BY ORDER COMMANDER US FLEET FORCES COMMAND.

*** MESSAGE ENDS***

An evac craft? Schelling had never even seen one, but he'd heard of something similar. Air Force one was equipped with two escape pods, but they were not much more than a padded cell on the end of a parachute. And now the country was at DEFCON Three? That was almost a shooting war. He keyed the intercom.

'How's our VIP doing?'

'Target is thirty-five clicks out and descending. Estimate splash down in four minutes, eight hundred meters off our port bow, heading of zero-one-three degrees. Closest surface traffic is zero-eight-three nautical miles south-southwest. We're on our own, Sir.'

'Roger.' Schelling turned to his number two. 'Mr Andrews, order the launch to close to that position and prepare the ship for high-speed run.'

'Aye, aye, sir.'

Schelling stepped down towards the wide, sloping bridge windows and looked out over the ocean, a vast sea of steel grey water beneath a cloudy, leaden sky. He lifted a pair of powerful lowlight binoculars and scanned the horizon. 'All ahead slow, Mr Andrews. Hold our present course.'

The California sliced noiselessly through the water. Sonar sounded over the PA.

'Bridge, Sonar. Target is two miles out and closing. Altitude is 262 feet. Estimate splashdown in fifteen seconds.'

Schelling tracked the binoculars to his left and then he saw it, skimming low across the sky. So that's what an evac craft looks like. It was smaller than he imagined, like a tiny fighter jet with a pair of stubby wings and a tail fin.

As he watched, its nose dipped towards the waves, then lifted, skimming across the surface in a plume of white water. It slowed rapidly, and Schelling saw buoyancy aids deploy around the fuselage. He switched views and saw the rescue launch bouncing across the waves towards it. Schelling ordered the California to close the gap.

The boat sped away and he gave another order—scuttle the evac craft. With the rescue launch safely out of the way, an unseen gunner opened up with a Vulcan 20mm cannon. Tungsten sabot rounds tore the craft to pieces and seconds later, what was left slipped beneath the waves. Schelling made sure the main body had sunk to the deep before heading for the sick bay.

When he got there, he saw the newly arrived VIP was a man in his mid-forties. Dirt streaked his face, and his eyes were dull and red-rimmed. He wore a pair of black trousers that were ripped at the knees and his once-white shirt was filthy and speckled with dried blood. His thick grey hair was messy and unkempt and there was a fresh dressing on his neck. He offered a hand.

'Captain Frank Schelling, United States Navy. Welcome aboard the California.'

The VIP took it. 'Terry Fitzgerald, US Ambassador to the United Kingdom.'

Schelling frowned. This was getting weirder by the second. Cleared by the ship's surgeon, Schelling escorted Fitzgerald to his compact, comfortable quarters. He invited the new arrival to take a seat and handed him a generous glass of Kentucky bourbon. The diplomat emptied it in two quick swallows.'

'Thank you, captain. That was some experience, and not one I'd like to repeat.'

'You'll have to excuse me,' said Schelling, 'but why are you here?'

'London is under attack. It was chaos. I mean real anarchy. No power, no cops, nothing. And there was talk or airliners being shot down. Terrorists assaulted the embassy with heavy weapons. And they weren't brainwashed kids. These were experienced fighters employing infantry tactics. Soldiers is my guess. The last I knew, they were inside the building. We lost a lot of people.'

'We've been tracking missile launches from the North African coast. Ships and aircraft too, all heading for Europe. I'm guessing this is something to do with Wazir's war games?'

Fitzgerald nodded. 'Used as cover. It's obvious now.'

'We're at DEFCON Three.'

Fitzgerald paled again. 'Jesus Christ.'

Schelling stood and picked up a bulkhead phone. 'Mr Andrews, rig the ship for a high-speed run. And send a steward to my quarters, asap.' He put the phone down and turned back to the ambassador. 'Mr Fitzgerald, I need to get you squared away before we get underway.'

There was a knock at the door, and a Schelling opened it. A Petty Officer waited outside. 'This is Mr Perry. He'll show you to your quarters. Now, if you'll excuse me, I have work to do.'

'Of course.' He shook Schelling's hand again and headed for the door. At the bulkhead, he paused and turned. 'This is one of those new stealth ships, isn't it?'

'That's correct,' said Schelling.

'Is she as fast as they say she is?'

Schelling smiled like a proud parent. 'You're about to find out.'

CHAPTER 48
BREACHER UP

'What's the problem, Mike?'

Harry and Forsythe were standing over Reynolds as he flipped switches and pressed buttons.

'Train carriage won't move,' replied the soldier. 'We've got a green light on the panel, but nothing's happening.' Behind him, Brooks and Sherman were back from their recce and were thumbing through several technical binders spread across the table.

'Have you tried re-setting the breakers?' Brooks asked.

'Tried and failed,' Reynolds told him.

'Here comes Cole,' Harry said, pointing through the glass. They all paused as Cole vaulted the tracks and barged into the control room.

'We've got to move. There are people in the basement. Someone's trying to get access to the generator room.'

'Maybe they're stragglers,' Sherman said. 'Shall we go topside and check?'

'Stragglers?' Harry echoed, horrified at the thought that people could be trapped up there, injured, desperate for help.

Forsythe shook his head. 'Doubtful. No one knows about this tunnel system apart from a very small group of people with the highest clearance.'

'Maybe it's one of them,' Sherman suggested.

'One way to find out,' Forsythe said. 'There should be a CCTV system here. Power everything up, quickly.'

Harry stood back as the others went to work, flipping switches and booting systems. The lights overhead dimmed momentarily, then blazed bright again, and he wondered just how long those solar batteries would last. He swallowed. Without lights, they would be blind, and Harry felt a ripple of panic.

'Found it!'

Harry turned. Brooks stood back and everyone gathered around the monitor he'd just powered up. It was filled with a chessboard of images that appeared the cover the whole subterranean complex. Reynolds pointed to one of the small squares.

'There's the train, boss.'

Forsythe touched the screen, and the feed filled the monitor. Harry saw a large, open train carriage with rows of seats, but it looked dim, foggy. 'What's wrong with the picture?'

'That's smoke,' said Reynolds. 'He tried remotely calling the train again. On the screen, a flurry of sparks spat across the track and white smoke drifted into the air. The train didn't move.

'Maybe a burned-out transformer. Or the electric motor itself.'

'Let's have a look upstairs,' Forsythe said. He leaned over and touched the screen again, selecting the generator room feed. The camera was set at a high angle at the other end of the room, above the workbench, Harry guessed. He saw the steel door, the ramp, and the emergency generators. The room was empty.

'All quiet on the western front,' Harry said, forcing a smile.

'Detonate!'

Mousa stopped his ears with gloved fingers as the combat engineer depressed the rubberised switch on his control unit. The resulting explosion shook the ground beneath his boots and a thick cloud of dust rolled up the staircase into Number Ten, where everyone had taken cover. Mousa turned to the hallway, now jammed with combat troops. He waved his arm.

'Get down there and clear that basement. Go!'

The troops, wearing dust masks and goggles, filed past him, slowing as they negotiated the stairs, their red-dot laser sights cutting through the smog. They disappeared down the stairs and into the basement. Mousa gestured to Allawi behind him. 'We'll give the dust a chance to clear, and then we go down.'

'Yes, general.'

Mousa's heart hammered. Adrenaline surged. He couldn't recall a time when he'd been as excited as he was now, standing in Ten Downing Street, hunting the British Prime Minister. The ground radar had revealed a cavern below the building, and Mousa knew that Beecham and his entourage had fled there. It wouldn't be long before they captured the man, and he looked forward to when he would report that news to the caliph himself.

'Jesus!' Harry said, flinching.

The tremor penetrated the cavern walls, rolling down them and across the floor. Harry saw a plastic cup of water on the console and watched its surface rippling. On the CCTV screen, the generator room was briefly obscured, but then right-angled shapes reformed as the dust cleared. To the right of the screen, he saw a thin beam of red light, then the room lit up with flashes. Somewhere above, he heard a sound like firecrackers.

'Assault team,' Reynolds said. 'They're clearing the room.'

And then they were inside, thin red beams sweeping around the room, the bulky shadows behind them spreading out. Portable lights lit up the walls and more troops entered the room. Forsythe leaned closer to the screen.

'What is it, Clive?'

The brigadier pointed to the screen. 'This man. He's in charge.'

Harry watched the figure standing on the ramp, taking in his surroundings. A couple of soldiers and a limping man accompanied him. Harry recognised the poise and authority that Forsythe had spotted, and he watched this new arrival explore the room, running a hand over the power units, reading a display panel, staring at the pipes and conduit trays that ran across the ceiling.

Harry could barely believe it. Foreign troops, right here in the heart of London. In *his* house. He felt a spike of anger that faded as the man strolled towards the workbench beneath the camera. Harry watched him as the trespasser fingered the tools and rags on the workbench, and then he raised his eyes, cold and hard beneath the rim of his ballistic helmet. Eyes that stared straight into the camera lens.

Harry swallowed. 'He knows.'

Mousa called over his shoulder. 'Major Allawi!'

A moment later, Allawi limped next to Mousa. The general pointed at the camera above them. 'Look.'

The major saw the camera mounted near the ceiling below some overhead pipework.

'Painted the same colour as the walls,' Mousa observed. 'They're probably watching us right now.' He picked up a wrench and smashed the camera with a solid blow. Plastic circuitry shattered across the workbench. He turned around and pointed to the power generators. 'I want those things ripped apart. The entrance is here, somewhere. Where's the SERTRACK team?'

'Fifteen minutes out.'

'Make it ten.' He clapped his hands. 'Clear the room! Make way for the engineers!'

Forty feet below Mousa's boots, Harry and the others saw that hard face and the raised wrench before the picture turned black. The words *No Signal* followed a moment later.

'Time to leave,' Forsythe said. He turned to the SAS soldiers. 'Storeroom, now. Grab rations, water, anything else that might be useful. Regroup outside in three minutes.'

As the soldiers moved away, one of them barged into Harry, knocking him off his feet. Sherman apologised, helping Harry up with firm hands.

'My bad,' Sherman said, dusting Harry down.

Harry grimaced. 'No problem,' he told the soldier.

Is this how it would be? he wondered, always in the way, always saying and doing the wrong thing. He felt like a fifth wheel.

Forsythe slapped a hand on Beecham's shoulder. 'How's your fitness, Harry? We'll be moving on foot, which will involve some running.'

Harry felt his stomach churn. 'I'll be fine. What I want to know is how those soldiers got here so quickly.'

'They're paratroopers. Probably landed close by, maybe Hyde Park. Or maybe they've been here for months and smuggled their equipment in. The how's and why's are not important right now. What I know is they're here, and my guess is you're their target.'

'Jesus Christ,' Harry muttered, suddenly aware that Forsythe was probably right, and the thought of being hunted by foreign troops was a terrifying one. 'I'll keep up, don't worry.'

'You'll need to. Those are special forces up there. They'll be fit and very determined, like Mike and his boys. It's all about speed and distance now.' Forsythe glanced up as Reynolds and his team assembled outside. He motioned the sergeant to join them.

'Mike, cut all the video feeds and the train's remote controls. But you need to be subtle. I want our pursuers to waste time trying to figure things out.'

Reynolds and his men got to work, unscrewing panels, tracing cables, and cutting them. They were done in under a minute.

'Outside,' Forsythe said. They gathered in the mouth of the westbound tunnel. 'Okay, we've got to get away from here as fast as we can, get to Kensington Gardens and contact Northstar from there. It's just over half-a-mile to the Buckingham Palace interchange and another two miles from there to the disused building in Kensington Gardens. Shouldn't take long, even on foot.'

Harry swallowed, his heart rate already climbing. He didn't want to die in these tunnels, but he didn't want to be a burden to the others, either. He knew they wouldn't abandon him, that protecting him was their duty, and that meant he was putting their lives in danger. All he had to do was keep up the pace and they might all get out of this in one piece.

'Mike, we need a diversion.'

Reynolds nodded. 'I'm thinking diversions, plural.' He turned to Cole. 'Gaz, get upstairs as quick as you can. We need booby traps. Set 'em up and get back down here pronto.'

Cole set off at speed towards the gantry stairs. Reynolds turned to Brooks and Sherman.

'You two are the decoy team. Take the foot tunnel, but don't make it too obvious. Move as fast as you can for a couple of miles, then find an exit and circle back to Kensington Gardens.'

The SAS sergeant checked his watch.

'I guesstimate you've got three hours, tops, before we exfil the city. If you don't make the RV, head west and linkup with friendly forces.'

'Sounds easy enough,' Sherman grinned. Sweat beaded on his ebony skin.

'Let's go,' Brooks said, and they headed off.

'Good luck,' Harry called after them.

The two soldiers disappeared behind the foot tunnel door and slammed it behind them. A loud metallic clang echoed off the cavern walls.

'Ready?' Forsythe asked him.

Harry nodded. 'As I'll ever be.'

Reynolds pointed. 'Standby. Gaz is on his way down.'

Harry saw Cole coming down the metal stairs two at a time. He ran across the platform and joined them at the tunnel mouth.

'I've rigged a shaped charge to the room behind the access panel, and another, bigger one under the gantry itself. Should buy us some time.'

'Nice work,' Reynolds told him.

'Mike, kill the platform lights,' Forsythe said, pointing to a fuse box on the platform.

Reynolds jogged across and flipped open the grey metal door. A moment later, the large banks of ceiling lights went out, and darkness swallowed the complex. Harry felt that panic again but took comfort from the blue lights still operating in the tunnel.

'Take point, Mike.'

Reynolds nodded. 'Gaz, watch our six.'

Cole fell in a few meters behind Forsythe. Harry watched Reynolds move off, and then he felt the brigadier's hand on his shoulder, heard the whispered words behind him.

'Let's go, Harry. Quick as you can.'

Harry didn't answer. Instead, he followed Reynolds into the dark mouth of the westbound tunnel.

CHAPTER 49
AFGHAN MASSIV

'What's taking so long? Find it! Hurry!'

Mousa was growing increasingly impatient. The engineers had been searching the dusty generator room for thirty minutes, trying to isolate the power units and dismantle them. What they'd discovered so far was that the units were encased in a single sheet of formed metal. There were no screw holes, no seams, vents, nothing except the iPad-sized digital display panels.

The engineer corps captain standing before Mousa mopped his brow, and not because the room was growing increasingly stuffy.

'The casing retention screws must be behind the units, general, but we can't get to them without heavy equipment. Crowbars won't do the job, sir.'

'Explosives will, no?'

'Not advisable. If the cavern is below us, the shock wave could cause serious damage. That might hinder your mission.'

Mousa glared at him. 'Then get what you need. Now.'

'It's on its way.'

Mousa turned on his heel. Paratroopers jammed the basement corridor, ready to enter the tunnel system. They parted like the Red Sea as Mousa made his way up into Number Ten. He sat down in the wrecked Cabinet Room and lit a cigarette as he studied a T-BIS console. *So, Al-Bitruji had made it to London.*

Although Mousa and Al-Bitruji both held the rank of general, Mousa's long-standing and personal relationship with the caliph ensured an unspoken seniority over his fellow officers and anyone on the Military High Command in Baghdad. The computer told him that Al-Bitruji was setting up his headquarters in Buckingham Palace. A vain but wise choice. It would be hard for the British to strike at such a culturally significant landmark.

Major Allawi limped into the room. 'General, the SERTRAK team is restless. Their commander asks permission to be redeployed.'

Mousa stubbed out his cigarette and went out into the main hallway where the Afghans had gathered. The SERTRAK teams (Search and Track), all Afghans, were the best at what they did. Drawn from former Taliban units, they were fearsome fighters, especially in dark, confined spaces, a skill learned in the hills and mountains of Afghanistan.

Of all the Islamic State forces, SERTRAK teams were feared the most, and were lethal with guns, knives, and their bare hands. They were fanatics, cold-blooded killers loyal only to each other, and seconded to the caliphate as irregular forces. They were a law until themselves and took orders only from the highest authorities.

Mousa watched them from the corridor as they loitered in the entrance hall, fifteen men who picked through the rubble, jabbering as they passed objects of interest amongst each other. Their uniforms were a mix of modern battledress and traditional Afghan clothing, and despite the sticky weather, they wore full battle-order webbing and equipment packs festooned with ropes, clamps, and collapsible ladders. Each man carried at least two weapons, and all of them had knives on display. Mousa had heard they were more skilled with them than the best of Baghdad's surgeons.

'Who's in charge here?' Mousa barked the words, stamping his authority. The Afghans stared at him. Mousa stared back.

'I am.'

The man discarded the antique carriage clock and approached Mousa. He was an inch taller than the general, and his pockmarked face was heavily scarred. He sported a shaved head and a thick beard, and he wore a sleeveless goatskin jerkin over US Army issue combat jacket and trousers. The weapon slung over his shoulder was an AK-12 with end-to-end taped magazines and an American EOTech holographic sight mounted on the top rail. Mousa would show him the required respect, but in the general's eyes, he was still a subordinate.

'Name?'

'Haseeb,' the Afghan said.

'I'm told you want to be redeployed?'

'There is much work to be done elsewhere.'

Mousa tapped his own chest. 'I decide when and where you'll be deployed. Do you understand?' He glared at Haseeb. The Afghan had unusual blue eyes, a genetic legacy of historic European bloodlines that ran through many Afghan tribes. The blue eyes never wavered, but after a moment, Haseeb's bushy beard bobbed.

'As you command, General Mousa.'

'Good.' Mousa spent the next few minutes briefing Haseeb. The Afghan listened until Mousa had finished.

'Questions?' Haseeb shook his head. 'Be ready,' Mousa told him. He turned, almost colliding with Allawi. 'What is it?'

'The engineers have exposed a crawl space. And we're picking up something else. A transmitter signal, one of ours, faint, but steady. The kind used by deep cover operatives.'

'Show me.'

Down in the basement, the waiting paratroopers watched Mousa lead the SERTRAK into the generator room. The facia of one unit had been peeled back like a banana, revealing a crawl space inside. A couple of signallers were hunched over a laptop and signal receiver, its long aerial poking into the crawl space.

The engineer looked pleased with himself. 'We found it, general.'

'What's on the other side?'

The captain frowned. 'I don't know, sir. We're waiting for instruction.'

Mousa approached the signallers. They snapped to attention. 'Tell me about this signal.'

'It's a high frequency radio wave transmitter signal, operating between 25 and 30 Megahertz. That means it's one of our, general.'

'The type issued to individuals close to the seat of power,' Allawi explained.

Mousa studied the aerial cable snaking into the dark crawl space. Haseeb crouched down next to him. 'If we're hunting a high-value target, they will leave booby traps in their wake. We need a penal squad.'

It was a valid request. Haseeb could lose his whole team to such traps. Mousa got to his feet. 'Major Allawi, send for a squad of penal troops. Quickly.'

Allawi spoke into his radio. Ten minutes later, whistles and jeers followed a dozen frightened caliphate soldiers into the generator room. They had been stripped of their weapons and equipment and they wore the black armbands of penal troops. All of them had broken military laws, but on the battlefield, there was no time for courts martial. Instead, transgressors were pooled together and formed into penal squads. Mousa waved a hand.

'They're all yours,' he told Haseeb. 'Let's get on with it.'

The penal troops lined up across the generator room, watching the big Afghan with wide, frightened eyes. Haseeb picked out two men, gave them each a torch, and ordered them inside the crawl space. One dropped to his knees and disappeared. The other looked the Afghan squarely in the eye and refused, claiming to be a victim of mistaken identity.

With surprising speed, Haseeb drew a curved knife and slit the man's throat. As blood sprayed, Haseeb pulled him from the line and threw him across the room. The prisoner tried to get to his feet, his hands red with blood, then fell to the ground. Haseeb gave the torch to another, and he scuttled into the dark chamber.

Mousa watched the man on the floor as he stared at the low ceiling, his hands clamped around the wide gash across his throat. He gurgled, choking on blood, and then his hands went limp as he gave up the fight. Mousa saw his lips moving soundlessly. Then he died—

An explosion rocked the floor beneath them, and a cloud spewed from the crawl space and filled the generator room. When it settled,

Haseeb bundled another prisoner inside. He came back a minute later, his uniform covered in blood.

Haseeb turned to Mousa. 'Just as I suspected, general. There will be others.'

Mousa clapped his hands. 'Then clear them! Let's go!'

Minutes later, Haseeb reported what Mousa already knew: the presence of an underground cavern, albeit shrouded in total darkness. Night vision equipment was issued, and the rest of the penal troops were ordered down onto the cavern floor. The explosion was much larger than the first and it shook the walls and floor. When Mousa crawled through and inspected the damage, he saw the gantry and staircase had been ripped away from the wall. Far below, the dead lay still and the injured moaned beneath the twisted, scorched metal. Mousa waved his torch around the cavern. He saw the train tracks and the tunnels, and he couldn't help but marvel at the engineering. He crawled back into the generator room.

'Major Allawi, I want our paratroopers down on the cavern floor asap. They'll need their roping gear. When they get down there, they must secure the immediate area. Send the signallers down with them and locate that signal.' As Allawi issued his orders to the waiting para commanders, Mousa turned to the Afghan. 'Split your men into two groups and send one up each tunnel. I want to know in which direction they lead. We've run out of penal troops and time is against us, so you must take your own precautions.'

'I understand.'

'I want Beecham alive. Remember that.'

He watched Haseeb and his men file into the crawl space. 'Major!' Allawi limped back to Mousa's side.

'Yes, general?'

'Get the engineers to widen that gap. This is all taking too long. And we'll need power and light down in those tunnels.'

'At once.'

'One last thing. I want a Quick Reaction Force on standby. Once we find out where those tunnels go, we need to intercept Beecham's escape route. Have the vehicles assemble in St. James' Park.'

Allawi nodded and left. Mousa folded his arms, his fists bunched in frustration. They'd wasted so much time already, and with each passing second, he knew Beecham was getting further away.

CHAPTER 50
POWER STATION

FAZ POUNDED DOWN THE STAIRS AND BURST THROUGH THE DOORS INTO THE Park Heights lobby. He saw a man behind the reception desk. The man looked startled and threw up his hands. Faz clocked the dark clothing, the black beanie, the rucksack on his back, and he raised the barrel of his gun.

'Get out,' he told the thief.

The man didn't argue. He backed away and disappeared out through the glass doors and onto the mezzanine level. Faz checked there were no more opportunities hiding in the reception area and followed the man outside. Shouts echoed inside the power station and Faz took a careful step towards the glass balustrade.

Down on the ground floor, armed shadows milled around, playing their torches over deserted shops and restaurants, and he heard shouts and laughter, much of it in English. Like their friends on the Wandsworth Road, they appeared confident, untroubled. Maybe they were the same people and had teamed up with a similar group. Or maybe there were groups like this all over the place. The only thing Faz knew for sure was that he had to get out of there.

He crept back into the service staircase and listened carefully. Nothing. He made his way downstairs and out through the service entrance. He loitered in the shadows of the doorway and weighed up his options. Heading south wasn't an option. A vast swathe of housing estates lay in his path and traversing them could prove deadly. Instinct told him he would be safer north of the river, but the view from the tower gave him little hope.

Faz knew about the emergency bunkers and government shelters, and he reasoned soldiers, senior police officers and civil servants would be there right now, managing this crisis from deep underground. A voice inside him whispered a warning—*there's no one there*, it said. They were the first targets. They're all dead.

Indecision rooted his feet to the ground. He needed somewhere to wait out the immediate crisis. Things would look better in the morning.

In the cold light of day, sanity and order would once again prevail. He would find an empty apartment, somewhere with running water and a locked door, and rest. When the sun rose, things would be better. He flipped up his hood and stepped out of the shadows.

He'd taken a dozen steps across the access road when the truck barrelled around the corner, catching Faz in its headlights. The engine roared, and the Faz heard the horn tooting. He shielded his eyes, knowing he was completely exposed, and in that moment, he realised he'd been mistaken for one of their own.

He held the AK by his right leg and forced himself to relax, employing the tactics he'd learned as a deep-cover agent. Breathe. Relax. Think.

He waved, and the trucks hissed to a stop next to him. The driver leaned an arm on the door frame and shouted something over the idling engines. On the flatbed behind him, two armed men leaned on the roof of the cab, watching. They were relaxed. Complacent.

'Who're you with?' the driver asked him. He was older, in his forties, with a crinkly black beard streaked with grey.

'What?'

The driver raised his voice. 'Which group?'

'Yours,' Faz said.

The older man stared at him, his eyes catching the ballistic vest, the

AK, the hoodie, jeans and sneakers. *I'm one of you,* Faz's body language screamed.

The driver's eyes narrowed. 'I don't recognise you.'

'Neither do I,' said the shadow in the passenger seat. 'What's your name?'

The driver switched off the engine. Inky darkness rushed in and swallowed the access road beneath the vast power station. Faz blinked his eyes shut. He needed his night vision. Fast.

'What was your activation word?' the driver asked him.

Faz's hopes faded. Activation words were the language of espionage and deep cover agents, of spymasters, and governments. Not truck drivers.

Faz snapped his fingers. 'I remember,' he said, raising the AK. 'It's don't fucking move.' He swung the barrel and covered the two figures on the flatbed. 'Drop the guns over the side. Now!'

He heard a door open, and feet dropping to the ground. The passenger. One of flatbed shadows ducked, and in that moment Faz knew he'd lost control.

He opened fire, a three-round burst that shredded the truck's tyre, and then he turned and ran for the landscaped grounds across the road. He weaved left, then left again, cringing as the guns behind him opened fire. Rounds zipped past him, and he dodged right, praying he wasn't running into the path of a bullet.

He made the trees, a thick cluster of silver birches, and leaves fell around him as bullets shredded the foliage. He threw himself onto the grass and crawled between the trunks. The gunfire stopped, replaced by running feet. Faz got to his and kept moving through the trees. Shouts echoed in the dark, and a gun fired, but the rounds were wild and distant.

The man-made copse ended abruptly, and Faz found himself on a wide footpath flanked by towering apartment blocks marching towards the river. There would be shops and play areas and ornamental gardens. That meant cover, and if he kept moving fast enough, he could outpace his pursuers.

He heard them shouting behind him, more voices now, and a burst of radio traffic. That frightened him. Ahead, he saw a dark channel between two apartment blocks, and he sprinted for it, his heart pounding, the assault rifle and ballistic vest plates weighing him down as he headed north towards the River Thames.

CHAPTER 51
BANGED UP

DAVE GREENWOOD NURSED HIS SECOND CUP OF TEA SINCE FINDING SHELTER in the basement flat.

He sat on a comfortable chair in a darkened drawing room lit by sweet-smelling candles. His saviour, Stuart Murray, sipped his own brew as he studied Dave from a creaky leather wing-back.

The white-haired gent's unruffled manner had impressed Dave, ever since he'd barged the old fella out of the way and bolted the front door. And that's where Dave had stayed for several minutes, ear pressed against the thick wood, listening to the shouts and footfalls on the pavement above.

He'd expected to hear those feet pounding down the basement steps towards Stuart's front door. He expected to hear thumping, and threats, and then gunfire.

Instead, the hunters' passage faded, and the shouts grew thin and distant. Dave had escaped by the skin of his teeth, and it was thanks to the man opposite him.

Now he felt safe. The front door was secure, and, like most basement flats, the street-facing windows protected with heavy security grills and thick drapes.

If they both stayed quiet and didn't move around too much, they should be safe enough. The room they occupied now was halfway along the apartment corridor and had no windows, just a wall of books and an unlit fireplace. Stuart smiled at him from the opposite chair.

'Feeling better?'

Dave studied his unruffled host. He must've been in his seventies, with thin white hair and a lined face that showed no fear. 'How are you so calm about all of this?'

'I've seen this kind of thing before,' the older man said. 'It'll blow over.'

Dave felt a flash of irritation. 'Blow over? Do you have any idea what's happening out there? It's absolute carnage.'

'You think we should be afraid?'

'Too right we should!' Dave bit his lip. 'I'm sorry. I didn't mean to shout. My nerves are shot.'

'Drink your tea. We're quite safe.' Stuart took another sip of his brew and set the cup down on the coffee table between them. He plucked a tobacco pouch from his cardigan pocket and rolled a thin cigarette.

A distant rumble rattled the montage of framed photographs on the mantle above the fireplace, and Dave's eye was drawn to one, a black-and-white shot of a much younger Stuart standing in front of a towering pile of rubble. He'd been captured in deep conversation with several others, men with beards, radios, and guns. Just like the men who'd stalked Dave.

'Where was that?'

'Syria, a long time ago,' Stuart said. He held up his cigarette. 'Do you mind?'

Dave shook his head. 'What were you doing out there?'

'I used to work for a charity, BBC Media Action. I was there during the war, assisting with the humanitarian crisis.'

Dave pointed to the gunmen. 'Those guys don't look so friendly.'

'One has to cooperate with all sides in a conflict,' Stuart told him, lighting his roll-up, and blowing smoke towards the ceiling. 'It's not always palatable, but one has to build relationships to get help to where it's needed.'

Who's going to help us? Dave wondered. He finished his tea and stood up. 'I'm going to the front door. See what's happening.'

'Be careful.'

Dave stepped out into the hallway. Night had fallen, and the corridor was dark. He felt his way along the wall to the front door and knelt at the brass letterbox. When he lifted the flap, cool air wafted into the apartment, tinged with smoke, and burnt timber. He heard distant gunfire and what sounded like an aircraft, also a long way off. There were no voices up on the pavement, no running feet. Things had settled down, but Dave wasn't going to stick his head above the parapet just yet.

Back in the drawing room, Stuart was tapping cigarette ash into a large glass ashtray. He saw Dave and raised an eyebrow. 'Well?'

'Nothing,' the policeman said, slumping back into his chair. 'It's dead out there.' He winced at his choice of words. 'Sorry.' Stuart smiled, and Dave felt another flash of irritation. 'You seem to be taking all of this in your stride.'

'I've learned to accept the things I cannot change,' Stuart said with a shrug of his thin shoulders. 'This situation is an extreme one, far beyond the experience of most people. My instinct tells me that things will get worse before they get better, so the prudent strategy is to wait it out.' He pointed to the hallway. 'As a police officer, your instinct is to get out there and help people. To restore the rule of law. Given your recent encounters, that might prove dangerous, if not lethal.'

'No shit,' Dave said.

'Exactly. Things are chaotic right now, so we must focus on our immediate requirements. Food, water, shelter. All of that we have here, minus gas and electricity, but we don't need heating and I have lots of supplies, including a portable camping stove.' He winked. 'Old habits die hard. So, we're relatively comfortable, in which case I suggest we ride out this storm and see how things look in the morning.'

Dave massaged his jawline. 'I have a wife at home in Guilford. She'll be worried sick.'

'Guilford is a long way from London. Things could be relatively normal there.'

'It doesn't feel like that. This is big. Huge. And what about those planes we heard earlier? It sounded like they were landing on the street outside. And the explosions.'

'They reminded me of Syria,' Stuart said. 'Except bigger.'

Dave shook his head. 'I just can't believe this. How could things have fallen apart so quickly?'

'I don't know, but I'm sure your wife would want you to be safe. What's her name?'

'Rebecca.'

'If she were here, she'd tell you to stay put. There's no sense in exposing yourself to danger.' Stuart got to his feet. He left the room and returned a minute later with a bottle and two tumblers. He poured something dark into both and handed one to Dave. 'For those nerves.'

Dave caught the scent of malt whiskey and downed it in a single swallow. It burned his throat, but it felt good. 'Thank you.'

Stuart raised his glass and sipped. 'Help yourself.'

Dave poured another stiff measure and sat back down, staring into the flickering candle flames. 'I've never killed anyone before.'

'It was self-defence, you said.'

'I shot them in the back.'

'What choice did you have?'

'I could've turned around, got out of there.'

'You were trying to help. Trying to stop the bloodshed.'

'I achieved nothing.'

'You saved your own life. Rebecca will be grateful for that.' Stuart poured another measure into his own glass. 'Try not to think about it. It doesn't help, believe me.'

Dave looked up. 'Have you ever killed anyone?'

'No,' Stuart said, shaking his head. 'But people have died because we couldn't get to them in time. They died because we bedded them down in buildings that were later bombed. Or because the food didn't get through the battle lines. These events happen in war. They're heartbreaking, and they can eat you alive if you over-analyse them. My advice is, focus on your intentions. You set out to do good. That's what's important—'

The whistle shrilled through the hallway. Dave snapped out of his chair and stood. 'Someone's outside.' He took the Glock from his belt clip and made sure he had a round chambered. 'Stay here.'

'I'm not comfortable with guns,' Stuart said, his eyes fixed on the automatic in Dave's hands.

'Don't worry,' he said, slipping it back into its holster. 'I won't use it unless I have to.'

'Leave it, David. You can't do any good by yourself and you certainly don't want to draw any attention. That could get us both killed.'

'I have to see what's happening. It could be important.'

'Then be careful. Please.'

Dave crept back down the hallway, his eyes focussed on the dim outline of the front door. When he got there, he took a step to the right and entered a pitch-black guest bedroom. Dave felt the unmade bed with an outstretched hand and worked his way towards the window. Slowly, he parted a thick drape and peered through a sliver of a gap, the curtain material soft against his cheek. Now he had a better view of the pavement above.

Beyond the black spiked railings, he saw the dark outline of a parked car, and the houses across the street. Above them, a red glow painted the sky. He heard the whistle again, long, and loud, like a referee signalling full time. Then he heard the drum of running boots and dark silhouettes flashed past the railings.

Dave watched them, saw their Kevlar helmets, their night vision equipment, their foreign weapons, assault rifles and belt-fed guns. One man carried a dark tube on his shoulder, and Dave knew instantly that he was looking at some kind of missile launcher.

He waited until the last man had passed, until there were no more whistles, and the street became quiet again. He eased the curtain back into place and re-joined Stuart back in the drawing room.

'Well?' the older man asked him, arching a white eyebrow.

'They were soldiers. Not ours.'

'You must be mistaken,' Stuart said.

'I don't think so.' Dave sat down and clasped his hands together.

Stuart set his glass down. 'Are you saying there are foreign troops here in London? That's impossible.'

Dave waved a hand towards the hallway. 'D'you hear any shooting out there? If they were our boys, they would've engaged those terrorists by now.'

'Maybe they surrendered.'

Dave cocked his chin towards the photograph on the mantlepiece. 'You think those guys would've surrendered? No chance.' Dave's eyes widened. 'They're Islamic State troops! They must be!'

'Impossible,' Stuart said.

Dave scowled. 'You keep saying that.'

'Because what you're suggesting makes little sense.'

'Really? Think about it. Every year, they hold these huge military exercises. This year was supposed to be the biggest ever. And there's been a lot of tension on the streets here in the UK. Protests over that prison riot, the asylum seekers washed up on the beaches of Kent—'

Stuart rolled his eyes. 'Come on, David. That's absurd.'

Dave took a breath. 'I agree. It sounds mad, but it's not beyond the realm of possibility, is it? Wazir has a lot of clout in Europe. He'd been making his voice heard for a long time now, stirring things up with all those inflammatory speeches.'

Stuart's nostrils flared, as if he'd caught a whiff of something rotten. 'That's borderline offensive. His people have suffered for decades, in conflicts all over the world. I've seen it at first hand and it's ugly. He has every right to demand justice and to protect people's basic human rights. Surely, as a policeman, you would agree?'

He stared at Dave, unblinking. Dave held up his hands. 'I'm not saying he shouldn't jump to the defence of others, I'm just saying…'

His voice trailed off. Dave hadn't climbed the Metropolitan Police ladder without constant self-censoring. Stuart might be getting on in years, but he probably had connections at the BBC. He could make trouble for Dave when all this was over. Because it would end, wouldn't it? Right now, Dave couldn't be sure. He changed the subject.

'You might be right about Guilford,' he said, embarrassed by his crude deflection. 'I think we should get out of London.'

'Really? How?'

'By car, probably. If we wait until the early hours, we can get out of the immediate area at least. Do you own a car?'

Stuart scoffed. 'Absolutely not. I'd need to re-mortgage this place if I wanted to drive around London.'

'What about your neighbours?'

Stuart shook his head. 'The apartment above us is a recruitment agency. The one above that is almost always empty. And before you ask, I can't speak for the neighbours. I barely see them.'

'I can't just sit here!' Dave snapped. He felt restless and frightened, and the urge to bolt was overwhelming. 'I'll find a bike, cycle across the river. Maybe the trains are running out of Clapham Junction.'

'And maybe they're not,' Stuart said. 'You could find yourself horribly exposed. My advice is to stay, wait things out. Let's see what the morning brings. Maybe the power will come back on. Maybe the mobile phone network will start working again. You'll be able to call Rebecca—'

Stuart frowned, then got to his feet. Dave looked up at him. 'Are you okay?'

The older man hurried from the room. When he returned, he was holding a small device. He held it out like a trophy. 'I forgot I had this.'

'What is it?'

'A radio. The wind-up variety. Let's see if we can get it working, shall we?' He cranked the small handle for several seconds, then switched it on. Static filled the room and Stuart dialled down the volume. Then he began scrolling through the wavebands. 'We'll try Medium Wave first,' he said. His eyes narrowed as he focussed, and Dave listened to the steady hiss that filled the room. They heard squawks and clicks, but no voices. 'Strange,' Stuart said. 'We'll try FM.'

Dave leaned in closer, his ears straining to pick up any sound other than static. Where had all the stations gone? He could understand the London broadcasters being out of business, but the national ones? What about pirate stations—

'*—and stay away from windows. Conserve food and water. Do not use your mobile or landline telephones. Some areas of the country are experiencing power outages. Do not be alarmed. Unplug all electrical appliances until power is restored. Stay tuned to this frequency. This has been a government broadcast.*'

The message was followed by a brief interlude of music, and then it started again. Dave and Stuart listened to it two more times before Stuart clicked the radio off.

'So, this is nationwide,' Dave said, feeling the blood drain from his face. 'I've got to get home. Get back to Becks.'

'You heard the message. We must stay here.'

'I can't fucking stay!' Dave bit his tongue. 'Sorry. I'm stressed out.'

'It's alright,' Stuart said in a soothing voice. 'How are your neighbours? In Guilford?'

'Decent people, level-headed. We get on well.'

'Then your wife will have someone to support her.'

'I suppose,' Dave said, and the more he thought about it, the more reassured he felt. His house was on the outskirts of town, close to the fields and woods. It was quiet and pretty and should be far from any trouble. 'Yeah. She'll be okay. She's a smart lady.'

Stuart smiled. 'There you go, then. I suggest we get comfortable. Let me top you up.'

Stuart refilled their tumblers, and Dave unclipped his gun and slipped it beneath his chair. He kicked his legs out and felt himself relax a little. It had been a long day, and a longer evening. He didn't want to think about the men he'd killed, so he shut the event out of his mind. Stuart interrupted his thoughts.

'So, where do you think the government people will be?'

'I've no idea,' Dave said, shrugging. 'I thought about a stint in the PDP—that's Parliamentary and Diplomatic Protection—but I never pursued it.'

'If you had, you might be in danger now. Trapped beneath ground in a bunker somewhere. I'm sure they're all over the place. Have you ever heard of such things?'

'There's one under Admiralty Arch. I'm sure there are others. Leftovers from the Cold War.'

Stuart frowned. 'We must pray the Prime Minister and his Cabinet are safe. They could be the only chance we have of resolving this thing peacefully. It's all about diplomacy in the end.'

'What if they're all dead? What then?'

Stuart stared at him, his face lit by the flame of a flickering candle. 'The consequences of that scenario don't bear thinking about.'

Dave looked away, his stomach sick with fear.

CHAPTER 52
ALL ABOARD

Harry couldn't run anymore. He stopped, hands on his knees, while he gulped the stale air of the tunnel. His head spun, and he retched loudly. Nothing came up except bile.

He heard Reynolds ordering Cole back down the tunnel to cover their rear. Progress had been too slow for the soldiers' liking, and they'd only just passed the broken train carriage. Forsythe had called a halt by the open car and Reynolds had gone to work, cutting the control cables, and disabling the thing for good.

How Harry would've loved to ride that car all the way to Kensington Gardens. Instead, his heart beat like a rabbit's as he coughed and retched. It was sheer exhaustion, but he felt something else too—fear. Borderline terror. The thought of capture turned his leg muscles to mush, and he prayed the electric carriage at Buckingham Palace was still there, and in service. Running all the way to Kensington Gardens might just kill him. He felt a hand on his shoulder.

'Are you alright?'

Harry cuffed his mouth dry with the sleeve of his jacket and stood up. Forsythe looked troubled. He was also breathing hard. Both had spent too long behind a desk.

'I'm fine,' Harry said between breaths. 'Out of shape, that's all. I'll do better.'

'Drink this,' Reynolds said, handing over a sports drink. 'It'll give you a little more energy.' Harry emptied half of the contents in one hit. Reynolds snatched it back. 'That'll do for now, sir. We'll top you up further down the line.'

'You make me sound like a clapped-out car,' Harry said, managing a tired smile. It disappeared when he heard running feet echoing off the tunnel walls.

Cole appeared from out of the gloom, barely out of breath. 'They're down on the cavern floor.'

Harry felt sick again. 'Already?'

'We've got to move faster,' Forsythe said.

'Then lead on.' Harry watched Cole turn back down the tunnel. 'Where's he going?'

'To slow the bad guys down,' Reynolds explained.

'Let's move.'

Forsythe started jogging up the tunnel. Harry followed, moving from a fast walk to a steady jog. Harry felt a little more energised. Maybe it was the fluid intake, or maybe it was the thought of soldiers chasing them. Either way, he was moving, and that was a good thing. It wasn't long before Cole caught them up again.

'Two trip-wires set,' the soldier informed Reynolds as they ran.

'Nice. Take point and recce the platform.'

Platform. The word was sweet music to Harry's ears, but still the tunnel stretched away, a subterranean world of stuffy air, faint blue lights, and inky black shadows. They ran for another ten minutes, until the t-shirt beneath Harry's combat jacket clung to his body and his breath came in ragged, irregular gasps.

'I have to stop,' he said with some difficulty. As he came to a halt, Reynolds grabbed his shoulder and walked him forward.

'No stopping,' he said. 'If you can stand, you can walk. Keep moving.'

Harry moved his legs, forcing himself to put one in front of the other. He took no offence at being manhandled or barked at. Like the others, he knew what was at stake. He also knew he was a potential liability.

'Keep your head up,' Reynolds ordered, marching by Harry's side. 'Breathe in through the nose, out through the mouth. Keep your eyes on the boss and don't think about anything else.'

'Roger,' Harry puffed, borrowing their military terminology. He focussed on the Forsythe's silhouette, striding ahead of him. After several more minutes, Harry felt his body rebelling against the exertion and his head dropped. He saw his shoes, handmade by George Cleverly's of London, now scuffed and covered in dust and grime, and he wondered how much longer he could put one in front of the other.

He lifted his chin, and then he saw something else, something beyond Forsythe's helmeted head.

A pale glow on the tunnel wall—

Reynolds jogged by his side. 'That's Buck House dead ahead. We're almost there, boss. Keep moving.'

Light at the end of the tunnel. Literally. Harry found a new, untapped seam of energy.

'It's clear,' Reynolds reported, a finger pressed against his earpiece. 'Let's move.'

Harry's lungs were heaving by the time he trudged up the sloping ramp to the dimly lit platform beneath Buckingham Palace. The facility here was much smaller than the Downing Street complex. It was like a small tube station, with several metal benches along its length and a single steel door built into the rough concrete wall. Harry assumed the door led up to the palace itself.

Cole was standing behind the window of a small alcove cut into the wall. He tapped on the glass as Harry as the others gathered outside. Harry heard a sound like an electric car and a few moments later, an open train carriage emerged from the westbound tunnel and glided to a stop midway along the platform. Cole joined them and addressed the soldiers. Harry reminded himself that right now, he was nothing more than baggage.

'I called it down from Kensington. No drama at all. Looks like everything from here westwards is working okay.'

'Let's hope so,' Forsythe said. 'Harry, step aboard please.'

Harry climbed inside the carriage and dropped onto one of several thick bench seats, his body rejoicing in the moment. Reynolds sat up front behind a small digital control panel with a single lever. He turned to Cole.

'How many grenades have you got left?'

'One.'

'Set it in the tunnel behind us. Quick as you can.'

Harry watched Cole disappear into the tunnel, praying he would hurry. He turned back to the brigadier. 'What happens if we get to the next stop, and we can't reach Northstar?'

'In that case, we find a vehicle and head west.'

'That sounds dangerous.'

'We have to get clear of the city while we still can.' Forsythe checked his watch. 'It's after midnight. Time is against us.'

Harry pointed a finger at the ceiling. 'Do you think there's anyone up there? Maybe they need our help?'

'The King and his family are in Balmoral.'

'I'm talking about the staff.'

Forsythe turned and faced Harry. 'We can't risk being swamped by a frightened mob. There're on their own, I'm afraid.'

Harry looked away. He didn't argue. He wanted to get to safety more than anything. Running feet echoed across the platform, and Cole scrambled aboard the carriage.

'All set.'

'Hold tight,' said Reynolds.

He pushed the control lever forward, and the carriage moved away from the platform. They entered the tunnel and sped up. Harry turned around and watched the dim lights of the station fade from view.

A moment later, darkness swallowed them. He turned back, feeling the breeze on his face, and watching the blur of blue wall lights as they headed west below the war-torn streets of London.

CHAPTER 53
TUNNEL RATS

Mousa switched off the portable battery lamp as light flooded the main cavern.

He looked down and saw the control panel was lifeless. Sabotaged, no doubt. It's what Mousa would've done.

All around him, engineering troops had exposed wiring cabinets and ducting panels and were busy ferreting away inside them. Mousa left the room. Outside on the platform, his paratroopers were assembling into sections. He looked up to the bomb-damaged gantry and saw a continuous stream of soldiers fast-roping down to the cavern floor—

BOOM!

Mousa squatted down, pistol gripped his gloved hand. Moments later, an enormous cloud of dust billowed from the westbound tunnel. The paras took up positions on either side, guns ready. From out of the dust, Mousa saw Haseeb emerge, jabbing into his radio.

'Well?'

'My men found a transportation carriage. It was booby trapped. Three dead, one seriously wounded. I need more penal troops, general. My men are too precious to waste on trip wires.'

Mousa gave him a hard look. 'You're the experts. Get your people up that tunnel and find Beecham. Go!' Haseeb doubled away. Mousa waved a para captain over. 'Take two sections and back up the Afghans. But don't get too close. Let them do their job.' The captain nodded and turned away.

'Allawi!' bellowed Mousa, his deep voice echoing off the cavern walls. The major appeared a moment later. 'Status?'

'The other tunnel heads north,' Allawi told him. 'The recce platoon is already two kilometres inside. No exits to be found. And no signs of passage. They found a train carriage, but it's unworkable.'

Mousa grunted. More confirmation that Beecham had headed west. 'And the foot tunnel?'

'Fresh prints in the dust. Two sets. I think it's a decoy team.'

'Maybe. Send a squad anyway. And where are my drones?'

'General Al-Bitruji has sent three over. They should be here any minute.'

'And he's set up in the palace?'

'Yes, general,' Allawi confirmed.

'He always had a taste for the opulent. Perhaps he's installed himself as the new King of England.' Mousa froze. *The palace.* It was close. Due west, in fact. 'The map. Quickly.'

Allawi returned a few moments later. Mousa laid it on the floor and studied it. How could he have missed the connection?

'The westbound tunnel leads to Buckingham Palace. If this is a VIP escape system, it would surely cater to the King and his people, no?' Allawi nodded. 'Get Al-Bitruji on the radio,' Mousa told him. 'Tell him to rip the place apart and find the entrance to that tunnel. If we're quick enough, we might trap them.'

Mousa folded the map and shoved it in his pocket. 'Have transport waiting for me upstairs,' he told his 2IC. 'I'm going to the palace. Call me when the drones are ready to fly. And stay close to the radio, Major. You're my eyes and ears.'

'Yes, general.'

Mousa walked over to the shattered steel gantry and got himself winched up to the generator room. He hurried through the basement of Downing Street, his paratrooper close protection team carving a path through the press of uniforms. He picked his way through the rubble of Whitehall, where the air was still heavy with smoke and distant gunfire echoed over the shattered rooftops.

Out in Whitehall, a three-vehicle convoy of Humvees waited, engines idling. Mousa hopped aboard the second jeep while his paras climbed aboard all three. A moment late the convoy headed off, snaking around burning cars and dead bodies.

Mousa looked up and saw the Foreign Office building engulfed in flames that reached high into the night sky. In Parliament Square, Big Ben had a clock face shattered and the Houses of Parliament burned fiercely. Gathered on the square itself, hundreds of individuals sat on the ground, their hands clasped on their heads. Mousa saw uniforms, police, and military, but most were civilians. And he saw defeat on their faces.

The convoy swung around Horseguards Parade and turned left onto The Mall, weaving to avoid the sea of discarded parachutes rising and falling in the night breeze.

Arriving at the gates of Buckingham Palace, Mousa noted the shattered stone plinths, the bent and broken black iron gates, and the two AFVs squatting on the parade ground, tracking the convoy with their 40mm guns. Mousa knew he was in no danger—the T-BIS system would've alerted those crews to Mousa's impending arrival, and more troops waved them through the arched portico into the central courtyard of the palace. Mousa climbed out and saw a waiting staff officer in full battle gear.

'An honour, General Mousa. Follow me, please.'

Close protection team in tow, Mousa trailed the orderly through the red-carpeted hallways of Buckingham Palace. As they passed, be-wigged and long dead royals, caught in the glare of torchlight, watched them from gilded frames.

They turned a corner and entered what Mousa assumed was the servants' section of the building. The hallway walls were devoid of expensive oils and object d'art, and the carpet looked worn and discoloured. They passed a room with several easy chairs and a lifeless TV screen. Mousa saw a woman in one chair, her head covered with a coat, her legs splayed out, her arms dangling beside her. A heart attack, he presumed, noting a lack of blood. Either way, her days of waiting on others were over.

The staff officer led them down a narrow flight of smooth stone steps to the palace basement, and Mousa found himself in another corridor with several doors along its length. There was much more activity here, with temporary lights and cables running along the walls. The officer led them into a large, low-ceilinged room that stank of mouldy vegetables.

So, this was Al-Bitruji's command post. It was a good choice, Mousa had to agree; below ground, easy access to the floors above and, if he was not mistaken, an exit to the grounds of the palace itself, covered with a heavy blackout drape and a light discipline warning sign. A large, clear-glass T-BIS screen dominated the centre of the room, surrounded by operators and senior staff. As Mousa approached, Al-Bitruji detached himself from a group of officers.

'Ah! General Mousa! Good to see you!'

Al-Bitruji shook Mousa's and kissed his cheeks. They had known each other for many years, each man's steady rise up the ladder mirrored by the other. But the similarities ended there. Although both men held the rank of general, it was only Mousa who had the ear of the caliph. It was why Al-Bitruji wore a greasy smile beneath his thick moustache as he steered Mousa by the elbow out of earshot. He gave Mousa a conspiratorial wink.

'Still jumping out of planes with the young bucks, eh, Faris?'

Mousa remained stony-faced. 'You received my message, yes?'

Al-Bitruji's grin collapsed. 'Follow me.'

He led Mousa to the T-BIS display, which was currently showing a large area of central London. Mousa saw all major junctions and river crossings had at least one IS element stationed there. He barked a command to the operators, and the display changed to an orbiting drone feed of Buckingham Palace and its immediate area.

Mousa watched as a row of ghostly white figures moved through the grey and black shadows.

'Those are combat engineers,' Al-Bitruji explained. 'They're using ground radar to look for voids. Other teams are searching every basement and cellar in this complex. If there's a tunnel here, we'll find it.'

Mousa nodded. He couldn't fault Al-Bitruji's efforts. He softened his tone. 'How goes the invasion?'

Al-Bitruji changed the display feed to show an overview of England and Wales. IS forces were represented by green icons and the southern half of England showed large concentrations of them, particularly in the South-East and the Midlands.

'It goes as planned,' replied Al-Bitruji. 'Strategic targets have been seized or destroyed. Our ships are docking unopposed in docks and shipyards along the south coast. An armoured brigade has almost reached the outskirts of the capital... here.'

Al-Bitruji pointed to a long line of green icons that stretched along the M3 motorway.

'The brigade will give our ground forces support where it's required. And their psychological impact on the public cannot be overstated.'

Mousa's eye drifted down towards the city of Portsmouth, on the south coast, a few kilometres from Southampton. There, an extensive collection of green icons was still at sea. Clustered along a small stretch of coastline, he saw several red icons.

'What's this?'

'A British frigate opened fire from its moorings, sinking at least three cargo ships before it was disabled.' Al-Bitruji cleared his throat. 'Yet the bloody thing is still firing, even though it's half sunk. And there are Royal Marines all over the city, causing problems. Ambushes, section attacks, sniping, you name it. They are troublesome, but their numbers are few. Soon the city will be flooded with our own troops and armour. They will end it.'

'No prisoners,' Mousa ordered. 'We must nip rebellion in the bud.'

'Of course.'

'What about organised resistance? And where is their air force?'

'Running, by the look of it. The sleeper teams did a good job on the RAF bases, and a lot of planes and equipment were destroyed. It doesn't take much to cripple a modern fighter, Faris. You and I could do it with half a can of gasoline.' He waved a hand at clusters of red icons across the map of England. 'As for their land forces, they're running for the Scottish border. It's an attempt to regroup, of course, but it suits our purposes...' He paused as a junior officer came to a halt in front a few steps away. 'Yes, what is it?'

'General, we have found the entrance to the tunnel system.'

'Show me,' Mousa told him. They made their way by torchlight across the palace gardens towards Constitution Hill, where the trees and shrubbery were thickest. Mousa set the pace, and he heard Al-Bitruji puffing behind him. In the darkness ahead, Mousa saw several soldiers gathered around a small vine-covered blockhouse, its green steel door forced open. The junior officer pointed his torch beam inside and addressed the generals.

'There's a staircase inside that leads down to a train platform.'

Mousa let his bodyguards take point and followed them down. A minute later, he found himself in a small terminus, like the one beneath Downing Street, but smaller. Troops swarmed all around it, torches piercing the darkness of the tunnels.

'This is amazing,' Al-Bitruji said, his jaw slack as his eyes wandered across the facility. 'I wonder how far it goes?'

Mousa ignored the question and jumped down onto the tracks. The smooth concrete between the rails was spotted with oil. Mousa dipped his finger into a small stain and rubbed it between thumb and forefinger; fresh. They'd missed them. That meant another train. He stared into the westbound tunnel and echoed Al-Bitruji's question—how far did it go?

He heard shouts behind him and saw Haseeb and his SERTRAK team emerge from the eastbound tunnel. They were panting hard. Haseeb saw Mousa and cocked a thumb over his shoulder.

'We've just defused another booby-trap. It was a rush job. My guess is, they can't be too far ahead.'

Al-Bitruji joined them. 'Tell me what you need, Faris. I have an entire battle group at your disposal.'

Mousa was about to answer when he heard a low humming noise coming from the westbound tunnel, and a grey, multi-rotored surveillance drone glided into the cavern. It slowed, then hovered eight feet off the ground. Allawi's voice hissed in Mousa's earpiece.

'General! I have you on audio and visual.'

Mousa saw the drone's cameras clustered on its nose. It resembled a flying spider, ready to pounce. He pointed to his right. 'Get up that tunnel, fast as you can. Find them!'

The drone's nose dipped, and it flew into the tunnel. A moment later, it was lost in the darkness. Mousa turned to the big Afghan. 'What are you waiting for? Get after it. And remember, I want Beecham alive.'

The Afghan nodded his bald, sweaty head. 'As you wish.'

Haseeb and his people set off after the drone. Mousa watched their red torches bouncing across the tunnel walls until they, too, disappeared.

'So, that's a SERTRAK team,' Al-Bitruji said, watching them go. 'They have quite a reputation.'

Mousa glared at his fellow general. 'Fuck reputation. All I care about is results. Let's get back upstairs.'

He led the way, as Al-Bitruji puffed and panted up the stairs behind him.

CHAPTER 54
KINGFISHER

FAZ RAN FOR HIS LIFE TOWARDS THE RIVER THAMES. SHADOWS CHASED him, too many to count, their voices overlapping, echoing off the surrounding buildings. He caught snatches though—

Cut him off!
Get the fucker!
Go left!
Go right!

His legs and lungs ached. His head twisted left and right as he looked for an escape route. They were driving him east along the riverbank, exactly where he *didn't* want to go.

Maybe they were pushing him towards another group, waiting somewhere ahead. Behind him, the whoops and shouts rebounded like radar off the high-rises. They were coming from all directions. Faz was frightened, more than he'd ever been. He couldn't think clearly. He didn't have a plan. What he needed was a bolt hole, where he could go to ground and wait out the storm of vengeance behind him.

He turned a corner, keeping to the shadows of another high-rise. The ground floor was all shops, and he tried the doors of each one, pushing and pulling, but to no avail. He couldn't break the glass, couldn't make any more noise. All he could do was hope.

He reached the last door, an upmarket beauty parlour. Flawless models smiled from the window display. He shook the door, but it wouldn't budge. The cardboard beauties smiled wider, mocking him— *they're going to catch you! You're going to die!*

He spun around, eyes moving left and right. There had to be somewhere—

Then he saw them, towering above another ornamental copse. Masts.

The marina!

He exploded out of the shadows, sprinting across grass borders and meandering paths. Behind him, the voices grew louder, calling to each other, but the tone and urgency remained the same. He hadn't been spotted. Yet.

He plunged into the darkness of the trees. Low branches whipped his face, plucked at his hoodie, snared his sling. Mother Nature was against him. He ducked his head and forced his way through the trees and bushes, and then he was free.

The footpath overlooked a huge, manmade harbour filled with boats of all shapes and sizes, from small skiffs to huge gin palaces. He climbed over the gate and hurried down a flight of steps to the wooden jetties.

His eyes searched the darkness. He ruled out anything with a sail. Too much effort to get underway and far too slow. He dismissed the smaller pleasure cruisers too—a gleaming white craft might make an irresistible target. No, he needed something else. He moved up and down the maze of jetties until he found it.

It was a Targa, a 25-footer, tied off between a single-masted yacht and a narrowboat. It was a working vessel, painted a dull grey, its flanks scuffed by the constant rub of jetty tyres. Someone had made a perfect job of tying off the mooring lines. That was a good sign. It meant the owner knew what he or she was doing, and that meant the boat would be well serviced. Faz hoped. If he could start it, she'd be perfect.

She was called *Kingfisher*, and she wobbled on the water as Faz jumped aboard. The shouts behind him were louder now, more urgent. They'd lost their prey, and they were angry. It was only a matter of time before they found the marina. That was a fish-in-a-barrel type situation, one that Faz wouldn't survive. He stepped into the small wheelhouse.

'Hello?'

No reply. He clicked on his barrel torch and checked the cabins below, two cramped rooms and a toilet. Empty. In the wheelhouse, he flipped open the chart table and saw a river map clipped to its surface. He unslung his rifle and searched for an ignition key. Nothing. He heard a shout close by and ducked. His eyes scanned the ground above the marina, but he saw nothing. He didn't have much time.

Beneath the wheel, he saw a small cupboard. Inside was a tool wrap, and he rolled it out on the floor. The medium-sized screwdriver looked like it would do the job and he jammed it into the ignition barrel, working it down, twisting it left and right—

Ignition lights glowed red and amber. The fuel needle crept up towards a full tank and the oil pressure gauge levelled out. As Faz suspected, *Kingfisher* was well maintained. He turned the screwdriver another notch and the powerful inboard rumbled into life. He ducked outside and let go the mooring ropes, jamming his foot against the jetty and pushing off.

In the wheelhouse, he eased the throttle forward a notch. The propeller bit into the water and *Kingfisher* moved away from the jetty. Ahead, he saw the harbour entrance and the black, drifting mass of the river beyond. He eased back the throttle, allowing the boat's momentum to carry him towards it. Passing the marina entrance, the current caught the bow and turned the boat downstream. Faz increased power and turned her back to starboard, his eyes scanning the riverbank above him. Nothing.

Ahead of him, in the darkness, two bridges spanned the Thames. The first was Grosvenor Bridge, the crossing used by commuter trains heading in and out of Victoria Station north of the river. A hundred meters beyond that was Chelsea Bridge, the span used by cars and pedestrians. Faz couldn't see any movement on either, but it was hard to tell from the water. He had no choice but to keep going.

The *Kingfisher's* engine echoed off the damp walls of the Grosvenor Bridge pier as the boat slid under its wide iron span. The noise sounded deafening, and he gunned the engine, desperate to put some distance between him and the power station complex.

Chelsea Bridge passed above him as he headed towards the middle of the river. He cut the power again, allowing the white wake behind him to dissipate. Red light blazed as a flare popped high overhead. It flickered and fizzed, casting the dark, looming towers behind him into sharp, crimson relief. The flare drifted out over the water, but it was a long way behind him, and then it died on the river. He was clear.

Faz looked left, watching the shadowy expanse of Battersea Park drift by. Dotted around the horizon, parts of the sky glowed red. Carnage and violence had engulfed London since yesterday evening, but here, in the wheelhouse of a small boat on a wide, black river, Faz felt a little safer. Not much, but a little.

And there was something else, too. *Kingfisher* had planted a seed of an idea, one that was forming into a plan. A plan that would take him upriver and out of the city.

CHAPTER 55
BAIT

Sherman trudged along the foot tunnel, leading both him and Brooks further away from the Downing Street complex.

They'd heard and felt some seismic rumbles on their journey north, and dust was a constant companion in the stale air, causing both men to sweat, cough and spit.

Despite being over six feet and weighing in at ninety-plus kilos, the low ceiling and the narrow concrete tunnel did not bother Sherman. Instead, he was bothered by this fruitless task, this time-wasting mission he had embarked upon. Orders were orders, he knew that, but his days of taking them from British troops were over.

In his mind, he's already revealed himself as the spy he was. No, not a spy—they were usually posh white dudes with Oxbridge educations. The ones he'd met on past ops were all like that. No, Sherman considered himself to be more like a secret weapon, like a tactical nuke buried beneath an enemy city, lying in wait until the call came. Sherman had heard that call loud and clear. And answered it.

Yet he ached to return to his brothers back at the complex. He wanted to join the hunt for Beecham, to see the surprise on his face when he laid eyes on his former bodyguard. Instead, he was here, diverting precious caliphate resources away from that hunt. But not for much longer, he decided.

The concrete shaft was lit by tiny overhead lights recessed into the curved ceiling every ten meters, creating deep pools of gloom in between each one. When Brooks stopped every so often to check their six, he did so in those shadows. Sherman would also use them for cover. When the time was right. And that time was fast approaching.

Exits from the stuffy tunnel were few. The first one, a few hundred meters behind them, was a steel ladder built into an escape tube cut into the ceiling. Neither man knew where it led to; a government basement somewhere, or a storm drain perhaps. Sherman had argued a case for using it, but Brooks was adamant. They were decoys, he explained, at that meant leaving a long trail that could be followed.

Sherman had fumed. Scaling that ladder would've been the perfect opportunity to drop Brooks and get back to Downing Street. Now, another opportunity presented itself. One that Sherman wouldn't squander.

He stopped beneath one of those tiny ceiling lights and held up his hand.

'What is it?' Brooks whispered, closing the gap between them.

Sherman sniffed the stuffy air. 'You smell that? It's like diesel.'

'It's aviation fuel. From the plane crash.'

'It stinks down here. We should head back to that escape ladder.'

'We keep moving,' Brooks said. 'Chances are they've found this tunnel. They'll be chasing us soon enough, and I don't want to be stuck in this pipe when the shooting starts.'

Sherman turned and faced his comrade. Brooks was staring ahead at the tiny string of lights that disappeared around a distant curve. 'And I don't want to be stuck in here if that fuel vapour ignites.'

Brooks looked up at his taller teammate. 'We keep going. And pick the pace up, would you? I'm champing at the bit back here.'

Sherman stepped aside, squeezing his big frame against the curved wall. 'You take point, then. There's no fucking oxygen down here.'

'Lightweight.' Brooks winked and shuffled past him. As he did, Sherman jammed a gun against Brook's t-shirt, just under his ballistic vest, and pulled the trigger.

The report was deafening in the cramped tunnel, and Sherman's ears rang as he watched Brooks stagger forward, his hands outstretched like something from a zombie film. The soldier fell to the ground, pinning his assault rifle beneath him. Sherman stepped forward and knelt by his side. Brooks was lying face down, his skin already chalk white as the shock hit him. He turned his head.

'I'm... hit. Take... cover...'

Sherman saw a dark pool of blood spreading through the dust. 'It was me, you daft cunt. I shot you.'

The wounded soldier's eyes fluttered and settled on the pistol in Sherman's hand. His lips moved, and Sherman had to lean closer to hear him.

'Why?'

Sherman watched the blood soaking up the dust around his boots. Brooks didn't have long.

'Why? Because I'm not one of you, mate.' He pointed a gloved finger at the wall. 'I was born overseas, in the Emirates, but you wouldn't know that. No one does. I came here as a kid, and getting the right documents is so much easier when you're a nipper. I had people looking out for me, guiding me. They wanted me in the army, so I answered that call. Then they told me to go for selection, and years later, here I am. We're everywhere, mate. All you had to do was open your eyes.'

Sherman wanted to say more, the urge to spill his guts almost overpowering. He wanted to tell the dying man of the sacrifices he'd made, the disgusting, depraved life the army had forced him to live. He wanted to explain how leading a double life for so long was more exhausting than any SAS selection process. How it took a special strength to make it this far. Sherman had achieved everything they'd asked of him, and for that, the rewards were far greater than anything this wretched country could offer him.

'I've bugged the PM,' Sherman said, as he wrapped a green scarf around his head. 'I slipped a transmitter in his pocket. My people will track him all the way to this Northstar location, or whatever rat's nest he'll try to hide in. Reynolds, Cole, they'll be dead soon too. I'll be the only one left, and that's because I picked the winning side. Actually, they picked me.'

He grinned, his black skin shiny with sweat. He thought about what came next. The fight would continue until British forces were defeated and then he would go home, back to the Emirates, for the first time since he was a child. There was a spot, just north of the town of Dayah, a sheltered cove of white sands and warm waters, a place where he would build a home, and then a family. After years of sacrifice, it was what he deserved.

He frowned. Brooks had died at his feet, his eyes lifeless. Sherman knew his former comrade wasn't a wicked man, so he closed his own eyes and offered a quick prayer. Then he stood up, his boots planted either side of the body. What Sherman needed was Brooks' weapons and ammunition, and anything else of value. Once he had them, he'd head back down the tunnel to Downing Street and the warm embrace of his brothers. He grabbed Brooks' webbing straps and heaved, flipping the dead soldier onto his back—

Brooks grunted.

Sherman heard a metallic *zing*.

He looked down and saw Brooks' face, saw the blood leaking from his smiling lips. In his hands he held two high-explosive fragmentation grenades, the pins and levers lying somewhere in the shadows. Sherman's time was up. Heaven awaited, and he hoped he'd done enough to be allowed in.

He looked into Brooks' eyes. 'You sneaky fucker—'

The grenades detonated, shredding both soldiers to pieces.

CHAPTER 56
THE BATTLE OF KEW BRIDGE

Ross and Lara stayed hidden inside a thick clump of bushes beside the towpath, a hundred meters short of Kew Bridge.

They sat with their rucksacks on, leaning against the tidal wall, waiting for the soldiers on the bridge above them to move off.

Ross cursed their luck. They'd only covered half a mile when he'd spotted movement on the bridge ahead of them. They'd watched from the shadows of an overgrown thicket as two silhouettes became three, then four.

Then a truck had stopped dead centre, disgorging several more figures, and Ross was relieved to see the new arrivals were soldiers. They wore helmets and packs and carried rifles, and Ross's hopes soared, thinking that the army had been deployed to restore order.

But that hope was short-lived when he heard their voices carried on the night air. They were foreign troops, and they spoke something like Arabic, he thought.

Lara was having trouble coping with the information, and Ross had to tell her to lower her voice several times. His own nerves were frayed, especially when a powerful beam of light flashed over their hiding place, lingering for a moment before sweeping across the water to the opposite bank.

Later, they saw the pin-prick glow of cigarettes and heard their voices again, relaxed voices, and even some laughter. As far as Ross was concerned, the soldiers weren't going anywhere, which meant he had to come up with another plan.

He checked his watch. It was after two am, and there were only a couple of hours of darkness left. If they didn't move, they'd have to stay hidden in the thicket for another day. Ross didn't like that idea. Those soldiers might decide to patrol the riverbanks, and they would catch them for sure. They had to find another way out, and fast.

Ross had a terrible feeling, like a noose was tightening around them. Things were going to get worse, he was certain of that. As a column of military vehicles rumbled northwards over Kew Bridge, he knew that noose would soon bite.

He felt Lara's hand reach for his, and he gave it a gentle squeeze. She hadn't said a single word for some time, and Ross wasn't sure if that was a good or bad thing. He didn't know her well enough, but that was changing. He knew she was cold, tired, and scared, but earlier she'd told him she had faith, that he would get them both out of trouble. No pressure then—

She squeezed his fingers, hard this time. He winced, and she placed a finger to her lips. She pointed to her ear, then back upriver. Ross peered into the darkness, and then he heard the faint chug of a motor.

Ross motioned Lara to head back down the path. They eased themselves out of the thicket and headed back the way they came. After rounding a slight curve, the bridge was lost behind them.

Ross stopped when he heard the engine again. Now he heard another sound, the slap of water against a boat hull. He saw movement in his peripheral vision and then the vessel glided out from behind the dark bulk of Oliver's Island in the centre of the river.

It looked like a tugboat, the shape of the wheelhouse distinctive. It approached slowly, barely making headway, and Ross had the feeling that whoever was behind the wheel was trying to avoid contact.

Ross turned and spoke to Lara. 'Stay out of sight until I see what this is.'

'Be careful,' she said, then disappeared into the bushes.

Ross knew he was taking a chance, but he did it, anyway. Using the red filter of his torch, he flashed the pilot, flicking the beam, on and off, on and off. *Come on, mate. Look over here.*

Suddenly, the boat's engine died, and the bow turned towards the riverbank. As it drew closer, Ross stepped down to the weed-choked water's edge. A dark form emerged from the cabin onto the open deck. A man.

'I'm throwing you a line,' he said, hissing in the darkness.

A snake of rope landed on the bank a few feet away. Ross threw the assault rifle over his back and yanked the rope, heaving the vessel towards the shore as the figure ducked back into the wheelhouse.

As the boat drew alongside the bank, Ross tied the rope off around the arm of a wooden bench behind him. The man who stepped out of the wheelhouse was also armed, the gun slung over his back.

'What's your name?'

'Ross Taylor. I'm a police officer.' His hand rested on the butt of his pistol.

Faz flashed his ID. 'Faz Shafiq. I'm Five.' He held out a hand. 'Why don't you both step aboard?'

So, he knew Lara was there, which meant he'd seen them before Ross used his torch. Good skills, but then again, he was MI5. Ross beckoned Lara down to the water's edge and they climbed into the boat. The pilot beckoned them into the wheelhouse.

'This is my neighbour, Lara Bevan,' Ross said. Lara nodded, her smile wary. 'We're trying to get out of the city.'

Faz gestured to Ross's black clothing and weapons. 'You're dressed for it.'

'Ditto.'

Faz tapped the barrel of his gun. 'I liberated this thing from a terrorist in south London.'

'Ditto,' Ross said again, and both men smiled.

'What's your take on all this?'

Ross shrugged. 'I was off duty when it all kicked off, and since then I can't raise a soul on any network. All I can tell you is what I've seen and heard, and none of it is good.'

'They shot down a plane. From behind our apartment block,' Lara said, her voice a little steadier.

'I saw explosions in central London,' Ross added. 'I think they were cruise missiles.' He pointed through the cabin windshield. 'Foreign troops have taken Kew Bridge. A military convoy passed over it a short while ago. It feels like an all-out war to me.'

'It's an invasion,' Faz said.

'Where's the army, for Chrissakes?'

Faz shook his head. 'No idea. I'm guessing they would've been hit first.'

'How's that possible?' Ross said, struggling to get his head around the idea. 'This is Wazir, right?' Faz nodded. 'But how could he get troops here so fast?'

'Ships. Trains. Planes. Who knows? But my guess is, it's happening all over Europe.'

'Fuck,' Ross whispered.

Lara cut in. 'Can we save the debates for later? How are we going to get past that bridge?'

Faz looked at them both. 'Where are you headed?'

Ross briefed him on his plan to get to Wiltshire. Faz thought it was a good one. 'So, I've got the boat and you've got a destination. I suggest we team up. That's if you don't mind me tagging along to your brother's place.'

'No problem,' Ross said. 'We should go.'

Faz agreed. 'Untie us, would you?'

Ross hopped back onto the riverbank and slipped the mooring line. He climbed back into the boat and curled it up. Faz placed his boot against the bank and pushed. The boat drifted out into the dark waters, and they gathered in the wheelhouse. Faz pointed to the stairs that led down into the small cabin.

'One of you stay down there out of sight. The less movement up here, the better.'

'You should go,' Ross told Lara. 'Just in case.'

'Don't do anything stupid,' she said, and headed below.

'Okay, here's the plan,' Faz said. 'I'm going to start the engine and pick up a few knots. When we get to within two hundred meters of the bridge, I'll cut the engine and let the tide take us underneath. It's changed in the last two hours, and it'll run fast enough to give us steerage.'

'Maybe we should wait for another convoy,' Ross said.

'That would work, but can we wait that long? What if they put more troops on that bridge? Or patrols on the riverbank? They're too many unknowns. I say we go now.'

Ross nodded, grim faced. 'Fuck it. Let's do it.'

'Get out on deck,' Faz told him. 'Get ready to return fire if they spot us. Otherwise, we're sitting ducks.'

Ross checked the HK and made sure he had a round chambered and the safety on.

'Hang onto something back there,' Faz told him. 'If I have to go full-throttle, I don't want you going overboard because I won't be able to swing around and pick you up. Got it?'

'Understood,' Ross said. 'Just get us under that bloody bridge.'

Faz punched the ignition button, and the engine growled into life before settling down into a low gurgle. Out on deck, Ross lay down and braced himself against the bulkhead, the HK gripped across his chest. He felt the boat beneath him change course, heard the slap of water against the hull, and he prayed those soldiers on Kew Bridge would be blind and deaf to the vessel that was headed straight towards them.

FOR THE SECOND time that night, the mob gathered beneath the concrete towers of the sprawling housing estate. They congregated quietly, herded by local gang leaders, men with well-known reputations for violence. Unlike the first time they'd assembled, this time they were armed. Their weapons were crude, petrol bombs, knives, machetes, baseball bats and clubs. The gang leaders, they carried guns. Their aim was to get more.

Some had seen the passenger jet nosedive into the streets across the river. They saw the old 'uns on the balconies, ringing Five-O and the paramedics for help, but no one had any service. Rumours swept through the estate like a wildfire—terrorist attacks had hit London. The Prime Minister was dead. So was the Royal Family.

From their high-rises, they saw the chaos on the roads, the

accidents, the carnage. They saw police cars and fire engines. They saw black smoke over the West End. When night fell, the fires grew, and still no one came to help. As the grey brigade barricaded themselves inside the homes, the young ones were drawn to the lawlessness that was taking over their streets. Older men arrived, local men with reputations for drug dealing, violence, and intimidation. Some carried weapons, automatic pistols, and sawn-off shotguns.

They rounded up the youngsters and sent them away. *Arm up*, they said, *and get back here quick*. By the time they'd assembled beneath the tower blocks, they numbered over six hundred. And now they had a purpose, a target.

The soldiers who guarded Kew Bridge.

They split into two groups, each commanded by older boys armed with battery operated walkie-talkies. A smaller unit, the mob leaders, broke into the Express Tavern pub and climbed up on to the flat roof overlooking Kew Bridge. From their vantage point, they saw two military trucks parked side on, blocking access to the bridge from the south. They watched the soldiers, strolling and smoking, confident in their supremacy. It was a mistake.

Orders were issued, and the two primary groups moved quickly, using the unlit back streets to get into position. The first group approached to within 50 meters of the roadblock, crouching behind parked cars and massing along the darkened pavements. The other group looped around to Spring Road until they were also in position. Two armies of street soldiers hiding in the shadows, hungry for excitement and ready to spill blood.

All they needed was the signal.

THE SOLDIERS GUARDING the northern end of the bridge smoked and chatted and watched the distant skies over central London. The next convoy was due in thirty minutes and none of them were expecting trouble. They spoke of their journey as soldiers, and the events that brought them here, from the desert lands to a bridge across the Thames in London's capital. They discussed rumours of British forces in retreat, of an already vanquished Europe, and prayed they were true.

After hundreds of years of western imperialism and exploitation, the rise of the caliphate and its glorious expansion were long overdue—

Petrol bombs swarmed through the air towards them. The closest soldiers were too slow to react. The makeshift bombs exploded all around them and engulfed the men in a sheet of flame.

They screamed and ran, human torches cannoning into each other, into the parapet. One soldier fell into the water below. Their comrades from the southern end came running and saw their friends on the ground, burning, blackened like coal. Then came the roar, a spine-tingling howling, and they saw the mobs, left and right, running for the bridge, clutching sticks and knives and machetes.

Bricks, stones, and petrol bombs sailed through the air, but the soldiers were already running for their lives.

Watching the main assault, the gang leaders scrambled down to the street and advanced towards the action. They stayed low, hiding in the shadows, waiting for the right moment. They saw the two groups converge and charge the bridge, but the soldiers spread out across the middle of it started firing.

The noise was deafening as a dozen automatic weapons opened up. The leaders saw the first wave catch the opening salvo and fall to the ground. Others stumbled over the casualties and were caught by the next wave of fire. The gang leaders closed in on the bridge and began shooting with their own weapons, but their pistols and shotguns were of no use. They were too far away and too conscious of the risk to their own lives, so their rounds fell short, and they killed and wounded their own.

Yet still they watched, revelling in the naked violence, thrilled by the terrible screams and deafening thunder of automatic weapons. This was the biggest tear-up they'd ever seen.

Proper blood and guts.

The roar of the charging mob woke the platoon officer from a fitful sleep in his Humvee.

His 2IC, a sergeant also from his hometown of Riyadh, wrenched open the door of the jeep, fear stamped all over his bearded face.

Approaching from behind a block of smart apartments overlooking the river, they watched as the mob stampeded up onto the bridge, waving their clubs and blades. The officer knew if they were spotted, the rioters would hack them both to pieces, no question.

They raced back to the Humvee, and the officer broke open a box of anti-personnel grenades. Both men stuffed their pockets before returning to the bridge. The roar of the mob deafened and frightened them, but the officer knew he had the advantage of surprise. They crouched low and crabbed across the slip road until they squatted in the shadows with their backs against the bridge.

The screams were deafening, terrible screams of rage, of pain. On the opposite bank, he saw some of his men retreating, firing wildly as they ran. Tracer rounds zipped and ricocheted into the night sky. His men were losing the fight.

It was time to act.

Nodding to his sergeant, the officer started pulling pins and lobbing grenades over the parapet of the bridge. Some he dropped just over the lip, and others he lobbed into the middle of the crowd. The explosions ripped through the mob, and now the screams were louder, visceral, and multiplying after each explosion. Both soldiers kept throwing until they were out of grenades, then the officer scurried to the corner of the bridge, keeping to the shadows. Slowly, he peered over the parapet—and saw absolute carnage.

The mob were in full flight now, running back towards the streets, leaving behind scores of dead and wounded. More dropped to the ground as his men beat them back over the bridge with sustained fire. The officer watched them, firing from the hip, spraying rounds across the width of the bridge, and he kept low, just in case. When they were close enough to be recognised, the officer broke cover and stepped out. He waved his men forward, and they fired as one into the retreating mob, cutting them down like wheat beneath a sharp scythe. Then they were gone.

The officer lowered his AK and looked around him. He stepped over the bodies, horrified to see that the attackers were young, some barely in their teens. The wounded sobbed and wailed for help, but the officer ignored them. Instead, he inspected the bodies of his men, the charred corpses, and those who'd been hacked and beaten to death. He knew them all, personally. They'd trained together, travelled together, and now they'd met their end, not with honour, fighting the enemy, but torn to pieces by children. He failed to recognise any of them, such was the extent of their injuries.

It was no way for a man to die.

He heard the smack of water, and he peered over the parapet. Waves lapped against the riverbank below.

He looked downriver and saw nothing.

FAZ'S HEART skipped a beat when the roar of the mob reached his ears. On the still night air, it sounded like an express train thundering towards them. He saw the deluge of petrol bombs and ducked when the guns opened up, the flashes lighting up the buildings along the northern bank. At first, Faz pulled back on the throttle, but when the grenades exploded up on the bridge, he changed tactics.

'Hold on!' he yelled over his shoulder. 'We're making a run for it!'

Faz pushed the throttle forward and the bow lifted out of the water. He steered for the middle span, aiming for a point beyond the bridge. On it, a battle raged, and the firing and explosions seemed to go on forever. And the screams too, shrill, and filled with pain.

He gripped the wheel as they approached the middle span, and then the roar of the engine boomed off the damp brickwork. Faz cut the power, and *Kingfisher* sailed beneath the bridge and out the other side, her wide, white wake dissipating fast.

He kept the revs down and rode the current until the sounds of battle receded, and the bridge was far behind them. Only when they were drifting past the dark, silent expanse of Kew Gardens did he speak.

'We're good,' he said, and Lara appeared from the cabin below. 'You okay?'

Lara nodded. 'What was that awful noise?'

'Trouble. It's behind us now.'

Ross appeared in the cabin doorway. 'Everyone alright?' Faz noticed he was looking at Lara. 'We're fine,' Faz told him. He pointed through the wheelhouse window. 'I'm going to take us a little further upstream, nice and slow. Ross, can you go forward and watch for trouble? Debris in the water, unknowns on the shore, that sort of thing. Take the binos.'

'Sure,' Ross said, taking the low-light binoculars.

'I'll go with you,' Lara said.

Faz watched them ease past the wheelhouse and stand together at the bow. Ross had one hand on the rail. The other was holding Lara's. Faz turned to look behind *Kingfisher*.

All he saw was darkness, and all he could hear were the calls of night birds screeching unseen in the surrounding trees.

BACK ON KEW BRIDGE, the mob had cleared the streets, disappearing into the rat-runs of the nearby high-rise estate, leaving half their number behind them. They were now littered across the road, dead, dying, or wounded. The officer could not have cared less.

Eight of his men were also dead and three seriously injured, and he was furious. Pistol in hand, he shot six mortally wounded rioters as they lay on the road. He would've shot more, but his signaller told him that another convoy was en route and every major bridge across the Thames was to be defended with armoured vehicles and at least one mobile anti-aircraft unit. The reinforcements would be there at sunrise. Too late to save my men, the officer fumed.

He looked to the east, where the sky still glowed red. Dawn was still some way off, and the streets around the bridge were a warren of dark passages filled with potential enemies. He looked around him and saw streetlamps lining the road, sentinel and powerless. He made his decision. It was distasteful, but that was the nature of deterrence. And he had to avenge the lives of his fallen comrades.

The prisoners lay face down on the pavement close to the northern end of the bridge, hands secured behind their backs, and watched over by his fuming men. Walking along the line, the officer counted thirty-two captives, males and females, the youngest sobbing like babies. The older ones stared and snarled.

Pacing along their prone rank, the officer saw a young man eyeballing him. Then the man spat and muttered something. That pleased the officer, because choosing the first was always difficult.

He pointed, and two soldiers dragged the man to his feet. The officer stepped forward and stared at him. The prisoner was young, with a shaved head, pimply skin, and crooked teeth. Singled out, the adolescent has lost some of his defiance.

The officer nodded, and the soldiers frog-marched him towards a nearby streetlight. That's when reality kicked in.

'Hey, what the fuck is this? What're doing?' He pushed back against his captors, but they marched him forward. 'Let me go! You can't do this!' The soldiers spun him around and slammed him back against the streetlight. He shouted at the officer. 'They made me do it!'

The officer barked an order, and the prisoners were made to watch.

'Stop!' the boy pleaded, tears streaming down his face. 'Please don't do this! Please!!' The soldiers coiled a thin rope around his neck. 'Help me, someone! Help me!!'

And then they hoisted him off his feet, securing the rope above his head. The youth kicked out his sneakers, his legs swinging wildly, but with every exertion the thin nylon cord bit deeper into his throat. He gurgled and choked, his face contorted like a gargoyle.

The officer watched him, watched the other prisoners, and he revelled in their fear. As the young rioter died, his men hauled another one up.

Her screams echoed around the concrete towers and drifted over the black waters of the Thames.

CHAPTER 57
DARK EAGLE

MIKE REYNOLDS EASED BACK ON THE CONTROL LEVER, SLOWING THE electric carriage to a crawl.

Up ahead, faint lights beckoned. He turned to Gaz Cole and cocked his head. Both men stepped out of the carriage and advanced towards the dim light, hugging the tunnel wall. The brigadier spoke in a low voice.

'They're making sure the terminus is safe.'

Harry nodded, too tired to speak. The bursts of adrenaline kept him mobile and alert, but when they dissipated, exhaustion returned like a fast-moving tide. He'd lapsed into silence, the momentary respite from danger and the movement of the train carriage rocking him to the verge of sleep. And he felt useless, and not a little guilty. Here he was, being shuttled to safety (he hoped), while the people of London suffered and died. He couldn't contemplate casualty numbers.

And then he thought of Ellen, her smiling face consuming him. It was dangerous to think of her now, to accept that his life with her was over. The speed of events had helped, if help was the right word, to focus Harry's mind on his own survival.

But now, as tiredness assaulted his consciousness, he failed to keep her image at bay. Her body was back there somewhere, broken and burned, left to rot like discarded meat. Who would recover her? Would they treat her with respect and compassion? Would there be a funeral, her life recognised and celebrated by family and friends? And would Harry ever find out what happened to her?

His throat tightened as the pain threatened to overwhelm him. The sound of someone approaching brought him back to the present. Two black shadows came running around the curve of the tunnel.

'They're back,' Forsythe said, stepping out of the carriage. Reynolds cocked a thumb over his shoulder.

'The station's all clear, boss. There's a single exit door on the platform and the staircase leads to the surface. Dust on the floor up there must be an inch thick.'

'Good work, Mike—'

Forsythe held up a hand for silence as he stared back down the tunnel. Reynolds and Cole brought their weapons up and squinted through their sights. Another wave of adrenaline washed away the weariness that threatened to cripple him. Harry spun around in his seat.

'What is it, Clive?'

'Quiet.'

Harry heard it then, a very faint hum. Getting louder.

'Drone,' Reynolds said. 'Let's go.'

The soldiers piled aboard, and Reynolds jammed the lever to the stop. The train sped up along the tunnel, and Harry couldn't help glancing over his shoulder, watching the blue wall lights flash past, trying to spot the chasing drone. His tingling hands gripped the seat in front of him, and Harry wondered if his heart would take much more of this.

Light bloomed along the walls, and Harry saw the tracks end at a solid concrete wall. The train shuddered to a halt, and they all decamped to the platform. Reynolds pointed to the open steel door.

'Go, Gaz! I'll follow!'

Cole pushed Harry as Reynolds headed back into the tunnel. Forsythe called after him.

'Mike! Where are you going?'

'To disable that drone.'

Harry shrugged off Cole's hand and walked towards Reynolds. 'Don't be stupid.'

'They don't know where this tunnel ends,' Reynolds explained. 'Could go all the way to New York as far as they know. If that drone catches up, they'll know where we are, and we need to buy every second we can. Go,' he said, pointing to the steel door.

Forsythe pulled his pistol. He marched past Reynolds, then turned, walking backwards. 'I need you on that radio, Mike. If you can't raise Northstar, you'll need to get the PM out another way. I'll take care of that drone.' He pointed to the platform. 'Kill those lights and get upstairs. I'll be right behind you.'

Forsythe jogged into the tunnel. Harry watched him go, then Cole was marching him towards the door. As he stepped into the stairwell, the lights went out behind him, and the darkness was complete.

CLIVE FORSYTHE LOPED along the tunnel wall. He could hear the drone, still some way off, but he was closing the gap fast. Something caught his eye, and he stopped. A narrow alcove set into the tunnel wall, some sort of expansion gap. He could hide in its shadows. Forsythe took off his helmet and threw it inside, turning sideways and squeezing in after it.

The buzzing noise filled the tunnel, and Forsythe's hand tightened around his Glock. He didn't want to shoot it—too much noise—but if it got away from him, he'd have no choice.

The buzz morphed into a hum and then he saw it, bouncing on the air like a giant spider, its multiple legs fitted with tiny rotors. It flew past him, six feet off the ground, and Forsythe squeezed out of the tunnel.

He holstered his pistol and ran after it, catching its back legs in a few strides. It was light, and the rotors screamed in protest. Forsythe swung it around and ran it straight into the tunnel wall. Plastic housing broke away, and Forsythe smashed it again and again. The rotors spun, then died, but Forsythe didn't stop until his hands were bleeding and the drone was lying dead at his boots.

The brigadier smiled. *I just killed a drone. That's a first.*

He heard another noise, and the smile faded.

'W E'VE LOST contact with the bird!'

Mousa marched towards the operator. Al-Bitruji followed him.

'Show me,' ordered Mousa. The operator re-ran the digital footage. The drone's low-light camera picked out the curve of the empty tunnel, the smooth concrete floor, and the inlaid train tracks. Then the machine took a hard left turn and drove into the wall. Again, and again. The sound of someone exerting themselves was plain for everyone to hear.

Mousa turned to Al-Bitruji. 'Tell Haseeb he's walking into a trap. Now!'

Al-Bitruji repeated the order to a nearby signaller. Mousa studied the T-BIS screen. In the glass reflection, he saw Al-Bitruji staring at the back of his head, fury in his eyes. Maybe he'd been too hard on the man, embarrassing him in front of his people. Maybe. But Mousa didn't have time to worry about hurt feelings. Al-Bitruji would get over it, take his frustration out on some poor subordinate.

The privileges of rank often proved to be its own soothing balm.

FORSYTHE STAMPED his boot on the drone's circuitry, making sure the thing was dead. One couldn't take chances with modern tech. He raised his leg for the coup de grâce, then froze. He stared back down the tunnel toward the palace. The scraping and rustling were unmistakable. People approaching fast.

He squeezed back into the alcove. The seconds passed, and he held his breath. A shadow appeared across the tunnel wall, then another. Then another, much closer. He heard the rattle of weapons. Soldiers, but none wore helmets. Mercenaries, maybe. He eased the gun from its holster and dropped his chin to shield his pale face. Another figure strode past, a tall shadow, and Forsythe glimpsed a bald head and beard.

The footfalls stopped. He heard voices and the scrape of plastic on the ground. They were picking over the drone's corpse. Forsythe was outgunned, but he couldn't allow them to continue. If he did, they would find the platform. Forsythe cursed, realising he should've ordered Mike to seal the door. This should've been a one-way trip, but he hadn't thought it through. He felt a stab of shame, of failure. He was a brigadier, but like most senior officers and general staff, he'd forgotten how to lead. The mission was now in danger, and that was his fault. He wasn't a soldier. He'd become a civil servant, a bureaucrat. And he never saw it coming.

Time to rediscover your inner infantryman, he told himself. Otherwise, the others were doomed, and Clive Forsythe refused to go to his grave carrying that burden.

He reached into his chest rig and eased the single fragmentation grenade from its pouch. He also had a smoke canister, which he was saving for a helicopter evac, but it wouldn't matter now. It was doubtful he'd make it back to the surface. He crossed his arms and pulled the pins one at a time, letting them dangle from his fingers. There was no going back now. He was going to die like a soldier.

What better way was there?

HASEEB PUSHED the fragments of the drone around with the toe of his boot. His men stood around him, curious looks on their faces. Haseeb didn't like drones, or smart weapons, or any of the technology that enabled a man (or to his lasting horror, a woman) to wage war on his homeland from an American airbase. The Great Satan had done so for decades, and it was always his own people who paid with their lives for such devilment. It wasn't true warfare.

If the soldiers of America met his people on the hot plains of Afghanistan armed with swords and shields, there would be only one victor.

So instead, they killed from afar. Haseeb liked to take a life up close, so he could feel warm blood on his hands, and watch the life fade from his opponent's eyes. And even though the Islamic State forces now employed such tools as the drone at his feet, it wasn't how a warrior should fight. And Haseeb had been born a warrior—

His earpiece hissed. Haseeb listened to the transmission, to the urgent voice. And the warning.

'—*Enemy troops in your location!'*

He registered the metallic ring of steel on concrete, the pop and fizz of the smoke grenade—

THE DETONATION BURST Forsythe's eardrums, the pain shooting through his head. He stepped out of the alcove, pistol in hand, into a cloud of thick green smoke. Screams echoed off the tunnel walls.

He took three steps and saw the bodies at his feet, two of them, bearded men bristling with equipment and weapons. He shot them both, then ducked as a burst of machine gun fire exploded close by. Forsythe saw the muzzle flash and fired twice. He heard a grunt, then the clatter of the weapon.

Another sound to his left, coughing, then a shout. Green smoke billowed and swirled. Forsythe ran into the figure, and he fired twice into the man's chest. The body dropped, and Forsythe crouched low, reaching for the tunnel wall with his left hand.

His boot kicked something heavy, and he saw an AK at his feet. He picked it up, flipped the selector to full auto and opened fire, spraying rounds in a semi-circle. A scream pierced the thick smoke, then another. The gun clicked empty.

He dropped it and felt his way along the wall, towards Kensington Gardens. As the smoke thinned, hope surged.

He might just make it.

Another AK fired, chewing the concrete behind him. He heard a grunt of pain, then a voice yelled out, angry, urgent. A blue-on-blue. *Good.* Confusion was his friend now. And speed. Faint blue lights pierced the smog. The smoke was clearing. It was time to throw caution to the wind.

Forsythe took three loping strides and tripped, falling hard onto the concrete. His pistol slipped out of his hand and skittered into the green mist. He was about to get up when a vice-like hand grabbed his leg, just above his boot.

Forsythe looked over his shoulder and saw a bald, bearded giant lying on the ground behind him, his face running with blood, his teeth bared in fury. The giant screamed something unintelligible and raised his hand. Forsythe watched the knife come down and bury itself in his calf.

Their screams filled the tunnel, anger and pain combined, and Forsythe couldn't stop the giant as the knife stabbed his legs again and again. He felt the blade slicing his flesh apart and screamed as it scraped and sheared his bones.

The giant crawled up his body, stabbing his thighs, his buttocks, his kidneys, spitting fury and curses. An unstoppable monster. Forsythe was frightened. He wanted it to be over.

The air left his lungs as the giant lay on top of him. He felt the blade sink into his right side and his body turned to ice. He felt a hand in his hair and then his head snapped backwards, exposing his throat. *Make it quick, please God.* He felt the blade on his neck and then the agonising sawing of his flesh.

He saw his own blood spray, cutting off his scream.

The darkness rushed in.

HASEEB ROLLED OFF THE CORPSE, exhausted. He could feel blood beneath his clothes, warm and sticky. He'd taken revenge, but he needed medical help fast. Shrapnel had lacerated his body, and the pain pulsed in ever-stronger waves. He heard movement close by. Two of his men emerged from the thin green haze and knelt by his side. He heard Velcro pouches ripped open and the tear of medical wrappers. Haseeb cursed. His wounds would keep him out of the action for a while—

Blood sprayed, and one man slumped across Haseeb's chest. Then the other one died, falling backwards. He heard brass rolling across the concrete and a figure emerged from the haze. A white man, wearing a dark jacket. But there was no mistaking the sophistication of the equipment he wore, or the gun he carried. A soldier. Haseeb smiled.

Better to die at the hands of an enemy than by an explosive metal egg.

. . .

REYNOLDS SAW the butchered corpse of Brigadier Forsythe and winced. He was a decent guy and didn't deserve to go out like that.

The SAS man looked down at the grinning, bearded hulk at his feet and fired a suppressed round through his forehead.

He checked the other bodies, firing safety rounds into each of them. Satisfied they were all dead, he went to work booby-trapping the corpses with their own grenades.

He backed away, gun barrel sweeping left and right across the tunnel before snatching a single dog-tag from around Forsythe's partly severed neck.

He slipped it into his pocket, then turned and ran back to the platform.

MOUSA STOOD OVER THE SIGNALLER. 'Try them again.'

The signaller obeyed, hailing the SERTRAK team several times. 'Nothing, general. We've lost contact.'

Mousa picked up an empty chair and hurled it against the wall. No one in the packed room moved. No one spoke. The air chattered with radio traffic. Mousa spun around and yelled at Al-Bitruji. 'Tell Allawi to send everyone into the westbound tunnel! Now!'

Mousa suffered a rare and fleeting flutter of panic. Despite their overwhelming numbers, Beecham might escape. He imagined reporting the news to the caliph, and he felt nauseous. He'd never failed the caliph. Ever. The sun would be up soon. When it rose, the British Prime Minister would either be in his custody or lost to him, maybe for good. He couldn't explain why he felt that way. A soldier's instinct, one that told him he was racing against the dawn.

He studied the map board. Kensington Palace lay to the west. Another palace, another point of entry to the tunnel system, perhaps. He snapped an order. 'General, send the QRF to Kensington Palace. I want the entire area flooded with our troops. And tell the engineers to take the place apart.'

He turned and glared at Al-Bitruji.

'Now!'

. . .

AL-BITRUJI RELAYED THE ORDERS, stung by the barb of Mousa's tone. How many times had the man humiliated him in front of his staff? Once was too many, Al-Bitruji decided. And yet, he'd heard something in Mousa's voice, a tone that was unfamiliar. It sounded like panic.

This mission was everything to his fellow general. Perhaps the caliph would not look kindly on his failure? Perhaps it might prove to be Mousa's downfall, in which case there was still a hand to be played here. And if he played that hand correctly, maybe Al-Bitruji would one day stand at the caliph's side.

He checked the T-BIS screen and saw the green dots of the QRF force rolling up Constitution Hill towards the dark expanse of Hyde Park, quietly praying their mission would fail.

HARRY HEARD the steel door clang shut far below. Cole stepped outside the small comms room and peered over the rail. 'It's Mike,' he told Harry. 'He's on his own.'

'Where's the brigadier?'

Cole said nothing and returned to the radio set. Reynolds entered the room a minute later, breathing hard.

'Where's the brigadier?' Harry asked him.

'He didn't make it. Went down swinging, though. Took out the guys hunting us.' The SAS sergeant crossed the small room and stood over Cole. 'Anything?'

Cole shook his head. 'Negative.'

Harry stared at Reynolds. 'That's all you've got to say? *He didn't make it?*'

'We don't have time for eulogies,' Reynolds told him. 'The job is to get you to safety. That's what the brigadier wanted. We won't let him down, right, sir?' The soldier stared at Harry, eyebrows raised.

Harry bit his tongue. 'No, we won't.' He stepped away and flopped on a plastic chair, one of several lined along the wall. The room was windowless and stuffy and lit by a single gooseneck lamp on the radio table. The only other equipment in the room was a CCTV monitor with a black-and-white external feed. Harry stared at it, but nothing moved in the dark copse outside the steel door.

Reynolds squatted in front of Harry, his assault rifle balanced across his thighs. 'Sunrise is in one hour. If we can't reach Northstar in the next thirty minutes, we bug out, find some transport, and head west. We lay up by day, move by night.'

'That's the plan?'

Reynolds smiled. 'Unless you've got another?'

'I wish I did.'

'Contact!' Cole blurted from across the room. He spoke into the headset. 'Northstar, we are receiving you, over.'

Harry took the radio mic and confirmed his voice print. ID's established, Reynolds had a brief conversation, much of it military jargon that was another language as far as Harry was concerned.

'Trash it,' Reynolds told Cole, and the blond soldier used a battery-powered screwdriver to take off the radio's cover and rip out its intestinal wires. 'We've got an RV and very little time,' Reynolds told Harry. 'We have to move right now.'

'What about the other two? Your colleagues?'

'They'll be alright. They're trained for this type of work. Probably see them at Northstar in a few days.'

Cole turned off the lamp and the CCTV monitor. He cracked the steel door and a temperate breeze rushed in. Harry took a deep breath, relishing the fresh air and the scent of the park outside.

'More running ahead,' Reynolds told Harry. 'Are you up for it?'

Harry swallowed and nodded. 'Good. Let's move.'

They filed out of the blockhouse and into the trees. Harry looked behind him and saw the disguised building squatting in the dark, overgrown with flowering creepers. The escape system, planned in secret and clearly built to the tune of hundreds of millions, had served its purpose. But Harry was still here, in the heart of central London, and he wondered why those planners hadn't kept going, all the way out west.

Reynolds pushed on through the trees, with Harry behind him and Cole trailing. As they moved through the shadows, the first melodic notes echoed across Kensington Gardens. Dawn was approaching fast, and the unseen birds rose in chorus to greet it.

• • •

AL-BITRUJI TOOK the message slip and dismissed the operator. His next move needed to be quick and decisive. He glanced at Mousa, now glued to the T-BIS display, as he monitored the QRF racing towards Kensington Gardens. The message in Al-Bitruji's hand was from Mousa's 2IC, Allawi—the tunnel was a dead end. There was no platform beneath Kensington Palace, but Mousa didn't know that yet. Which meant Al-Bitruji had a card to play.

As the minutes ticked by, the British Prime Minister was getting further away. Al-Bitruji watched Mousa's knuckle tapping on the table as the general followed the action on T-BIS. He was nervous, and that was good. Al-Bitruji suppressed a smile. Maybe this was the moment things changed.

He waited another sixty seconds, then crossed the room. He held out the message slip. 'General, this has just come in from Major Allawi. The tunnel is a dead end.'

Mousa snatched the note and scanned the message. 'When did you get this?'

'A moment ago.'

Mousa keyed his radio, then frowned. He checked the display, popped out the battery, and hurled it against the wall.

'Bring General Mousa a fresh radio battery!' Al-Bitruji yelled to no one in particular. A young soldier hurried forward, head bowed, a battery in hand.

Mousa snapped it in and hailed Allawi. 'Sitrep, Major.' He listened for a few seconds, then spoke. 'They're in the park, which means they're on foot. Find them!'

Al-Bitruji fired off his own orders, sending more troops towards Kensington Gardens. He stood back and watched Mousa. His arms were folded, and his fists bunched as he watched T-BIS. A man in crisis, Al-Bitruji observed.

Oh, what webs we weave...

HARRY RAN, grateful the path sloped downwards towards Kensington High Street. He tried to stretch his legs, lengthen his pace, but his shoes weren't designed for running and his feet were suffering. It was eerie, running across dark, open spaces like this, the lifeless buildings ahead towering and ominous.

Reynolds led the way. Cole was behind Harry, urging him forward. Beneath his combat jacket, the t-shirt clung to his damp skin. His lungs were running on empty again. He really wasn't sure how much longer he could keep moving. No matter the danger, a car ride sounded like heaven right now.

Reynolds veered towards the trees and stopped beneath a large oak. Cole leapfrogged them, disappearing through the black iron gates.

'He's going to recce the route ahead. Make sure we're good,' Reynolds whispered.

Harry could barely get the words out. 'Where are we going?'

Reynolds pointed to the inky black canyon. 'Kensington High Street. We've got transport waiting. A helicopter. I know you're tired, but you've got to dig deep—'

'Lights!' Harry said, looking over Reynolds' shoulder. The SAS soldier spun around. He grabbed a small eyepiece from his kit and looked east.

'Trouble,' he said. 'Let's go, no stopping!' He pushed Harry ahead and spoke into his radio. 'Convoy approaching from the east. How are we looking?'

As they scuttled through the tall black gates of the park. Harry looked left. To the east, the sky was tinged with a thin band of blue. Beneath it, a column of headlights blazed.

'Let's move!'

Harry followed Reynolds as they dodged between a sea of abandoned vehicles on Kensington High Street. He saw vague lumps on the pavement outside the Royal Garden Hotel and knew they were bodies. Even here, in one of London's famous shopping areas, death had struck. The scale of the attack staggered Harry. And he feared what might come next.

Glass crunched beneath his shoes. They kept moving, the lights behind them getting brighter, flooding the canyon of buildings ahead with light. Shadows rose and fell. Vehicle engines roared, thundering off the towers as the enemy convoy closed in.

Reynolds shoved Harry forward. 'Run towards the light! Go!'

He followed Reynolds' pointing finger and saw a red light glowing in the shadows of a wide canopy. It was the Barkers building, Harry realised, a significant landmark in this part of London. Behind the light, Cole waited. The soldiers conferred in the dark.

'Chopper's on the roof,' Cole said. 'They can't wait. Sun's coming up.'

Reynolds nodded. 'Move.'

Cole turned and disappeared inside an open door. Harry found himself inside a cool, dark lobby. Cole's red torch flashed over a staircase with an ornate handrail. Harry saw a figure on the landing above, wearing a flight helmet, black jumpsuit and carrying an automatic rifle. The figure turned and headed up the stairs ahead of them.

They'd only just made it onto the first landing when the doors below them shattered. The thunder of guns was deafening, and Harry felt the weight of Reynolds as he lay on top of him. Harry heard the bullets cracking and ricocheting around them and squeezed his eyes shut. *I'm going to die, right here in a stairwell*. The gunfire paused. He felt Reynolds' hands drag him upright and shove him.

'Move! Gaz, get him on board! I'm gonna buy us some time!'

The adrenaline was flowing through Harry's system. He followed Cole and the flight suit upwards, running, stumbling, pulling himself up by the rail. As he rounded the switchback, he saw Reynolds heading back down.

THE SAS OPERATOR reached the bottom of the stairs. On the pavement outside he heard low voices, urgent commands. He waited until they were close, then he lobbed two grenades and turned away. The three-second fuses burned out and the high-explosives detonated, one after the other.

As shrapnel pinged against the walls of the lobby, Reynolds was already moving, jamming his Sig Sauer MCX Spear assault rifle against the shattered door frame and opening fire, the landscape as clear as day through his Vortex combat optics. He dropped targets with 6.8mm double-taps, switching left, switching right. He'd been in firefights before, but not like this, not alone, unsupported by the vast NATO military machine that managed combat operations all over the world.

But it didn't matter. His mission was the safe extraction of the British Prime Minister, a mission he was determined to complete successfully.

He changed magazines with the hand speed and dexterity of a Las Vegas blackjack dealer. He heard the enemy beyond the shattered lobby doors.

Mike Reynolds stepped outside and into the fight.

HARRY HAD one hand on the stair rail. The other was holding Cole's arm as the soldier helped him reach the eighth-floor landing. As they mounted the last step, the figure in the black flight suit opened the fire escape door, and a blast of rotor-wash assaulted Harry.

Cole shoved him outside and Harry saw it then, a black, angular helicopter squatting on the rooftop. There was no whine and thunder of jet engines, just a faint *whupping* noise, like a helicopter heard from some distance away.

The flight suit helped Harry inside the aircraft and strapped him in to a large, comfortable seat. The cabin resembled that of an executive jet. Harry slipped on a headset and the next voice he heard was the pilot's.

'Good to have you aboard, Prime Minister. Is that everyone?'

Harry could only see the pilot's nose and mouth. His visored flight helmet covered the rest, and the futuristic touch-screen display threw a multicoloured wash over the man's skin. 'There's one more,' Harry told him. 'He's on his way.'

'He's got two minutes,' the pilot replied before turning away.

Harry felt powerless, and he hated it. The idea of abandoning Reynolds to his fate was unthinkable. Sitting in the open door to the helicopter, Cole had his gun trained on the fire escape. Harry leaned over and slapped him on the shoulder.

'They're leaving in two minutes, with or without Reynolds.'

Cole dropped from the doorway and ran for the fire escape, talking into his radio.

Reynolds stabbed the soldier twice, once in the groin and then, as his head came off the ground, in the neck. He took a grenade from the dying man's pouch, pulled the pin, and threw it towards his buddies, who were still searching for the enemy in their midst. The grenade clattered off a car roof and then exploded. He heard a scream, and more angry commands. He took the rest of the grenades and threw them one by one in a wide arc, hoping they'd take out a few more—

Night turned to day.

Reynolds winced as the searchlight swept across the abandoned cars littering Kensington High Street. He crawled over the fresh corpse and peered around an open car door. Through his gun sight he saw dozens of troops heading his way, not charging, but taking their time, using cover.

Behind them, engines roared and growled as the convoy came to a halt and more troops deployed. He should hear the leaders now, shouting orders, their voices booming off the dark buildings.

Above his head, the sky was a lighter shade of blue. But the searchlight was a problem. Reynolds waited until it swept past his position, then he fired—one, two, three suppressed shots. They missed.

A grenade landed somewhere to his left, then another. He squatted behind the car's engine block, and then there was an almighty bang as the fuel tank of another vehicle exploded, shooting flames up into the sky.

Reynolds rested his Sig on the window frame of the open car door and fired again. Glass shattered, and the searchlight went out.

He heard Gaz in his ear. *'Mike, transport's leaving. You've got sixty seconds, or we both stay.'* Reynolds knew that would mean certain death for him and his friend.

He rolled away from the car as another weapon opened up, a 20mm cannon that ripped through the pre-dawn air like a giant buzz-saw. Glass, metal, asphalt, and concrete erupted all around him, and he stayed low until the storm had passed. When it did, he was on his feet and running.

He heard more shouts, and more weapons opened fire. He crashed through the shattered lobby doors and pounded upon the stairs as the 20mm zeroed in on his position, chewing up the walls of the lobby and filling the air with choking dust. But Reynolds was already one floor up and moving fast.

He saw Cole ahead of him, heading back up the stairs. Four flights up, he heard gunfire in the lobby and nervous war cries. These weren't frontline troops, Reynolds knew, but they all carried guns and were ready to use them.

The stampede of boots chased the SAS men up the stairwell. Reynolds reached into his pouch—two grenades left. He plucked one out, taped it to the handrail, and ran the wire across the stairs. He heard them puffing below, heard them whispering, heard a magazine being changed, the empty one clattering on the steps below.

'For fuck's sake, Mike! Move!'

Not on the radio this time. Gaz was yelling from the floor above. Reynolds ran, taking the stairs two at a time.

On the top floor, he felt the wash of the rotors. Gaz disappeared onto the roof. Mike crashed through the door five seconds later. Below him, someone tripped the wire, and the grenade detonated with a sharp crack. Screams of pain chased him across the roof.

He saw the Dark Eagle, landing gear up and hovering, and he leapt into the cabin. He dropped into the seat next to the PM. Gaz was strapping in, and the crewman was getting rounds downrange, into the stairwell.

The world spun as the Dark Eagle twisted beneath its humming rotors and then they were moving across the rooftops, low and fast, so low that Reynolds felt himself gripping the armrest with one hand while the other held the Sig between his knees.

He felt a hand patting the sleeve of his jacket. The Prime Minister was speaking, and Reynolds clamped on a headset.

'Say again, sir?'

'I said, it's good to have you back. Thank you.'

'Don't mention it.'

The PM turned away and stared out of the window. As the Dark Eagle dipped and twisted across the rooftops of west London, Reynolds made eye contact with Gaz and gave him the thumbs up. Gaz grinned. Reynolds grinned, too. They'd made it by the skin of their teeth, but that was the job and they both knew it.

Reynolds had never felt so alive.

CHAPTER 58
LAND HO!

K‍INGFISHER GLIDED ALONG THE THAMES UNDER A PATCHY MOON AND minimal power.

The last few hours were the most traumatic any of them had experienced, but the low throb of the boat's engine and the dark, empty riverbanks helped to calm their ragged nerves.

While Faz steered the boat, Ross perched himself on the bow, keeping forward watch. Lara sat at the stern rail, where the pulsing red sky had paled a fraction. The horrors of London slipped further behind them.

The river carried them past a dark and deserted Syon Park and under a traffic-free Twickenham Bridge. As they approached Richmond-Upon-Thames, they saw a large Victorian house burning on the hill. Fire engulfed the top floors, and as they passed beneath the bridge, one of those floors collapsed in a roar of crashing bricks and timbers, sending a blizzard of embers into the sky. Everyone on board heard the shouting and screams.

'Oh my God.'

Ross saw Lara standing beside him, her arms folded tight across her chest.

'That screaming. It's horrible.'

'They probably lost someone. No fire brigade, you see.'

Fiery embers swirled in their wake, dying on the water's surface. 'It's like the end of the world,' Lara said.

Her eyes were wide and frightened. Ross was frightened too, but they had supplies, weapons, and transport out of the city. Right now, they were better off than most. 'We're going to be okay,' he told her. 'The further west we go, the safer it will be. Lots of army camps out that way.'

'I hope you're right.'

'Of course, I am.' He smiled in the darkness and Lara smiled too. She didn't quite pull it off.

Passing Eel Pie Island, the river turned south towards Kingston. As they motored through Thames Ditton towards Sunbury, Ross raided the boat's galley and made them all a hot drink. He stayed in the wheelhouse and kept Faz company, swapping theories and trying to work out what had happened and how. In reality, it was more about keeping each other awake. Both men were exhausted. Lara was catching some sleep in the cabin below.

Sailing beneath Walton Bridge, Faz steered the boat along the arrow-straight Desborough Cut, shortening their journey by a couple of kilometres. Faz handed his empty mug to Ross.

'Make a couple more coffees, would you? Strong ones. There're a lot of shallows and tricky turns ahead. I need to be on top of my game.'

Ross boiled the kettle in the galley area behind the pilot's seat. 'Where did you learn to drive a boat?'

'Sail,' Faz corrected him, smiling. 'I got hooked at Uni. Did my skipper's ticket, offshore racing, sailboats mainly. I also worked covert cases with Border Force and Customs and Excise down in Kent. Drugs, illegals, firearms, you name it. I ran my own boat team. We were always out on the Channel.'

Ross handed Faz a coffee. 'You saved us, you know. I was looking to grab a boat myself, but now I realise I wouldn't have got far. Probably drowned us both.'

'The water can be treacherous,' Faz agreed. 'Even this far upriver. It's all about respect.' He stepped back from the wheel. 'Here, take her for a minute, would you? I want to check the charts. Just keep her straight.'

Ross stepped up and gripped the polished wooden wheel. He couldn't see much through the windows, but the sliver of moon helped, reflecting off the water and throwing the riverbanks into deep shadow.

He glanced at the controls. The navigation display had him dead centre of the river, which was reassuring, and there was a depth finder too. Maybe if he'd found a boat like this, him and Lara might've made it on their own. Maybe.

He watched Faz working beside him, a small adjustable lamp throwing light over the charts that looked way too complicated for Ross to understand. 'How far can we go? Realistically?'

'Henley, further maybe, but I don't intend to spend the next few days on this boat. We need to get off the water, find help, a base of operations. If there's a fight, we need to get back into it.'

Ross checked the river ahead, then the display. All clear. He whispered. 'What about Lara? I can't leave her.'

'We'll find a civil emergency centre, something like that. She'll be safe enough.'

Ross thought about that for less than a second. 'I promised I'd take her to safety. That's my brother's place. I'll take her there first, get her settled. After that, we'll find out where we need to go.'

Faz snapped off the light. 'Your brother's in Wiltshire, right?' Ross nodded. 'From where we are now, that's about forty miles. Doable, while it's still dark. Risky, though.'

'My gut tells me, the longer we wait, the worse this will get.' Ross stared at Faz. 'I saw cruise missiles, and a passenger plane shot down over my apartment. The countryside is our best bet until we can find out what's going on.'

Faz said nothing. Instead, he studied the chart for another minute, then he took the wheel. 'I've found a spot ahead where we can put ashore. It's just after Chertsey Bridge. We find a car, then we get to your brother's place as fast as possible.'

That was music to Ross's ears. Three heads were better than two. And two guns better than one. 'What do you want me to do?'

'Get Lara up and get a coffee inside her. Stack your gear on the deck and stand by the lines, fore and aft. When we hit the shore, we need to move fast.'

'What about a car?'

Faz pointed off into the darkness. 'There's a caravan site ahead, close to the M3 bridge. It's summer. There'll be lots of cars.'

Ross knew what that meant. It didn't sit well with him, but they didn't have a choice.

Kingfisher slipped past Pharaoh's Island towards the town of Chertsey. Lara was up and helped Ross stack their rucksacks on the aft deck. The noise rose and faded, a muted roar that rose again as they passed beneath Chertsey Bridge. Ross stood at the bow, listening. It was louder now, humming—

Traffic. Lots of it, passing over the M3 bridge spanning the Thames. He used the binos to get a better look. The traffic was heading east, towards London, and it was all military; trucks, jeeps, six-wheeled things with big guns. And he heard helicopters too, the sound rising and falling. He ducked into the wheelhouse.

'Trouble up ahead.'

Faz took the binos and stepped outside. 'Holy shit,' he muttered, before taking the wheel again. 'Get up front, Ross. We're heading into shore.'

Ross returned to the bow as the boat chased course, heading towards the bank. He found a long pole secured to the bulkhead and pulled it from its rubber clamps. They were heading into a dark channel beneath a stand of huge willows overhanging the water. He heard the engine stop and then they were drifting, slipping beneath the overhang. Ross brushed the leafy canopy out of his face, and he used the pole to brace against the bank. The engine rumbled, and the boat came to a shuddering stop.

'Tie us off!' Faz said from the wheelhouse. Ross jumped ashore, a mooring line in his hand. At the stern, he saw Lara had beaten him to it, wrapping her line around a willow trunk. They carried their gear and weapons ashore. Ross looped the HK over his head while Faz checked the lines.

A minute later, they were hiding in the trees, surveying the ground ahead. Ross peered into the darkness and saw caravans and motor homes scattered amongst the trees and open spaces.

'What now?' Lara whispered.

'We steal a car,' Ross told her. The shadows couldn't hide the look on Lara's face. 'I don't like it either, but it's the only way.' Through the trees, the sky was paler now, a beautiful shade of lighter blue. 'We need to move,' he said. 'Sun's coming up behind us.'

They walked through the trees, passing caravans and motor homes. They discussed taking one of those but decided against it. Stealing a car was bad enough, but not someone's temporary home. It was Faz who saw it first.

'There,' he whispered, pointing to a stand of trees. Beneath it, a large luxury lodge. Parked next to it were three cars. 'I'll go,' Ross said. 'Just cover me, okay? Just in case.'

Faz took up position close by as Ross whipped the HK around his back and rapped on the lodge door. He did it several times before a voice answered from inside.

'Who's there?'

'Police,' Ross said, holding up his warrant card. Several pairs of eyes watched him from behind the blinds. The door cracked open. The man was in his sixties, his thin grey hair unkempt, his voice deep and middle-class.

'What's going on?' he said. 'We've heard all sorts of rumours about terrorist attacks. The power's out. Phones too.'

'There's a national emergency underway. My name is Sergeant Ross Taylor, Metropolitan Police. We need to commandeer one of your vehicles.'

The man spluttered. 'Commandeer? Out of the question.'

'He's not asking.'

Ross turned around. Faz appeared out of the darkness, the AK slung across his chest, one hand on the pistol grip. 'We need the Range Rover. The Porsche is too small, and the VW won't cut it.'

Ross saw the cars parked in a neat row on the hard standing next to the lodge. A cable snaked from the VW's charging point.

'Keys,' Faz said, holding out his hand. 'Now.'

'Get the bloody keys!' the man hissed over his shoulder.

Ross heard the thump of someone moving around inside. He took out his notebook and pen and scribbled his details, handing the page to the owner. 'That's me. Don't worry, you'll be compensated. This is official government business.'

'I won't hold my breath,' the man said, dangling the key. Ross took it and the lodge door slammed shut.

They packed their gear aboard. Lara settled in behind the wheel and Ross sat next to her.

'Can you drive one of these?' Faz asked her through the open window. She raised a sardonic eyebrow in reply, firing up the engine. It settled into a soft purr. The instrument panel was all digital, and Ross noticed the fuel tank was almost full.

'Perfect,' he said, tapping his brother's postcode into the satnav.

The route flowed across the large central screen. Forty-nine miles, avoiding the M3, which showed lots of traffic. Every other road looked clear. Fifty-eight minutes to their destination, the computer calculated.

'At least the satellites are still working,' Ross said.

'That's a good sign,' Faz said from the back seat. 'Let's go, shall we?'

Ross turned around. 'I would've got that key, you know. The man needed a little reassurance, that's all.'

Faz rested the AK across his lap. 'He would've argued with you all night. I get it, you're a cop, but diplomacy might get us killed. Just an observation,' he added.

Ross turned and settled in his seat as Lara pulled away. She kept the headlights off, navigating the narrow road that twisted through the trees and open spaces of the park. They saw camping lights glowing behind caravan and lodge windows, and a group of people with torches watched them leave.

Ross had his window powered down in case he needed to use his gun. Behind him, Faz did the same with both windows. The cool, pre-dawn air flowed through the car, and then they were pulling out onto the main road.

'Not too fast,' Ross said. 'Let's just get there in one piece.'

Lara put her foot down and the Range Rover purred along the

empty road. Ross glanced in the wing mirror and saw the sky brightening behind them. 'Not too slow, either.'

'Let me do the driving,' Lara snapped.

They settled into an uneasy silence as the eastern horizon heralded the start of a new, uncertain day.

CHAPTER 59
BODY COUNT

Mousa leaned against his Humvee and watched the QRF troops milling around the Royal Garden Hotel forecourt.

Further along the road, vehicles burned outside the Barkers building, a result of the engagement with Beecham's security team.

At least, that's what Mousa assumed. There was evidence of transit through the tunnel. There was a gutted radio set in a disguised blockhouse in Kensington Gardens, and there were bodies, all of them IS forces.

But no Beecham.

'One fucking man,' Mousa spat, recalling the grainy body-cam footage of the engagement. 'One man held them off long enough to get Beecham on that chopper.'

'A ballsy move too,' Allawi said, staring up at the Barkers rooftop. 'It's tight up there.' The major shook his head. 'If our paras had got here first, it would've been a different story.'

Mousa fumed. He knew he should abandon the hunt and focus on the invasion, but the desire to deliver the British Prime Minister to the caliph burned inside him. And there was still a straw to be grasped.

'Ground all aircraft west of the city and divert any flights inbound to Heathrow,' he told his 2IC. 'As of now, the whole of western

England is a no-fly zone. Have every mobile search radar west of here start sweeping the skies. And I want a Big Eye in the air immediately.'

Mousa pulled a map out of his pocket and spread it across the hood of the Humvee.

'Move a company of paras to Heathrow and have them ready to deploy by helicopter on my order. And I want the first available armoured brigade landing at Southampton to divert northwest towards...' he traced his finger across the map. 'Swindon. When we find Beecham again, I want them snapping at his heels.'

Allawi stared at the map, then at the general. He frowned. 'There are reports of enemy troop concentrations to the west. Scattered British forces out of Tidworth and Aldershot garrisons. Any engagement could prove costly.'

'It's worth the risk.'

Allawi lowered his voice. 'Forgive me, general, but this goes against the invasion plans. The priority now is to secure the major cities in the south-east and consolidate our positions before we advance west. Beecham might be in the wind, but we've taken London. That alone is prize enough.'

Mousa watched a crocodile of body bags being loaded onto a waiting truck. When the struggling soldiers had heaved the last corpse aboard, they slammed the tailgate shut. Mousa lowered his voice.

'I know you're right, Reza. But the opportunity to capture Beecham still exists. At the very least, we can locate the aircraft and find out where he's going. And having a brigade move out west is a prudent move. It will disrupt the enemy's plans and force them to react.'

Allawi bit his lip. 'Can I be frank?' Mousa nodded. 'This is a mistake.'

Mousa understood what Allawi was saying. It wasn't just Mousa's career and reputation that was on the line. He slapped his 2IC on the shoulder. 'I'll make you a promise, Reza. If we fail, I'll take the blame. Just me. You'll walk away with your career and reputation intact. I'll make sure of it.'

He saw the relief on Allawi's face. And the embarrassment. 'I serve at your pleasure, general,' was all the man could say.

Mousa smiled. He hadn't known Allawi that long, but his 2IC had proved himself to be a highly competent officer and valuable ally. The caliph had chosen well, Mousa admitted, another sign that the great man was also a great chess master. That Allawi might be the caliph's mole inside Mousa's command had crossed his mind several times. Such was the Byzantine nature of Baghdad politics. If that were the case—and Mousa didn't think it was—then it was prudent that Allawi remain onside.

'We should leave,' Allawi said, looking up at the pale morning sky. 'We're exposed here.'

Mousa took a last look along Kensington High Street. Vehicles still burned, the smoke spiralling up over the Barkers building and into the lightening sky. Yesterday, Londoners were going about their business. On this morning, they would wake to a new world, a paradigm shift in their reality. The shock would be seismic, but acceptance of that reality would soon follow. Decades of decadence had weakened the spine of Europe.

Most would have no stomach for a fight, only for the resumption of normality. That was a certainty in Mousa's mind. Victory in Europe was practically assured, and the caliphate's empire now stretched from London to the Chinese border. The caliph would be more than pleased. And he would forgive the impulsiveness of his favourite general.

Mousa climbed inside the Humvee, and the driver started the engine. Allawi sat next to him, radio in hand.

'Send the orders, major. Find Beecham. Let's bring the bastard back to Baghdad in chains.'

CHAPTER 60
SALISBURY PLAIN

THE AIRBUS 330 BIG EYE SURVEILLANCE AIRCRAFT ROTATED OFF THE runway at Heathrow and climbed into the dawn sky, headed due west.

The flight crew had been in-country for less than two hours when the call came to scramble, but the ground crew had already turned the aircraft around for rapid deployment and the Big Eye's technicians and specialists were eager to get to work.

The captain's name was Al-Sadir, and he pushed the throttles to their stops as the Airbus rumbled towards its operating altitude of thirty-thousand feet. The pre-flight mission briefing had been urgent and succinct—locate and track a stealth helicopter headed west. But Al-Sadir knew that finding a tiny helicopter cloaked with stealth technology was going to be difficult, even for the formidable electronic capabilities of the Big Eye.

As he dipped the nose and levelled out, he flexed his fingers inside his flying gloves. The military push to the north and west of England was supposed to begin after they had secured the major cities and before the enemy mustered their remaining forces. Al-Sadir expected to be patrolling the skies above London, protecting newly acquired caliphate airspace, but something had happened. Plans had changed. That is the nature of warfare, Al-Sadir knew. Besides, he liked a challenge, and this mission was important. Allegedly, the orders came from General Mousa himself.

If that was true, this was an opportunity to impress, and so the 42-year-old captain considered the advantages of the tactical situation. Electricity supplies were still cut off, which meant electronic ground emissions would be minimal. The cloudless skies had also been cleared of traffic, further de-cluttering the electronic landscape. The ground below, stretching towards the distant western horizon, was reasonably flat and lit by the rising sun behind him.

Conditions were almost perfect.

Yet Al-Sadir was a careful man, and the absence of enemy radar emissions troubled him. British armed forces had been dealt a massive blow, intelligence reported. Their communications had been crippled. Counter attacks had been few and disorganised. The RAF had been neutralised, and any surviving enemy aircraft were operating far to the north.

Al-Sadir wouldn't dream of questioning military intelligence—not publicly—but as the Big Eye headed west, he felt the rush to deploy was a mistake, that potential threats had been considered and dismissed too easily. His feelings were irrelevant, however. The job was to find a rogue helicopter, and Al-Sadir intended to do that as fast as humanly possible.

The huge, grey Airbus was flying at just under thirty-thousand feet, level and smooth. It was time to go to work. He keyed his helmet mic.

'This is the captain. We've achieved optimal speed and altitude.'

Behind him, inside the sophisticated main cabin, the Big Eye's crew of eighteen technicians had calibrated their instruments and activated their search radars, sweeping the airspace and ground to the west.

Computers filtered the avalanche of information from multiple radar returns and sorted them into categories. Within 30 seconds, the techs interrogated several contacts. The software identified them as flocks of birds or similar anomalies, and the sweep continued.

Positive returns were whittled down. Ground targets were identified as clusters of enemy vehicles and random armour. These returns were plotted, and the information fed into T-BIS. Then they were ignored.

The Big Eye pushed on.

The assumed target was a Dark Eagle, and it possessed a specific electronic signature that was not recorded in any known database. But the mystery aircraft had a maximum speed, so the techs had tweaked their search algorithms to ignore any target travelling at under 180 kilometres per hour.

After radars had bombarded the empty skies for nineteen minutes, another positive return was detected. The signal was weak, fading in and out on the radar display, but its speed, altitude, and direction were plotted anyway. And there was no transponder signal, which was also underpinned the case for possible interdiction. The target was tracked for another sixty seconds.

Al-Sadir heard the message inside his headset.

'Primary target acquired, bearing 272 degrees, speed, 230 kilometres, altitude 240 feet.'

Al-Sadir banked the Big Eye over a few degrees and increased power. He radioed the Forward Air Controllers at Heathrow. 'Ground Station Hotel-One-One, this is Bravo-Echo-Niner. I have target acquisition. Request fighter vector.'

'Vector approved, Bravo-Echo-Niner. You have tactical command,' Heathrow replied.

Al-Sadir contacted the fighters directly, two F-22 Raptors, callsigns Dagger-33 and Dagger-34. The planes were bracketing the Big Eye a kilometre out, and the pilots fed the target track to their onboard computers.

He heard the Raptors acknowledge the information, and Al-Sadir felt a brief stab of envy. He'd never made the grade for fast jets and imagined the thrill of piloting a F-22, of receiving the orders he'd just transmitted, then going to full afterburner. Beneath his helmet, Al-Sadir smiled.

Lucky bastards.

SIXTY-EIGHT MILES ahead of the Big Eye, above the western edge of Salisbury Plain, Harry heard the pilots conversing through his headset.

The language of military aviation was another dialect Harry didn't fully understand. Voice chatter had been almost non-existent as the Dark Eagle headed west, snaking around towns and villages, and using the terrain to stay low and undetected. It made for a bumpy and nerve-wracking ride, but Harry's nerves were shot already.

The pilot's next words didn't help.

'We've been pinged by an enemy surveillance platform. Looks like a Big Eye, operating to the east. Two bandits are inbound. Time to contact less than ninety seconds. We're taking evasive action, so buckle up and hang on.'

Harry swallowed, his hand reaching for the overhead handle. He looked down and saw a patchwork of golden wheat fields bordered by green hedges. He saw farm buildings to the west, and several clusters of thick woods. It was better than dying in a dark tunnel—

The helicopter's nose tipped upwards, pressing Harry back in his seat. The aircraft stopped in mid-air, then twisted and fell towards the ground. Harry swallowed a frightened whimper as he left his stomach behind.

Outside the window, the wheat field rushed up to meet them before disappearing in a cloud of chaff. They hit the ground hard, then settled, the quiet hum of the engines fading as the rotors slowed.

The chaff cleared, and Harry saw they'd landed behind a thick copse at the edge of the wheat field.

'Here they come,' the pilot said.

'CONTACT LOST.'

Al-Sadir heard the transmission and noted the loss of signal on his own display. No doubt the enemy helicopter had detected the incoming threat, which meant one of two scenarios had taken place. Either the aircraft had gone to ground, or it had used its stealth technology to disappear completely. Al-Sadir put his money on the latter.

Going to ground was a dangerous move. The Raptors were armed with 20mm canon that could rip any aircraft to pieces. They could also pin-point the enemy helicopter's position and vector ground forces to that location. He heard the traffic inside his helmet—a company of paras was already being airlifted off the tarmac at Heathrow. He was curious to know how this one would turn out.

If the mission was a success, perhaps General Mousa might offer his personal congratulations.

HARRY WINCED as the thunder grew louder. It sounded like an approaching express train, or a violent lightning storm, or an earthquake, getting louder with each passing second—

The roar grew to an ear-splitting crescendo, and then a shadow flashed overhead. The thunder rolled away, leaving a mild vibration in its wake. Around the horizon, the sky rumbled. Harry watched the pilots as they watched their instruments. He depressed his microphone switch.

'Did they see us?'

'DID YOU SEE THEM?'

Dagger-33 registered the negative response of his wingman. Where the hell were they? The Big Eye had vectored them to a point where Dagger-33 had the target on his scope, but that lasted for less than two seconds. Now it was gone. The Raptors had covered the separation distance at full speed, so the chopper—or whatever it was—must've gone to ground. But where?

It would be difficult enough to hide a helicopter in all this open countryside. Maybe they were somewhere ahead, flying low. If it was Dagger-33 flying a chopper, he'd head for the nearest built-up area and set her down between two buildings. Or in the clearing of a wood. He pulled back on his joystick and climbed for height.

What Dagger flight needed was a better view.

'POWER OFF! NOW!'

The radar operator flipped the switch and shut down his equipment. He'd done it so often in the last ten minutes, his thumb ached. 'We're dark,' he said.

The radar op was one of three men, all British soldiers, all gunners of the Royal Artillery, sweating inside their Stormer armoured vehicle. The commander, a corporal, joked that they were the last line of defence—Rourke's bloody Drift, he'd laughed—as they'd sat inside the cramped confines of their tracked vehicle. Waiting.

They'd been out on Salisbury Plain for five days as part of a scheduled exercise. At six pm the previous evening, they'd lost contact with their platoon commander. The radio net was dead and so were their mobile phones. Something was wrong, but the corporal decided to remain at their current location. Eventually, someone would come looking.

The Stormer was parked in a small but well-camouflaged depression that ran through a patch of scrubby woodland. They had no idea where the rest of the battery was, or any of the other mechanised units taking part in the exercise.

At first, the corporal thought it was a joke. Yesterday was his 26th birthday, and his platoon commander liked to pull the occasional prank. As the evening drew in, they stood outside the Stormer and watched the light and sound show on the horizon. That wasn't unusual for Salisbury Plain, but the pulses of light and long bursts of fire were coming from the east.

So they watched and waited in the dark, armed with nothing except blank rounds for their Colt M4 carbines. They listened to the radio, and at one point, just after 3am, there was a burst of static and a desperate call for help, and then the transmission failed. That voice had shaken them all up.

At 4am the cavalry arrived in the shape of a MAN flatbed truck, bouncing through the scrub. Four Husky patrol vehicles and a couple of quad bikes escorted it, and every soldier looked seriously pissed off. They were also geared up for combat.

They didn't stay long, but in that short time, they told the Stormer crew everything that had happened. Islamic State forces had attacked the UK. London had fallen to an airborne assault. Tidworth Garrison was gone. All British land forces were ordered to regroup to the west or north, whichever was closer. The Stormer crew were told to head west, to a marshalling area south of Exeter. There were no friendlies to the east, they were warned.

Then came the good news. The armouries of Tidworth had been emptied, and the convoy had brought ammunition and ordinance. The corporal and his men unloaded crates of Starstreak 2 anti-aircraft missiles and a couple of thousand rounds of 5.56mm ammunition, plus grenades, both smoke and HE. Handshakes were exchanged in the dark and the convoy saddled up and headed west. To the east, the sun was rising.

As his crew loaded the missile tubes, the corporal had watched the night sky fade and thought long and hard about their next move. An inner voice told him to go now, escape beneath the blanket of darkness that was fast receding to the west. But their air-search radar blinked with potential targets…

He gathered his crew. They spoke, weighed up the pros and cons. They could run before the sun rose, but if IS forces owned the skies, they could be dead before lunchtime without firing a single shot. Or they could stay, monitor the air traffic, record the data for the boffins and intelligence types. Retreating didn't sit well with the corporal, but they were a team, and this had to be a unanimous decision. His crew grinned in the darkness. Fuck it, they'd stay, do some damage, record the data, then bug out.

So, the Stormer's air-search radar watched and listened, dumping everything to its computer's hard drives. As the sun breached the horizon, the traffic thinned out until the skies cleared.

Then they saw the Big Eye and its Raptor escort. The emission sweep lit the Stormer up, and the corporal ordered everything to be shut down. The driver tore up the ground as they raced to another position. Then they sweated inside their vehicle, listening for the scream of an incoming jet or missile. It never came.

After a few minutes, the crew breathed again. The Big Eye had either missed or ignored them.

Big Eye. Big Mistake.

The corporal ordered the radar op to switch his equipment on and off intermittently. That would limit their electronic exposure, while still feeding the Stormer's targeting system with a tactical picture. Now it was time for another look. The corporal stood over the radar op. They watched the blank radar screen.

'Light 'em up,' the corporal said.

INSIDE THE BIG EYE's command cabin, a female technician noted the emission flare on her screen and pressed the transmit button of her headset. 'Contact, surface target, air-search radar, military spec.'

Her supervisor, patrolling the central gangway, approached, and leaned over her shoulder. His breath stank of cigarettes and garlic. 'Where?'

She rewound her track and pointed to the screen. 'There. Salisbury Plain, an intermittent signal. Recommend a sideband sweep.'

'Negative,' snapped the supervisor, straightening. 'Our target is further west. Maintain your watch.'

Fool! The supervisor didn't take her seriously because she was a woman. He often berated the females in her unit, especially when there were other men around. She recalled the incident during her training, when the pot-bellied gargoyle had told her—in a gust of bad breath—how much he wanted to bed her.

The thought of it made her nauseous. She'd rejected him, and not diplomatically, because she was good at her job and the other senior instructors had said so. They'd called her an asset.

Now the gargoyle simply ignored or dismissed her. If there was another supervisor on board, she would be carrying out that sideband sweep right now. Instead, she sat and stewed, and watched her screen, trying to ignore the alarm bell that was ringing inside her.

TWENTY-NINE THOUSAND FEET below the Big Eye, the radar op flipped off the power switch, and the corporal saw the emerging pattern. Like all expensive surveillance platforms, the Big Eye was supposed to stay out of trouble. Losing one would be a serious blow, and not just in equipment. It took years to train the right crew, who were often considered more valuable than the aircraft itself. And this one was headed straight for them.

The opportunity was too good to miss.

'Prepare to engage,' said the corporal. He turned to the driver who sat squeezed inside his compartment. 'When I say move, floor it.'

The driver raised his thumb. 'Roger.' The six-litre diesel engine roared into life.

The corporal settled in the command seat next to the radar op. 'Ready?'

The younger man nodded, sweating beneath his helmet. 'Ready.'

The corporal slapped him on the shoulder. 'Do it.'

The radar operator flipped the switches, and the fire control systems hummed and bleeped into life. The air-search radar swept the skies. Red buttons flashed—

'Contact air! Bearing zero-nine-three—' He gripped his launch controls. 'Target acquired, hostile air—'

'Engage!' yelled the corporal.

'Firing!'

Mounted on top of the Stormer, four missiles exploded from their tubes, enveloping the vehicle in a cloud of white smoke.

'Missiles away!'

'Shut it all down! Let's move!'

The corporal stood up in the hatch as the driver slammed the tracked vehicle in reverse and roared backwards out of the small depression. As they headed for fresh cover, he watched the missiles rocketing into the clear blue sky. Hunting the hunters,

'Go, you fucking beauties! Go!'

'Missile launch!' cried the tech, her console alarms buzzing and flashing red. 'Four missiles inbound and locked!'

The point of origin was the suspicious signal she'd seen only moments before. The sideband sweep would've confirmed the danger, but now it was out of the operator's hands. She pulled her safety belt a little tighter as the Big Eye's automated defence systems took over. An air-to-ground missile dropped from a hard point on the starboard wing, its target the coordinates of the enemy missile launch. Chaff pods fell away and dropped a thousand feet below the aircraft before exploding in a glittering cloud of aluminium. From the A300's fuselage storage rails, IR flares spat out at three-second intervals, burning through the sky to lure the incoming missiles.

Inside the cockpit, Al-Sadir banked the plane and dived for the ground, launching more flares in his steep wake. He'd never had to evade a real missile before. Simulated, yes. That was easy. Keeping cool, no problem. Now? He was shitting himself.

The sweat ran beneath his flight suit and his hands trembled as he eased the Airbus into a steep dive. Four missiles were homing in on his plane. He fired off more countermeasures in the hope there'd be no leakers.

Through the cockpit windows, the sky titled and disappeared. Now all he saw was a chessboard of English fields.

He gripped his shaking controls and prayed.

THE STORMER CRASHED into a thick copse, crushing saplings, and churning up the loamy soil before lurching to a halt. 'Sitrep!' shouted the corporal.

'It's lost track. Going to miss us.' A moment later, the anti-radar missile exploded beyond a nearby rise. 'No other inbounds,' the radar op reported.

'How are our birds doing?'

'We've lost one to chaff. The others are locked on and singing.'

THE TECH GLARED at her supervisor across the aisle. He'd strapped himself into a spare seat, his face drained of colour, his jowls flapping as he looked left and right. Like he was looking for a way out.

'You idiot!' she yelled, unable to control her anger. 'I warned you. Now you've doomed us all.'

He looked as if he were about to cry. 'Shut up, bitch!' He sobbed as a wet stain ran down the leg of his flight suit.

She turned away and grabbed the safety rail beneath her console. She felt the plane twist and yaw, headed ever downwards. How much room did they have to manoeuvre? She didn't know. Her console shook but the incoming missiles were still there, three quivering, fast-moving red dots heading straight for them. The plane had seconds to live.

She hoped paradise was all they said it would be.

'LET'S MOVE! We're going for the Raptors!'

The driver gunned the engine until they were clear of the trees. The tubes had been reloaded and a full complement of Starstreak 2 missiles awaited the F-22s that were now to the west of them.

'Clear us a path,' the corporal said. 'Take them fuckers out!'

'Target acquired, hostile air—'

'Engage!' yelled the corporal.

'Firing!'

Thump, whoosh! Thump, whoosh!

'Missiles away!'

The weapons launched at half-second intervals until the tubes were empty. 'Let's get to cover and reload,' the corporal said. The Stormer's engine roared, barrelling across the bumpy ground to the next cover point.

AL-SADIR BRACED himself for missile impact, knowing he had almost zero chance of survival.

Outside the Big Eye, the three surviving Starstreak missiles closed in, separating from their main rocket tubes to form nine, 40cm tungsten-alloy darts, each topped with an impact fuse and 450 grams of high explosive. All nine darts sliced through the thin skin of the airbus and detonated, shredding the cockpit and the cabin, and everyone in it.

The Airbus fell from the sky, trailing black smoke and fire, engines screaming as it twisted through the air before diving into the soft earth of a rapeseed field and exploding, scattering expensive technology and human remains across the English countryside.

THE RAPTORS TURNED to evade the incoming swarm of Starstreak missiles. In the cockpit of Dagger-33, the pilot knew he had only seconds to act as the F-22s and the British missiles accelerated towards each other with a closing speed of over Mach 5. Dagger-33 broke left, heading for the deck. His wingman wasn't as quick to react. Two missiles sliced through his cockpit and exploded the fighter in mid-air.

Dagger-33 circled back and saw the black smudge hanging in the sky. The swarm was still tracking him, six deadly missiles he had no chance of evading. He banked left and right, up, and down, torturing the airframe. He flew as low as he dared, but still the missiles chased him, closing the gap, moving at speeds that the Raptor could not match let alone outrun. What Dagger-33 needed now was height and just a little more speed.

He turned due east and jammed his throttles to the stops, spending every countermeasure his plane carried. Ahead, he saw the black asphalt ribbon of the M4 motorway, and he sent out a mayday call. He kept heading east, towards friendly forces, and then, with the first missile only seconds away, he cut power and pulled the aircraft into a shallow climb. Then he reached between his legs and blasted himself out of the cockpit.

After a short, rocket-assisted flight, his parachute deployed. A mile away across the sky, a ripple of detonations destroyed his F-22 and sent the smoking remains crashing to the ground, narrowly missing the deserted motorway.

The field rushed up to meet him and he flared his parachute before stumbling into a thick green crop. After shaking off his harness, he picked himself up. He took a careful look above the waist-high crop and saw nothing but swaying vegetation. Pulling his pistol, he chambered a round before slipping it back into its underarm holster. He doubted he would need it, unless a bunch of angry farmers confronted him, and that didn't seem likely.

He left his chute and helmet where they lay, hidden by the swaying crop. He lit a cigarette and headed east across the field.

THE CORPORAL AND the radar op watched the display for several minutes, but there were no more targets. The Big Eye and the Raptors were gone. They looked at each other and smiled. All the training, all the drills and the exercises, had paid off. One engagement, three kills. Two Raptors and a Big Eye, all captured on the computer's hard drives. Not bad for a day's work.

The corporal plotted a course through Salisbury Plain, where they would cross the border into Somerset just south of Trowbridge. Hopefully, they'd link up other stragglers, find out what was going on elsewhere.

'Let's get the hell out of Dodge,' the corporal said.

The driver spun the Stormer spun on its tracks and headed west, the three crude aircraft silhouettes chalked on its armoured flanks visible for all to see. And when someone asked what they meant—because some would definitely ask, the corporal said, laughing—they'd get the whole heroic story, blow by bloody blow.

'ALL CONTACT LOST,' the Dark Eagle pilot said, and Harry deflated, closing his eyes.

The experience had been yet another nerve shredder, but someone, somewhere, had downed the enemy aircraft with missiles, and now the skies were clear. If Harry ever met those men, he'd pin the medals on himself.

'Everything alright?' Reynolds said as the helicopter's rotors began their quiet chop.

Harry nodded. 'I'm okay. Be glad when we reach Northstar.'

'Shouldn't be long now,' Reynolds told him with a smile of reassurance.

Harry felt the ground drop away, and they hovered above the field for a few moments, whipping up a storm of chaff. The helicopter's nose dipped, and their journey resumed. Harry prayed they would get to Northstar without further incident. He heard the pilot's voice inside his headset.

'Looks like we're in the clear, Prime Minister. We should be home and dry within the hour.'

'Amen to that,' Harry said, forcing a tight smile.

He folded his arms, hoping no one would notice his shaking hands.

CHAPTER 61
AFTER-ACTION

Mousa listened to the verbal updates and heard the radio chatter, but his eyes were glued to the T-BIS screen.

He was worried, because his dark mood had deepened and now, he felt homicidal. One wrong look from a subordinate, one off-the-cuff remark and Mousa might just pull his gun and shoot someone.

He'd lost a Big Eye and two Raptors. That was borderline incompetence. The Big Eye he could chalk up to a missed enemy anti-air vehicle. That had been confirmed by a transmission from the Big Eye. So, he had a scapegoat for that, and the captain of the Airbus had vectored the Raptors himself, which resulted in their liquidation. He would speak to the surviving F-22 pilot personally and confirm.

Officially, events had moved too quickly, and decisions were made outside the chain of command. Mousa was certain the fighter pilot would corroborate the story.

'Where's the Raptor pilot now?' he asked no one in particular. It was Al-Bitruji who answered him.

'Still in the field. He wants to recover the body of his colleague.'

'Put him on a chopper and get him back to Heathrow asap. When he gets there, let me know. I will debrief him personally.' Mousa turned and stared at Al-Bitruji as he waited for an answer. After a moment, his fellow general nodded.

'I'll see to it.'

'Good. I'll be in my quarters.'

Mousa headed upstairs and crossed the palace courtyard. Al-Bitruji had allocated a suite of rooms in the King's private wing, but Mousa had refused the offer. The flagrant ostentatiousness of the so-called royals made his stomach churn, and he'd told Al-Bitruji so, knowing the man had already settled himself in such gilded accommodations. Instead, Mousa had commandeered the modest residence of a private secretary in another basement, one guarded by his paratroopers.

He took the stairs below ground and closed the office door. He requested a video call to the command-and-control centre in the Jabal Sawda mountains and waited.

A few minutes later, his laptop feed stuttered and settled. Mousa saw an ornate but empty chair in front of a rough-hewn rock wall. The caliph's private chambers, he knew. He'd been there himself when he was always at the man's right shoulder. Now he was thousands of kilometres away, and the caliph would no doubt seek counsel elsewhere. Mousa didn't like that.

The great man himself entered the frame and sat down. He wore a white, full-length gown with light blue silk piping around the cuffs and high collar. His white hair and beard had been trimmed, and he looked healthier than Mousa had ever seen him. The observation was not reciprocated.

'You look tired,' said Wazir.

Mousa bowed his head. 'My apologies for not contacting you sooner. An opportunity presented itself. One I felt we could not ignore.'

Wazir raised a thick white eyebrow. 'Oh?'

'Prime Minister Beecham survived the attack on Downing Street.'

The caliph nodded but said nothing. Mousa continued.

'He escaped into a tunnel system below Whitehall, a facility we knew nothing about. He was close, so I prioritised his capture. Beecham was accompanied by a team of special forces soldiers, and their knowledge of the tunnel system gave them the advantage. He escaped by helicopter before we could apprehend him.'

'A pity,' Wazir said. 'But there are other priorities now.'

'There's more,' Mousa said, steeling himself. 'I pressed the hunt, diverted valuable resources. This resulted in the loss of a Big Eye and two fighter jets. Mistakes were made by certain individuals that were beyond my control and contributed to the loss of all three aircraft.' Mousa took a deep breath and exhaled, running a hand through his thick dark hair. 'I wanted to deliver Beecham to you, personally. Bring him back to Baghdad in chains. I'm truly sorry.'

On the screen, the caliph cleared his throat and dabbed at his lips with a matching blue silk handkerchief. He tucked it into the folds of his sleeve

'Perhaps Beecham will prove himself as a wartime leader, or perhaps he will capitulate like so many of Europe's politicians. His future is uncertain. What is certain is that you did your best, but now there is other work to be done. European resistance continues to buckle before our armies. Britain will do the same, but we must consolidate our hold on their cities, shore up our defences, continue to flood the country with men and munitions.'

Wazir leaned forward in his chair. 'Give them no opportunity to strike back, and if they do, crush them.' He smiled. 'You can do that for me, Faris, can't you?'

Mousa smiled too. 'Your word is my command.'

CHAPTER 62
THE SHIRE

SO FAR, SO GOOD, FAZ THOUGHT, AS THEY MOTORED ALONG YET ANOTHER deserted rural road.

He was happy to admit that Lara had proved him wrong about driving the Range Rover. Despite her diminutive frame, she threw it around like she'd driven one for years.

And Ross knew his way around Hampshire, knew the small towns and villages, knew the roads that linked them.

Passing beneath the M3 motorway had been nerve-wracking. On the outskirts of Chertsey, they'd found a quiet road that took them under a narrow bridge. The noise of the passing traffic overhead had been tremendous, and Faz asked Lara to stop the car once they were beyond the motorway and out of sight.

Then he doubled back and climbed the embankment. Hidden in the undergrowth, he used his mobile phone to film an endless convoy of IS military traffic heading north along the M3. He came to the obvious conclusion. *They've taken Southampton. Portsmouth too. How? When?*

Back in the car, he'd studied the footage, the composition of the convoy, the vehicle types. He didn't know that much, but he saw armour and missile pods and large-barrelled weapons platforms. How was this possible? Had the ships already docked in Southampton days, maybe weeks before? Impossible. Border and customs officials would've known. UK ports were secure. Except when they weren't. Faz had been involved in enough investigations to know that nothing was impossible.

The countryside passed by, but Faz barely noticed. The implications of what he'd seen since yesterday evening shocked him. An invasion force, massive and spearheaded by multiple terror attacks that appeared to have crippled any government response. How far had the crisis spread? Were they headed into deeper trouble? Faz didn't think so.

Maybe it was localised to the south-east. Maybe Wazir was staking a claim. Faz tutted. A stupid theory. The caliph didn't operate like that. He'd unified entire countries and brought warring factions to the table. He'd brokered peace in ancient lands soaked in generational blood by the sheer force of his personality. If he was extending the borders of the caliphate, would he stop at the M25? Of course not.

'There's a crowd ahead.' Ross pointed through the windshield.

They were on a long, straight road, bordered to the right by high hedges and fields beyond. To the left, a long row of houses, set back from the road. Faz saw well-tended gardens and nice cars. He also saw people gathered in the car park of a local pub. Lara slowed the Range Rover.

'Shall we stop?'

'Keep going,' Faz said. 'There's nothing we can do to help.'

Ross turned around. 'We could tell them what's happening, give them a heads-up. They've a right to know.'

'I'd advise against it. It'll cause panic. Some of them might set off to find family members. That could be lethal for them. Right now, fear and uncertainty will give them pause. It might save their lives.'

Lara looked at him in the mirror. 'So, keep going then?'

'Don't stop,' Faz told her.

They drove by the crowd, twenty or thirty people, men and women, gathered around their cars. They saw the Range Rover and stared. Ross waved his hand. A couple of people waved back.

'Poor bastards,' Ross muttered. 'They've got a shock coming.'

'Let's avoid any more people if we can,' Faz said.

With Ross navigating, they kept to the back roads, always heading west. The only life they saw were pheasants and rabbits loitering on deserted country lanes.

Every so often, Faz would turn around and watch the road behind, looking for tails. In times of crisis, some people lost their minds, while others saw opportunity. They were travelling in an expensive car. That might tempt certain individuals to consider jacking them. If that happened, Faz would fire warning shots first. But he hoped it wouldn't come to that. He hoped people would stay in their homes, wait for the TV and—

'Ross, turn the radio on, would you?'

'Good thinking,' the cop said, tapping the car's big screen. The vehicle filled with a low hiss. 'Let's try scanning.'

Five seconds passed. Then—

'This is an emergency broadcast. Do not leave your homes or workplace. Lock all doors and keep away from the windows...'

Lara pulled onto the grass verge. Ross cranked the volume.

'Conserve food and water. Do not use your mobile or landline telephones. Some areas of the country are experiencing power outages. Do not be alarmed. Unplug all electrical appliances until power is restored. Stay tuned to this frequency. This has been a government broadcast.'

'Thank God,' Lara said. 'That means they're getting things under control. Back to normal.'

Ross turned in his seat. 'Sounds legit, right?'

'Sounds like they want everyone off the streets. If I was trying to take control, that's what I would do. Reassure and pacify.'

Faz saw the hope fade from Ross's face. Lara's voice rose a notch. 'What do you mean? This is fake? We're going to be okay, aren't we?'

Faz winked. 'Of course, we are. But we should get going.'

'He's right, Lara,' Ross said, squeezing her shoulder. 'Let's get to my brother's place. We'll find out more there. And we'll be safe.'

Lara dropped the Range Rover back into gear and sped up the lane. A few minutes later, they arrived at a junction. Ahead of them was a weather-beaten signpost and beyond that, a line of distant hills dissected by a black ribbon of road. Ross pointed.

'That's Wiltshire. If we stick to the back roads, we'll be there in less than an hour.'

The Range Rover powered across the junction and headed towards the distant hills. Faz checked the roads—nothing left or right. Behind them, the road was empty.

This was the lull, he knew, a period of fear and uncertainty. London was gone, a death trap, and clearly a target for IS forces. He looked up into the clear blue sky. How long before they headed west? Or maybe they'd already landed in Bristol, Swansea, and Liverpool? There were too many unknowns, but they'd learn more in the next few days.

Faz hoped that somewhere, the UK government was preparing a response, that Britain's armed forces were rallying, and the UK's allies had already mobilised to help repel the invaders and defend her shores. Faz hoped for all of that and more.

Yet he couldn't shake the terrible feeling that the war was already lost.

CHAPTER 63
NORTHSTAR

THE DARK EAGLE SKIMMED THE SOUTHERN EDGE OF FROME IN SOMERSET, and Harry saw an enormous bottleneck of vehicles cramming both sides of the town's ring road.

He saw tanks and tracked vehicles, jeeps and trucks of all sizes, and huge engineering monsters, the function of which Harry could only guess at. Quad bikes and motorcycles buzzed across adjacent playing fields to navigate the huge traffic jam.

And there were soldiers, too, hundreds of them, maybe thousands, milling around by the side of the road. He saw their faces, tilted up towards the morning sky as the Dark Eagle flew low over the playing fields.

'They'd better sort that out fast,' Reynolds said. 'Make a nice target.'

Then the chaos was behind them, and selfishly, Harry felt a little safer now that a bigger target stood between him and their destination. That made him feel a little ashamed, but he couldn't help it. He was exhausted, his nerves were in pieces, and his wife was dead. He didn't know how or what to think. Rest was what he needed, a chance to close his eyes. To breathe. If only the world would slow down long enough.

The helicopter hummed westwards. Ahead, the Mendip Hills rose steeply above the flat Somerset plain, a range of valleys and gorges, of rolling hills and precipitous escarpments. At its centre, a plateau that was windswept and dotted with dense forests and ancient sinkholes that twisted deep into the limestone rock. It was a beautiful yet desolate area, and Harry recalled a couple of camping trips to the nearby Cheddar Gorge from his youth. Now he was headed there for different reasons, none of which would involve barbecues or swimming in lakes.

The Dark Eagle hugged the eastern foothills of the Mendips, sweeping up over the plateau and heading northeast towards Mendip Forest. After a few minutes, the helicopter slowed. Harry looked down and saw a dark, narrow valley, its rocky flanks thick with pine trees. It ran for a couple of miles, Harry guessed, and looked completely enclosed. As they neared the vertical rock face at the far end, the Dark Eagle descended towards the treetops.

'One minute to landing,' the pilot's voice hissed in his headset.

Harry could see only treetops. Then they thinned a little, and he saw a large clearing directly below. After hovering for a few seconds, the aircraft descended below the treetops. The morning sun barely penetrated the surrounding forest, and the world was transformed into shadow pierced with bars of sunlight. The Dark Eagle touched down, then rolled forward along a hard-deck runway between the trees.

Camouflaged uniforms appeared, ground crew and security troops. The aircraft stopped alongside another Dark Eagle, and beneath a vast rooftop of camouflage netting. The quiet engines shut down. Harry stepped outside, relieved to be back on terra firma. A dozen soldiers emerged from the trees, all wearing green berets and carrying guns. The leader, a tall man, his face striped with camouflage cream and wearing an equipment vest stuffed with magazines, stepped forward.

'Welcome to Northstar, Prime Minister. My name is Major Monroe, Second Rifles. I'm the security officer here. Would you follow me, please?'

He turned and led the way through the trees. The other green berets fell in around Harry and his SAS escort as they followed. The hard deck cut deeper into the hillside, and the sloping ground on either side rose to form rough-hewn dirt walls.

Harry felt and heard a deep rumbling, and a section of the rock face ahead moved, sliding to the right and revealing a black cavern beyond. Harry was impressed. The door must've been twenty feet high, and it blended in with the surrounding rock face perfectly, even down to the moss and rivulets of water running off it as it rolled open.

'Like something out of a Bond film,' Reynolds said beside him.

Inside, the cavern was dark, but to his right, Harry saw lights and storage areas behind high chicken-wire fencing. Soldiers passed through the low-wattage pools like ghosts. The rock face door closed behind them with a deep boom, shutting out the daylight. Torch beams waved around the darkness.

'This way,' Monroe said.

His green berets peeled off into the shadows, and now it was just the four of them. They passed through a thick steel door and the light returned. Harry felt his heart rate pick up. *Another bloody tunnel*. A single white line ran down the middle of a smooth concrete road. Monroe invited them aboard an electric buggy. The motor clicked and whined, and then they were moving.

'How big is this place?' Harry said, impressed by yet another secret engineering project. Impressed and mildly irritated, he corrected himself. Why didn't he know of these things?

Monroe's voice echoed off the curved tunnel walls as he steered around a gentle curve. 'Northstar—we refer to it by its callsign—isn't huge. Most of it is here under this one hillside.'

'What about the valley?' Reynolds asked him from the front seat. 'I didn't see any roads in or out.'

'There's a tunnel at the southern end that runs under the valley wall. The entrance is concealed, and it's on government property, anyway. It's very secure.'

The buggy whined around another bend, and the tunnel emptied into an enormous cavern. Monroe stopped the vehicle. 'This is the assembly area. We're on foot from here.'

The cavern was a hive of activity, and troops criss-crossed the cavern floor, disappearing and reappearing from various tunnels around the craggy limestone walls. Soldiers swarmed over piles of supplies as forklift trucks shuttled back and forth. The sight of such fevered industry gave Harry some hope. As they continued across the cavern, some of those soldiers stopped and stared.

'How many people are here?' inquired Harry.

'Right now? Around six hundred. Mostly military personnel.'

'What about my ministers?'

'It all happened very quickly, Prime Minister.' Monroe walked ahead without looking back. 'Your quarters are just up ahead. You'll have a chance to freshen up before the briefing.'

They passed through a guarded door into a small corridor. They twisted and turned through more passageways and into another smaller cavern. Four numbered doors led off it, two on either side. Monroe gestured to the two on the right.

'These are your quarters. You're in number one, Prime Minister. There's running hot water, and we've provided a change of clothes.' He glanced at his watch. 'I'll be back to fetch you in thirty minutes.'

The room looked reasonably comfortable, if a little cramped. Beneath its low ceiling, Harry inspected the two single beds and the free-standing wardrobe with a full-length mirror. Inside it, Harry found clothes, trousers, shirts, a couple of fleeces, a dark green outdoor coat, boots, and shoes. In the drawers, underwear, sealed in plastic wrappers. Everything was his size or looked to be. There was a small en-suite bathroom behind another door. Harry twisted the shower tap and a powerful jet of hot water drummed on the flagstone floor. He undressed quickly.

A breakfast tray was delivered to his door. Wrapped in a thick robe, Harry polished off the sausages, scrambled eggs and toast in short order. A large black coffee also helped keep the nagging exhaustion at bay. By the time Monroe came to collect him, Harry had changed into dark Berghaus trousers, a navy shirt, and a green fleece. It wasn't a ministerial look by any stretch, but it was clean and functional, and Harry felt a little better. There was no sign of Reynolds and Cole.

'Where's my security detail?'

'They're being re-tasked, sir.'

Harry shook his head. 'Out of the question. I want them assigned to me. As my close protection team.' He saw the hesitation on Monroe's face. 'I'm not asking, major.'

'I'll see to it,' the soldier said. 'Follow me, please.'

Harry trailed Monroe through the complex, feeling naked without Reynolds and Cole. Right now, everyone was a stranger, and that made him feel uneasy.

They turned into another tunnel, this one bathed in red light. Loops of thick cables ran along the walls, and armed soldiers guarded a set of steel double doors. As they approached, one of them opened and white light spilled across the corridor. A young girl in combat uniform hurried past him, clutching a laptop. She didn't even look at him.

He followed Monroe into a long and cavernous room that stretched away beneath a rugged limestone ceiling. He saw huge TV displays and digital maps of the UK and Europe, and soldiers sat at rows of tables, hunched over their computers. Officers gathered in conference, poring over table maps and talking into radios.

As Harry passed them, all conversation stopped, and all eyes turned towards him. There were smiles and nods, and Harry thought he saw hope on some of the younger faces. There would be a lot of expectation on him, and he felt the pressure building once again.

Monroe led him towards the other end of the room, to a vast conference table set beneath a bank of bright lights. Perhaps thirty men and women sat around it, soldiers, and civilians, deep in conversation. As he approached, Harry's eyes swept the table for familiar faces, but he didn't see many. He recognised a few senior civil servants and their aides, and a couple of military figures from the general staff.

Two men, both civilians, got to their feet and crossed the floor to meet him. One was Tom Armstrong, the current Chief Secretary to the Treasury, the other Brendan Lewis, Harry's Secretary of State for Transport. Monroe peeled away as hands were shaken. Armstrong pumped Harry's a little too enthusiastically.

'Prime Minister, it's so good to see you.'

'And you, Tom.'

'Welcome, Prime Minister,' said Lewis, cutting in diplomatically. 'We're glad you made it.'

'Are there any other ministers here?'

Lewis shook his head. 'I'm afraid this is it. For now, at least. Things happened so fast.'

Armstrong bit his lip. 'We know about Ellen. I'm so sorry.'

Harry swallowed a knot of grief. 'Thank you.'

'Clare's missing. And the children.'

Harry gripped the man's arm. 'You mustn't think the worst, Tom. They're probably fine. Keeping out of trouble. They'll have friends, neighbours. People come together in times like these.' The words sounded hollow even as he said them.

Lewis stepped closer and lowered his voice. 'There's been a lot of talk about designated survivors and lines of succession. Much of it from First Minister Gower.'

Harry glanced over Lewis's shoulder. The leader of the devolved Welsh government remained in his seat, locked in quiet conversation with another strange face. 'What's he doing here?'

'He came to offer his leadership. As interim Prime Minister.'

'That's generous of him.'

Lewis grinned. 'And moot since your arrival.'

'Leo Tubbs is here too,' Armstrong said.

Harry took another look around the table and saw Tubbs at the far end, squeezed into a chair. Beneath the bright lights, the overweight Shadow Home Secretary dabbed his neck with a handkerchief as he stared at Harry with unblinking eyes. Harry turned away. 'Let's get started, shall we?'

Lewis and Armstrong retook their seats. Harry took his, reserved for him at the centre of the table. Introductions were made, and Harry realised that the government he knew had ceased to exist. In its place, a collection of ministers, civil servants, bag-carriers, military staff, and civil emergency people, most of whom were unknown to him. One person he knew—although they'd never met—was the uniformed man sitting opposite. Major-General Julian Bashford, Chief of Joint Operations at Northwood. He sported an old-fashioned moustache beneath thick grey eyebrows and thinning hair. When he spoke, his voice was deep and authoritative.

'It's good to see you, Prime Minister.' The sentiment echoed around the table. 'I'm told your escape was a close-run thing.'

'To say the least,' Harry said, not wanting to think about it.

'Where's the rest of your team? And what's the situation at Northwood?'

'Northwood has been compromised,' Bashford said. 'Some of the Strategic Command staff made it here, but many did not.' He glanced at his watch. 'Let's bring you up to speed, but I must warn you, good news is thin on the ground—'

'That's an understatement.'

All eyes turned towards Tubbs at the far end of the table. The man glowered as he rolled a pen between his thick fingers. Bashford continued.

'Europe and the UK have been invaded by Islamic State and Russian forces, although the latter has restricted its incursions to the Bay of Greifswald on the German Baltic coast.'

'They're securing Nord Stream,' Harry said.

'That will be their justification,' Bashford said. 'There's been no official statement from Baghdad or Moscow. Protests have been lodged in the United Nations, and President Mitchell has summoned the caliphate and Russian ambassadors to the White House, but it seems they're in the dark too.'

'What's the situation on the ground. Here in the UK?' Harry wanted to know.

Bashford checked his notes and continued. 'The invasion was preceded by multiple terrorist attacks against government and military targets. The assault began at 6pm local time yesterday evening, and most of those attacks were concentrated in the south-east. However, since then, we have received—and continue to receive—reports of enemy activity across the Home Counties, the Midlands and the north-west. The picture is confused and evolving rapidly. Our problem is data—we're not getting enough of it.'

'What about casualties?' Harry asked him.

'Again, we don't have the numbers. But we must brace ourselves.'

'They cut off power supplies to the major cities,' Lewis added. 'Gas, electricity, phones, all of it. And they're broadcasting an official-sounding emergency message. It's created a lot of fear and confusion.'

'I heard it myself,' Harry said, and then he felt an icy chill shoot up his spine. He turned to Bashford. 'What about our nuclear plants? And our weapons facilities?'

'As far as we can tell, the power stations are untouched,' Bashford told him. 'Aldermaston and Porton Down escaped any direct attack and those facilities have very strict and well-rehearsed evacuation protocols. Much of the material stored there has already left the country for the United States. Burn procedures are still ongoing at both locations and will be completed in the next few hours. Sensitive areas will be sealed, and the sites abandoned. They'll be of little strategic use to anyone.'

Harry sat back in his seat. 'You make it sound as if we've given up already.'

Bashford's gaze was unblinking. 'Given the absence of prior intelligence, our lack of military preparedness, and the size of the force we're facing, nuclear and bio-security must be our priority.'

'I'd call it a total intelligence failure,' Tubbs grumbled. 'Which means we're dealing with either gross incompetence on an unprecedented scale. Or something else.'

Harry ignored the barb. 'What about communications? Are they working? And are they secure?'

'We're using satellites and encrypted channels. GCHQ is being evacuated, which means we're mothballing the Critical National Infrastructure. Many of the exchanges and data hubs were disabled when the attacks began—'

'By spies and sleeper cells,' Tubbs interrupted again. 'I prefer the word *traitors*.'

Harry glared along the table. 'You're not helping, Leo.'

Tubbs grumbled as Bashford continued. 'We must assume the CNI is compromised, so our comms people are rigging up secure channels using fresh encryption algorithms. The new software will piggy-back onto our existing equipment here and deploy it to surviving formations in the field. It could be some time before it's all up and running.'

'And how soon can we strike back?' Harry asked. He ignored Tubbs' derisory snort at the end of the table.

Bashford pinched his chin with a thumb and forefinger. 'Right now, we're unable to mount offensive operations. Our posture is purely defensive, and our priority is to protect what we have. Before IS forces press their advantage.'

Harry felt a flutter of panic. 'We can't fight them?'

Bashford shook his head. The other uniforms around the table lowered theirs. 'Not without adding to our losses. We need to take inventory, Prime Minister. Surviving units are scattered across the country without the means to communicate. Most personnel were off duty at the time of the attacks. Some don't have any weapons or equipment at all. We have very little idea of our strength right now.'

'How can that be the case?' Harry asked him, folding his arms on the table. 'Surely we have combat-ready aircraft, tanks and infantry on standby? Reaction forces. Where are they?'

'You scrapped them, remember?'

Tubbs again. Harry glimpsed the faces of the men and women seated opposite him. They weren't looking at Tubbs. Their eyes were fixed on Harry. Waiting for answers. Tubbs was still talking.

'Our armed forces have been combat-incapable for years,' he said. He tapped his chubby fingers one by one. 'We're talking about scrapped programs for new missile systems and mechanised armour. About aircraft carriers and frigates that can't put to sea because of design faults and a lack of spares. We've got bases full of outdated equipment that's falling apart. Some of that armour is over fifty years old, for crying out loud. It's a joke.'

Harry stuttered. 'We have some of the finest soldiers in the world—'

'I don't doubt that for a second,' Tubbs said. 'But at the last inspection, the British Army could deploy eighteen thousand fully trained and equipped combat-ready troops. And that's a peacetime mobilisation figure. Christ knows how many we can muster right now. Don't you read anything from the National Audit Office?'

Harry felt his face flush. He turned back to Bashford. 'Is that true?'

The major-general frowned. 'Sadly, yes. And I suspect the speed and ferocity of yesterday's attacks has further depleted that number. We must consolidate and reorganise. And we need to do it fast.'

Tubbs snorted. 'Our troops may not have guns or uniforms right now, but they can fall back on their diversity training. That'll send a ripple of fear through the invaders.' There were awkward grumbles around the table. Tubbs spread his hands. 'Did I say something wrong?' No one answered, and Tubbs wagged a finger at Harry. 'You were warned, time and time again. Your predecessor, too. And this is where it's led to. Tell him about Colchester, general.'

Harry braced himself as the senior officer spoke. 'The garrison at Colchester was attacked by a sleeper cell of British soldiers. They gained access to the armoury and mounted an attack on Merville barracks. Reported casualties are in the hundreds.'

'The victims were paras,' Tubbs said. 'Some of our best soldiers. Now decimated. They did the same at Plymouth. Suicide bombers in the cookhouse. Blew a hundred Royal Marines to pieces.'

'Dear God,' Harry muttered, stunned. 'Where are they now? The survivors.'

'Colchester has been evacuated and all personnel are headed for the Thetford training area. They'll regroup there. The attack at Plymouth was isolated, thank God, and other commando units in the region have been ordered to head for the naval base at Devonport.'

'Those poor bastards were stabbed in the back by their own colleagues,' Tubbs said, pointing at Harry. 'And you gave them the knife.' He pushed his chair back and stood. 'My apologies, but I'm struggling to contribute anything positive right now, so if you'll excuse me.'

Harry watched the man leave. Was he right? Was Harry culpable? He'd inherited most of the defence policies from former administrations. He knew about the shortages, especially in personnel. Despite internal reviews and changes of culture, the armed forces struggled to find recruits, and found it even harder to hang on to them. So, the UK government opened the door to the Commonwealth. Numbers ticked up. That was a good thing, surely?

A rumbling interrupted his thoughts, and he watched two young soldiers wheel a large display screen to the head of the table. They powered it up, and a map of Britain glowed on the screen. The graphic was dissected by a swathe of red from Manchester to Ipswich, effectively dividing it in half. The whole of the south-east, including London, was also red.

'It's pretty self-explanatory,' Bashford said. 'The red areas signify the known conflict zones. As you can see, Scotland has suffered a single attack. A team of suicide bombers entered the debating chamber in Holyrood and detonated their devices. They killed the First Minister and most of his cabinet.'

Harry struggled to keep up. Everything was moving so fast. 'Who's in charge up there?'

'Lord Advocate Matheson. He's forming an emergency administration. We have a direct link with SCOTFOR military HQ outside of Edinburgh and they are ramping up their comms and sat link capacity as we speak. Scottish regiments are being deployed along the border and a general call-up has been issued to Territorial and reservist personnel. I have ordered all surviving British units to head for Scotland. Most intact RAF aircraft and ground crews are already there and are dispersing around its military airfields.' Bashford indicated the area beneath the red swathe. 'Anyone south of the line will head here, to Northstar. We'll regroup temporarily and set up a defensive line, while everyone else boards the ships in Devonport, Teignmouth, and elsewhere.'

Harry couldn't believe his ears. 'We're running away?'

'Consolidating,' Bashford said. 'We need somewhere large enough to accommodate the rest of the British armed forces. Scotland has secure ports, barracks and airbases, and a lot of difficult terrain and airspace that is easier to defend. The plan is to withdraw behind her borders, take stock, rebuild, and rearm. Then we fight.'

Fight. The word made Harry nauseous. 'What about the civilian population?' he said. 'We can't just abandon them.'

'We have no choice,' Bashford said.

Transport Secretary Lewis spoke next. 'We've gone over this, Prime Minister. When the Islamic State forces advance west—and the consensus is they will—we face the prospect of all-out war across the countryside. Towns and cities will be flattened. Thousands will die. Maybe hundreds of thousands.'

'And where will the refugees go?' First Minister Gower said, slapping an angry hand on the table. 'They'll flood into Wales, won't they? I can't imagine the chaos that will cause. I urge you to listen to General Bashford and his team, Prime Minister. And take his advice.'

Not angry. Gower was frightened. Harry was too. And looking around the table, so were many of the others.

'As I said, good news is thin on the ground,' Bashford continued. 'If we dig our heels in and engage the enemy here, what's left of our ground forces could be decimated. The rest of the country would then be at the mercy of the invaders.' Bashford took a deep breath and exhaled. 'While our armed forces still exist, there is hope. If they are defeated on a battlefield not of our choosing, that hope dies. For all of us.'

No one spoke, and once again, all eyes were focussed on Harry. 'What about their air force?' he asked, remembering the roar and thunder of the jets only a short time ago. 'How much of a threat are they?'

'A significant one,' Bashford told him. 'Combat formations have been tracked flying over the Channel into the UK. However, we have had some minor success in that regard. Our anti-air capability has already proved itself to be a danger, and it's given the enemy pause. Right now, they're keeping their distance. But our missile inventory is low,' Bashford warned. 'We're emptying the defence munitions complexes in Plymouth and elsewhere. There's already a fully stocked site at Beith in Scotland, but the problem is getting munitions into the field. Logistics and supply lines have yet to be established, but we're prioritising those units on the defensive line.'

'This line of yours,' Harry asked. 'How will that work, exactly?'

Bashford tapped the map display and zoomed into an area of the West Country. A crooked blue line ran from Cirencester in Gloucestershire to Poole in Dorset. Bashford pointed to the clusters of blue dots along its length. 'We've stationed pickets at these locations, comprising mixed armour and SAM assets. They're watching the skies and major road junctions. UAVs are filling the gaps.'

Harry frowned. 'It looks thin.'

'It is,' Bashford told him. 'But it's a trade-off. The priority is to get the bulk of our people and materiel onto the ships and send them north into the Irish Sea.' He tapped the map. 'These brave souls will hold position until the last ships have rounded Land's End. Then they'll make a run for it.'

Gower spoke next. 'How much time do we have?'

Bashford shrugged. 'Hard to say. The IS commanders will know we're in disarray and struggling to organise. Despite their recent losses, they'll want to press their advantage. If I were in charge, I wouldn't wait. I'd hit us hard and fast.'

Harry felt fear bubbling in his stomach. He stood up, and the table stood with him. He waved them back into their seats and helped himself to a coffee from a refreshments table set against the wall. It was a distraction because he needed to buy himself a moment to think. To phrase the question without sounding like a man desperate to save his own skin. He sipped his brew, dark and bitter. He remained standing as he found the words.

'And what about this place? What happens to the people here?'

'Everyone leaves, Prime Minister.' Bashford waved his arm. 'What you see represents what's left of the UK civil and military command structure. If we're attacked, we lose the ability to function. As unpalatable as it is, we must abandon England and relocate to Scotland. There is no other choice.'

'But the people out there, the civilian population. What will they do? What will happen to them?'

It was Lewis who answered the question. 'That broadcast we spoke about. Most people are obeying, staying in their homes, keeping off the streets. Yes, they'll be frightened, but we can't help them right now. General Bashford is right, Prime Minister. We have no choice.'

'I'm briefing senior officers this afternoon,' Bashford announced. 'We've implemented a phased withdrawal plan. And it needs to happen fast because we're losing people. Desertions, mostly. There have been hundreds already. We can't afford to lose any more. We need to get those ships loaded and away, while convincing the enemy we're holding position. That won't last long, of course. We're pretty sure our ports and military facilities are being watched.'

'Do we have enough ships?' Harry asked him.

'We have budget constraints to thank for that,' Bashford said.

'There are several auxiliary vessels in dock at Devonport, and they're being loaded with as many supplies and munitions as possible. Frigates and destroyers are already at sea, providing security. As for the troops, we'll load them during the hours of darkness and set sail when each ship is full. Their destination is the naval base at Faslane.'

'So, we're leaving by sea,' Harry said, not thrilled by the prospect.

'The leadership team are flying north in helicopters. The Dark Eagle has been assigned to you, Prime Minister.'

Harry's spirits lifted, but he kept his poker face. 'I see. What about our other naval assets?'

Further along the table, the Royal Navy admiral cleared his throat and spoke. Harry struggled to remember his name.

'The navy has fared rather better than our sister services, Prime Minister, but we've lost all contact with our ships in the Mediterranean. Thankfully, they were few. I never thought I'd hear myself say this but spending cuts have saved lives.' He glanced at a tablet in front of him. 'All four Vanguard nuclear subs, each with a full complement of Trident missiles, are intact. Three are on patrol in international waters and have been placed on alert. One is still in dock at Faslane. She'll put to sea this evening.'

'That's good,' Harry said. Having four nuclear missile boats roaming undetected beneath the world's oceans would certainly give Baghdad something to think about. And that's where Harry wanted to be, seated at the negotiating table. Thrashing out a solution. Not running from bunker to bunker, waiting for the bombs to fall. 'What's the word from President Mitchell?'

'We have open lines of communication to Washington and the Pentagon,' Bashford explained. 'President Mitchell has ordered US forces to DEFCON Three and has closed her borders. General Mulford at the Pentagon is our military liaison, and SCOTFOR has conferenced with several others in the White House and State Department. And we're getting lots of intelligence from them, mostly satellite imagery and SIGINT. Look.'

Bashford tapped and swiped a tablet. On the big display, Harry saw aerial shots of dockyards, crammed with ships of all sizes.

'This is the latest satellite imagery from the Americans. These were taken less than two hours ago.'

'Where is it?'

'Southampton,' Bashford said. He pointed to the screen. 'You can see armoured vehicles, tanks, logistics vehicles here, lined up along the quay. And these are helicopters having their rotors fitted. There are more ships at sea, waiting to dock. And more shuttling between France and the south coast.'

'My God,' Harry said, his voice low. 'Can't we hit them? Precision strikes?'

Bashford pointed to several white ships dotted between the military vessels. 'Those are cruise ships. There are passengers still aboard, clearly being held as hostages. Then there are the dock workers. They'll be locals, press-ganged into service. Yes, we can hit them with cruise missiles, but there would be significant collateral damage. And if you wanted to put the docks out of commission, we'd have to obliterate half of Southampton.'

'So, we hit them at sea,' Harry said. 'Sink them before they can dock.'

'That's why the sub at Faslane is heading south this evening,' the admiral said. 'However, it appears the caliphate is using civilian ships under flags of convenience. We'll have to tread carefully, make sure that if we sink vessels, they're full of military supplies and not food destined for a neutral country.'

Bashford was scrolling through more images of dockyards. 'This is Portsmouth, Dover, Harwich, and this is Lowestoft. Sinking a few ships won't make much difference at this stage.'

'This is a bloody outrage,' Harry stuttered, feeling an icy fist of panic grip his insides. He hoped the catch in his throat was interpreted as anger, and not the mounting fear that he thought might soon overwhelm him. 'What's our timeframe here?'

Bashford waved a hand at the far end of the room. Harry saw equipment being wrapped and packed into crates by busy uniforms.

'We're dismantling anything of use and loading it into waiting vehicles. They'll use the south tunnel to leave the valley and head for the coast. We're broadcasting pre-recorded exercise radio traffic to convince IS forces we're up and running, but we're evacuating this entire facility ASAP. You'll leave tonight once the sun has set. The Dark Eagle is called that for a reason.'

'And go direct to SCOTFOR?'

Bashford shook his head. 'A secure location. I'll brief you later.'

Harry said nothing. He was rather glad he wasn't heading for another underground bunker. But where was he going?

Bashford looked at his watch and addressed the table. 'The time now is 10:30. Last light is in approximately 11 hours. I suggest you all prepare for departure at the earliest opportunity. And grab a meal, while the cookhouse is still in operation. When you're summoned to the assembly area, go immediately. We won't be waiting for anyone. Understood?'

There were nods and affirmative murmurs around the table. Harry studied the display screen, and the millions of tons of equipment being unloaded at the UK's southern ports. How would they fight such an army? What would happen next? And how much danger was he in right now? He rubbed his jaw, hoping that anyone watching would believe he was absorbing the tactical picture. The truth was, he was trying to compose himself, appear cool and collected, while inside, all he wanted to do was run and hide.

They'd hunted him like an animal in London. Would they try again now that he was relatively safe? Harry doubted it. Politicians were consumed by self-importance, but they were all expendable, even Harry. Especially Harry. Because at this moment, he had nothing to offer, no leadership, no words of wisdom, no Churchillian speeches. He was a run-of-the-mill Prime Minister, like so many of his predecessors, and that gave Harry Beecham some comfort.

He doubted anyone would be interested in his location.

THE ORDERLY SCOOPED up the filthy combat jacket and trousers and threw them in the green rubbish bag. He plucked the bloodied shirt, underpants, and socks from off the bathroom floor and bagged them too. He emptied the bathroom wastebasket and noticed the Prime Minister had used a disposable razor, some balled-up tissues, and a couple of cotton buds. Weighing the bag in his hand, he wondered how much he could get for the lot. Not soon, of course, but one day, when this bullshit was all over, and things went back to normal. It would probably be worth something.

He remembered visiting the Cabinet War Rooms in London as a kid. Behind a sheet of glass was Winston Churchill's cot, where, during WW2, the Big Man had occasionally bedded down. His pyjamas were there, folded on the bed, and a cigar butt balanced on a tin ashtray, as if he'd just left the room. Living history, they called it.

Maybe Beecham's dirty ear buds and bloody shirt would be put on display somewhere down the line. Maybe Northstar would become a museum of the future, and Beecham's room a major attraction. Then again, maybe this was it, the end of western civilisation. That's what some were saying.

He scanned the room and left, closing the door. Outside, he picked up another rubbish sack and set off at a brisk pace. He couldn't hang about. Earlier, they'd paraded in the assembly area where a tooled-up infantry officer had asked for volunteers to stay behind and keep the place running until the last moment, whatever that meant.

While others had raised their hands, the Orderly had kept his firmly by his side. Then they'd queued up and received their transport orders. As luck would have it, they'd assigned him a place on the first wave of transports out of Northstar. That would take them into the nearby town of Wells, and from there, after loading more evacuees, down to Plymouth and the ships.

The Orderly was desperate to leave. He'd only just escaped from Tidworth Garrison with his life. Terrorists had attacked his accommodation block, throwing grenades along the corridors and into rooms. The Orderly had escaped by dropping from his first-floor window and running for the fences. He'd seen others cut down, including the bloke who ran beside him. The Orderly could hear him screaming as he rolled under the perimeter fence. Could still hear him screaming.

He left the senior staff quarters and made his way through the warren of passageways to the service shafts. Being an orderly made a person invisible, and since arriving at Northstar, he'd been privy to conversations not normally overheard by privates like him.

But what he'd heard had frightened him. London had fallen. IS soldiers were pouring into the country on planes and ships. The British army was in disarray. The Orderly could attest to that. Tidworth had been a nightmare, all gunfire, explosions, and burning buildings.

He'd seen some terrible things too, like the Challenger tank careering around Mooltan barracks, hunting the terrorists, and crushing them under its tracks. More screams he'd never forget. But he'd made it to Northstar, and now he had a place on the first wave of transports.

There was no way the Orderly was going to miss his slot, orders be damned.

The waste and recycling centre was at the other end of the complex but going there would add another thirty minutes to his day. He needed to eat before his journey, load up on supplies, get his kit squared away. No one knew when the next meal might be, and the Orderly didn't want to go hungry.

So instead of heading down to the lower levels, he headed up.

Two minutes later, he was on the observation level. As he turned left and right through the limestone tunnels, he caught the scent of pine. He turned another corner and saw the warning signs on the walls about noise and light discipline. One more turn and he was there, in an observation post, a narrow opening cut into the rock face that looked all the way down the valley.

He approached the cut and peered over the edge. Below him, he saw the entrance to Northstar, the enormous door sealed tight. Nothing moved, but the Orderly knew there were people down there in the forest. No one would be looking up.

He picked up the first rubbish sack and shoved it through the opening. It fell away, into the treetops, where it caught in the thick cover. He did the same with the other bag, the one with Beecham's dirty clothes and earbuds, and watched it split as it hit the trees.

No matter. It was done, and he'd saved himself a good half-hour.

He'd make that transport now, no problem.

• • •

CAUGHT AMONGST THE UPPERMOST BRANCHES, Harry Beecham's combat jacket swayed and twisted with the lazy movement of the treetops.

As the morning sun blazed across the hidden valley, the unseen jacket clung to the highest branches of a tall pine, the micro-transmitter inside the pocket announcing its presence to anyone that cared to listen.

CHAPTER 64
THE CRASH OF '47

NINE NAUTICAL MILES SHY OF THE MID-ATLANTIC SHELF, THE *CALIFORNIA* pitched and rolled in heavy seas beneath a steel grey sky.

'Here she comes.'

Schelling pointed through the sloping bridge windows and handed Terry Fitzgerald his binoculars. The ambassador pressed them to his eyes and watched the Seahawk helicopter heading for the *California*. A mile behind it, the *USS Arizona*, a nuclear-powered aircraft carrier, rode the swells of an unseasonal North Atlantic storm.

The *California* wasn't faring much better. *Like a toy in a bathtub*, Fitzgerald thought, as his breakfast of muffins and coffee threatened to make a reappearance. Still, he felt better than he did yesterday. The medics had cleaned him up and jabbed him, and now he wore clean underwear and a baggy navy flight suit.

Last night, the stealth ship had made a record-breaking start to its run, but the worsening sea conditions had curtailed its speed and progress. Schelling made a call, and now naval aviation was inbound to take Fitzgerald to the *Arizona* and complete the journey home.

He handed the binoculars back to the captain. 'What d'you think? A day to make land. Maybe two?'

'They have an aircraft waiting to take you Stateside,' Schelling explained. He motioned to a waiting officer. 'Lieutenant Andrews will escort you to the transfer deck.' He held out his hand. 'Good luck, sir.'

'Likewise, captain. And thank you.'

Andrews escorted Fitzgerald off the bridge. He followed the sailor up through narrow gangways and into a cargo bay at the top of the ship. The noise was tremendous, and Fitzgerald looked up to see a wide section of the sliding roof had rolled back to reveal the low grey skies above.

Twin assaults of wind and rising helicopter chop filled the bay. Waiting seamen hurried forward and dressed Fitzgerald in a red survival suit, helmet, and harness. They hurried him towards a large, orange hazard square painted on the deck, directly beneath the open roof, and ordered him to stand still.

Fitzgerald looked up. Dark clouds galloped overhead, and the unseen helicopter's engines roared. Andrews approached Fitzgerald and leaned into his ear to make himself heard.

'The chopper will winch you straight up. It's fast, but it's safe, so just relax. You'll be on the *Arizona* in a few minutes.'

'Thank you,' shouted Fitzgerald, registering the quiver in his voice. He hated it when people said *relax*.

Then the sky darkened as the Seahawk nosed across the open roof thirty feet above his head, whipping salt spray around the bay. It all happened fast after that. Fitzgerald watched a crewman run towards him and grab a dangling cable hook. He attached it to a strong point somewhere around Fitzgerald's upper back, gave him the thumbs up, then titled his head towards the helicopter hovering directly overhead and did the same—

The deck fell away, and Fitzgerald felt the wind and rain flailing him. It took his breath away, and powerful hands yanked him inside the helicopter. He caught a final glimpse of the *California* as the Seahawk banked hard over the ocean and levelled off.

A few minutes later, Fitzgerald jumped down to the noisy deck of the *USS Arizona*. Four armed Marines escorted him through a dizzying maze of gangways to the captain's quarters. A large, shaven-headed man rose from behind his desk and met Fitzgerald as he entered the cabin.

'Mister Ambassador, I'm Captain Purcell, commanding officer. Welcome aboard the *Arizona*.' He gestured to a chair, and the men sat down. 'I wouldn't get too comfortable. There's a TR-51 on the flight-deck prepped and ready to take you directly to DC.'

'Okay,' Fitzgerald said, then he swallowed. 'Wait, isn't that a drone?'

'It's a UCAS-TR. That's an Unmanned Combat Air System, Tactical Reconnaissance variant,' Purcell told him. 'It flies fast and high and is completely automated. A little like the EV that got you out of London, just bigger and more comfortable. This one is configured for VIP transport. That's you.'

Fitzgerald felt his heart rate climb. 'So, there's no crew? No pilot?'

Purcell smiled. 'Don't worry, it's perfectly safe. And the view should be pretty good. The east coast is clear from Labrador to Key West.'

A white-coated steward tapped and entered with and a tray of coffee. The young man's balancing skills impressed Fitzgerald as the carrier nosed into another trough. A low boom rippled through the ship as the ocean made its powerful presence known.

'How was London?' Purcell asked after the steward had departed.

Fitzgerald sipped his coffee. 'It was terrifying. Chaotic. By the time I launched from the roof, they'd already breached the building. Is there any news?'

'Europe has gone dark,' Purcell told him. He spent the next few minutes updating Fitzgerald, and what the ambassador heard wasn't good. 'They want you in the White House for a full-court press event,' Purcell said. 'Lone survivor out of London, a personal account of what happened, that kind of thing.'

'I can't be the only one. There must be prisoners.'

'I sure hope so.'

'What about the Russians?'

'Sticking to the self-defence narrative, protecting their Nord Stream pipeline.'

There was another tap at the door. Purcell barked permission to enter, and the door opened to reveal the same Marine escort. 'The guys will escort you to the ready room, get you prepped for launch.'

Fitzgerald stood, and the men shook hands. 'Good luck, Mister Ambassador.'

'You too, captain.'

They escorted Fitzgerald to a huge hangar bay below the flight deck. Squatting on a giant elevator was one of the strangest, yet beautiful craft that Fitzgerald had ever seen.

The TR-51 reminded him of a scaled down B2 bomber, only sleeker and infinitely more compact. It was light grey, with black US Navy signage on its fat body, and it rested on three spindly looking legs. The wings tapered towards the single jet engine at the rear, its exhaust vent not round but rectangular. It looked like a classic-shaped UFO, Fitzgerald thought.

It was a comparison that was no longer absurd.

Several crewmen closed in and prepped him for the flight. He couldn't see their faces, hidden behind the black visors of their helmets, and they had to shout above the noise of the giant hangar that was crawling with crew and jammed with aircraft.

They guided him up the aircraft's ladder and settled him inside, securing his seat harness and plugging him into the aircraft's support and comms systems. The seat was of the first-class commercial variety, black leather, large and comfortable. *Relax*, the guys in black jumpsuits told him, *just enjoy the ride*. Fitzgerald wanted to ask if any of them had ever been a passenger on a pilotless plane over a vast and empty ocean but decided against it.

Purcell was right, though—the TR-51 was far more comfortable than the evac craft, and when they lowered the hatch, the constant roar of carrier noise disappeared, replaced by the quiet hum of the TR-51's internal systems.

Fitzgerald swallowed to clear his ears, then felt a shudder as the elevator cranked upwards towards the flight deck, followed by a solid boom as it locked into position. Rain lashed the shifting deck as personnel swarmed around the aircraft.

After a minute, they jogged away, gathering behind the safety line to watch. The engine whined into life and the digital display lit up, the screens scrolling with indecipherable data. Fitzgerald looked out through the windshield. Rain dribbled down the acrylic canopy that wrapped itself around the cockpit, giving Fitzgerald an all-round view. He looked down the nose of the craft and all the way along the deck to the end of the runway. He watched the bow pitch as it rode the Atlantic swell, the sky above dark and oppressive. His heart raced.

Here we go again.

He heard a voice inside his helmet. 'Mister Ambassador, my name is Captain Sommers, 432 Operations Group, 14th Reconnaissance Squadron, and I'll be piloting your aircraft today. To respond, key the transmit button on the left arm of your seat, sir.'

Fitzgerald did just that. 'Thank you, captain. Did we just meet down in the hangar?'

'No sir, I'm talking to you from Creech Air Force Base. In Nevada.'

'Right,' Fitzgerald said, amazed and terrified that his safety was in the hands of a man sitting in a desert compound four thousand miles away. Sommers' next words were a little more comforting.

'We've got a room full of people here, all monitoring your flight. So, you can relax, sir. You're in excellent hands.'

'Appreciate that, captain.'

'Launch in 60 seconds.'

The craft shuddered on its spindly legs, and he felt his seat vibrating. On the deck to his right, Fitzgerald saw a white-vested crewman give him the thumbs-up—

He grunted, the g-forces slamming him back into his seat. He saw the carrier superstructure flash by, and the rolling ocean rise up to swallow him. Then the bow fell away—along with Fitzgerald's stomach—as the craft nosed upwards at a steep angle.

Fitzgerald gripped his seat as the TR-51 bucked and vibrated through a world of solid grey. He glanced at the TV screens and saw the altimeter rising. At nineteen thousand feet, the aircraft punched through the cloud layer into blue skies. The vibration stopped, but the aircraft kept climbing until the altimeter read fifty-eight thousand feet. Engine noise faded, and the nose settled. The craft flew onwards, smooth as a ride in a Tesla. And the view was breathtaking.

An ocean of white cloud stretched across the horizon as the TR-51 hummed through the sky. Fitzgerald craned his neck and observed the dark atmosphere above him. That was space up there. It didn't seem far away. He was in awe of the sheer beauty of the world outside the canopy. Captain Sommers' voice broke the spell.

'How's the ride, Mister Ambassador?'

'Pretty awesome. I can barely hear the engine.'

'That's the point of the TR-51, sir. High and quiet. And she's flying herself right now. Outlying naval pickets have your transponder, but we'll be watching, anyway. Weather looks good all the way into Andrews AFB. You should be on the deck in under two hours. If you have questions, just ask.'

'Thanks, captain.'

'Roger that.'

Fitzgerald felt his body relax a little, and when it did, exhaustion weighed heavy on his body. He took a small bottle of water from the cool box by his seat and sipped it.

Two hours to DC. Two hours in which to compose his thoughts and try to make sense of what had happened.

He'd spent a couple of hours on the *California* recording the sequence of events in London, the people he knew, where he'd seen them, who they were with, what they were doing. He catalogued the attackers—numbers, physical descriptions, voices, weapons, equipment, anything he could remember. Then he'd emailed it to his State and personal email addresses. When he got home, he'd go over it again and make sure it was as accurate as possible. Truth and clarity were key.

He let his mind drift and speculated on how things had come to this.

Purcell had said that Europe had gone dark. An operation of that magnitude had inside help, of that Fitzgerald had no doubt. He'd seen it before, at home and abroad, when western politicians had kowtowed to their Middle Eastern and Chinese counterparts. Everyone respected strength, and both the caliphate and the Chinese were not afraid to project that power.

Wazir had demanded the closure of US bases in every country he'd annexed, including Saudi Arabia. The domino effect spread right across the Middle East as Britain and the EU cosied up to Baghdad, determined not to follow America's example of expulsion, diplomatic protest, and grudging acceptance.

Instead, they played host to Wazir, and allowed him to address the people of Europe and the UK. Shackled by the chains of self-censorship, no one had the courage to call out the caliph's message—that Europe was sick and wallowed in sin. Western leaders were weak and corrupt. Europe's capitals were the devil's playground. Wazir said what he wanted, his message unfiltered. And often amplified.

And so, America found itself increasingly isolated. The international markets began trading in roubles, yuan, riyals, rupees, and precious metals. The dollar faltered, undermined by the collective power of emerging, burgeoning markets. As the economy tanked, defence spending fell for the first time since the outbreak of WW2.

The administration ordered borders controls to be tightened, and the visa programme suspended. Exports slowed to a trickle. Factories closed and welfare programmes collapsed. Against a backdrop of ever-tightening budgets and political infighting, two long and bitter winters bled into a couple of punishingly hot summers, heaping tremendous pressure on America's energy infrastructure.

Oil imports doubled, and so did the price of a barrel. Inflation soared. Keeping warm in winter and cool in summer became a blood sport. Across America, blackouts followed brownouts. The supply chain faltered, and supermarkets ran dry. Major riots erupted in New York, Chicago, Baltimore, Oakland, Los Angeles, Seattle, and a dozen other cities. Times were hard, and another Great Depression loomed like a towering tsunami, only this time it would be so much worse. People sought the comfort of their faith and church attendances soared.

They prayed hard for a miracle.

And then those prayers were answered.

THE DELEGATION ARRIVED in DC the day after fourteen people were killed during disturbances in the Washington suburb of Columbia Heights and black smoke stained the capital's skyline.

The three men and one woman arrived in an unescorted, unmarked minivan, and all of them were in possession of security clearances several levels above Top Secret. When Secret Service agents ushered them into the Oval Office, President Bob Mitchell, then Chief of Staff Trey Palmer, and Eliot Bird, the president's national security advisor, were waiting. Introductions were made, and seats were taken around the sofas.

The meeting began.

Mitchell assumed the last-minute appointment referred to a national security matter. He was right, but also unaware of the specific subject of the meeting. Palmer and Bird were equally nonplussed. It fell to the head of the delegation, an air force general by the name of Huffman, who told the President exactly why they were there.

What happened next is still shrouded in mystery and conjecture. Fitzgerald was privy to it only because of his lifelong friendship with Mitchell's former chief of staff. Naturally, Palmer was sworn to secrecy, but eventually, he confided in Fitzgerald during a round of golf whilst their families were vacationing together in Arizona. The reason? Because his old college roommate needed to tell someone. To share the burden. Someone he could trust with his life. And when he did, he kept it breezy, like a humorous dinner party yarn.

But while he spoke, Palmer's face had paled…

HUFFMAN: *Mister President, we accessed the White House servers to create this appointment today. We apologise for the security breach, but our mission is one of both necessity and national urgency. We're here for the sake of the nation.*

Mitchell: *Wait a minute, you hacked the White House?*

Huffman: *Yes, sir. Our visit, and the subject of this meeting, must remain totally and unequivocally confidential. To that effect, you've all been pre-cleared for Sensitive Compartmented Information in relation to what we're about to discuss. Only you three.*

At that point, Mitchell had held up his hand.

Mitchell: *Stop right there, general. Before you say another word, let me make myself absolutely clear, because I'm this close to calling the Secret*

Service in here and ordering them to detain you all. Criminal trespass for starters—

The President stopped talking as the lady arranged a series of photographs across the table between them. Mitchell examined the photographs one by one, his eyes shifting back and forth between the images of a silver disc buried into the side of a desert mesa, between the charred and childlike bodies lying side by side on a green tarpaulin, and back to the stone-faced delegation staring at him from the opposite sofas.

Mitchell: *These can't be real.*

Huffman: *The New Mexico crash is not a myth, Mister President. We have studied the recovered hardware for decades. With each new breakthrough, human technology took a similar leap forward. Some time ago we made another fundamental discovery. Zero-point energy.*

Mitchell: *Which is…?*

Huffman: *A discovery on par with man's ability to make fire. A game changer of such unimaginable proportions that it could entirely disrupt and destabilise global wealth and power structures overnight. For that reason, it must remain hidden beneath the veil of total secrecy.*

Mitchell learned that Las Vegas had been running on zero-point power converters for over a month, to the increasing bemusement and concern of the Nevada Energy board. Questions were being asked, and it was the President's job to sell the story. A new processor, capable of providing low-cost energy…

The TR-51 hit a pocket of turbulence, shaking the craft.

Trey Palmer's tale had ended there, and Fitzgerald had kept his friend's secret. Mitchell sold the miracle to the country as a breakthrough in power conduction and storage. Transition would be slow, but the economy would stabilise. Then grow.

Palmer left the White House to become CEO of the newly formed Domestic Energy Commission that oversaw the rollout of the technology, starting with regional power providers. The lights stayed on, with no impact on the environment. Where they went from there,

Fitzgerald didn't know. He was out of the loop now, and his friend never spoke about that meeting again.

Except for one time, when Fitzgerald asked him about the future. Palmer had shrugged and smiled, and said he knew nothing about the development of new public transport systems, an automation revolution, and potential propulsion plants that might push the boundaries of space travel and human endeavour.

Fitzgerald's recollections and his flight through the heavens had improved his mood. Europe may be dark right now, but Lady Liberty's torch shone brighter than ever.

He heard Sommers' voice inside his helmet. 'Mister Ambassador, we're about to start our descent into Andrews. ETA is twenty minutes. Just relax and enjoy the rest of the flight, sir.'

'Thank you, captain.'

The TR-51 dipped its nose and began its controlled glide over the eastern seaboard. Fitzgerald took another look at the world outside the cockpit. The sun was rising behind him, and ahead, the cluster of lights of Atlantic City were still visible as dawn rolled across America. He was almost home.

He sat a little straighter in his seat. Once he hit the ground, it would be all business. Before anything, he would demand an update on the embassy in London. He needed to know the numbers, the living, the wounded, and the dead. He prayed that the number would be low, but in his heart, he knew it would be devastating.

The TR-51's nose dipped, and the aircraft dropped almost silently through the sky. Fitzgerald saw the shimmering scoop of Delaware Bay below, and beyond it, another cluster of lights. His destination, Washington DC. It was going to be a long day, the longest in his career. And when he was done, he'd take a room at the Hyatt-Regency and try to get some rest.

Fitzgerald knew that sleep wouldn't come easy.

CHAPTER 65
FALCON

THE UMBILICAL CABLES WERE DETACHED FROM THE UAV'S FUSELAGE AND the battery cart wheeled away.

Its Turkish ground crew had checked all on-board systems and the remote pilot/operator in the ground station flexed his fingers to prepare for the flight.

The TAI-4 *Dogan* (Falcon) was a low altitude, medium endurance aircraft designed and built by Turkish Aerospace Industries for tactical surveillance and reconnaissance missions. It squatted on the runway at Heathrow Airport like a giant black insect, its fuel-efficient turbo prop engine idling while it awaited its launch command.

Inside the nearby ground station, the pilot received the green light and advanced the bird's throttles, watching the runway roll beneath one of the Falcon's nose-mounted cameras as it gathered speed. At V1, he eased back the joystick, and the UAV lifted into the air and climbed into the morning sky, heading due west.

The pilot had a general brief—to probe the airspace to the west, to monitor and record enemy traffic movements and send all captured footage and SIGINT data back to London for analysis. There were other UAVs in the air, and they would do the same on a broad, fifty-mile-wide front, but the pilot of the Falcon intended to push his bird to the limits of its operability.

It was designed for low-level work, and the pilot had proved his flying skills in the mountainous regions of Kurdistan. He was aware of the loss of a Big Eye and two Raptors, which meant the British had serious SAM capability. The pilot considered this a challenge and intended to test the enemy ground crews while hoovering up as much visual and electronic data as possible. The Falcon flew low and fast, and the pilot was adept at squeezing her through craggy ravines and shallow valleys.

But now, on his curved display screen, he saw only green fields and low, undulating hills passing beneath his bird. He sat a little straighter in his ergonomic chair and rested his right hand on the joystick. The HUD flight data feed in the corner of his display told him that all flight systems were nominal, and all sensors were functioning. It was time to go to work.

The pilot eased his joystick back a touch, and the Falcon climbed to two thousand feet. He didn't have to wait long for the data to flow. The first contact was a long column of armour, troop transports and support vehicles moving northeast up the M3 motorway.

As the Falcon crossed Salisbury Plain, it registered enemy air-search radars and electronic returns from other clusters of military vehicles scattered across its western borders. The pilot targeted the air-search radars and updated T-BIS with their locations as the Falcon continued westwards.

Above the town of Frome, it ran into a virtual wall of electronic noise, forcing the Falcon to reset its sensors and pinpoint the dozens of tracked and hand-held radars sweeping the sky. An alarm buzzed on The pilot's console as his bird detected a launch, then an incoming missile. He fired off an IR chaff pod and dipped the nose, banking around to face the incoming threat, then glimpsing the fast-moving dart as it shot past the Falcon's starboard wing.

Trimming power, he brought the UAV around in a slow turn and headed for the treetops. The missile disappeared from his threat display and the Falcon continued its mission.

Tapping his keyboard, the pilot started the Falcon's low-level reconnaissance program, an advanced algorithm he helped design. The aircraft received the command and ran the program. The pilot let go of the joystick as the UAV began flying itself. In the low-lit ground station, others gathered around to watch the unfolding scene on the curved display.

They saw the English countryside race beneath the nose of the Falcon as it interrogated the ground ahead, making subtle course corrections as it hunted for enemy signals. They saw villages and towns, soldiers and civilians, their pale faces turned up to the sky as the UAV skimmed low over rooftops and fields, banking left and right, moving too fast to intercept and too low and slow for missile lock.

As it swept over the village of Bathway in Somerset, a burst of anti-aircraft fire angled past the nose and up into the blue sky. Whoever the gunner was, he was fast, but not nearly fast enough.

Ahead, the black ribbon of a major road cut across the countryside and the Falcon changed course towards it. On his display, the pilot watched the data feed and was satisfied the bird's onboard cameras were recording the enemy convoy's direction, speed, and composition.

It was a big one too, the pilot noticed, and it was heading south. He saw puffs of ground fire but the Falcon, flying a parallel course to the road and partly shielded by trees, made itself a hard target. Then it banked away behind a wooded rise, leaving the convoy behind.

The ground gave way to steeper hills and limestone bluffs. The Falcon pushed westwards, climbing over the undulating countryside, and flying low above a desolate plateau. Electronic noise fell away behind it.

The pilot retook control, eager to explore this strange, rugged formation. It wasn't Kurdistan, not by any stretch, but he saw ridges and deep gorges, and he knew from experience what they might mean. Hiding places. He flew low and slow over forests and barren moorland. The jagged teeth of a rocky outcrop loomed to his right, and the pilot banked over to take a look. What lay beyond those strange formations?

The outcrop flashed beneath the nose cameras, and a long, steep-sided valley stretched ahead, the ground below covered with a dark and impenetrable forest of pines.

. . .

HARRY'S DISCARDED combat jacket still clung to the uppermost branches of the pine tree. In its pocket, the micro-transmitter, its signal weakening by the minute, continued to broadcast its presence.

Beep, beep, beep...

'WHAT WAS THAT?'

As the watchers pressed closer around him, the pilot's fingers flew across the keyboard and isolated the new signal. Across the room, sophisticated processing servers interrogated the broadcast against its vast database.

'It's a micro-transmitter,' a colleague announced. 'One of ours.'

'Out here?' The pilot brought the Falcon around for another pass, flying his bird low over the valley. All he could see were bluffs and trees. Nothing moved below. There were no masts, no satellite dishes, no structures, except for a nearby farm on the other side of the valley, and that looked deserted.

'It's a Mark 3 dedicated signal transmitter,' said the technician behind him. 'Used by special forces and infiltration units for HVT target identification.'

'There's nothing here,' said another onlooker.

'Nothing we can see,' the pilot said. 'And the thing didn't fly out here on its own. Upload it to T-BIS.'

Maybe someone in London could shed a little light on the mystery.

'HE'S COMING AROUND AGAIN,' the missile defence operator reported. 'We're locked on.'

Bashford stood over the young man's shoulder, watching the TV screen. The camera was tracking the UAV, watching it circle overhead like a bird of prey.

Goddam you.

Another day and the evacuation would've been completed. Now there was an enemy UAV above them, and it had clearly found something. What it had found didn't matter. Northstar was now compromised, and Bashford had two choices—destroy the UAV, and give away their position, or wait for it to fly away. But if it flew south and spotted the convoys and the waiting ships—well, that was unthinkable.

So, no choice at all.

'Take it out,' ordered Bashford.

'WHAT THE HELL?'

The display flashed, then went blank. The HUD feed failed, as well as the Falcon's data streams. 'She's gone,' the pilot said.

'Did you hit something?' asked a colleague. The pilot gave him a scornful look.

'Rewinding footage,' another tech said.

The pilot got up and stood over the other tech's workstation. He saw a flare of light just below the ridgeline. 'That's a missile. Or a disruption laser, maybe. Either way, this valley is important. Probably a storage depot beneath the hill, or a command bunker. Tell London, right now.'

'Roger.'

The EWOPs scurried back to their terminals and began collating the data for transmission. The pilot studied his blank screens for less than three seconds.

'And someone get me a replacement bird, asap!'

MOUSA WOKE to the sound of persistent knocking. He checked his watch—he'd been sleeping for just over an hour. Cursing, he threw the sleeping bag aside and rolled off the sofa. He stepped into his boots and laced them. 'Enter!' he bellowed.

Major Allawi entered the room. Mousa snatched the message slip from his outstretched hand.

'A UAV has located an enemy signal. It's a micro-transmitter, the same frequency as the one found in Downing Street—'

'Beecham,' Mousa said.

'A probability.' Allawi spread out a map on the office desk and pointed. 'Right there.'

Mousa studied the location. The signal was broadcasting from deep in the west country, just north of a town called Wells. 'What is this place?'

'A tourist area. And a geological Swiss cheese. A lot of sinkholes and caverns. A good place to hide a Prime Minister on the run.'

'You think there's a government facility there?'

Allawi spread his hands. 'Why not? We didn't know about the tunnels beneath Downing Street.'

'So, we've found another rat's nest.' Mousa woke up his T-BIS terminal, and the screen glowed with coloured icons. He studied it for several seconds as it updated itself with the Falcon's data. Mousa's eye was drawn to the clusters of red icons running north to south. He traced a finger across the map.

'You see it, Reza? That's a defensive front. Look at the overlay, the roads, and junctions. They intend to stand and fight.'

Allawi rubbed his jaw. 'They don't have the numbers.'

'So it would seem, but they've been full of surprises so far. Get the reconnaissance units moving west. I want to know what kind of resistance to expect. And I want my field commanders on-line asap. This may be our chance to decapitate their leadership and capture Beecham.'

Allawi hurried from the room, already issuing orders on his radio. Mousa had to act fast. He would need permission to launch an unplanned assault. He tapped at his laptop and established a link with the caliph's distant desert base. Wazir entered the frame a few moments later and sat down.

'General Mousa. You have news?'

'A significant development, in fact. We've discovered a secret command post, and the likelihood of Beecham being there is high. I'm seeking permission to launch as assault, one that could cripple the enemy leadership team and shorten our campaign.'

Intrigued, the caliph sat forward in his chair.

'Go on, general.'

CHAPTER 66
THE FARM

FAZ REACHED ACROSS THE BED AND SWITCHED OFF THE PORTABLE RADIO. The emergency message was still broadcasting, and the TV was devoid of any programmes. He stood up and stretched, yawning, and wondered if the public heeded that advice. Most would, and those that didn't wouldn't venture too far from their homes.

But there would be others, opportunists, criminals, political activists, who would rejoice in the collapse of order. Wazir's military high command and his intelligence networks in Europe and Britain had probably war-gamed the same scenario, and Faz imagined how it might play out. Many of those opportunists would head out into the streets, to loot and burn, to exact vengeance on rivals, to assassinate political opponents.

Somewhere down the line—days rather than weeks, Faz reckoned —order would be restored at the barrel of a gun. An interim government would be formed, made up of senior IS military personnel, British collaborators, and senior figures from religious councils across England and Wales. Calm would return to the cities. Life would begin again, albeit under new management.

Would people care? Some would, but Faz believed that a vast majority of people would accept the new regime. There would be resistance, and that would take many forms, but the caliphate would implement its laws and punishments, and those would keep the majority in line. Eventually, life would return to some sort of normality.

In the bathroom, Faz splashed tepid water on his face. He'd just imagined a cowed Britain, and a new European order. Was he being over-pessimistic? Would it be that simple? Or would the British armed forces push the invaders back into the sea?

He dried his face and re-watched the footage on his phone. The convoy stretched for miles along the M3, headed north to London. He saw SAM vehicles and big tracked guns and lots of troop trucks. And no one was opposing them. Did that mean that the British Army had collapsed? Already? Or was a fightback about to begin, one that would roll across the south-east, laying waste to towns and cities? Faz wasn't so sure. Everything had happened too fast. Whatever was left of the government would still be reeling.

At least they were safe here, at the farm. They'd arrived yesterday, after weaving through deserted country lanes and turning onto a narrow, gated track. The Range Rover climbed between steep-sided banks of tall grass and through a field of wildflowers. Beyond it lay a cluster of farm buildings, perfectly secluded. Geese scattered as they stopped outside the main house, a large, well-maintained building with small windows and a red-tiled roof. The scattered geese had regrouped and eyed the newcomers with suspicion.

Helen—Ross's sister-in-law—had greeted them with hugs and told them Rob—or Bob—as he preferred, was overnighting at a farm a few miles away, helping another farmer plant for the autumn harvest. She invited them into the kitchen, where the open windows looked out over an orchard. A black retriever puppy yelped around them, leaping and licking, then chasing its tail in excitement at their arrival.

Helen called, and the kids came running, six-year-old Hugo and Daisy, four, who were overjoyed to see their Uncle Ross. She fed them, and showed them to their rooms, but there was no mention of the invasion, or the dangers any of them had faced on their journey to the farm. Helen wanted to wait until Bob returned. Then they would talk.

Faz was invited to stay in the self-contained flat over the barn and he slept reasonably well, knowing it was exhaustion that kept him under for seven straight hours.

He woke with the sunrise, then dozed for a couple more hours. The radio on the bedside table provided no clues other than the looping emergency message. Now dressed in some of Bob's old cast-offs that Helen had provided, Faz wandered across to the main house.

The morning sun reflected off the solar panel arrays on every roof. Faz saw a wind turbine a short distance away and water butts at every building corner. A nearby barn had a Land Rover and a quad bike parked inside, and other machinery Faz didn't recognise.

Beyond a stone wall, he saw pigs snuffling around in the mud, and chickens ranged around the buildings, pecking at the dirt. There was an orchard and a crop field too, stretching all the way out to where the land met the sky. This was a good spot, he realised. No matter where he stood, he couldn't see another settlement. Which meant they couldn't be seen either.

Ross and Lara were already at the kitchen table eating breakfast. The food smelled so good, Faz's stomach grumbled instantly. Bob, who'd returned from his overnight planting, introduced himself. He was older and greyer than Ross, but Faz noticed the tanned skin and thick forearms beneath his rolled-up shirtsleeves. A big, no-nonsense guy, who could prove to be a useful ally like his brother.

Helen handed him a plate of scrambled eggs and toast and shooed the kids outside. The food didn't last long, and after a second helping and a fresh pot of coffee, they all settled around the big dining table. Ross had already brought his brother up to speed, and Helen asked the obvious question.

'So, what happens now?'

It was Ross who spoke first. 'Me and Faz need to link up with the authorities. We'll be needed.'

'Doing what?' Lara asked him. They were getting close, Faz noticed. It didn't take much to throw people together in times of conflict, and there was a connection between them that even a blind man could see.

'My job,' Ross told her. 'I can't stay, Lara.'

'He's right,' Faz said. 'We must find a military camp, a government facility, something like that. There'll be people there, civil emergency types. We need to get organised.'

Bob shook his head. 'You can forget Tidworth. The place is in turmoil, apparently. A lot of dead bodies and burning buildings. The army emptied everything and headed out onto Salisbury Plain. Same goes for Bulford.'

Faz thought that one over. 'Salisbury Plain seems a bit exposed. Tactically, I mean.'

'Someone in the village just got back from Marlborough,' Helen said. 'The town has seen no violence, but half the British army drove through it, apparently. They're heading west.'

Bob raised an eyebrow. 'So, what's that about, then?' He was looking at Faz.

'They're regrouping, I imagine,' Faz told him. 'I'm no military expert, but after what's happened, that would be the thing to do.'

'Who's in charge?' Bob asked.

Faz shrugged again. 'Beecham's probably dead. It'll be someone else, a Cabinet member, a senior civil servant maybe. God knows where they might be or how they're deciding things.'

'What about nuclear weapons?' Helen's eye was drawn to the kids' laughter drifting through the kitchen door. 'Please tell me no one will be insane enough to press the button.'

'I doubt it,' Faz said, but he knew that in war, anything could happen. Especially if the line of succession goes far enough down the ladder. 'Look, this situation is unprecedented and unpredictable. All I know is, they planned it to such a degree that regime change looks inevitable. The video footage I shot backs that theory up. You can see how much firepower the invaders have brought with them, and so far, their advance has been unopposed. We should prepare for a power shift. How long it might last is anyone's guess.'

'We need to focus on security,' Ross said. 'The power is out everywhere, and that will impact food and water supplies. If this crisis continues, people will get desperate. Food shops will be emptied if they aren't already. And if there's fighting in the cities, many people will head for the countryside.'

'Refugees,' Helen said, and Faz imagined immense columns of people pouring into the countryside.

'Any sign of the police?' Ross asked. 'Any patrols come through? Community cops?'

Helen glanced at Bob, and the man's face darkened.

'Yesterday, I saw Ritchie Drummond and a few of the other lads. Apparently, there's been a lot of trouble in Swindon, and our local uniforms headed off there. No one's seen 'em since. One of Ritchie's cousins turned up with his wife and kids in tow. He said Swindon town centre was on fire and there'd been a lot of shooting.'

Bob paused for a moment. 'He saw bodies too, cops, lying on the ground outside the police station on Princes Street. As if they'd been executed.'

'Jesus,' Ross muttered. 'Where's this cousin now? I need to speak to him.'

'Gone,' Bob said. 'He's going west. Told us we should do the same.'

'How far is the village?' Faz asked him.

'Just under a mile away. It's more of a hamlet, really. A church, community shop, a school, village hall.' He stared at Faz. 'What are you thinking?'

'I think you should consider security for the entire village. They need to know the potential dangers out there. You're okay up here, isolated, but I would recommend you act as a community, protect each other, make sure you have enough resources to ride out this crisis. I'm talking weeks, months, maybe a year. We like to think of ourselves as civilised, but it doesn't take much to descend into Lord of the Flies territory.'

'You're right.' He rapped a knuckle on the table and stood. 'The village needs to be told. I'm going to run down there, talk to the parish council, arrange a meeting.'

'When?' Helen asked him.

'As soon as possible.' He turned to Faz. 'Care to join me? You should meet the council. They'll listen to you.'

Faz shook his head. 'Not yet. I need to gather some intel that might help you plan your way through this.' He looked at Ross. 'Can you take me on a tour of the area around the village?'

Ross nodded. 'Sure.'

'I'll join you,' Lara said.

Outside the house, they waved Bob off and gathered around the Range Rover, now parked beneath a metal shed. The sun was warm and the sky a cloudless blue. Insects danced on a warm breeze that whispered through the surrounding trees.

'This is a lovely place,' Faz said, shielding his eyes from the sun. 'Remote too. Hard to spot from the road.'

'What's this mission we're on then?' Ross asked. He opened the rear tailgate and checked the weapons inside.

'How well do you know the area?'

'Like the back of my hand. Why?'

'I've been looking at the map,' Faz told him. 'The geography is quite interesting. Let's take a tour, shall we? I'll tell you all about it as we go. Lara, you drive, okay?'

She climbed behind the wheel and the Range Rover purred into life. Ross pressed the button, and the tailgate lowered and closed with a soft thump. As he stepped away, Faz grabbed his arm, his voice low.

'I hate to sound dramatic, Ross, but if the stories we've heard are true, we're officially behind enemy lines. Now they're shooting cops in Swindon. The people who did it might head in this direction. Others may come from elsewhere. We're going to have to think fast if we want to survive. I take it the village knows you're a cop?'

Ross nodded. 'Pretty much.'

'So, you've got a choice. *We've* got a choice. We stay, take our chances, or we keep moving west and link up with the military.'

Ross thought about it for less than five seconds. 'My family's here. Lara too. I can't abandon them, not now. I need to make sure they're safe before I go anywhere.' He scratched his head and said, 'I don't have to decide right now, do I?'

'No,' Faz said. He bit off his next words. The sound rose and fell in the summer sky. They listened to the muted roar in silence as they watched the horizon. Then the roar faded to nothing.

'You know what that was?' Faz asked.

'Helicopters. Lots of them.'

Faz shook his head. 'That was the sound of time running out. If you're going to go, you need to do it sooner rather than later.'

Ross nodded. 'I understand.'

Faz climbed into the Range Rover and powered down the window. Ross sat next to Lara, and they drove off. No one spoke.

Faz cradled the AK across his lap and watched the sky.

CHAPTER 67
THE WILTSHIRE BACKWOODS

SEATED INSIDE THE LOW-FLYING BLACK HAWK TRANSPORT HELICOPTER, Mousa tapped his boot on the deck as he watched the fields and treetops flash beneath the aircraft.

The caliph had granted him a further twenty-four hours to capture Beecham, a last opportunity to succeed where he'd failed before. Time was of the essence.

Eight other helicopters flew in a loose box formation around his own. Some were loaded with his own paratroopers, and the outer pickets were Apaches, ready to intercept trouble. Mousa thought he might well need the paras. This wasn't London, where thousands of IS troops were pouring into the capital every hour. Out here he was chasing the tail of the enemy, and British forces intended to stop any advance.

Mousa doubted that was possible given the numbers, but they would try. He hoped so. He'd come for a fight.

The Black Hawk slowed and dropped beneath the treetops. As the Apaches circled above, the troop carriers landed in a forest clearing in a storm of dry brush and twigs.

Grovely Wood was a series of undulating hills dominating the skyline to the west of Salisbury. Advance units had already secured the site and mobile anti-aircraft batteries swept the skies above them.

The paras dropped from their helicopters and spread out, securing a path beneath the thick overhead canopy. Mousa and Allawi followed them into the trees and down a slope towards the recently excavated command bunkers. A small delegation waited to greet them. Mousa returned the salutes and ducked inside the bunker. He followed the corridor of log walls and swept the blackout curtain aside.

His first impression was favourable. The low-ceilinged bunker was spacious and dominated by an enormous glass T-BIS screen alive with coloured icons and graphical map overlays. Rows of operators sat hunched over their consoles and more electronic maps glowed around the shadowy walls. The atmosphere was one of quiet intensity which would serve him and the mission well.

Mousa headed for the T-BIS screen, where a gaggle of army and aviation group commanders were locked in quiet discussion. They turned as one as Mousa approached.

'How far west have we pushed the recce units?' he asked no-one in particular.

A senior army group commander cleared his throat and pointed to the screen. 'To the outskirts of Trowbridge, General Mousa. I've ordered them to withdraw and wait for support. They've lost three light-armoured vehicles to anti-tank and small arms fire.'

Mousa glared at the commander. 'Order them back into action. Press the attack.' He saw the snake of red icons moving to the southwest. It was the convoy detected by the missing Falcon UAV. 'Do we know where they're headed yet?'

'No, general. The British are jamming the skies and disrupting our UAV surveillance. They might try to loop around and move against our southern flank. I recommend we shift our threat axis to counter any potential counterattack.'

'Agreed. And send up another Big Eye to burn through those jammers.'

'There's one on station already, general. We should have some data soon.'

Mousa growled an acknowledgement. He knew the decision to commit his ground forces without adequate air cover could prove costly. And British SAM units still operating to the west also threatened his air assets. This operation was risky but waiting might allow Beecham and his leadership team to escape. He noticed an Air Force commander hovering close by. 'What is it?'

'We're getting intel from the Big Eye, general. Something interesting.'

'Show me.'

The blue-uniformed commander flipped the T-BIS display into air-mode. Immediately, Mousa saw a multitude of cone-like radar washes on the map, pulsing from dull to bright yellow and back again.

'These are the enemy search-radars,' the commander explained. 'And these are the same radars an hour ago.' He loaded a historical view and Mousa noticed the red dots had changed position, but the radar envelopes had remained steady. 'It's a pattern, general. They're moving their vehicles at irregular intervals and overlapping their search patterns.'

'They're trying to fool us,' Mousa realised.

The Air Force commander nodded. 'They have far fewer assets than we think.'

'Good work, colonel...?'

'Ahmed,' the man beamed.

'Firm up the data and plot their positions.'

'I've already sent the order,' Ahmed told him. 'I have two squadrons of fully loaded ground-attack aircraft idling on the tarmac at Heathrow. An air assault brigade is also on standby, waiting to follow the bombers in.'

'Excellent.' He flipped T-BIS back to surface mode. 'Where's my armour?'

The infantry commander took his cue and circled several positions with a laser pointer. 'We have combat formations ready to roll west along these routes here, here, and here. They await your order, general.'

Mousa nodded in satisfaction. 'Good. When I give that order, they must push hard and fast. If anything gets in their way, destroy it.'

The senior officers responded in unison. 'Yes, general.'

'And remind your people that failure will not be tolerated. The penal battalions are always looking for new recruits.'

He marched outside. Allawi waited as Mousa found a tree to empty his bladder against. His strike force was in place. All he had to do was pinpoint those British SAM assets and take them out. Then the path would be clear, all the way to the rat's nest in the Mendip Hills. He would drive a wedge through the West Country and scatter the surviving British forces. Scatter and destroy. And if they caught Beecham into the bargain, so much the better.

He zipped himself up, and Allawi fell in beside him as they paced around the command bunker.

'What do you think?' Mousa asked his 2IC.

'It's doable, general. If we can take out those missile systems fast enough.'

Mousa looked at his watch and smiled. 'We will. And with nothing to stop us, we'll drive what's left into the sea.'

CHAPTER 68
BLAME GAME

Harry pressed himself against the tunnel wall as a crocodile of young soldiers left the operations room, some loaded with boxes, while others wheeled flight cases and trolleys.

None of them paid any attention to Harry, and he supposed they were all worried about their own survival. He didn't blame them. So was he.

As the last one hurried by, Harry stepped into the ops room. There were more soldiers here, dismantling equipment and throwing cables into crates. There were papers strewn across the floor, and chairs and tables stacked against the wall. The command group was elsewhere, it seemed.

At the far end of the room, he saw a lone figure sat at the conference table, and Harry wandered over. As he got closer, he saw it was Leon Tubbs, and he hesitated. Tubbs was toying with a mobile phone, spinning it on the table like a toy. He looked lost in another world. Harry was about to walk away when Tubbs saw him.

'Come and join me, Prime Minister. The coffee's still warm.'

Harry cursed under his breath, but he couldn't walk away. There would be others like Tubbs out there, with the same intransigent mindset. He couldn't avoid all of them, so he poured himself a coffee and sat across the table. The soldiers at the other end of the room were too busy and too far away to eavesdrop on their conversation. Tubbs wore a green flight suit, the sleeves rolled to the elbow. It bulged at the seams.

'It's all they could find,' he explained. 'Not a good look, is it?' The smile melted from his face. 'Alice wanted me to lose weight. She said voters didn't respond positively to fat blokes like me, even though we're the most obese nation in Europe. I thought the fatties might rally around me, but no. That's the trouble with politics these days. It's all about image. She even bought me a treadmill. I think I used it twice.' He held up the phone. 'I keep expecting her to ring, despite the network failures. Pathetic, eh?'

Harry shook his head. 'No, Leon. It's not.' Earlier, Harry had tried to sleep, but Ellen's nightmarish screams kept waking him.

'I'm sorry about your wife. A truck bomb, they said.'

Harry nodded. 'Right outside Downing Street.'

'You were lucky.'

'She wasn't.'

'No.' Tubbs bowed his head. 'Alice is abroad. In Brussels. God knows where she is now.'

'Safe, I would imagine.'

Tubbs looked up. 'You can't possibly know that.'

'It's best to be positive.'

Tubbs scowled and sipped his coffee. When he looked at Harry again, his eyes had hardened. 'I stand by what I said. Your administration must bear some responsibility for this. For the lives lost.'

'Now's not the time, Leon.' Harry took a careful sip of coffee. Tubbs' emotions were all over the place, just like Harry's. Now he could sense a growing anger across the table.

'You enabled Wazir,' Tubbs said, his eyes narrowing. 'You let him spread his message without a scintilla of criticism. Your Home Secretary turned a blind eye to the boats crossing the Channel. You allowed hundreds of thousands of people to come here from countries that are indifferent or openly hostile to our way of life, and you didn't carry out a single background check.'

'I didn't think—'

Tubbs slammed his hand on the table. Coffee spilled, black and steaming.

'There it is! You didn't think! And you didn't listen! You ignored all the studies, all the warnings. You looked the other way.' His eyes narrowed. 'No, that's wrong. You knew what you were doing, didn't you? The question is, why?'

Harry didn't know what to say because he didn't have an answer. Not one that would satisfy Tubbs.

The Shadow Home Secretary used his napkin to wipe the spilled coffee.

'When I was a boy, we had a corner shop at the end of our road. The owners were Indians, a pleasant couple, friendly. Hard workers too. They gave me my first job, a paper round. I was always up at the crack of sparrows, and that bloody bag weighed a ton, too. Especially on Sundays.' Tubbs snorted. 'Can you imagine a twelve-year-old doing that today? Anyway, the point of the story is this—the proudest day of their lives was the day they became British citizens. It took them thirty years to get there, thirty years of hard work, of paying taxes, and playing by the rules.'

Tubbs balled up the napkin and tossed it aside. 'A British passport used to mean something. Now we hand them out like free newspapers at a tube station.'

'That's not true,' Harry countered.

'What you've done is nothing short of criminal.'

Harry took a breath and counted to three before replying.

'We've had problems for decades, Leon. And look what's happened in these last few months. Racist attacks in our prisons. Dinghies rammed in the English Channel. And all those bodies washed up on the beaches of Kent—'

'You mean the prison fires that started themselves?' Tubbs said, mocking Harry. 'And those boats that did the ramming, where did they disappear to, eh? The Bermuda Triangle?'

Tubbs shook his head, jowls flapping. 'For a smart man, you can be pretty stupid. They were false-flag events, and they were happening all over Europe, to stir up hatred and division. My guess is, Wazir was behind it all.'

Harry leaned forward and raised his eyebrows. 'Conspiracy theories, Leon? Really? I didn't think you'd stoop so low.'

Tubbs didn't blink. 'When all this is over, you're going to have to explain yourself. And I'll be pushing for criminal charges too.'

'How dare you—'

Both men turned at the sound of approaching footsteps. Major-General Bashford, flanked by Reynolds and Cole, stepped into the light. Harry saw the look on Bashford's face and stood up.

'What is it?'

'The outlying pickets are under sustained electronic attack and enemy radio chatter is spiking. An offensive is imminent, as we must assume this facility is their primary target.'

Harry frowned. 'How? I thought it was secret.'

'That's irrelevant. It's time to go, Prime Minister.'

Reynolds and Cole stood to one side, waiting to escort Harry. All eyes turned to Tubbs as he struggled to his feet. 'What about the rest of us, General Bashford?'

'You're leaving too. You should make your way to the main assembly area.'

Tubbs nodded and walked away, staring at Harry, and shaking his head. Bashford watched him go.

'Everything alright, Prime Minister?'

Harry ignored the question. 'What happens now?'

'I've ordered the evacuation to begin immediately. We're loading the ships as fast as we can, but it's going to take time. Those troops on the defensive line will need to slow the enemy down.'

'How many troops are we talking about?'

'About a thousand.' He saw the look on Harry's face. 'Without them, we're dead in the water. Literally.'

'What are their chances of survival?'

Bashford didn't sugar-coat it. 'Low to zero.'

Tubbs's words still stung. Whatever Harry's political motivations, he never wanted this. And those people on the defensive line, they were willing to sacrifice themselves so the rest of them could escape. Was that fair? Was it right? Harry didn't think so.

'Let's get them out, general. All of them.'

'That's not an option. It's unpalatable, I know, but there's no other way.'

'Maybe there is.'

All eyes turned to Reynolds. Harry saw the rifle magazines arranged in pouches across his chest, and the ugly, upside-down knife on his equipment harness. Both he and Cole were prepared for war, one that was headed their way. Harry was glad they were on his side.

'Explain,' Bashford said.

Reynolds pointed off into the distance. 'We've got Sky Sabre, Stormers and some old Rapiers out there on the line. All three platforms can run automated. Detect and fire. The Rapier is a little cranky, but the other two should work okay. The guys could bug out long before the Hajis zero in on them.'

'Is that true?' Harry asked Bashford.

The general rubbed his jaw. 'Technically, yes, but the automation software isn't perfect. Ideally, there should be human intervention, otherwise we're gambling the safety of the evacuation on computers.'

'We're going to lose that hardware, anyway, are we not?'

Bashford nodded. 'Yes, but not the Sabres. They're too valuable. We'll use them to engage the enemy from beyond visual range. If they do so at the first sign of trouble, we can withdraw them before they're targeted.'

'So, we sacrifice the Stormers and the Rapiers,' Harry said. 'Set them to automatic and leave them. Surely that's preferable to losing more troops? Those crews are skilled soldiers, yes? Why waste them when we can buy them some time, as Mike suggested?'

Bashford mulled it over. Harry glanced at Reynolds, and the SAS sergeant winked. *Never underestimate the lower ranks*, Harry reminded himself. Often, their input was as just as valuable as the men and women behind the big desks.

'It's too risky,' Bashford said.

Harry was a seasoned politician. He knew what Bashford really meant. 'I'll take full responsibility,' Harry told him. 'This is my decision, and if I'm not mistaken, I still have operational authority. The buck stops with me, yes?'

Bashford nodded. 'That's correct.'

Harry clapped his hands together. 'Good. So, how best to proceed?'

Bashford had already thought about that. 'We can pull all four Sky Sabres back a further ten miles. Then they'll watch the skies. When the enemy launches their air assets, the Sabres will fire first. We're low on ordinance for those platforms, but a swarm of supersonic missiles headed east will make the enemy think twice. The Sabres will then head for the ships at Plymouth.'

'What about the soldiers on the defensive line?'

'We'll ask for volunteers to drive out to them in civilian vehicles. The anti-air crews can set their automation and then they'll all head north, via the SAS lines at Credenhill. They can resupply there while the camp is being evacuated.'

'Sounds good,' Harry said with some relief.

'The tank crews will have to wait until the very last moment,' Bashford warned. 'They're already dug in at several key westward junctions, and we must stall the IS ground advance any way we can. The nearest enemy formations are less than fifty miles away. They could be here within the hour if we don't stop them.'

Harry's momentary optimism faded. 'Will we have enough time?'

'If everyone does their job, and if the Gods are on our side, then maybe. But this will be a close-run thing, Prime Minister. So, we should set the plans in motion right now. And send you on your way.'

INSIDE NORTHSTAR, the evacuation gathered pace. Most of the Rifles security force climbed aboard their transports and left the facility, bumping and winding through the wooded valley and passing through the limestone tunnel. On the other side, the trucks stopped at the farm to pick up more evacuees, and then they were moving again, heading south towards the commercial shipping port of Teignmouth.

Reynolds and Cole escorted Harry through the tunnels. Major Monroe and his skeleton security team waited at the concealed rock wall entrance and formed a protective box as Harry and the SAS men boarded one of the Dark Eagle helicopters squatting beneath the camouflage nets. The other aircraft waited for General Bashford and his team. Harry wasn't sure how far behind Bashford would be, but he hoped he would leave soon.

The frantic activity, the threat of a massive assault, and his own exhaustion combined to further shred his nerves. As he buckled up inside the helicopter, Harry's hands shook so badly he struggled to secure his safety belt. Then the aircraft was moving, rolling along the hard standing.

Clear of the camouflage nets, the Dark Eagle lifted off the ground and climbed until it was hovering just above the trees. The nose dipped, and the forest slipped beneath the belly of the aircraft.

A few moments later they were clear of the valley and heading north-west and bracketed by a pair of Apache helicopters. Their route would take them away from major population centres and up the rugged spine of Wales before crossing the Irish Sea to Scotland.

Safe inside the stealth helicopter, the urgency of the evacuation melted away, and Harry's hands stopped shaking. He was lucky, he knew that much. His chances of making it to Scotland without incident were high. For the men and women left behind, it would be a different story.

Thousands of lives hung by a thread.

Harry prayed they'd escape in time.

To the west, scattered along the defensive line, dozens of Challenger 3 tanks, Stormer anti-aircraft crews, Rapier teams and mixed infantry units armed with Javelin anti-tank missiles waited for the IS advance.

Many were hidden amongst tree lines and hedgerows, or camped behind buildings, overlooking bridges and traffic bottlenecks. They waited and watched the ground and skies to the east. For most of those soldiers, adrenaline ran high, a mixture of excitement and fear. Weapons were locked and loaded, and eyes pressed against binoculars and targeting scopes. Personal equipment had been piled into nearby vehicles driven by volunteers wearing a wide variety of cap badges. Those vehicles waited a short distance away.

The plan was to fire everything they had and bug out as fast as possible before counter fire took them out. The Javelin crews would go hunting in their fast-moving Jackals and Coyotes, hoping to get their punches in before escaping.

Those at the southern end of the defensive line would head to their designated port of departure. The rest would go north to the hills of Wales and the port of Holyhead. Ships would transport them to Scotland from there. Intelligence warned that the road routes through the Midlands and the Northwest were unsafe.

As the day wore on and the evacuation proceeded in haste, the Challenger and Javelin crews sent up their reconnaissance drones and watched the roads to the east. The Stormers and Rapiers scanned the skies. Much closer to the southern ports, the Sky Sabres did the same. Everyone was edgy, watching, waiting.

But it was the soldiers on the ground, those closest to the enemy's line of advance, who would bear the brunt of the coming assault.

Jim Jakes was one such soldier. A Royal Anglian infantryman by trade, Jim's base in Aldershot had been attacked while he'd been eating pizza in a town restaurant. By the time he got back to camp, buildings were burning, and vehicles were loading up and heading out.

He'd hitched a ride to Blandford, and from there to Wells, in the Mendips. There, they'd issued him with a weapon (an M4 with a sweet EOTech holographic sight), a plate-carrier with three mag pouches, and a pack with water and rations. He still wore his civvy gear, Berghaus trousers and a Nike t-shirt beneath a tactical-issue fleece, but now he had a waterproof jacket and wore a black assault helmet.

When they asked for volunteers to drive out to the eastern units, Jim had raised his hand.

Now he was sitting in a brand new, navy blue, 7-seater Toyota Land Cruiser on an industrial estate to the east of the town of Shaftesbury. Close by, hidden inside an empty warehouse, a Challenger 3 battle tank, running on diesel fumes, watched the nearby A30 road for the enemy to show itself.

The warehouse, one of several, was on elevated ground overlooking a shallow valley and the road to be defended. Its walls were made of cinderblock and the half-raised metal shutter gave the tank crew a wide arc of fire without exposing them.

The tank itself was parked deep inside the unlit warehouse, and as the sun began its downward slide to the western horizon, it would be in the eyes of anyone heading up the road towards them.

But Jim Jakes wasn't thinking about the sun or about the advancing IS formations heading their way. Instead, he was watching the nearby perimeter fence and the ever-expanding crowd behind it.

The chain-link and barbed wire was all that separated the industrial estate from a sprawling, scruffy housing project. The crowd stood idle, smoking, and chatting, their sullen eyes watching Jim.

Earlier, the roar of the Challenger's twin diesels had drawn them, and now they watched with idle curiosity, but not fear, Jim noticed. Behind the crowd, the housing estate stretched away, rows of small, scruffy red brick dwellings that might've been nice once upon a time. Now all Jim could see were old model cars, filthy windows, and kids in hoodies pulling wheelies on mountain bikes.

The grown-ups stared at Jim and his Toyota.

The M4 lay across his lap, a round in the pipe, the safety on. He had three, thirty-round mags, so he was in better shape than he was in Aldershot. That was a horrible feeling, to be an unarmed soldier in a combat zone, but now his radar was telling him that this current situation could be just as bad.

As he watched, the crowd was still growing, as more men and women streamed towards the fence. Even the kids had joined them, glaring from beneath their hoodies. Jim estimated the crowd size. A hundred at least.

He saw a ripple and watched another group of men push their way to the fence. The new arrivals were older, 30s and 40s, Jim guessed, with hard faces and weapons in their hands. Jim saw a hammer and at least three baseball bats.

The rule of law had broken down, and men like the ones staring at Jim always filled such voids.

Some of them started shouting. Jim's heart beat a little faster. The stand-off had just cranked up a notch.

'Oi! What's happening?'

'What's that tank doing round here, then?'

'What's happened to the bloody internet? And the power?'

Jim said nothing, his elbow resting on the open window. He'd already recced two escape routes, and he was confident that when the enemy came, he would have enough time and room to get away.

He glanced at the map again, making sure he'd memorised the route north. Back roads and country lanes, that was the trick. Urban areas and busy traffic junctions were to be avoided. And so were mobs, like the one a short distance away.

Now there were fingers in the chain link, shaking it, testing its strength. He heard jeers and laughter.

Jim knew that wouldn't last long.

FAR TO THE WEST, the Sky Sabre units watched the skies and detected the spike in enemy airborne signals. Missile tubes were loaded, and each Sabre could launch twenty-four anti-aircraft missiles at once. They would fill the sky with munitions, then dismantle and head for the ships.

Closer to the front, the Stormers were already running their automatic detect-and-launch programs, but most of the crews stayed with their vehicles, determined to ensure the missiles launched successfully.

No one wanted to run without giving the enemy a good, hard kick in the bollocks.

'GENERAL!'

Mousa saw Allawi limping towards him through the trees. He was taking another toilet break, the result of too much coffee as he waited for the coming assault. He zipped up as Allawi approached.

'What is it?'

'The enemy anti-aircraft units have been located and pin-pointed. They're not moving, and their search radar patters are regular and predictable.'

Mousa followed Allawi back to the bunker. He ducked inside and approached the T-BIS display. On it, yellow radar washes glowed and faded with mathematical predictability.

'They're out of fuel or out of ammunition. Either way, those units are static.'

When Mousa spoke, he addressed the entire bunker.

'Engage the enemy SAM units. Order the assault force west and release the fighter-bombers as soon as eighty percent of the enemy's air defences have been degraded. Get the ground units moving and tell the field commanders to push west as hard as they can. No one stops for anything. Am I understood?'

A chorus of *yes, general*, filled the bunker.

Mousa watched the T-BIS display, and the faint pulse of the transmitter deep in the Mendip Hills.

Beecham was there. If they moved fast enough, if his forces punched a hole all the way to the Mendips, the British Prime Minister could be in his custody by nightfall.

'Have my helicopter fuelled and ready,' he told Allawi. 'We're heading west as soon as the route is clear.'

IN THE GROUNDS of Great Windsor Park, a dozen multiple-launch anti-radar rocket batteries waited for the order.

The co-ordinates of the British SAM units had been plotted, and sensitive instruments mounted on the roofs of the armoured vehicles tracked wind speed, humidity, and air temperature, all of which were fed into the missiles' on-board targeting computers.

Inside the command vehicle, the battery commander leapt to his feet as an incoming message chattered inside his headset.

He listened for less than five seconds, then turned to his second-in-command.

'Execute launch order! All units! Now!'

CHAPTER 69
BEHIND THE LINES

THE HALL WAS FULL, EVERY FOLDING SEAT TAKEN, EVERY NARROW AISLE packed, the small lobby jammed tight.

Dust drifted through warm bars of late afternoon sunlight, and a faded Union Jack hung limply from the rafters above the villagers' heads.

Yet despite over a hundred faces watching him, Faz could've heard a pin drop as he finished his talk, and he wondered if telling them was the right move. Maybe, in this case, ignorance was bliss.

Eventually, the invaders would arrive, but there was no strategic value to be had out here in the countryside. This was farming country, England's breadbasket. Maybe these people would be left alone to do what they did best, which was to grow, harvest, and sell their crop. Or their herds. Or flocks. Whatever. Even invading armies had to eat, and no good ever came from starving populations.

But if Faz were in their shoes, he'd want to know the bigger picture. As he took his seat alongside the parish council members, a storm of raised voices erupted from the floor.

'What'll happen now?'

'How much danger are we in?'

'What about our livestock? And the crops?'

Next to Faz, Andy Metcalfe, a burly, no-nonsense farmer in his fifties, got to his feet and held up his big, calloused hands for silence. The hall settled and Metcalfe spoke.

'Our friend here hasn't got any answers, and we've all got lots of questions, but we must do what's right for the village, and that means working together. Our priorities are food and water, and even though it's mid-summer, we should start thinking about stockpiling reserves for light and heat. God knows how long the power will be out, and when it comes back, who's saying it won't go out again? So, we should make a plan. Combine our resources. Work out a rationing system and be ready to implement it. And we'll need to meet more often. Regular, like.'

There were nods and murmurs around the hall.

'Good. Now, has anyone got any suggestions for the short term?'

Before anyone could speak, Faz got to his feet again.

'There is one other thing you can do. As I said, a lot of people have died since this war kicked off—'

The hall trembled with the sound of distant thunder. The rumbling lasted for several moments before fading away.

Faz shared a look with Ross and Lara, standing by the side of the stage. That was no summer storm.

'So, what can we do, then?' a voice at the back of the hall asked.

'You can hide the village,' Faz told them.

The silence that followed told Faz that more detail was required.

'London is a black hole. No power, no water, buildings burning everywhere, plane crashes, armed gangs on the streets—dangerous is an understatement. And look what's happened in Swindon. More fires, looting, police officers executed—'

There were several sharp intakes of breath around the hall. Word hadn't spread as far as Faz had imagined.

'My advice would be to avoid all contact with the world outside this village and the surrounding area. For as long as possible. Until things settle. Bob?'

Ross's brother wheeled a large white board onto the stage. Drawn on its surface was a crude map of the village and the surrounding countryside. Faz tapped the squares at the centre.

'Okay, this is the village here. You all know the area, so I won't need to elaborate too much. But there are only two roads that lead into this village, one from the south and this one here that heads northeast towards Lockeridge itself. Everything in between is farmland or woods. In fact, this village is a small island in a sea of rolling hills. If you weren't looking for it, you'd never know it was here.'

He looked around the room.

'Has anyone got a digger, something with a big blade and a bucket scoop?' Half the hands in the hall went up. Faz smiled. 'You've got to love farmers.'

The laughter faded quickly. Faz continued.

'It's all high-sided banks and hedgerows along almost every road. Especially where the village roads connect to the bigger roads. So, my suggestion is this—cut the village off from the outside world by blocking the only two roads in and out. You build earth walls and camouflage them with trees and shrubs and grass. While some of you do that, others should drive further out and take down every road sign they can find.'

'How do we get in and out if the roads are blocked?' asked a voice in the crowd.

'I would suggest you don't travel around, but if you do, use fields and public footpaths to get back onto the road. But only if it's necessary.'

He studied the faces around the room. He saw fear there, but he sensed a quiet determination too.

'They'll find you, eventually. When they do, don't resist. You'll be okay. But right now, the biggest threat is refugees from the cities. Many will try to leave, seek safety and shelter in the countryside. They'll be scared, hungry, thirsty. And they could be armed. Think about that when you're blocking those roads. Make them look at natural as possible, okay?'

Metcalfe's voice boomed around the hall.

'You heard the man. We might not have a lot of time, so let's get to work.'

The hall stood as one, and the rafters filled with excited chatter. Metcalfe's voice was the loudest of all as he gathered people together and thrashed out the details. Faz stepped down off the stage. 'I thought that went well,' he told Ross.

The policeman nodded towards the sizeable group gathered around Metcalfe on the stage.

'Andy will sort them out. He's the biggest landowner around here, and the Metcalfe's have farmed these lands forever. If anyone can get the job done, it's him.'

'Good.' Faz looked around. 'Where's Lara?' Then he spotted her, squeezing through the slow-moving tide of bodies as the hall emptied. Something was wrong. He walked towards her, and Ross followed.

'What is it, Lara?'

She cocked her head. 'There's someone outside you should talk to. A soldier.'

They followed her to the main door. Around the green, people and vehicles were heading off in all directions. Except for one man, stood by the war memorial, smoking. He wore baggy cargo shorts, and a faded red Adidas t-shirt. He was young too, Faz observed. Late teens, early twenties, tops.

When he saw them approach, the soldier stepped on his cigarette and pocketed the butt.

Faz held out his hand. 'I'm Faz. I'm with the intelligence services. This is Ross. He's Met police.'

'Gary,' the young man said, shaking hands. 'I heard you talk.' The soldier scratched his close-cropped head. 'Good idea, hiding the village. They'll spot us from the air soon enough, but it might buy us time to get organised.'

'Lara said you're a soldier,' Faz said.

'I am. Was.' Gary shrugged. 'I deserted yesterday.'

'Why?' Ross asked him.

'Because I'm not suicidal.' He looked at each of them. 'They sent us west, to watch the roads. I was with a mixed group of infantry out of Aldershot and Tidworth. They gave us a few Javelins and told us to slow the IS advance as best we could.'

Faz brightened. 'We're fighting back?'

Gary shook his head. 'The opposite. We're running. To Scotland, of all places. Can you believe that shit?'

Ross frowned. 'Why?'

'We don't have the manpower. They attacked almost every base, every camp. Big attacks, small attacks. They went for the vehicles and the armouries. And the accommodation blocks. We got a lot of gear out, but we lost a lot too. Including troops. The whole thing's a complete shit-show. So the word came down from on high—get the fuck out. They're leaving on ships, from Plymouth and other places out west. I think they're worried they'd get trapped down in Cornwall. Backs to the sea and all that. Makes sense, I suppose.'

Ross tried and failed to suppress the edge to his voice. 'And you thought it best to desert?'

Gary didn't blink. 'My wife has just had twins. They're a month old, and I can't leave them, not while all this shit is going on. So I handed over my weapon and ammunition and headed cross-country. The lads didn't stop me. They understood. And I'm not the only one.'

'What exactly are you telling us?' Faz asked him.

Gary pointed to the eastern sky. 'There's a big push coming. Huge, I heard. We've got no chance of stopping it either. Do you know how big this invasion is?'

Faz remembered the endless convoy on the M3. 'I've got a good idea.'

'So, you know, then.'

'What if we need to get out of here?' Ross asked him. 'Where do we go? How do we link up with friendly forces?'

Gary shrugged. 'You could take your chances, drive north to Wales. There are ships in Holyhead. I wouldn't recommend you go due west. There's a lot of very jumpy guys with guns out there, and they're watching the roads.' He looked at Faz. 'No offence, but if you drove up to a roadblock, they might shoot first and ask questions later.'

'None taken.' The kid was right, though. In times of war, nerves were frayed, and fingers rested on triggers. It didn't take much to apply that pressure.

'You should stay here in the village,' Gary warned. 'It's too dangerous out there. And besides, it's all gone to shit. There's no government, that's what I heard. Beecham's alive—'

'He made it?' Faz asked, hope soaring again.

'He's pretty much on his own. That's what I heard. The military are in charge now.'

'Where are they?' Ross asked him. 'The invaders, I mean. How far?'

Another roll of thunder rumbled around the horizon, deep and ominous. Faz couldn't work out what direction it was coming from. It was Gary who spoke next.

'There's your answer,' he said, walking away. 'They're everywhere. Which means we're now behind enemy lines. If you're going to run, you'd better go now.'

No one said anything as they watched him head off down the lane.

BUCKLING up aboard his Black Hawk, Mousa clamped a headset on and twirled his finger, ordering the pilot to lift off. The aircraft leapt into the sky, surrounded by the other troop transports and the Apache escort. The flight cleared the treetops and banked to the west. Next to Mousa, Allawi studied his T-BIS laptop.

'Over eighty-five percent of enemy SAMs confirmed as destroyed, general. Ground forces and air mobile assault units are now on the move.'

Mousa keyed his mic.

'Send in the bombers.'

TO THE EAST, a flight of ten F-15 Strike Eagles of the Islamic State Air Force turned to their new headings and went to full afterburner, rocketing low across the English countryside.

The SAM threat had been all but neutralised and they were now free to engage any targets they could find. Their wings were heavy with ordinance, and their sensors scanned the ground ahead for military targets.

In each aircraft, the two-man crews flipped down their anti-glare visors as they thundered into the setting sun.

CHAPTER 70
NOT QUIET ON THE WESTERN FRONT

It was a gamble, one that might cost them their lives, but the British Stormer crews were determined to make it work.

They'd received the order to set their systems to automatic detect-and-launch, and their escape vehicles waited nearby, two luxury Range Rovers liberated from an abandoned dealership in Yeovil, but the Stormer commanders knew the targeting software was flaky.

In their view, too much depended on the British anti-aircraft deterrent to take such a gamble. Down on the coast, ships were still being loaded with troops and munitions. Enemy fighter bombers could wreak havoc if they made it that far.

And so the commanders and their crews remained in situ, their Stormers shut down and hidden behind two huge grain silos on a farm just north of Salisbury.

A few minutes earlier, an IS armoured convoy had roared past them on the distant A30. The lookouts had lost count at fifty tanks and AFVs, so now the Stormer crews were officially behind enemy lines. They would worry about that later. What mattered now was finding targets for their missiles.

The distant rumble grew louder. Then the commanders heard the message from the lookouts lying on top of the grain silos, their binoculars scanning the skies...

'Enemy aircraft approaching from the east, fast movers—'

The Stormers' engines roared into life, spewing clouds of grey diesel exhaust. Both tracked vehicles lurched forward and away from the surrounding farm buildings. The lookouts scampered down the silo ladders and ran for the Range Rovers parked inside a nearby vehicle shed. They started the engines and drove towards the farm entrance and the main road. Then they waited for the music to begin.

The rumble became a roar. The ground shook, and then they were there, a tight flight of F-15's passing low to the north. Inside the Stormers, the crews were already working.

'Contact air! Multiple contacts! Bearing two-seven-one—'

'Targets acquired, hostile air—'

'Engage!'

'Firing!'

One after the other, sixteen Starstreak missiles launched into the sky, blanketing the farmyard in dense white smoke.

'Missiles away!'

'Let's move!'

The crews scrambled from the Stormers and plunged into the smoke. They ran for the Range Rovers and piled in, lowering the windows and holding their weapons ready. Engines gunned, and the vehicles fishtailed out of the farm, spraying gravel. Then they were heading north.

Behind them, the Stormers were still operating, still tracking their missiles as the Starstreaks chased the F-15's.

BLINDED by the low sun and knowing that British SAM capability had been significantly degraded, the F-15 pilots focused solely on spending their own ordinance as they scanned the horizon for targets. When ten threat receivers lit up and ten cockpit alarms warbled, the F-15 crews were surprised, then shocked by the speed and proximity of the incoming threat. Missiles, lots of them, closing fast—

Two F-15's banked hard over and collided, shattering wings and tail fins. Both planes fell from the sky. Then the missiles were amongst them, detonating around the low-flying aircraft, the explosions rippling across the summer sky. Thousands of metal shards sliced through metal and flesh, killing another five planes.

Now there were three aircraft left, and all of them fired off chaff pods and IR reflectors, filling the sky behind them with countermeasures. The alarms stopped and the threat board cleared. There were no more missiles.

One plane was badly damaged and limped back towards Heathrow, black smoke trailing from one of its engines. One of the two surviving F-15's banked hard over and headed for the probable launch site. In the distance, the pilot saw a cloud of white smoke hanging low on the ground and his sensors told him that two military-spec vehicles were still operating there.

He flipped his weapons control and selected cluster munitions. A moment later, the F-15 thundered over the Stormers, spilling bomblets all over the farmyard. The resulting fireball swallowed the farm in a storm of fire and shrapnel. The F-15 continued back east, leaking fuel from a punctured wing.

Inside the cockpit of the surviving F-15, Captain Ibrahim Tasman raged. A flight of ten planes reduced to one in a matter of seconds. He needed a target to vent his rage, and Sami, his Weapon-Systems Officer, gave him several potential sites, but Tasman wanted something big, something that would seriously degrade British military capability. And he wanted revenge for his pilot brothers, too.

What he didn't want was to run into another ambush, so he flew a low-altitude racetrack pattern and listened to the chatter.

The sky to the west was alive with incoming missiles, fired from beyond visual range. He heard screams and bursts of static and knew that more planes had been downed. Tasman controlled his breathing and his temper. Behind him, Sami interrogated the sky and ground to the west. Quiet again. Tasman checked his instruments. They were good for fuel and the sun had dipped below the horizon.

Now he could see.

There was a convoy out there somewhere, detected by a Falcon drone earlier that day. Convoys were excellent targets, perfect for his cluster munitions. Sami fed him the convoy's last known position, and Tasman doubted it was still on the road, but intelligence suggested that the British were evacuating from ports along the south coast. Tasman imagined dropping his bombs all over an enemy dockyard and watching ships and warehouses burn.

But if he headed south, he might run into serious trouble. Anti-air crews would protect those ports. Still, Tasman thought it was worth the risk. The desire for revenge remained an unquenchable flame.

He turned to his left and looked below. The F-15 was flying parallel to a main road packed with armour and troop carriers. Tasman checked the terrain ahead. He saw a collection of warehouses and a housing estate beyond that. Sami reported no immediate threats.

Tasman dipped his wings in salute and turned away, heading for bigger and better targets.

Jim Jakes flinched as the F-15 banked overhead and disappeared to the south-west. Enemy aircraft could mean only one thing—British SAM coverage had been neutralised. And that meant ground forces were heading their way.

But enemy armour wasn't Jim's only concern. The mob on the other side of the chain-link fence had grown to at least a couple of hundred, and now the older men were helping the kids shake it loose. The barbed wire crown whipped back and forth as the chain-link rippled beneath the onslaught of violent hands. Others were pulling at the ground stakes, yanking the bottom of the fence towards them.

Jim cursed as he saw some of the smaller kids roll under and breach the perimeter. They held up their side and now more people—adults this time—joined them, making the gap bigger and spilling onto the industrial estate.

The younger kids wandered off to explore. The older ones, the teenagers, and adults, loitered, weapons held in their hands, their eyes fixed on Jim and his Toyota. There was going to be trouble.

The radio hissed on the seat beside him. 'Jim, come in.'

It was the tank commander, speaking in clear. Jim snatched the radio. 'Send.'

'We've got eyes on. Stand by, mate. Contact is imminent.'

'When you bug out, do it fast,' Jim told him. 'The natives are getting restless.'

The radio squawked, and Jim tossed it back on the seat. He fired up the engine and watched the digital display settle. The mob on the estate numbered well over a hundred. Most of them were poking around the nearest warehouse and trying the doors of the commercial vans. Others—the older guys—walked towards the Toyota. Jim left the engine running and hopped out of the vehicle.

'Stay where you are!' he shouted, brandishing his M4 and hoping it would be enough to deter them. 'This is a national emergency! Go back to your homes!'

Some of the younger men stopped short at the sight of the gun. The older ones didn't. They kept moving, spreading out. Behind them, dozens more headed his way, drawn to the confrontation. Another few seconds and they'd surround the Toyota.

Jim knew what mobs could do to someone caught at the sharp end of their rage. There was no way he was going out like that. He brought his weapon up and the shirtless torso of a beefed-up, tattooed man jumped into his EOTech. The target looked to be in his mid-forties, possibly a leader. If Jim dropped him, the others might falter. Then again, they may go fucking ballistic. Jim's heart pounded. This wasn't the ranges and paper targets. This was the real deal, and he might be about to take a man's life. Still, if it was a choice between tattoo man and Jim—

Boom!

The sharp concussion rang around the industrial estate. Jim ducked as the Challenger's 120mm gun roared close by. He heard screams and saw several people scrambling back under the fence. The tattooed man, crouching on the ground like a sprinter, stood up and turned towards Jim.

'What the fuck's going on?' he yelled. Another cannon blast echoed around the estate, followed by two more in rapid succession.

'Go home!' Jim yelled back, his weapon still levelled at the man's chest.

'Fuck that! Gimme a gun! You must have more in there.' He

pointed to the Toyota. His friends were moving closer too, an ever-shrinking circle.

'Don't come any closer!' Jim shouted as the Challenger's gun roared again. 'Can't you see what's happening? We're at war! Go back home!'

'Fuck you! Gimme a shooter!'

Tattoo man scrambled towards Jim, ducking left and right. Jim shot him, the round taking him through a mess of blue tattoos on his chest and spinning him around. Jim swivelled and shot another man with a raised claw hammer charging around the hood of the Toyota. Another attacker yanked open the passenger door and Jim swivelled left, double-tapping him in the chest. He saw life leave the man's face in an instant and the body dropped out of sight.

A nearby warehouse exploded, and Jim hit the deck. Enormous sheets of twisted and blackened roofing fluttered in the air before crashing to the ground nearby. The enemy had found their range. Another incoming round blew apart a wall of the adjacent building. Chunks of cinderblock rained down like hail in a storm.

As the crowd scattered and ran for the fence, Jim saw a warehouse fire escape door fly open and the tank crew charging towards him. He climbed back behind the wheel as the breathless crew bundled inside. They all saw the bodies sprawled around the Toyota.

'Let's go!' The tank commander yelled.

Jim dropped the 4x4 into drive and floored the accelerator, bouncing over the tattooed man. He swerved around a couple of corners and headed for the main entrance. Behind them, explosions blew apart the industrial estate. Infantry would be close behind.

Jim stopped at the main gate and looked both ways. To the right, thick columns of black smoke roiled into the air from the valley below. He yanked the wheel left, away from the carnage behind them.

'How many did you get?' he asked, his eyes glued to the road.

'A couple of APCs and three tanks,' the commander told him. 'Their convoy discipline is shit. What happened back there?'

Jim shook his head. 'I wish I knew.'

He saw the right turn ahead and swung into it. He gunned the engine, putting distance between themselves and the enemy. The road twisted and turned through fields and hedgerows.

Jim slowed down, and the world became quiet again. He wondered how many crews along the defensive line had made it out. All of them, he hoped, though that hope may be in vain.

He slowed for another junction and turned left, heading deeper into the countryside, pursued only by the gathering darkness as the Toyota headed for the Welsh border and the dark hills beyond.

TASMAN SKIMMED his F-15 low over the English countryside. Fuel state was adequate, enough for 30 minutes of high-speed manoeuvres before he had to make the run for Heathrow. Behind him, Sami also scanned his instruments. *Come on, brother, give me something to shoot at.*

Tasman's rage had subsided, replaced by his trademark composure. One sobering thought had occurred to him—the loss of nine multi-strike aircraft would require some explanation. And when that was done, someone would have to pay.

Tasman was the flight leader, and he knew they'd been flying too close together. He should've corrected that, but he hadn't, such was his desire to engage the enemy. Now he needed to atone for his mistake, take something back to his squadron commander and hope to assuage the man's fury at the loss of over half of his planes.

'Got something.'

Tasman tilted his head. 'Talk to me.'

'Air-search radar, range thirty-eight kilometres south-southwest. Recommend new heading of one-eight-zero degrees. We could lose a few feet in altitude too.'

'Roger.' Tasman banked to the left and took the plane due south out to sea, thundering over the coastal town of Seaton and out into Lyme Bay.

'Okay, I'm seeing three air-search sets, all low frequency. Designate signals as mobile anti-aircraft batteries, probably in passive mode. Locations are static.'

Tasman maintained his heading, heading further out into the English Channel, watching his fuel, altitude, and threat displays. Then he banked the aircraft around in a long, shallow turn. He was burning juice at a rapid rate. He couldn't remain on station for much longer. Nor could he go back empty-handed.

He keyed his microphone. 'Do we have a target?'

'Not sure. We've got three mobile SAM units, all in close proximity, but they're not watching us. They're looking east.'

'They're guarding something,' Tasman said. 'What is it?' He didn't have to wait long for an answer.

'The port of Teignmouth. Civilian commercial facility, warehouses, storage areas, sheltered harbour, good links to the M5 motorway. The military must be using it.'

'Those mobile AA units are on the high ground, providing cover,' Tasman said.

'Recommend new heading zero-one-niner degrees.'

'Roger.' Tasman banked the F-15 around and settled on the new heading. He had two, 1000-pound bombs and one canister of cluster munitions, plus 500 rounds of 20mm. What he needed was a target to spend it on.

'Come on, Sami. Talk to me.'

'Can't see a thing from down here. Take us up to two-fifty.'

Tasman eased back the yoke—

'Contact!'

He levelled off at one hundred feet, watching his instruments carefully. The sun had set, and the world was turning blue and grey. The sea was calm, no whitecaps to give Tasman any point of reference. These were tricky flying conditions, especially at high speed. He heard Sami talking.

'Registering two ship-borne radar signatures. First contact is a military set, and it's on the move. Second target is stationary—standard sea-set signature, no air-search. Possibly a cargo ship. Looks like the navy is guarding the port entrance. Nothing incoming.'

Tasman shifted in his seat. 'We're going for the cargo ship. We'll come in fast and low, and with any luck, it'll be packed to the gills with ammunition and equipment. Dial up the GBUs for simultaneous drop.'

'Roger.'

'Prep the clusters as well. I'll hit the westernmost AA unit on exfil.'

'Received.'

As Sami programmed the Guided Bomb Unit for low-altitude release, Tasman flexed his fingers inside his flight gloves and increased power.

'Here we go.'

THE ORDERLY HATED SHIPS. In fact, he hated boats of any kind. They made him sick, and that included the smell of the docks.

He remembered a trip with his mum and dad when he was a kid, from Portsmouth to Bilbao in Spain. They'd hit some rough weather in the Bay of Biscay and the Orderly thought he was going to die. The boom of the waves and the clanking and groaning from the car decks had terrified him, as if the rusty old ferry was tearing itself apart. It was night-time too, and all he could see through the window were the white caps rising and falling and seawater pounding the windows. His mum had wrapped him in her arms. His dad had laughed and called him a *poofter*. When they'd left the boat the next morning, he almost cried with relief. And as it turned out, his dad was right.

Now he was about to do it all again, only this time it was around Land's End and up into the Irish Sea. Sheltered waters, he'd heard. And it was summer too. How bad could it be? The priority was to get out of harm's way, and he was prepared to suffer a night or two in a cramped cabin for that.

'You lot! On your feet!'

The Orderly turned his head. The sergeant was pointing at his group. Finally! He heaved the backpack over his shoulder, his SA80 rifle bumping painfully against his ribs. There had to be at least a couple of thousand troops still waiting to board the last cargo ship. The other ships had already left, and service families had besieged Plymouth, desperate to escape the advancing Islamic State forces, forcing more convoys to divert to the small port of Teignmouth.

Now the last boat had to take everyone, and there were still people arriving, abandoning their vehicles at the gate, and streaming into the warehouse. The Orderly wondered where he'd be if he hadn't dumped the Prime Minister's clothes.

Back of the queue, that's where you'd be.

Outside the warehouse, the sun had set, and although the sky was a wonderful shade of deepening blue, the shadows on the dockside were deep and dark. There were soldiers everywhere, from every unit in the army, and there seemed to be a constant, disjointed chorus of shouts and whistles.

He joined one of several queues snaking around the damp quay. The gigantic ship loomed above him, its red and black flanks streaked with rust. Civvy sailors herded them up onto a gangway and the Orderly stepped over the threshold. Inside, the air stank of oil, metal, and saltwater. He struggled up several cramped stairwells, cursing the rifle banging against his knees, and the backpack that was almost as big as he was.

Fresh air blasted away the dank stench, and he found himself back outside. He was facing aft, looking directly at the ship's main superstructure. He saw figures moving inside the bridge and higher up, a thin column of black smoke rose from the boiler stack into the darkening sky. Above it, seagulls wheeled and screeched.

'Keep moving,' a voice growled.

He followed the man in front, his eyes down, his mind elsewhere. Scotland, in fact. On arrival, he figured they would redeploy him, and he prayed it wouldn't be to an infantry unit. He didn't join the army to fight. He wanted a trade and a career in civvy street. Doing what, he wasn't sure. He was still working on that.

The Orderly collided with the man in front as the column rippled to a halt.

'Careful,' the man growled beneath his helmet.

'Sorry.' The Orderly craned his neck. 'What's going on?'

'Looks like we're going down there.'

The man pointed. Ahead, the dark line of figures snaked around a huge, open hatch. The column moved forward, and the Orderly found himself alongside the vast square opening in the deck. He peered over the edge and saw a sea of faces turned up towards the sky. Figures climbed down ladders to join them in the giant hold. Horrified, the Orderly backed away. Someone shoved him.

'Back in line. Keep moving.'

The Orderly turned to see a group of Royal Marines policing the queue. The one who'd manhandled him scowled beneath his green beret, his camouflaged face barely visible against the fading sky behind him.

'I thought we had cabins,' the Orderly protested.

White teeth grinned in the dark. 'I'll get right on it. In the meantime, your arse goes down there.'

'I'm claustrophobic,' the Orderly whined.

Another Marine shoved him forward. 'Get fucking moving!'

'Don't touch me!' the Orderly snapped. The Marines closed in. The Orderly frowned and pointed. 'What's that?'

He saw the dark silhouette of a warship, maybe a mile away, the sea churning to white foam in its wake as it keeled hard over. There was something else out there too, a black dot on the horizon, growing larger.

'Look,' the Orderly said, pointing. 'What is that? What is it?'

The Marines turned and looked. And started yelling.

'Cover!'

'Arm GBUs!' Tasman ordered.

The F-15 was rocketing across the sea, the cargo ship growing with every passing second. A big ship too. Off his starboard wing, the frigate had seen them and was turning to bear. Probably trying to use its Close-In-Weapons-Systems, Tasman guessed. Too late, buddy.

'Arming failed! Arming failed!'

Tasman felt his blood freeze. 'Try again!'

'Arming failed,' Samir repeated. 'Same for the cluster. The system keeps recycling. Must've been damaged by the missile blasts. Maybe the control pods took a shrapnel hit.'

Tasman shook his head. So, his plane had been taken out just like the others, but not so dramatically. Either way, they'd failed. They couldn't go back now, not with their friends dead, their squadron decimated, and with all their weapons intact. 'What about the cannon?'

'She's good. Full mag of tracer and explosive.'

Tasman raised his hand and reached behind his seat. He felt Samir take it, squeeze it. 'I'm sorry, my friend.'

'Don't be. *Inshallah.*'

'See you in Paradise.'

Tasman gripped his flight controls and pushed the throttles to the stops. From the corner of his eye, he saw a flash of tracer, but it fell away behind them.

Ahead, the dark hull of the cargo ship loomed. Nothing could stop them now. Tasman squeezed the trigger and felt the aircraft shudder as his own tracer cut through the hull like a blowtorch.

He kept his eyes open and his finger on the trigger as the enemy vessel loomed large in his cockpit canopy.

THE TERRIFYING RIPPING sound echoed across the bay. On the deck of the ship, hundreds of faces turned towards the sea. Like the Orderly, some saw the speeding dark object seconds before heavy-calibre rounds impacted across the crowded deck. The Orderly cringed as explosive rounds tore people apart all around him. Severed limbs spun crazily through the air. He clamped his hands over his ears as the incoming plane screamed, and then there was an almighty bang. A fireball belched from the open hatch as the ship lurched against the quayside.

The Orderly lost his balance and screamed. He fell backwards into the smoke and flame, his ears filled with the cries of those burning in the fires of hell below.

But his descent into the underworld was short-lived. The twin, 1000-pound GBU bombs detonated, vaporising the Orderly and lifting the ship out of the water, breaking its back.

The double explosion obliterated the vessel and most of the quayside, hurling steel, concrete, and bodies all over the town of Teignmouth.

CHAPTER 71
MAC IN BLACK

THE DARK EAGLE CAME IN LOW OVER THE TREETOPS AND LANDED IN A clearing carved from the thick forest of Norwegian pines that surrounded McIntyre Castle.

The rotor blades wound down, and Reynolds and Cole disembarked first.

Harry stayed put, watching them head towards a small party waiting beneath the trees. More men with guns, Harry observed, although they too were wearing civilian clothes. Reynolds waved, and Harry stepped out onto some sort of green rubber matting. Above his head, a camouflage net was rolling back into place across the clearing.

'Security team,' Reynolds explained. 'They'll escort us to the main house.'

Harry greeted them with a nod and a tight smile and followed them through the trees. Here in Scotland the air was cooler, the sky through the treetops dusted with early evening stars, and Harry felt himself relax a little more.

The flight had been uneventful, and after they'd refuelled on the Isle of Man, the Dark Eagle had continued its journey alone, leaving the Apache escort behind. Wrapped in its invisible cloak, the helicopter took them across the Irish Sea and into Scotland, hugging the rugged west coast and avoiding population centres.

And now they were here, on a private estate in the wilds of western Scotland. Nobody was rushing him here and there, there was no shouting or desperate urgency, just the call of night birds and the breeze between the pines.

The woodland path emptied onto a wide lawn, and a baronial mansion loomed in the darkness, its short conical towers jutting into the sky. There were no lights to be seen, but as he crossed a gravel drive towards the main entrance, Harry noticed another figure waiting.

The escort party peeled away and disappeared into the dark. The figure stepped forward and held out his hand. Harry took it, feeling the calloused skin and firm grip.

'Welcome to McIntyre Castle, Prime Minister. My name is Bill Kerr and I'm the duty keeper here. Please follow me.'

Harry followed the man into the light of the entrance hall. Kerr looked to be in his sixties, and his short grey hair and physical bearing screamed ex-military. The hall was lit by a brass oil lamp, throwing the stone walls into shadow. Clan flags and regimental colours hung from the rafters of the vaulted ceiling, and to Harry's right, a wide stone staircase wound its way up to the floor above. The building was quiet. Silent, in fact.

'Where is everyone?'

Kerr closed the heavy wooden door behind them. 'There's a skeleton staff here, Prime Minister, and a small security force—'

'I'm referring to my leadership team,' Harry told him.

'I'm told there will be others arriving shortly. In the meantime, may I show you to your room so you can freshen up?'

Harry nodded, feeling vaguely irritated. He was tired, exhausted in fact, but this surreal transition from war to some sort of hotel in a Scottish forest grated on his nerves. And there was no one here to greet him, to brief him, to connect him to other world leaders and the UN Security Council.

And more than anything, he wanted to know if those troops on the defensive line got out. He wanted confirmation that his contribution had been a successful one.

He followed Kerr up the stairs, Reynolds and Cole trailing behind.

Harry's suite was on the first floor. Kerr showed him around the large, comfortable lounge, the bedroom, and the vast ensuite. The Scot billeted Reynolds and Cole further along the corridor.

'There are strict blackout protocols to be followed,' Kerr told him. 'Everything's in the briefing packet on your writing desk. I shall let you know when the others arrive. If you need food and drink, just pick up the telephone.'

'Thank you, Bill.'

Kerr closed the door behind him. Harry slumped onto the sofa and stared into the fire glowing in the grate. He didn't know how much time had passed when he jerked awake to the sound of tapping on the door. Kerr poked his head around it.

'The others are here, Prime Minister. I'll escort you downstairs in thirty minutes.'

Harry took a long shower, flipping the lever from hot to cold for the last few seconds. Just like at Northstar, there were fresh clothes and underwear in the huge bedroom wardrobe. He selected a pale blue shirt, dark slacks, and a navy pullover, and inspected himself in the full-length mirror. Presentable, at least. Kerr arrived a few minutes later. He told Harry that Reynolds and Cole were liaising with McIntyre's security team and familiarising themselves with the layout of the estate. Then he led the way downstairs.

The reception room was an impressive one, its stone walls decorated with heraldic shields and oil paintings of local wildlife. Arranged in front of an enormous fireplace were a collection of large sofas and chairs, half of which were occupied when Harry approached.

The people waiting there stood as one, and Harry shook hands with Major-General Bashford and two of his senior officers, and with Treasury Secretary Tom Armstrong and Transport Secretary Brendan Lewis. And finally, with the glowering Leon Tubbs, still wearing his ridiculous flight suit.

No one spoke as silent, waist-coated staff carried refreshments to a sideboard and retreated from the room, ushered out by Kerr. The door closed. Harry poured himself a black coffee and sat down. The fire crackled and spat, threatening to ignite the tension in the air.

'What is it?' Harry asked, looking at the surrounding faces. Except

Tubbs.

Bashford sat on the edge of his seat, his hands clasped in front of him. 'An enemy fighter-bomber hit a ship at Teignmouth. The loss of life has been considerable.'

Harry deflated. 'Define *considerable*.'

'A thousand, at least. The wounded have been evacuated to local hospitals and the survivors are heading for Plymouth, although most of our air cover has now been destroyed or withdrawn, so they'll be lucky if they find a boat. We can't afford another loss like Teignmouth, which is why the remaining ships have been ordered to make all possible haste for the Irish Sea.'

'And those soldiers on the defensive line? Did they get out?'

'We'll know in the next twenty-four hours.'

'What about my Cabinet? Are there any other survivors?'

It was Armstrong who answered. 'It's just us, Prime Minister.'

'There will be others,' Lewis said. 'But I suspect the numbers will be low.'

'We'll have to form some sort of government,' Tubbs said.

Harry forced himself to look at the man, now squeezed into an armchair. '*We*, Leon?'

Tubbs cocked a defiant chin. 'This is no time for political games. Moving forward, all decisions should be made by committee, not just by you. Your administration has been wiped out. The same goes for my side of the House. We need to find others, lawyers, civil servants, judges, what's left of the establishment, and form some sort of working government.'

'That's unconstitutional,' Harry explained.

'We can get into the legalities later. We need a new administration, and quickly. Our allies will expect a reorganisation.'

'He's got a point,' Lewis said, an eyebrow raised in Harry's direction.

'I'll consider it,' Harry told him.

'It's not a request,' Tubbs said, pointing his finger. 'After the mistakes you've made, and the lives already lost, you're not the man to lead us. You should stay on for now, for continuity, but at the earliest possible opportunity, you should resign.'

It took a moment for Harry to recover. He felt his anger rising and struggled to control it. 'People have died,' he said. 'And you want to engineer some sort of coup? You should be ashamed, Leon.'

Tubbs smiled, but there was no humour in his voice. 'Nice try. But you know what you've done. Your position as leader is untenable.'

Harry glanced around at the other faces. Bashford and his officers looked mortified. Lewis and Armstrong were equally embarrassed. Harry prided himself on the ability to read a room, and this one was telling him that things were not going his way.

The anger he felt had subsided and now another emotion surfaced—panic. It was bubbling in his stomach, and he felt his heart rate climbing. He needed to get it under control, and fast. He refocussed on his antagonist, keeping his tone conciliatory.

'Your strong opinions are noted, Leon. We should talk, all of us, when things have settled. And I promise you all that we will come to a mutual agreement. But for now, we must focus on the military situation. Do I have your support?' He directed the question at Tubbs. After a few seconds, the man nodded.

'I agree. For now.'

'Thank you, Leon.' Harry glanced at Lewis and Armstrong. Both men were also in agreement. The panic subsided. 'Good. Well, it's been a long and terrible day. I suggest we call it a night, get some much-needed rest. We'll pick this up first thing.'

No one argued. Harry got to his feet and shook hands with everyone, even the reluctant Tubbs. *Kill 'em with kindness*, as a former Prime Minister once told him. As they filed from the room, Harry said, 'General Bashford, could I have a word?'

Harry closed the door and sat back down. Bashford sat opposite and waited. 'I apologise for that,' Harry began. 'As you know, politics is a grubby business.'

'I understand, Prime Minister.'

Harry stared and smiled, but Bashford was a closed book. Had the soldier quietly agreed with Tubbs? Was Harry's position really in jeopardy? There was only one way to find out.

'I don't think my political colleagues can contribute much as this stage,' he said. 'Armstrong is struggling mentally, and Lewis is a recent appointee. He's keen, but new to Cabinet. As for Tubbs...' Harry shook his head. 'We've never seen eye to eye, and this vendetta he has against me is not helping matters.'

'I can see that,' Bashford said.

'Good. Because until I can form a new administration, I think all decisions should come from me. With your help,' he added quickly. 'May I call you Julian?'

'Of course, Prime Minister.'

'Harry is fine. Out of earshot of others, you understand?' Harry settled back in his seat, feeling more in control. 'I believe the best way forward in the short term is for you and I to liaise directly. If there are too many voices around the table, too much political infighting, it will jeopardise the decision-making process. And that could cost lives.'

'That's a possibility,' Bashford said.

'So, we're in agreement. Can I count on your support, Julian?'

The man in the combat uniform nodded. 'With so much uncertainty right now, a power struggle helps no one. Yes, you have my support.'

Harry exhaled. 'Thank you. And with that in mind, I think my political colleagues would be more useful if they were relocated to SCOTFOR in Edinburgh. They'll just be a distraction if they're here.'

It was blunt and clumsy, but Harry's gift for political subtlety had deserted him. Yet he had to derail Tubbs before the man could do some serious damage and threaten his leadership.

Bashford nodded. 'I'll arrange for your people—and Mr Tubbs—to be flown to Edinburgh tonight.'

'Your help in this matter will not go unrewarded,' Harry told him, feeling a lot better. Faint flutters of panic persisted, but Harry could control them. 'Now, what's the situation on the ground?'

'The good news is the Scottish border is not directly threatened. We've had a report of IS aircraft landing at Leeds International, but that's unconfirmed. We have two ASTOR aircraft—that's Airborne Stand-Off Radar—patrolling the airspace to the south, and we've diverted over half of our operational UAVs to Scotland. With the Sky Sabres intact, and augmented by our remaining Stormers and Rapiers, we'll have significant anti-air capability in place and operational within the next twenty-four to forty-eight hours.'

'Along the whole border?'

'Yes. And Royal Navy ships will widen that envelope from the Irish Sea.'

'So, we're quite safe for now?'

'Yes, Harry.'

He took a deep breath and exhaled. 'It's been a hell of a journey from Downing Street,' Harry said. 'And now I find myself in yet another unknown location. What exactly is this place?'

'A former MI6 debriefing facility last used a decade ago. Since then, it's been mothballed. It's off the books, remote, and well-guarded by the usual tech and a company of infantry, most of whom are in civilian clothes. We're also very close to Kerrera Sound, which means we can get you out by boat should the need arise.'

The birds of panic took to wing in Harry's gut. 'Do you think that's likely?'

'We must prepare for all eventualities. But you're safe here. For now. You should make the most of it. Try to rest.'

'Good idea.' Harry pushed himself off the chair. 'What's next?'

'I'm leaving tonight, with my staff. We'll reconvene in the morning by video link. I'll be at SCOTFOR from this point on, along with the rest of Strategic Command. There'll be much work to do in the coming days, with the primary focus on the defence of Scotland and its land, sea, and air borders. I suggest you try to get as much rest as possible in the next couple of days, Harry.'

'That's a good idea. Good luck, Julian. Keep me posted.'

They shook hands, and Harry left the room. Kerr was waiting outside and escorted him to his suite. Safely locked inside, Harry headed for the drinks cabinet and poured himself a large scotch. He downed it in one and poured another, hoping it would stop his hands from shaking. No one had noticed downstairs, or so he hoped.

He sat down on the edge of the bed, then lay back, staring at the ceiling. He debated throwing another log on the fire, maybe having another drink. Anything to avoid sleeping in the dark.

Because he knew that when sleep came, he would dream of Ellen.

And hear her terrible screams.

CHAPTER 72
STAND AND DELIVER

MOUSA COULD FEEL THE RUMBLING BENEATH HIS FEET AS THE ATTACK ON the enemy's underground installation continued.

The surrounding area had been secured with a heavy military cordon, and tanks had gained access to the enclosed valley via an abandoned farm just beyond its steep flanks. Those tanks had found a concealed entrance and blasted it to pieces. Mousa's paratroopers had entered the complex in force and had been fighting for over an hour.

In the nearby town of Wells, British stragglers were engaging IS forces in house-to-house fighting, and there were reports of more enemy troops roaming the countryside with anti-tank weapons.

Yet Mousa knew that these were nothing more than the tired punches thrown by an already defeated opponent. The British were on the run, heading for Scotland. That pleased Mousa. All his eggs in one basket. Allawi acknowledged an incoming radio message.

'Well?' Mousa said.

'Enemy forces have surrendered, general. There are several prisoners.'

Mousa climbed into his Humvee. They drove through the valley, escorted by six-wheeled AFVs and a platoon of paratroopers. At the shattered entrance to the complex, Mousa and Allawi dismounted and followed the paras on foot through a series of tunnels.

A few minutes later, Mousa found himself in the main assembly area. Debris and bodies littered the huge cavern, and the air was thick with cordite. At its centre, a small group of prisoners squatted on the floor, their hands secured with plastic ties and watched over by his paras. Mousa spied an officer in the huddle and had him hauled to his feet.

'Name?'

'Major Monroe, 2nd Rifles. And you are?'

Mousa folded his arms, smiling. One had to admire the defiance of the British. 'My name is General Mousa. Where is your Prime Minister, major? I know he was here.'

Monroe shifted his weight to compensate for the calf wound that soaked his bandage with blood. 'Under the Geneva convention, I'm only obliged to give you my name, rank—'

Mousa held up his hand and Monroe stopped talking. 'You and your men have fought well,' he told the British officer. 'But I need to know the location of your Prime Minister. Right now.' He stared at Monroe. He saw pain and defiance, yes, but he also saw fear. 'Tell me, and you and your men will be treated with dignity and respect.'

Monroe's bloodshot eyes didn't blink. 'And if I don't?'

'Is he still hiding here somewhere? Or has he left? If so, where did he go? North, with the rest of your people? Or a ship, perhaps? We know your navy is skulking in the Irish Sea.'

Monroe tapped the rank tab on his chest. 'I'm a major. They tell me what to do. They don't tell me their plans.'

Mousa gestured to his 2IC. 'This is Major Allawi. He knows everything I know. So, I'll ask you for the last time—where has Beecham fled to?'

Monroe swallowed. 'I don't know.'

Mousa pulled his sidearm and cocked it. The sound echoed around the chamber. 'Last chance.'

Monroe closed his eyes. Mousa raised his gun.

'He's gone to Scotland,' said another voice.

Mousa looked past Monroe. Another bloodied prisoner stared with sullen eyes.

'He left long before you got here.'

'Be quiet!' Monroe snapped.

The soldier on the ground looked at his superior. 'They know already.' He turned back to Mousa. 'You're too late. He beat you.'

Mousa felt a spike of anger. He gripped the pistol, his knuckles turning white, but then the anger passed. He barked at his paratroopers. 'Have their wounds treated and interrogate every one of them.' He pointed at the sullen soldier on the ground. 'Starting with him.'

Mousa turned and headed back through the tunnels to the valley. 'Have the engineers pull this place apart,' he told his 2IC. 'It may tell us in what hole Beecham is hiding.'

'You think he's in Scotland?'

'That's where they're regrouping. It's where I would hide, way beyond our present reach. Right now, we need to get back to London and refocus on the wider campaign.'

The convoy took them back to the farm beyond the valley, and a cool night breeze gusted across the grassy landing zone Mousa waited for his helicopter.

He'd failed, of course. There weren't many times in his career when he would freely admit to it, but this was one of them. And the price had been heavy. They'd lost planes and armour, and the British had evacuated a significant force north. *We should've hit their ports first*, Mousa realised. Britain was a sea-faring nation and possessed the ability to mobilise a naval force in short order.

Now he would have to fight those same troops in the future, and on a battleground of the enemy's choosing. The Military High Command would bear responsibility, Mousa knew. And he would ram that point home when he spoke to the caliph.

There were some plus points, however. A lot of British anti-air capability had been destroyed, and a troopship had been sunk somewhere to the south. The caliph understood about omelettes and eggs.

The chop of distant rotors disturbed the quiet night air as Mousa's Black Hawk and its Apache escort headed towards them. He helped Allawi inside, and they strapped in. Mousa jerked his thumb at the pilot and the helicopter lifted into the air, twisting beneath its rotors, and heading east.

Mousa stared down into the darkness. How lucky he was to be here, living this life. Generals tended to reside far to the rear, to conference and debate in the relative comfort and safety of command posts and commandeered facilities. But not Mousa. No, he was a soldier prepared to face the same dangers as his lowliest private.

And now he was here, riding a helicopter across territory where angry Englishmen with shoulder-launched SAMs might still be hiding. Yet Mousa was unconcerned. Only God would decide when and where death finally caught up with him. When it did, he would face that day with no regrets.

Before then, there was much work to be done, and Mousa considered the days ahead. With the enemy scattered and running for the Scottish hills, the invasion operation would ramp up to full speed, and his forces would continue to spread across the country. That must be his only priority now.

The helicopter continued east, skimming across the dark countryside towards London, where the black flag of the Islamic State was already flying over the ruins of Whitehall.

CHAPTER 73
THE ROAD SOUTH

THE SUN WAS WARM, THE SKY A CLOUDLESS BLUE, THE DAY QUIET.

Taking advantage of a lull, Faz took a ride out in the Range Rover. Ross sat next to him, his HK resting in the footwell. When they drove up to the northern junction, they saw the road that led south to the village had been blocked with a wall of dirt eight feet high. Some villagers were still working on it, tamping down the soil around thick clumps of shrubs and bushes.

Faz parked the Range Rover, and they climbed out, taking a detour through a copse and crawling through a deer run out onto the main road. From the other side, the berm looked natural, blending in with the high grass banks on either side. The villagers had covered the dirt with transplanted turfs of wild grasses and the road markings were hidden beneath the dirt wall. Nearby signs had been uprooted and taken away.

The villagers had done a better job than Faz had imagined, and they told him that work was still ongoing at the southernmost junction. The village was now inaccessible by road, except for several concealed access points scattered around the surrounding farms and public footpaths.

Back in the Range Rover, Faz powered down the window and let the warm air swirl around the car. No one spoke for several minutes, each of them lost in their own thoughts. It was Faz who broke the silence.

'I'm leaving,' he said.

Ross turned in his seat. 'You heard what that kid said. We're behind the lines now. Leaving is way too dangerous.'

'Hiding the village will buy this community time to make plans and prepare for what comes next. And that's my problem—no one knows what that might be.'

'If you stay here, you'll be safe, at least.'

Faz glanced at Ross as the road cut through a vast wheat field. 'Will I? I stand out like a sore thumb. Questions will be asked. Someone will talk. If they find out I'm MI5, it's game over. Same for you, you know. You heard what they did to those cops in Swindon.'

'I can't leave the family. Or Lara. Her folks are in Bedfordshire. I'm all she's got right now.'

'If you stay, things could go badly.'

'And if we go?'

Faz thought about the answer. He'd been thinking about it for some time. 'I know a place further south. With luck, we could be there in a couple of hours.'

'And then what?'

'I've got a plan.'

'So, when are thinking of going?'

'Tonight. After sunset.'

'Jesus. You're not giving me much notice, buddy.'

Faz shrugged. 'I know, but I'm getting a bad feeling. I think staying is a mistake.'

Ross said nothing. Instead, he turned away and looked out at the rolling landscape, lost in his own thoughts. It was easy to be fooled, Faz knew. The day was beautiful, the sky warm and clear. There was no hint of trouble on the horizon, and they hadn't seen a single aircraft all morning. Yet it could all change in a heartbeat, and he wouldn't wait around for that.

Back at Bob and Helen's place, Faz gathered a few things together while Ross broke the news to the others. Faz scrounged an old rucksack and stuffed it with a few of Bob's castoffs and a decent raincoat. He loaded a box of perishables, fruit, jam, and bread, and packed it into the Range Rover, then he checked the tyres and levels. While the others were out of sight, he gave the AK-15 and his sidearm to Ross and told him to hide it where it couldn't be found but where he could get to it in a hurry.

'There's still time for you to join me,' Faz told him.

Ross shook his head. 'Lara's been through enough. I can't drag her back on the road even if I wanted to. Besides, Bob will need help if things get tough.' He looked around the farm, peaceful beneath the clear blue sky. 'It's a better place than most to wait things out. Until our boys come back.'

'That could be a while. Months. Maybe years.'

Ross smiled. 'With a little luck, we'll be here when they do.'

As the sun passed its zenith, Faz ate lunch, then took a nap. When the shadows lengthened, he joined the others in the farmhouse kitchen and drank coffee. They made small talk around the table and shared a couple of laughs, but Faz felt it was all a little too strained.

The reality of war was sinking in. The village had yet to be touched by it, but when it came, Faz knew the shock would be seismic. Yet he said nothing, instead enjoying the company and wondering—hoping—that somewhere down the line he would see them all again.

The sun set behind the distant horizon, and Faz waited another thirty minutes before heading for the Range Rover. Bob had topped her up with a jerry can of diesel, and Faz had already plotted his route into the satnav. He would keep to the country roads as far as possible, but when he got close to his destination, he would have no choice but to risk the busier routes. He was heading into the lion's den, but if his luck held, it might be worth it. If things didn't pan out, he had a Plan B ready to go.

After a few last-minute checks, he walked around the vehicle and stood by the open driver's door. Lara stepped forward and kissed his cheek.

'Thank you for saving us.'

Faz smiled. 'You saved me too.' He turned to Bob and Helen. 'Thanks for everything. I hope things work out for you all. Just remember, when they come, don't resist. They'll know farms are important and I suspect they'll leave you alone.'

'Let's hope so.' Helen said, her smile replaced by a worried frown. Then she pulled out her phone and arranged Faz, Lara, and Ross into a group shot. 'For posterity,' she said.

They stood together with frozen half-smiles as Helen snapped away, then Ross patted Faz on the shoulder. 'I'll go with you as far as the southern roadblock.'

Faz climbed in and powered down the window. He hit the start button and the diesel hybrid engine hummed into life. 'Take care,' he told the others, then he dropped the vehicle into gear and pulled away.

They made the ride to the southern roadblock on side lights and low speeds. Not much was said, and Faz was distracted by the journey ahead and the dangers he might face. Arriving at the barricade he saw some people still working by torchlight. A pale arm waved in the growing darkness. Faz braked to a halt.

'Come to admire our handiwork?' Metcalfe asked, standing at Faz's window.

'I'm heading out. Probably be back in a few days,' Faz told him.

Metcalfe frowned. 'Where are you going, then?'

'West,' Faz said, and left it at that. In the awkward silence that followed, the sound of distant helicopters clattered around the horizon, then faded. 'Time to go. Good luck, Andy.'

Metcalfe shook his hand, and Faz could feel the strength there. The burly farmer pointed into the darkness. 'There's a track to your right. Follow it along the hedge until you get to a public footpath. Turn left and you're on the asphalt. Make sure you cover your tracks, okay?'

'Will do.' Faz pulled away and bumped onto the track, following the hedgerow.

'You lied,' Ross said. 'Why?'

'The less anyone knows about me and where I'm going, the better for them.' Faz was quiet for a moment. 'Don't take this the wrong way but keep an eye on Metcalfe. Guys like him, big personalities, intimidating physical presence, they can go either way in situations like this.'

'What do you mean?'

'Just be careful. That's all I'm saying.'

Ross smiled in the darkness. 'Jesus, you spooks are a paranoid lot.'

Faz steered the Range Rover towards the end of the hedgerow and onto a narrow, tree-lined path. He turned left and followed it to the tarmac road. Ross climbed out and walked around the car. He put his hand through the window and Faz shook it.

'Lara was right. You saved our arses back on that riverbank.'

'It was a team effort.'

'Come back and see us. When this is all over.'

'I will.'

Ross stepped back, his face lit by the red wash of the Range Rover's brake lights. Faz pulled away and sped up along the lane. He checked his rear-view mirror, but darkness had already swallowed the road behind him.

He never saw Ross or Lara again.

THE INITIAL THIRTY miles were uneventful. Faz followed the route mapped out on the dashboard's big screen, sticking to the country roads, and avoiding population centres, but he knew his luck wouldn't last. He carried his driving license with a London address in his pocket and he'd memorised the name of a street on a Fareham housing estate on the south coast. He was hoping his name and skin colour would do the rest.

The night was silent, and the road empty when he turned on to the A338 and headed south towards Tidworth. The miles slipped by, and the only life he saw were bugs in his headlights and a lone deer on a narrow road that skirted Tidworth town. Faz saw the distant orange sky and knew that big fires were burning there. The garrison, he guessed. Or what was left of it. He kept moving, eager to put the town behind him.

At the junction with the A303, Faz circled an empty roundabout and headed south on a quiet back road that would take him as far as Romsey in Hampshire. From there, it was roughly ten miles to Southampton, but Faz had programmed the satnav to skirt the city centre and loop around the eastern side of Southampton Water. Where he hoped she was still there—

He stamped on the brakes and the Range Rover decelerated, throwing Faz against his seat belt. The vehicle came to a stop less than a meter from the from the front grill of an Oshkosh M-ATV reconnaissance vehicle squatting in the centre of the narrow country lane.

Soldiers yanked the driver's door open. They dragged Faz out and slammed him against the car, tying his hands with plastic loops and rifling his pockets. They found his driver's license, and he heard a mumbled conversation, but it was difficult to catch anything specific over the rumble of the M-ATV's engine.

Faz saw the vehicle turret mounted with a 40mm grenade launcher, a belt-fed weapon, and secured to the vehicle's hood, the black flag of the Islamic State. And there wasn't just one vehicle, he noticed, but at least three others behind it. Islamic State soldiers milled around, and cigarettes glowed in the dark.

Hands spun him around and he found himself face to face with a helmeted soldier.

'There's a curfew in place,' the man growled in decent English. 'And you're breaking it.'

'My apologies, sir.' The soldier would be an officer, after all.

He studied Faz's driving license. 'You are Pakistani?' he asked, switching to Urdu.

'I was born here,' Faz replied in the same tongue. 'My family is from Islamabad.'

'Where are you going?'

'I was at a conference in Swindon. When the troubles began, I became stranded. I'm trying to get home to Fareham, on the coast. My wife has two young daughters. The youngest, Ayesha, has a heart condition. I'm very worried.'

The officer studied Faz's driving licence. 'It says you live in London.'

'We moved a six months ago. I haven't changed it yet.'

The officer peered inside the driver's door. 'Nice car.'

'It's not mine,' Faz told him, still speaking in Urdu. He grimaced. 'I stole it. I was desperate.'

The officer stared at the licence for another few moments, then he snapped an order. Another soldier cut off his restraints, and the officer handed his license back.

'Thank you, sir.'

'My advice is to stay off the roads. If you get stopped, show this.' He handed Faz a plastic card with the IS flag on one side. On the other, it said *Permission to Travel* in multiple languages.

'You're most kind.'

'On your way. And good luck.'

Faz climbed back into the Range Rover. He heard a whistle and saw the soldiers clearing the road. He drove past them slowly, nodding and smiling. Most of them were looking at the car. He counted eight M-ATVs in all. A reconnaissance unit, Faz assumed, though he had no idea why they were idling on a back country road.

But it didn't matter. What mattered was forward progress, and though the permit they'd given him now sat on the dash, the black flag in full view, Faz decided to stick to his plan and stay away from the main roads. He'd been lucky once. And good luck rarely lasted.

Just outside Southampton, he saw the M27 motorway jammed with military traffic. The scale of the invasion was staggering, confirming what Faz had already suspected—that this was about regime change, nothing more. And it had to be happening all over Europe, too.

Skirting Southampton airport, he saw a transport plane on final approach. Beyond the perimeter fence, more military planes jammed the aprons. Faz kept driving southeast, to the river mouth he knew well. Where he hoped she would be waiting. And if she wasn't, there would be others.

Thirty minutes later, Faz stopped the Range Rover beneath a large stand of trees on School Lane just outside Hamble Point Marina.

He left the food in the car, making sure his hands were free, and he walked the rest of the way, keeping to the shadows. Like everywhere else, the marina was in darkness, the power still out. The red and white security barrier was lowered in place, but the checkpoint had been abandoned, the door lying wide open.

Faz ducked under the barrier and headed into the complex. He knew where he was going, and so he avoided the warehouses, the shops, and office buildings. Instead, he headed for the forest of white masts sprouting beyond the waterside rooftops.

As he moved through the shadows, stopping every few moments to watch and listen, he saw other people. The first contact was a man and a woman. They hurried by him, oblivious, wheeling heavy suitcases.

The second contact was more troubling. A group of men, maybe a dozen, ransacking the first-floor office of a marine brokers, their torches waving in the darkness. Keeping watch outside were two others, both armed with shotguns and standing alongside two dark coloured Ford Transit vans. Faz diverted around another building and continued unseen towards the cluster of masts.

At the edge of the marina, a vast network of moorings spread out before him, and where boats of every kind floated on black, oily water. A night breeze whistled through the masts, covering his quiet passage along the puzzle of wooden jetties.

When he reached the farthest one, he stopped at the steel security gate. Faz held his breath and punched in the code, hoping it hadn't changed since his last visit, otherwise it would mean a chilly night swim. He stabbed the metal buttons and twisted the handle. The gate opened on well-oiled hinges, and he breathed again.

He closed the gate behind him and listened. There were no voices, no shouts, no alarms. He saw more boats tied against their moorings, some familiar, some not. His eyes searched the darkness, his feet moving faster along the boards. He saw a recent addition, a Princess luxury cruiser, looming out of the dark, but as tempted as he was, Faz ignored it.

He took another ten paces and stopped. Somewhere a dog barked, and he heard the faint roar of a distant aircraft. But at that moment, none of it mattered.

Because she was there.

And she was waiting for him.

CHAPTER 74
DEMONS

Harry tramped along the narrow woodland path, the thick green ferns soaking his trousers.

A bird of prey screeched high overhead, and Harry's heart skipped a beat. He craned his neck, searching for it, but the canopy was too thick and the morning sun barely above the horizon. The screeching faded into the distance, but Harry's heart never slowed. He picked up the pace, eager to escape this thing that was chasing him.

He'd woken before dawn and breakfasted alone. Armstrong, Lewis, and Tubbs were gone, choppered away to Edinburgh the night before. Harry had listened by his open door as Tubbs had protested, the ensuing ruckus carried around the stone walls of McIntyre. He'd called Harry names too, like coward and traitor, and any self-respecting leader would've confronted such slurs, but not Harry. Not now. He didn't feel strong enough. His confidence was shredded, along with his nerves.

He'd pushed his breakfast eggs around his plate and drank three cups of black coffee. The walls of the dining room had squeezed closer, and Harry felt the sweat running down his body. He took a coat from a peg by the main door and stepped out into the crisp Scottish air. Men with radios watched him from doorways and windows, their lips moving soundlessly, conspiring against him, just like Tubbs.

Harry ran for the trees and didn't stop until he was beneath the dark canopy. His lungs burned but he kept moving, following a narrow woodland path that wound away from McIntyre.

Harry didn't know where he was going, only that he wanted to be alone, to process the avalanche of thoughts and emotions that threatened to engulf him. He'd dreamt of Ellen again, only this time she was in his bedroom, a blackened ghoul with bared teeth and charcoaled skin. She'd stepped out of the shadows and held out her arms, begging for help, screaming in agony. Harry had woken, shouting, struggling with the duvet. The dream had been so real.

As he hurried along the fern-lined path, he wondered again about the fate of her remains. Probably scraped off the road with a shovel, then tossed into a plastic bin like so much rubbish. There would be thousands of bodies lying across London, and in the summer, there was no time for niceties. But Harry didn't care about them, or even David Fuller. He cared about Ellen—

Something moved in the gloom behind him. Harry spun around and saw a shadow between the trees. He turned and ran, his boots pounding the path, his soaking trousers clinging to his skin. He heard a roar behind him and saw the monster crashing through the undergrowth, burned and blackened, just like Ellen. Harry sobbed in fear, and he tripped and fell into the ferns. He crawled on all fours as the monster closed in, its roar echoing through the surrounding forest. It stamped closer, and Harry felt the tremors through his body.

'Please don't hurt me! Please!'

He gasped and panted, and then he collapsed. The sobs came then, like waves beating the shoreline, incessant, unstoppable. Harry gave in to the onslaught, the thin veneer of stability he'd portrayed for so long shattering into a thousand pieces. The sky darkened, and the monster loomed above him.

He closed his eyes and curled up into a ball on the damp earth, sobbing, muttering incoherently, until he was spent and the only emotion that remained was exhaustion…

HARRY ROLLED onto his back and looked up at the sky.

The sun had given way to grey clouds, and he watched them pass overhead, watched the trees swaying in the wind, the birds floating high on the breeze. A chill ran through his body, and he sat up, brushing the dirt from his hands, his hair.

He wasn't sure how he felt. Better, he thought. As if a valve had opened and the pressure released. He got to his feet, one hand braced against a tree trunk. A wave of light-headedness passed. He slapped more dirt from his hands. He looked around and realised he was still alone. Good.

He returned to the path, the panic gone. He knew it would come again, but maybe not for a while and maybe not as overwhelming. His focus turned to the world around him, cold and green, the towering pines reaching into the sky. He saw the occasional rabbit scampering before him, and a small herd of deer that saw him too, before bolting deeper into the forest.

The trees gave way to the shoreline of Kerrera Sound, and Harry followed the waters' edge, invigorated by the beauty of the surrounding hills, their sharp flanks dotted with swathes of purple heather. A mile away, the island of Kerrera was shrouded in an early morning mist, like a slumbering giant rising from the slate-coloured sea.

Harry stopped and looked around him. There were no boats on the water, no aircraft in the skies, not a soul for as far as he could see. He was truly alone, maybe for the first time in decades. Just him and the quiet world around him. He needed to savour that isolation for a while longer.

He pushed on, past the Sound and towards those purple hills. The ground rose through the rocks, ever steeper, but Harry pushed himself. Or was it punishment? Maybe that was it. Maybe he deserved it. That's why Ellen haunted him. He scrambled up between a couple of enormous boulders and found a flat escarpment that overlooked the Sound.

Harry stopped to catch his breath. The view was magnificent, and beyond the vast swathe of forest, he saw the turrets of McIntyre. He'd travelled some distance, he realised. What was he thinking? He was up here, high on a rock, alone, unprotected. He had no phone, no way of letting anyone know he was okay. They would be looking for him. He had to get back—

'Nice view, eh?'

Harry spun around. Mike Reynolds sat several feet above him, his legs dangling over the edge of a boulder. He was dressed in waterproof camouflage trousers and a green fleece jacket, and he cradled a black rifle across his lap. 'Mike. How the hell did you—?'

Harry stopped talking. He'd also stopped thinking. They'd kept tabs on him from the moment he'd stepped outside the castle. They'd followed him, discreetly, of course, and they'd seen everything. These people were professionals and Harry was still the Prime Minister. It remained to be seen for how long.

Reynolds pointed up the escarpment behind him. 'There's an anti-aircraft battery near the summit. Didn't want you stumbling into them, not while everyone's twitchy.'

Harry bit his lip. 'Yes, of course. Stupid of me. My apologies.' There was an awkward silence between them. 'I take it you saw that little incident in the woods?' Reynolds nodded. 'I feel fine now,' Harry told him. 'It was the pressure. And my wife's death. The thought of her remains, still there back at Downing Street. It's been haunting me. This morning it became too much.'

'I get it. Everyone's grieving in some way.'

'Prime Ministers are supposed to be made of sterner stuff.'

Reynolds grinned. 'Not exactly been a normal week, has it?' He slipped down from the rocks with the grace of a younger, much fitter man. Harry saw he was wearing his usual kit, the gun magazines arranged across his chest, the knife, the pistol. And his radio.

'Who knows about my breakdown, Mike?'

'Just me and Gaz.'

Harry looked around for Cole. 'Where is he?'

'Watching the path below.'

Harry tried to gauge Reynolds but failed. Lately, his political instincts had deserted him. He couldn't read people or rooms, not like he used to. But Reynolds was SAS, and Harry knew those men were often used to project British power across the globe. He'd personally authorised several operations in the past, and maybe Reynolds had been involved in those deployments.

He studied the man now, square jawed and hard-eyed. A killer, really. But that's why such men joined the SAS and the SBS, wasn't it? To kill people. What else could it be? The foreign travel? Parachuting? Snorkelling? Of course not. No, what men like Reynolds wanted was the proverbial green light.

And it was men like Harry who gave it to them.

'I would consider it a personal favour if we kept this matter between us,' Harry said. 'Unlike you, I'm ill-equipped to deal with sudden and violent death. What you saw was my way of exorcising the demons that have stalked me since this all started. I feel stronger now, more able to cope with what lies ahead. Dark times, I'm sure.'

'You're probably right. I can't see this ending anytime soon.'

'So, Mike. Do we have a deal?'

Reynolds shrugged. 'All this is above my pay grade. You tell me you're okay, great, I'll take your word for it. If it happens again, I might not have a choice.'

'So that's a yes, then?'

'Sure,' the soldier said.

'Thank you. And be assured, it won't happen again.'

Even as he said the words, Harry felt them to be true. He felt better, more in control. Here, in the Scottish Highlands, far from trouble and protected by what remained of the UK's armed forces, he could take a moment to breathe. To find his centre. To steady his boat. And it wouldn't hurt to have a quiet word with the doctor, ask for something to help him sleep.

Harry looked out across the Sound. He saw two boats, black dinghies, racing across the smooth surface of the water, leaving wide, white wakes behind them.

'Patrol craft,' Reynolds explained. 'You're well protected here, boss. Air, land and sea, nothing's getting through. You can relax for a bit.'

'Good to know. Thank you, Mike.'

Confirmation, then. He was safe, and he would use the time to improve his fitness, to sharpen mind and body for the task ahead. He was a wartime leader now, and there would be certain expectations.

That reality caused a mild flutter of anxiety, but it soon melted away. He would cope, he felt sure of it. It was time to step up.

'We should head back to McIntyre. Let them know we're on our way, would you?'

As Reynolds reached for his radio. Harry set off, heading down the hillside, treading carefully between the rocks. Once more, he'd had a lucky escape. Not only from the physical threats to his life but also this morning's mental health crisis. Now he felt a little stronger, and that was a good sign.

'They're sending a vehicle,' Reynolds told him. 'They'll meet us at the bottom.'

'Thank you, Mike.'

The wind whipped across the hill. Harry kept moving, grateful that he still had both hands on the reins of power.

CHAPTER 75
SUNFLOWER

She stood at the end of the mooring, tall and beautiful, wrapped in navy blue, and she called to Faz like a siren from the rocks. When he reached her, he ran an admiring hand along her stainless-steel rail.

'Hello, baby,' he whispered.

Sunflower was an Oyster 675, a 70-foot oceangoing yacht, sleek and superbly appointed, a top-of-the-range addition to the British government's covert fleet of boats and one used as a stage where the performances of deep cover security agents had deceived many a drug importer, most of whom were now languishing in British jails. Or were they? Faz wondered what was happening inside those jails right now, especially the ones in and around London. Anarchy, he imagined.

He looked around the moorings and saw he was still alone. He stepped aboard, and his first impression was a good one. The deck was clean, and the ropes tied off and stored where they should be. The hydraulic sails lay furled inside their booms, and the twin helm stations secured beneath their protective covers. All the hatches were sealed, including the lower deck companionway situated amidships.

Or was it?

Faz stepped closer. Just past the cockpit seating, he saw a gap in the sliding top hatch. He eased his fingers inside and pushed it open. The cabin below was in complete darkness. He reached for the torch in his pocket and flicked it on, waving it around the large, luxurious saloon. The blinds on the wraparound windows were lowered and the dining area was empty. Faz crept down the steps. The air below was muffled and silent. His torch picked out the navigation station, the equipment lifeless. Except for a single red light—

The blow caught him across the back, knocking the wind from his lungs and sending the torch spinning across the solid wooden floor.

Someone kicked his legs away, and he dropped to his knees. Strong arms wrapped around his neck and squeezed. Faz felt himself choking and tapped out, but the pressure remained, and the dark cabin grew darker still. He felt himself slipping away, and then his head slammed against the floor. He coughed violently and tasted blood. His hands were shackled with plastic ties, then his attacker's hands rifled through his pockets. After a thorough search, a light shone on Faz's face and a male voice, full of menace, hissed in the darkness.

'Who the fuck are you and what are you doing on this boat?'

Faz took several deep breaths before he answered. 'My name is Faz Shafiq. I'm Five. I've been here before, on this boat. Sailed her.'

'Where's your warrant card?'

'I ditched it. They're shooting cops out there.'

'What's your ID number?'

'Nine-five-four-one-seven-five.'

'Who's your line manager?'

'Jane Horton, G Branch, 9C.'

'Why are you here?'

Faz didn't hesitate. 'To steal this boat.'

The torch clicked off. The man switched on a battery-operated lamp sat beneath the polished oak dining table. Whoever this guy was, he was making sure he kept a low profile, too. The stranger stood over Faz and cut his plastic ties off.

Faz sat up and coughed, rubbing his throat. His attacker wore khaki trousers, a dark polo shirt, and Musto deck shoes. His dark hair was pulled back off his forehead and tied in a small bun at the back of his scalp. Faz saw the knife sheath on his belt, a blade with a black handle. He reckoned the thirty-something man knew how to use it, too.

The stranger held out his hand and yanked Faz to his feet, handing back his torch.

'Grab yourself a bottle of water out of the fridge.'

It was a test, Faz knew, so he turned around and stepped into the galley. The fridge light spilled across the saloon. Faz saw it was full of food and water. He grabbed a small plastic bottle and took several gulps.

'Mind if I sit?' The man nodded and Faz sat on the L-shaped bench sofa. 'Did I pass your test? Or do you want me to show you where the service bay is?' He tapped the floor with his trainer. 'It's right underneath this deck. And the covert firearms cabinet is behind a blank facia panel on the starboard side of the two-bunk cabin. Just through there.'

Faz pointed into the dark corridor beyond the saloon. 'There's also a pistol stowed in the engine compartment, accessed via the aft passageway.'

'Not anymore.'

The man grinned as he turned his body and showed Faz the Glock clipped to his belt. 'I'm Ben Francis, Hamble Security Officer. I look after the moorings.' He offered Faz his MI5 warrant card.

'Faz Shafiq. My real name, by the way.' He cocked his head. 'What's happening around here? I've seen some movement. Not all of it encouraging.'

'It's been quiet. But it's only a matter of time before they come for this boat,' Ben said.

'Who's *they*?'

The younger man shrugged. 'Thieves. Opportunists. Locals with a keen eye. I thought you might be one of them.' He got to his feet and twisted the blind handle. Faz stood too. Outside, beyond the boat's rail, the moorings were silent, deserted.

'I've been here since it started,' Ben said. 'I've seen tracer fire and missile launches over Southampton. A cop stopped by, a local, knows we're here. He wanted to use our comms, but I told him they were down.'

'Everything's down,' Faz said. 'Even the government. Beecham's alive, but the armed forces have abandoned England and Wales and are heading north.' Faz spent the next fifteen minutes briefing Ben on his own movements, and what he'd seen and heard since the invasion began.

'So, you can sail this thing?' Ben asked him.

Faz nodded. 'She sails herself, almost. We used it in joint ops with the National Crime Agency to lure the big dealers in. Worked every time. I knew she was moored here, so I took a chance. If it didn't work out, Plan B was to steal something else and put to sea.' He pointed to the red light on the navigation station. 'She's drawing power, right?'

Ben nodded. 'From a solar generator at the boathouse. She's sucked the thing dry, but the batteries are charged up and both fuel and freshwater tanks are full. I do all the turnarounds when the boats come in.'

'You don't sail?'

'I was in the Marines for nine years. Got my powerboat qualification. I was supposed to get my offshore skippers' ticket here, as part of my posting, but I guess that's on the back burner now.' He rubbed his hands together. 'So, where are we headed?'

'It's a good question.' Faz took another drink of water before continuing. 'My original plan was to take *Sunflower* around Land's End and up into the Irish Sea, but now that our troops have retreated north and IS forces have filled the void, we risk direct confrontation with either side, or getting caught in the middle of a full-on naval engagement. We could be boarded and captured or sunk with no questions asked. I'm assuming the Irish Sea will be defended, and that could mean mines. Or if we wander into a free-fire zone, UAVs with Hellfire missiles.'

Faz shrugged.

'And we know nothing about Ireland itself. Are they neutral? Has there been trouble? Given their policies over the last couple of decades, I'm guessing the answer is *yes*. So, we could take a wide detour, sail around the west coast of Ireland, reach Scotland that way, but again, any initial contact with our military could be a risky one.'

'We've got a radio,' Ben said. 'We tell them we're coming. Identify ourselves.'

'And if those comms are intercepted? A caliphate boat could pick us up. Or they might use *Sunflower* for target practise. Imagine what a 20mm gun would do to her.'

Ben held up his hands. 'Enough. I'm convinced. So, what's the plan, then?'

'We sail straight out into the Atlantic, destination, the US eastern seaboard. *Sunflower* is a blue-water boat, so getting there won't be a problem. Once we're there, the embassy will take care of the rest. Getting back to Scotland won't be a problem. I'm sure they're plenty of UK military personnel over there on postings or training in Canada. They'll want to get back into the fight asap.'

Ben scratched his chin. 'A trans-Atlantic crossing, eh? Good training for my skipper's ticket. Though, it's the wrong time of year, right?'

'Correct, but it's not impossible. *Sunflower* is a big, sturdy boat, with the latest weather and navigation tech. The routing program is like having your own captain onboard. But I'm not saying it'll be easy. If we take the northern route, avoiding the Canaries, we risk bigger seas and stronger winds, and at this time of year, squalls, and hurricanes. Though if things start to look bad, we can always head south for the equator.'

'Sounds safer than 20mm.'

'What about our food supplies?' Faz asked him. 'The crossing could take four weeks. I suggest we stock for double that. We need to stay independent for as long as possible.'

'In that case, we'll need to top up our dried goods. There's a supply store on the marina.'

Faz peered through the blind again. It was still quiet, but they needed to move fast. The sun would be up in a few hours, and Faz wanted to be out at sea by then. Waiting another full day could mean the end of his plan. 'We should go now.'

Ben disappeared forward. When he returned, he was carrying an HK-417 marksman rifle. The Glock was now in a plastic holster clipped to his belt. 'I'll take point, provide cover. You grab the gear.'

'Roger.'

They secured the boat and left through the security gate, navigating the network of moorings. When they reached the shore, Ben led the way, using hand and head signals. They kept to the shadows of several buildings until they reached the marine supplies shop further along the road. Faz felt horribly exposed. They were more than two hundred meters away from the moorings, with a lot of open ground between them and *Sunflower*.

Ben reached the shop door first. He tried the handle, but predictably, the business was locked up. 'Stand back,' he said. He raised the HK and fired a couple of suppressed rounds at each of the top and bottom locks. Faz barged it open. Glass shattered and crashed to the floor. The noise made Faz wince.

'Move fast,' Ben whispered, taking up position between two parked cars.

Faz went inside and used his torch, sweeping it across the shelves, all of which were still full. Maybe the reality of the situation hadn't sunk in amongst the Hamble sailing community, Faz thought. Or maybe there weren't as many risk-takers as he imagined. He wheeled a shopping trolley towards the dried goods section and filled it with boxes of freeze-dried meals and energy foods. Filled to the brim, he ran it towards the door, stopping only to grab an extra item that caught his eye…

'Let's go!' Faz said, shoving the trolley across the broken glass. Bright light flared. Ben spun around and flipped down the HK's bipod, resting it on the boot of a parked car. 'Don't move,' he said.

Faz saw the van approaching. No, two vans, he realised. The same two vans from earlier. 'They're armed,' Faz warned. 'I saw them ransacking an office on my way in.'

Faz flinched as Ben squinted through his sight and opened fire. Brass spiralled through the air. The lead vehicle slewed across the road and crashed into a parked car. Steam vented from its ruptured radiator.

Ben fired again, steady shots, the rifle kicking in his shoulder. Then he turned to Faz.

'Go! I'll be right behind you!'

Faz ran, pushing the trolley ahead of him, staying close to the buildings and swerving into the road when he saw the mooring entrance up ahead. Behind him, he heard shouts and gunshots.

He kept moving, the trolley wheels screeching in protest as he slammed it onto the wooden pontoon. He turned around and saw Ben running towards him. Behind him, a mob of figures, all pounding feet and vengeful voices. He pushed ahead, navigating the moorings until he reached the security gate. He punched in the code and held the door open.

Ben caught him up seconds later.

'Must be a dozen of 'em at least! I dropped two shooters, but they're not stopping. Let's go!'

Faz ran with the trolley, the wheels slipping close to the pontoon's edge. When he reached *Sunflower*, he emptied the trolley, throwing the boxes aboard without ceremony.

'Untie her!' he told Ben. Faz ran the trolley back to the gate and left it blocking the pontoon. Leaping aboard the *Sunflower*, he scuttled below and powered up the systems. Indicators glowed blue and green. He kept the cabin lights off and ran back upstairs to the cockpit.

Ben was aft, the HK in his shoulder, his eye at the sight. The rifle coughed once, twice.

'They've reached the moorings. They can't see us yet, but you'd better move fast. I'll try to get clean shots.'

Faz dragged off the waterproof covers to reveal the engine controls. He punched the starter button, and the Volvo rumbled into life beneath his feet. He let the levels settle, then used the bow thrusters to ease the boat away from the mooring.

Then they were moving, caught by the Hamble's current. Faz advanced the throttle, watching the depth finder, seeking the deeper water mid-river. He kept the running lights off, but the white mast would be easy to spot moving through the darkness.

He heard gunshots behind him, and not the HK. The sound echoed over the river. Ben returned fire.

'How are we looking?' Faz asked.

'They've seen us, but they've got nothing heavier than shotguns. Just get us out onto Southampton Water. I'll cover our six.'

Faz increased power and felt the engine respond with smooth precision. Their speed increased, and Faz steered the boat towards the river mouth.

Ahead, a giant car transporter vessel was steaming north towards Southampton docks. The river spilled them out into deeper water, and Ben packed up the rifle. Faz looked beyond him, but the marina was lost in the darkness.

Ben grinned. 'That was easy enough.' The grin faded when he saw the car transporter, a giant, rust-streaked monster sailing towards the distant docks. 'Jesus Christ, that's big.'

'And packed with troops and armour, I suspect.'

Faz pulled the helm to the left, turning south. The breeze picked up immediately, but Faz kept the sails furled. He stayed out of the shipping lanes, but all the traffic was headed north, anyway. Nothing was sailing in their direction.

'Stow that weapon,' he told Ben.

The security officer threaded through the cockpit seating area and disappeared downstairs. Faz flipped on the autopilot and went aft. Ben returned a few moments later.

'Secured,' he said. 'What now?'

'We use engine power to take us to the turn at the Isle of Wight. I don't want to raise any big white sails yet. Once we're clear of Hurst Castle, we'll open her up to the wind.'

'What about enemy naval traffic?'

Faz pointed. 'It's all coming through the eastern Solent. My guess is, they're hugging the French coast for as long as possible before turning north for England. Which is good news for us.' He pointed to the boxes of supplies scattered across the deck. 'Stow that lot, would you? And tie off those mooring ropes.'

'Aye-aye, cap'n,' Ben winked, and set to work.

Faz was glad he'd run into the security officer, despite almost being choked out. The guy knew what he was doing, and thanks to him, they had everything they needed to make the crossing.

A lot of luck wouldn't go amiss, either.

. . .

FORTY MINUTES LATER, Faz was still at the helm, watching the instruments as they approached Calshot Castle, a medieval fort on a prominent finger of land that jutted out into Southampton Water.

Faz timed his run across the paths of two large freighters a mile apart, bouncing over the wake of the first and pushing the engine to full speed to avoid the massive bow of the second. *Sunflower* was not in any danger, but Faz was more concerned about being spotted, and having to deal with the threat of an IS patrol vessel stopping them.

The castle slipped by to starboard. Faz kept as close to shore as he could, grateful for the continuing power cuts that blanketed the coastline and the Isle of Wight. Except for the docks back at Southampton.

Ben was watching aft, where the distant quays glowed white beneath powerful arc lights. Clearly, the invaders had no fear of a British counterattack, at least not by air, and that spoke volumes. Once again, Faz felt relieved he'd followed his instincts.

Twelve miles to go, he pondered. Twelve miles through the narrow western channel of the Solent, where *Sunflower* was well within range of shore-based guns. Yet the tide was with them, and he calculated it would take less than two hours under engine power to get to Hurst Spit.

Beyond that was the Needles Fairway Buoy, and then the open waters of the English Channel—

The helicopter came in from the north as the *Sunflower* glided past the Beaulieu Estuary. In a few seconds, the distant throbbing had turned into a thunderous hammer-beat. He shoved Ben forward.

'Get below! Move!'

The former Marine scuttled down the stairs. Faz turned away, shielding his eyes as a powerful searchlight zeroed in on *Sunflower*. He engaged the autopilot and then he saw the helicopter, flying without navigation lights, a huge, black shape silhouetted against the night sky, circling the yacht like a giant, deadly hornet, and lashing the deck with sea spray. Faz raised his hand and waved. With the other, he yanked the rope behind him.

The green flag of the former Kingdom of Saudi Arabia unfurled on the pole and snapped and cracked in the helicopter's downwash.

Faz continued to wave, battered by wind and spray, praying that the helicopter would leave them alone.

'What do you think?' asked the pilot of the Black Hawk.

'Nice boat,' the co-pilot remarked. 'Old flag, though. Think he's one of the Saud princes?'

'If he was, he wouldn't advertise it.'

'True.'

The door gunner spoke next. 'Want me to put a few rounds into the water, get him to heave to?'

The pilot considered that option as he watched his on-board camera system. The man was still waving, still squinting as the Black Hawk's massive rotors lashed the sea. Luckily, the guy didn't have his sails raised, otherwise the down-draught would've driven his boat onto the rocks.

'It's a bit late to be out sailing, no?'

'Agreed,' said the co-pilot. 'I can call up a patrol boat, get them to check him out?'

The pilot studied the man for another few seconds. 'Forget it. Fuel state is low, and we've got enough work to do. Besides, I need a coffee and some food.'

'Sounds like a plan,' the co-pilot said.

'Hold tight. We're heading back.'

The pilot switched off the searchlight, slammed his pedals to bring the nose around, then dipped it, cranking up the power and heading east.

White spots danced around the back of Faz's eyeballs as the searchlight blinked out and the helicopter banked away. Moments later, it was lost in the darkness, the thunder receding as quickly as it had arrived. He closed his eyes, and the dance faded. He heard Ben's voice above the sound of the sea.

'How are we looking?'

'All clear.'

Faz's heart rate slowed, and he wondered how the conversation went inside that helicopter. Whatever was said, they decided *Sunflower* was no threat. As Ben approached, he saw the flag whipping in the breeze and grinned.

'Good thinking. Did you get it from the store?'

Faz nodded. 'Grabbed it on the way out. An impulse buy, you might say.'

'That's why they pay you spooks the big bucks.'

'Let's get the Bimini raised over the cockpit. It'll give us a little more cover.'

'No probs. And once I've done that, I'll get a brew on.'

Sunflower continued westwards, cutting quietly through the dark channel. As the winds freshened, Faz used the hydraulic system to unfurl the jib, and *Sunflower* sliced a little faster through the waves.

An hour passed and they saw nothing ahead of them. Off the port bow, the dark mass of the Isle of Wight tapered towards the open sea. Ben appeared with another round of coffees. Both men stood at the twin helms, watching the sea and the digital displays.

'Hurst Spit is dead ahead,' Ben said, pointing. 'After that, we're in the channel proper.'

'Open water at last,' said Faz. 'As soon as we're clear of the Spit, we'll cut the engine and set the sails. Then we'll program our course into the navigation system.'

'What are thinking? A westerly heading? Stay out of the shipping lanes and away from the coast?'

'Exactly that,' he told Ben.

The wind picked up then, and Faz cut the engine. He estimated it would take another 24 hours to clear the Channel and reach true open water. The dangers after that would be familiar ones, the threats of wind and bad weather, of vast waves and bottomless oceans, and the sheer physical isolation of an Atlantic crossing.

But they had a boat that could cope with all of it, a boat packed with enough technology to get them across the world with little human intervention.

Faz raised the sails, and he felt the wind catch them, fill them, and

Sunflower surged forward. As Ben hooked on his safety line, Faz did the same and spread his feet, his hands on the helm.

He tasted the salt on his tongue, felt the spray on his skin, and listened to the wind whistling through the sail. He was alive, and that was all that mattered.

Sunflower headed west, leaving the dark and troubled shores of England in its wake.

CHAPTER 76
BLUEY

DEAREST BROTHER,

I hope this letter finds you and the family well. Yes, we are back to writing letters because all emails are banned for the moment. Security, you understand. Or so they tell us.

At long last, they have given us some R&R, so I thought I would write and tell you of the things I have seen during my time here in England. Let me start by saying that the parachute drop over London was one of the most exciting things I have ever done, and to see one of the most famous cities in the world blacked out from horizon to horizon was a surreal experience. My platoon was the first into Downing Street, and the destruction was unbelievable. I can't tell you much about what happened after that, only that there was so much more to that place than you can imagine.

We didn't stay in London for long. We moved out west, to Heathrow Airport, and later we stormed an enemy installation buried beneath a hillside. You remember my friend Abu, from Mosul? He was killed by a British grenade during the fighting, and his loss was a real blow to us all. Such a funny guy, always joking. We've missed him a lot since then.

We won the battle though, and now the British have fled north, to Scotland. Some say they're preparing for a fight, but others think they may strike a deal at the United Nations. No one really knows. Our forces have pushed as far north as Newcastle and Carlisle, which is about twenty kilometres from the Scottish border. (Funny names, I know. Look them up on a map.) For now, we're keeping our distance, which is good because it's always raining here. It's such a change from the desert, and much of it is beautiful. You must all come and visit when the troubles are over.

For now, it feels like we've turned from soldiers into policemen. The daytime curfew in London has been lifted, and the Shahada flies from buildings and rooftops right across the city. Many British people have joined our ranks, running government offices, manning roadblocks, and policing the streets, in exchange for extra food and better accommodation. It's surprising how quickly many of them turned on their fellow citizens.

Some of the British are sullen and angry, though. You can see it in their faces, and it makes me think they have yet to accept defeat. Some have carried out attacks, and terrorists are hanged and beheaded in Hyde Park every week. They've put other troublemakers to work, clearing rubble, collecting bodies, that sort of thing. A building near St. Paul's collapsed a few days ago, killing over a hundred people. Corpses are a real problem here. You can smell them everywhere. Trucks take them to a big incinerator in east London. Gas and electricity supplies are still patchy, but the utility companies are back up to speed and repairs are being carried out. I think most people just want things to go back to normal.

They posted us to Wembley Stadium for a week, which is now a registration centre. In exchange for registering, they give the local population ID cards which allow them to buy food and receive medical care. Most are compliant. But not everyone.

There was much trouble in Brixton, a district in south London. The invasion triggered a huge uprising there, and they burned the town centre to the ground. By the time we arrived on scene, hundreds had already been killed, and bodies were lying all over the place. The gangs had been pushed back into an area of tower blocks and surrounded by armour. We spent a couple of days negotiating, and when that failed, we shelled them, and picked them off with sniper fire, but patience wore thin and the word came down from on high. It was time to end matters.

So, they pulled us back from our positions. A short while later, an air force transport plane flew over and dropped something. When I first saw it floating down under several parachutes, I thought they were dropping supplies or something. Then whistles blew, and we took cover. Have you ever seen a

MOAB bomb go off? The detonation was the loudest thing I've ever heard, and it seemed to last for ages. When the noise finally died down, all you could hear were dogs barking and car alarms going off all over the place. And when we got back to our positions, guess what? The tower blocks had gone, little brother. Vanished, vaporised. When the dust settled, all that was left were gigantic mountains of rubble, every building flattened like pitta bread.

Believe it or not, some rebels survived. They looked like ghosts, covered head to toe in dust, and they staggered all over the place, like zombies in a movie. It was funny to watch them. Only a few made it out, and that night the bulldozers came in. It took another two days but, by the time they ordered us to withdraw, the roads had been cleared and the rubble piled high. The smell was bad though, so it was a relief to leave. There's been no trouble since.

I guess that's because a lot of troops and equipment have arrived since June. Every plane and helicopter in the skies is one of ours, every ship at anchor offloading more caliphate troops and supplies. If there was any doubt that England has been conquered, that doubt has been laid to rest. And of course, Europe, has already fallen.

I got talking to a guy recently, a military policeman, who'd just arrived in London. He'd been in England from the beginning and had seen quite a lot of action, mostly around the city of Birmingham. Shortly after the British fled, they tasked his unit with prisoner admin, not POWs, but the ones in England's gaols. It was a tough and gruesome job, by his account.

Some prisons had been abandoned by the staff, and many prisoners had died of thirst and malnutrition. Other prisons were destroyed, the escapees leaving a trail of corpses in their wake. Those that remained were processed and formed into work groups to clear roads around the cities or remove bodies. They were the lucky ones.

They took thousands of prisoners into custody, but what to do with them? So, the top brass made a decision. The very worst offenders—thousands of them—were bound in chains and transported to the east coast, where they were loaded onto a giant freighter. The ship put to sea after dark. Thirty kilometres off the coast, the engines were cut and the crew, plus the cop and his escort team, climbed down on to a waiting navy boat. Once they were out of the way, they blew the hull out of the freighter.

The cop saw it go down. He said it sounded awful, a terrible screech of metal, and he could hear the screams of those still aboard. He said the noise *would haunt him for a long time, but true justice had been served. Anyway, I'm sure it's for the best.*

As for the other prisoners, the soldiers, and policemen, they're also being ferried out of the country, but those ships are sailing back home. I wonder what will happen to them. If you find out, let me know.

So now we wait, little brother. Hopefully, we will soon begin preparations for the assault on Scotland. Right now, curfew sirens are wailing across the city, so I must finish up and prepare for tonight's patrol. I will write to you again if I get the chance. And remember, not a word of this to anyone!

Give my love to mother and father, tell them not to worry and tell them I will see them again.

In this life, or the next.
Your loving brother,
Rahman

CHAPTER 77
RUSH HOUR

The sound of a key rattling in the front door woke Dave Greenwood from a dreamless sleep.

He sat up, rubbed his tired eyes, and checked his watch. It was just after seven pm. He'd fallen asleep again, this time in the drawing room chair. Out in the hallway, he heard the front door close and the bolt slam home. Stuart appeared a moment later, a plastic carrier back in his hand. He held it up.

'Supplies,' he said, smiling.

Dave rubbed his hands together. 'Great. I'm starving.'

'I'll get dinner started.'

Stuart left the room, and Dave followed him to the kitchen.

'How was it out there?'

Stuart emptied his bag onto the kitchen counter. 'Same as usual. Fewer soldiers and more police.'

Dave snarled. 'Traitors.'

'They're very aggressive,' the older man said, placing cans in the overhead cupboards.

Dave saw tins of minced meat and chicken curry, pasta and rice, and his stomach grumbled.

'Power corrupts absolutely,' the older man continued. 'In the past, the police were always bound by regulations. Those days have gone.

Four officers beat a man to death outside Westminster tube station, last week. What have we become?'

Dave was still staring at the tins. 'I vote for curry tonight. What about you?'

'Curry is fine.' Stuart coughed violently, and his hands grasped the counter. Dave helped him to a kitchen chair. 'Thank you, David. I must confess, I'm not feeling all that well.'

Dave ran a glass of water under the tap and handed it to him. 'You need a decent meal, for God's sake. We're eating like birds here.'

Stuart gulped some water and wiped his mouth. 'Perhaps it's time for you to register with the authorities.'

Dave's eyes widened. 'Are you mad? You know what they're doing to hideaways out there.'

'Many have recanted their former allegiances and taken the caliphate oath. If you did the same, they would feed you, give you a uniform. Maybe they'd let you travel to Guilford. To see Rebecca.'

'She'll think I'm dead by now,' Dave told him, peeling back the tin lid of the curry. He licked it clean and threw it in the bin. 'Besides, they're not letting anyone travel, are they?'

'Not without authority, no. But that will change in time.'

'You talk like the war's over. That Wazir has won.'

'Hasn't he? Or are those British soldiers on our streets? I don't think so.'

'Our boys will be back, you'll see. This occupation can't go on forever.' Dave emptied the curry into a pot. He ran a finger around the inside of the empty tin and licked cold curry paste. His stomach grumbled in anticipation. 'And I'm not swearing any allegiance, not to Wazir.'

'We can't live on a single person's food allowance, David. Look at us. We're wasting away.'

Dave measured out a cup of rice and placed another pan on the stove. He put the rice back in the cupboard. 'Is it my imagination or have we got more food this week?'

'I think the manager of the supermarket took pity on me.'

'Well done you,' Dave said.

Maybe they could have a little extra tonight. Stuart was the thrifty type, measuring rice and pasta down to the last grain and shell, using only level spoons for coffee and reusing tea bags. Dave didn't mind at first—this was Stuart's place and Stuart's rations—but lately the old man's scrimping and scraping was getting on Dave's nerves. He was restless, and he wanted to go home, get back to Becks. He needed to see her face, to hold her. To tell her he loved her.

And perhaps things weren't so bad down in Surrey. In London, the situation was worsening. Hostilities may have ended, but the war against freedom continued, and if Stuart was right, a lot of Londoners were helping the invaders.

The old man coughed again and wiped his mouth with a handkerchief. 'You don't have to mean it.'

'What?'

'Becoming a policeman again. You can take the oath but not believe the words or sentiment. You could work from within to change things. It's what we did at BBC Media Action. Abroad, I mean. In Syria, Ukraine, countless other places. We worked to undermine certain regimes, take control of the narrative. Stir the pot, so to speak.'

Dave was confused. 'I thought you did charity work?'

Stuart raised an unkempt white eyebrow. 'How's that curry coming along?'

'Almost there.'

Dave took the hint, stirring the simmering sauce with a wooden spoon. The smell filled his nostrils, and it took all his willpower not to shovel it into his mouth. He stirred the rice with the same spoon, then sucked down a couple of errant grains clinging to the spoon's edge.

'I'll serve.'

Stuart got to his feet and took over, as he always did. Dave ran a couple of glasses under the cold tap and set them on the table. He watched Stuart spoon the rice into bowls, then top it with a blob of curry, scraping the pots for every grain, every smear of juice. He shuffled back to the dining table and set Dave's bowl in front of him.

By the time Stuart had taken his seat, Dave had wolfed down two large mouthfuls. Stuart tutted as he picked at his food.

'I really wish you'd wait. It's rude.'

'I'm starving,' Dave said, running his spoon around the bowl. Then he picked his bowl up and licked it. Stuart slapped a bony hand on the table.

'David! Please!'

Stuart glared, and Dave pushed his spotless bowl to one side and took a gulp of water. 'I'm sorry. I'm a pig.' Then he chuckled at his own joke.

'Just say the words, and then you can eat all you want.'

'No way,' Dave said, the smile fading. 'If I did, they might make me take part in those executions. I won't do that. It's barbaric.'

'The police carry out prisoner escort duties, that's all. They have dedicated executioners, you know.'

'And that makes it alright, does it? You said it yourself—police officers take them all the way to the gallows. Or the chopping block. They stand and watch while their own people are butchered.'

'They're terrorists.'

'Bullshit. They're freedom fighters. And they're better people than you and I. They're taking the fight to the invaders. Look at us, cowering down here like church mice.' Dave stared at the table. 'I'm ashamed of myself.'

Stuart waved his spoon. 'Then go. Join this so-called resistance.'

'How? Is there a recruiting office somewhere?' He lowered his voice. 'That guy you saw beaten to death at the tube station—do you think those officers should get away with it? What about the victim's family? Don't they deserve justice? And if the state won't do it, why shouldn't they take matters into their own hands?'

Stuart sighed, long and loud. 'I just want peace, David. That's all. I'm too old to fight.'

'Well, sometimes a man must stand up and be counted. At any age.'

'Not me. Not anymore.' Stuart picked at his food.

Dave watched him, his stomach still grumbling. 'Are you going to eat that?'

Stuart looked across the table. 'Of course I am—'

Thump! Thump! Thump!

Dave's pulse raced. Since he'd been hiding, Stuart hadn't received a single visitor. Flyers had been shoved through the letterbox, demanding people register at local halls and government buildings (what was left of them), or info-leaflets outlining new community regulations, but no one had ever knocked or rung the bell.

Until now.

Thump! Thump! Thump!

'Who is it?' Dave whispered.

'Let's find out, shall we?'

Stuart got up from the table. Dave pushed back his chair and grabbed the older man's arm.

'Where are you going?'

'Relax, David. It's probably the supermarket manager. I left my wallet on the counter.'

'You did?'

'A *senior moment*, I think they call it. Sit down, please.'

Dave did as he was told. He heard Stuart shuffle down the corridor and the sound of the bolt sliding back. Then he heard low, muffled voices.

Dave couldn't help himself. He leaned across the table and picked up Stuart's bowl, spooning curry and rice into his mouth. He heard the bolt slide home and set the bowl back on the table, making sure the spoon was in the right position. Or as near as dammit.

He heard footfalls on the hallway carpet and swallowed the food as fast as he could, cuffing his mouth with the back of his hand. He folded his arms and stared at the table, feigning distraction, and hoping the old man wouldn't notice the missing food.

The footfalls stopped at the kitchen door.

Dave cringed, knowing Stuart was staring at his bowl, at the bird-like portion that was suddenly smaller. Then they would argue. Again. Dave felt he'd outstayed his welcome, and he reckoned Stuart felt the same. It was time for a talk. Time for Dave to make a proper plan. He looked up.

It wasn't Stuart watching him from the doorway.

The man was short, well under six feet, with receding red hair and heavily tattooed arms. A tactical vest strained at his big belly, adorned with Islamic State Velcro patches and Ginger's blood group. But what frightened Dave most was the Sig automatic held in the man's hand and levelled at Dave's chest.

'Don't move. Not a single muscle.'

Ginger stepped into the room, his eyes never leaving Dave's. Two people followed him in, a cropped-haired white woman and a muscular black man, both wearing the same tac vests with the same patches. They all wore jeans, t-shirts, and sneakers, and sneering faces. Dave reckoned if he ran any of them through PNC, he'd get hits. But he doubted PNC existed anymore. And it was people like these who held the whip hand now.

'Who are you?' Dave asked.

The black man punched him in the side of the head. Dave saw stars, and his left ear rang. 'We ask the questions.'

'I ask 'em,' ginger reminded his colleague. The black man scowled. Ginger rounded on Dave. 'Where's the gun?'

'He hides it under the washing machine.' Stuart had stepped into the room. He stared at Dave without a trace of embarrassment.

'Stuart? What the fuck?'

The old man didn't answer. Dave watched the black man ease the Glock out from behind the kick-board beneath the built-in appliance.

'There's a spare magazine down there, too.'

Dave glared at Stuart. 'Shut the fuck up!'

The woman slapped Dave's face. 'Keep your mouth shut,' she warned, her pierced nose an inch from Dave's.

The pockets of her tac vest were filled with all sorts of crap. Notebooks, pens, leaflets, a torch, a first-aid kit. She had a pistol strapped to her bulging thigh, the flap undone. These people hadn't been trained properly, not like Dave and his former colleagues. These were scumbags, recruited from the gutter to do the regime's dirty work. But that didn't make them any less dangerous.

'You should try brushing your teeth,' Dave told the woman, and that earned him another slap.

'The accuser should now speak,' Ginger said, as if he were making an official announcement.

Stuart stood on the other side of the table. He raised a finger, then his voice, enunciating like a high court judge.

'This man was a police officer. He has expressed support for the corrupt Beecham regime. Now he wants to join the terrorists. He refers to them as freedom fighters.'

'They're the real traitors,' Ginger snarled.

Dave looked at him. 'How do you work that out, Einstein?'

Ginger placed a warning finger against his lips. Stuart continued, as if Dave wasn't there.

'I've frequently encouraged him to contact the traitors so they could be identified and denounced, but instead, he has remained in hiding. Like a coward. Eating his way through my rations.'

The black man sneered at Dave. 'Taking food out of the old geezer's mouth. What a hero.'

They all laughed.

Dave looked up at them and knew his days were numbered. Fear made him nauseous as he considered how things might play out. Hideaways like Dave were treated as criminals, and anyone suspected of any connection to the resistance would be tortured. Dave was under no illusions about that. Guilty or otherwise, tortured people would admit to anything.

And that's what terrified Dave the most, what made his stomach churn and his heart race. He would end up on some gallows somewhere, a noose around his neck. Or worse, on his knees, staring into the blood-stained basket that would catch his decapitated head.

His skin turned cold. He was never going home, he knew that now. His life would end in a cell, or on a scaffold, and the horror of being killed in front of a crowd was too much for Dave to imagine.

Slowly, he raised his arm and pointed his finger at Stuart.

'It's not me you should be questioning. It's him.'

The laughter faded. All eyes shifted from Dave to Stuart. The old man frowned.

'What did you say?'

'I said they should investigate you.' Dave turned to Ginger. 'Yes, I'm a cop, and yes, I've been hiding, because he told me they were arresting former cops on sight.'

Dave pointed at Stuart again.

'He's got a radio somewhere. Sometimes at night I can hear him whispering. He wanted me to join you lot, to find out how it all works. *Infiltrate*, that's the word he used.'

Stuart's voice was filled with outrage. 'He's lying,' he told Ginger.

Dave registered the confusion on the three interlopers' faces. 'It's a double bluff,' he told them. 'He denounces me on fake charges, makes himself look like a pillar of the community, but all the while he's gathering intelligence. He'll probably try to befriend you, find out your names, where you live. Then he'll pass that intel to his mates in the resistance. Target your families.'

Dave shook his head.

'People like him look down their noses at people like us. They think they're superior. Look at his face,' Dave said, jabbing a finger in Stuart's direction. 'He thinks he's got you fooled, that you're too stupid to see through his bullshit. Ask him about the radio. And the gold coins he's got stashed. Worth a fortune, he told me. A family heirloom. All my dad ever left were debts.'

Stuart looked like a deer caught in the headlights of a fast-approaching truck. 'Surely you don't believe this fairy tale?'

'See? Calling you stupid again.' Dave almost smiled. The old twat had just dug his hole a little deeper. The three thugs glared at Stuart, arms folded. Ginger took a step closer to him.

'Maybe you should show us where this radio is.'

'And the gold,' the black man added.

They turned their backs on him. Dave stood up, quiet as a ninja, then he lunged, whipping his arm around the woman's neck, dragging her backwards, knocking over his chair as he reached for the loose holster flap, for the gun strapped to her fat thigh. He pulled it, aimed, and prayed she was as sloppy as he hoped.

In the basement kitchen, the gun roared, the bullet punching through Ginger's right cheek and out through his skull in a puff of red mist. The black man fumbled for his own gun, a curse on his lips, and Dave shot him twice in the chest. He hit the wall and fell sideways, burying Ginger beneath his muscular frame.

'Please don't kill me!' the woman begged.

Dave pushed her away and levelled the gun at her. She raised her hands.

'Please, I've got kids! I only took this job so I could feed 'em! Please!'

Dave pulled the trigger, and the round took her through the forehead. She was dead before she hit the floor.

Dave's heart pounded, his breath coming in quick gasps, the barrel of the Sig waving between all three bodies. After a moment, he lowered the gun. They were all dead. Across the table, Stuart stood open-mouthed.

Dave waved his hand. 'Sit.'

The old man flopped into his chair. Dave reached across the table and took Stuart's bowl. He put the pistol down and spooned the rest of the old man's food into his mouth. When he'd finished, he burped, long and loud, then he picked up the gun and smiled.

'Well, that didn't go the way you thought it would, did it?'

'I won't say anything,' Stuart said, talking fast. 'You have my word.'

'Really? That's nice of you. How will you explain the bodies?'

'I'll tell them you barged your way in, held me hostage.' He leaned forward. 'I won't tell them your name, or where you live, and I certainly won't mention Rebecca—'

Dave extended his arm across the table and shot Stuart in the face. Blood sprayed across the wall, and the old man slumped sideways, blood leaking from a hole above his right eyebrow. His body slipped off the chair and fell beneath the table.

Dave put the gun down. If Stuart was prepared to give Dave up, he would've told anyone who cared to listen about Guilford and Rebecca, and Dave couldn't allow that.

THE RADIO SPEWED a sudden burst of chatter, waking Dave from a deep sleep. He sat upright, his heart rate climbing, but he heard no hammering at the door, no pounding of boots, no shouting. The apartment was peaceful. He could hear birds singing and saw sunlight out in the hallway. The night had passed without incident and that gave Dave some hope.

After shooting Stuart, Dave had gathered the guns and spare

magazines from the three stooges and sat at the kitchen table, listening to radio traffic, and waiting for their buddies to arrive. He ate more food and drunk half a bottle of Stuart's best pinot noir, and later, as the night dragged on and his eyelids drooped, he retired to the drawing room and lay on the couch, where he quickly fell asleep.

Now, with the rising of the sun, the radio had burst into life. He heard their voices chattering across the airwaves, much of it undisciplined traffic, a mixture of callsigns and first names. Yet there was no urgency there, just people checking in.

To Dave's surprise, no one was looking for the stooges, and he wondered why. Bad admin? Or maybe they'd just clocked off when blabbermouth accosted them? Either way, this period of grace wouldn't last. Someone would notice three missing guns and radios. If they hadn't already.

Dave got to his feet and went to work.

AT ONE MINUTE PAST NINE, he stepped out onto the pavement of Queen Anne's Gate, his heart racing.

Part of him expected to see a police cordon at both ends of the street, and guns trained in his direction, but the street was clear and the other pedestrians uninterested.

As he headed towards the tube station at St. James's Park, Dave noticed that people barely glanced at him. He wore a liberated militia vest and a gun on his hip, so maybe that was the reason. If so, good. All Dave needed to do was get to Victoria Station.

It felt good to be out in the fresh air after weeks of being cooped up in Stuart's flat. His legs were a little weak, but the recent calorie intake had helped in that regard.

The real shock came when he reached the corner of Tothill Street, and he saw the broken stone teeth of what used to be Westminster Abbey. Even as he watched, a thousand years of history was being levelled by a wrecking ball, sending rubble crashing to the ground in vast clouds of ancient dust.

Dave felt his anger rising. He wanted to rage at the invaders, at the obscenity of what he was witnessing, but he turned away, reminding himself not to draw attention. Home, that must be his priority now.

He waved to a couple of militia patrols standing outside St. James's Park tube station, and they waved back without a second glance. On Victoria Street Dave watched a convoy of military Humvees rumble past, and he waved again, but none of the top-mounted soldiers returned his greeting.

As he neared Victoria Station, he saw hundreds of people streaming in and out of the entrances and exits. Many of them descended into the underground and more waited in long queues for buses at the terminus outside the station.

There were more Humvees here, two in fact, parked one behind the other right outside the main entrance, both mounted with heavy machine guns, but the military crews looked relaxed enough, smoking and chatting, and eyeing passing women.

Dave found the entire experience bizarre. The crowds were smaller than pre-invasion, but they were still significant. Which could only mean one thing—a relaxation of travel restrictions.

Beneath the vast glass roof of the station, thousands of people flowed back and forth, streaming through barriers, and heading for the exists just like a pre-invasion commuter crowd.

As he made a beeline for the train departure boards mounted above the platform barriers, Dave saw people queuing for coffee and pastries and gathered around tables, surrounded by luggage. It felt normal, and Dave's anger bubbled again.

He stopped beneath the departure boards, and the word jumped out at him from the digital display:

GUILFORD

The train was leaving in eleven minutes. Plenty of time.

'Oi, you!'

Dave turned, and his heart sank. A man marched towards him, a big Asian man with a bushy beard and a carbine rifle slung across his chest. He wore a black uniform with an Islamic State patch on one shoulder and a Union flag on the other. Not a soldier, not like the troops outside, but he wasn't a militia either. He was somewhere in between. Neither one nor the other, but doubly dangerous. And he reeked of authority. Dave's heart pounded.

'What are you doing?'

'Going home,' Dave said without pause. 'I've been on shift all night.'

'Tough luck, mate. You're coming with me.'

Dave swallowed. 'Why?'

The Asian took a step closer. 'Never question me again, understand?' He tapped the Union flag on his shoulder, and on closer inspection, Dave saw crossed swords had replaced the saltires. 'British Division, which means you're outranked. So shut the fuck up and follow me.'

The man must've been ten years younger than Dave, but he wielded his authority like a stick. Dave looked back at the barriers and the waiting trains beyond. He was so close now.

'My kid, she's sick,' Dave blurted. 'I really need to get home. Please.'

The Asian shook his head. 'No chance. We're raiding an address in Pimlico. It's a rush job, and we need bodies to surround the building. Let's go. Transport's waiting outside.'

Dave scrambled. 'Let me use the toilet first.' He pointed to the facility across the concourse.

The Asian nodded. 'Okay. I need a piss too.'

He marched ahead of Dave, and people moved out of their way. Dave's mind raced. If he got on that transport, he was finished, and that meant execution. He couldn't risk it. What he needed was a diversion.

The men's toilet was a big facility, brightly lit and tended by Africans who mopped floors and cleaned mirrors. The Asian veered right to the urinals. Dave turned left to the cubicles. He locked the door, his mind racing. Now what? He pulled the Sig and checked it. Ready to go—

Bang! Bang! Bang!

'Hurry it up in there! We haven't got all day.'

'Give me a sec.'

Dave glanced under the door. The Asian was standing directly outside, the toes of his boots pointed towards the cubicle. Which meant his face would be about the same height as the coat hook on the door…

He jammed the Sig against the thin wood and fired, the gunshot deafening inside the tiled walls. Dave yanked the door open and saw the Asian on the ground, clutching his throat, the blood pumping through his fingers, his eyes wide and wild.

Dave vaulted him and hurried outside with everyone else. People scattered. Dave pretended to make a radio call as he walked towards the platforms. A scream shrilled across the concourse and Dave saw militia and soldiers streaming into the station, all heading for the men's toilets.

Dave picked up the pace. He hurried beneath the departure boards, losing himself in the crowd. He saw frightened faces, and heads turning left and right, like a herd of skittish deer. Some stared at him as he passed—running *away* from trouble.

He checked the board above.

Two minutes to departure.

When he reached the ticket barriers, he beckoned a railway employee.

'Open the gate.'

Dave saw the train on platform twelve, its doors open. Waiting. The announcement boomed across the station.

'This is a security alert—'

Dave spun around and saw a tremor ripple through the crowd. Hands pointed in his direction. He saw guns and helmets barging people out of the way, running towards the barriers.

He turned back and drew his gun. 'Open that fucking gate!'

The man sprinted away, arms and legs pounding.

'You! Stop!'

Dave didn't look back. Instead, he leapt over the barrier, his boot catching the edge. He fell to the ground on the other side, the Sig skittering away.

A whistle blew.

Dave crawled after the gun, grabbed it, and stood up. He ran for the train, saw the orange lights above the doors, heard another whistle.

Departure imminent.

He ran faster, racing against the warning beeps, knowing the doors were about to close. He reached out—

Something took away his left leg, and Dave fell to the ground. He tried to get up and fell again. Putting the weight on his other leg, he stood and hopped towards the open doors.

They rumbled and closed with a thump.

With a screech of wheels, the train started moving. Dave hopped alongside, banging on the windows as it gathered speed, but he couldn't keep up. He watched it snake out from beneath the platform roof and into the sunlight.

He'd almost made it.

Paper exploded like confetti as a bullet ripped through the notebook in his tac vest pocket.

His legs failed him, and he collapsed onto the platform as gunfire hammered all around him. He looked down at his body. *Oh, no*. Blood ran across the ground, so much blood. *Must've nicked an artery*, he realised, and the thought occurred to him that he couldn't be saved.

And they wouldn't be able to execute him.

Through a narrowing tunnel of vision, he saw the helmets and guns approaching. His breath came in short, quick gasps now, and he closed his eyes and thought of Rebecca. He'd never see her again, and that hurt more than the bullet holes in his body.

But he'd tried at least.

He opened his eyes and saw the shadows creeping closer, their guns pointed at him.

With the last of his strength, he lifted the Sig—

Dave Greenwood never heard the shots that killed him.

CHAPTER 78
BLUE WATER HORIZON

S*UNFLOWER* SLICED THROUGH CALM BLUE WATERS AS IT HEADED TOWARDS the eastern seaboard of the United States at a steady six knots.

She was still over 100 nautical miles from the South Carolina coast, but her orders were to maintain a specific course and speed, and *Sunflower* was adhering rigidly to those instructions.

For Faz and Ben, it was their thirty-third day at sea and, given their initial northerly routing, the Atlantic crossing had gone better than both men had hoped. *Sunflower* had performed well in the moderate to heavy seas they'd encountered in the first week, and the sophisticated navigation and weather systems had guided them away from serious trouble.

The automated sail-rigging systems had been easy to use, and after passing north of the Azores, the weather had improved, and *Sunflower* had turned her bow and filled her sails with the prevailing eastern trade winds.

After that, she'd made steady progress.

Despite the sophisticated onboard technology, one of them was always standing watch on deck, and Faz reflected on his good fortune that he'd run into Ben. It was an intimidating experience to be standing at the helm of a sailing vessel, alone, in the dead of night, a thousand miles from any ship and any shore, between the cold, star-lit heavens above and the restless, fathomless sea below, and Faz wasn't sure if he would've risked such a northerly route on his own. But Ben had proved himself to be a capable sailor, and he'd performed well against the occasional heavy seas they'd encountered.

So, they'd ridden the trade winds all the way to Antigua, but Faz had avoided making landfall, unsure of the political situation in the Caribbean and the Bahamas, and troubled by the huge flashes of light on the western horizon that the weather computer confirmed was not a storm.

Instead, they steered northwest, using the North Equatorial Current to track past the Turks and Caicos and head for a point somewhere between Bermuda and the South Carolina coast before turning west for the coastal city of Charlestown.

The aircraft had appeared in the eastern sky just after midday, a rapidly approaching dot that morphed into a US Navy surveillance UAV. As it circled above them, Faz had answered the subsequent radio inquiry and told the operator the name of the boat, registration, port of origin, and crew details. The interrogation lasted for ten minutes, ending with an instruction to maintain their heading.

After the UAV had disappeared over the horizon, Faz went below and made two mugs of coffee. Bringing them back up on deck, both men sat in the cockpit as the boat sailed on auto-pilot, eating up the hours as she headed west. The next morning, Faz woke to find *Sunflower* shrouded in a sea fog. Ben stood at the helm, monitoring their course and surface radar. Wrapped in a fleece to keep out the dawn chill, Faz joined him as they studied the radar.

'He's still there,' Faz noted. The radar echo had appeared thirty minutes ago, and continued to shadow *Sunflower*, often steering away before heading back towards them, but never closer than a mile or two.

'She's big,' Ben said. 'Bigger than us, at least. I'm guessing Coast Guard or navy.'

'Agreed. Looks like she's headed our way again.'

Faz stared out into the fog, a wispy grey cloak that restricted their visibility to a couple of hundred meters. Faz watched the radar, troubled by the ship's apparent collision course. As he slopped the dregs of his coffee over the side, the console radio hissed.

'*Sunflower, Sunflower,* this is US Navy ship *Augusta* requesting you heave-to immediately.'

'Roger, heaving-to now,' replied Ben. He turned to Faz. 'Here we go, then.'

Faz used the touch screen to furl the sails. After a few moments, *Sunflower* was drifting with the current and riding the gentle swell of the Atlantic. The mist surrounded them, dampening any sound except the slap of water against the hull.

'You hear that?' Faz said. Ben nodded, his hands on the wheel. The hiss grew louder, coming from somewhere off the port bow. Faz took an involuntary step back as a long, battle-grey bow knifed through the mist and cruised past them. He saw several armed Marines watching them from a flight deck at the rear, and then the haze swallowed the fast-moving vessel.

'That's a littoral combat ship,' Ben said. 'A trimaran. The yanks use them for shallow water gigs, coastal patrols, that sort of thing. Brace!'

The wake hit them, rolling *Sunflower* back and forth, until she steadied herself and the silence returned, broken only by the southern twang of the voice behind them.

'Hands where I can see 'em, gentlemen.'

Faz and Ben turned to see two US Marines in combat gear pointing short-barrelled weapons at them. At the stern, three more boarders were clambering out of a black assault boat as it bobbed up and down on the swell. *Crafty bastards*, thought Faz, using the big ship to mask their approach.

'I'm losing my edge,' Ben grumbled, his hands clasped behind his head. Faz held his at shoulder level, palms open, legs wide as he rode the swell. Two Marines searched them while the others went below. Faz and Ben were told to sit on the cockpit seats, and even though they were watched over by a gun-toting Marine in helmet, goggles and a dark grey uniform, their hands remained unbound.

'VBSS, team,' Ben said. 'They're good. Slick.'

The search took some time, especially after Ben told the boarding party officer there were weapons and ammunition aboard. *Sunflower*'s armoury was duly confiscated, and after another thorough search, the officer approached them.

'Thank you for your cooperation,' he said. 'The boat is clean, and I have to say, pretty damn impressive. But we will impound it while your IDs are checked. There'll be a period of detention too, but I doubt that will last long, given what you've told me.' He gestured to the cockpit controls. 'We've programmed an alternative course for you. It'll take you west, and a Coast Guard vessel will meet you a few miles offshore.'

His friendly countenance darkened.

'I warn you now, if you stray off course or fail to respond to instructions, you'll be intercepted and sunk. Understood?' Faz and Ben nodded. The Marine rapped a gloved knuckle on a handrail. 'Good, because she's a beauty and I'd hate to see her scuttled.'

Faz heard the growl of outboards and saw the assault boat loitering off the starboard bow. The Marines climbed aboard, then the boat sped up and was swallowed by the mist. Faz and Ben turned to each other and shook hands.

'We made it,' Faz said, smiling.

'Good job,' Ben replied, resting a gentle hand on the cockpit console. 'She didn't let us down, did she?'

'I knew she wouldn't.'

'I'll get breakfast on.'

Ben disappeared below, and Faz retook his seat. It was the end of a nightmare that had started in south London. But it wasn't over, not by a long stretch.

He heard a screech and saw a pair of gulls sliding above the mainmast. Soon, he would step onto US soil. He'd been lucky. He didn't know what the future held for him, but at least he had one.

He turned and stared back out over the stern. He couldn't say the same for those still trapped in war-torn Europe.

CHAPTER 79
BORDERLANDS

ONE BY ONE, THE BLACK HAWK HELICOPTERS CAME IN LOW ACROSS THE fields of Old Castleton and touched down in a large rectangle of pasture bordered by roughhewn, grey stone walls.

The Apache escort whirled in the sky above, and when all four transport helicopters were safely on the ground, the Apaches headed east to their own landing zone.

Harry didn't wait for the rotors to wind down. Instead, he jumped into the whirlwind and jogged towards the waiting convoy of green Humvees parked on the B6357 road beside the pasture. Reynolds and Cole kept pace beside him and waiting soldiers in full battle gear formed a protective ring around them all.

As he climbed into the third Humvee, Harry sat and watched the others stumbling through the tufty grass. They had taken his lead, of course, too afraid of the negative optics, and now he saw them battered by the rotor blast, hair and ties flapping in the down-draught.

Harry smiled when he saw Leon Tubbs trip and fall to the ground. His bag carriers helped the overweight politician back up on his feet as he struggled after the others. Welsh First Minister Gower led the pack, a beanpole of a man, striding ahead, lifting his legs like a stork lest he befall the same fate as Tubbs.

The man looked ridiculous, Harry observed, and his media team would catch it all on camera. A carefully timed and embarrassing leak was a card that every canny politician should have up their sleeve.

Tom Armstrong and Brendan Lewis, his former ministers, brought up the rear, struggling in their suits and shiny shoes, and Harry felt a little sorry for them. They were collateral damage in the battle for overall authority, a battle that Harry had to win.

Tubbs and Gower were the genuine threats. The fat man continued to brief behind his back, trying to blame Harry for the succession of security failures prior to the invasion. Meanwhile, the post of First Minister of Wales had gone to Griffith's head, calling press conferences at will, imagining himself capable of leading a nation at war.

So, when Harry had suggested an impromptu visit to the frontline, it caught both men off-guard. Neither had declined for fear of those dreaded optics, and now they were floundering in their corporate attire, their equally inappropriately-garbed aides lumbering behind them.

Naturally, Harry had dressed for the occasion. He wore Merrill hiking boots (recommended by Reynolds), baggy green cargo pants, a black fleece, and a camouflaged waterproof smock. On his head he wore a dark baseball cap with a black and grey Union Jack Velcro patch, and as a finishing touch, he wore a sky-blue silk scarf tucked around his neck. Rather flamboyant, he knew, but the public warmed to these things. It set him apart from the others and made him look like a wartime Prime Minister. Watching the spectacle outside, his rivals looked anything but.

A few moments later the convoy lurched forward, driving only a hundred metres along the blacktop before turning right onto a farm track that disappeared into distant hills crowned with thick forests.

Lately, Harry's appetite for public appearances and prolonged meetings had returned. The nervous breakdown was behind him now, and even though he felt an occasional flutter of anxiety, it was easily controlled with some basic mental affirmation mantras. He'd come to terms with Ellen's death, and with the imagined abuse of her remains.

The sudden, violent whirlwind of war that had befallen London would have left many such victims. Too many to count, Harry knew. Children had died too, which was the ultimate obscenity. In the grand scheme of things, Harry's loss barely registered. Ellen had died instantaneously. She was lucky. Harry had been lucky, too.

He was still here, alive and kicking.

The snake of Humvees drove up and over the hills, bouncing and swaying along densely wooded tracks towards the English border. As it wound to a halt beneath vast drapes of camouflage netting strung across the treetops, doors opened and waiting soldiers spread out along the track. Harry stepped down.

'Prime Minister! Welcome!'

A group of officers headed towards Harry, led by a brigadier named Duggan. Like every other uniform, his tired face was smeared with dark war paint, and his shoulders struggled beneath the weight of exhaustion. Harry felt a flash of guilt. He had access to every comfort. These men had been working non-stop for weeks, racing against time. He shook their hands.

'Thank you, brigadier. Lead on.'

Harry turned, watching the rest of the visitors stamping along the track, a gaggle of muddy trousers and ruined shoes. He registered anger on Griffith's face and simmering resentment on Tubbs's rotund countenance. Both men had been robbed of an introduction and relegated to mere bystanders in the eyes of the military men surrounding Harry, and he glanced at his media people, now stood in the shadows, training their compact cameras on the procession as they made their way down the hillside. *Perfect.*

'Almost there,' said Duggan, pointing ahead.

Harry saw the tunnel entrance, where soldiers were piling bags of hard-packed dirt around a timber-framed black rectangle. It looked more like a mine shaft than anything else. The soldiers paused and nodded silent hellos. Harry smiled and projected his voice.

'Good afternoon,' he said, making eye contact with as many tired young faces as possible. 'Thank you all. Keep up the good work. Stay safe.'

And then he was ducking inside, and the log walls and ceilings pressed in beneath the hellish red lighting. The tunnel sloped down and ended at another tightly packed log wall. A wide corridor split left and right, and passing soldiers stopped and stood to attention as Duggan led them into a large room.

Harry watched his political colleagues file inside the low-ceilinged bunker, saw their noses wrinkling at the smell of damp earth and rotting vegetation, saw the unease in their eyes as they absorbed their stark surroundings. Portable lamps threw cold light across a cluster of wooden picnic tables covered with maps, and cables hung on nails looped around the log walls and disappeared into the corridor outside.

It was a sharp departure from the brutalised concrete shelter of SCOTFOR, with its digitised command centre, comfortable seating, and refreshments on tap. Yet Harry was in his element because he knew he was in no real danger. Coming here was all theatre, designed to diminish the reputation of his colleagues and bolster his own, and Harry stood centre stage.

As the last of the aides pressed into the room and the door thumped shut, Duggan and his officers gathered on one side of the wooden tables, whilst Harry, Tubbs, Gower, and assorted chiefs-of-staff and aides, clustered around the other side. All eyes were on the maps that covered the tables. Some were topographical, while others resembled engineering drawings. Harry wasn't sure what he was looking at, but Duggan was about to fill in the blanks.

The brigadier cleared his throat and pointed to a large, colour-coded map.

'I'd like to welcome you all to Sector Four. We are located here, to the west of the Kielderhead National Park. Each sector along the border has its own unique circumstances and geography, so for the purposes of this briefing, I will explain only what's happening here, although much of what I'm about to tell you is replicated in the other sectors.'

'How many sectors are there?' Harry asked.

'Twenty-five, each approximately three miles wide.'

'We don't have enough troops,' Tubbs observed from the far end of the table.

Harry shot him an irritated look. Duggan turned in Tubbs's direction.

'You're right, sir. So let me explain.' The brigadier ran a finger along the map. 'As you know, all road routes into Scotland have been blocked and fortified, so when Islamic State forces advance, they'll have to circumvent the roads and use the countryside. I'm talking about farm tracks, hiking trails, bridle paths, and everything in between. They have the same maps as we do, and they'll attempt to exploit any potential weak points they can find.'

'I take it you've gamed this out?' Tubbs said. 'The weak points, I mean.'

Duggan nodded. 'We have. In fact, we've run over two hundred simulations. We even brought in the Southeast Scotland Wargamers Club.'

Harry raised an eyebrow. 'The what?'

'Wargamers,' Duggan repeated. 'Civilians mostly, but don't let that fool you. They game out battles as a hobby, recreating and fighting them again over table-top exercises. Mostly historical stuff, but they run speculative conflicts too.'

'And these are grown men?' Harry said, failing to keep a note of scorn from his voice.

Duggan nodded. 'And women. I wouldn't dismiss their input, Prime Minister. Their local knowledge is impressive, and their strategic and tactical awareness would put some of my own officers to shame. They've contributed significantly to our preparations.'

'No doubt,' Harry said rather too quickly. From the corner of his eye, he saw Tubbs watching him.

Duggan continued, tracing a finger across the map.

'The closest IS formations are eleven miles away, the larger ones further south and east. And they are gathering in strength—'

'Then let's attack them,' blurted Gower, eager to make himself heard.

Duggan frowned. 'It's not that simple. They're using housing estates, hospitals, and schools as assembly areas—anywhere with large concentrations of civilians. Life goes on in the occupied zone, First Minister.'

Gower's face turned pink. 'What about smart weapons? Cruise missiles and suchlike.'

As expected, Gower had just doubled down on his stupidity. Harry opened his mouth to speak, but Tubbs beat him to the punch.

'A smart weapon can't differentiate between an enemy soldier and twenty kids in a school playground, for God's sake.'

'I didn't mean that,' the First Minister snapped, but the damage had been done. The Welshman knew it too, his face puce with rage.

Duggan continued. 'Targeting enemy formations is off the table, for obvious reasons. So, when they decide to advance, our job is to limit their tactical options. They can't use the west coast routes towards the Solway Firth because we control the Irish Sea, and our naval assets can do a great deal of damage. So, their main thrust will be here, in this central section, all the way out to Newcastle and the eastern coast, which we don't control but is well defended. In summary, the war-gaming exercises have revealed less than a dozen potential routes across the border suitable for mass armoured formations. That's where we'll concentrate our defences.'

Harry leaned on the table, his eyes scanning the maps before him. 'Where are these points? They're not marked.'

'Because they're probably classified,' Tubbs said.

'Correct,' Duggan said, and Harry felt his own face redden. He waved a hand over the table.

'I was referring to general regions. I'm trying to get an idea of how many towns and villages are in the enemy's path, and the potential for collateral damage.'

'Good point,' Duggan said. He raised an eyebrow. 'Perhaps that's a conversation for another time?' He glanced at the suits across the table. 'A smaller audience.'

'Clear the room,' Harry said over his shoulder. He didn't elaborate. Instead, he wondered who would relegate themselves to also-rans. From the corner of his eye, he saw the aides staring at each other while the bag carriers headed for the now open door. Tubbs stood his ground. Gower too.

Harry might be Prime Minister, but behind the scenes, a constitutional battle was playing out. Exiled lawyers were talking to exiled judges, and Lord Advocate Matheson's interim Scottish administration was ignoring all of them, demanding Scotland adopt a neutral position and act as negotiators in a peace deal. Harry had pointed out that Wazir wasn't listening, and most Scots were busy preparing to defend their homeland, not surrender it. Politically, Matheson was a dead duck, but he continued to snipe from the side lines.

The last of the aides, and most of the soldiers, left the room, and the door thumped closed again. Harry stood alongside Tubbs and Gower. Of the two men, Harry considered Tubbs to be the only real threat to his position as Prime Minister. Gower was a tiny king without a tiny throne, a regional lightweight controlled by his own biases and driven by a hatred of anything to do with Westminster. The longer he spent in the company of his contemporaries, the more the man's reputation diminished. Soon he would fade into the background, and Harry would make sure his contribution today, or lack thereof, would leak out. Gower was done, cooked.

Tubbs was a wholly unique problem.

Wherever Tubbs went, he was treated with the respect of a serious politician. He was popular with the average citizen and squaddie, and his tough stance on immigration had been well-documented long before the bomb exploded outside Downing Street. Tubbs laid the pre-invasion security failures at Harry's door, and that argument had traction. People listened to Tubbs.

And worse, the White House had heard of him too. Harry believed that Tubbs's people had reached out to the Mitchell administration. Perhaps Tubbs would try to undermine him. Maybe the Americans would insist on the fat man's involvement in the decision-making process.

Unlike the rest of the team, Tubbs had rejected all of Harry's offers of a post in his administration, arguing that Harry had yet to receive consent to lead any interim government under such unique and tragic circumstances. And he believed Harry wasn't up to the job, a belief he shared with anyone who cared to listen—

'Prime Minister?'

Duggan's voice pulled Harry back into the room. 'I'm sorry,' he said. 'Go on.'

The brigadier nodded. 'As I was saying, come the assault, the enemy's offensive options will be limited. We'll know in advance where they intend to concentrate their efforts.'

'What kind of numbers could we be facing?' Tubbs asked.

'We estimate fifty thousand infantry, with another fifty thousand in reserve, supported by hundreds of tanks and fighting vehicles, long-range missile systems, artillery, UAVs and the kitchen sink if they can throw it at us. Once our arsenals have been depleted, they'll launch an airborne assault, fixed wing, and rotor, and seize the ground beyond the border.'

None of the politicians said a word as the sheer scale of the impending attack sunk in. Harry was the first to react.

'Those numbers have jumped since my last briefing.'

'Dozens of ferries have been docking at east coast ports for the last twenty-four hours. Satellite imagery has revealed huge concentrations of IS troops and armour disembarking at Sunderland and Newcastle. All of it is headed north towards the border.'

'I take it they're using major road routes,' Griffith said. 'If there's little chance of collateral damage, why can't we hit them while they're on the move?'

'As well as troops and armour, IS forces have increased their anti-air capability in the region,' Duggan explained. 'They have a formidable envelope that stretches from coast to coast. A manned fighter-bomber attack would be suicidal and given the amount of hardware spread out across the road network, it would have little effect.'

Duggan spread his hand out on the map.

'As I've said, we've gamed their options to less than a dozen points of entry. Of those, we calculate only four have the potential to funnel the thousands of troops and armour needed to secure a bridgehead. After they breach, they'll link those bridgeheads—including airfields—and use them to surge more assets into Scotland.'

'You talk as if it's already happened,' Gower said.

Duggan waved a hand around the bunker. 'All this only slows them down. The point is to lure them onto open ground, where we can strike a significant blow. What we don't have is the manpower or materiel to stop them. Unless there's a political option?'

'Wazir has the UN in his pocket,' Harry told him. 'Baghdad is demanding the arrest of all British politicians for war crimes. Can you believe it?'

'He's got some nerve,' Tubbs growled.

Gower stared at the table. He was the only man in the room to have flown to Baghdad on an official visit, though he'd never met Wazir in person, just a few of the man's flunkeys. Gower was an embarrassment to his nation, Harry remembered thinking. Not much had changed—

The overhead lights flickered, and the door flew open. Harry glimpsed running uniforms. Warning shouts filled the dead air.

'Incoming!' yelled the soldier in the doorway.

He was barged aside as Reynolds and Cole charged towards Harry, knocking him down to the floor and piling on top of him.

Harry cringed and closed his eyes as a terrible screaming filled his ears—

He felt the impacts through his body as explosions shook the earth. Something hit his leg, but Harry gritted his teeth and kept his eyes closed as the barrage continued. He heard timber cracking and the hiss of falling dirt.

The explosions continued, rattling Harry's teeth, and at one point it felt like the ground beneath him would give way. He heard Reynolds and Cole grunting and swearing, and Harry felt suffocated by their weight. He prayed the ceiling would hold, that he wouldn't be buried alive—

BOOM!

Harry felt his body tossed around, and his ears and mouth filled with dirt. The world turned black...

THE VOICES WERE DISTANT, desperate.

'Here's here!'

'Get him out! Pull his arms, for fuck's sake!'

'Prime Minister! Can you hear me?'

Harry could, just about, but he couldn't speak, couldn't move. There was a dead weight on his back, and he found it hard to breathe. He tasted dirt and spluttered. That hurt his back, his lungs. *I'm dying,*

Harry realised, and his heart raced. He didn't want to die, not here, not in this underground tomb.

And then he felt a hand on his, and another wrapping around his wrist, and then he was being pulled and the weight from his back lifted…

Harry coughed, then choked. Fingers dug into his mouth and then his airway was clear. He vomited. Through watery eyes he saw uniforms everywhere, digging, scraping at the dirt, shouting commands.

'Move him! Now!'

It was Reynolds' voice, loud and hard-edged, and full of authority. The sergeant gripped his left arm, Cole on his right. Soldiers in helmets and brandishing guns cleared the way, scrambling over disorderly piles of fallen logs and mounds of dirt. Harry spat and coughed and moved his legs as he tried to keep up.

'Make a hole!'

The air reeked of cordite and burning timber. Red light turned to grey and then Harry was outside, the breeze cool on his face. He looked down, saw his hands were bloody and filthy, his clothes covered in dirt and mud.

He was surrounded now, a dozen uniforms packed around him, carrying him uphill. Flames reached up into the air as splintered trees burned and smoke churned. He saw bodies lying everywhere, shredded by bright spears of jagged timber. The screams of the wounded echoed across the smoking hillside.

They bundled him into a Humvee, and it sped away, all caution thrown to the wind. Reynolds poured water over Harry's face, and Harry snatched the plastic bottle and swirled the dirt from his mouth, spitting the gritty wash onto the floor.

The vehicle raced down the other side of the hill and towards the pasture. Doors flew open and chopping rotor blades battered Harry as they bundled him into the helicopter. The aircraft lifted off, twisting around, and flying low over grey stone walls and scattering sheep. The side door slammed shut and a helmeted crewman examined him, but Harry was okay. There was no pain, not really. His throat hurt and his muscles ached, and maybe he'd twisted his ankle a little. Maybe.

But the attack had frightened him. All he wanted now was to reach safety. He gestured for a headset and the crewman handed him one. Harry plugged in and adjusted the mic.

'Take me to McIntyre,' he said.

A disembodied voice answered him. Harry assumed it was the pilot. 'That's a negative, sir. Our orders are to transport you to Edinburgh—'

'To hell with your orders! Take me to McIntyre! Now!'

'Stand by.' He saw the pilot talking into his own mic. After a moment, he heard the man's voice in his headset. 'Phoenix is cleared for reroute.'

'Thank you,' Harry said, his tone a little more conciliatory. *Phoenix* was his callsign, and Harry would be the first to admit that he'd risen from the ashes on more than one occasion. Today was a case in point. He saw an Apache slide alongside the Black Hawk and he sat back in his seat. With every passing second, he was further away from danger.

In less than an hour, he'd be home.

IT TOOK a twenty-minute shower and a long, hot bath before Harry convinced himself he'd washed away every microbe of dirt from his body. Doctors had poked and prodded him and treated his cuts and scrapes.

Now, fed, and watered, he sat alone in front of the drawing room fire with a large malt whiskey and reflected on the day.

The bunker had received a direct hit from a random salvo of IS missiles. It didn't happen often but given that senior members of the interim British administration had been on site, an inquiry was already underway to determine blame.

The trip had been Harry's idea, of course, but not his fault. A head would roll, obviously. But Harry would come out of this smelling of roses. So far, the enemy had bombed him, hunted him, shot at him, and buried him alive, but Harry Beecham was still here, still putting himself in harm's way and leading from the front. Or something like that. His PR team would work out the text.

Others were not so lucky.

Brigadier Duggan was in a coma, and Gower and Tubbs were both dead. Harry couldn't help but feel relieved. Gower had been killed by a falling log that had caved in his empty head. Tubbs, however, had escaped with barely a scratch, but it was the shock and the subsequent heart attack that killed him.

So, not such a suitable candidate after all, Harry thought. The briefings against him would lose their impetus, and his near-death experience would be milked to bolster his reputation as a wartime leader.

And he had Wazir's army to thank for that.

Reading the daily summary, Harry saw there was more good news.

The Nord Stream 2 pipeline was open once more, pumping gas into Europe, and although Russian forces now occupied a significant tract of German real estate, they had publicly declared that Mother Russia harboured no hostile intentions other than protecting its own energy infrastructure. As long as the money was pouring into the Kremlin's coffers, they would take a back seat.

So, what lay ahead was another invasion, one that threatened the Scottish border. A hundred thousand troops, Duggan had said. Facing what? Thirty thousand? And those included volunteers ranging from sixteen-year-old schoolboys to sixty-year-old bus drivers.

Dad's bloody army, Harry mused, sipping his drink. British forces had already suffered a surge in desertions, estimated to be somewhere between five and ten percent of total numbers, and Harry didn't blame them. This would not be like past conflicts, where laser-guided bombs were dropped on goat-herders and tribal weddings. The coming conflict was shaping up to be more like World War One. Trench warfare, and hand-to-hand fighting with bayonets and rifle butts. That's if anyone survived the artillery storm that was sure to fall upon the defensive line. Harry shuddered at the thought of what those British troops would soon face.

The border was a land of darkness, a stage set for war. One that British forces would lose. Many would die and die horribly. The thought of more death troubled Harry. He was tired of it, tired of reacting, tired of running. But run they must if they wanted to survive.

A sharp tap interrupted his dark chain of thought and Harry saw Bill Kerr peer around the door.

'Sir, would like something else before I retire for the evening?'

'No, thank you, Bill. Early call tomorrow, please. Six am.'

Kerr nodded and closed the door behind him. The fire in the grate had died a little, and Harry debated throwing on another log. He decided against it, and as the wood burned and the smoke funnelled up the chimney, it reminded Harry of the day's events. The death and destruction. The young kids skewered by exploding trees. Terrible stuff.

And while British soldiers dug trenches, no one was talking about ceasefires and peace deals. Governments of the world remained silent. The UN made noises but failed to criticise Wazir's strong arm and strong words. Nations looked the other way, many relishing in the fall of their former colonial masters, despite Britain bending its knee at the altar of progressive ideology for several decades. Some people, some nations, would never forgive, nor forget. Harry couldn't blame them.

So, they were on their own, and it was time to ask for help. Harry wasn't sure if he'd get it, but it was his duty to ask. Those same friends had been called on before when another enemy had gathered on England's doorstep. They'd answered that call and together they'd been victorious. But this time there would be no D-Day, and certainly no VE day. Crowds would not descend on Trafalgar Square to sing and dance.

No. The only option now was to escape the coming maelstrom that threatened to engulf them all and lay waste to a land that Harry now called home.

He tipped the rest of the alcohol down his throat and picked up the phone beside him.

'I need to speak to President Mitchell. ASAP.'

CHAPTER 80
NEWKY BROWN

GENERAL MOUSA AND HIS CLOSE-PROTECTION TEAM HEADED FOR THE entrance of the Forth Banks police station—now temporary headquarters of the Islamic State's Northern Army Group—as the helicopter behind him leapt back into the air and twisted away over the elevated train tracks.

Mousa took the stairs two at a time to the third-floor and marched along the busy corridor to the newly promoted Colonel Allawi's office, ignoring the salutes around him. While his CP team guarded the outer room, Mousa shook Allawi's hand and closed the door. He dropped into a swivel chair and stretched out his legs. Allawi poured them both a coffee and handed one to Mousa.

'How was the field inspection, general?'

Mousa thanked him and sipped the dark, bitter brew. 'There's another delay. Al-Bitruji is still waiting for his precious LDDs. Right now, they're on a ship, steaming up the Portuguese coast.' Mousa saw Allawi grimace. 'Spit it out, Reza.'

'The longer Al-Bitruji waits, the more time the British have to strengthen their line.'

'They can't be everywhere. They don't have the manpower.'

'The Americans are sending them weapons and ammunition. We've captured dozens of British deserters and they're all telling the same story. The assault could be tougher than we imagine.'

'Have you expressed these doubts with the general?'

'He's not receptive to alternate viewpoints.'

Mousa wagged a finger. 'A good general should always listen to his subordinates.'

'He thinks the LDDs will make a difference.'

'It's possible,' Mousa responded.

The Layered Defence Destroyers were enormous, armoured bulldozers, powered by turbo-charged diesel engines and fitted with giant blades. They were armed with machine guns and grenade launchers and could deliver an impressive storm of fire while demolishing enemy positions, be they buildings or bunkers. The internal troop bay, accessed by a hydraulic ramp at the rear, could hold a platoon of infantry who would then storm the breached fortifications.

'The border defences are formidable,' Mousa said. 'The LDDs might open them up.'

Allawi shrugged. 'They might, but there's not a single, serviceable road between England and Scotland. If they haven't been dug up and mined, the Brits have demolished whole buildings to block them. We're talking rubble several stories high. They're forcing us onto softer, slower ground, which is a concern, especially now that winter has arrived.'

'Does it ever leave these Godforsaken shores?'

'I fear not. Did you visit the frontline?'

Mousa nodded. 'Their engineers have been busy.'

'And they continue to work,' Allawi said. 'These delays only strengthen the British hand.'

'Al-Bitruji assures me they can avoid the major obstacles. His plans are workable.'

Allawi winced. 'Really? Did you see them?'

'The general and I had a robust discussion, in full view of his officers. Al-Bitruji is adamant he can deliver victory. I must take the man at his word.'

Before Allawi could respond, Mousa got to his feet and stood at the window. Down on the street he saw cars, taxis and buses driving by, and people hurrying along the pavements, shoulders hunched, heads bowed. Defeated, Mousa observed.

'I expected more from the British. The caliph did too. In fact, Britain was his chief concern, yet all I've seen from their people is compliance. Especially amongst their political class. Many are so craven, so hungry for power, it turns one's stomach.'

'There's a growing resistance movement. We've had problems here in the city. A couple of shootings, several stabbings.'

'Yet nothing like I imagined.'

Allawi's chair creaked as he leaned back and folded his arms. 'I suspect the cancellation of all individual debt and the favourable dollar exchange rate has much to do with it. We're offering good paying jobs, especially for the unqualified. We need police on the streets, gaolers, security people. The recruitment figures are impressive.'

'Yes, they seem to relish cracking the skulls of their fellow countrymen.' Mousa shook his head. 'Past generations would never have laid down like this.'

'You seem disappointed, general.'

Mousa turned away from the window. 'Life in Britain is returning to normal. We've overhauled their institutions and people have gone back to work. Shops, restaurants, and cinemas are open, and the TV networks are broadcasting once more. Sky and the BBC are feeding the population what we give them, especially revelations of past government corruption and lies. There are fewer soldiers on the streets and more of their own people, albeit in service to the caliphate. They've exchanged one flag for another without so much as a murmur. So yes, Reza. I'm disappointed.'

'A child rapist was executed a few days ago,' Allawi told him. 'Publicly, in a place called Bigg Market. The crowd was far larger than expected. They cheered while the man dangled from the scaffold.'

Mousa took a deep breath and exhaled. 'I rest my case. They have been deprived of true justice for too long. Except for a few disruptive elements, the British have been subjugated. I expected better from them.'

Allawi smiled. 'Maybe the battle for Scotland will cheer you up. How long before you give General Al-Bitruji the green light?'

'Three weeks. Four, tops. Then we'll let him loose. Until then, I want you here, with your eyes and ears open.'

'A month?' Allawi glanced at the window where rain tapped against the glass. 'Wonderful.'

'Keep your chin up, Reza. You'll feel the warm desert sun on your back soon enough. After Scotland.'

'The place will be empty when we get there.'

'People are on the move everywhere. Jews are leaving Israel and our own people are leaving the United States and returning to the caliphate. It's a realignment on a scale we've never witnessed before. These are historic times, Reza. You'll remember them with fondness and tell tall tales to your grandchildren. Never failing to mention the great General Mousa, of course.'

'Naturally,' Allawi smiled. He got to his feet as Mousa paused by the door.

'I'll be back when Al-Bitruji is ready to launch his attack. I'll see you then, Reza.'

His subordinate snapped up a smart salute. 'Stay safe, general.'

Mousa returned it and left the room. 'Summon the chopper,' he ordered his CP team leader. 'We're heading back to London.'

CHAPTER 81
CAMP DAVID

ROBERT MITCHELL PEERED THROUGH THE FROST-CRUSTED WINDOW OF HIS presidential lodge and watched the departing SUV wind its way out of the high-security compound.

Further down the hill, a helicopter waited, its rotors chopping the cold air, the roar of its jet turbines rolling across the wooded slopes. The SUV's brake lights bloomed crimson in the darkness, and then it was lost, sinking behind a thick stand of black birch marching across the ridgeline.

Mitchell's recent guest, British Prime Minister Harry Beecham, sat in the rear of that SUV, returning to Andrews AFB, and from there, to Scotland. And for now, he would travel in ignorance, because his request for help had yet to receive a definitive answer. Mitchell turned away from the window and sank into the deep cushions of his sofa.

Sat opposite him were White House Chief of Staff Zack Radanovich and Eliot Bird, the president's national security advisor. They waited in silence as Mitchell fished into his trouser pocket and extracted a pill from a small plastic box. He popped it on his tongue, then washed it down with lukewarm coffee.

'Blood pressure's up again,' he said, grimacing. He set down his coffee mug emblazoned with the presidential seal. 'Jesus, what a mess.'

'We have options here,' Radanovich told him. 'Saying *no* is one of them.' The chief of staff ran a tired hand through his thick red hair. 'The fact is, the old Europe has gone, and the UK with it. So, what are we really defending? And what if Beecham asks for more? Boots on the ground, maybe? The truth is this country is tired of war. Israel needs to be our primary focus now.'

'Zack has a point,' Bird said. 'Militarily, their position is untenable, and Wazir isn't negotiating. We should give the Israeli situation our fullest attention, because it has the potential for a global disaster.' Bird paused. 'We can't just ignore the situation in Scotland, either. We must do something.'

'What are we giving them now?'

'Satellite data, mostly. Some low-grade human intel from our assets in Baghdad and elsewhere. As much as we can without tipping our hand.'

'What a mess,' Mitchell repeated, shaking his head.

'Question is, can we afford to escalate things with Baghdad right now?' Bird opined. 'Diplomatically they've reached out to us, kept the channels open, left most of our embassies intact, repatriated US citizens from Europe—'

'Half of them in coffins,' Radanovich growled. 'We have to look at the bigger picture here, Mr President. The Islamic State has inherited France's nukes, and the way Europe folded has given their military high command a huge confidence boost. Right now, they think they're invincible. How long before they settle their crosshairs on Israel? Any help we offer Beecham could give Wazir the excuse to make his move.'

'He wouldn't dare,' Mitchell countered, but his words lacked conviction.

The caliphate now stretched from the North Sea to the foothills of the Himalayas. If the worst happened, if old hatreds prevailed and Baghdad launched against America's only remaining ally in the Middle East, then any retaliatory nuclear strike against Baghdad or Islamabad wouldn't make any difference. The destruction of Israel would be total. He pondered the scenario for a moment, the crushing tension in the bunker far below ground, the grave faces of the assembled military personnel, the loud snapping of plastic, the confirmation of the codes.

The order to launch.

Mitchell's blood ran cold. Bird's voice interrupted his dark vision.

'You heard what Beecham said. They're prepared to place their nuke subs under our command should things deteriorate. That's gutsy talk for a guy who's staring down the barrel of a gun.' He glanced at Radanovich, the only Jew in the room. 'The real question is, do we desert our friends when they need us most? If we do, what does that say about us?'

'Damn it,' cursed Mitchell. 'We can't help one without compromising the other. What's the latest out of Jerusalem?'

'Sec State's brief is right there,' Radanovich told him, sliding a buff-coloured *RESTRICTED* folder across the table. 'Baghdad is attempting to maintain cordial relationships with Israel. All diplomatic channels are open, and Wazir has assured the Knesset it harbours no hostile intentions towards its neighbour. They're insisting it's a European problem. Meanwhile, the IDF is on full alert, and Israeli citizens are digging bunkers and stocking up on ammunition and tinned goods. It's precarious.'

Radanovich got to his feet and crossed to the refreshments table. He poured three coffees into white enamel mugs emblazoned with the logo of the United States Marine Corps and handed them around. The president took his, watching Radanovich, noting the worry lines around his red-rimmed eyes, and the runner's frame that appeared to have shrunk even further over the last few weeks. Mitchell recognised the signs. Fear and stress gnawed away at all of them.

'You okay, Zack?'

Radanovich put down his mug. 'Israel will be next, Mr President. We all know it. Fifteen hundred years of anti-Semitism doesn't disappear overnight. Synagogues have been burned to the ground all over Europe. Baghdad is saying it's localised, mob rule, whatever, but it's clear what's really happening.' He took a breath. 'That's how it started in pre-war Germany.'

Mitchell felt the New Yorker's pain. The reports coming out of Europe were indeed ominous. As well as the destruction of synagogues, there were unsubstantiated rumours of mass disappearances and deportations. The fact was, Israel was surrounded by her historical enemy, one that had now conquered Europe. The wagons were circling. No wonder Zack felt troubled. They all were.

'Israel is expecting an attack,' Radanovich continued. 'If Baghdad makes a single, questionable move, the IDF will throw the first punch. That means we'll be sucked into a nuclear shooting war. If that happens, it's game over.'

'Let's pray it doesn't,' replied Mitchell.

'Prayers might not be enough.'

'Then keep a lid on the rumours,' the president growled. 'Do what you have to do. Call the media in, get them onside. We can't let this thing gain momentum, or God knows where it will lead us.'

'Baghdad thinks we're a busted flush,' Radanovich said. 'Our disengagement from Europe and the Middle East has opened up this goddam Pandora's box, and now we'll be lucky if we get the lid halfway closed.'

'Take it easy,' Bird warned his colleague.

'No, he's right,' Mitchell said.

The president stood up and crossed to the stone fireplace. He used a poker to tease the burning logs, dislodging one and sending a shower of tiny embers billowing up the chimney.

Mitchell stared into the flames. He was approaching the end of his first term, and the economy was recovering fast, along with his approval rating, as the media continued to debate the unprecedented economic uptick. Mitchell couldn't take credit for that. He was at the right place at the right time, that's all. Wasn't that the difference between success and failure in life? Luck and good timing?

He took the White House just as they made the breakthrough, and later he'd travelled to the top-secret facility deep in the Nevada desert to witness the energy miracle made possible by the tireless work of generations of faceless men and women after the crash of '47. It was a discovery that could change every life on the planet for the better.

Yet once again, war had raised its ugly head in Europe, threatening that future. Mitchell shook his head. When would humanity learn?

The heat of the fire wrapped Mitchell in its comforting embrace and warmed his bones. At sixty-seven, he wasn't getting any younger. He'd won the party nomination by a slim margin, the presidency by even less. No one had been more honoured, or prouder to serve, than Bob Mitchell on inauguration day. Since then, he hadn't given the American people much to cheer about, but finally, things were turning around.

And now this. What a goddam mess.

His eyes wandered up to the oil painting that hung over the fireplace, a Leutze reproduction of General George Washington crossing the Delaware, leading his troops through the icy river to surprise and defeat the British at Trenton. The physical hardship back then was unimaginable, the sacrifices too many to mention. For Mitchell, the picture said more about the American spirit than any Independence Day speech or schmaltzy movie. He stared at those tiny boats, crammed with revolutionary musket men, as frigid waters broke over wooden bows. The solution was there, right in front of him.

'What were the figures Beecham gave us?'

Bird reached for a printout on the table. 'Ten thousand military casualties in the first twenty-four hours of the caliphate's assault. Civilian refugees, a million at least, all heading north to avoid the conflict. Which they won't be able to. When their backs are finally against the sea, there'll be nowhere left to run.'

'Nowhere,' Mitchell echoed quietly. He studied the painting a moment longer, then he turned to the men on the sofa.

'For as long as I can remember, Britain has been a close friend and ally of the United States. It's been a complex relationship, but what isn't in doubt is the history we share. The blood that ran through the veins of the folks at Jamestown runs through us today, blood that's been spilt on battlefields for centuries, as friends and enemies. It's my belief we're bound by that blood. The United States is tied to Britain in fundamental ways that transcend politics. It's a relationship we cannot ignore.'

'You're going to help them,' Bird said.

Mitchell nodded. 'Not just the Brits. Let me tell you what I have in mind...'

The president spoke for several minutes, and by the time he'd finished, both the chief of staff and the national security advisor were stunned into silence.

'Jesus Christ, that's a big ask, Mr President,' Radanovich said when he finally found his tongue.

'But doable, right Eli?'

'I believe so,' Bird agreed.

'There's a lot to consider,' Radanovich added. 'Security and diplomatic issues, statements of intent—'

'Let's not forget the rules of engagement,' Bird reminded them. 'International waters and air corridors are dangerous places. Anything could spark an incident.'

'Work it out with Sec Def and the NSC. Zack, you speak to State and Justice. I'll speak to the Israeli ambassador and the attorney general myself. And keep Connie up to speed. When the news breaks, the UN and Baghdad will demand answers. She'll need to dismantle any protest from legal counsel. Our case must be airtight, got it? And make sure she reminds the Security Council that American lives have been lost during this conflict. Remind them we won't tolerate the loss of another.' He clapped his hands together. 'Let's get to it.'

As Radanovich scooped up his jacket and left the cabin, the president turned to Bird.

'The military aspect will be delicate. Time is running out, Eli, so we'll have to move fast.'

'We're already at DEFCON Three, Mr President. Mobilisation shouldn't be an issue.'

'Good. I'll need to speak to the NMCC. We'll also need time with Langley and Fort Meade.'

'I'll set it up.'

'The commercial shipping aspect is crucial. I want a conference with the owners of all major lines by the morning. We can't do this without them, Eli, so be nice.'

Bird left the lodge, leaving Mitchell alone. He studied the painting once more. Washington at the bow of the lead boat, wrapped in a thick cloak, his jaw set, heading towards an enemy that was both numerically stronger and technically superior. *And still they followed him.*

That was the true nature of the American spirit right there. Risking life for freedom, and protecting those same liberties paid for by the blood of millions. Now the people of England and Wales laboured beneath the yoke of oppression, while those in Scotland faced an uncertain future. It was time to remind the world exactly what America stood for.

He crossed the room and picked up the phone on the table.

'Patch me through to Prime Minister Beecham.'

CHAPTER 82
EXODUS

HARRY STOOD IN THE CONTROL TOWER OF GLASGOW INTERNATIONAL Airport, watching through binoculars as a US Air Force C-5 Galaxy rotated off the runway and clawed its way up into a leaden sky, its General Electric turbofan engines powering the giant transport aircraft through low cloud until it was out of sight.

'That's departure number eight,' General Bashford told Harry. 'There are fourteen more flights scheduled for today here at Glasgow, and we're seeing the similar numbers at Edinburgh. We're also utilising civilian airliners out of Dundee and Aberdeen, and military transports from the RAF bases at Kinloss and Lossiemouth. Total daily air transport evacuees are roughly forty thousand.'

Harry did the math. The evacuation had been running for seventeen days, which meant almost 680,000 people had already left the shores of Britain. And then there were the ships. The sea routes to the west were a lot slower, but they carried more people, especially the seven giant car transporter vessels supplied by the Americans for the duration of the evacuation.

The smaller ships would head for Iceland, where the evacuees —*refugees*, Harry reminded himself—would board planes bound for the US and Canada. So far, almost 300,000 civilians had left by sea, an astounding feat of logistics by any measure.

The threat of imminent invasion did much to sharpen the mind and lend power to one's elbow, Harry recognised. He focussed his binoculars on a distant C-17 as it taxied for take-off.

'How are things at the border?' he asked Bashford, who'd recently been promoted to full general.

'The enemy has ramped up their surveillance. We've neutralised a lot of UAVs, but they just keep coming. And we're now seeing human assets probing the border defences. They're pretty clumsy, so the thinking is penal troops, kitted out with cameras and mini-drones. They keep our snipers busy, but we've lost some of our long guns too. Their own snipers are proving just as capable.'

Harry hadn't returned to the border, nor did he have any intention of doing so. His near-death experience had been the most terrifying yet, and he had no wish to repeat it. And so, he watched the preparations from afar, by video at McIntyre and SCOTFOR, and he marvelled at the feats of engineering that had taken place from coast to coast.

Particular attention had been paid to the regions where it was predicted Wazir's army would attack, and much effort had been carried out in preparation. That work was almost complete, and not before time. Because war was coming, and all British forces could do was slow the advance.

It was the reason Harry had flown to the US, why he'd sat with President Mitchell at Camp David and pleaded for his help. After a nail-biting wait, the president had called Harry a few moments before wheels-up at Andrews AFB and told him the good news.

And the plan was an audacious one—evacuate every living soul possible from the shores of Scotland. Even now, vast resettlement centres were being constructed across the US and Canada to receive the refugees. But the ships and planes that Mitchell was sending across the Atlantic to collect them were not empty.

'Are the troops getting everything they need?' Harry asked Bashford.

The general nodded. 'It's quite a haul they're sending us, too. Ammunition, grenades, thousands of man-portable anti-tank and surface-to-air weapons, artillery munitions, mines, flares, medical supplies, and it's all being distributed along the front as we speak. The White House is taking quite a risk. Politically, I mean.'

'There's no public support for war over there,' Harry said. 'They're coming out of a long and painful recession. The last thing the US needs now is another pointless, drawn-out military conflict. But we'll take all the bombs and bullets we can get.'

Bashford shook his head. 'It still won't be enough to stop them. The army we're facing is huge.'

'Wazir knows we're evacuating.'

'The entire world knows.'

Harry's no-frills address aired on Scotland's only remaining public network, STV, three weeks ago. He delivered the news that everyone north of the border had feared—England was lost and Scotland would be next. Attempts at diplomacy had failed, and IS troops were massing south of the border. War was inevitable. Whatever the outcome, the future for the civilian population was worse than bleak.

Harry told the public that the US and Canada had opened their doors and were offering the chance of a new life. He urged everyone to register for evacuation. Public demonstrations followed Harry's speech, and much anger was directed at Wazir. So much would be lost by so many; homes, businesses, jobs, friends, relatives, personal property, hopes, and dreams. And the land itself. So, it came down to a simple choice—stay, and face a dangerous and uncertain future, or go, cramming whatever was left of one's life into two standard sized pieces of luggage.

The first to leave were those who lived near docks and airports, evacuated early to clear the approaches for the rest. Women, and children under sixteen were prioritised, along with pensioners, the disabled, and hospital and care home patients. When they had been safely transported offshore, the main evacuation began in earnest.

Hundreds of thousands packed up and drove their vehicles north, east, and west, abandoning them near designated ports and airports. At departure points across Scotland, confiscated luggage filled whole car parks, and flocks of opportunists and thieves picked over the discarded mountains like gulls at a landfill. No one paid them any notice. All that mattered was escape.

The airports themselves had become eerie places, Harry reflected, much like the one he was visiting now. Glasgow International's shops were closed and shuttered, and all lights were extinguished, transforming lounges and departure gates into dark, cheerless halls, where evacuees made their way across windswept tarmacs towards the gaping mouths of US transport planes that swallowed them like plankton.

Other refugees departed on vessels from all around the rugged coast of Scotland, cramming into container ships, rust-stained ferries, and huge white cruise ships. Some of those ships would cross the Irish Sea and dock in Belfast and Larne, collecting evacuees who believed that Wazir wouldn't stop at England's west coast.

As the weeks had passed, more and more people made their way to Ireland's ports and airports, before making the journey into the stormy North Atlantic. The trickle grew to a deluge, which then became a flood. And ultimately, an exodus.

'I'm told many Scots are staying,' Bashford said, watching another US transport plane rotating off the runway and thundering into the grey sky. 'Almost forty percent of the population have yet to register.'

'Many have family trapped south of the border,' Harry told him. 'They want to be here when they make it back.'

'I admire their optimism,' Bashford said. 'I'd probably stay myself if I could.'

'I'll need you in Massachusetts,' Harry told him. 'We'll have to rebuild, reorganise.'

Bashford grimaced. 'The task ahead is going to be huge. The US and Canadian economies will take a hit, trying to absorb three million refugees.'

'Four and a half million, if we factor in the Irish numbers.'

'And all of them will need to be processed, housed, fed. Will the shelter provided be adequate? And what about healthcare and schooling? And jobs?'

Harry offered Bashford a grim smile. 'Welcome to my world.'

'This is way beyond anything we've known.'

'We'll all muck in, Julian. I'll be counting on you and your team to help organise.'

'We'll do our best,' Bashford replied, though he didn't sound confident.

Harry put down his binoculars. 'We should go, head back to SCOTFOR. I want to hear this evening's briefing. Get an update on the border situation.'

They left the tower after shaking hands and Reynolds and Cole fell in by Harry's side as they headed for the waiting Merlin helicopter.

As he strapped in and the aircraft lifted off the tarmac, Harry reflected on the help already given by their North American cousins. And soon the US Navy's 2nd Fleet would head out into the Atlantic to provide support when the attack began. No one knew when that would be, not exactly, but everyone agreed that the pressure was building. Like a storm on the horizon.

Beyond the dark, fortified hills to the south, the invading armies were massing. Soon, the guns would roar, and the battle would begin.

Harry hoped and prayed the evacuation would be complete before it did.

CHAPTER 83
PORKY PIES

ALMOST FIVE MONTHS HAD PASSED BEFORE IS TROOPS GATHERED IN strength at both the northern and southern barricades.

The deception was over, but the troops' arrival wasn't unexpected. Military UAVs and helicopters had overflown the village several times in the past month, and Ross, watching the assembled IS troops at the southern roadblock from a wooded rise, steeled himself for what was coming next. What that might be, no one really knew.

He ran the binoculars over the articulated lorry, and the bulldozer that was reversing off its low-loader ramp in a belch of blue diesel fumes. He scanned the assembled troops, milling around their trucks and Humvees, chatting and smoking, then handed the binoculars to Andy Metcalfe.

'They looked pretty relaxed,' the burly farmer noted.

'Agreed. They could've bypassed those blockades a long time ago, sent helicopters in, but they didn't. I think we might be alright.'

'There's still time for you and the missus to hide out in one of my barns.'

The missus. Ross was still getting his head around the fact that he was married. As the long, hot summer had rolled by, he'd grown much closer to Lara, and their feelings for each other were obvious to everyone around them. The pregnancy was unexpected, but Lara was happy enough, and when Ross went down on one knee, it made her even happier.

The entire village had turned out for the wedding, and the village pub exhausted most of its alcohol supply. Later, in the cold light of day, Ross wondered if it was all happening too fast, if bringing a child into a dangerous and uncertain world was the right thing to do. Now that world had come to them.

'I appreciate it, Andy, but we'll take our chances.'

'They'll make us all register. That's what they're doing all over the place.'

'I know.'

People had passed through South Lockeridge, friends and relatives who'd escaped the cities for a less oppressive life in the countryside. They told tales of Draconian laws and public executions, and the compulsory registration of every single person, man, woman, or child.

Some of those people had kept going, headed for the coast, where passage could be bought on boats heading across the Atlantic or down to sub-Saharan Africa. Or so the rumours went.

Ross had heard those stories too, though no one knew of anyone who'd made a successful journey. The country was cut off from the outside world—no international calls, no internet links outside the UK, no unscrambled satellite networks, and no snail mail. And the news was a constant stream of pro-Wazir propaganda.

'Are you sure you won't hide?' Metcalfe pressed him. 'There's still time.'

Ross shook his head. 'We can't stay hidden forever. Lara will need medical care at some point. We can't risk the kid being born in a barn.'

'It was good enough for Jesus,' Metcalfe winked. 'But you're right. Get registered, get yourselves on the system, and with any luck, they'll leave you alone.' He slapped Ross on the shoulder. 'C'mon. Let's go. The council needs to prepare.'

They rode back to the village in Metcalfe's Land Rover, where the parish council had gathered, along with a dozen other villagers.

The self-appointed reception committee all wore their Sunday best, and all flags and other national symbols had been taken down from every house, shop, and building. Outside the church, poppy wreaths had been removed from the base of the war memorial, and within the boundary of its stone walls, the graves of fallen relatives and ancestors had also been stripped of all symbols of remembrance.

Ross caught a lift back to the farm with Bob, and that night, they'd all eaten an early supper and debated what would happen next.

The shots echoed across the hills just after sunset, the sound rippling away on a cold, gusting wind.

After that, Ross lay awake for most of the night, holding Lara close, listening to the world outside. He expected to hear approaching Humvee engines, to see lights blazing across the windows, but nothing happened, and Ross fell asleep after four am.

At eight o'clock, as everyone was eating breakfast, the geese sounded the alarm as a vehicle bounced along the track. Ross and Bob leapt to their feet and tears welled in Lara's eyes. Helen ushered her upstairs, and Ross and Bob went to the door.

'It's Dale, one of Metcalfe's boys,' Bob said.

He ushered the twenty-something inside, and Ross noticed the kid didn't wipe his feet. Dale Metcalfe wore an old Barbour jacket and jeans tucked into green wellies. His hair was short and spiky, and receding at the temples. Like his three brothers, Dale possessed a surly disposition, and he barely glanced at Ross as he stood in the kitchen. Instead, he looked around the room, his eyes missing nothing.

Bob closed the door. 'What can we do you for, Dale?'

'They want everyone down at the village hall. To register.'

'What about you?' Ross asked him.

Dale turned and stared at Ross. 'What about me?'

'Have you registered?'

Dale shrugged. 'Yeah. So?'

'Is that why they gave you that armband?' Ross hadn't noticed it when Dale first walked in. It was only when the kid turned his body that he saw the black armband with white crossed swords.

'That's so I can travel about. They want me to go to all the outlying farms, get everyone to report to the village hall. ASAP, they said.'

'What shall we bring?' Bob asked him.

'Driving license or passport.'

'So, everything's okay?'

Dale turned back to Ross. 'Course it is.'

'We heard shooting last night.'

'A stray dog bit one of the soldiers.' He cocked his head. 'You'd best get down there. The ladies too, and the little 'uns. And you're to bring all firearms and ammunition. No exceptions.'

After Dale left, Helen and Lara came back downstairs. 'We heard most of it,' Helen said. 'What d'you think, Ross?'

'Sounds okay, I suppose. We shouldn't keep them waiting, though.'

'You get the guns, I'll get our IDs,' Helen told Bob.

Ross pulled Lara to one side. He could see the fear in her eyes. 'Don't worry, it'll be okay. It's doesn't say *policeman* on my passport.'

'What about the guns? The one's you and Faz brought with you.'

'They stay hidden. If they find them, we're done for.'

Lara bit her lip. 'I always knew this day would come, but now it's here, I feel sick.'

'That's the baby.' Ross took her hand and kissed it. 'Maybe you'll find out if your parents have registered. They might let us go and see them.'

Lara brightened. 'D'you think?'

'Why not? You've heard the same stories as me. Life is getting back to normal out there. Under new management, obviously, but the fighting's over. At least for now.'

Lara stepped close and slipped her arms around his waist. 'Tell me it's all going to be okay.'

'It'll be fine,' Ross said, smiling. 'Let's go, get this over with.' As she walked away, he grabbed her hand. 'Just remember what we spoke about, okay?'

'You think—'

'No,' he said, cutting her off. 'But just in case.' He kissed her again. 'Go.'

They drove down to the village in Helen's people-carrier. Ross saw a long queue snaking around the central green and into the hall, which was now a *REGISTRATION CENTRE*, according to the newly strung banner above the doors.

As they climbed out, soldiers searched their vehicle and Bob's shotgun and .22 rifle were added to the pile on the grass, along with the ammunition. They all joined the queue, shuffling past more soldiers perched along the church wall, who smoked and stared at the females. Their weapons were slung or propped against the stone, but the two guards flanking the hall entrance were alert and held their weapons tight.

Inside, more soldiers lined the walls, watching the crowd of villagers. Beneath the stage, tables stretched across the room, and Ross remembered Faz standing on that same stage and talking about hiding the village. That felt like a lifetime ago, and he wondered where Faz was now. Wherever it was, he hoped his plan had worked.

Bob, Helen, and the kids stood in another queue, and Ross saw them issued with freshly printed ID cards. Bob winked as they headed back outside, and Ross gave him a nod. Ten minutes later, it was the Taylor's turn.

Ross and Lara handed over their passports. The clerk sitting behind the table was in his fifties, with pale, freckly skin. He wore an IS military uniform with red epaulettes, and he studied their passports through thick, black-rimmed glasses. When he spoke, he did so with a west country accent.

'I hope these are kosher. I've seen a lot of forgeries. The punishments are severe.'

'They're real,' Ross told him with a smile, wondering how this man could side with the enemy.

The clerk's fingers hovered over a laptop. 'Occupations?'

'Housewife.'

'Farmhand.'

Ross watched the clerk type with stabbing fingers, then he ordered Lara to sit in a chair beside the table. She stared into the camera, and a few moments later the clerk's printer spat out a plastic ID card. He handed it to Lara, and Ross took her place in the chair. The clerk looked at him over the top of his glasses.

'No one told you to sit.'

'I'm sorry. I thought I—'

'Stand up!'

Heads turned in their direction. Ross felt his cheeks flush, part embarrassment, part anger. He felt like dragging the bootlicker over the table. The clerk glared.

'Occupation?'

'I told you, farmhand.'

'Occupation?'

Ross frowned. The clerk must've heard him the first time. He glanced at Lara and saw a puzzled look on her face. In the queue beyond her, other faces turned his way as the clerk's voice rose several notches.

'Occupation?'

'Farmhand.'

The clerk thumped his fist on the table. Blank ID cards spilled onto the floor.

'Last chance! Occupation!'

'I'm a farmhand—'

The clerk snapped out of his chair. 'Liar!'

Soldiers pushed through the queues towards him. Amongst them, he saw another face, a familiar one. One he'd thought of as a friend and ally.

'That's him! That's the one I told you about!' Andy Metcalfe pointed his finger at Ross. 'He's a copper from London. Worked in some fancy control centre. Thought he was Billy Big Bollocks when he first came here. Had a friend with him, a spy or something. Ask him.'

Ross stared at Metcalfe. Every fibre of his being screamed at him to tear the man's face off, but he kept his feet rooted to the floor.

'Walk away,' he whispered to Lara. 'Do it now.'

She backed off, tears streaming down her face, and melted into the crowd. They might talk to her later, squeeze her for information, but Ross had never spoken about his job to her, not in any detail. He'd assumed—correctly—that his profession would be revealed at some point. How that information would be received was always going to be guesswork, but now he knew. Things were about to go downhill. What he needed to do was limit the fallout.

He turned to the clerk.

'He's right, I was a policeman, and I worked in the Operations

Control Centre at Scotland Yard. I came here to escape the fighting, and since then I've done nothing but help around the farms.'

He glanced at Metcalfe, now stood to Ross's left, hands on his hips, a cross-swords armband around his coat sleeve.

Faz had been right about Metcalfe all along. Maybe it was the training, or maybe that's why Faz was MI5 and not a copper like Ross. Because his instincts about people were more sharply honed than Ross's.

Metcalfe had always got his own way around the village, but the big farmer knew the caliphate authorities would never stand for his bullshit. So, he'd sided with them, and Ross wondered how long it would be before Metcalfe was running the village on behalf of his new bosses. Life in South Lockeridge was about to change, and not for the better.

The soldiers twisted his arms behind his back and cuffed them with plastic ties. Ross gritted his teeth. The clerk came around the table and slapped Ross's face.

'Liar!' he repeated.

Ross kicked him between the legs as hard as he could. The clerk went down, and so did Ross as the soldiers beat him. As he curled into a ball, he caught glimpses of angry faces; the soldiers as they rained rifle butts on his body, the clerk, purple faced and writhing in agony, and Metcalfe, enjoying himself as he circled Ross, whacking him with a wooden truncheon. The pain shot through Ross's body, but they never went for his unprotected head, just his arms and legs. *They want me conscious,* Ross realised.

Screams shrieked through the hall. He heard whistles blowing outside and prayed that Lara was still walking away. Rough hands dragged him upright, and pain shot through his bones. The clerk was rolling around the floor, moaning, his hands cupped over his genitals. Metcalfe stepped in front of Ross. He poked the truncheon into Ross's stomach.

'Don't take it personal, lad. The other villagers need to know who's in charge.'

Ross wanted to spit in the man's face, but he restrained himself. Tonight, Lara would be on her own. She was the prettiest girl in the village—in the world, as far as Ross was concerned—and the news that Ross was out of the picture would spread. When it did, some might consider paying her a nocturnal visit. Bob would try to step in, but he had Helen and the kids to think about.

No, with Ross gone, Lara and the baby would be on their own, and knowing that was more painful than any beating.

'Silence!'

The shout echoed around the hall. More soldiers appeared, surrounding an IS officer who wore a green beret and a pistol on his hip. They formed a loose circle around Ross and the writhing clerk.

The officer pointed at the groaning official. 'Get him out of here.'

Soldiers dragged the clerk away. The entire hall was watching, listening. The officer stared at Ross.

'What happened?'

'He's a police officer, sir,' said one of the other clerks. 'He lied about it.'

The officer stared at Ross. 'Is this true?'

'Yes.'

'I already told your people about him,' Metcalfe chipped in. 'I'm claiming the bounty.'

'You'll get it,' the officer said. He raised his voice and addressed the entire hall. 'We'll pay good money for useful information of any kind. Spread the word.' He turned back to Ross. 'So, you're a policeman.'

'Was. I haven't worn a uniform since the invasion.'

'Liberation.'

'Whatever,' Ross replied with a shrug. 'Look, I don't want trouble. I just want to forget the past, get on with my life. My wife's pregnant. I need to be here.'

'He can't be trusted,' Metcalfe said. The officer stared at him until Metcalfe dropped his eyes. He turned his attention back to Ross.

'It's out of my hands,' he said. 'All former police officers must be processed back in London. It's the law.'

'Can't you make an exception? Please?' The officer wavered, and in that moment, Ross's hopes lifted. But the silence of expectation bore heavy on the man's shoulders, and Ross saw his eyes flick to the watching crowd.

'I don't have the authority,' he said in a low voice before turning away. 'Put him in the truck.'

Ross was escorted from the hall, passing people he knew and liked, but none of them made eye contact.

As they marched him across the green towards a waiting truck, Ross searched for Helen's people-carrier and saw it had disappeared. They'd gone home, he hoped, and Lara had gone with them. He saw villagers gathered outside the pub, watching the proceedings, and muttering in each other's ears like conspirators.

The soldiers helped him up and made him behind the cab. It was gloomy beneath the tarpaulin, but Ross recognised the man sat opposite. He'd seen him around the village, but he didn't know his name.

'Scott,' the man told Ross. He had shoulder-length blond hair and wore a British Army combat jacket over jeans. Like Ross, they'd tied his hands behind his back.

'Why are you here?'

Scott winced. 'Thought I was being clever, wearing this. An act of rebellion, see? Andy Metcalfe grassed me up, told 'em I'm ex-army. Didn't matter that I left twelve years ago.'

'He dropped me in it, too. I spent all morning with him, watching that lot gather outside the barricades. He must've chosen a side long before then.'

'He had us all fooled,' Scott grumbled. 'Piece of shit. Still, we're lucky.'

'How so?'

'Last night, Metcalfe and his boys went after Gary Blake, an ex-soldier. The kid deserted a while back, came home to his family.'

Ross remembered meeting the youngster outside the village hall, all those months ago. 'What happened?'

'Metcalfe tried to make a citizen's arrest. He must've known the invaders were coming, see? I guess he had it all planned. Anyway, word is Gary fought back, so Metcalfe shot him. Left his body in a ditch by the road.'

That explained the shots Ross had heard the previous evening, and any hope he had for the future of South Lockeridge faded.

A whistle blew, and several soldiers climbed aboard. The tailgate slammed shut, and the truck roared into life. Scott raised his voice above the growling engine.

'Where are we going?'

'London,' Ross said. 'That's what they told me.'

He caught a look of anguish on Scott's face, then he slumped against the flapping tarpaulin. 'That's us done, then. Cooked.'

'Maybe. Maybe not,' Ross replied, though he didn't feel optimistic. What was in London? How would they be processed? What would their treatment be like? So many questions and Ross had no answers.

The truck crunched into gear and lurched forward, making a slow loop around the village. Ross looked beyond the heads of the soldiers and over the tailgate, catching glimpses of the hall, the snaking queue, the churchyard, and its tumble-down graves. He saw the war memorial and the pub, and the gathered faces staring after the departing truck.

And then they were heading up the lane towards the northern barricade, except the barricade would be gone. South Lockeridge was finally exposed to a new and brutal world, and Ross prayed Lara would be safe in that world. His child too.

The hedgerows flashed by, and the tyres hissed on the tarmac as a heavy rain fell. He saw the distant thatched roofs of the outlying houses disappear as the lane twisted up a gentle rise.

'Think we'll be back?' Scott said.

Ross pretended not to hear, because the voice inside him was a frightening one. It told him to look long and hard at the passing countryside he'd grown to love, to capture its sights and sounds and smells and hold them in his heart for as long as he could.

The same voice that said, *you're never coming back.*

CHAPTER 84
PRE-APOCALYPSE

ACROSS SCOTLAND, THE EVACUATION WAS COMPLETE.

City centres were devoid of human life, the shops, pubs, and restaurants all closed and shuttered against the elements, and the coming storm of war.

Darkened buildings towered over empty pavements. Dead traffic lights watched over desolate roads and thoroughfares, and streetlights stood dark and sentinel. Flurries of snow fell across the landscape of a lost civilisation.

Beyond those once-bustling central hubs, the outlying suburbs looked much the same. Across vast tracts of terraced housing and sprawling local authority estates, homes lay open and abandoned to the elements. The winter winds whistled through open doors and broken windows, and litter scraped and tumbled along deserted roads. Doors and gates thumped and screeched in the icy gusts.

On a Parkhead street in Glasgow, a lone fox, emboldened by its lifeless surroundings, sniffed the air outside an open front door, then disappeared inside, emerging several minutes later with the remnants of a garbage bag hanging from its jaws. There was no-one to chase him away, no objects hurled in its direction. Everyone had left. The fox snuffled amongst the garbage for a few moments, then loped off into the darkness.

Further along the street, faint notes of music carried on the wind, from a home recently vacated, where no one had time to secure the windows or close the front door, nor collect the small, battery-operated TV screen still broadcasting on the kitchen table.

The music stopped. The screen and the room went dark. Then a title card appeared—*IMPORTANT ANNOUNCEMENT*—and remained on the screen for several seconds before a storm of interference blotted out the words. The digital blizzard faded, revealing Harry Beecham sitting in a wing-backed chair, wearing an open-necked shirt and pullover. He looked off-camera, nodded, then stared into the lens. He spoke with a measured voice, his gaze strong and resolute.

'My fellow citizens. This may be the last time I speak to you from here in the British Isles. There was much I had planned for our nation, and for you, its people. My dreams, and yours, were shattered on the eleventh of June. Now, thanks to our friends across the ocean, we can rebuild our lives. We are pilgrims once more, seeking a new life in the New World. The weeks and months ahead will be challenging, but our indomitable British spirit will see us through the turbulent times ahead.'

On the screen, Harry paused and looked down. He seemed to struggle with some inner emotion before continuing.

'Yet many have stayed. Some have gone south to join the men and women of the British armed forces who stand shoulder to shoulder along the border, ready to repel the invaders. We are all humbled by their courage. And the courage of those civilians who refuse to leave, who wait for missing loved ones, who stay by the bedsides of those unable to make the journey west. And the many who simply refuse to give up their birth right.'

He cleared his throat and sipped water from a glass beside him.

'The opportunity to evacuate has now passed. The last ships and transport planes have left. As of midnight tonight, remaining power and communications networks will be shut down for the foreseeable future—'

The TV signal dropped, the screen a brief snowstorm of static. Then the picture and sound returned. Harry's voice was heavy, his brow furrowed.

'Darkness will descend upon us tonight, and it is uncertain when the light of freedom will shine across these islands again. So, I ask all of you to pray for each other, for our brave armed forces on the front line, and for those who have

crossed the ocean to salvage a new life from the remnants of the one left behind. And remember, this is not the end, merely the end of the beginning. Good night, and God be with us all.'

Mousa scooped up the remote control and turned off the TV set. 'Nice speech.'

Allawi shook his head. 'Just another actor reading a script.'

'A decent performance, though.' Mousa used the remote to dial up the T-BIS screen and a map of the border, where large clusters of blue icons faced off against smaller and more widely dispersed red icons. 'I see Al-Bitruji is sticking to his battle plan.'

'Without a single deviation,' Allawi confirmed.

'He smells victory. He dreams of ticker tape parades and cheering Baghdad crowds.' Mousa took a step closer to the screen and studied the icons in greater detail. 'The LDDs are in place?'

Allawi stood next to him and pointed. 'Two at each of the four attack points.'

'Quite a gamble,' Mousa said, scratching the dark stubble around his jaw. 'Come on, let's get some air.'

Mousa switched the lights to red and threw open the door of the command vehicle. He stepped down and breathed in the cold air. His small, four-vehicle command element was hidden below a steep, wooded hillside at the southern edge of Kershope Forest, nine miles south of the Scottish border. All the vehicles were well-camouflaged and none of them were broadcasting on any frequency.

A single relay unit on a distant hill was sending microbursts of digital T-BIS information every thirty seconds. It was no way to direct forces in a major battle, but that was not Mousa's job tonight. For this engagement, he was an observer, nothing more. It was General Al-Bitruji who stood centre stage.

Walking through the trees to the top of a low rise, Mousa and Allawi stopped short of the open ground and looked north, watching the black, rolling landscape. Just then, the wind gusted, bringing with it a few flakes of snow.

Allawi shivered. 'I hate it here. It's always cold, wet, and miserable.'

Mousa smiled in the darkness. 'Now you know how the Romans felt.'

'What on earth possessed them to travel this far north? Their troops were wholly unsuited to the climate.'

'It was more than that,' Mousa said, pointing out into the darkness. 'They feared the warriors who lived over those hills. So, they built a wall instead.'

Allawi turned to his superior. He kept his voice low, mindful of the security team spread out through the surrounding trees. 'Perhaps someone should table such a notion to the caliph. Someone who has his ear.'

'We must let things run their course, Reza. Al-Bitruji is confident he can conquer Scotland. We should give the man the opportunity to prove himself.' He checked his watch. 'Not long now. Let's head back. We don't want to miss the show, do we?'

Allawi led the way back down the rise. Mousa lingered for a moment longer, watching those dark, distant hills to the north.

Then he turned away and followed Allawi into the trees.

INSIDE BRITISH MILITARY HEADQUARTERS, now relocated from SCOTFOR to the Camphill water treatment plant located twenty miles to the west of Glasgow, General Bashford monitored the bank of TV screens broadcasting multiple live feeds from UAVs and static blimps tethered high over the British lines. Around him in the sub surface room, his staff watched too, as bursts of radio traffic from the front filled the stale air. There was nothing any of them could do except wait for the attack to begin.

Bashford knew his troops stood no chance of stopping the caliphate army. The best they could do was slow it down long enough for the survivors to withdraw and head north for the ships, and he prayed there would be enough of them to fill the vessels moored at Greenock harbour to the west of Glasgow—

'Contact! Grid four, sector two!'

The sound of gunfire filled the underground bunker. On one monitor, muzzle flashes flickered like strobes. A red icon glowed on the digital screen, and a female ops sergeant moved a numbered marker across the huge table map. Around him, Bashford's command team spoke in low, calm voices.

'It's another probe.'

'That's twelve in the last hour.'

'Special forces or suicide teams?'

'They'll save their best for the main assault.'

Bashford let them talk and speculate. It helped with the stress, although Bashford's own coping mechanisms had failed some time ago. He was now reliant on pills to combat the strain on his heart. This would be his last action as overall commander. He'd debated stepping down earlier, but he wanted to see it through to the end. His doctor had advised against it, but Bashford's sense of duty forbade bowing out before the final curtain fell.

Yet there was some hope. The IS military machine would be devoid of air cover, at least in the short term. The Americans had delivered two thousand man-portable Stinger missiles, plus hundreds of extra missiles for the Stormer, Rapier and Sky Sabre air defence systems ranged all along the front line and were now cooking the skies to the south with their air-search radars.

In the last three weeks, every IS aircraft that had flown within five miles of the border had been attacked with extreme prejudice. The stubborn defence left flaming wreckage scattered across English hills and IS commanders in no doubt that British air space was an impenetrable wall. When the enemy finally advanced, they'd have to fight their way across the border without significant air support.

And that moment was almost upon them.

As Bashford watched the monitors, he saw flares popping high over the undulating terrain, painting the empty hills and valleys with ghostly white light, and exposing shimmering seas of razor wire, before darkness swallowed the landscape once more. Bashford knew those valleys wouldn't be dark or empty for much longer.

'General Bashford? It's time, sir.'

Bashford turned to the young sergeant at the end of the map table, child-like in her baggy combat uniform. He nodded.

'Send the order. Start the withdrawal.'

ON THE HIGH ground overlooking the abandoned English hamlet of Deadwater, Jim Jakes watched the valley below, one hand covering his right eye as the flare flickered and fizzed to the ground. The light died, and a curtain of darkness rolled back across the steep-sided valley.

Jim's fire bay was buried in the hillside, just below a thick forest of pines that crowned the top of the hill. The cramped bay, constructed of thick pine trunks, gave him a good view of the ground below.

Into the valley of death rode the six hundred...

Jim didn't know who wrote those words, but when the Hajis attacked, they would advance straight at Jim's trench line, and he didn't fancy their chances.

Directly in front of his fire bay, the muddy ground sloped down towards the B6357, a minor, cross-border road that the engineers had broken into pieces a long time ago. They'd also scooped out gigantic pits on either side that had filled with black water over the last few weeks.

The sodden ground around them was sown with tank traps and steel obstacles, so any attacking force would have to veer off the inaccessible road and head straight up a valley that was less than five-hundred meters wide and surrounded by steep, open flanks of gorse and thick stands of trees.

Waiting at the top would be Jim Jakes and another thousand British troops, all manning an extensive trench system of hardened fire bays, rat runs, ammunition storage bunkers, grenade and anti-tank firing points, mortar pits, and casualty evacuation routes.

Jim looked down the slope at the killing ground below, a field of certain death punctured with metal anti-tank stakes and covered in the largest carpet of razor wire Jim had ever seen. Even now he could hear the wind whistling through its layers, a sea of sharp metal sown with anti-personnel mines.

No, he didn't fancy the Haji's chances at all.

Jim brought his Sig Sauer 516 G2 carbine up to his shoulder and squinted through the Trijicon LED combat scope. His adrenaline was pumping, like it did down south, when the mob had stormed the fence of that industrial estate and the Haji armour headed up the road towards them.

Back then, he'd been caught between a rock and a hard place, but he'd survived. Would he be so lucky this time?

He heard a muted roar, then a thump and a crunch somewhere down the slope. He scanned the sea of wire through his scope.

'It's another drone,' the soldier standing next to him said, a low-light scope pressed to his eye. Kyle was a recent addition to Jim's fire bay, and Jim was glad of the company. Both men had spent the day shoring up the log roof, loading magazines and sharpening their combat knives.

Kyle was armed with an M4 assault rifle, and both men had piles of magazines stacked on a rough timber shelf just below the firing slit. They had grenades too, and in boxes against the back wall, more ammunition. The other soldiers along the trench line—specifically, grid four, sector two—also enjoyed a glut of ammunition and weapons, most of it courtesy of Uncle Sam.

'I can see it down the hill, ten o'clock, two hundred meters.'

Jim looked through his scope and saw it, too. The UAV's body was broken in two and smoke belched from its engine. Anti-aircraft teams had been taking them out all day using signal-blocking transmitters, while the enemy did the same to Brit drones, so both sides were pretty much in the dark when it came to low-level surveillance.

The wind blew, and Jim saw the sea of wire shimmer. He looked at his watch. 'Think it'll be tonight? The tension's killing me.'

'No idea,' Kyle said. 'But it's got to be soon.'

Jim heard running feet in the trench outside. A camouflaged face appeared in the small, reinforced doorway. 'Grab your gear. We're pulling back to the shelters.'

Kyle grabbed his day sack and magazines. 'Here we go.'

'Could be another drill,' Jim said, stuffing mags inside his patrol bag.

'I hope not.'

They picked up their weapons and gear and headed out into the trench, pushing into the long line of troops filing through the deep, log-lined trench system.

'Keep moving! No talking!'

The whispers were sharp and urgent, and no one needed telling twice. Jim followed Kyle, turning left and right at corners lit by fluorescent green chem sticks. There were other colours too; red for ammo stores, purple for med supplies, orange for the anti-tank runs—the tunnels that led further down the hill. At the end of each one was an open hole with a log step, where Javelin teams would pop up, fire their weapons, and take cover again. Jim was glad he wasn't one of them.

They turned another corner, passing the now-empty mortar pits, and headed deep beneath the hill. In cramped side tunnels, Jim saw the dead-eyed, mud-streaked faces of a Royal Engineer team digging with shovels. Since Jim had first seen them, those teams hadn't stopped working.

'Watch your feet,' a voice hissed in the semi-darkness. 'Trip hazard.'

Jim looked down and saw the black and yellow striped covers on the floor. He stepped over them, and the tumble of thick wires sprouting beneath them.

Heads ducked as the trench became a tunnel that cut beneath the hill. When they emerged on the other side, it angled down into a vast underground bunker. Jim saw the bodies crammed in there, but there was no choice. When the artillery storm came, it was better to be below ground.

As they packed inside, Jim felt his breathing quicken, and he worked on slowing it down, taking deep, measured breaths. The air became thick and stuffy as more soldiers pressed inside, and then, for the first time since they'd drilled the trench evacuation, someone sealed the heavy pine door with an airless *thump*.

No one said a word. All Jim heard were a few coughs and a couple of confused whispers.

'Quiet,' said an authoritative voice near the door.

Jim heard the hiss of a radio, and a faint, garbled message. Kyle nudged him with an elbow. Jim held his breath. The passing seconds felt like hours. The tension in the bunker stretched to breaking point.

Then that same voice spoke again.

'This is it, lads. They're coming.'

Harry Beecham hurried across the gravel courtyard of McIntyre Castle, an overnight bag in his hand.

There was no moon, only the reflected light of a recent dusting of snow, and an icy wind gusted through the surrounding forest. He veered away from the small party waiting for him and headed towards two figures dressed in full combat gear.

Harry set his bag down and thrust his hands inside his coat pockets. The two men stood before him were barely recognisable, their bodies covered with equipment and weaponry, their faces streaked with dark camouflage paint.

'Gentlemen,' Harry said, unnerved by their appearance. Reynolds and Cole smiled and nodded their heads.

'Evening, boss.'

Harry tried to smile too but failed. 'Well, this is it then.' He studied his shoes for several moments, unsure of his words. 'Thank you just doesn't seem enough. I owe you both my life.'

Reynolds shrugged. 'That's the job.'

Harry shook their hands. As he did, he kept his voice low. 'I could order you to stay with me, get you both out of this God-awful mess.'

Reynolds shook his head in the darkness, his breath fogging on the cold air. 'Tempting, but not this time. Not while the rest of them are holding the line.'

Harry knew they needed every uniform on the border. Offering a way out to men like Reynolds and Cole was almost insulting. 'I had to ask, you understand?'

'Sure.'

'Take care of yourselves. And try not to do anything too brave or too stupid, okay?'

'Can't guarantee that,' Cole smirked.

'Good luck, then.'

'Likewise,' Reynolds said.

Harry turned and walked away. Ahead of him, shadowy figures waited, breath freezing in the frigid air. Beyond them, the Dark Eagle idled on the lawn, its rotors spinning slowly as it prepared for imminent departure.

The figures closed in around Harry as he approached. Two of them were soldiers, replacements for Reynolds and Cole. The other two were military officers whom Harry had only just met.

'We really must push on, prime minister. The attack could start at any time now.'

Harry nodded. The troops around McIntyre had left an hour ago to bolster the defensive line, leaving only a single platoon of soldiers behind to provide security. As soon as Harry was airborne, they'd head south too.

Harry turned to look for Cole and Reynolds, but they'd disappeared into the woods, where troop trucks idled on the road beyond the trees. All that remained were their boot prints in the snow.

Harry's eyes travelled across the familiar silhouette of McIntyre Castle, a place he now called home, and a place he doubted he would ever see again. He struggled with a sudden knot of sadness. Time passes, and things change, even more so in wartime.

'I'll look after her,' Kerr said. 'She'll still be here in another five hundred years.'

'You read my mind.' Harry forced a smile. 'You can still join us, Bill. There's plenty of room on the chopper.'

Kerr shook his head. 'This is my home, my country. I'll not desert them.'

Harry couldn't help but feel the sting of the old Scot's words. Still, he gripped the man's hand. 'Take care of yourself, please. Stay safe.'

'Come back and see us,' Kerr said with a smile.

Harry turned and stamped towards the helicopter. A few moments later, the aircraft lifted off and headed north. He caught a final glimpse of a tower, and then she was gone.

Harry left McIntyre Castle as he'd found her, in the black of night, by the windswept shores of Kerrera Sound.

CHAPTER 85
CONTACT FRONT!

'Steady, lads. Steady, now…'

Jim heard that same calm, comforting voice, full of experience and authority. A Warrant Officer, probably, with a couple of decades of ops under his belt.

Jim closed his eyes and focussed on that voice as the earth shook beneath his boots and the log ceiling threatened to collapse onto his Kevlar helmet. The only light in the room was a green chem stick above the sealed door, and Jim wanted to push his way over to that door, because any moment now, the bunker would take a direct hit and that would be game over. No need for burial teams, just plant a cross in the ground and walk away. Instant mass grave. Or worse, survive the impact and die of suffocation beneath tons of earth and corpses—

'They're shifting fire. Switching targets,' the voice said. 'Feel that? Them's rockets. Small stuff, lighter, not like the big arty shells. Won't be long now, lads. Then we'll show 'em, make 'em bleed.'

The voice was right. The detonations were not as powerful, and the tremors now lower on the Richter scale. Jim looked at the surrounding soldiers. Kyle's face was streaked with dirt and cammo cream. He winked and grinned, and other helmets started tilting up, no longer staring at the ground that threatened to swallow them.

Thump! BOOM!

Dirt rained down from above. Jim's heart rate took off like a rocket. He bit his tongue as other voices cursed and whimpered.

'A lucky round,' the voice said, still so calm. 'Close, but no cigar, fuckers.'

Jim heard muted, strained laughter. He smiled as he stared down at his boots, but it didn't last long. The log door opened and the smell of burning timber reached Jim's nostrils. Outside, he saw a red glow.

'This is it, lads! Back to your positions! Go!'

Jim shuffled with the crowd towards the door. He passed the Warrant Officer, saw a grizzled face beneath the rim of his helmet, and a serious, old-school moustache beneath a hooked nose.

'Keep moving, boys! Look after each other! And when come, give 'em hell!

He slapped Jim on the shoulder as he shuffled past, and then Jim was outside. Above the walls of the trench, trees burned across the ridgeline. Smoke trails raced across the sky, heading north to south.

'Counter batteries,' Kyle said, looking up. 'They're getting a taste of their own fucking medicine.'

They passed through the tunnel where the engineers were still working. The crowd packing the trench walls thinned out as troops disappeared into their defensive positions, clambering over collapsed log walls and smoking shell craters.

Jim hurried down the line until he reached his fire bay and saw it was still intact. He ducked through the doorway, emptied out the magazines from his daysack, and threw it in the corner. Stooping beneath the low ceiling, he set himself up at the fire slit, setting the barrel of his Sig on a sandbag, and placing his mags on the shelf. Kyle did the same, and both men peered out through the narrow aperture.

'Oh Jesus,' Jim said.

'Oh fuck,' Kyle whispered.

The artillery storm had shredded the sea of razor wire as far as they could see, which wasn't that far given the pall of white smoke covering the whole valley. All they saw now was a muddy slope dotted with slivers of silver wire and a moonscape of smoking craters. The booby traps, the tank obstacles, they were all gone, and neither soldier could see more than a hundred meters.

They stared through their scopes, searching for an enemy they knew was out there. Nothing moved except the twisting, curling smoke, and the only sound Jim could hear was his own breathing as his breath fogged in the chilly air.

Boots ran past their fire bay, then faded, and the oppressive silence rushed in once more.

'Maybe they're not coming,' Kyle whispered.

'They're coming, trust me.'

That's when Jim heard it, a distant clanking of steel, the roar of diesel engines, and the grind of caterpillar tracks echoing over the hills.

'Game on,' Kyle said, his eye pressed to his scope.

Flares popped overhead, but their white light only reflected off the smoke, throwing shadows across the open ground, shadows that moved—

The fire bays to Jim's left opened up, and Jim fired too. He had no targets, but the tension was too much. Kyle had his spotter scope pressed to his eye.

'I can't see shit!'

The noise grew louder, a demonic screeching that filled the valley and rolled up the slope towards them. Jim felt a sudden urge to urinate. He stared down the hill and saw only broken twists of razor wire and mud. But that dreadful sound was growing. And now, accompanying it, the blast of whistles and the screams of men.

Not screams, Jim realised. Battle cries. It was like a tsunami coming towards them, one that neither man could see.

Kyle yelled in Jim's ear. 'We should've opened fire by now!'

'Stand by,' Jim told him. He rested his grenades in a neat line on the shelf. He touched his knives, one on his right thigh and one in a scabbard on his tactical vest. His Sig pistol was cocked and chambered. It was going to get ugly. Hand to hand shit.

Jim was ready.

'C'mon you fuckers,' Kyle muttered, moving his barrel left and right. 'Show yourselves.'

Jim saw the smoke swirl again, violently this time. A sudden wind whipped around the fire bay, and then, across the slope below, the fog of war lifted, like a curtain being pulled back…

Jim's mouth dropped open, and his heart hammered in fear as he watched two monstrous bulldozers climbing up the slope towards the trench line, each the size of an articulated lorry and twice as wide. Behind them, spread out across the entire width of the valley, tanks and tracked gun platforms twisted and turned, firing smoke. Behind the armour, more troops than Jim had ever seen. The scene was like an ancient battle.

Kyle opened fire.

The entire sector opened fire.

Tracers lit up the night, a constant stream of red lasers that pinged and ricocheted off the blades of the giant dozers. Mortars rained down, exploding with little effect amongst the armour.

Jim fired at the infantry scrambling through the cratered terrain, but it was difficult to tell if he was making a dent. There were thousands of them, using the armour as cover, the outliers firing their own guns.

Incoming rounds raked the trench line, everything from 30mm cannon, 20mm mini-guns, and small arms. A storm of gunfire chewed up the mud in front of their trench and both men hit the deck.

Jim scrambled back up and continued to fire, targeting the infantry through his LED scope, aiming for their legs. He watched some fall, tripping those behind them, but still they marched on, relentless.

From the anti-tank murder holes, Javelin missiles thumped and whooshed as their crews launched round after round at the approaching dozers, but the missile ricocheted off the enormous blades in dizzying trails of smoke and sparks.

The metal monsters kept coming, their giant caterpillar tracks whipping up rooster tails of dirt as the closest one headed directly for Jim's fire bay. Packed behind it, hundreds more troops, and beyond them, more tanks and armour. And still more troops.

The sky was alive with flares, the battlefield bright beneath their harsh light.

'They got one!' Kyle said, grinning.

Jim followed his gloved finger and saw an Abrams tank two

hundred meters out, spinning around on one working track as Javelin missiles rained down onto its thinner turret armour. The tank blew, a spectacular explosion that took out two passing mobile guns.

The slope was now a quagmire of mud, blood, burning vehicles and thousands of screaming, yelling troops. Jim heard the calls over the radio, the orders to target the armour. Outgoing rounds swarmed all over the dozers and battle tanks, but there were too many of them, too many troops—

Boom! Boom! Boom! Boom! Boom! Boom!

Great geysers of earth erupted into the sky as British artillery rained down across the valley, obliterating vehicles and sending bodies spinning through the air. The barrage lasted for thirty seconds, then stopped.

As the thunder echoed away across the hills, enemy troops picked themselves up and marched on, scrambling to keep up with the giant dozers, now scarred and blackened, but still advancing towards the British trench line.

Jim's heart was in his mouth, but his mind was calm, his movements smooth. He changed magazines with practised speed, and when the dozers were less than a hundred meters away, he ducked outside the trench and threw grenades as far as he could. He knew he was going to die, but he was so jacked up on adrenaline he didn't care.

Beneath the flickering light of multiple flares, fresh snow fell in violent flurries. The slope immediately below their position was an undulating mass of caliphate troops and tracked vehicles, crossing the cratered earth towards them.

Jim looked to his left. All along the sector, the enemy was edging closer, and tank and grenade rounds began chewing up the British lines. The noise was tremendous, the screams ugly and terrifying. Jim targeted a mob of infantry massed behind a six-wheeled AFV sliding through the mud. He emptied one magazine into their massed ranks, then two, watching the Hajis falling like skittles, losing their momentum, returning wild fire.

But they were close now. So close, Jim could hear their commanders yelling orders.

He kept shooting.

. . .

Thirty-two RAF Typhoon fighters thundered south, hugging the earth at dangerously low altitudes. They were split into four groups of eight aircraft, and each formation headed for one of the four sectors where IS commanders had concentrated their attack.

As they approached the combat zone, British anti-aircraft teams shut down their air-search radars, opening up the sky to enemy aircraft.

The Typhoon pilots knew they were playing a deadly game, so they flew their planes at two hundred feet above the ground—and often lower—to avoid enemy radar and mobile SAM teams.

The pilots pushed on, rocketing across the Highlands, thundering through dark valleys and over black lochs. Roads, buildings, and forests flashed beneath them, barely visible in the darkness.

'Reaper flight, one minute to target.'

The flight leader banked his aircraft to port, watching his altimeter, noting the new contacts on his threat receiver. Enemy fighters were headed their way now that the British air envelope had been shut down, but that wouldn't last long. Just enough time for Reaper flight, and the three other flights, to complete their mission.

He levelled out his aircraft and flew parallel to the border. A few miles ahead, he saw the white glow of the target and pressed his mic switch.

'Climbing.' The other planes followed him up to five-hundred feet. Ahead, he saw tracer and flares filling the sky ahead. 'Arming weapons.' As the plane thundered over Deadwater, the pilot glimpsed the carnage in the valley below. He pressed the trigger. 'Bombs gone!'

He felt the *clunk* of the weapons' release, felt the aircraft nose up, and he pushed his stick forward, banking over the ridgeline before heading north on full afterburner. One by one, his flight weathered the storm, dropped their munitions, and followed him out.

The pilot's threat receiver was alive with hostile contacts.

. . .

THE HEAVENS ROARED, and thunder ripped the sky apart. Jim barely registered the aircraft overhead before the slope erupted in fire and mud. He hit the floor and Kyle fell on top of him. The earth shook and bright light pierced Jim's tightly closed eyelids. He felt the detonations through his body, and then the thunder rippled away, and all Jim could hear was the roar and clanking of the approaching monster.

He scrambled to his feet. Kyle was already up and firing.

'Air strike!' he yelled. 'One of ours!'

Jim saw the devastation across the slope below—burning armour, thick black smoke, swirling snow, but the enemy was still advancing, screaming now, bayonets fixed on their weapons.

He looked up and saw missiles criss-crossing the sky. It felt like the end of the world. He aimed, fired, switched aim, fired. Enemy soldiers were hard-targeting towards him, shooting, throwing grenades. Jim's gun clicked empty. He ducked down to change magazines, and the fire bay filled with white light—

BANG!

Dirt and splintered wood rained down on his back and legs. The firing bay had collapsed, the support logs shredded. He dragged himself free and got to his knees, coughing, spitting, scrambling for the grenades scattered on the muddy ground. He snatched them up and pulled the pins, throwing them out through a gap between the collapsed timbers. Sharp bangs and terrible screams told him he was doing damage. Then he heard something else—whistles, lots of them, shrill and insistent, ringing out over the ridgeline.

That was the signal.

Loose dirt fell like rain. Timber logs trembled. Jim saw the dozer, as big as a house, less than twenty meters away, roaring up the slope towards them.

'Move, Kyle! Go!'

But Kyle was dead on the floor, his face and throat ripped away, his sightless eyes staring into nothing. Jim scrambled outside and into the fast-moving current of British troops. Behind him, he heard the sharp crack of detonating grenades as the enemy closed in on the line.

He turned a corner, then another. Hands ripped off the green chem sticks as they made good their escape beneath the ridge. Jim funnelled down the other side, towards the waving, shouting figures who told them to run for the trees.

To keep running.

And don't stop.

THE LDD BORE down on Jim's abandoned trench and crushed it beneath its tremendous weight. Inside his cramped seat, the driver heard the on-board gunners firing as the vehicle shuddered to a halt.

The sound of battle leaked into his headphones, but the angry voice of his commander was louder, ordering him further up the hill, away from the open ground. He didn't need telling twice. The British planes had come from nowhere, cooking dozens of vehicles and hundreds of men.

The driver jammed his boot on the accelerator. The giant bulldozer roared and shuddered, but it didn't move. He heard cursing voices from the troop bay behind him, and he cursed them back. This wasn't like the war games on the hard-baked earth of the North African desert. Here, the slope was rising steeply, and the ground was a quagmire.

As he de-clutched, the driver felt the LDD slipping sideways. On his rear camera, he saw his tracks thick with cloying mud as he slipped further along the hill. The commander was shouting in his earphones and the soldiers yelled more abuse. He heard screams through the thick armour and glanced at his monitors. Outside, he saw men falling beneath its giant tracks, screaming as their bodies were chewed and pulped.

He cursed and dropped gears, gunning the engine, and then the LDD gained a little purchase, accelerating once more, bouncing over broken logs and a dozen more of his comrades before he reached the crest. The blade reared up, and the LDD crashed down to earth at the top of the ridgeline with a deep, seismic concussion.

He heard the rear ramp fall and the infantry stampede outside, splitting left and right, ready to engage the British.

The driver frowned as he looked at his TV screens.

The trenches were empty.

. . .

IN THE SKIES above the border, IS planes pushed their throttles to the stops and chased after the British aircraft. Within seconds, their threat receivers lit up as the Stormer, Rapier and Sky Sabre air defence systems positioned behind the border came back online.

More British troops, stationed on high ground overlooking the battle zones, heard the frantic warble of their Stinger missile targeting systems and launched their weapons.

Seconds later, the vengeful IS pilots were banking hard over and running south as the air filled with more incoming missiles than their systems and reactions could cope with. They fired flares and decoys, but the swarm headed towards would not be deterred.

Less than five minutes after crossing into Scotland, over thirty IS planes were blotted from the sky and fell to earth.

The survivors raced at low level for the safety of the hills to the south.

'ALL SECTORS HAVE ACKNOWLEDGED the withdrawal, general.'

'Pull the Sky Sabre and Stormer units out. Tell them to head for the ships. Leave the Rapiers on autopilot. And pull the Stinger teams, too.'

Bashford turned his attention to the remaining working feeds on the monitors. Most were broadcasting live footage of IS troops spilling into the vacated British positions, but Bashford focussed on one particular feed.

On that screen, he could see stranded British troops fighting hand to hand in a trench. No one spoke as the silent, grisly scene played out in real-time. Someone reached up to turn it off. Bashford barked.

'Leave it! We owe them that much.'

He watched the fight play out, saw gunfire, watched men stabbing each other, swinging rifles and shovels. He saw enemy troops gather above the trench and fire down into it until all the British were dead. It was Bashford who broke the silence.

'Status?'

The young female sergeant answered him. 'Hard to say, sir. Some sectors are reporting fifty percent casualties. We won't have a final count until everyone gets to the ships.'

Bashford turned to the Royal Engineers colonel.

'Are you ready?'

The man nodded. 'Green lights across the board, all four targets.'

Bashford turned back to the monitors.

'Let's give them a moment to savour their victory.'

IN THE FOREST of Brunshiel Hill near the Cumbrian border, Mike Reynolds ducked low as rounds whizzed and cracked above his trench.

For the last twenty minutes, Reynolds and his fellow defenders had kept a superior enemy force at bay with sustained heavy weapons fire, mortars, and anti-tank rounds, but the line had been breached somewhere to the west, and now the enemy were behind him, and in force.

He could hear them shouting, firing, throwing grenades. He no longer heard anyone talking English.

He'd joined a small SF element amongst a mixed group of Paras and Rangers, and they'd fought hard, but now they were all dead. Reynolds found himself at the end of the trench line, the forest close behind him. He'd heard the whistles, the signal to withdraw, but the enemy was too close and the incoming too heavy.

So, they'd stayed and fought until the first Haji had jumped into the trench and detonated his suicide vest. Then another wave had charged, spilling into the trench, and they'd fought toe-to-toe. Reynolds had his pistol in one hand and a knife in another, and he'd killed four of them, but he'd been wounded, the round shattering his ankle. It hurt like a bitch too, but that didn't matter. The pain wouldn't last much longer.

Now he was alone, surrounded by the dead. He leaned against the rear wall of the trench and listened. In the trees behind him he could hear gunfire, but it was petering out, replaced by the voices of the enemy, calling to each other, sounding off.

Reynolds looked down at Gaz Cole, his head connected to his body by just a few tendons. A screaming Haji had done that with a machete. Reynolds had shot the man and stabbed him in the eye. Reynolds hopped towards the end of the trench, his ankle a hot iron of pain. He tried his radio, but he couldn't raise anyone.

A dark shape loomed above him. Reynolds fired twice, and the figure dropped out of sight. He heard boots pounding and twigs snapping behind him. He spun around and raked two dark figures heading right for him. They went down, one silent, one screaming in pain. Reynolds raised himself up and shot him again. The screaming stopped—

The punch struck his back, slamming him against the trench wall. He twisted around and saw a silhouette charging out of the snow flurries. Raising his carbine, he fired a single round and missed. The gun clicked empty. He dropped it at his feet and drew his pistol. A round zipped past his head. He double-tapped the guy and his attacker fell dead.

Reynolds collapsed against the trench wall. His chest hurt and he was having trouble breathing. He yanked off his glove and felt under his left armpit. His fingers came back wet and sticky. He didn't bother picking the glove back up. It was too much trouble.

His legs gave way and he slid down the log wall. As he sat on the dirt floor, he struggled to take a deep breath, and a vice squeezed his chest. He heard movement close by. With the last of his strength, Reynolds pulled the pin from a grenade and lobbed it over the top. The weapon blew, and he heard a scream.

Then things got very quiet.

Snow drifted through the pines, white flakes against black shadows. He'd had a good run, better than most. He'd been places, seen and done things that most people—including his fellow soldiers —would never see or do. He'd been lucky, but now his luck had run out. That was fine with him.

Never look back, his dad had once told him. Now, as his life ended, he wondered what was next.

He heard whispers above the trench. He tried to raise his pistol, but for the first time in his life, Mike Reynolds had nothing left to give.

The grenade landed in the mud next to him.

He closed his eyes.

ON THE RIDGELINE ABOVE DEADWATER, the driver of the LDD lit a cigarette and inspected the hole in the ground into which his giant bulldozer had sunk nose-first.

The collapse wasn't an immediate one, and the driver hadn't noticed the ground giving way until he saw the rear ramp in the troop bay rising into the air. By the time he'd got the engine started again, the ground had deflated, and the giant blade was dragging the whole damn thing below the earth.

The driver had promptly abandoned ship and now stood, scratching his head, as the LDD angled into the ground like a dog burrowing in a rabbit hole.

It wasn't his fault. He'd simply followed orders, but the problem still needed solving, and that was above his pay grade. He looked around for an officer, but all he saw were columns of muddy troops trudging up from the valley below and crossing the ridgeline before heading down the other side.

As he took in the scene around him, the driver realised how lucky he'd been. Across the narrow valley, vehicles burned, and some of them were still exploding as the fires ignited ammunition. Closer to the British trench line, the ground was thick with mud and bodies, and he thanked God he drove an LDD.

He watched long columns of soldiers heading down through the forest of decapitated trees into Scotland and wondered how many of them it would take to drag his baby out of the hole. A lot, he reckoned.

As he walked around the edge of the crater, his boot caught something, and he fell headfirst into the mud. Passing soldiers laughed and jeered, and the driver got back to his feet, flicking freezing mud from his hands, and wiping them on his trousers. Never again would he complain about sand and heat.

He saw the offending loop sticking out of the ground and crouched down, running the thick, rubber-coated cable through his fingers. Maybe they were telephone wires? Or data cables? He plied and twisted the thick black sheathing. It was tough, and probably too strong for telephone wire. What was it then?

He yanked at it, and a long length sprang up out of the hole made by the LDD. He skirted the cave-in, tugging at the mystery cable, exposing more of it.

As snow fell in fierce flurries, the driver followed the cable across the hilltop and found a big, rubberised junction box half-buried in a shell crater. From its tough, green body, more mud-covered cables led off in different directions.

Strange, the driver thought.

The cables ran all over the ridgeline.

On a wooded rise seven miles to the north-west, a Royal Engineer captain, riding shotgun in a Foxhound patrol vehicle, ended the brief satellite phone call. He turned to his sergeant sitting in the rear compartment. 'Now.'

The sergeant nodded. 'Firing.'

He tapped the green icon on his REACHER satellite-enabled command unit, and an x-band comms packet fired from the small dish on the roof of the Foxhound and bounced off a Skynet satellite to a waiting receiver mast camouflaged in Scottish woods close to Deadwater. The comms packet was a firing command, and within three seconds of its transmission, the order was received and executed.

The sky to the south lit up with the intensity of a nuclear detonation, a pulse of white light that bloomed and shrank, then bloomed again, followed a second or two later by the loudest explosion any of the engineers had ever heard. Beyond the horizon, similar flashes flared and died, and the sky rumbled with manmade thunder.

'So, that's what two hundred tons of TNT looks like when it blows,' said the sergeant, standing outside the rear door of the Foxhound.

Beside him, the captain pointed into the distance. 'That's four successful detonations. Solid work, Sergeant P.'

'We should go, sir. Those ships won't wait.'

The engineers climbed aboard and slammed the doors shut. The driver started the Foxhound's engine and drove off down a firebreak, re-joining the tarmac and heading west to link up with the A74 that would take them north to Glasgow.

Behind them, the sky above the border glowed red.

MOUSA STARED at the T-BIS screen. Specifically, he was staring at the four dark areas where a short while ago there had existed large clusters of blue and green icons.

'How many?' Mousa asked, his boots perched on the console.

Allawi tapped the screen. 'All four penetration points have been obliterated, general. First reports suggest they used pre-buried, non-nuclear munitions. The attack has stalled.'

'So, it wasn't just trenches they were digging.' Mousa checked his watch. 'Is he here yet?'

'On his way.' Allawi glanced at the two operators sweating at their consoles. It wasn't the stuffy heat inside the vehicle that was making them perspire. 'We've also lost over thirty aircraft—'

Mousa held up has hand, cutting Allawi off. 'Let's walk.' He swung his boots to the floor and stepped outside, wrapping a black winter parka over his uniform. Allawi joined him, and together, that wandered away from the camouflaged vehicles as snow continued to fall in fat, fluffy flakes.

Mousa lit a small cigar and flipped up his fur-lined hood. He smoked in silence for a while, listening to the wind stirring the trees and watching the snow swirl and eddy. To the east, the sky had lightened. Soon it would be a new day. And a new beginning.

'How many casualties, Reza? Ball park.'

Allawi shrugged. 'Thousands. Maybe Ten. Wounded? Three times that number.' He cleared his throat. 'Permission to be speak frankly.' Mousa waved his cigar. 'The plan was flawed from the start. I expressed my doubts to you on several occasions.'

'Relax. You won't get caught in the fallout.'

'But we could've stopped it.'

Mousa shook his head. 'Omelettes and eggs, my friend.'

Neither man spoke for a moment. Allawi rubbed his hands together. 'It's cold.'

'Put in a leave request, Reza. Make it a month. You've earned it.'

'But there's so much work to do, general. The after-action reports, the re-org. We need a plan.'

'We have one,' Mousa said, cigar smoke leaking from beneath his hood. 'We're going to hold position and dig in. Defend the line.'

Allawi frowned. 'Defend? General, we have the momentum.'

'Do we? I'm not so sure, Reza.' He waved an arm at the surrounding landscape. 'Have you ever been to Scotland?' Allawi shook his head. 'No, neither have I, but I know it's a cold, dark land of mountains and lakes, of impenetrable valleys and remote, offshore islands, and a coastline we couldn't possibly secure even with an army twice our size.'

'What are you saying?'

'I'm staying we hold position and consider our options.'

A figure jogged towards them from out of the snow. He stopped short and threw up a salute. 'General Mousa, General Al-Bitruji has arrived.'

'Send him over.'

They waited in silence. General Umar Al-Bitruji appeared a few moments later, wrapped in a thick coat and wearing a Russian-style fur Ushanka on his head. He wore the earflaps down and the hat's silver crossed swords insignia reflected the snow light. Another officer accompanied him. Mousa raised an eyebrow.

'This is Colonel Farad,' Al-Bitruji explained. 'My 2IC.'

Mousa exhaled a mouthful of cigar smoke and ground the butt beneath his boot. 'What happened?'

Al-Bitruji fumed. 'You didn't see? They blew half my army to pieces!'

'*Your* army? We serve at the pleasure of the caliph, general.'

'Of course,' Al-Bitruji said quickly. 'The rats must've worked for weeks to build those voids.'

'Perhaps you showed your hand, Umar? Massing your spearhead divisions so close to the penetration points. A blind man could've seen what you were planning.'

Al-Bitruji said nothing for several moments. When he spoke again, his anger had faded a little. 'We have superior numbers and equipment. We must push on, take Glasgow and Edinburgh.'

'It's a mistake.'

Al-Bitruji stepped closer. 'I'm still the overall commander of the invasion forces. I expect your support, Faris.'

'You should think again.'

'Perhaps the caliph would like to weigh in on the debate?' Al-Bitruji said. 'Maybe it's time he listened to other voices.'

'We have already spoken.' Mousa told him. 'He's aware of what happened here. Of the lives lost. That's on you.'

Al-Bitruji stabbed a finger into Mousa's chest. 'You were there in my command post! You knew of the plan, sanctioned it!'

Mousa saw Allawi's eyes widen. No one had ever laid a hand on Mousa, not in anger, and not for years. But Mousa didn't react immediately. Instead, he turned to Al-Bitruji's 2IC.

'Colonel Farad, did you hear me sanction General Al-Bitruji's plan?'

Farad's eyes flicked from Mousa to his boss, and then to Allawi. He shook his head. 'Not that I recall, general.'

Al-Bitruji spun around. 'Traitor!' When he turned back, he saw the pistol in Mousa's hand, held by his side. Al-Bitruji paled beneath his fur hat.

'Maybe I underestimated the British, I'll admit to that, but the border is now wide open. We can march all the way to Glasgow, add another chunk of real estate to the caliph's portfolio.'

Mousa shook his head. 'The caliph isn't interested. British forces have fled the country, along with much of the population.'

'But we've created a void,' Al-Bitruji blustered. 'If we don't fill it, they will. Then we're back to square one.'

'It's no longer your decision.' Mousa raised the gun. Al-Bitruji shook his head.

'Please, Faris. There must be another way.'

'Better by my hand than a firing squad.'

Al-Bitruji stared at his boots and nodded. 'I have a final request—'

The pistol cracked, and the round took Al-Bitruji through the heart.

He dropped to the snow at Mousa's feet and rolled over, dead. Mousa holstered his pistol and addressed a trembling Farad.

'Colonel, I'm promoting you to Brigadier, effective immediately. You are now in charge of the UK invasion force until we can find a suitable replacement. You'll report directly to me. Is that understood?'

A relieved Farad whipped up a smart salute. 'Yes, General Mousa.'

Mousa gestured to Al-Bitruji's body. The dead man's arms were spread wide, his fur hat lying in the snow. 'A quick, quiet burial with full military honours for our friend here. Then send a press release to Baghdad. It was a heart attack.'

Farad nodded. 'Consider it done.'

Mousa and Allawi walked away. As they reached the command vehicle, the 2IC turned to his superior.

'What now, general?'

Mousa stopped and looked around him. The snow fell, drifting through the trees. Further away, the peaks of the surrounding hills were dusted white. It was cold, and the eastern sky had turned grey. Soon the sun would rise, but the earth beneath their feet would remain frozen.

'The caliph once told me that Britain was a strange land, and he was right.' He turned to his 2IC. 'The story doesn't end here, Reza. But when it does, it can have only one ending.'

Allawi raised an eyebrow. 'What kind, exactly?'

Mousa didn't answer him. Instead, he opened the door to the command vehicle and stepped out of the cold.

CHAPTER 86
FAREWELL AND ADIEU

THE GREY-GREEN US MARINE CORPS MV-22 OSPREY CIRCLED THE VALLEY before making its final approach, its big prop-rotors rotating upwards, allowing the aircraft to settle vertically on the frozen scrub in a blast of powdered snow.

From the cover of a nearby tree line, Harry watched two aircraft rumble past the white hump of a distant snow-covered hill. Those would be the fighters, providing cover. And there were navy frigates patrolling the neighbouring coast, combing the skies with search-radars, and small teams on the surrounding hills with man-portable missiles.

Yet despite all the precautions, Harry didn't feel very safe. Similar missiles had brought down scores of aircraft all over southern Scotland, many of them far more sophisticated than the strange-looking, unarmed turbo prop waiting to transport him over the sea.

Harry shivered as melting snow dripped from the peak of his baseball cap. Fretting about being shot down was not the best way to start the day, but he had to remind himself that this was a historic moment.

An invading army had finally conquered England and Wales. The monarchy, and what remained of the UK's constitutional government, were being forced into exile overseas, and future historians would debate Harry's role in this seismic event.

Which was fine with Harry. Good or bad, it was better to be talked about than forgotten. And how many sitting Prime Ministers had experienced what he had these last six months? Exactly zero. Harry Beecham had a story to tell, and one day it would be told. If he ever made it off these bloody islands.

He shivered again, his hands thrust deep into the pockets of his camouflaged parka. A short distance away, a tired-looking General Bashford stood in silence beside his staff officers, watching the Osprey. A week had passed since the battle at the border, and most of the surviving British forces had escaped across the sea in ships and transport aircraft. The docks had finally emptied, and the airports lay abandoned.

It was over.

But not for everyone.

Some of Bashford's uniformed colleagues had volunteered to stay behind. They would have no offensive capability, and their role would be to monitor enemy movements and harass them where they could, but right now that enemy had advanced no further than a couple of miles into Scotland.

Intelligence sources hypothesised that Wazir had tired of the campaign, that the caliph's gaze had now turned to the Himalayas, but staying remained a risk, Harry had been told. And with so many ordinary people starting new lives in the US and Canada, the Prime Minister's place was with them, across the Atlantic. Harry couldn't argue with that logic.

And Scotland was still a dangerous place to be. Shells and missiles continued to rain down indiscriminately across the mostly empty cities of Glasgow and Edinburgh, and SCOTFOR had suffered significant damage from precision weapons. Bashford had argued that enemy spies must still be at work. It was another reason Harry and his administration had to go.

He watched the Osprey's rear ramp drop to the ground and four heavily armed US Marines in white winter combat uniforms jogged towards them. Harry's escort team stepped out from the tree-line and met them, shaking hands, and talking in each other's ears over the roar of the turboprops. Then they all marched towards Harry. The lead Marine was a tough-looking man in his mid-forties.

'Prime Minister, my name is Captain Van Buren, and we're here to fly you out to the *Arizona*. Are you ready to leave, sir? Do you have everything you need?'

Harry nodded. 'Yes, captain.' He turned and shook hands with the escort party. 'Good luck,' he told them.

The British soldiers, also wearing winter whites, melted into the trees. Harry watched them go, still perplexed by their decision to stay.

Van Buren waved a gloved hand. 'Sir, we have to leave. Right now.'

Harry didn't need telling twice. Accompanied by Bashford and his people, he headed towards the Osprey, one hand clamped on his baseball cap, his eyes narrowed against the blizzard of snow and ice kicked up by the huge rotors.

When everyone was safely aboard, the Osprey lifted off the ground, dipping its nose as its rotors tilted and it became a fixed-wing aircraft once more.

As they cleared the valley's snow-capped hills, Harry couldn't help thinking about those hand-held missiles, but his apprehension abated a little when a flight of grey attack helicopters appeared and formed a protective box around the Osprey.

Harry twisted around in his seat and stared out of the window. He was leaving behind a nation that had changed irrevocably and not for the better.

Beyond the English Channel, Europe had suffered the same fate, and the British mainstream media were running with the narrative that life had returned to normal. In London and Paris, Madrid and Rome, the scars of war were being erased, and most people had returned to their former lives.

Many of them were Harry's former colleagues from both sides of the House, men and women who had embraced the new regime and now played prominent roles in its radical new administration.

In Brussels, other familiar political faces were enforcing Wazir's laws with shocking vigour. And here was Harry, running away. Defeated. Exiled. But alive, and still in the game.

The hills and peaks fell away, and he watched rolling green waves pound themselves to white spray along the jagged coastline.

Harry felt the aircraft climbing as they headed for the safety of the sea, and he relaxed a little more. Soon they would land on the USS *Arizona* and a new chapter of Harry's life and career would begin.

Where it would take him, he didn't know. The future was uncertain, but it was clear to Harry and everyone around him that such an audacious and devastating military campaign against Europe could not go unchallenged.

For now, he had time to regroup, to gather his thoughts. President Bob Mitchell held all the cards, and so much would depend on that man's worldview. Old debates would rage once more—is Europe worth saving (again)? Is political compromise and grudging acceptance preferred to a long and bloody fight for freedom? Only time would tell, and that's what Harry had now. Time.

He turned away from the rugged shoreline and closed his eyes. His thoughts turned to Ellen, and he said a silent goodbye. He thought about the countless people who'd died, and those young and brave soldiers who'd sacrificed themselves so that others may live. It was bravery on a scale that Harry could barely imagine, and it needed to be remembered. And honoured.

That would be his mantra going forward, Harry decided. *Lest we forget*, etcetera. The sentiment always played well with the public, and he'd enjoyed playing the role of a wartime leader, but such leaders needed armed conflict to survive, not years spent in frustrated exile, and inevitably, political oblivion.

Any military operation to recapture Britain would be America's decision. Yet they were already in the fight, and Harry felt confident he could persuade President Mitchell to go that one step further.

The aircraft bucked and shuddered through a pocket of turbulence, and Harry opened his eyes.

He turned to the window.

Britain was no longer there.

CHAPTER 87
WHITE SANDS

Ross stepped outside the tent and straightened up, stretching his limbs and scratching at the lice beneath his armpits.

He wiped his hands on the loose black smock hanging from his thin frame and set off, trudging between the endless rows of white canvas tents that stretched in every direction across the flat, sun-baked desert.

The British contingent called the place *Baghdad Butlins*, but there was no joy to be had here. A former military padre billeted next door to Ross's tent had likened the camp to purgatory, a featureless, transitory world between heaven and hell, but no one was listening to his increasingly illogical sermons.

Because this place *was* hell.

Ross kept walking, passing groups of other British prisoners, some of whom caught his eye and nodded. Most were cops, or community support officers, and there were lots of civvies too, many of whom worked for regional forces.

Whenever a bunch of them arrived, they protested their innocence the loudest. *We're not police*, they'd wail, and after a week of back-breaking labour and minimal rations, the camp administrators gave them a choice—continue to wear the black uniform of a prisoner, or the white dishdasha robe and Tuareg head dress of a kapo.

Most chose the latter, which offered them accommodations in their own compound, better food and more of it, and no break-backing work. In exchange, they policed their fellow inmates with their *sjamboks*, long leather whips that could take the skin off a man's back like a razor.

Many prisoners had died at the hands of the kapos, including some of Ross's friends, until the Haji commandant had clamped down on such murders. Labourers were a valuable resource, after all.

As he kept moving through the European quarter, Ross recalled his first day at the construction site.

A few kilometres away, beyond a range of low, rocky hills, a huge city was being built, a place of marbled mosques and soaring minarets, of residential complexes, shopping malls and luxury hotels, all surrounded by irrigated crop fields, orchards, and man-made lagoons.

When Ross had arrived at the site by truck, the sheer scale had taken his breath away. In a wide, shallow valley ringed by craggy hills, tens of thousands of workers scurried like black ants across an enormous pattern of excavations.

It had reminded Ross of what ancient Egypt must have looked like during the rule of the pharaohs—without the security drones, guns, and heavy plant machinery, of course.

They put him to work on the canals, two enormous trenches thirty feet deep and forty wide, running parallel to each other. The canals carved the site in two and stretched out beyond the western edge of the excavations. Ross's job was to follow the giant mechanical diggers as they tore at the earth and guide the liquid concrete hoses used to form the canal walls.

Beneath the brutal desert sun, the work was exhausting, and the kapos, leaning on their long sjamboks, constantly eyed the prisoners, seeking every opportunity to use their whips. After the first two days of work, Ross thought he might die. Two weeks later, he knew it was a certainty. The only question was, when and how.

Eventually, the canals would need water, and rumour had it, the two enormous channels were headed straight for the sea. Debates raged around the evening cooking fires, but most people were convinced they were nowhere near water.

The twitchers amongst the British contingent had seen no gulls or coastal birds of any kind. There was no tinge of salt carried on coastal winds, only the dry desert atmosphere. Yet some had seen the architects' plans and confirmed the 3D renditions of a gleaming city dissected by two blue-water canals. So where would the water come from?

It was one of many questions that remained unanswered, and after six brutal months in the desert, Ross had given up caring. The fact was, no one knew where they were.

Maybe they were in Iraq, maybe southern Egypt, or possibly Sudan. Wherever it was, it was a long way from civilisation. Yet there was one certainty about life in this place—it was going to end here, for all of them.

It was the only question never debated because everyone knew the answer. If they all survived the build—which most of them wouldn't—what then? Would they be congratulated for their soul-crushing efforts and set free? No. Freedom was a concept many of the prisoners could no longer imagine. Ross wasn't one of them.

Not yet.

Skirting the African quarter, he heard a sudden commotion and saw a sizeable group of prisoners fighting in a sandy area between the tents.

There must've been thirty men involved, throwing punches, and swinging lengths of timber. When Ross heard the first chilling scream, he knew the knives were out, and the brawl had turned deadly.

More Africans joined in the fight, and the screams multiplied. Ross ducked between two tents as a large team of black kapos ran towards the fray, their sjamboks held ready.

He kept moving, away from the fringes of their territory, as fast as the heat would allow, weaving through narrow passages between tents and marquees.

The shrill screams faded into the distance, and Ross slowed his pace. He stopped for a moment, fighting for breath, the sweat dripping off his dark, bushy beard. He heard voices in the tent beside him and pushed on towards the outer limits of the camp.

It was more like a city than a jail, with its own suburbs, its places of worship, its town squares, and avenues. And like most big European cities, it also had its fair share of no-go areas, gang violence and ethnic tensions. As far as Ross was concerned, it was a city of the dead.

He remembered seeing it for the first time as the Airbus banked overhead and levelled out for landing at the remote airstrip. Initially, he thought he was looking at a vast area of solar panels, or sunshades, not a city of slaves. On reflection, what else could he have expected?

His mind drifted further back in time, to England, and to South Lockeridge. In the wake of his arrest, the truck had stopped at other villages, and more men and women had climbed aboard. They were prisoners like Ross, all of them as confused and angry as he was.

Those feelings turned to apprehension as the truck joined a larger convoy headed along the M4 motorway towards London. Ross didn't catch many glimpses of the outside world beyond the truck's canvas sides, but when he did, he saw well-lit carriageways and plenty of vehicular traffic. As if life had returned to normal. Later, he discovered that for many people, it had.

He stayed for several months in the capital, billeted inside a warehouse at a rank-smelling recycling centre in east London. Much of his time was spent in work gangs, clearing war damage across the city and the West End, and Ross lost count of the corpses he'd found and scraped into body bags.

As winter set in and a flu virus swept through the prisoner accommodations, Ross and some of the younger, healthier inmates were shipped further up the Thames in rusting barges. The ex-soldier he'd met on the truck at South Lockeridge, Scott, had fallen ill, and stayed behind.

He never saw Scott or any of the recycling centre prisoners again.

From the barges, they were cross-loaded onto a large commercial ship and transported up the Thames Estuary and into the English Channel. No one told them where they were headed, and as night fell, he watched the lights of the Cornish coastline sink beneath the dark horizon.

At that moment, Ross thought he might never see England again.

The boat docked in Gibraltar, and along with a thousand other prisoners, Ross spent several months in a Marbella clean-up crew. He'd been there once before, on a stag weekend, but much of it was gone now.

The tourist shops, bars and restaurants had been torn down, the streets and buildings south of the A7 motorway bulldozed flat. The former Euro playground was to be rebuilt as a summer retreat for the caliphate's elites, expanding the former Saudi royal family's vacation complex in the Marbella hills.

When the gang bosses stood his crew down and sent them to Malaga airport, Ross thought his luck had changed. After landing in the desert some hours later—and spending his first day being whipped and cooked beneath a harsher, unrelenting sun—he realised it had changed for the worse.

THOSE MEMORIES all seemed so long ago now, and he wondered if the desert heat was sapping not just his physical strength, but also his mind.

The sun was dipping towards the horizon when Ross reached the outlying tents that marked the edge of the canvas city. Beyond them, the sun-baked earth stretched away to a quivering horizon.

There were no guard towers here, no barbed wire, no security lights, nothing but an empty desert. The Hajis didn't bother to fence them in because there was nowhere to go. At least that was the theory, and it was one that made sense. Sometimes a truck or two would drive out into the nothingness and return with black-clad corpses. The trucks were never gone for long because none of the escapees ever got very far, and they always dumped the bodies at the edge of the cemetery for the burial teams to take care of.

Sometimes the corpses lay there for days, pecked over by carrion birds before the grave diggers arrived. It was a reminder to those who might contemplate escaping that only death awaited them out beyond the empty horizon.

The cemetery was located a mile across the flat earth, a sprawling collection of sun-bleached grave markers covering a wide area of sandy dunes and scrubby dirt.

As he shielded his eyes against the setting sun, Ross saw other prisoners heading back to the canvas city. The graveyard wasn't a safe place at night, and it wasn't only the dead who occupied it. Gangs of grave robbers prowled the area, digging up and mutilating fresh corpses for tooth fillings and replacement hip and knee joints, for metal of any kind.

And there were others who lurked in the darkness; sadists, rapists, and murderers, and often all three. In a camp of over 150,000 prisoners, there were no women, and some inmates could not silence the insistent voices inside them.

By the time Ross reached the cemetery, his elongated shadow stretched across the hard-packed earth behind him. He tramped past the untidy graves with the names of the dead etched into the bleached wood markers, the bones below them from every country in Europe and beyond.

Ross kept going, towards the far western edge of the burial ground, to the grave of a fellow Brit, a man called Price. Waiting by that grave was a kapo, a thin-faced Dutchman called Boeker, a former Rotterdam cop who'd fallen foul of that city's new blasphemy laws.

Boeker was as corrupt as they came and had whipped the backs of many, including Ross, but he was always looking for an angle, a way to make his own life more bearable.

He smiled beneath his white Tuareg when he saw Ross approaching.

'Ah! Englishman! You've kept me waiting. We may have to renegotiate.'

'Did you bring the food and water?'

Boeker kicked the hessian sack at his feet. 'It's all there. You and your friends will eat like princes. For a couple of days at least.' He tapped the wooden grave marker with the toe of his sjambok. 'This is him, yes? Your friend?'

Ross nodded. 'Liam Price, an old mate of mine from the Met police. He made me jimmy out three of his gold fillings after he arrived. Frightened of getting robbed, see? He kept them hidden between his toes. When he died, I helped bury him, but I couldn't take the teeth. There were others nosing around.'

Ross turned and looked across the vast, empty graveyard. 'Looks like we're on our own.'

'I chased them all away, Englishman. Now, get on with it. I've got a card game tonight and I need my stake.'

Boeker threw a long-handled shovel at Ross. He caught it and started digging, piling the loose sand to one side, and attacking the tougher dirt beneath. Boeker sat a short distance away, watching the setting sun and smoking a hand-rolled cigarette.

After ten minutes, the Dutchman flicked his cigarette away and got to his feet, dusting the sand from his white dishdasha. He leaned on his sjambok like a staff.

'Hurry up, English. It's getting dark.'

Ross straightened up and cuffed the sweat from his brow with a black sleeve. His eyes roamed the graveyard. Boeker was right. The place was empty, but one could never be sure.

As the light faded, the black linen smocks and baggy trousers became an asset for those with murder in mind. Ross raised the shovel and slammed it into the dirt. The blade thumped as it hit a hard object. Ross scraped the top of it with his shovel.

'What's this?'

Boeker stepped towards the grave and saw the flat planks of wood beneath the ground. 'Looks like a crate or something,' Ross said.

'Dig it out.'

Ross dropped to his knees and started slapping the dirt away, uncovering more worn planks of wood. 'Give me a hand, would you?'

Boeker tutted and dropped his sjambok behind him. He got down on his knees and together they scraped the dirt from the top of the crate.

'It's big,' Ross said, standing up. 'I'll dig down the sides while you ease it out.'

Boeker looked around, then jammed his fingers in the gaps between the planks. 'Let's make this quick, dammit.'

As Boeker tugged at the wooden planks, Ross picked up the shovel, scooped up a blade full of sand and tossed it in the kapo's face. The Dutchman roared with anger, clawing at his eyes.

'You clumsy bastard!'

Ross swung the shovel with all his strength, cracking it over the man's head. Boeker crawled away, groaning, his hand reaching for his long whip. Ross dodged around him and lifted the shovel, bringing the blade down with such force that it severed three of Boeker's fingers.

The kapo roared, fury and pain, and pushed himself to his feet. Ross panicked and swung again, catching Boeker on the side of the head, and opening up his cheek to the bone. The bigger man dropped to his knees, clutching his mangled hand, his face running with bright blood.

The fight had left him, and he looked up at Ross with watery eyes.

'Please, stop it! Please!'

Ross steeled himself and swung the shovel. Boeker raised his wounded hand and Ross heard the snap of his arm breaking. The Dutchman was wailing now, begging and pleading, but Ross didn't stop. Couldn't stop. He was committed, and with each wild and desperate blow, Boeker's protestations waned.

Ross kept hitting him until the man lay still, and the sand beneath his head ran red. He threw aside the shovel and sat breathless on the dirt. He was exhausted and sickened by what he'd done. Boeker had been a brutal, sadistic kapo, but he'd been better than most, and the whipping he'd given Ross hadn't been that bad. More importantly, the man liked to bargain.

And now, Ross had what he needed.

He got to his feet and looked around. The sun was below the horizon, and across the canvas city, cooking fires bloomed like fireflies in the gathering darkness. Ross squinted. Was that a group of figures at the edge of the camp?

He dropped to his knees and stripped Boeker of his white headdress and gown. He attacked the wooden planks arranged across the grave. There was no crate, and no corpse, and no one called Price. It had been a ruse all along, and Ross had groomed Boeker long enough for the man to fall for it.

From the open grave, he retrieved a large square of white canvas cut from a tent, along with coils of thin rope, a couple of bungee cords, wooden pegs, and plastic bottles of water.

Boeker had brought more water and food for their trade, and Ross stashed it all in the hessian sack. With the Dutchman's liberated belt knife, he made two holes in the sack and ran a length of rope through them, tying off both ends with thick knots. He rolled up the white dishdasha and Tuareg and stuffed them in the sack, too.

The men he'd seen earlier were heading for the graveyard, and Ross counted at least ten silhouettes.

Moving fast, he rolled Boeker into the grave and heaped dirt and sand on top of the semi-naked body. It wasn't the best job, but the surrounding graves were some of the first to be dug, and he didn't think many people would visit this part of the cemetery.

Ross watched the small band of shadows as they entered the far side of the cemetery. They hadn't seen him, and Ross turned and headed down the rise on the other side, taking a moment to hurl the shovel as far as possible. He didn't hear it land.

Looping the hessian sack over his head, he tightened the ropes around his body and walked away, Boeker's sjambok in his hand. He headed west, towards the thin sliver of pale sky that was all that remained of the day.

As he strode out into the semidarkness, the cooler air invigorated him. In the sack, he carried dried meats, salt, sugar, and grain. He had plenty of water, powdered milk and salt tablets. And to combat the worst of the daytime heat, he had Boeker's dishdasha and Tuareg, plus a sheet of white canvas to shelter beneath.

And he had a plan—continue west, in the same direction as those dreaded canals, until he reached the sea. Because Ross believed it was out there, beyond the horizon. It *had* to be.

And if it wasn't, if the others were right, he would die in the desert, alone.

But the prospect held no fear for him, because he was a father now. His son was growing up without him and Ross couldn't bear that.

He didn't know the child was a boy. It was just a feeling, but it had given him the strength to endure. He knew he was lucky, because real memories had driven many fathers to despair and suicide.

Instead, Ross could only dream of the child, of how he looked, the colour of his eyes, the scent of his soft, flawless skin. He imagined holding him, and Lara too, both wrapped in his arms.

Their faces would be the wind in his sails as he headed west beneath a star-filled sky.

EPILOGUE
THE FAR FUTURE

THE EMIR LED THE TWO YOUNG MEN DOWN A NARROW STAIRCASE INTO A large basement area, brightly lit with overhead strips.

The brothers had been well-fed and were now eager to begin their mission. They'd already completed a dangerous task—entering the city after dark—but the rest of the operation would require their full commitment.

These were brave boys, and the emir knew their courage would not falter, and with luck, their future was assured. His own future was uncertain, though. The smallest mistake, a wrong word, and his life would be in grave danger. If that happened, well, the emir had a plan for that too.

He led the boys to the end of the corridor, where he opened a cupboard crammed with cleaning supplies. Hanging amongst the rags and overalls—hidden in plain sight—was a black t-shirt. He took it to a workbench in the centre of the room and ordered the older boy to put it on. The boy obeyed, swinging his arms, testing the garment's flexibility.

'It's the latest technology from the Americas,' the emir told him.

The boys shared an excited look. Soon, they would call that country home. Their acceptance of the mission had earned them passage on a ship to the New World, a place where food was plentiful, where intelligent homes cooled themselves in the summer and glowed warm through the winter months. A world where electrical power was plentiful and silent vehicles flew across the skies. Where poverty was non-existent, and people were free to roam from sea to shining sea.

Paradise.

But to get to Paradise, one must first sacrifice, the emir told them.

The attack would remind their overlords there was still fight left in this nation, that its people remembered a history that successive regimes had tried to erase and bury.

The boys would strike a blow for freedom, and word of their bravery would spread all the way to the Borderlands, where soldiers patrolled high walls, lashed by wind, snow and rain, as they watched the dark hills to the north. And from the densely wooded slopes of those hills, free men and women stared back from the shadows.

The emir spent the rest of the night teaching the boys how to use the garment, how to connect it to the tiny battery pack, where to place it for maximum effect, their entry and exit, scratching maps and diagrams on a chalkboard.

They rehearsed the practical side of the operation until they'd satisfied the emir. Then it was time to leave, as the sun rose above the city.

The emir snapped new security bands around their wrists, pre-loaded with check-in markers for today's journey into the city. He ushered them through the kitchen and into a large vehicle garage. The boys gawped as they came face to face with the emir's vehicle, a silver Bentley limousine. His manservant, Ali, had already removed the rear seat. Beneath it was a large, rubber-lined void.

'You won't be in there for long,' the emir told them. 'Here are your tools.' He handed the younger boy a small black bag and helped them both into the void.

After Ali had locked the thick leather seat back into position, the emir sat on top of it. The garage door opened with a press of a button, and at 6.30 am, the car glided out into Warwick Square and turned east towards the River Thames. There was little traffic to speak of and few pedestrians on the streets.

The car continued its journey, sweeping along the wide, empty riverside avenue before turning north past the enormous glass and marble edifice of the Grand Halls of Justice.

The emir looked beyond its immaculate gardens and palm-lined walkways to the bronze dome high above, now reflecting the morning sun. So many oppressive laws had been passed under that dome, the emir reflected. It was time those that lurked beneath it were given cause to regret that oppression.

Half a kilometre north, Ali steered the Bentley into the kerb and stopped.

The emir looked to his right and knew the lush riverside park stood on the site of the British Ministry of Defence. To his left, across the wide avenue, the granite statue of General Faris Mousa towered over Victory Park.

Mousa was one of the first soldiers to land on these shores during the Great Liberation, and his heroic effigy—hands on hips, his chin jutting forward beneath the rim of his helmet—had been erected on the spot where Mousa was said to have landed by parachute on that fateful day.

The general had died, along with thousands of others, when Chinese special forces had detonated a tactical nuclear weapon directly beneath Mousa's headquarters in New Delhi, shortly before his planned incursion into the Chinese province of Nepal.

In the shadow of the granite general stood the Downing Street monument, now rebuilt as a tourist attraction. The emir's eyes narrowed as the sun flared off the dome of the Gold Mosque beyond it, a vast hall of prayer that dwarfed the site where Buckingham Palace had once stood, its 100-meter-tall minarets reaching up into the sky.

Soon the call to prayer would begin, and the emir intended to be in his usual spot inside that mosque before the muezzin's first notes echoed across London.

He powered down the interior's connecting glass partition.

'Are we in position?' he asked Ali.

The driver nodded in his rear-view mirror. 'Yes. They can proceed.'

Ali had lined up his front tyre with the faint chalk mark on the kerbstone. As his manservant got out and feigned concern over the car's tyre, the emir heard the boys shifting the storm drain cover on the road below the Bentley. He heard them moving around, heard their whispers, and then the two sharp knuckle raps beneath his seat.

The emir waited until he heard the scrape of the cover and the metallic ring as the boys re-seated it. He watched Ali shake his head theatrically and climb back behind the wheel.

Seconds later, the Bentley pulled away from the kerb before making the left turn onto Victory Mall, where the *Shahada* hung from every flagpole all the way along the palm-lined avenue to the gates of the Gold Mosque.

'We must pray for their success,' the emir said.

Ali nodded, his eyes on the road ahead. 'God will decide if justice is to be served this day.'

'Indeed, He will.'

THE BOYS CLIMBED down the storm drain's access ladder to a wide, dry intersection of rainwater tunnels.

The monsoon season was still some months off, so they were relatively safe from the annual deluges that London endured. Above them, daylight shone down in bright bars.

'Hand me the compass,' the older boy said. His name was Shev, and he held his hand out as his younger brother Jax rummaged in the bag the emir had given them. He handed the compass to his sibling, and they studied the hand-drawn map. Shev took a bearing. 'There,' he whispered, his voice echoing off the concrete walls.

Shev nodded and led the way into the southbound drain, a smooth, circular concrete tube. During the monsoon season, it would dump millions of gallons of rainwater into the Thames. Now, thankfully, it was dry, and it would stay that way until the first rains in October.

They kept moving, darting through shafts of sunlight. They walked for two hundred meters until they reached another intersection and found the rusted steel cover set into the floor. Shev studied the map. 'This is it.'

They prised the cover off and Jax shone his torch inside. This shaft was much older, the walls constructed of crumbling red brick. The rusted ladder shook as they descended ten meters to another junction, where smaller, unlit tunnels stretched into inky blackness.

The smell of the river was strong down here. Shev took another bearing and led the way. When they reached the rusted steel door, they sprayed the lock and hinges with the solution in the bag and waited for two minutes. Then they threw the metal handles, and the door swung open with barely a sound.

Jax closed it behind him, and the boys stood on an unlit platform. Shev shone his torch down on the train tracks. 'This is the spur,' he whispered. 'The platform will be right up there.' He pointed along the tunnel, where a dim light shone in the distance. 'Come on.'

They moved quickly, hugging the wall, watching their feet now. Neither boy wanted to break an ankle. They heard a rumbling that grew into a shaking, rattling thunder, and a huge tube train clattered past the spur ahead and shuddered to a halt beneath the bright platform lights of Justice Station. Shev held up a hand. 'We wait here for the next one.'

They didn't have long to wait. As another train rumbled past, Jax ditched the bag, and both boys ran for the bright lights of the station. Hundreds of passengers disembarked from the train, filling the platform.

The boys hurried from the shadows and into the light, melting into the crowd, slapping dust from their coveralls, and washing their hands and faces with bottled water. The tide of Lowborns carried them towards the escalators. They scanned their bracelets at the travel gates, and then they were inside the basement level of the Great Halls of Justice.

They reported for duty and collected their work cart. Before they left the maintenance area, Shev stopped to use the washroom. When he emerged, he stuffed the black vest in a bucket of rags beneath the cart.

The hours passed as they went about their chores. In the late afternoon, they headed for the inner chamber, where an important debate was scheduled to take place later that evening. Sticking to a routine that rendered them almost invisible, they entered the chamber and started cleaning, while the guard below them leaned against the wall and dined on his fingernails.

Shev swept the floor of the terraced seating, and Jax focussed on cleaning the carved wooden lectern on the raised central podium.

The younger boy polished the autocue and the long, twin microphones jutting from the lectern. He moved around the lectern, and with one eye on the guard, he dropped to his knees and opened the small electrical inspection hatch just below the document shelf...

Shev's broom caught a bucket, and soapy water washed down the terrace steps. The guard cursed, running up the steps and dancing around the spillage.

'Clumsy fool! What happened?'

'An accident. It's just water,' Shev told him, reaching for his rags.

The guard turned around just as Jax stepped down from the podium. 'You! Help this idiot clean up!'

It took another thirty minutes to dry the steps and finish cleaning the chamber. Out in the hallway, Shev's lips barely moved as they steered the cart.

'Well? Are we good?'

Jax had jammed the black t-shirt inside the inspection hatch, stuffing it down into the lectern's recess. He attached one metal clip to the material and the other to a microphone wire. The battery would last for several days, but the emir told them it wouldn't take that long. A continuous thirty seconds of vocal vibrations transmitted through the lectern's microphones would be enough to trigger an electrical pulse that would change the chemical composition of the material and transform it into a block of powerful explosive.

Enough to destroy the inner chamber and everyone in it.

Jax winked at his older brother. 'We're good.'

Later that evening, the scheduled debate would require the attendance of all one hundred members of the Supreme Judicial Council.

THEY RETURNED to the Lowborn enclave in Vauxhall, but neither boy could relax.

If they brought the meeting forward and the bomb triggered

prematurely, the authorities would surround the enclaves, and the bloodletting would begin.

Shev and Jax would be among the first to be lifted, and neither boy could resist the torture. The emir's name would be known, and the names of others who had guided them on their path of resistance. Being captured wasn't an option.

When he heard the quiet tapping on the door, Shev opened it. A toothless old woman dressed in rags stepped inside. From beneath her tatty raincoat, she handed Shev a small rucksack. Then she removed both of their security bands with a tool only ever used by the authorities.

After kissing their hands, she left. Inside the rucksack were two bottles of water, some energy bars, wire cutters, plastic ties, and a list of instructions printed on a piece of paper. The first one was in bold and underlined.

Leave immediately. Talk to no one. Walk, don't run. And don't miss your ride.

Less than a minute later they left their apartment for the last time, taking the stairs down to the rubble filled yard, skirting the rusted skeletons of long abandoned cars, and avoiding the usual clusters of residents gathered around their fires.

They kept their hoods up, and Shev wore the rucksack over a dark coat. Using the shadows, they arrived at the security fence. Beyond were the railway lines that led in and out of Waterloo Station.

Shev went to work with the cutters while Jax watched for trouble. The fence ran for several kilometres along the edge of the enclaves, where buildings stood empty and weeds grew taller than men, and CCTV and floodlight coverage was intermittent.

It took Shev less than a minute to cut enough links for them both to squeeze through. On the other side, Jax used the plastic ties to secure the fence, and they scrambled down to the edge of the tracks.

They stepped carefully over the multitude of rails, making use of a pool of darkness between the wash of security lights. Shev headed for the signalling control box halfway across the landscape of tracks and the boys squatted behind it. The minutes passed, and then the rails closest to them sang.

The autonomous cargo train rumbled towards them, its driverless engine clanking by, the two dozen box cars and flatbeds rattling over the rails. Shev and Jax got to their feet and waited for the last flat bed.

As it passed, Shev urged Jax up the ladder, then followed him. They scrambled over the edge and under the tarpaulin, squeezing past the cargo and settling at the rear of the train.

They sat with their backs against a wooden crate and stared out at the passing world from beneath the tarp. Shev reached out and squeezed his brother's hand.

The train picked up speed, thundering through a deserted Clapham Junction station. It was an exhilarating experience for both boys, travelling at speed, heading for a world beyond the city that neither had any experience of.

The train continued south, rattling through the darkness, and for the first time they saw the wastelands beyond the city, where nature had reclaimed crumbling warehouses, office blocks and endless stretches of suburban homes, now barely visible beneath a landscape of weeds, grass, vines, and trees. The wild countryside seemed to last forever.

Later, the train decelerated until it was moving at walking speed. Outside, the wilderness ended at a tall security fence lit by powerful lights, and the train crawled past a military compound. The brothers shrunk lower beneath the tarp until the night had swallowed the lights of the border post.

They were now travelling through the Southern District.

Around them, the untamed world had morphed into trimmed hedges and cultivated fields. Occasional headlights carved through the darkness along black tarmac roads. Shev pulled the tarp back and let the warm night air wash over them. It was Jax who saw the lights first.

'We're here,' he said, pointing.

The train slowed again. Up ahead, Petersfield Station glowed in the darkness, and lines of commercial trucks queued in bays alongside the tracks. This is where the train would unload its cargo. It was also the place where the boys were told to get off before it reached the pool of distant light.

The train was still moving, but much slower now, and the boys jumped down onto the trackside. Keeping low, they scurried into the overgrown grass and watched the train continue its journey until it shunted and clattered to a halt.

Shev led the way through the undergrowth until they stepped out onto a gravel path. They rechecked the instructions and headed west, following the path through a shadowy copse that ended in a large, square clearing.

A vehicle park, they realised, with only a single, dark-coloured occupant. Jax checked the plate number, noting the black, crossed-swords emblem before the six-digit number. It matched the information on their instructions.

Still, they were careful, approaching the car from an angle. They froze when the driver's door opened, and a dark-skinned man climbed out. White teeth smiled in the shadows.

'Shev, Jax. I am a friend of the emir. Please.' He held open the rear door.

Jax hesitated. 'What do we do?' he whispered.

Shev turned to his younger brother. 'We've come this far. We must trust the emir.'

He walked towards the open door, and Jax followed. They climbed inside, and the driver steered the car out of the gravel turnaround and onto the smoothest tarmac road the boys had ever travelled on. The vehicle was a hybrid, running almost silently, the speed and direction glowing in the windscreen.

'Congratulations,' the driver said.

The boys looked at each other. 'What?'

'You have struck a blow. Many of the supreme council are dead. A gas explosion, they say. That will change by morning.'

The boys looked at each other, unsure how to react. 'Where are we going?'

The driver shrugged. 'Not far.'

Shev sat back and Jax did the same, watching the world pass by. They saw magnificent houses and quaint, pristine villages. They passed endless vineyards that rolled across dark hills, and they saw forests and fields of cattle. It was a different world to the one they knew.

As the car crested another rise, it pulled to the side of the road. 'This is it,' said the driver. 'You should go, quickly, before someone comes.'

'Thank you.'

The boys climbed out and watched the car disappear into the distance. Shev turned all the way around and didn't see a single light. He studied the instructions. 'There's the wood,' he said, pointing to the only thick cluster of trees nearby.

'Looks dark,' Jax said, wary.

'The moon will show us the way.'

'I don't like it.'

Shev turned on his sibling. 'You want to go back to Vauxhall? Wait for them to kick the door in?' Jax stared at his sneakers. Shev squeezed his shoulder. 'Come on. It's not much further.'

They crossed an open field, watching and listening. The wood closed in around them, splintering the moon's guiding light. Ancient timbers creaked and leaves hissed as a gentle breeze filtered through the trees. A bird screeched overhead, frightening the boys, but only for a moment.

Shev stopped and re-read the instructions by shielded torchlight. He hadn't made a mistake, of that he was certain.

Follow the field into the wood and keep walking.

He couldn't help feeling the same fear his brother was feeling. Was it a trap? He didn't think it was possible. Why wait until now? Why not take them back in Vauxhall?

They pushed on, and after a few more minutes, the trees thinned out. Jax saw a clearing ahead and Shev picked up the pace. As they reached the edge of the woods, they saw it and stopped dead.

Bathed in silver moonlight, a huge black egg squatted in the centre of the clearing—

'Don't move,' said the voice behind them.

Silhouettes appeared out of the gloom, surrounding them. Gloved hands gripped their arms, but neither boy felt any pain. Shev's heart pounded. A red light shone in his eye and a soldier interrogated a hand-held device. He did the same to Jax.

'ID confirmed,' he said.

'Let's move.'

The soldiers hurried them into the clearing. The elongated egg was much bigger than a helicopter, but smaller than a transport plane. There were no tail fins, only two stubby wings that protruded from a fat, windowless body that rode high on three thin black legs.

The soldiers escorted them up the ramp at the rear of the craft. Inside, red lights glowed around a cabin filled with seats, just like the airliners the boys had seen in history books and films. They were made to sit at the front and other men strapped them in, slipping headphones over their ears. To their surprise, they found they could see through a large window to their right.

And even more surprising, the craft was already moving, rising straight up in the air with barely a sound.

Jax found his brother's hand and squeezed it tight. Now the ship was hovering just below the treetops. Shev let go as a weight pressed down on his shoulders and squeezed him back into his seat. He turned to the window in time to see the ground falling away.

The craft hummed, climbing higher, and he saw the sea far below. The land—their home—slipped out of view. He heard a voice in his headset.

'This is the captain. We'll be crossing the eastern seaboard in thirty-seven minutes, so relax, sit back, and enjoy the ride.'

The boys looked at each other. Shev turned to the nearest soldier, strapped in across the aisle.

'What does it mean? *Eastern seaboard?*'

The soldier smiled beneath his black helmet. He pointed to his arm patch, the delta wing symbol embossed over the Stars and Stripes, and the words *United States Space Force*.

'America,' the soldier told him.

Shev bit his lip. 'Thank you.'

He gripped Jax's hand again, overwhelmed.

When he looked at his little brother, he was crying too.

THE EMIR CROSSED the room and threw open the balcony doors, inviting the cool sea air into his first-floor study.

He'd travelled down to his luxury coastal villa after prayers, as did most of the well-heeled citizens who lived in the capital. He hoped to find similar accommodations in the Americas when he made the jump.

He stood on the terrace and breathed in the salty air, watching the breakers boom and hiss along the shore.

The gas blast narrative wouldn't last long, not with so many prominent figures dead. The mission had been a success, as the emir prayed it would be. He'd seen the TV news, and the gaping hole where the dome above the inner chamber used to be. Now it belched black smoke.

The death toll had yet to be announced, but it was likely to include most of the brutal tyrants who'd attended the meeting. There would be innocents among the dead too, and the emir had prayed for their souls. Revenge would be high on the regime's list of priorities, and they would execute as many prisoners as it took to satiate their bloodlust. But the message had been sent—if the oppressed can strike at the heart of the regime, then no one was safe.

Eventually, the boys would become the prime suspects. Their home would be raided, but the police would discover that they'd spoken to no one, that they had no friends or relatives, that their employment at the Great Halls of Justice had been secured by a man who'd died in a tragic accident over a year ago, when Ali pushed him in front of a tube train.

CCTV might place the emir at the kerbside that morning, but any investigation would discover that Ali had driven the Bentley to a garage to have the punctured tyre repaired. There was nothing to connect the boys to the emir.

And if the worst happened, and they came for him, he would know. Then he would activate the distress beacon and the ship would come for him. As it had for the boys.

The wind picked up, and the emir stepped back inside the study and closed the doors. He poured himself a glass of Malbec and retired to his favourite chair.

As he sipped the rich red, he closed his eyes and recalled his own long-buried past, how his parents were killed during the New Forest battles, and how he'd been plucked from the child markets by a wealthy couple from Damascus who'd passed the dark-haired child off as their own.

He'd inherited his adopted father's title and wealth, and after his mother died, her personal possessions. Among them was the key to a past he never knew existed. And as he discovered the truth of his identity, the embers of rebellion fanned to flame.

The emir used his wealth and influence to become a valuable friend and patron to his enemies. As his status grew, so did his network of fellow rebels, until it included a trusted connection with the Americans.

Today, all those years of hard work had paid off. But it wouldn't end there. It took many such battles to win a war, and the emir imagined this one would rumble on long after he had departed this earth.

He crossed to the bookshelves and used the ladder to pluck the thesaurus from a higher shelf. Sitting back in his chair, he sipped his wine and opened the thick reference volume, skipping to the back sleeve.

Carefully, he peeled away the inside jacket cover and retrieved the clear plastic envelope secreted within. He placed the book to one side and extracted the photograph and the faded hand-written letter.

The missive explained much yet left many questions unanswered. He laid his birth mother's words to one side and held up the photograph, a digital printout of the only family members he had ever seen.

He reached for a magnifying glass. The emir was approaching his sixtieth year and had scrutinised every pixel hundreds of times, yet it never failed to fascinate him. It was a tangible link to his ancestors, and a world he could barely imagine.

The photo was a group portrait, taken in front of a farmhouse during the Great Liberation. The woman was attractive, and the man strong jawed and handsome. There was another man in the photo, an Asian, and the emir could only guess why he was there.

All three smiled for the unknown photographer, yet the emir always felt those smiles were strained, and the eyes somewhat sad.

As if they were saying goodbye.

Ross and Lara Taylor. Those were the names of his long-dead ancestors. Taylor was a proud English name, too. The emir was fortunate to be born with such a rich heritage.

He slipped the treasures back inside their hiding place and returned the thesaurus to its home on the shelf. He sat down, swirling his wine around the glass as he considered the day that was almost at an end.

The boys would live in America, where they would learn new skills, languages, and proficiencies they could only dream of. And one day they would return, as teachers, as fighters, and they would pass their skills to others.

The war would continue, as it must, because freedom was a fragile concept, paid for in blood and easily surrendered by apathy and deceit.

That's what had happened to Britain. To Europe. Their civilisation had ended because their leaders had lost the will to defend it. The people had been betrayed. The emir would not do the same.

He didn't consider himself a terrorist. History was littered with struggles against oppression, against the ruthless power of tyrannical states. Almost every country on the planet had witnessed such struggles, and many had led to the downfall of despotic regimes. The emir's cause was no different.

He was a student of history, and he knew those who ignored it were doomed to repeat it. The emir would never make that mistake.

Instead, he would stand and fight for freedom until he took his last breath.

And where was the crime in that?

HAVE YOUR SAY

Did you enjoy *Invasion: Redux*?
I hope you did.

If you have a moment, would you mind rating it, or leaving a review?

It would be hugely helpful.

Rate this book!

And many thanks for your time.

THE INVASION UK SERIES

The original version of *Invasion* ended with an epilogue set in the far future.

Since that first release back in 2006, I was inspired to write further adventures because of the interest shown by readers and their desire for a continuation of the story.

So, I wrote another three novels, following the lives of Harry Beecham and a fresh intake of new characters on their post-invasion journeys.

I also wanted to explore the technological advances made by the Americans after their world-changing discovery, and how that might translate into military capability.

Most of all, I wanted to write about ordinary people, and how their lives might be affected when democracy is replaced by tyranny.

And beneath that brutal heel of oppression, how easily friends, relatives and neighbours can become dangerous enemies.

The following chapter is the current epilogue to *Invasion: Downfall*, book #1 of the *Invasion UK series.*

As always, I hope you enjoy it.

SAVING PRIVATE NOVAK

THREE YEARS AFTER THE INVASION...

'ON YOUR FEET. LET'S GO.'

Eddie Novak heard the words echo through the shifting fog of his dream. He didn't want to let go, not just yet. He was dreaming of home, of the day he'd left.

It felt so real, like it was yesterday.

He'd risen early that morning, long before the sun came up. His combat uniform was laid out on the other bed, the unmade one that his twin brother Kyle would never sleep in again. The newly issued uniform was the flame-retardant type with the IR patches and a Union Jack flag on the left shoulder. Eddie had earned the right to wear it because he'd passed the fourteen-week Basic and Advanced Combat Training courses at Fort Benning in Georgia, and now he was a fiercely proud soldier in the King's Continental Army. He'd dressed in that uniform in the dark of his bedroom. The darkness was his friend, the ACT course had taught him.

He'd eaten breakfast with his dad, while his mum fussed around the kitchen, fighting back the tears and refusing to look at him. When she did, she broke down. Dad battled hard, but he cried too. That was the last time he'd seen his parents.

He trudged through the snows of New London, past the neat

streets of single-storey housing pods that stretched from the outskirts of South Lancaster all the way out to the I-190, a little corner of England now located thirty miles outside of downtown Boston. On the way up to Trafalgar Square people had opened their doors, braving the bitter cold to shake his hand and wish him luck, but the dream had blurred their faces and distorted their voices. He remembered the words, though...

Good luck, son.
Take care, God bless.
Give 'em hell...

The square wasn't as impressive as the one back in London, where Lord Nelson had long been removed from his column by a wrecking ball. That wasn't so bad, though; no one wanted to bear witness to the executions they held there, not even sightless statues. No, the public square in Brit Town was more of an oversized vehicle turnaround, flanked on all sides by banks of ploughed snow and portacabins that served as schools, grocery stores and makeshift pubs.

There was a huge granite memorial in the middle of the square, commemorating the soldiers, sailors and airmen who'd died during the Great Invasion. At its base, frozen wreaths of red poppies poked through the snow, and a Union Jack flag fluttered from the pole above. The square was normally lit up, but not that morning. That morning it lay shrouded in darkness because there were four hundred uniformed men and boys gathered there, all aged between seventeen and fifty, and all proud members of the newly formed Second Massachusetts Battalion.

Proud and apprehensive.

Hundreds of family and friends stood with them in the predawn darkness, wrapped in coats and hats, stamping their feet and making awkward conversation. There was a lot of crying mum's and stern-faced dad's trying to hold it together, but everyone knew this might be it, the final last time they'd ever see each other. Eddie was glad his parents had stayed back at the pod.

In his dream, Mac, Steve and Digger stood with him. They chatted quietly, and then they'd watched a huge flight of aircraft pass overhead, their collision lights winking in the darkness. Bombers, or transports, heading for the bases on Greenland or Iceland. Like the Second Mass, they were on the move.

The crying jumped a notch when distant headlights signalled the arrival of the transport, a convoy of Greyhound buses that crawled through the thick snow along The Mall before turning into the square. Tears flowed as the soldiers prised themselves from the vice-like embraces of their loved ones, stowed their rucks in the luggage bays and climbed aboard.

Eddie found a window seat and watched those anguished goodbyes, the soldiers' hollow reassurances, the desperate helplessness of those left behind. He wondered how many families would get the email from the Department of Defence, the one that informed the recipient that their relative had been killed in service to the King's Continental Army. Some. Maybe half. Only time would tell.

When the doors hissed closed and the buses began to move, Eddie saw his brother in the crowd. Kyle's uniform was shredded, his face caked in dark blood. His breath escaped from the jagged hole in his neck and steamed on the cold air. He smiled, mouthing the same words over and over again. It was only after they'd left Brit Town and turned onto the interstate that Eddie realised what Kyle was saying.

See you soon, bruv...

'On your feet!'
No. Just a few more minutes...

The Greyhounds had headed south, then west, covering the seventy miles to Westover Air Force base in a little under ninety minutes. There were thousands of other soldiers there, many of them the British and Irish volunteer battalions from New York, Maine, Pennsylvania, Massachusetts and New Hampshire. Union flags and Irish Tricolours snapped in the frigid breeze as Prime Minister Beecham made a rousing speech about settling scores and reclaiming ancient homelands.

Then the bands had struck up, the brass, pipes and drums, and they'd marched across the taxiway towards a huge fleet of waiting aircraft. Eddie's heart had soared.

Along with the rest of the Second Mass, he'd boarded the Boeing 747 and flew south to Virginia, where another fleet of buses ferried them to Naval Station Norfolk. In his dream the base was an industrial city by the sea, the warehouses, cranes and ships towering far above him like rusted iron skyscrapers. Soldiers, sailors and Marines crammed the cobbled dockside waiting to board their respective ships, and when the whistles shrilled and neon wands waved, Eddie followed the others up a crowded gangway onto the *USS Arlington*, a San Antonio-class amphibious transport vessel.

He passed four grey Osprey aircraft on the flight deck and then he was stepping over a bulkhead and into the darkened ship. He followed his buddies below, past the tactical hovercraft, the fighting vehicles and mountains of supplies, deep into the damp, salty bowels, where all four hundred of the Second Mass crammed into a dark cargo bay. In the adjacent bay, a battalion of US Marine Corps Raiders was settling in, but the Brits kept out of their way. This was their ship, their turf. God willing, Eddie and the others wouldn't have to wait long before they could say the same.

The ship shuddered and then they were moving out into the Chesapeake Bay. Confined to their damp quarters, the Brits could only imagine the size of the armada that was waiting for them far out to sea.

It had taken a week to sail to Reykjavik in Iceland, and in his dream, Eddie had laughed as they'd tottered ashore like newborn foals. The laughter didn't last, though. Iceland was all about sharpening combat skills, and they trained for days, expending thousands of rounds on the ranges, zeroing their M27 assault rifles and getting cosy with their Sig Sauer sidearms. They'd brushed up on first aid and map reading skills, and then the dream skipped forward again.

Eddie was back on the ship, heading south now, into the dark, restless waters of the North Atlantic. He dreamed of the final briefings and the quiet orders, of pulling his gear on and checking his equipment, of filing silently down into the submerged well-deck, of cramming into the landing craft, then reversing out onto the deep, dark ocean.

The surrounding ships were black against the night sky, a ghostly armada twisting and turning in the pitching seas. The landing craft's engines roared but Eddie could see nothing apart from the bobbing, swaying men around him. He braced his legs against the motion, against the Atlantic swell that slammed into the forward ramp and dumped wave after wave of cold spray over them. Yet in his dream, Eddie hadn't cared; bigger waves meant shallower waters.

They were getting close.

The engines slowed. Above the ramp, a dark, rugged coastline loomed. Spectral seagulls whirled in the sky.

The ramp slapped into the water and then they were moving, wading through the shallows and hard-targeting up a shallow beach towards the foot of the cliffs. Not cliffs, Eddie saw. Bluffs crowned with tufts of wind-bent grass. He dreamed of reaching down, of grabbing a handful of wet sand, working it through his gloved fingers, holding it beneath his nose. He didn't know why. This wasn't England, the country of his birth. It was Ireland, but the land and its people had been a part of Britain's history for as long as anyone could remember.

At that moment, right there and then, Eddie felt he'd come home. And he wouldn't be leaving, not until they'd taken it all back.

Every square inch...

'Novak, wake the fuck up!'

McAllister's urgent whisper banished the dream and brought Eddie back into the world. Just for good measure, the big Scot gave his rucksack a kick.

'This might be a caravan park but it's nae fucking holiday. Get your shit together. We're moving in five.'

'Aye,' Eddie muttered, rolling to his knees.

He'd only come off watch an hour ago. He'd eaten an energy bar and then tried to sleep, only managing twenty minutes. The dream had been intense, like a replay of everything that had happened up until that point, but now it was gone, banished by the urgent tones and sharp boot of his section commander.

He watched Mac disappear into the darkness of the overgrown drainage ditch they were sheltering in. They'd been there for over fourteen hours, the grey waves pounding the shore behind them, the westerly gales buffeting the deserted caravan park ahead of them.

Beyond the park, enemy troops were pouring into the nearby settlement of Milltown, the rumble of their vehicles rising and fading as the wind rose and fell. They were rushing troops in to defend a coastline that was over six hundred miles long, abandoning strategic locations further to the north and east. The plan was working, but it was still dangerously early days.

And the Second Mass was up shit creek. Strong winds and stronger currents had pushed some landing craft south, delaying the main offensive around the strategically important coastal city of Galway. Now, positioned to the south of the Marine Raider battalion and the Brits of the First Penn, they were spread way too thin along a two-mile front with their backs to the sea and the enemy massing in front of them. Occasional flashes lit up the sky to the north, but everywhere else was quiet.

'Cards on the table,' Steve whispered behind him in the dark. 'Who's shitting themselves right now?'

Eddie smiled, grateful for the fleeting release in tension. The screech and clank of distant tracked vehicles wiped the smile from his face.

'Fuck. That's tanks.'

'Maybe APCs,' Digger countered, squatting behind Steve. He patted the Javelin anti-armour weapon at his feet. 'Either way, they're the ones getting fucked.'

Steve smiled beneath his helmet. 'This ain't *Call of Duty*, nipper. Ain't the ranges either. Targets move. And they shoot back too.'

'Who asked you, grandad? Worry about your own shit.'

Digger Barnes was a seventeen-year-old Mancunian who'd been messing around with his school pals in the Trafford Centre in Manchester when the first car bomb obliterated the main entrance. His family had made it to Liverpool before boarding a ship to Ireland. They'd been lucky. Digger's dad was a cop, and he'd seen the writing on the wall. He'd enlisted too and was somewhere out on the Atlantic as the armada carved its way south.

Digger was fearless and eager to get blooded. Eddie knew that their first contact would change them all for life.

He slipped off his helmet and inched his head up over the ditch. Tall thickets of coastal grass whipped backwards and forwards in the wind. The ground ahead was a graveyard of white boxes, abandoned holiday caravans creaking before the strong westerlies. There was little to see, no lights, no movement, just the odd snatches of distant, urgent commotion.

'They know we're coming.'

'Bullshit,' Digger countered. 'They'd be dropping munitions on us if they did.'

'I meant Baghdad. They know.'

Steve snorted in the dark. 'Course they do. Half of Virginia waved us off.'

Steve Palmer was the oldest man in their section and the only one who'd been a soldier when it'd all kicked off, though only just. He was a few days away from his pass-off parade when the truck bomb had levelled Whitehall. He had family somewhere outside of Middlesbrough, a wife and kid, and he hadn't seen or heard from them since, but Steve was an optimist. They were waiting for him, he'd told them. He could feel it.

Eddie pulled a night vision scope from his tactical vest and held it to his eye. He made a slow sweep of the horizon, but all he saw were distant hedgerows and rabbits hopping between the caravans.

'Gaffer's incoming,' Steve whispered.

Mac loomed out of the darkness. He glared at Eddie.

'Get your fucking lid on.' He squatted beside them, and they gathered closer. 'Right, listen in. Hajis are massing in town, Eritreans, and they must've come straight off the boat 'cos they haven't got a fucking clue. All their armour's parked right next to the supermarket and the troops are standing around with their hands in their pockets freezing their fucking nuts off. Navy's got a targeting drone right on top of them, so they're about to get fucked. Second Mass is going to assault from the south, Raiders from the east. First Penn is gonna chop down runners to the north.' Mac jabbed a finger into the darkness. 'We're gonna rescue them poor bastards in that town and they're gonna be the first of many. It's Liberation Day boys, so gear up and get ready.'

The word went down the line, passed from man to man. Eddie pulled his straps tight and flexed his gloved fingers. Like everyone else, he had rounds chambered in his M27 and his Sig. Both had full magazines. His chest rig was stuffed with more mags, grenades and smoke. His combat knife was in its sheath just above his right hip. His radio was dialled in, his face striped with cammo cream, and his helmet was fixed on tight. He was ready. His heart raced.

Crouched in front of him, Mac half turned his head. 'That you whispering sweet nothings in my ear?'

That's when Eddie realised he was breathing fast. Too fast.

'Deep breaths, Eddie lad, nice and easy. You're gonna be fine. Just listen to my voice and trust in your training.'

'Roger that.'

Mac was a natural leader, tough and resourceful. Like the rest of them, the Scot was yet to be blooded by battle, but he possessed a calmness and strength that Eddie found deeply reassuring. He felt safe around Mac. The man had probably been a soldier in another life.

He saw Mac glance at his watch, heard his voice in his headset.

'Prepare to move.'

Eddie gripped his M27 a little tighter. He'd dreamed about this day since he'd learned that Kyle had been killed. Everything he'd done since then, the training, the enlistment, the hardship of basic, his graduation and mobilisation, the voyage across the ocean, had brought him to this point, this very moment.

Now he banished it all, the memories, the thoughts of home, his parents, Kyle. He cleared his mind. There could be no distractions, no hesitation, not now.

This was it.

He felt Steve's hand on his shoulder, heard his whispered words.

'Good luck, brother.'

The wind gusted again, whipping the tall grass, moaning between the caravans. Mac twisted around.

'Move.'

Eddie took a deep breath and scrambled out of the ditch, moving quickly between the caravans, advancing to contact. His heart hammered like the rabbits scattering before him. He'd never felt so alive.

He charged into the darkness and into the unknown.

INVASION: UPRISING
BOOK 2 OF THE INVASION UK SERIES

Three years long years of tyranny and bloodshed have passed since the invasion of Europe. Now a new dawn rises…

A nuclear attack shatters the fragile peace between Beijing and Baghdad. In Europe, caliphate forces are driven across a war-torn Ireland and into the sea.

As the tide turns and hope rises, hard decisions are about to be made.

Learn more

Get the complete **Invasion UK series box** set plus **bonus content** and save **44%**!

Get offer

NEVER MISS A NEW RELEASE

To learn more about my writing and filmmaking life, and to receive all the latest book news and updates, please visit my official website and sign up for my occasional newsletter.

Sign up!

ALSO BY DC ALDEN

Invasion: Downfall
Invasion: Uprising
Invasion: Frontline
Invasion: Deliverance
Invasion: Chronicles
Invasion: The Lost Chapters
Invasion: Redux
The Horse at the Gates
The Angola Deception
Fortress
End Zone
The Rogue State Trilogy
UFO Down

Join the conversation on social media:

Printed in Great Britain
by Amazon